WARM WELCOME

The enraged Cotton charged, waving his gun and snarling.

"Damn! Can't get a clear shot! Move aside, Trench!"

Bowman raised his double-barreled derringer at Cotton as he came crashing into the room. Cotton saw it, but not fast enough to do anything about it before Bowman fired.

A single shot took Cotton square in the middle of the face, dropping him.

Shaking off his paralysis, Trench clawed for his gun. Pulling his knife out of Sid's lifeless belly, Grimes side-stepped, and in one smooth flowing motion slung the blade in an underhanded throw at Trench. It pierced his throat, lodging in the center of his bull neck. Trench swayed, gun forgotten, massive hands fluttering helplessly around his chest. He leaned forward, choking and sputtering, blood filling his gaping mouth.

Lurching sideways, he staggered toward the side door. Shouldering into it, he knocked it off its hinges and out the doorway. He followed, trampling it underfoot. A half-dozen paces more, and Trench collapsed, falling facedown in the snow.

Inside, Cotton and Sid lay sprawled on the dirt floor.

To no one in particular, Grimes said, "Nice friendly folks you got around h...

BIG IRON

Book One in the Golden Spike Trilogy

JAKE LANCER

POCKET **STAR** BOOKS
New York   London   Toronto   Sydney

An *Original* Publication of POCKET BOOKS

 A Pocket Star Book published by
POCKET BOOKS, a division of Simon & Schuster, Inc.
1230 Avenue of the Americas, New York, NY 10020

ISBN: 0-7434-6493-1

First Pocket Books printing March 2004

10 9 8 7 6 5 4 3 2 1

POCKET STAR BOOKS and colophon are registered trademarks of Simon & Schuster, Inc.

Manufactured in the United States of America

For information regarding special discounts for bulk purchases, please contact Simon & Schuster Special Sales at 1-800-456-6798 or business@simonandschuster.com.

BIG
IRON

PROLOGUE

In 1866, on a winter's day, the Majestic Hotel was the scene of an emergency meeting of the board of directors of the Union Pacific Railroad. One of the finest hotels in Manhattan, the monumental structure presented an image of four-square solidity and rock-ribbed respectability. Behind closed doors, however, the meeting was something less than a model of decorum, with the directors on the verge of open revolt.

The conference room was long, narrow, and high-ceilinged, like the central aisle of a church. At one end, the wall was pierced by a row of three tall, narrow windows with rounded tops. Wind and cold rain beat at the glass panes.

It was a dark day. Globed gas lamps lightened the gloom, shouldering shadows aside to the far corners of the room. Blue with cigar smoke, the air was close, thick, overheated.

Mounted on one of the long walls was a bedsheet-sized map of the United States. Drawn on it in thick red lines was the proposed route of a transcontinental railroad.

A long, narrow table occupied the center of the room. Grouped around it on three sides, fitfully contained in high-backed chairs, sat a dozen board directors. Some were physically powerful, hard-fisted; others were soft-bodied, with smooth, plump hands. All were shrewd, tough, and successful enough to have won a hard-fought place at the table.

Opposite them, at the head of the table, stood the president of the line. He and these twelve others were principals of a company that was building the westward-driving branch of the cross-country railroad.

In the event of success, each of them stood to make a fortune. If failure was the result, ruin awaited them.

A black-bearded magnate put the question of the hour: "What about Kansas?"

The others stirred, disturbed, restive. They took up the cry.

"Yes, what about Kansas?" "It's criminal!" "Kansas!" "Damned outrage!" "Kansas, Kansas!"

Some of them were actually shaking their fists.

When the clamor lessened, the black-bearded one continued. "The Kansas Division branch is stopped dead in its tracks, and we all know why. The lawless element has got the road dead in its sights. Outlaws rob our pay-rolls, shoot our people, burn bridges, and tear up the track. It's war down there! And we're losing!"

Others assented, nodding, grumbling.

"Let me remind the board of the stakes we're playing for here," Blackbeard said, his tone that of a prosecutor delivering the closing argument in a capital case. "The government pays us in completion bonds for every mile of track that's laid. Those revenues are vital for financing the transcontinental road. If the Kansas line isn't com-pleted—and quick!—we'll be out of money, and the whole transcontinental venture will come crashing down for lack of operating expenses.

"And if that happens, gentlemen, we're sunk."

The directors nodded again. They knew the shaky financial structure on which the company rested. A weakness in any one spot could send the whole house of cards toppling.

Throughout, the president of the company had stood at his place at the head of the table Neat, smooth, and self-composed, he now spoke.

"I agree, gentlemen. The situation in Kansas is intolerable," he said. "That's why I've already taken measures to correct it. Strong measures. We're going to fight fire with—gunfire." He smiled thinly.

Whatever they saw in that icy smile, the directors were content to affirm their confidence in the leader and to move quickly to other matters.

1

Beyond the end of the line—the railroad line—lay Black Creek, Kansas. To that country, on a day in late March 1866, came a lone rider, Dane Bowman. Mounted on a gray horse, he rode west.

Ahead lay vast, well-watered plains, above them an oncoming storm. Clouds massed, charcoal gray with lead-colored outlines, streaming, churning, dimming the late-afternoon light.

A cold wind blew up, flicking a handful of cold raindrops onto Bowman. A big, square-built man, he huddled inside the folds of a dark brown greatcoat, hunched forward on the horse, leaning into the rising wind.

Jammed squarely on top of his head was a well-worn Union cavalry hat. His coat was open and unbuttoned at the bottom, and he'd need only to sweep back the flaps to get to his gun fast. He wore the gun on his left hip, butt facing out—a cross-belly draw, a cavalry-style draw that was especially fast on horseback.

The saddle scabbard held a carbine rifle. In the saddlebags were other weapons and ammunition.

Tools of the trade.

The gunman's trade.

• • •

The sprawling Kansas flat was divided by a dirt road running east-west, all the way to the horizon line. Beside it was a telegraph line, wires and poles receding into the distance.

This was Telegraph Road, drawing Bowman deeper into Black Creek country. From afar, it looked like tableland, but, once entered, it revealed itself to be a place of rolling grasslands and wooded ridges, honeycombed by streams and rivulets.

Good farming land but not so good for farmers, not lately.

Here and there, widely scattered along the road, stood the burned-out remnants of stone chimneys and foundations, marking the sites of abandoned homesteads, cleared planting fields now returned to the weeds, brambles, and thickets.

These were the only signs of human habitation.

For this was Kansas, bleeding Kansas. For four years, the nation had been wracked by the Civil War. But long before that, since 1854, the border states of Kansas and neighboring Missouri had been the scene of unrestricted guerrilla warfare between proslavery and antislavery forces, with the luckless civilians getting it from both sides. It was a war of mounted bands, raids, counterraids, theft, arson, shooting, the killing of unarmed men and boys.

In 1861, when the Civil War was declared, it came almost as a relief for denizens of the border states. But not for long, not with the likes of Missouri's William Clarke Quantrill and Bill Anderson, and Kansas's Jim Lane and Doc Jennison leading their private armies into battle with a wartime level of slaughter and plunder.

This was the soil that had spawned Dane Bowman and, for better or for worse, had made him what he was.

For him, this was a kind of homecoming.

The road crested a long, low rise, spilling into a broad shallow valley. On both sides of the path lay weedy fields and, beyond them, woods. The dried, dead weeds were bronze-colored. Trees were bare, their trunks gray-black, and their intertwined branches silver and white.

Winter was no friend to bushwhackers—less cover for ambushers to hide behind. But spring was near, Bowman noted, only a few weeks off.

"Have to get my business done fast," he said under his breath.

The gray horse paced along steadily, moving at an easy, sure-footed gait. The rider kept a sure, light touch on the reins. Saddle leather creaked.

He rode up out of the valley, cresting the lip. Wind gusted, spattering him with big, fat raindrops. Squinting against windblown chaff, he fixed his scarf so that it covered his face below the eyes.

Not wanting to be skylined, he quickly descended the other side, pausing when he was below the summit. Reining in the gray, he paused to survey the landscape laid out below him in the day's last light.

A wide, easy slope ambled down to a grassy plain cut by a thin, dark snake, a lesser branch of Black Creek. Entering from the northwest, the stream switchbacked across the plain before exiting at the south.

On the far side of the stream, in the middle ground on a rise, stood a blocky structure whose cubed windows were dimly glowing amber squares.

Far to the west, somewhere beyond the ridgeline, too distant to be seen, lay Black Creek town.

Bowman started downhill. The tempo of the rain quickened. Mixed with it were big, fat, wet snowflakes.

Cold winds blew, turning the rain to snow. Silver-dollar-sized flakes fell with soft plopping sounds on his hat and shoulders.

Daylight was closing when Bowman reached the flat. Telegraph Road crossed the creek at one of its widest, shallowest parts. At the crossing, the stream was spanned by a wooden plank bridge whose boards echoed hollowly to the tread of the gray's hoofbeats. Black water swirled, gurgling around the piles holding up the bridge.

On the creek's west bank stood a stone blockhouse, a corral, and some outbuildings.

The site was a combination stagecoach station, stopping place for travelers, and trading post. Telegraph Road followed the course of the old prewar stagecoach and mail route. The coming railroad, too, was designed to follow that route.

The main building was set back about a hundred feet from the road, to which it was connected by a horseshoe-shaped drive. It was a square, flat-roofed, cabin-sized blockhouse. Spaced along the stone walls were tall, thin windows. The chimney vented a line of woolly gray smoke, blown into vertical streamers by the wind.

Behind and to one side of it was a barn, some sheds, and a corral. The corral was now empty. The barn doors were open. Inside, a lamp burned, and shadows moved. One of those shadows resolved itself into a figure, holding a lantern in one hand. He exited the barn and went to Bowman, who'd reined to a halt nearby.

At first, Bowman thought it was a boy, but as the other neared, he was revealed by the lamplight to be an adult man, jockey-sized, with a thin, pointy, middle-aged face. Looking up at Bowman, he squinted against the pelting snowflakes.

He said, "Climb down, mister. I'll take care of your horse."

Bowman said, "Who're you?"

"I'm Johnny—Herk's hand."

"Herk?"

"Mr. Herkimer. He owns the place," Johnny said, jerking a thumb toward the blockhouse.

Bowman shrugged. "I'll walk the horse down to the barn. Lead on."

Turning, Johnny started back the way he had come, holding the lantern high. His footprints were brown against the thin layer of wet snow covering the ground.

A stone's throw away from the blockhouse, the unpainted wooden barn was a two-story structure with a peaked roof. After scuttling inside, Johnny hung the lantern on a pole peg and adjusted the flame, brightening the barn's gloomy interior.

An open center space was flanked on both sides by stable stalls lining the walls. Five stalls were occupied by horses, two on one side of the barn, three on the other. In the open area stood an unhitched buckboard wagon, its wheels and undersides mud-spattered.

Dismounting, Bowman gentled the gray, patting its muscular neck, making murmurous sounds. Hefting his weighty saddlebags, he draped them over one shoulder. He shucked his rifle out of the saddle scabbard and held it in one hand, muzzle down.

He said, "Give him a good rubdown; then put on the feedbag."

Johnny nodded, busying himself with unsaddling the animal. Seeing a heaped pile of feedsacks, Bowman said, "Those oats fresh?"

"They ain't rotten, mister. See for yourself," Johnny said, not looking up.

"I'll take your word for it." Bowman fished a coin out of a pocket. Johnny looked up. Bowman tossed him the coin, and he plucked it out of the air.

Bowman said, "Take good care of my horse."

Johnny, eyes hot, unsmiling, said, "I'd 'a taken good care of him anyhow, mister."

"I like a man who likes horses."

"I got more use for 'em than I do for some people."

"Me, too," Bowman said. "If you don't want the coin, you can toss it back."

"I'll keep it," Johnny said quickly, making the coin disappear into one of his pockets. "Thanks."

Bowman nodded, going out into the yard. On one side, a path went down the side of the rise, descending about twenty yards to the creek. It was sunken several inches and could be seen despite the snow.

Another slightly sunken path connected the barnyard to the blockhouse. Bowman followed it. About halfway to the station building, he passed a covered well. The path forked, one branch connecting to a side door in the blockhouse, the other going around to the front.

Bowman went to the front and entered through the main door.

A dim, shedlike space was broken by gnarled, smoke-blackened wooden posts holding up a low-ceilinged, flat roof. It was lit by firelight and by several lanterns hanging on nails driven into poles. The dirt floor was hard-packed, clayey. To the left, running parallel to the wall, stood a crude bar, consisting of a couple of upright hogshead wooden barrels with plank boards nailed across their tops.

To the right, toward the rear of the building, were some tables and chairs. Dominating the rear wall was a massive stone chimney and fireplace, its hearth glowing with sooty, orange-red firelight.

Two women, one young, one old, sat huddled by the fire, warming themselves Nearby were their wet coats and scarves, hung up to dry.

Across from the women, behind the bar, leaning against the wall, stood a balding, bearded, potbellied man in buckskins.

When Bowman entered, the wind blew in through the open doorway, causing the hearth fire to flutter. A beat after he closed the door behind him, the flames lost their agitation.

The other three turned to look at him. The man pushed off the wall, turning to face Bowman. Beckoning, smiling widely, he said, "Howdy, stranger! Come on in."

Bowman crossed to the middle of the room, pausing to look around.

The man behind the bar was sixtyish, with a wispy, white, goatish beard. His buckskins were dark and grimy. His belly overhung a worn, frayed gunbelt slung low on his hips, a holstered gun worn on his right side.

"I'm Herkimer, station manager and proprietor of this establishment," he said. "Call me Herk, everybody does."

"Glad to know you, Herk. The name's Bowman."

"Make yourself to home, Mr. Bowman. That fire's good and hot."

Bowman nodded. He crossed toward the fire, moving in the space between the two seated females and the tables and chairs. They turned to look at him, the older woman with disapproval, the younger with interest.

The senior of the two was severe, sour-faced, and sinewy, her graying hair worn in a tight, prim bun. She wore a heavy, long-sleeved dress and sensible, high-topped shoes. A black crocheted shawl wrapped her bony shoulders and upper body. Her white, blue-veined hands were wrapped around a tin cup filled with steaming coffee.

Her crabbed face pinched tighter when she got a good look at Bowman.

Her youthful companion looked to be around sixteen, with a heart-shaped face, sulky but pretty. Strawberry-blond hair, cut in bangs across her forehead, fell past her shoulders. Her pink-lipped mouth was full, pouting. Her face still showed traces of baby fat, but the rest of her looked all grown up. Twisting around in her chair, she pulled her dress taut against her lithe, shapely young body.

Touching his hat with thumb and forefinger, Bowman nodded toward the duo, said, "Ladies . . ."

The elder, scornful, said, "Hmmph!"

The other looked up at him from the tops of her eyes, her face smooth, pink, doll-like.

As he made his way to a table near the wall, Bowman shrugged the saddlebags off his shoulder, setting them down with a thump on the tabletop. They were heavy with guns and ammunition. He laid the carbine flat on its side on the table. The table and chairs were crudely fashioned from rough-hewn wood.

He shook wet snow off his hat and used the hat to beat the snow off his shoulders and upper body before taking off his greatcoat. Beneath it he wore a pale blue denim jacket over a dark flannel shirt, brown pants tucked into the tops of leather boots.

He draped the coat over the back of a chair, then sank down into another chair. He sat with his back to the wall, half turned toward the fire.

Mounted above the mantle, high in the middle of the

chimney, was a buffalo skull. The air was thick with the smells of tangy woodsmoke, wet stone and earth, wet animal hides, raw whiskey fumes, coffee, and cooking smells.

On an iron spit over the hearth embers hung a bubbling pot of stew or something like it. It smelled pretty good.

Bowman's empty stomach rumbled. He licked his lips.

The blond teen must have thought that was meant for her. Wriggling a turned-up nose, she stuck out her tongue at Bowman. High, firm breasts thrust against the front of her blue-and-white gingham dress.

The older woman tugged at her sleeve. "Don't stare at the man, Francine. It's not polite."

"I'm not staring at him, Miz Abigail. He's staring at me," Francine said.

He was staring, Bowman realized, and quickly looked elsewhere. Miz Abigail wasn't about to let it pass so easily.

She rose, turning to face Bowman, her posture erect, spine ramrod-straight. "I am Abigail Cuttle," she announced.

Unsure of what to do, Bowman rose to his feet. "Pleased to meet you—"

Holding up a hand for silence, she said, "This is not by way of being a social introduction. I'm a plainspoken woman who likes to know who's who and what's what."

Bowman froze, halfway between sitting and standing.

Francine heaved a heavy sigh, further outlining her breasts against the gingham. Glancing at Cuttle, she rolled her eyes.

Indicating the teenager, Abigail Cuttle said, "This is Miss Francine Leland. I'm escorting her to Black Creek, where she's going to live with her uncle. His name is Vestry, Lucas Vestry. He's one of Marshal Bragg's deputies."

She said Bragg's name as if she were invoking a deity.

Bowman, thoughtful, said, "I've heard of Bragg."

"I daresay," the Cuttle woman said, sniffing. "You just keep that in mind and keep to yourself and don't go bothering young women, and there won't be any trouble."

"Yes, ma'am," Bowman said.

Abigail Cuttle gave him a hard look, skeptical of his ready assent. "Just so we understand each other," she said.

Francine smiled weakly, shrugging. Distancing herself.

Abigail Cuttle sat down, pointedly turning her back on Bowman. Placing a clawlike hand on Francine's shoulder, she physically turned the girl away from him so that she, too, now faced the hearth.

Shaking his head, Bowman circled the table, putting it between him and the women, before he crossed to the bar. Behind it stood Herkimer, genial, waiting.

Bowman said, "Who's she, one of the local characters?"

"Heh heh," Herkimer said, not chuckling but actually saying the words. All the lines on his moon face curved upward, giving an appearance of good fellowship. "What'll you have?"

"Whiskey. If that won't get me in trouble with Marshal Bragg."

"Heh heh." From a shelf on the wall, Herkimer took down a half-gallon brown jug. He popped the cork and poured a splash into a tin cup, setting it down on the bar.

Bowman said, "This Bragg supposed to be somebody?"

"Bad man to cross, they say," Herkimer said, nodding.

"Well, here's how." Bowman drank up, tossing it back. A heartbeat later, it hit, detonating a fireball in his belly that skyrocketed through to the top of his head. He shuddered. He slapped a coin down on the bar, shaking it.

"Not bad!" he said, gasping, eyes tearing.

Herkimer said, "Another?"

"Let me catch my breath first. Whew!" Bowman wiped the tears from his eyes with the back of his hand.

After a pause, he said, "What happened to Sinclair?"

"Who? Oh, you must mean the fellow who built this place. Sinclair, sure," Herkimer said. "He's long gone. Dead. Shot during the war—a holdup. A Dutchman took it over until his health went back on him, and I took it over from him. This Sinclair fellow a friend of yours?"

Bowman shook his head. "Just to say hello to once or twice."

"Never met him myself." Herkimer placed his hands flat on the plank bartop, leaning forward. It sagged under his weight. "You from these parts, Mr. Bowman?"

"From around Paola way."

"A native Kansan, eh?"

"Came out here with my folks when I was a boy."

"Must have been pretty rough in those days, thanks to those Missouri raiders."

"We made it rough right back at them," Bowman said. "I hear it's still pretty rough right around here, what with outlaws, bushwhackers, and what-all."

"Some might say so." Herkimer was elaborately non-committal.

"What do you say?"

"Nothing. Not a thing! Can't get into trouble that way."

"You might have something there," Bowman said. "Let's have another drink."

Herkimer refilled the tin cup. Bowman said, "Have one for yourself."

"Thanks, don't mind if I do."

Another tin cup appeared on the bartop, to be filled

with clear liquid from the brown clay jug. The cups were gripped, raised, clinked, and quaffed.

This time, Bowman swallowed only a mouthful. It sent shivers along his spine. Herkimer set down a drained cup, his round face red and shining. He smacked his lips.

Bowman said, "Why doesn't Bragg clean up on the bandits?"

"He would, if they came to Black Creek," Herkimer said.

"Not sure I get your drift."

"He's a town marshal. If it happens outside city limits, he and his deputies won't lift a finger," Herkimer said, looking owlish. "Anyway, they've got their hands full. Black Creek is filling up with bad ones."

"I could use some filling up myself," Bowman said. "What're the chances of getting a hot meal?"

"Got a stewpot boiling on the fire."

"Any good?"

"It's fresh."

"I'll take some."

"Coming right up," Herkimer said.

In the rear wall, to the left of the fireplace, was a doorway covered by a tacked-up blanket. Ducking under it, Herkimer disappeared into a back room, emerging a moment later with a bowl and some utensils.

Cup in hand, Bowman returned to his table and sat down. Taking a cloth square from his pocket, he wiped dry the scattered droplets of melted snow that were beaded up on the carbine.

Among Abigail Cuttle's possessions was an octagonal wicker sewing basket. From it she now took out a pair of long knitting needles and a ball of yarn and began knitting. The click and tap of the needles performing their intricate rounds had a kind of lulling clockwork sound.

Gusty winds rattled the windows in their casements. No matter how solidly built those stone walls seemed, there were plenty of cracks and crannies that let the cold blasts get inside.

Herkimer stood bustling at the hearth, ladling out a mess of stew into a dark wooden bowl. Steam rose from it, moistening his pink cheeks, as he brought it to Bowman. Along with the bowl, he set out a couple of biscuits.

Bowman went to work on the meal. The stew wasn't bad; there were even a few actual scraps and strings of meat mixed in with the soupy broth of potatoes and carrots. After a minute or two spent soaking in the gravy, the biscuits softened up enough so that he could gnaw on them without breaking a tooth.

Bowman polished off two bowls and some more biscuits. The booze had set his teeth to buzzing. The food soaked up some of it. He washed it down with about a quart of strong black coffee.

Herkimer said, "Good, huh? It's made with well water, not creek water."

The coffee was okay, no more, but Bowman kept his opinion to himself. Instead, he said, "I noticed you had a well. What's wrong with the creek water?"

"Nothing's wrong with it; it's perfectly safe to drink. It's just got an off taste. Too many minerals in the water, they say. But there's nothing wrong with it. It's been tested by doctors, who all gave it a clean bill of health," Herkimer said.

The side door opened, and in came Johnny, snow matting his head and shoulders. Standing in one place, he brushed off the snow with his hands, stamping it off his boots.

Herkimer said, "What's it doing out there, Johnny? This storm going to amount to anything?"

"Nope. It'll turn to rain before midnight."

"Well, that's that," Herkimer announced to the three travelers. "If Johnny says so, that's how it'll be. He ain't hardly ever wrong about the weather."

Johnny nodded, head bobbing. "I know a storm when I see it."

"Go get yourself some hot coffee, and warm up by the fire."

Johnny hefted the coffee pot. He lifted the lid and looked aside. "There ain't none."

"Well, make some," Herkimer said

Johnny pulled off his jacket, muttering. He brewed up a fresh pot, making it cowboy-style, with handfuls of the coffee thrown directly into the pot of boiling water.

Bowman dipped two fingers into his jacket's inside left breast pocket and pulled out a half-smoked cigar he'd been saving all day. Burning the end with a lit match, he puffed it into glowing life.

The mechanical punctuation of the knitting needles abruptly ceased. Abigail Cuttle swung around in her chair, glaring. Her neck was a taut tangle of cords, veins, and sinews. She said, "A gentleman would first ask the ladies for permission to smoke." She put particular emphasis on the word *gentleman*.

"Sorry, ma'am," Bowman said, face wreathed with smoke. "Guess I forgot my manners—too much time on the trail."

"Too much liquor at the bar, you mean!"

"I see there's no getting on your good side, ma'am."

Abigail Cuttle waved a hand in front of her face, dispelling invisible smoke clouds. She coughed, choked, her face reddening. "Tobacco is the devil's weed. And liquor's worse!"

Bowman rose. "I'll smoke it outside. Otherwise Marshal Bragg might not like it."

"I'd like to see you say that to his face," she said.

Bowman turned, crossing to the front door. He stuck his head outside, cigar clamped between his teeth. It was snowing hard, a vortex of whirling white flakes. An inch or two of wet, glistening whiteness covered the landscape.

He stepped outside, closing the door behind him, cutting off Abigail Cuttle's continuing protest in mid-squawk. Overhead, a rooflike overhang above the entrance provided some protection from the elements.

He stood to one side of the door, back to the wall. It was cold but not so cold that he couldn't stand it for the short time it'd take him to finish the cigar.

Light from inside shone out through the windows flanking the door, spotlighting swirling, spiraling columns of wind-whipped snow. Gusts blew into his face, stinging it with icy needles. His eyes were slitted, and his head turned down and to one side, to avoid facing directly into it.

He puffed away, the orange disk of the cigar tip winking. This was no time for a leisurely smoke. He smoked the cigar down to a stub and flicked it away. It splashed down in the snow in a burst of embers which were quickly extinguished.

Turning toward the door, Bowman paused with his hand on the latch. Something he'd seen in the corner of his eye made him look back.

Out there, on the road east of the station, there was movement. Barely visible through streaming curtains of snow was a patch of blackness. Darker than the backdrop of night, gliding upward from the crossing along the sunken trail, the black blur continued its advance toward the station.

Nearing, it resolved itself into three separate black blurs. Three riders.

2

On came the riders, horses trudging along, making for the station. Snow dulled the sound of hoofbeats, muffling them.

Bowman went inside to the bar. "Company's coming."

Herkimer said, "How's that?"

"Three riders coming this way."

"That's fine. I can use the business." Looking pleased, Herkimer rubbed his hands together. He turned to look for Johnny, but the latter was already in motion, pulling on his hat and coat.

"I'll tend to the horses," Johnny said. He picked up a lantern and exited by the side door.

Bowman had Herkimer refill his cup from the brown jug. He set down the cup at his table and went to the fire. He stood facing it, warming his hands. He chafed them, flexing the fingers, working feeling and flexibility back into them.

Abigail Cuttle remained silent, but her knitting needles clicked and popped like the sender's key of an ace telegrapher. They only slowed into moderate quicktime when Bowman went away.

His chair had its back to the wall. He moved it a few feet to one side, into the shadows cast by the junction of an upright post and a rafter beam. He pulled on his greatcoat, draping it cape-style over his shoulders and arms, wrapping himself in it.

After a while, from outside came the sound of voices and heavy boot treads.

Flung open, the front door swung back on its hinges, fetching up against the inner wall with a crash.

Through the open doorway, cold wind came streaming in, triggering an uproar at the hearth, whipping up the flames.

In came three men, their outlines fuzzy with clinging snow. Where not covered by beards or scarves, their faces were red and shiny. They brushed off the snow, stamping booted feet.

One was huge, hulking, oafish. Another was dandyish, with curly silver hair framing a clean-shaven face. A third, built like a blacksmith, had an anvil-shaped jaw. All wore belt guns. They looked like a rough bunch.

Abigail Cuttle's knitting fell silent.

For an instant, as he got a good look at the newcomers, Herkimer's face fell. Shaking himself out of it, he formed the lower half of his face into a toothy smile, freezing it in place.

He said, "Howdy, gents!"

None of them returned his greeting.

Wind rushed through the door, flailing the flames in the hearth. It sounded like flags flapping in a stiff breeze.

Huddled into her shawl, shivering, Abigail Cuttle said, "Close that door! Were you raised in a barn?"

That set the strangers back on their heels.

The curly-topped dandy started, staring in disbelief at her, then burst into braying laughter. The blacksmith-looking one said, "Get the door, Trench."

The oaf, Trench, shambled to the door and closed it.

"Thank you very much!" Abigail Cuttle said, her tone saying, *Damn you to hell very much.* Turning her back to them, she once more faced the fire.

Curly-top laughed, a jackass bray. "She sure told us, Cotton!"

The blacksmith-looking one was Cotton. "You talk too much, Sid," he said, without rancor or warmth.

"I don't mean nothing by it. I'm just funning," said Sid, the curly-topped dandy. "Anyhow, I got to carry the weight for Trench. He don't talk at all. Ain't that right, Trench?"

Trench grunted. "Unh."

Sid grinned, showing a set of yellowed horse teeth. The grin turned into a leer when he caught sight of Francine.

She sat turned around in her chair, eyeing the strangers. Firelight gave her face a rosy golden glow. Her eyes were wide, her lips parted in a tiny O shape.

Abigail Cuttle thumped her hand on Francine's shoulder. "Turn around, and keep your eyes to yourself, missy."

Sid vented his jackass bray. "Looky that! Honey—and vinegar."

He crossed to the fire, Trench trailing after. Bellying up close to the hearth, Sid opened his coat, spreading its flaps like batwings. Basking in the firelight, he showily warmed himself.

Rigid with speechless indignation, Abigail Cuttle sat with her fists in her lap, knitting needles jutting with their points up from each hand.

Turning around in a circle, preening, Sid caught sight of Bowman sitting in the shadows. He started, scowling. It was the first he'd noticed of the other.

Trench, too, had been equally oblivious until now.

But not Cotton. Upon entering, he'd seen Bowman

and since then had been keeping an eye on him. When the other two went to the fire, Cotton had stayed in place near the bar, where he had a clear view of Bowman.

Bowman knew that because he'd been watching Cotton right from the start, too. And the others.

Watching without looking as if he were watching.

Between the end of the bar and the blanket-covered back-room door stood a vertical wooden pillar. A nail had been driven into it at head height, and from it hung a dimly glowing lantern. Within the clouded glass shone a ball of beer-colored light.

Sid went to it, swaggering. His boots were built up with four-inch heels that made him look taller. He looked as if he were walking on tiptoes.

He took down the lantern from its post and approached Bowman, halting on the other side of the table. After setting the lamp down on the table, he turned up the wick, increasing the brightness of its murky bronze glow.

Sid's silver hair was as curly as sheep's wool. His face was pointy, wizened, with moist, dark eyes peering out from behind paperlike skin. Underlit by lantern light, he looked fey, almost elfin.

He wore two guns in a showy black leather rig decorated with silver stitching. The holstered weapons were tied down, gunfighter-style.

Bowman looked up, lamplight reflected as two yellow pinpoints glinting in the darks of his eyes.

Whatever Sid was looking for, he didn't find it.

"That ain't him," he said over his shoulder to the others. "He's wearing a Union Army hat. The one we're looking for wouldn't be caught dead in no Yankee blue."

With some sharpness, Cotton said, "Shut up, Sid."

"Besides," Sid continued, as if he hadn't heard, "this

one's too old. Thirty if he's a day. The one we're looking for ain't hardly more than twenty-one." Trench, bored, returned to warming his slablike hands before the fire. Cotton kept on watching, stonily, steadily.

Sid reached out, bony forefinger pointing, its tip inches from Bowman's hat brim. He said, "You a soldier?"

Bowman said, "Not since the war."

"Then what are you wearing the hat for?"

"It's a good hat, broken in the way I like it."

"Is that a fact. What do you think about all this?" Sid said, gesturing to include Trench and Cotton.

"Not much," Bowman said. "I don't mix in things that don't concern me."

Sid thought it over, then nodded, his mop of tight curls bobbing. "Keep thinking like that."

Bowman said nothing. Sid snickered. Hefting the light, he turned and crossed to the bar, hanging the lantern back on the pole.

Cotton said, "I still say you talk too damned much, Sid."

"You worry too much," Sid said. "Besides, I like to talk. I'm a friendly fellow."

Trench snorted. Sid went to the fire, circling Abigail Cuttle and Francine and coming up in front of them.

Cotton said, "Sid."

Not looking at him, Sid waved a hand in his direction, waving him off. Facing the women, he made a deep bow, bending from the waist so deeply that his hat fell off. He caught it before it hit the floor.

"Fast, huh?" He straightened, showing his yellowed horse teeth in what was supposed to be a smile. Eyeing Francine, he said, "What's your name, pretty girl?"

Francine looked at the floor, fidgeted. Abigail Cuttle held her chin up. She said, "Her uncle's a deputy for Walcott Bragg. That's all you need to know." Her voice was clear, firm, direct.

Sid turned to her, his smile undiminished. "My, my. Walcott Bragg. Is that a fact?"

"Yes, it's a fact. Let a word to the wise be sufficient."

Sid shook his head. "You speak right up, don't you, lady?"

"That's my way."

"You're a long way off from Black Creek, and I don't see no marshal and no deputies around," Sid said. "You see, I speak right up, too," he added.

Cotton said, "Quit pestering those folks, Sid."

Sid was the picture of aggrieved innocence. He held his hands out palms up, as if in appeal. "Pestering? Who's pestering? I'm not pestering you folks, am I?"

Abigail Cuttle said, "Indeed you are!"

Cotton said, "I'm not going to tell you twice, Sid."

"Well, all right!" Abruptly breaking off, Sid went to the bar.

Abigail Cuttle said, "Well, I never!"

"I believe it," Sid said to her over his shoulder.

"Hmmph!"

Cotton said, "Sorry, ma'am."

"Is the man mad? Drunk, more likely!"

Francine, anxious, plucked at the older woman's sleeve. "Miz Abigail, please! Let it go."

"Good-for-nothing saddle tramps—"

"Please!"

At the bar, Cotton said, "Don't make complications, Sid."

Sid said, "What're we doing standing here talking instead of drinking? Set 'em up, station man!"

Herkimer set out three cups and poured the whiskey.

Trench, Sid, and Cotton drank up. The cups were refilled. Sid slapped down a coin on the bar.

Herkimer said, "You fellows looking for someone?"

Sid leaned toward him, mean-faced. "What's it to you? I mean, why do you ask?"

Taken aback, Herkimer said, "I don't mean nothing. I was just making conversation, that's all."

"Well, don't. Just shut up and keep the drinks coming."

Indicating the blanket-covered archway, Cotton said, "What's back there?"

"Storeroom," Herkimer said.

Strolling past the end of the bar, Cotton lifted the edge of the blanket covering the doorway. Beyond lay a dark, cold storeroom.

Letting the blanket fall, he went back to the bar. From where he stood at the end of the bar, he could keep the whole room in view.

After a while, the side door opened, and Johnny came in. "Your horses are all squared away in the barn."

"Good," Cotton said.

Johnny took off his hat and coat and stood by the fire, warming himself. Abigail Cuttle and Francine sat huddled together, backs turned to the rest of the room. Bowman sat in his shadow zone, hat pulled down over his eyes, as if he were sleeping.

Sid set fire to a long, gnarly cigarillo that looked like a brown twig and puffed away. Abigail Cuttle made a throat-clearing noise but otherwise kept her peace. Her chin-high posture and rigidly upright spine radiated contempt.

The fire burned low, drawing the darkness in. Cold followed. Herkimer said, "Toss another log on the fire, Johnny."

Johnny complied, and soon yellow rags and streamers

of flame curled around the fresh log, which popped and crackled as it burned.

The wind rose and fell. Now, in the lull between gusting blasts, Bowman thought he heard something.

Hoofbeats.

He remained motionless, betraying his discovery by no action, not even a twitch—if it *was* a discovery and not his hearing playing tricks on him. It might have been the sound of his pulse, thudding in his ears.

When the wind once more died down, he heard it again. At the bar, Cotton stiffened, then turned his head, cocking an ear toward the front of the building. He listened, intent.

Trench said, "What?"

Cotton motioned him to silence. "Hear that?"

Trench shook his oxlike head. "I don't hear nothing."

Abruptly, Sid pushed off from the bar, starting toward the door. He opened it and stuck his head outside, cold drafts rushing in. Squinting against wind-driven snow, he held up a hand over his eyes to shield them.

Trench said, "You see anything, Sid?"

"I don't know," Sid said over his shoulder. "Wait a minute . . . wait a minute! Rider's coming."

Cotton said, "One rider? Alone?"

"As near as I can see in this slop. He's coming on toward the station, be here in a minute."

Johnny rose, starting forward. Cotton said, "Where're you going?"

Johnny said, "If somebody's coming, I've got to take care of his horse."

"Never mind about that. Sit down."

"But—"

Cotton drew his gun, leveling it. "Sit down."

Johnny sat down.

Abigail Cuttle started. Francine gasped. Herkimer raised his hands in the hands-up position. He said, "Mister, if this is a holdup—"

Abigail Cuttle said, "A holdup? Oh, Lord!"

"—you came to the wrong place. I ain't got but a few coins," Herkimer said.

Sid said, "Quit your poor-mouthing."

Cotton said, "Get his gun, Trench."

Trench went around behind the bar, lifting Herkimer's gun from its holster and sticking it in the top of his own waistband.

Cotton's gun was trained on Bowman, who sat with both hands resting on the tabletop. "Keep those hands where I can see 'em."

"Like I said, I don't mix into things that aren't my business," Bowman said.

"Fine. Don't make it your business, if you want to keep on living." Cotton crossed over to him. Pointing the gun at Bowman's head, he circled behind him, lifting his holstered gun and dropping it into a deep side pocket of his coat. He picked up Bowman's carbine and moved it about eight feet away, well out of Bowman's reach, leaning it upright against the wall.

Some of the tension seemed to have left him now that Bowman had been disarmed. He looked at Johnny. Johnny said, "I ain't got no gun!"

"I believe it," Cotton said. "You ladies ain't armed, are you?"

Abigail Cuttle said, "Certainly not!"

"Good, because things are going to start breaking fast, and I'd hate to have to shoot a woman for trying to play a man's game."

Sid said, "Maybe we should search them anyway. Especially the young one."

"I bet you'd like that," Cotton said.

"She would, too."

"Keep your mind on your work, dammit." Wagging his gun muzzle in Herkimer's direction, Cotton said, "You can put your hands down now."

Herkimer obeyed, gripping the edge of the bar to steady himself.

"This is no holdup," Cotton said. "It's got nothing to do with you—with any of you folks. Just do like you're told, and nobody'll get hurt."

Abigail Cuttle looked mad enough to spit. "Filthy ruffians!"

Sid held a finger before his lips. "Shhh."

Cotton went to the blanket-covered doorway, standing with his back to it. "Everybody act natural, and don't go cutting up any capers. Remember—I'll be watching." Lifting the blanket, he stepped behind it, into the dark storeroom, and let the blanket drop.

Outside, a horse whinnied; footfalls crunched through the snow, approaching. The front door opened, admitting a scarecrow-like figure.

3

A rangy, raggedy man, the newcomer carried a long rifle, an old-fashioned single-shot musket, what was called a squirrel rifle. His hat was weathered to the point of colorlessness and battered to near shapelessness. Wrapped around his shoulders and upper body, serape-style, was a dark green horse blanket. Beneath it could be seen a threadbare gray military tunic—Confederate gray.

He wore no belt gun, no sidearm. In its place, worn over his hip, was an outsized Bowie-style knife with a foot-long blade buried in its leather sheath.

Standing at the bar, Sid and Trench eyed him. The stranger beat his arms and stamped his feet, shaking off snow. He looked as if he'd done some hard traveling.

He wavered, blank-faced, eyes fogging. The spell passed, and his vision cleared, focusing on the bar and the brown half-gallon jug set atop it. He made a beeline for it, stumbling forward, one arm extended, hand reaching.

He stood at the end of the bar nearer the front door, putting Sid between him and Trench and the two of them between him and the blanket-covered storeroom doorway. He leaned the upright musket against the bar.

His voice a croak, he said, "Whiskey!"

Herkimer looked at Sid, who nodded. Herkimer shuffled forward, smiling weakly. Setting a tin cup on the bar, he fumbled with the jug. His hands shook.

"Hell, man, let me have it before you spill some," the stranger said in a Texas twang that buzzed like a sawmill.

Hooking a finger through the neckhole, he hefted the jug, bending his forearm under it to support the weight. He tilted it back, gulping greedily.

When he put down the jug, he was red-faced, breathless. He looked up, as if taking note of his surroundings for the first time.

He was young, in his early twenties. His face was long, sharp-featured, with a knife-blade nose. Guileless-seeming sky-blue eyes contrasted with something in the set of his mouth and chin that was both hard and sly.

Surveying the scene, his gaze flickered across Sid and Trench, gliding past Abigail Cuttle to fall on Francine. It stayed there, eyes widening, then narrowing in appraisal, looking her up and down. He grinned, showing a mouthful of white teeth. Francine looked away. The stranger glanced at Johnny, then took a longer look at Bowman, sitting with his hands folded on the table.

When he looked back at the bar, Sid was sidling up, ready to get in his face. Trench pressed in, crowding behind him.

Smiling nastily, too casual, Sid said, "You know, mister, I don't appreciate your slobbering all over that jug. Others have to drink from it, too."

The stranger used the edge of his sleeve to wipe off the mouth of the jug. He slid the jug across the bar toward Sid.

"I don't want to drink something that's got your spit in it," Sid said.

The stranger slid the jug back toward himself. "Sounds like you're spoiling for a fight, *hombre*."

"You got one?"

"More'n you can handle."

Sid's grin widened, his eyes ringed by a net of wrinkles. "You talk big."

"I'm through talking."

"You don't know how right you are, Grimes. That's your name, ain't it? Grimes?"

"Who wants to know?"

"Shofter. Sid Shofter. Maybe you heard of me."

"Nope," the stranger said, shaking his head.

"If you had, you'd be quaking in your boots right now," Sid went on.

Grimes said, "I never heard of you, but you heard of me. How is that?"

"Then you are Grimes," Sid pressed

"That's right."

"I heard of you, Grimes. Somebody told me you've been living too long."

"Who?"

"Never mind who. You can wonder about it on your way to hell," Sid said.

His right hand flashed for his gun, even as Grimes was jostling the musket, shoving it at him. For an instant, Sid got tangled up in it, stalling his draw.

The big woodsman's knife in hand, Grimes closed with Sid. His free hand clamped down atop Sid's gun hand, keeping him from pulling his gun from his holster. He stepped on one of Sid's feet, pinning him in place while he knifed him in the belly, burying the blade deep.

It was done before the musket hit the floor.

Grimes worked in close, so that his face and Sid's were inches apart. Sid's eyes bulged as if they were going to pop out of his head. He would have fallen if Grimes had not been holding him up with the knife.

Trench stared, slack-jawed with stupefaction. Cursing,

Cotton charged out of the back room, entangling himself in the blanket. He tore wildly at it, stepping forward, waving his gun.

"Damn! Can't get a clear shot! Move aside, Trench!"

As before, Bowman continued sitting with his hands placed backs up on the table. Cupped in the palm of his hand was the squat lump of a double-barreled derringer. Earlier, when Grimes had first entered, Bowman had used the distraction to free the concealed weapon from its inner-sleeve holster, palming it.

Now, he raised his hand off the table, bringing the derringer into play, pointing it at Cotton as he came crashing through the doorway. Cotton saw it but not fast enough to do anything about it before Bowman fired.

A single shot took Cotton square in the middle of the face, dropping him.

Shaking off his paralysis, Trench clawed for his gun. Pulling his knife out of Sid, Grimes sidestepped and in one smooth flowing motion slung the blade in an underhanded throw at Trench.

It pierced his throat, lodging in the center of his bull neck. Trench swayed, gun forgotten, massive hands fluttering helplessly around his chest. He leaned forward, choking and sputtering, blood filling his gaping mouth.

Lurching sideways, he staggered toward the side door. Shouldering into it, he knocked it off its hinges and out the doorway. He followed, trampling it underfoot. A half-dozen paces more, and Trench collapsed, falling facedown in the snow.

Inside, Cotton and Sid lay sprawled on the dirt floor.

To no one in particular, Grimes said, "Nice friendly folks you got around here!"

4

Cold air rushed through the open doorway into the station, breaking up the puff of gunsmoke from Bowman's derringer, scattering it to the far corners of the room. Breaking up the stink of cordite, blood, and worse.

Abigail Cuttle and Francine stood holding on to each other. Francine was white-faced, trembling. The older woman was pale, but her expression was grimly satisfied. She looked like a bird of prey. Johnny stood blank-faced, cracking his knuckles, fidgeting. Herkimer's face was dripping with sweat, and he panted for breath as if he'd just run a race.

Bowman moved forward into the light. For the first time, Grimes focused on Bowman's cavalry hat. His lips quivered with distaste.

Grimes said, "Saved by a Yankee—and a bluebelly at that!"

"I won't tell Jeff Davis if you won't," Bowman said.

Grimes scowled. "Careful how you toss around that name, mister."

"The war's over—or hadn't you heard?"

Bowman stood, arm at his side, holding the derringer muzzle down.

Grimes said, "Who were they?"

Picking up a filthy bar rag, oblivious to its condition,

Herkimer used it to mop his sweaty face. "Who were they? Don't you know?"

Grimes shook his head. "Never saw them before in my life."

"They sure seemed to know you!"

"That they did," Grimes said, looking thoughtful. "Now, why do you suppose that is?"

Bowman went to Cotton, dropping to one knee beside him. He reached into the dead man's coat pocket and removed the gun that Cotton had taken from him. Not wanting to reveal the secret of his inner-sleeve holder, he dropped the derringer into an inside breast pocket of his jacket. He rose, holstering the big gun.

The body lay on its side. Bowman toed it, flipping Cotton over onto his back. The wet red wreck of his face drew winces from Herkimer and a shuddered intake of breath from Francine. Nodding, Grimes smiled encouragingly at her.

Hunkering down, Bowman began going through the dead man's pockets, turning them out. Somewhere in the folds of his garments metal clinked.

A buttoned-down vest pocket yielded a plum-sized rawhide pouch, secured at the mouth by a pulled drawstring. Bowman held it in his palm, weighing it. It had a nice heft to it.

Opening the pouch, he spilled some gold coins into his hand. The coins glinted, molten with reflected firelight, glimmering. All eyes in the room were on that gold.

The pouch also held some silver coins and greenbacks. All told, there was about two hundred dollars in gold and another fifty or so in silver and paper money.

Bowman put it all back into the pouch, stowing it out

of sight in an inside pocket. The absence of the gleaming coins made the room seem darker.

Huffing and puffing, Abigail Cuttle said, "Well, I never! Robbing the dead!"

"He's got no use for it," Bowman said. "Besides, he probably robbed it from somebody else."

Grimes took a step forward. "You know him?"

"Only from wanted posters. He's Dawes Cotton—or at least, he was. He's wanted for killing a man in Black Creek." Bowman turned to Abigail Cuttle. "That ought to put me in Bragg's good graces. Or is that *gold* graces? There's a price on Cotton's head, what's left of it, and I mean to collect it. Maybe you can handle the introductions, ma'am."

She said, "Bah!"

"Well, I wasn't really counting on it," Bowman said.

Grimes snickered. "I was wondering why you tied into something that wasn't your fight. Now it all makes sense. You killed him to collect the bounty on him."

"Maybe so."

"No maybes about it."

"The big question is, why did he want to kill you?" Bowman asked.

"He's an outlaw, a killer. That's what his kind do."

"They were waiting for you. Knew you were coming. Knew your name."

"It's a mystery." Pushing back his hat, Grimes scratched his head. "Well, this one's mine," he said, squatting down beside Sid "Whew, what a mess! Good thing this is a dirt floor, to soak up all that blood."

Sid's gun was in its holster. Much of the fancy rig was blood-soaked but not the gun and holster. Grimes reached for the gun, starting to slide it clear of the holster.

In an eyeblink, Bowman's gun was in his hand, covering Grimes.

Grimes froze, holding the gun halfway out of the holster. Eyes wide, he said, "Whew! Fast!"

Herkimer cleared his throat, rasped, "Walk soft, gents. There's been enough killing for one night."

"Easy, mister, easy," Grimes said, letting go of the gun. His hand came up empty. "I'm just relieving this poor sinner of his burdens, starting with his gun. You know, like you did with yours."

Bowman said, "I get jumpy when somebody pulls a gun when I'm not looking."

Grimes colored, starting to get hot. "If I pull a gun on you, mister, it won't be behind your back. I'll be looking right straight at you."

"That's a comfort," Bowman said dryly. "Even so, I'd hate to have to shoot you after saving your life."

Grimes frowned, his lynx eyes narrowed, calculating. Resentful. "Who says you saved my life?"

Bowman glanced at Cotton. "He does."

"That's a matter of opinion. The way I see it, I could've handled all three of them by myself," Grimes said.

"That how you see it?"

"That's right." Grimes's face set in hard, stubborn lines. "Anyhow, I don't recall asking you to go mixing in my fight. You got in, that's your choice. You just did it to collect the bounty."

"I could've shot him after he shot you. Would've been safer that way for me."

"Why didn't you?"

"Maybe I like the idea of having a Johnny Reb owe his

life to a damned Yankee." Bowman's eyes glittered, his grin sardonic.

"From where I sit, Mr. Bluebelly, I don't owe you nothing!"

Bowman eased down the hammer, reholstering the gun. "Go on, take the gun. The way you make friends, you're going to need it."

Some of the quivering tension had left Grimes's frame when Bowman put away the gun. Grimes said, "I'll take it, but not on your say-so. This one's mine. Everything he owns belongs to me. Same goes for the one outside, the big man."

Bowman said nothing. Grimes said, "I'm going to pick up the gun right now. I'm telling you first, so you won't get jumpy."

"Much obliged."

Gingerly, eyes on the other, Grimes drew the gun, careful not to point it in Bowman's direction. But Bowman had already turned away and was moving toward the bar. Grimes returned to plundering Sid.

Abigail Cuttle said, looking from Bowman to Grimes and back again, "A fine pair of ghouls! Robbing the dead!"

"Hell, I didn't even like him when he was alive," Grimes said. "Not that I got to know him too well, in the short time we had together."

Three tin cups filled with varying amounts of whiskey stood upright on the bar, where they'd been set down for the last time by Cotton, Sid, and Trench. Trench's cup was empty, drained of every drop.

Ignoring them, Bowman said, "Whiskey."

Behind the bar, Herkimer shook off his torpor and began moving clumsily, heavily, thick-fingered hands groping.

Bowman said, "Give me a clean cup." Herkimer fumbled around behind the bar until Bowman pointed out a cup on a shelf. The station master set it down on the bar. Bowman picked it up, eyeing it. "Okay." Reaching for the jug, he patted it fondly. "Thank God this wasn't spilt."

"Amen," Herkimer said, licking his lips.

Glancing at Grimes, Bowman wiped his sleeve against the bottle mouth before pouring. Grimes was too busy picking over Sid's belongings to notice. Bowman poured and drank.

Grimes went through Sid's pockets with a light touch, a fine hand. With wild tufts of hair jutting out above his ears under his hat, his feral eyes, and nimble hands, he reminded Bowman more and more of a lynx.

The discovery of several gold coins forced from Grimes a cry that was somewhere between a yelp and a whoop. His joyful expression flattened when a further search failed to discover anything more than a handful of silver.

Bowman said casually, "Those gold coins looked new."

Grimes glanced up. "What's it to you?"

"What's it to you, that's the question. Cotton had some some brand shiny new gold coins on him, too. Most likely, those coins came from the same source. Could be that's the money they were paid to kill you."

Grimes scoffed, but his eyes were wary. "Why would anybody pay to kill me?"

"You tell me," Bowman said.

"Mister, I wouldn't tell you nothing, even if I did know, which I don't." Still, Grimes looked troubled. After a pause, he shook it off.

He rose from where he was hunkered down beside Sid. His hands were red-stained. He started to wipe them against the side of his pants, saw Francine was watching him, and decided not to.

He crossed to the side door, exiting. Bowman followed, standing in the doorway. The storm had broken, the snow tapering off to a light dusting of flakes falling lazily from the skies. The clouds were thinning, coming apart.

A pale crescent moon floated into view, veiled by rushing clouds. Its horns ripped open a seam in the cloud canopy, venting moonlight on a glazed landscape of wet whiteness and blue shadows.

A half-dozen paces from the doorway lay Trench, stretched out facedown in the snow. Beside him, down on one knee, Grimes was retrieving his knife. Loosing it from Trench's neck, he wiped both sides of the blade clean on the big man's shoulder, then slipped it into its belt sheath.

Using one of Trench's arms as a lever, Grimes flipped him over onto his back. The dead man's eyes were open, staring.

Grimes turned out Trench's pockets, finding only a handful of coins and some paper money. After pocketing that, he washed his hands in the snow, cleaning them as best he could, then wiping them dry on his pants.

He came back inside. At the bar stood Johnny, draining what was left in the dead men's cups, gulping it down. Catching his eye, Grimes said, "My horse is tied up to the rail out front. How about taking care of him?"

Johnny hesitated, looking at Herkimer. Grimes jingled the coins in his pocket, said, "I can pay—now."

Herkimer nodded. Johnny pulled on his hat and coat, picked up a lantern.

Standing beside the seated Francine, Abigail Cuttle pointed a bony forefinger at the corpses. Looking at

Herkimer, she said, "What're you going to do about them?"

"There's nothing to do, ma'am. They're dead."

"I know that, you idiot! But you can't just leave them there. It's heathen, ungodly."

"Reckon you're right. They'll keep in the shed out back." Herkimer came out from behind the bar. "Give me a hand, Johnny."

Grimes said, "What about Buttercup?"

Herkimer said, "Buttercup? Who's Buttercup?"

"That's my horse."

"We'll take care of it as soon as we get these two squared away."

"They're dead, Buttercup's not. It ain't right to keep that poor horse shivering out there in the cold and snow. Besides, I'm paying. Those stiffs ain't."

Herkimer said thoughtfully, "Well, when you put it that way . . ."

Stepping forward, Abigail Cuttle said, "If you don't get those two dead bodies out of my sight right now, I'll take a horsewhip to you!"

"That tears it," Herkimer said. "We'll get rid of this mess, and then Johnny'll stable your horse, friend."

Grimes said, "I'll help with the toting, while Johnny tends to Buttercup."

"All right."

Johnny picked up the lamp and went outside. Herkimer circled around, standing at Cotton's feet. "Let's start with him."

Indicating Sid, Grimes said, "He's closer to the door."

"This one's less messy."

Grimes moved to Cotton's head. Looking at Bowman, he said, "How about pitching in and helping? Hell, you killed him."

"I don't care if he stays here or not. It doesn't bother me," Bowman said.

Herkimer grabbed Cotton's ankles, and Grimes grabbed his wrists. Together, they hefted the body off the floor, straining.

"Heavy bastard," Grimes muttered.

Pushing off from the bar, Bowman picked up Cotton's hat off the floor, covering the dead man's face with it. "Now the decencies have been observed," he said.

Grimes shot him a dirty look. Staggering under the weight, he and Herkimer made for the door, lugging Cotton outside and dropping him just beyond the sight-lines of the open doorway.

Herkimer said, "We'll put 'em in the shed later. For now, let's just get them outside, to quiet that old crow."

From inside, Abigail Cuttle cried, "I heard that!"

Voice low, talking under his breath, Grimes said, "I do believe she would've taken a horsewhip to you at that."

"I never doubted it," Herkimer said.

From around the front corner of the building came Johnny, lamp in hand, leading by the reins a tough, rangy yellow pony. He and the animal ambled across the yard to the barn.

Herkimer and Grimes entered the station, emerging a moment later with Sid's body borne between them. Sid was much lighter than Cotton, enabling them to move more quickly. After dumping him beside Cotton, they went back inside.

They were met by Abigail Cuttle, who demanded, "Now, fix that door! It's freezing in here!"

5

The side door had been torn from its frame but was otherwise intact. Herkimer had wedged it back in place, driving fresh nails through the leather hinges fastening it to the jambs. Cold air seeped in through the cracks where the door failed to butt up perfectly against the frame, but the fire in the hearth kept it at bay.

The door was on the east side of the building, while the wind blew mostly from the northwest. Still, every now and then, a stray gust shivered the door against its frame.

As the night wore on, the fire burned low, and the station room got darker and colder.

Bowman slept lightly, bobbing restlessly in the shallows of sleep. He sat slumped in a wooden chair near the fire, wrapped in a greatcoat whose folds served to cushion somewhat the rigors of the unpadded chair. His hat was pulled down over his face, in such a manner that he could still peer out from below the brim.

The wind, the crackling of the fire, the noises of the station settling on its foundation, and the sounds of the other sleepers grouped around the hearth all made a pattern. A lulling pattern.

Every now and then, Bowman would start awake, listening intently for the source of what had stirred him. A sleeper's groan, an ember popping, the creak of a floorboard. Always the sounds were of a piece, part of the pattern, signaling no imminent threat. Eventually, he would drift back into that floating twilight of half wakefulness, half sleep.

Cold closed in around Bowman, his limbs stiffening, forcing him up from the dark. He stirred, sat up, wincing, sore and uncomfortable. Tilting up his hat brim, he looked around. The fire had burned low, its pale embers shedding a muted, murky orange-brown glow. In it he could see the subtly molded forms of the others.

Occupying a nearby table, Grimes sat leaning forward, arms folded on the tabletop, head pillowed atop them. His face was hidden, his breathing slow, regular.

Standing against the east wall, near the fire, was a long wooden bench shared by Abigail Cuttle and Francine. The bench's hardness was softened by a rug that had been thrown over it and by blankets that wrapped the women's sleeping forms. They sat at opposite ends of the bench. Francine lay curled on her side with her legs together, knees bent. Abigail Cuttle lay with her back propped up against an arm of the bench, with one foot on the seat and the other on the floor.

Out of sight behind the blanketed doorway, in a small room opposite the storeroom, Herkimer slept on a cot, snoring away. Earlier, when the sleeping arrangements were being made, he'd offered to let the women use his room, a suggestion that had been nixed after Abigail Cuttle had taken a quick, hard look at the space, a small, sooty cubicle warmed by a smoky wood-burning stove.

Johnny was bunking out in the barn, where he had a little place fixed up for himself.

Shrugging his coat off his shoulders and onto the

back of the chair, Bowman rose. His back was stiff, his limbs heavy. He stretched, trying to work out some of the kinks.

He crossed to the fire, soft-footing it, the dirt floor further muffling his light tread. Taking up a poker, he stirred up the ashy embers, coaxing a handful of smoldering coals into hot brightness. On them he placed a few split logs. Hunkered down by the fire, he tended it until the logs were blazing nicely, then stacked some more fresh logs atop them.

Basking warmth radiated from the flames in waves. He rose, standing with a hand resting on the slab-rock mantle.

Abigail Cuttle sat at the far end of the bench, facing him. Her back was braced against the bench arm, her raised legs bent at the knees, the soles of her shoes planted on the seat. Her head was tilted back, cording her neck so that it looked like a slim, vine-wrapped tree trunk. Her long face was taut, leathery, like a piece of sun-dried fruit.

She was snoring, her knife-blade nose vibrating, nostrils quivering. It was a high-pitched sound, irritated and waspish.

At the near end of the bench slept Francine. Her folded arm rested on the blanket-cushioned armrest, her head in her hand. Masses of honeyed hair, gilded by firelight, spilled across her shoulders and upper arms. In sleep, her ripe mouth had lost its sullen pout.

Glancing at Grimes, he saw that the other's face was no longer buried in his folded arms but was turned to one side, toward Bowman. From behind long, spiky tendrils of hair that fell across his face, Grimes's eyes were glittering slits. They were so narrowed that they might have been mistaken for being closed, if not for the betraying gleam of firelight reflected by the orbs.

He was motionless, the monotous rhythm of his deep, slow breathing continuing uninterrupted.

The fire was burning good and hot now. Bowman crossed to his chair and sat down, wrapping himself in his coat. Slumping, resting the back of his head against the top of the back of the chair, Bowman tilted his hat over his face, again leaving a space through which he could peer.

Grimes's head had moved so that his face was still turned toward Bowman. His eyes were almost closed, slitted. His breathing rose and fell, counterfeiting the rhythms of sleep.

Time passed. The fire burned brightly, toasty warm.

After a while, Grimes's eyes closed all the way.

When Bowman next awoke, the fire had once again burned low, bringing a return of the cold. But the darkness had lessened. Shuttered east windows were outlined with pearly gray-white light. Outside, a bird chirped, its cries harsh yet plaintive. A lonesome sound.

The side door opened, and Johnny came in, carrying a bucket of water. For an instant, the open doorway showed cheerless predawn light before Johnny closed the door behind him.

After setting the bucket down on the hearth's stone apron, he went around the room, opening the shutters. The interior's charcoal-colored gloom lightened to ash gray.

From behind the blanket-covered doorway emerged Herkimer, hastily pulling on a shirt, covering the upper half of the red woolen long underwear that could be seen above the top of his pants. Yawning, he scratched his pot-belly and flanks with both hands. "Good morning!"

As loudly as he boomed it, it was a wake-up call. The others stirred.

Grimes lifted his head from his folded arms, his lynx eyes bleary. Sitting back, he used his fingers as a comb to brush the long hair away from his face.

A groan announced the awakening of Abigail Cuttle. Herkimer started toward her. "You all right, ma'am?"

"Certainly not! I barely slept a wink all night," she said. "Who could sleep in this house of rogues, knaves, and fools, wondering every instant if we're going to have our throats cut!"

She swung her feet to the floor, sitting up. Pain spasmed across her face. She clapped a hand to the small of her back.

"Oh, my aching back! I'll be lucky if a night on this bench hasn't crippled me!"

Francine sat up, arms unfurling, hands raised over her head, stretching luxuriantly. The blankets fell to her waist. Her dress was pulled taut, outlining her shapely figure.

Stifling a moan, shaky, Abigail Cuttle rose. She lurched, shooting out a clawlike hand to clutch an arm-rest, steadying herself. Herkimer moved toward her, but she fended him off, holding out her free hand palm up.

"I can take care of myself very well, thank you," she said through clenched teeth.

Herkimer said, "Just trying to help out, ma'am."

"You can help by making it possible for us to be on our way as soon as possible!"

"It'll be a pleasure."

Abigail Cuttle gave him a sharp look. "I wonder what you meant by that."

"I don't mean nothing at all, ma'am, nothing at all," Herkimer said.

"I can well believe it."

"You can leave anytime you like. Say the word, and I'll have Johnny hitch up the carriage for you," Herkimer said. "But it'd be a whole lot safer if you had an escort taking you into town. Like last night showed, there's a lot of bad *hombres* in this part of the territory. Two women alone, well, if you ride into trouble again, there'd be no one to help you."

Grimes pushed back his chair and rose. "I'd be proud to see you two ladies safely to Black Creek."

"Hah!" Abigail Cuttle said. "And who's going to protect us from *you?*"

"Just the same, the offer's open," Grimes said, speaking directly to Francine. He smiled at her, a friendly enough smile but one that showed a little too much tooth in it. He looked hungry.

Francine looked interested.

Abigail Cuttle stepped between her and Grimes, breaking eye contact between the two.

Herkimer said, "Fellow named Pike Cobb runs a freight wagon between Zenith and Black Creek. He passes here most days, about an hour after sunup. You can ride in with him. You can trust him, Cobb's a good man."

"I was starting to despair of finding one in these parts," Abigail Cuttle said.

"While you're waiting, you can have breakfast. I'll have Johnny rustle some up."

Bowman said, "You can rustle some up for me, too."

"And me," Grimes said.

Johnny stoked the fire, feeding it. Casting a jaundiced

eye on the pile of split logs in the corner, Herkimer said, "You all sure used up a heap of firewood last night."

Nobody said anything. Johnny splashed some of the water from the bucket into an iron pot, putting it on to boil.

Bowman made for the side door. He wanted air and a chance to stretch his legs. Outside, it was wet and raw. The snow had all melted away, baring sodden ground. It was still cold, though. The sky was closed in by low clouds. Rain fell, a rain so fine it was like mist. Mist rose in curtains from the winding streambed, pouring upward from dark waters.

The dead bodies were nowhere in sight, having been moved the night before into one of the sheds behind the building.

Bowman walked around, shaking his arms and legs, trying to work out some of the stiffness. Halting, he held his hands out in front of him, studying them. They were steady enough.

"Not bad, after all that bad whiskey I soaked up last night," he said. Reaching for a cigar, he discovered he was all out of them. Too bad—he could have used a smoke.

He stamped around for another minute or two, then went inside.

Breakfast consisted of bacon, ham, fried potatoes, and fresh-brewed coffee. "Sorry, no eggs," Herkimer said. "Farmer comes by with 'em once or twice a week, but the last of them is all used up."

The women sat at one table, Grimes at another, Bowman at a third. Abigail Cuttle positioned Francine so that she was sitting with her back to Grimes.

One thing the older woman couldn't resist, however, was the call of nature. A whole lot of squirming and

fidgeting went by before she rose from the table and
crossed to where Herkimer sat. Uncharacteristically, she
put her mouth close to his ear and from behind her
hand whispered a question.

"It's out back," Herkimer boomed. Gesturing with his
thumb toward the blanketed doorway, he said, "Go
through there and out the back door. It's right outside."
Abigail Cuttle hastily departed the scene, scurrying
beyond the blanketed doorway, out of sight.

Grimes rose and went to Francine's table. "Howdy."

Not looking up, Francine picked at her food. "I'm not
supposed to talk to strangers."

"I can fix that. I'm Jed—Jed Grimes."

"Francine Leland."

"That wasn't so hard, was it? Now that we know each
other, mind if I sit down?" He rested a hand on the back
of the chair.

Francine said doubtfully, "I don't think Miz Abigail
would like that."

"I know she wouldn't," Grimes said.

Francine laughed. Encouraged, Grimes pulled out
the chair and sat down. Francine looked serious. "If Miz
Abigail catches you—"

"I guess we still got a minute or two before she comes
back," Grimes said. He moved his chair closer to hers,
leaning toward her. "She kin to you?"

Francine looked surprised, then burst out laughing.
"Miz Abigail kin to me? Not hardly! Does she look like
she could be kin to me?"

"No, she don't, and that's a fact. That's why I was asking. It didn't seem natural that she could be kin to a pretty
girl like you."

"You trying to sweet-talk me?"

"It ain't sweet-talking to tell the truth."

Francine shrugged. She glanced in the direction Abigail Cuttle had gone.

"If you don't mind my asking," Grimes said, "what's she to you, anyhow?"

"I don't mind," Francine said. "Miz Abigail lives in Black Creek. She's real big in the church, the Ladies Aid Society. They've got a branch in Black Creek and one in Zenith, where I come from. She's always running back and forth between the churches, doing good deeds and charity work and such."

"Meaning no disrespect, but from what I've seen of her, she don't exactly seem like she's overly charitable, if you get my drift."

"She's strict and set in her ways, but she means well, I guess," Francine said. "She does lots of volunteer work. She's taking me to Black Creek, to live with my aunt and uncle."

"What about your folks?" Grimes asked.

"My pa just died, a couple of weeks ago."

Grimes looked appropriately solemn. "I'm sorry to hear that."

Francine looked aside, sighing. "He'd been sick for a long time. As for my ma, she died a long time ago, when I was a little girl. When Pa died, the pastor said it wasn't fitting for me to live by myself. Aunt Hattie and Uncle Luke are taking me in. He was real good to me and Pa when Pa was sick. Aunt Hattie's kind of frail and not much for travel, so Uncle Luke used to ride over to Zenith regularly to make sure we were getting by all right. That's a long ride, especially in winter."

"You're going to live in Black Creek?"

Francine nodded. "Yes."

"Ain't that something," Grimes said, pleased. "I'm going to Black Creek, too."

"To live? Or just passing through?"

"I don't rightly know," Grimes said. "I've got some business to take care of there." He grinned. "I don't want to puff it up into more than it is. An uncle I didn't even know died and left me a little piece of property near town. It probably won't amount to much, but I'll take a look-see at it, find out what I got. Maybe I can sell it for a few dollars. Hey, I just thought of something. You're going to Black Creek on account of your uncle, and I'm going on account of mine. Now, that's what I call a coincidence!"

"Maybe it's fate," Francine said, giving him a sidelong glance.

"It's possible," Grimes said.

"Maybe you'll find something or someone that'll make you want to stay in Black Creek, hmmm?"

"Maybe I already have," Grimes said, moving his chair closer to hers.

Francine's gaze was downcast, her expression demure. "Oh?"

"Maybe I could call on you sometime, in Black Creek."

"You're not afraid of my uncle?"

"Francine, the only person I'm afraid of is that Cuttle woman!"

"Then you'd better get moving, because here she comes."

Emerging from behind the blanketed archway, Abigail Cuttle cast a cold eye on the two young people and bore down on them. Grimes rose, smiling, stepping back. Abigail Cuttle said, "What's all this?"

"Not a thing, ma'am, not a danged thing." Grimes held his hands in front of him, palms up.

"Hmph! Make sure that it stays that way," she said.

Francine's sullen pout, which had vanished during her chat with Grimes, had now returned. "I was thanking him for protecting us from those outlaws and killers last night, Miz Abigail."

Abigail Cuttle flashed a look of scorn. "Protecting us? You silly girl! He was the reason we were in danger in the first place. If he hadn't come here, none of this would have happened."

Francine wouldn't be moved. "I think he's very brave."

"Bah!"

Grimes retreated to his table. Approaching it, he saw Bowman looking at him and said, "What're you grinning at?"

Bowman said, "That arrow in your chest."

"Huh? What you talking 'bout?"

"Cupid's arrow. Right through the heart."

"What business is it of yours, anyhow?" Grimes asked hotly.

"None," Bowman said. He drank some coffee.

Grimes gripped the edge of Bowman's table, leaning across it, thrusting his face forward. "You shouldn't go around listening to other folks' conversations. Maybe it's time somebody taught you to mind your own business—"

"She seems like a nice girl," Bowman said. "I think she likes you."

"—and I'm just the fellow to do it, and—" Grimes did a take. "You think she likes me?"

"While you were talking to her, she stopped sulking and starting smiling, for the first time I've seen her," Bowman said.

"She did, didn't she?"

"She thinks you're a hero, Grimes. Well, she's young. Don't do anything to spoil the illusion."

"So you think she likes me," Grimes went on, dreamy-eyed.

"Yes," Bowman said. "And I think somebody *doesn't* like you, too."

"The Cuttle woman, but she ain't even kin to Francine, so that's no problem."

"Not her," Bowman said. "Whoever's trying to kill you."

"There is that," Grimes said. "But what do you care whether I get killed or not? I don't hardly figure you to be any more charitable than her." He indicated Abigail Cuttle.

Bowman said, "You're good for business, Grimes. My business."

"What business is that? Bounty hunting?" Grimes asked.

"It is for now, so long as it stays profitable. Someone wants you dead so bad that they're willing to pay a couple of hundred dollars in gold to some hired guns. You already flushed out Dawes Cotton, and he's worth cash money. For whatever reason, you're a magnet for bad-men. Maybe some more'll come out of the woodwork to try for your scalp, wanted men with big-money prices on their heads."

"And if they do," Grimes said, "you figure on being there to collect it."

"That's right."

"Be careful you don't get caught in the crossfire. You could get killed that way."

"I'll be very careful," Bowman said.

Grimes started to move away, then turned back. "Why would they want to kill me?"

"Remains to be seen," Bowman said. "If you live long enough, you might find out."

A rumble of hoofbeats and wagon wheels approached, clattering to a halt outside the front of the station.

Herkimer said, "That's Cobb now."

Through the front door came Pike Cobb. He was middle-aged, medium-sized, thick in the arms and chest, thicker in the belly. The front brim of his sand-colored hat was worn pinned back to the crown, wagoneer-style. Where it wasn't covered by bristly beard stubble the color and texture of steel wool, his face was ruddy, sun-seamed.

A brown corduroy coat was worn open, its big, round, brown leather buttons left unfastened. Baggy gray trousers were tucked into the tops of knee-high, brown leather lace-up work boots. Holstered on his right hip was a gun as big as a plow handle. Most of the rest of the gunbelt was hidden under his sloping belly.

He went to the bar. Raising a hand in greeting to Herkimer, he said, "Johnny tells me you had some excitement last night."

"Some," Herkimer said.

"Give me some of that good coffee and tell me about it," Cobb said.

Herkimer fetched a cup of steaming hot coffee, stiffening it with a generous splash from a brown jug of whiskey.

Cobb held it under his lumpy nose, inhaling, the whiskey-laden fumes bringing tears to his eyes. Gratefully, he sipped at it, smacking his lips. Herkimer put his head close to Cobb's and started talking, low-voiced, filling him in about what had happened the night before.

Cobb looked up, eyeing Bowman, then Grimes, then glancing away. As Herkimer continued, Cobb glanced at the duo a couple more times. Cobb drained his cup, and Herkimer refilled it.

Bowman rose, crossing to the bar. "Mr. Cobb? The name's Bowman."

Cobb nodded, said, "Howdy."

"I hear tell you're a freight hauler."

Cobb thought about it for a second before nodding yes.

"I've got a proposition for you," Bowman said. "A business proposition."

Cobb, wary, said, "As long as it don't cost me nothing to listen."

"I'll pay you to haul some freight for me," Bowman said.

"Freight? What kind of freight?" Cobb asked.

Bowman said, "Well . . ."

6

The rain had stopped, but moisture beaded all. The ground was soft, wet. A brisk west wind blew, breaking up the mist, driving it down to the bottom of the streambed, where the black waters swallowed it up.

In front of the station, a convoy of sorts was forming up. In the lead was Abigail Cuttle's carriage, a light, two-wheeled black gig drawn by a single horse. Behind it was Pike Cobb's wagon, long, deep, flat-bedded, with heavy reinforced springs and undercarriage, harnessed to a four-horse team yoked in tandem.

Hitched to a nearby rail was Bowman's gray gelding, Grimes's yellow horse, a black mare that had belonged to Sid, and Trench's chestnut gelding. Johnny had seen who of the trio had arrived on which horse, settling any potential arguments about rightful ownership.

A third horse, which had belonged to Cotton, remained in the barn. Bowman had sold it and the saddle gear to the station master.

Standing beside the two-wheeled carriage were Abigail Cuttle and Francine. At Francine's feet, a pair of traveling bags, faded and frayed, contained her belongings. The older woman picked up one of Francine's bags and slung it into the carriage, then stowed the other beside it.

Cobb was perched up on the wagon's high seat. Under

the seat, on the floor of the boot, lay a sawed-off, double-barreled shotgun. Biting off a plug of chewing tobacco, Cobb wadded it between his jaws, where it made a walnut-sized knob at the corner of his mouth. He set about chewing, grinding the plug between his teeth.

The wagon was laden with stacked wooden crates covered with tarpaulins and secured by ropes. At its rear, the tailgate was lowered to horizontal.

Cobb spat some tobacco juice onto the left side of the wagon. He was restless, fidgety.

Abigail Cuttle fitted her white, purple-veined, claw-like hands into a pair of thin, wrist-length black leather gloves. She tapped her foot. "What's keeping them?"

"Here they come now," Cobb said, glancing back over his shoulder, "and about time!"

Johnny, Herkimer, Grimes, and Bowman emerged from behind the back of the station, carrying a blanket-wrapped, man-sized bundle. At one end, below the bottom of the wrappings, a pair of booted feet stuck out, oversized clodhoppers.

There were four of them, but they labored to haul the bundle to the rear of the wagon with its lowered gate.

Smelling death, Cobb's team and the gig's lone horse became uneasy. Not so the animals owned by the gunmen. Sid's black mare, Trench's chestnut, Grimes's tawny yellow, and Bowman's gray were used to death; it was nothing new to them.

Crates had been moved to clear a space in the flatbed hopper. The quartet now hefted their bundle, loading it into the back of the wagon. It hit the floorboards with a leaden thud.

Up front, the team leaned into the traces, sidling and pawing the ground with their hooves. But the handbrake was set, and Cobb had a firm grip on the reins. Over his shoulder, he said, "Hurry up! Time's a-wasting."

The four headed back toward the shed. Panting, Herkimer said, "Trench was a big bastard—heavy as hell!"

Bowman said, "Cotton's no lightweight, either."

Cotton was the next wrapped bundle to be loaded into the hopper, followed by Sid.

"That's the last of them," Bowman said. He lifted the tailgate into place, slamming it home and fastening the catch.

After securing the reins, Cobb turned, climbing over the back of the seat into the wagon. With surprising nimbleness, he scrambled across the tops of tarpaulin-wrapped crates. He tugged at ropes and rattled the loading gate, testing the catch.

Grimes said, "I thought you were in a hurry, Cobb."

"I am!"

"Then what're you doing?"

"Making sure that the load is properly stowed and that everything's squared away. You can do real damage if cargo starts sliding and moving around during a run," Cobb said. His work done, he scrambled into the wagon's front seat. "Saddle up, and let's go. I've got a schedule to meet, and I'm already running late!"

Grimes said, "You're getting paid for it—five dollars from Bowman for his and ten for my two. Highway robbery, if you ask me."

"If you don't like it, sonny, take them out and haul them yourself. It's no picnic carting a couple of dead men on horseback from here to Black Creek," Cobb said. "Now, if you and your partner will mount up, we can get moving."

Indicating Bowman, Grimes said, "He's no partner of mine."

Bowman said, "That goes double for me."

Cobb said, "You fellows done jawing? Good, then we can get going."

Grimes said, "I've got to hitch the horses to the wagon."

"More delay!" Cobb complained.

Grimes uncoiled a length of rope, tying one end to the back of the wagon, using it to string along a two-horse file of Buttercup and the chestnut. He gave them a nice, long lead, so they wouldn't be too bunched up with the wagon or each other.

Bowman unhitched the gray from the rail and swung into the saddle.

Grimes stood beside the black, a hand on the saddle horn. Saddle and equipage were made of black leather inlaid with hand-tooled silver. He mounted up. Bowman said, "Changing horses?"

"Buttercup's a trusty little ol' pony, but this black's a thoroughbred," Grimes said.

"Fine-looking animal," Bowman noted. "Looks fast."

"She feels fast." Grimes patted the mare's sleek, well-muscled neck.

"That's some fancy rig, too."

"That Sid was some kind of showboat. Look at these conchos—solid silver. A man could get used to this. I'll sure cut me one fine figure when I ride into town."

Abigail Cuttle occupied the driver's seat in the gig, Francine beside her. The older woman took from a side-mounted iron holder a horsewhip, long, thin, and snaky, like a catfish's whisker. In her other gloved hand, she expertly held the reins.

Standing in front of the station were Johnny and Herkimer. Bowman halted beside them and said, "Watch out. Some friends of the dead men might come by, to find out what happened to them."

"Don't worry," Herkimer said. "I'll just tell them that it was you boys what done for them!"

Grimes said, "Make sure you get my name right: Grimes, Jed Grimes."

"I ain't likely to forget it," the station master affirmed.

This pleased Grimes. "If anybody wants me, tell them I'll be waiting for them in Black Creek."

Bowman pointed his horse toward the western road. "Let's ride."

Bowman and Grimes took the point, riding about a hundred yards ahead of the others. Next came the one-horse gig, followed by Cobb's wagon, with its two-horse string bringing up the rear.

Behind them, the sun climbed the eastern sky but failed to show itself, hiding behind gray clouds. But the weather was turning crisp, dry. The muddy road firmed, hardening, allowing the travelers to make better time.

Ahead lay a vast flat plain, veined by brooks and streams, bisected by Telegraph Road. Open country, grassy. The hardpacked, short-cropped grass was dry, colorless, winter-dormant. What few patches of brush there were grew low to the ground. Scattered across the tableland was a handful of thickets of thin, scraggly timber.

Riding side by side in advance of the others, scouting, were Grimes and Bowman. Bowman said, "This kind of country I like—no place for bushwhackers to hide in."

Grimes said, "A war party of Comanches could be hiding right beside us, and you wouldn't know they were there until they showed themselves."

"Good thing we're not in Comanche country," Bowman said. "Anyway, it's not the Comanches who're after your scalp."

Grimes fell silent, and the conversation lapsed. After a while, he turned his horse and rode back to the gig. Pointing his horse west, he rode abreast of the carriage, on the passenger side, beside Francine.

When he tried to talk with Francine, Abigail Cuttle flailed away at him with the horsewhip, driving him off. Laughing, Grimes urged the black forward, catching up with Bowman, once more falling into step beside him.

He said, "I'd rather tangle with Comanches than with that Cuttle woman!"

Bowman said, "You're a long way off from Texas, Grimes."

"Don't I know it!"

"What brings you to Black Creek?" Bowman asked.

Looking cagey, Grimes countered, "What brings you?"

"I come from around these parts," Bowman said. "You're a long way from home."

"The ol' family spread wasn't much before the war," Grimes said. "Now, it's less than nothing. The pickings are so slim that even Governor Davis and his thieving, carpetbagging Yankee cronies won't touch it. And they've stolen everything in the state that ain't nailed down. Mister, the only home I got is right here, under this hat."

"No kinfolk? What about your people?" Bowman asked.

"Gone. Scattered to the four winds or dead," Grimes

said. "Not that we ever liked each other much in the first place. I was the only one left around. That's why I got Uncle Marsh's inheritance."

"Who?"

"Obed Marsh. Distant kin, an uncle I didn't know I had until I got a letter from his lawyer saying he was dead."

"Well, you can't miss what you never had," Bowman said. "He leave you any money?"

"Not a cent," Grimes said cheerfully. "All I come into is a piece of property called Bittersink Basin."

"Never heard of it."

"Nobody has," Grimes said. "According to the lawyer, the land wasn't even being worked at the time of my uncle's death, which tells you what the property's worth."

Bowman said, "The railroad's coming through Black Creek. If your land's along the right of way, it could be valuable. Even if it's not, it could still be worth something. The line is going to put that town on the map."

"I thought of that. I already did some checking," Grimes said. "The land's about an hour's ride outside of town, out in the middle of nowhere, according to the map."

They rode on for a few more miles.

"Was anybody trying to kill you before you became an inheritor?" Bowman asked.

Grimes said, "No more than usual. You know, there's a lot of bad *hombres* around." He looked at Bowman. "Why?"

Bowman said, "A man inherits a piece of property, and suddenly strangers are trying to kill him. Paid gunman, hired killers. Seems like there could be a connection."

"Hmm . . . maybe that piece of property is worth something after all!"

• • •

The flat was broken by a ridge, a man-high hummock running north-south. More ridges appeared, all running north-south. They were low, neat, and widely spaced apart, land waves rippling across a sea of dun-brown dead grass.

As the group moved farther west, the ridges became higher and wider, the shallow troughs between the crests lessening. But the ridges were never too high, more mounds than hills. This was low, flat country.

No longer simply a straight line, the road curved right or left as needed, following the contours of the landscape, threading the gaps between the ridges. With some few exceptions, this was the route the railroad would eventually follow.

An hour before midday, the travelers topped a ridge, and Black Creek came into view. They halted, the two-wheeled gig, freight wagon, and riders all bunched up together.

Below lay a broad, saddle-shaped valley. Entering from the northwest, a river wound across the plain, exiting toward the southeast. It was the central trunk line of an extensive watercourse whose roots and branches were streams and rivulets honeycombing the floor of the divide.

In the middle distance, on the far side of the river, sited on a flat-topped rise, lay Black Creek town. A clock tower and church spire stuck out of the jumble of cubed buildings and peaked roofs.

A road ran downhill, across the valley, over a bridge spanning the river, and into town.

Grimes sat on his horse beside Cobb, perched on the high wagon seat. A hand-rolled cigarette dangled from Grimes's lower lip. He said, "What's that river down there?"

Cobb snorted. "Don't you know nothing? That's Black Creek!"

"That's no creek, it's a river."

"It's Black Creek all the same."

Grimes laughed, a harsh crow caw. "A river that thinks it's a creek! You Yankees can't even name a river straight."

"We whupped the South," Cobb said. "That's straight enough, ain't it?"

Grimes gave him a hard look. "You know, mister, you got a rough tongue on you. I don't know why I waste my time talking to you."

Cobb reminded him: "Because you wanted to borrow a match, remember?"

"Uh, right . . ."

Cobb fished a wooden match from his shirt pocket, extending it to Grimes, who had to lean out of the saddle to reach it. "Here."

"Thanks," Grimes said. He struck the white phosphorus-tipped match against a row of silver studs serving as part of the saddle's decorative border trim. It sputtered into flame, flaring, hissing. He set fire to the end of the cigarette.

On the seat beside Cobb lay a blacksnake whip, wound into several coils. He took hold of it, his body between Grimes and the whip, so the other couldn't see what he was doing. Grimes was looking elsewhere, anyway.

While Grimes puffed away, Cobb was stealthily easing the whip into position, shaking out the coils. Suddenly, he lashed out, cracking the whip, snapping it into an air-borne S curve, its forked tongue popping the cigarette out of Grimes's mouth and sending it flying.

Grimes jerked; the horse started, rearing. Grimes got the mare's four hooves back on the ground, gentled the animal.

Bowman rode up, reined in. "What's the trouble?"

"No trouble at all," Cobb said, grinning hugely. "I can make this snake dance to any tune I call."

He said to Grimes, "You weren't in any real danger, sonny. I never miss." Cobb held the whip so that its length trailed behind him, the snake stretched out across the back of the seat and some crates in the front of the hopper.

Grimes drew his knife and flipped it through the air, a windmilling silver blur. It thunked home point-first, lodging in the top of a crate behind Cobb.

It had cut the blacksnake in half, severing it cleanly.

The knife was still quivering with the impact. Cobb did some quivering himself. He sat there, looking stupidly at the piece of the whip he held, the handle and four or five feet of whip.

Grimes said, "Don't worry, mister. I never miss. Looks like your bullwhip just got short-horned."

Cobb sputtered, "I'll short-horn you, you dirty Reb—"

Bowman said, "Let it go. Both of you."

"Like hell!" Cobb said.

Grimes said, "That goes double for me."

"Back off," Bowman said. "I mean it. If I have to start showing off, somebody's going to get shot."

Cobb and Grimes backed off.

"That's better," Bowman said. Reaching over, he plucked the knife out of the crate top. It came loose with a twang. He handed it hilt first to Grimes, who sheathed it. Bowman said, "Keep it to yourself."

"I'll do what I damned well please," Grimes said. But he sheathed the knife.

"No more foolishness," Bowman said. "Black Creek awaits."

7

The river was wide and deep enough to allow for barge and flatboat traffic, and the bridge was built high enough to afford them free passage. Northeast of town was a landing, with docks, wharves, and a couple of warehouses. The western shoreline was bordered by River Road, which began at the landing and continued south.

On the west bank of the river, outside of town, Telegraph Road split off into two branches. One followed the actual telegraph line, swinging south of town and then west, which also marked the planned course of the railroad line. The other ran east-west through the center of town. This branch was called Trail Street.

The principal north-south thoroughfare, Market Road, connected the town with the farms and ranches of the southern valley.

At the crossroads of Market Road and Trail Street lay Black Creek town. In the northeast section was the courthouse square. The crossroads was the heart of the commercial district. A few blocks south of Trail Street lay Rowdytown, a cluster of saloons, dives, gambling and sporting houses, and shanties. The northwest section was mostly a residential area, a few square blocks of boardinghouses and single-family homes. West of that, on a knoll, stood a church, complete with its own graveyard.

Opposite, on the south side of Trail Street, was Boot Hill.

Its east side open, the town square's other three sides were enclosed by buildings, except where gaps opened at the corners of the square, allowing entrance and exit. Lining the north side was a hotel, a bank, and a tall, narrow, wedge-shaped office building. The west side was fronted by a two-story white wooden-frame courthouse with a square-sided, flat-roofed clock tower. On the same side, off by itself in the southwest corner of the square, was the jail. The south side was walled with a handful of stores, including a café, a dry goods and notions store, an apothecary shop, and a funeral parlor.

Like the jail, the funeral parlor stood slightly to one side from the rest of the row shops, physically separated from them.

Jail and funeral parlor sat cater-corner to each other, at the southwest corner of the square.

It was a little short of noon when the travelers entered the square. Above, the sun was a cool gray-white disk floating behind streaming clouds, its brightness continually waxing and waning, never quite breaking out into the open.

It was lunchtime, and people were abroad in the unpaved streets and square, some hurrying elsewhere, others idling in place.

The dirt streets were mucky, clayey. They'd dried out some but not enough. Wagon wheels and iron-shod hooves churned up mud gobs, sending them flying.

The black gig, the freight wagon, and the two riders all had the same destination: the town jail. They halted in front of it. The object of mildly curious glances cast by citizens moving about in the square, they as yet attracted no undue attention.

The newcomers were grouped facing the jail. On the right, in the black gig, were Abigail Cuttle and Francine. In the middle, freighter Cobb. On the left, on horseback, Grimes and Bowman.

In the rear of the wagon, high walls screened the dead bodies from sight.

The jail building was a flat-roofed, one-story stone rectangle, its short side fronting the square. About six feet in front of it was a hitching rail.

Two windows flanked an iron-banded, dark brown wooden front door. They were without bars. Set at shoulder height, they were long, narrow, and rectangular, with small, square glass panes set in wooden gridwork. Behind them, curtains veiled the interior of the building. The long walls and the short rear wall were pierced with high, small, square barred windows, open to the elements.

The buildings on the south side of the square were fronted by a boardwalk, a wooden plank sidewalk. So was the courthouse, but not the jail. It opened on dirt ground, hardpacked from heavy foot traffic. A pair of wooden steps linked the front doorsill to the earth.

Now, the door opened, venting a trio of lawmen. One, fiftyish, was as big as Trench had been but with more belly. Pinned to his massive chest was a marshal's badge. The other two wore deputies' badges that were simpler, plainer. One deputy was in his mid-thirties, bony and spare. The other, about ten years younger, was athletic, broad-shouldered, with a tapering torso.

In an aside to Bowman, Cobb said, "That's Bragg and two of his men, Vestry and Bailey. Vestry's the older one."

Scowling, the marshal said feelingly, "Damn! How I hate to get up out of my chair!"

This was Marshal Walcott T. Bragg. Perched atop a

head shaped like a cured ham was a hat that looked curiously undersized, a black hat curling up at the edges. It looked like a parson's hat. Below the brim, a close-cropped scalp was a bristly boar's hide. Small, widely set eyes, webbed in wrinkles, added to Bragg's whalelike appearance. A sickle-shaped mouth, curved with the ends pointing downward, was topped by a tobacco-colored walrus mustache.

He wore a black broadcloth suit, light gray flannel shirt, and string tie. Pinned to his left breast was a five-pointed tin star. A holstered gun rode high on his right hip. Compared with his oversized plowman's hands, the gun looked small.

Almost directly overhead, a rift opened in the clouds, letting the sun break through, shining into the square. In the sudden brightness, Bragg squinted, putting a hand over his eyes, shading them.

"What's all the commotion?" he asked.

Abigail Cuttle now began waving her hand, calling, "Lucas! Lucas Vestry!"

There was no ignoring that voice. All three lawmen turned to look at her.

The other two then glanced at the third, Vestry. He was thin-faced, sharp-featured, clean-shaven, with watery, bulging blue-gray eyes.

"Why, that's Miz Abigail with my niece, Francine," he said mildly, going to the carriage to greet Francine.

When it came to expressing his feelings, Vestry wasn't exactly the demonstrative type. He fidgeted, circling Francine, shoulders hunched, as if he were going to hug her. Instead, he settled for taking hold of both her hands and giving them a quick squeeze. "I'm mighty glad to see you, Francine, mighty glad."

She said, "Hi, Uncle Luke."

"Welcome to your new home."

"What, the jail?" she asked.

He was puzzled, then vexed. "No, of course not! I mean, Black Creek is your new home, where you'll be living with Aunt Hattie and me."

"It was just a joke, Uncle Luke," she said.

Abigail Cuttle said tartly, "Jail is no joking matter, miss."

The younger deputy, Bailey, was green-eyed, snub-nosed, alert. He faced Cobb, Grimes, and Bowman, but his head was toward Francine, whom he eyed appreciatively as she climbed down from the carriage, showing a flash of ankle.

Bragg said, "Eyes front, Bailey."

"Right, Marshal," Bailey said, turning his attention away from Francine's nubile form, focusing it on the two mounted strangers.

Vestry turned to Abigail Cuttle. "Much obliged to you for fetching Francine to us."

"It's nothing any God-fearing woman wouldn't do," she said, her tone implying the opposite, that what she'd done was pretty darned special. "But I don't mind telling you, Luke Vestry, that things have come to a pretty pass in the territory! What with all the outlaws and robbers plaguing the countryside, it's not safe for decent folk to go about their business. And it's just as bad right here in Black Creek!"

"Cobb," Bragg said, nodding to the freighter seated high up on the wagon. "Something I can do you for?"

Indicating Bowman, Cobb said, "Ask him."

Bragg eyed Bowman. What he saw failed to kindle in his expression any sign of warmth or fellowship. Putting his hands on his hips, he said, "And who might you be?"

"The name's Bowman."

If the name meant anything to Bragg, he didn't show it. It was the same with Bailey. Vestry, though, stopped talking to Francine and looked up, studying Bowman.

As he turned to Grimes, Bragg's scowl deepened. "And you?"

"I'm Grimes."

Bragg chewed on a corner of his mustache. "You ain't going to make many friends in town with that Rebel coat, Grimes."

"I can stand it, Marshal."

"Mebbe so, mebbe so," Bragg said, sounding doubtful. "What's your business in Black Creek?"

Bowman said, "I've got business with you, Marshal."

"Me, too," Grimes chimed in.

"Well, I'll tell you," Bragg said, "it better be worth it, now that you've hauled me out of my chair. I purely don't like to move from it, and that's a fact."

Bailey nodded, seconding his chief. Bowman said, "Cotton—Dawes Cotton."

"What about him?" Bragg asked.

"You want him," Bowman said.

Bragg spat. "He killed a man in my town. Shot him in the back, too, the skunk. You're derned right I want him."

"I've got him," Bowman said.

Bragg made a show of looking around. "I don't see him."

"He's in the back of the wagon."

Bragg looked at the freighter. "That so, Cobb?"

Cobb said, "There's three bodies in the wagon sure enough, Marshal."

"Three?"

Grimes said, "Two of them are mine."

Cobb said, "I don't know who they are, or what happened, but there's three deaders in the hopper, and these two put them there."

"Huh." Bragg pursed his lips thoughtfully, his small eyes far away, calculating.

Bailey said, "I thought there were a lot of flies buzzing around the wagon."

"Go take a look," Bragg said.

Bailey circled around behind Bowman and Grimes on their horses, approaching the rear of the wagon. The string of two horses, the chestnut and Buttercup, stretched from where the rope line was tied to the back of the wagon, out into the square. Instead of going around them, Bailey ducked under the rope.

Bragg caught Vestry's eye. "Knock off that family reunion for a minute, and start doing your job, Deputy."

Vestry nodded.

The wagon walls were higher than Bailey's head. Gripping the top of the tailgate, he chinned himself up, looking into the hopper. "Uh-oh. It's bodies, all right. Smells like it, too," he added, his nose wrinkling. He dropped to the ground.

"They're not getting any fresher out here under the sun," Cobb said. "The sooner they're out of my wagon, the better."

Bowman said, "It's Dawes Cotton and two of his sidemen, Marshal. Sid Shofter and a big man named Trench."

"Cotton? Dawes Cotton? He's dead?" Bragg asked.

"He's right there in the back of the wagon."

"Dawes Cotton?"

"I killed him," Bowman said. "Grimes did for the other two. Happened last night, out at the station crossing. Herkimer's place."

"Others? What others?"

"Shofter and Trench, like I just said."

"Don't mind me, son. I just got stuck on Cotton being dead. Fact is, I been wanting to put my hand on him real bad."

"Then this is your lucky day."

"Don't know as I'd go that far," Bragg said.

"You want Cotton, I've got him," Bowman said. "As for Sid and Trench, well, that's Grimes's business. He thought they might be worth something."

"Sid and Trench?" Bragg tugged at his lower lip, thinking. "Little monkey-faced fellow and a big dumb ox?"

"That's them."

"How about that?" Bragg said. "I had them two figured for a couple of no-goods. I didn't know they were in with Cotton, though. Hmm."

Vestry said, "They're in with that Gus Arnholt crowd, Marshal."

"I believe that is the case," Bragg said.

Bailey said, "That Taylor crowd, you mean."

Bragg said, "Makes you wonder if ol' Gussie knew Cotton."

"I wonder," Vestry said, thoughtful. He and Bragg exchanged looks.

"The next time I see him, I'll ask him that very thing," Bragg declared. "In the meantime, though, three killings is serious business. Even if they was all no-goods, which is a proposition that ain't in dispute."

Bowman said, "Three killings in self-defense, Marshal." He indicated Abigail Cuttle and Francine. "Ask them. They saw it."

Vestry, shocked, said, "My Lord, Francine!"

"I'm fine, Uncle Luke. Nothing happened," she said.

She turned toward Bragg. "That's right, Marshal. The others started it. They were mean men—killers."

Bragg said, "That how it was, Miz Abigail?"

"They were bad ones, all right, Marshal," Abigail Cuttle said. "It's lucky we weren't all killed! Or worse," she added, glancing meaningfully at Francine, her pointed tongue jabbing at thin, parched lips. "But we're none the worse for it, thanks to these two no-account saddle tramps," she said. "The Lord surely does move in a mysterious way."

"Yes, ma'am," Bragg said piously.

Bowman said, "Herkimer and his hand Johnny'll tell it that way, too."

Bragg took hold of his lower lip between thumb and forefinger, twisting and pinching it. After a moment, he said, "Let's see what we got here." Gesturing toward the back of the wagon, he said peevishly, "But first, get them animals out of the way. This's official business."

"Sure enough, Marshal," Grimes said. He climbed down from the saddle, hitching his horse to a rail in front of the building. Going around to the back of the wagon, he unfastened the lead rope, tying his end of it to the far end of the hitching rail. Bowman had already dismounted and fixed the gray's reins to the near end of the rail.

Vestry, Bailey, Bragg, Grimes, and Bowman grouped around the back of the wagon. Nearby stood Francine and Abigail Cuttle. Up front, Cobb sat perched on one hip, turned toward the rear of the vehicle.

Bailey unfastened the tailgate, lowering it to the horizontal. In a central space, piled up like a heap of rolled-up carpets, were three blanket-wrapped corpses.

Bragg's peevish expression remained unchanged. "They're bodies, all right. That much is true. Which one's supposed to be Cotton?"

Bowman said, "The one on top."

Grimes glanced at Bowman. "So that's why you had us load Cotton last!—Always thinking, ain't you."

Bowman shrugged. "It's a habit of mine."

"Scheming, more like."

Bragg looked at Bowman, then Grimes, then Bowman again. "You know I ain't climbing up into that wagon. Why, if I put my weight on that tailgate, it'd probably bust clean off."

Bowman pulled himself up into the wagon.

He'd rigged things so Cotton was on top of the pile, but during the long, bumpy ride, the bodies had gotten a pretty good jostling, mixing them up. They'd all been placed head-in. Bowman looked at the sets of booted feet emerging from under the blanket wrappings, finding Cotton's boots. Cotton had rolled off the top and was now wedged side by side with Sid.

A dozen or more fat black flies crawled over the bodies. Most of them took to the air when Bowman planted his feet on the boards, hunkered down, took hold of Cotton's blanket wrappings in both hands, and pulled.

The bodies thumped and bumped against each other, the tarpaulin-covered crates flanking them, and the wagon bed. With effort, Bowman yanked Cotton free from where he was stuck, wrestling him to the top of the pile, propping his blanketed head and shoulders up against the side of a crate.

He peeled back the blanket folds, baring Cotton's head. It was like husking corn.

Francine gasped. Vestry said, "You don't want to look at that."

"I don't mind," she said, staring avidly.

He put an arm around her shoulder, urging her away

from the sight. He nearly collided with Abigail Cuttle, who had also pressed in close to see.

Cobb said, matter-of-factly, "He ain't got much face left."

"It's Cotton, all right," Bragg said flatly, his tiny eyes glinting. Bailey stood there gaping, breathing hard. Noticing, Bragg frowned with annoyance. "Close your mouth, Deputy, you're catching flies."

Bailey's jaws clamped shut, his teeth clicking audibly.

Cotton's flesh was the color of dirty snow, making the dried blood and wounds stand out all the more starkly. His one intact eye had been closed before he went into the blanket. Flies fastened themselves to his upturned face. Studying it, Bragg said, "Well, well."

In the square, passersby halted, grouping in knots near the wagon, craning for a better look. It was hard for them to see inside the wagon, since the group standing there blocked the view.

Bowman said, "Seen enough?"

Bragg said, "Plenty."

"It's Cotton."

"Yes, it's him."

Bowman grinned. He lowered Cotton's head, shooing the flies, covering his face with the blanket. He wiped the palms of his hands on a crate's canvas wrapping.

Cobb said, "Hey!

"Sorry." Bowman clambered down from the wagon. "Looks like I saved you a ride to the crossing, Marshal."

"And don't think I don't appreciate it," Bragg said. "I like it when I don't have to get out of my chair."

"You can show your appreciation by paying me the reward."

"You'll get it."

"Two hundred dollars," Bowman said. "That's what the circular I saw in Zenith said."

"You'll get it," Bragg repeated. He tugged at his lower lip, studying Bowman. "Maybe there's a circular out on you."

Bowman laughed, a short, choppy sound. "Oh, no. You won't get out of paying me the money that easily. I stay on the right side of the law."

"Well, see that you do. Step out of line in my town, and I'll crack down as hard on you as I would anybody else," Bragg said. "Harder."

Pushing himself forward, Grimes said, "Hey! What about me?"

Bragg said, "That goes double for you. We got enough trouble in town without an unreconstructed Reb bulling in and throwing his weight around. I ain't gonna stand for it."

"No, I mean what about them? My two," Grimes said, indicating the bodies in the wagon.

"What about them?"

"Ain't you gonna take a look at them?"

"I will, when they're all properly laid out. Just for the record." Bragg was grave, ponderous. "But I believe it's Sid and Trench, all right."

"Good!" Grimes rubbed his hands together. "What're they worth?"

"To me—nothing. Not a red cent. And I'm speaking now in my official capacity as marshal of Black Creek township."

Vestry said, not unkindly, "They're not wanted for anything here."

Bragg said, "If they'd broken the law, I'd have thrown them in jail. But they didn't. And there were no outstanding warrants out on them, not to my knowledge."

Grimes was growing more desperate. "But they must be wanted for something somewhere!" He whipped off his hat and beat it against his thigh, raising up dust. "I killed them for nothing! Hell and damnation!"

Vestry's lips were pursed, disapproving. "Watch your language, there's ladies present. One of them's my niece."

Bowman said, "At least you've got the satisfaction of helping out the law, Grimes."

The other glared at him. "That's easy for you to say—you're in line for some of that reward money. Dang!"

"Watch it," Vestry cautioned.

Francine plucked at his sleeve and said, "He doesn't mean anything by it, Uncle Luke. And he did save our lives."

Vestry moved his lips in and out, as if he were sucking lemons. "I guess I could check the wanted circulars, see if there's anything on those two. If there is, we could help you file your claim for the reward—if any. That is, if it's all right with you, Marshal. Seeing as how he helped out Francine and Miz Abigail and all?"

"Sure, so long as it don't cost us nothing," Bragg said expansively. "If there's a price on their heads somewhere, it belongs to the man who brought them in. That's fair and proper."

Grimes perked up. "That's fine, just fine."

"What about my money?" Bowman asked.

"Right now, it's still the town's money," Bragg said. "I aim to keep the red tape to a minimum, but between the mayor and that pettifogging town council, the forms have got to be observed. I'll need a statement from you, Bowman. And one from your pal here."

"You'll get it," Bowman said.

Grimes said, "We ain't pals."

"He said it," Bowman said. "How's about I go make that statement now?"

Bragg goggled at him, with as much amazement as if he'd sprouted a second head. "Before lunch?"

"I could write it out to save time."

"Got to get a statement from Miz Cuttle and the girl, too."

"They're here now, Marshal."

"You're sure in an all-fired hurry, mister," Bragg said heavily. "I told you, you'll get your money."

Cobb spat. He hadn't moved from his perch high atop the wagon seat. "Hey, Marshal! What do you want to do with these bodies? I want 'em out of my wagon so I can go back to work."

Bragg said, "Hold your horses, Cobb."

"I can't sit around here and wait all day. I've got deliveries to make. Bad enough that my rig's been turned into a corpse wagon. I don't want to be late, too."

"This is the law's business, Cobb. It'll take as long as it takes."

"Tell that to those town merchants of yours when they start hollering about their deliveries being late."

"We'll get you out of here as soon as possible," Bragg said briskly. His eye fell on Bailey. "Run over to Knox's place; tell him he's got three coming."

"There he is now," Bailey said, pointing at a man who'd just emerged from the front door of the funeral parlor.

The two-story white wooden-frame building housed the parlor on its ground floor, while the upper floor held the private living quarters. Between the upper and lower levels was a long horizontal sign whose neatly painted letters read, "Knox Mortuary."

In front, the upper floor had two windows, each

fitted with a black canvas awning. A broad, tentlike awning, like a black canopy, overhung the top of the wide display window. From the sill to chest height, the display window was masked inside by a crinkly purple satin screen. The upper third was curtained by purple-black velvet drapes. Between the bottom of the curtain and the top of the screen, the narrow band of clear glass pane was further obscured by strategically placed potted plants. Above the door, an arched wooden panel was carved to depict the beams and orb of a rising—or was it setting?—sun.

Bragg motioned to Knox, beckoning. Knox came scurrying forward, crossing to the wagon.

Knox's melon-shaped head was crowned by a shiny charcoal-gray tophat. He had white tufted brows and woolly gray-white muttonchop sideburns. His pear-shaped body was clothed in a brown suit, with a green, yellow, and brown vest and a mustard-colored cravat.

Grimes said, "Looks more like a banker than an undertaker, don't he?"

"It's the hat that gives him away," Bowman said. "Who else but an undertaker would wear a tophat for everyday use?"

Trailing in Knox's wake were a half-dozen or more spectators eager to satisfy their curiosity. Bragg said, "Keep them citizens back, Bailey."

Bailey moved between them and Knox. Making shooing motions with his arms, he said, "Hold it, folks. Hold it!"

The advance halted.

Knox came over to the wagon. Bragg said, "Got some business for you, Knox." Knox tried not to look too pleased. "There's three of them," Bragg said.

Knox said, "Three! Anyone I know?"

"One of them is Dawes Cotton, that backshooter who did for Merrill Tinsley."

"Ah, yes, that was a tragedy," Knox said, the twinkle in his eye speaking of anything but tragedy. "Poor Mr. Merrill, his life cut tragically short. It was a lovely funeral, though. Really first-class." Knox's eyes had a distant look of fond reminiscence. "Dignity and elegance combined."

"Well, this ain't going to be no fancy deal like that," Bragg said. "It's Cotton and two other no-goods who got what was coming to them. Saves the town the cost of hanging them. This'll be the standard deal. The cheapest pine boxes you got and a quick burial on Boot Hill. All courtesy of the township of Black Creek."

Knox peered into the wagon, his head bobbing, tufted white eyebrows rising and falling. "Who got them?"

"Them two," Bragg said, pointing with his thumb at Grimes and Bowman.

Knox studied them with interest. "Very public-minded of them. I approve."

"You should. Not only did they do the killing, they even trucked in the bodies," Bragg said.

"Oh." Knox frowned, looked at him. "From where?"

"The station crossing."

Knox cleared his throat. "To broach a delicate matter . . . there won't be any trouble about payment, will there? The council might balk at paying to bury those killed outside town."

Bragg said, "Cotton was wanted by Black Creek for murder. The other two were siding him. That makes it official town business."

Knox looked doubtful. "Some of the members have been complaining about paying for so many funerals lately. Meager though those payments have been," he added.

"You'd think it was their own money," Bragg said. "Let them talk. They don't have a choice. What're they going to do, leave the bodies unburied?"

"Certainly not. That would be scandalous." Knox sounded scandalized.

"Well, what about these three? What do you want to do with them?" Bragg asked.

"Have the wagon bring them to the back of the shop," Knox said. "I'll tell my nephew Merwin to be ready for them." Touching his hat brim in parting salute, Knox turned and crossed to the funeral parlor.

People called out to him, asking him what it was all about, who'd gotten killed. He was silent, nodding his head and smiling as he walked along.

Standing at the edge of the boardwalk, scrutinizing the wagon, was Merwin, a lumpish, oversized man-boy, massive and sweaty. He crouched with his shoulders hunched, cutting inches off his height.

Knox spoke briefly to him, and the two disappeared inside the funeral parlor.

In front of the jail, tethered to the hitching post, some of the horses were acting up. Tied to the end of the lead rope, the chestnut gelding sidled around behind the black mare, tied separately to the hitching pole. The mare didn't like having the other behind it and was tossing its head, snorting, its front hooves pawing the ground.

Bragg, vexed, said, "Get them horses out of here before somebody gets hurt."

Grimes said, "I'm on my way, Marshal. Where's the livery stable?"

"Across Trail Street, about three blocks down," Bragg said, pointing.

At that moment, an excited man came running up the

side street that connected Trail Street to the square. Hatless and in disarray, the newcomer staggered toward the lawmen. Bailey said, "Why, it's Ward Newkirk!"

Bragg said, "Must be something pretty danged important to get him moving like that."

Newkirk was middle-aged, heavy-set. Most of his heaviness had settled in his middle. He wore the garb of a prosperous man of business. Clearly, his run had left him played out, near exhaustion. His hair was disordered, his eyes wide and staring. His face was red, his mouth a wide, sucking, black O. Red droplets speckled his face and front.

Bailey caught him by the arm, keeping him from falling. "What is it, Mr. Newkirk? What's wrong?"

Bragg said, "What's that on him? Blood?"

Before he could talk, Newkirk had to catch his breath. Chest heaving, his wracking coughs presently subsided into rasping wheezes. He blurted, "Yancey—Yancey's been shot!"

Bragg said, "Yancey? Harl Yancey?"

Newkirk nodded emphatically. "Shot dead!"

"Huh!" Bragg leaned in. "Who done it?"

"Drummer—Drummer McCray."

"Drummer! You sure?"

Newkirk drew himself up, swiping his fingertips across some red blotches staining his jacket and shirt. Smearing them, holding the fingers under Bragg's nose, he said, "See that? That's Yancey's blood. I was standing next to him when Drummer shot him full of holes. It was awful!"

"Well, well," Bragg said.

Bailey still held the other's arm, steadying him. "That's all right, Mr. Newkirk. You're safe now."

Bragg rubbed his blocky chin. "Where's Drummer now?"

Newkirk, distracted, said, "I don't know—still at the Pole Star, I guess. I didn't stick around to find out."

"What for did he kill Yancey?"

"They were quarreling, arguing over a woman. One of Lana's girls."

Leaning on Bailey's arm, Newkirk had recovered sufficiently from his shock and exhaustion to take note of his surroundings. For the first time, he caught sight of the bodies in the back of the wagon. Starting violently, he would have fallen had Bailey not continued to brace him.

Pointing at the bodies, Newkirk cried, "My God! Where did they come from?"

"We're shipping 'em in now," Cobb said.

"Never mind about that," Bragg said. "Bailey, take Mr. Newkirk into the office, where he can sit down."

Walking like a very old man, Newkirk was guided by the deputy into the jail building.

Vestry said, "You'd best be going, Francine. Aunt Hattie's waiting for you over to the house. She'll sure be glad to see you.

"Miz Abigail, would you be so good as to see that Francine gets home safely?"

"Certainly!" Abigail Cuttle bobbed her head, a tight, sharp bob, like a bird pecking at something. "Another killing at the Pole Star—and in broad daylight! That Crain woman should have been run out of town long ago. I hope you're going to arrest her, Lucas."

"If she broke the law, I will."

"You should arrest her anyway!"

Francine said, "You're not in any danger, are you, Uncle Luke?"

"Who, me? Pshaw," Vestry said. "This is just routine.

These animals shoot each other, but they fold up fast when the law shows up. I'll be fine."

Bragg made a beeline for the jail, disappearing inside.

"Got to go," Vestry said. "You, too, Francine. Miz Abigail, it'd be best if you go to my place by way of Commerce Street. Steer clear of Trail Street, especially around Miz Lana's place. It's liable to get a mite hot around there."

"That strumpet! It's not safe for a decent woman to go by that den of sin day or night."

"I don't know about that, Miz Abigail—"

"Well, I do, and if you were really doing your duty, Deputy, you'd have closed her down a long time ago!"

Vestry shrugged helplessly. Francine asked, "What place is that?"

"Never you mind," Abigail Cuttle said. Taking hold of the reins, she pointed the horse's head toward the north part of the square.

Francine said, "Be careful, Uncle Luke."

"Don't you worry about me, I'll be fine. We handle this kind of thing every day," Vestry said. "Tell your aunt that I'll be there when I can, but it might not be until dinner-time."

"I will," she said.

"Thanks again, Miz Abigail."

"You're welcome, Lucas."

"Now, you'd all best be going," Vestry said.

The carriage started forward, and Vestry started toward the jail. Francine turned in her seat, looking back, not at her uncle but at Grimes.

Seeing her leaving, Grimes waved to her. "So long, Francine!"

Smiling, she waved back.

"See you later!" Grimes said.

She nodded vigorously, still waving. Holding the reins in one hand, Abigail Cuttle caught her by the shoulder, turning her around so she was facing front. "The less you have to do with that no-account piece of Rebel trash, Miss Francine, the better!"

"He's so brave," Francine said, dreamy-eyed. "Handsome, too."

"You're a very foolish young girl," Abigail Cuttle said. At the top of the square, the gig turned left, exiting by the northwest corner, going west on Commerce Street.

The marshal and the two deputies came out of the jail, Bragg carrying a double-barreled shotgun, Vestry a lever-action rifle.

Slapping his knee, Cobb said, "They's loaded for bear."

Bragg spoke to the deputies. "I knew it was only a matter of time before Drummer hanged himself."

"Want me to round up Dick and Eb?" Vestry asked.

"What for? I can handle Drummer all by my lonesome," Bragg said.

"I was thinking about Rufe Taylor and that crowd. They're not going to like this much."

"To hell with what Taylor likes."

"Arnholt might make trouble," Vestry warned.

"Let him," Bragg said. "Ol' Gussie needs to be taken down a peg or two, and I'm just the man to do it. It's time to show the bunch of them who's boss. And Mr. High and Mighty Rufe Taylor needs to be taken down two pegs," he added, sounding as if he were looking forward to it.

Walking three abreast, with Bragg in the middle, the lawmen exited by the southwest corner of the square, turning right onto a sidewalk and walking west.

Several handfuls of people had gathered, first to gawk at the bodies and then for Newkirk's advent. Now, they streamed out of the square, trailing Bragg and company.

Bowman started after them. Grimes said, "Where you going?"

"To see the show," Bowman said.

"Wait for me!"

8

Running one block north of Trail Street and parallel to it was Franklin Street. Above that was Locust Way, more than a dirt path but less than a road. Where Locust and Franklin met Market Road, the immediate area was sparsely developed. Franklin Street bordered the backs of the rows of big commercial buildings fronting Trail Street. East of Market were some barns, a blacksmith's shop, stables, and storehouses.

On the northwest corner of Franklin Street and Market Road, fronting Market, stood a sprawling three-story white wooden-frame building, big and barnlike. The structure and its surrounding grounds occupied an entire block. On all sides but the west, the building was edged by a roofed-over veranda.

In front, mounted across the second-floor balcony railing, was a signboard reading, "Pole Star Saloon." The painted sign was blue, with yellow stars and planets, gauzy constellations, and a crescent moon floating around the lettering.

A pair of batwinged doors stood at the front entrance, flanked by long, low, curtained windows. Through them could be glimpsed a dim, cavernous interior, where one or two drop lights glimmered wanly through the murk.

No one could be seen inside. The veranda was similarly deserted. Behind the building was a yard, gardens, walkways, trees, and a small carriage house.

About sixty or seventy people had gathered. In Black Creek, that was quite a crowd. More were arriving every minute, massing in a loose-knit, kidney-shaped cluster facing the saloon's east and south sides.

The crowd mix made up a cross section of the town, the godly and the godless alike. There were the so-called respectables: men and a few women of substance, property holders, businessmen. Storekeepers, clerks, and handymen. A handful of farmers and ranchers who happened to be in town.

Less refined types were represented by a scattering of traveling salesmen, as well as the usual idlers and loafers.

No less well represented were the denizens of Black Creek's so-called sporting element: easy women and the men who lived off their earnings, gamblers, barkeeps, tinhorns, hard cases. Drifters who'd blown into town and were now stuck in place, going nowhere. Saddle bums, drabs, and drunks.

Most of them had come up from Rowdytown, south of Trail Street.

There was a carnival mood in the air.

Someone shouted, "Here comes Bragg!"

Walking west along Franklin, three abreast in the middle of the street, ominous, inexorable, came the lawmen. When they reached Market, the crowd opened a path for them.

Trailing along behind them were Grimes and Bowman. Grimes said, "They sure know to get out of Bragg's way!"

"Moses parting the Red Sea," Bowman said.

Pressing close to the lawmen, almost at their heels, the duo followed them to the front of the crowd.

At the intersection's southwest corner stood a group of about a dozen residents of the house. *Saloon gals* was the polite term. What they were was whores, open and unashamed—in fact, damned proud of their calling, and doubly proud to be working at the Pole Star, the highest-class house and saloon in town. The only such north of Trail Street, where the respectables dwelt. But none of them dwelt too near the Pole Star.

The females ranged in age from fifteen to thirty, with most in their early to midtwenties. Some were slim and willowy, others fat and buxom. They had plenty on display, since most of them had only had time to throw a robe or wrapper around themselves before running outside. A couple were barefoot.

Sleek robes were tightly belted around ripely curved figures. Deep, plunging cleavage and bare, shapely calves abounded, with red satin and black lace trimmings. Flesh and filigree.

The nearness of the Pole Star's scantily clad whores spiced the crowd's circus mood. Men and boys pressed close, ogling, leering.

Also temporarily evicted from the saloon were two bartenders, a couple of gamblers, and a gray-haired handyman.

Of the Pole Star insiders, males and females both showed a certain pallor that comes from not getting enough sun. They were night creatures, their work time the hours of darkness. Daytime was for sleeping.

Now, they looked like owls in daylight, stunned, shrunken.

A notable exception stood at the head of the group, a

slim, striking, redheaded beauty with green eyes and cream-colored skin. She looked to be in her mid-twenties. Her looks were clean, chiseled, cold. She wore no makeup, no lip rouge or powder.

Her form was lithe, willowy, long-legged. She wore a brown jacket with black frogging down the front and black borders at the cuff, a white ruffled-front blouse, an ankle-length brown skirt, and black leather ankle boots.

Her smooth, masklike face showed a certain hardness in the eyes, a tightness around the mouth. She looked as if she'd been around, Bowman thought, eyeing her. It was a look he liked.

Grimes and Bowman found that there was plenty of room at the head of the throng. The crowd members were leery of being exposed to the potential line of fire, without having a few extra bodies between them and a bullet from the saloon.

Bowman drew alongside a man who was regaling a knot of rapt listeners with an account of the shooting.

The speaker was round-faced, his high, shiny forehead fringed by long, curly yellow-brown hair. Perfectly round wire-rim glasses were fitted over slightly pop eyes. He was saying, "Then Drummer says, 'You're wearing a gun.' "

"Was Yancey wearing a gun, Joe?" somebody asked.

"He was!" Joe went on, "Then, before Yancey could reach, or even say anything, Drummer opened fire—he already had his gun out—filling Yancey full of lead. Gave it to him right square in the middle, derned near cutting him in half!"

Somebody said, "Did you see it, Joe?"

"Me? Hell, no!" Joe roared. "I'm a married man. If the missus ever caught me in the Pole Star, she'd come after me with an ax! But I got it on good authority, straight from the horse's mouth. That old-timer who empties out the spittoons—Swamper—he was there and seen it all, and he told me."

A voice said, "Aw, that rumdum don't even know the time of day!"

"He knows plenty, believe you me!" Joe insisted.

Bowman tapped him on the shoulder. "Hey, Joe, who's that redhead over there, the one talking to Bragg?"

Joe turned his head toward Bowman, his expression amiable but puzzled. "Do I know you, friend?"

Bowman said, "I'm new in town."

"Me, too," Grimes said, standing at Bowman's shoulder.

"You must be," Joe said, laughing, some of those around him joining in. "Why, everybody in town knows who that is. That's Lana Crain, owner of the Pole Star."

"Fine-looking woman," Bowman said.

"She's all of that, and then some," Joe agreed.

"Who're those two men with her?" Bowman asked.

"The big fellow with the black mustache is Moritz, the bartender. The wizened little fellow is Swamper, who sweeps up and cleans out the spittoons," Joe said. "You picked a fine time to arrive, friend. There's going to be plenty of fireworks!"

"What happened?"

"Drummer McCray gunned down Harl Yancey! Drummer's a fast gun Miz Lana keeps around the Pole Star for protection. He's come out on top of a couple of shooting scrapes, but he went too far this time, when he burned down one of the quality."

"What were they fighting about?"

Joe snickered. "It wasn't what you'd call a fight, friend. More like a killing. Drummer caught Yancey trying to move in on his woman, and he burned him down. Didn't give him a chance to go for his gun or nothing, just emptied his six-gun into Yancey's guts. Damn near cut him in half!" Joe smacked his lips, relishing the phrase.

A short, gray-bearded man with a derby hat and an unlit cigar butt stuck in the corner of his mouth spoke up. "You boys better watch what you say. If Miz Lana hears you calling her name out of turn, she's liable to up and shoot you herself."

Grimes said, "A sweet thing like that? Don't hardly seem likely."

Plenty of guffaws, smiles, and elbows in the ribs greeted Grimes's remark. The derby wearer said, "Don't let her looks fool you, son. She'd shoot a man easier'n spitting in his eye."

"They say she shot her first husband and used his money to buy the Pole Star," Joe said, his voice lowered to a confidential pitch.

Drifting away, Bowman eased closer to Bragg and Lana Crain, listening in on their conversation. Bragg was asking, "Anybody else inside?"

Lana Crain said, "No, we all got out while Drummer was gloating over the body, crowing about what a big man he was." Her speech was carefully enunciated, her voice sharp, metallic.

"Sounds like you don't like him much," Bragg said.

"I wish I'd shot him myself, when I had the chance," she said viciously. "Going and killing one of my best customers!"

"The fat's in the fire now," Bragg said. He started to move away, pausing when Lana laid a hand on his forearm.

She said, "Try not to do any more damage than you have to, that's all I ask."

"To Drummer?"

"To the place! I don't want to get stuck with any heavy repair bills."

"I'm afraid that's up to Drummer," Bragg said.

He stepped out in front, flanked by his two deputies. They stood there, looking at the building. Bragg said, "Luke, you come at him from the side. Keep an eye on the back, in case he tries to make a break that way. Bailey, you cover my back. I don't reckon Drummer has any friends in the crowd, but we've got plenty of enemies, and when the bullets start flying, somebody might want to try a little backshooting."

Rifle in hand, Vestry angled toward the south side of the building, avoiding the line of fire from any of the windows.

Bailey pushed the crowd back. Now that Vestry and Bragg were moving into position, with shooting imminent, not much persuasion was needed. Shrinking from the vicinity of the saloon, they flowed out of the intersection, leaving it empty.

Standing on the sidelines near a tree for cover were Grimes and Bowman. Grimes said, "I heard a lot about this here Bragg, and he sure does carry on like the bull of the woods. Now we'll see what he's got."

Standing in Market Road, facing the front of the saloon, Bragg called out, "Drummer!"

From inside came a ragged shout: "That you, Bragg? What kept you? I've been waiting for you!"

"You ain't gonna have to wait no more," Bragg said. "I'm giving you a chance, which is more than you gave Yancey. Throw out your gun, and come out with your hands up."

"Come on in! I'll buy you a drink!"

"I'm not playing, McCray."

"Me, neither."

Bragg said, "If I come in there, you're coming out feet first"

McCray opened fire, shooting through the open front entrance.

The crowd scattered, running for cover.

A shot hit Bragg's hat, lofting it backward into the air. The rest of the fusillade passed harmlessly overhead.

A half-beat later, the lawmen opened up. Leveling the shotgun, Bragg loosed a barrel at the doorway, blowing the batwing doors off their hinges. "You son of a bitch—"

Inside, a shadow that might have been McCray flickered in and out of view.

Dropping into a crouch, Bailey fired his six-gun at the window to the left of the doorway, disintegrating it.

Vestry's rifle blew out a side window, then fired through it into the building.

Bowman noticed Lana Crain standing in shelter behind the corner of a building. She stood hunched forward in a half crouch, elbows at her sides, fists held out in front of her. Each time another window exploded, she flinched.

She was saying something under her breath, and judging by her facial expression, it couldn't have been anything nice.

Bragg rushed the saloon, emptying another shotgun barrel through the doorway. Jumping up onto the veranda, he crashed against the front of the building, to the right of the doorway. He flattened his back against the wall, out of the line of fire.

The deputies continued to pour fire into the building.

Bragg broke the shotgun, shucked out the empties,

fitted à fresh pair of double-aught shells into the bores, and closed the weapon. Pivoting away from the doorway, he fired a blast through the window to the right of it. Glass shattered, sharded panes cascading inward.

Pausing a beat, he pivoted toward the doorway, sticking the shotgun muzzles inside.

The interior was filled with gunsmoke, haze, dust, chaos. To the right, parallel to the north wall, was a long wooden bar. In the center was an open space, at whose far end lay a stairway climbing to the second floor. To the left was a cluster of tables and chairs.

A figure popped up from behind the bar, where he had been hiding—McCray, holding a gun in each hand.

He threw lead at the front window that had just been blown out by Bragg. Laying down covering fire, he vaulted the bar, dropping down into a crouch on the other side.

A glimpse of motion at the doorway's edge caught McCray's eye. Too late, he realized that Bragg had faked him out, that he wasn't coming by the window after all, that it was only a feint.

Snarling, he snapped a shot at the doorway, diving away from the bar.

That's where Bragg caught him, tagging him in midair with his second shotgun blast, cutting off McCray's outcry in mid-shriek.

McCray dropped and rolled across the floorboards. He crashed into a table, knocking it over.

Shielded behind the door frame, Bragg let go of the empty shotgun, drawing his sidearm.

McCray half sat, half lay on the floor, leaning against an overturned table that helped prop him up. Clutching the table's upper rim with one hand, he pulled himself up on one hip.

Escaping the full force of the blast, he'd been tagged by the edge of the buckshot fan, chewing up his left side. His white ruffled-front shirt, fancy vest, and tight fawn-colored trousers were bloodsoaked, glistening. He was wild-eyed, furious, desperate. His right hand lay on the floor, holding a gun. Before he could lift it, Bragg stepped through the doorway.

Bragg emptied his gun into McCray, who jerked and shuddered under the impact as the life was shot out of him. He never did manage to raise his gun.

McCray's head turned to one side, eyes staring, mouth gaping. For an instant, the hand clutching the table rim in a death grip continued to hold him up. Gravity triumphed then, and he slumped over onto one side, falling to the floor.

Bragg shouted, "Cease fire!"

The deputies' guns fell silent. A glass shard worked loose from a busted window frame, falling to the floor, striking a crystalline note.

Empty brass cartridge shells jingled against the floor-boards as Bragg cleared the cylinder empties. Reloading, he started forward.

A blue-gray haze of gunsmoke drifted waist-high above the floor, eddying as Bragg moved through it, closing on McCray. He stepped on the wrist of McCray's gun hand, pinning it to the floor. He bent over and pried the weapon free, then kicked it a few paces away.

He grabbed a fistful of McCray's jet-black hair, pulling his head up and back, lifting his face off the floor. McCray's staring eyes were already glazing over. A line of blood ran from the corner of his mouth to his chin.

Bragg let go, causing McCray's head to flop facedown to the floor.

On Bragg's left, in an empty window frame on the south wall near the building's front, appeared Vestry's head, shoulders, and rifle barrel. Vestry said, "Did you get him?"

"He's got," Bragg said.

Outside, Grimes and Bowman exchanged glances.

"Now you know what Bragg's got," Bowman said. "Plenty!"

9

Alone in the saloon, Bragg went behind the bar, emerging with a bottle of whiskey and a glass. He poured himself a shot, drank it, and set the empty glass down on the bartop as Vestry and Bailey came in.

Bailey said, "You okay, Marshal?"

"Not a scratch," Bragg said.

Vestry and Bailey went to look at McCray. Bailey said, "Well, so much for him."

"He died game," Bragg said from where he was standing beside the bar. "I'll give him that."

Deeper into the space, sprawled near the foot of the stairs, lay another body. Vestry stood over it. "Here's Yancey."

Bailey said, "He had a lot to live for, a rich man like that. He shouldn't have tried to cut in on Drummer's woman."

Outside, Lana Crain crossed to the Pole Star. Trailing a pace or two behind her were Moritz and Swamper. Grimes said, "Man, that sure is a whole lot of woman!"

Bowman *tsk-tsk*ed. "What would Francine say if she heard you talking like that?"

Grimes gave him a hard look. "She ain't gonna hear it, as long as nobody goes telling tales out of school."

"She'll never hear it from me," Bowman assured him.

"Besides," Grimes said, "they're two different things, like whiskey and wine. That redhead's the whiskey, and Francine's the wine."

"Maybe you should stick to soda pop," Bowman said.

"Maybe you should stick to your own business."

"Okay, Grimesy."

"And don't call me that, I don't like it."

"Okay, Grimesy," Bowman said, starting toward the saloon.

"Hey, where you goin'?" Grimes started after him.

Lana Crain and the two men went into the saloon. She stood with her hands on her hips, looking around.

"Thanks for keeping the damage down, Bragg," she said sarcastically.

Bragg, conciliatory, said, "I gave him a chance to surrender. He didn't take it. After that, things just naturally took their course."

"You sure shot the hell out of the place. Too bad you couldn't take him in the street."

"If he'd of come out, I would have," Bragg said. "But he didn't, so what else could I do?"

"You can pay for that drink," Lana Crain said. "Take your post, Moritz, before anybody else gets the idea we're giving out free drinks here."

Bragg said, "Drummer said he'd buy me a drink. I was just taking him up on his offer."

Glancing at the corpse, Lana Crain said, "Drummer doesn't work here anymore."

Moritz nodded, going behind the bar. Weighing almost three hundred pounds, he was one of those big men who're light on their feet, floating along. He had black curly hair, parted in the middle, and a black handlebar mustache. He wore a fancy brocade vest over a white shirt with black sleeve garters.

He pulled on a white bib apron, knotting it behind his back. Once in position at his station, he stood opposite Bragg, looking at him unblinkingly with black button eyes.

"I forgot," Bragg said. "Nothing comes free around here."

"Not a thing," Lana Crain said, smirking.

Bragg slapped a coin down on the bartop. "Now we're even up."

"That's how you see it, eh? Who pays for the rest of the damages?"

"Yancey, since I'm sure he's already been plucked clean of his money, his watch, and anything else he might've had," Bragg said.

"I wouldn't know anything about that," she said guardedly. "Anybody who was in here when he was shot could've done it. For that matter, you or one of your deputies could've done it just now."

"Now, Miz Lana," Bragg said indulgently. Pushing off from the bar, he went between the two bodies and looked around.

"How're we doing back there, Moritz?" Lana Crain asked.

Behind the bar, a handsbreadth above the tops of the bottles racked on the uppermost shelf against the wall, the boards were pierced by several bulletholes.

"Not too bad, Miz Lana," Moritz said. "There's a couple of holes in the wall but no busted bottles."

"I knew there was a reason I didn't replace the mirror behind the bar after the last shooting," she said, looking pleased with herself. She turned to Swamper. "You can start cleaning up."

"Yes, Miz Lana," he said. "You want me to fetch a carpenter, too?"

"I'll send a boy to do that. You start cleaning," she said.

Swamper was short and wiry, all brown, leathery, sundried flesh stretched taut across a loom of sinews and bone. Long, shaggy silver hair and beard hid much of his wizened face. He wore a flannel shirt, red bandana, stovepipe liver-colored pants, and a pair of grimy moccasins.

To the left of the bar, in the rear wall, a doorway opened into the back rooms. Swamper went into the back, then came back with a wooden barrel about the size of a keg of nails. This barrel was filled with sawdust. Edging around Yancey's corpse, Swamper neared, holding a fistful of sawdust.

Before he could scatter it, he was stopped by Bragg, who said, "Hold off on that until the bodies are taken away."

Swamper looked at Lana Crain, who nodded. She said, "Start in on that broken glass."

"Yes'm."

"Lord knows there's enough of it," she said. "It's a miracle that there's a pane left unbroken."

Swamper set down the barrel of sawdust to one side of the foot of the stairs and trudged into the back room. Returning with an empty barrel and a push broom, he went to the front of the building, picking up the larger shards of glass from the shattered front windows and dumping them into the barrel.

"Don't cut yourself," Lana Crain said. "There's already enough blood on the floor. Put on some gloves."

Swamper yes'm-ed her, then went to get some gloves.

"Just to keep the record straight," Bragg said, "how did the deal go down?"

"There's not much to tell," Lana Crain said. "Yancey had it bad for Nelly Curry. He was seeing her during business hours, but that wasn't enough. He wanted her to leave Drummer and let him keep her."

"How did she feel about it?" Bragg asked.

"Oh, she was willing enough. Nelly's a lazy girl and doesn't like to work. She'd have gone if she wasn't afraid of Drummer. Not that Drummer gave a damn about her. They came here together; both started working here at the same time."

"Where'd they come from before that?"

"I don't know," she said. "End-of-Track, I believe, but I wouldn't swear to it. I don't like asking a lot of questions—or answering them, either." She continued, "They hadn't been here long before Drummer started playing some of the other girls."

Bragg said, "Including you?"

"I don't mix with the hired help, Marshal."

"Still, Drummer was your protector, wasn't he?"

"I can take care of myself," Lana Crain said. "My staff can handle unruly drunks and bar fights, but they're not gunfighters. To handle gunmen, you need a gunman. That was Drummer's job. He was nothing more to me than a hired hand."

"What for did he kill Yancey?" Bragg asked.

"Drummer was a dog in the manger," she said. "He was through with Nelly, he didn't want her anymore, but he wouldn't let anybody else have her."

"Sounds like that would've put a crimp into her earnings here."

"He didn't mind when she went with men in the course of her, shall we say, professional duties. That was business, and he was taking most of her money. But when it looked like she was going to get away from him, he stepped in."

"I see," Bragg said. "He didn't mind nobody getting milk from the cow, so long as it was in his pasture. But when she tried to jump the fence—"

"I don't know as I'd put it in quite that way, Marshal, but that's the sense of it, more or less," Lana Crain said.

"How'd the deal go down?" Bragg asked.

"Yancey dropped in a little while ago. It was our slack time, when the girls are off duty. He was down here talking to Nelly, trying yet again to persuade her to go with him."

"Seems to me you'd have something to say about that, Yancey trying to steal away one of your prize girls."

"They knew better than to talk about it in front of me," Lana Crain said. "When I was around, they talked about other things. But I knew what was going on. I've got eyes. This time, though, I was in my office upstairs, going over the accounts. Drummer was sleeping off last night's drunk. That's what Yancey and Nelly thought. Drummer caught them together. The first thing I knew about it was Drummer yelling and cursing, calling Yancey all kinds of dirty names. I came out of my office to the balcony, to see what was happening. While they were arguing—well, they weren't really arguing, it was just Drummer waving his gun and cussing out Yancey—Nelly slipped away, out the side door. Without a warning, Drummer shot Yancey, shot him down just like that." She illustrated her remark with a snap of her fingers. "Drummer went to the bar, got himself a bottle, and sat down to drink. By this time, the whole house was roused. The girls and I went down the back stairs and out through the back. Drummer wasn't interested in us. He was waiting for you, I guess.

"That's all of it," she said.

"Seems pretty open and shut," Bragg said. "Still, I'd like to talk to the girl. Nelly. Where's she?"

Lana Crain shrugged. "The last I saw of her, she was slipping out the side door while Drummer stood gloating over Yancey's body. I guess she's outside, with the rest of the girls."

"I'll want to talk with her," Bragg said. "Tough break for Yancey."

"If it wasn't him, it would've been someone else, someone big enough so that killing him would kick up a fuss that was too big to go away," she said. "Drummer was spoiling for a fight, any fight at all, so long as it made things go bust in a big way. Things were going too smoothly for him. He was getting bored."

Lana Crain stood facing the front of the building, talking to Bragg. Already intent, her gaze hardened as she caught sight of something over Bragg's slab shoulder. She said, "We're closed."

Bragg turned to see to whom she was speaking. Behind him, edging up toward the bar, were Grimes and Bowman. He said, "What do you want?"

Bowman said, "I just wanted to make sure you were all right, Marshal. I'd hate for something to happen to you. Especially before I collect my money."

"Don't you worry," Bragg said. "Nothing's going to happen to me. Nothing. Savvy?"

"That suits me fine."

Bragg frowned. "Who let you two in here, anyway?"

"I did," Bailey said, sheepish. "Bowman said it'd be okay with you."

"Well, it's not," Bragg said.

Circling for a better view, Bowman eyed McCray. "You sure shot the buttons off of him," he said, impressed.

Bragg said, "That's what happens when you break the law in Black Creek, Bowman."

"I'm not breaking any laws."

"See that you don't." Bragg looked at Grimes. "You, neither."

"Who, me?" Grimes asked.

"It's all over and done," Bragg said. "Nothing in it for you."

Eyeing Lana Crain's slim, lithe form, Bowman said, "Oh, I don't know about that."

Bragg made shooing motions. "Now, you two can march right straight out of here and—" He stopped, his eyes suddenly thoughtful. He squeezed his lower lip, tugging at it. "Wait a minute," he said. "Hold on, now. Don't you boys go rushing off so fast." His gaze went from the two to Lana Crain, then back again. "I'm commencing to get an idea here."

"You sure changed your mind fast," Grimes said.

Cagey now, Bragg said, "I got to think fast with two red-hots like you."

Bowman gave a short, dry chuckle, as if he was clearing his throat. "You wouldn't try to country-boy me, now, would you, Marshal?"

"Why not? I'm a country boy, myself."

"Me, too," Grimes said.

Bragg was doubtful. "I said country, not the back of beyond."

Grimes opened his mouth, but before he could speak, Bragg beat him to it.

"Now, don't get yourself in an uproar, Reb, not when I'm feeling all warm and friendly toward you two."

Bowman said, "I once saw a gator get the same friendly look that you've got on your face right now,

Marshal, right before it gobbled up a bird that was sitting on its nose."

Glaring at the newcomers, Lana Crain said, "Who're these clowns, Bragg?"

Stepping forward, Bowman touched the tip of his hat brim. "The name's Bowman, ma'am, Dane Bowman. Pleased to meet you."

"The pleasure is all yours, I'm sure," she said.

"Jed Grimes, ma'am," the other said. "Glad to know you."

"Nobody gets to know me," she said. "We're still closed. Now, get out."

"Um," Bragg said.

Lana Crain looked at him. "Or is there some reason why they shouldn't get out, Bragg?"

"Well, now, I'll tell you, Miz Lana. These fellows just rode into town, and already they've made their mark. They killed three men at the station crossing. All legal and aboveboard, natcherly, elsewise I'd've thrown them in jail. One of them was Dawes Cotton."

Her eyebrows rose a few millimeters, the only reaction visible on her white porcelain visage. "Cotton? Hard man to beat."

"Bowman took him," Bragg said.

"He give it to him in the back?" Lana Crain asked.

"I resent that," Bowman said, protesting mildly.

"No, straight on," Bragg said.

"Actually, sideways," Bowman said.

Lana Crain eyed him speculatively, an artisan scrutinizing a tool to determine its proper use and worth. "I don't care if you shot him in the back, the front, or upside down," she said.

"That's only half of it," Bragg continued. Jerking a

thumb at Grimes, he said, "Reb, here, killed two of Gus Arnholt's crowd."

More interested, she said, "Which ones?"

"Shofter and Trench. Little bitty weaselly fellow and a big galoot."

"I know them."

"You know everybody in town, Miz Lana."

"Sooner or later, they all come here," she said. She smiled a bright, wintry smile. "Two less of Taylor's bunch," she said. "That's something, anyway."

She turned to Grimes and Bowman. "We're closed for repairs. Come back in a couple of hours when we're open again, and I'll buy you a drink."

Bowman said, "I'm looking forward to it."

"Likewise," Grimes said.

Bragg said, "Clear out of here, you two. There's things to be done, and you're only in the way."

"What about my money?" Bowman asked.

"Damn it all," Bragg said. "You can see I'm busy, can't you? Don't bother me with that now."

"I'm not trying to rush you, Marshal," Bowman said. "It's just that I'd like to put some of those dollars to work, seeing as how there's such nice things to spend them on." He was looking at Lana Crain.

She said, "What money, Bragg?"

"The reward the town put up on Cotton for killing Merrill Tinsley," he said.

"Do tell," she said, eyeing Bowman in a new, more speculative light.

"Don't get too worked up. It's only a couple of hundred dollars," Bragg cautioned.

"In this town, that counts as a windfall," she said. "What're you waiting for, Bragg? Pay the man."

"There's a little matter of two killings done in your place that I've got to attend to first."

"One of them is yours," she pointed out.

Looking at Bowman and Grimes, Bragg said, "You still here? The longer you keep me from doing my job, the longer it'll be before you get paid."

"We're just leaving," Bowman said. He turned to Lana Crain. "I'll be by later, to spread some of that reward money around."

"You do that, sugar," she said.

Bragg snorted. "See how glad you are when you wake up tomorrow with empty pockets and a hangover."

"That's all right, Marshal," Bowman said. "This looks like a town where a fellow can make some money, as long as he shoots the right people."

"You better make damned sure they are the right people, or you'll answer to me."

"Like I said, I always stay on the right side of the law."

"Well, you're getting on the wrong side of me," Bragg said. "I'm sick of looking at you. Go on, get moving."

Bowman started for the door, Grimes a half-pace behind. At the threshold, Bowman paused, causing Grimes to stop short to keep from bumping into him. "Quit following me so close," Bowman said.

Grimes said, "Who's following? I ain't following nobody, least of all you."

Bowman turned, went out, Grimes following. When they were gone, Lana Crain shook her head. Bragg said, "I ain't sure what to make of them two yet."

"They're easy enough to figure out," Lana Crain said. "They're gunmen. You see a lot of that type since the war. The war stopped, but they didn't. One's a Yankee, and one's a Reb, but they're both the same. They don't want to work for a living. Being a gunman pays better than pushing a plow or punching cows, they think. Easy money—if they don't get killed. If they do, well, there's always plenty more to take their place. More now than ever. Since the war, it's a buyer's market."

"You're the expert on markets," Bragg said.

She said, "What I wonder about is what you're up to, Bragg."

"Just this," he said. "Those two are sure to wind up on Taylor's bad side. Shofter and Trench were part of Gus's bunch, doing Taylor's dirty work. The Reb killed them, but Bowman was part of the showdown, and I don't reckon Gus and the rest of them are going to draw too fine a line between the two. That puts them and you more or less on the same side, Miz Lana. Maybe some good'll come of it."

"Hmm, you might have something at that, Bragg. Come on, I'll buy you a drink."

Bragg and Lana Crain stood at the bar. She said, "Set them up for me and Bragg, Moritz." Moritz poured two drinks, placing the glasses on the bar.

Lana Crain said, "It's on the house, Bragg."

"I appreciate it."

Both tossed back their whiskey, neat, neither flinching. Empty glasses rapped sharply on the bartop.

Lana Crain turned to face Bragg. "And you, Marshal? What side are you on?"

"The side of the law."

"That's what Bowman said, too."

"But I mean it."

"I hope not; otherwise, we're all liable to be killed while you're worried over some pettifogging legal niceties," she said. "You've got just as much to worry about from Taylor as I do. That puts both of us on the same side of the fence. And that side's getting smaller every day. We've both got something Taylor wants: my place and your badge. Once he has them, he'll have Black Creek sewed up inside his vest pocket, right in time for when the railroad gets here. When are you going to make a stand against Taylor, Bragg?"

"When he gives me a good reason to."

She said, "I could name a half-dozen killings in the last six months that he's behind."

"I could, too, but proving it's a horse of a different color," Bragg said. "When you go up against a man like Taylor, you got to have proof that'll hold up in front of a court of law."

"If you don't move against him," she said, "he'll go on like he's been doing, picking us off one by one, getting rid of anybody who stands between him and owning the town. Sooner or later, Bragg, you'll have to get down off that fence you're sitting on and take a stand. And it better be sooner, because later there's not going to be enough people left on our side for it to make a difference."

There was a stir in the front of the building. Some of the whores were returning, grouped outside the entrance, looking in. They were huddled together, as if there was safety in numbers. Looking in, they were white-faced and wide-eyed, mouths small and tight. They spoke in hushed whispers.

"Which one of them's McCray's woman?" Bragg asked. "I want to talk with her."

"She's not there." Lana Crain crossed to the entryway. "Where's Nelly?"

None of the others knew where Nelly was. They said they guessed she was outside. Lana Crain slid past them, stepping outside, looking around.

The gunplay done, the crowd was coming back, massing closer to the saloon, its leading front lapping at the edge of the veranda.

Nelly Curry was nowhere to be seen. Looking around, Lana Crain saw Bowman leaning on the wall between the entryway and the broken window opening on the bar.

She said, "I suppose you've been eavesdropping on me and Bragg?"

"Is that what I've been doing?" Bowman asked.

"I suppose you can hear pretty good, with the window glass shot out," Lana Crain said.

"Not bad," he said. "Enough."

"Plenty, I'm sure," she said. "Nosy, aren't you?"

"I'm new in town. I've got a lot of catching up to do," he said. "You might say I'm just trying to get the lay of the land."

"You might say it—I wouldn't," Lana Crain said. "You're something of a sneak, aren't you, Bowman? No, don't bother to deny it," she added quickly. "You might have possibilities, Bowman. Come around later, and we'll talk." Turning, she went back inside.

10

The curious crowded close to the front of the Pole Star. Bailey came out on the boardwalk and kept them from getting too close. Now that the shooting was done, they wanted to see the results.

A stir rippled through the crowd. Somebody cried, "Here comes the corpse wagon!"

Approaching from the east on Franklin Street was a hearse drawn by two horses yoked in tandem. It was a long, narrow, high-sided black wagon. The varnished black wood was shiny in the sun.

On the front seat were Knox and his assistant, Merwin. Knox was handling the reins. The seat wasn't quite big enough for both of them, so Merwin sat crowded on one side, kind of sidesaddle, leaning on his hip, with part of his rear hanging over the side. There was plenty of padding there, cushioning the jouncing and bouncing on the spring undercarriage.

The hearse was reined to a halt in front of the building. Merwin climbed down, his weight compressing the springs, tilting the hearse slightly over on his side. When both of his feet were planted on firm ground, the springs decompressed, and the hearse returned to its upright position.

Knox set the handbrake and stepped down on his side of the hearse. Merwin went around to the back of the wagon and opened the door. It opened outward, like a pantry door. Inside were a stretcher, two long poles, and a canvas sling, all rolled up. Merwin shucked it out of the hearse and tucked it under an arm, following Knox toward the saloon door.

Knox's expression was carefully, guardedly neutral. Not happy but not unhappy, either. Briskly professional. Seeing Bowman, he beamed, nodding pleasantly to him. Bowman nodded back.

Knox rearranged his face into its dignified professional mien and went inside. Several minutes later, he emerged, holding up the tail end of the stretcher. At its head was Merwin. Between them, laid out on the stretcher, was a blanket-covered form, rising up in the middle like a hummock.

McCray was lean and wolfish, Yancey soft and paunchy, recalled Bowman. The body on the stretcher could only be Yancey.

The stretcher bearers descended the stairs. In a situation like that, the lead man does most of the heavy lifting, which is why Merwin had the lead. The air was cool, but he was sweating heavily. Knox broke no sweat, but his face had lost some of its carefully composed neutrality, showing signs of strain from carrying his share of the load.

Still on the stretcher, Yancey was loaded into the back of the hearse. The door closed. Merwin and Knox remounted the front seat of the vehicle.

Lana Crain appeared in the doorway. She said, "Be sure and come back for McCray."

Knox bobbed his head, nodding agreement. "We'll be right back, Miz Lana."

"Good," she said. "The sooner the trash is carted away, the sooner I can get back in business."

The hearse drove away. In the saloon, Swamper emptied out a whole keg of sawdust on the floor where Yancey had lain. The sawdust soaked up the blood. Swamper used a push broom to sweep it up.

Lana Crain stood in the front doorway, one hand resting on the frame. The door frame and adjacent walls were pocked with buckshot craters from where Bragg had blown the batwing doors off their hinges.

She peered left and right and at the crowd, frowning. Absently, her fingertips brushed lightly against the cratered shot marks, but her attention was elsewhere.

"Looking for somebody?" Bowman asked.

"One of my girls is missing," she said.

Coming up alongside her, Bragg said, "Where is she? Where's that Nelly gal?"

"I don't know," Lana Crain said. "She's not inside, and she's not out here. Nobody's seen her since the shooting."

Bragg said, "Was she hurt?"

"No. That is, I didn't see it myself, but those who did say that Drummer ignored her and just went after Yancey."

"Scared, most likely," Bragg said. "Give her time to get over her fright, and she'll come back. When she does, I want to talk to her." After a pause, he asked, "Did she love him?"

"She might have thought she did," Lana Crain said.

Seeing something in the corner of his eye, Bragg turned his head, discovering Bowman standing nearby. Bragg said, "You're still here?"

"Got nowhere else to go," Bowman said.

"Well, go there. Where's that Reb partner of yours, up to some new devilment?"

"He didn't think there'd be any more killings for a while, so he went back to see to the horses," Bowman said. "And quit calling him my partner. I'm no partner with Grimes."

"No? You are where these fellows are concerned," Bragg said, gesturing with his blocky jaw toward the north end of Market Road.

Riding south along it were a half-dozen horsemen and a carriage. In the lead was the carriage, a slick, spring-seated, four-wheeled job, drawn by two horses. In the front seat sat two men. It approached at a medium pace, not racing but brisk. A pair of riders flanked it. Behind the wagon were the others, coming four abreast.

People got out of the way, fast. The crowd scattered, scrambling for the sidelines, opening a space on Market Road. It was filled by the carriage and riders, which came to a halt in front of the Pole Star.

"Who's that?" Bowman asked.

"The Taylor bunch," Bragg said. "The fellow in the passenger seat is Rufe Taylor, the head honcho. The driver is his partner, Cord Gentry. The big, mean-looking fellow sitting his horse directly beside Taylor is Gus Arnholt, his ramrod.

"The others are Gussie's crew: Hauk, Griff, Dolan, Jeff, and Purdy," Bragg said, pointing them out.

"There's two of them missing," he said, looking at Bowman. "Sid and Trench. You know, the ones your partner killed."

"He's not my partner."

Bragg said, "Looks like Grimes left a little too soon, huh? If he'd stuck around long enough to meet these *hombres,* there might have been a few more killings. Might be a few more yet."

● ● ●

Taylor and Gentry wore business suits and guns. Arnholt and the others were more casually clad but more heavily armed.

Taylor looked like a wealthy rancher, mine owner, livestock buyer, or something similar, someone who had made a lot of money doing something outdoors. Big, powerfully built, he was in the prime of life.

Broad-brimmed as a planter's hat, his hat was made not from straw but from felt. Under it, his ruddy face was massive and square. Moist brown eyes glimmered from out of baggy pouches, the eyes of a basset hound. They looked faintly mournful. Thin sandy hair, a ginger-colored mustache, and a mouthful of white, shining teeth. He wasn't smiling, though. He was just showing his teeth. They were gritted.

He wore a light brown jacket with a dark brown leather shoulder yoke like a shooting jacket, trimmed with brown piping. Under it was a string tie and fancy gilt-brocade vest. On his right hip he wore a holstered gun.

Beside him, in the driver's seat, was Cord Gentry. In his early fifties, he was spare and lean, pale-eyed and clean-shaven, with a hawklike profile. Long, straggly gray-and-white hair fell past his collar. At his throat was a black ribbon tie, knotted into a bow, with twin ends trailing across the top of the front of his starched white shirt. Perched on the back of his head was a dark hat with a stiff, round brim and rounded crown, the type of hat associated with country parsons. He didn't look like a preacher. He looked like a hard, sharp, flinty man of business.

The jacket of his black broadcloth suit was worn open and unbuttoned, giving easy access to the gun on his left hip. Gunbelt and weapon alike appeared well worn, serviceable.

As for the riders, they were hard cases all, rough men, grizzled, sure of themselves. Garments and saddle leather were rugged, weathered, but their shiny guns were well tended, their horses sleek and fast-looking.

"Harl Yancey was my friend, Bragg," Taylor said. He had a fine, deep speaking voice, booming and resonant. "He's dead. What're you going to do about it?"

"Nothing," Bragg said.

Taylor flinched, his ruddy face darkening, jowls quivering. Gentry looked outraged. The riders bristled, scowling, shifting ominously in their saddles.

Taylor opened his mouth to speak, but before he could get it out, Gentry leaned across him and said, "Do I understand you properly, Marshal?" There was something in his tone of a schoolmaster questioning a miscreant pupil. "You say you will do nothing?" Gentry asked, frankly disbelieving the implicit dereliction of duty.

"Don't have to do nothing," Bragg said offhandedly. "It's been done."

"Eh? What's that?" Gentry said.

Taylor said, "I'm in no mood for games, Bragg."

"Me, neither," the marshal said. "Yancey's dead. McCray shot him. He's dead, too. It's over and done with, so you and your bunch can turn right around and head back the way you came from."

"Shooting was too good for the man who killed Harl Yancey," Taylor said, red-faced. "But let it pass. He's dead, but justice of a kind has been done. But that's only a half-measure. You've nipped the branch but not the root."

Bragg's face reflected bovine puzzlement. "How's that again, Mr. Taylor?"

"What good does it do to get rid of McCray, if only to have his place taken by another? These killings will go on as long as the Pole Star stays open. It's a haunt for drunkards, harlots, tinhorns, robbers, and killers, not safe for decent folk!"

"I don't know about that," Bragg said mildly. "Plenty of decent folk go in there all the time. Like your late pal, Yancey."

Gentry said chidingly, "Speak no ill of the dead, Marshal."

"Every night, there's a shooting in there," Taylor continued.

"Not every night," Bragg said.

"And all this taking place north of the Trail Street deadline! Bad enough, what's going on in Rowdytown, what with all the shootings and stabbings nightly. But at least it's contained down there," Taylor said.

He was speaking to the crowd now. "You can't allow these kinds of goings-on in this part of town, where respectable people live and work and go to church. The Pole Star should've been closed down long ago. And that woman should be run out of town!"

"That'd clear the way to you buying the place, like you been trying to," Bragg said shrewdly. He was playing to the crowd, too.

"Indeed I have," Taylor said, unabashed. "I'm a businessman and a believer in Black Creek. This town's got a big future, when the railroad comes in. The sooner it's cleansed of the trash element, the sooner that day will arrive."

"Miz Lana ain't breaking no laws," Bragg said. "If she does, I'll crack down on her, same as I'd do for anyone else who sets themselves up above the law."

"Meaning me, I suppose," Taylor said. His tone implied that Bragg's statement was proof positive of his unreasonableness, if not his outright lunacy.

Gus Arnholt said, "If you don't do something about this whore's nest, Bragg, we will." His flat statement hung in the air.

He was big and blocky, about Bowman's height and fifty pounds heavier, all of it solid. His squat, wide head was topped by a high-crowned hat whose brim curved upward on the sides, hornlike. The corners of his eyes were turned upward, while the corners of his mouth were turned downward. A cratered and pocked moon face was fringed by a straggly iron-gray beard.

He wore a knee-length brown rawhide coat with a wolf's-fur collar, coat worn open to expose the six-gun riding his hip. Gray trousers were tucked into hand-tooled cowboy boots with pointy toes and chunky heels.

"You say something, Gus?"

"You heard me, Bragg."

"You'd best move on while you're able," Bragg said.

Pushing back his coat, Arnholt rested his hand on the butt of his gun. Leaning forward across the saddle, he said, "Maybe I don't feel like moving on, Bragg." He gestured, his free hand indicating the riders. "Maybe we don't feel like moving on. What're you going to do about it?"

Bragg said, "Get your hand off that gun, unless you plan to use it."

"You going to shoot us all, Bragg?"

"Not all by my lonesome, Gus."

On either side of Bragg, inside the saloon, the empty window frames were filled by Vestry and Bailey. Vestry held a rifle, Bailey a shotgun—the same double-barreled job that Bragg had used against McCray.

Both weapons were leveled on Taylor and his men.

Arnholt didn't flinch, but some of the riders started, as did Taylor. Arnholt sat in place, hand resting on his gun, the sneer frozen on his face. His eyes were narrowed, calculating.

Slowly, carefully, he opened his gun hand, splaying his fingers wide apart, raising his hand to show it was empty.

"Say the word, chief," Bailey said, "and I'll cut loose with both barrels."

Bragg's hand hung down at his side, near his gun. "Try your luck, Gus?"

There was a silence, broken at last by Taylor.

"You've got that rifle pointed at me," he said to Vestry.

"Why, so I have," Vestry said.

Taylor forced his features into a smile. "Easy . . . let's all just slow down and back off here, before things get out of hand."

"I got them in hand," Bragg said. His thick-featured, stolid face was blank, his little whale eyes cool, distant.

Glancing back at the horsemen, Gentry said, "Nobody do anything stupid. Don't start shooting." His face was taut, stiff. The muscles at the corners of his jaws jutted, protuberant hinged knobs.

"There's not going to be any shooting," Taylor said. "You've got to excuse me and the boys, Marshal."

"Do I?"

"Naturally, we're all upset about Yancey's death. He was a good man and a good friend. In the heat of the moment, tempers flare, and people say and do things they shouldn't. All right. That's over and done with. We're backing off, if it makes you any happier to hear me say it. None of my men is going to reach. If there's any more trouble here, it's of your making." Taylor looked around, his gaze widening to include the crowd of onlookers. He said, "All of you folks are witnesses. I've said we want no trouble, and I mean it. I say it before you and the Lord God Almighty."

"How about you, Gussie? You feel that way, too?" Bragg asked.

"You heard Mr. Taylor," Gus said.

"You're not calling me out?"

"I ain't calling nobody out. That's all in your head. I'm just a law-abiding hired man working for wages. I ain't no killer with a badge. Now, I'm going, Bragg. I'm leaving. If you or your deputies shoot, it'll be cold-blooded murder. They even hang marshals for that," Arnholt said.

"The next time you put a hand on a gun in my presence, pull it," Bragg said. "Because I'll surely be trying to kill you."

Taylor said soothingly, "There won't be a next time, I'm sure."

Arnholt spat.

"You're lucky, Gus," Bragg said. "I already killed a man today, so that lets you off the hook. I don't like to bag more than my limit. It ain't sporting. Enough of the palavering," he said, his face hardening. "Now, git!"

They got.

"Let's go, men," Taylor said, motioning them forward. Gentry worked the reins, the horses starting forward, setting the carriage wheels spinning. It went south, down Market Road. Again, the riders paced it, with two flankers and four abreast bringing up the rear.

The carriage always had to be in the lead; Taylor wasn't eating anyone else's dust.

Riding past, Arnholt kept both hands folded on top of the saddle horn. He looked straight ahead, his head held as immobile as if it had been welded onto his neck. They turned left on Trail Street, going east, rounding a corner, and vanishing from sight.

"Whew!" Bowman said. "If I'd have known you were going to brace the whole bunch, I'd've stood somewhere else!"

"Those yellowbellies didn't have the stomach for a fight," Bragg said dismissively. "The odds were against them. They like a sure thing."

Vestry and Bailey put up their weapons and came out through the front entrance.

"Hey, Bailey, you load that shotgun?" Bragg asked, frowning.

Bailey said, "No."

"Me neither, not since I tangled with McCray," Bragg said. "You got an empty gun."

Bailey broke the shotgun and shucked out the two spent cartridges in the chamber. He looked green around the edges.

"Oh, my Lord."

11

Fronting the north side of Trail Street, in the middle of the block between Market Road on the west and Webster Street on the east, the Fremont Hotel was a prewar, three-story red-brick structure. Bowman took a room there.

Before the advent of the Liberty Hotel, the Fremont had been Black Creek's premium hostelry. Now the Liberty was the quality's first choice, while the Fremont's clientele were predominantly independent small businessmen, local ranchers and farmers staying overnight in town, and traveling salesmen of the more or less honest variety. A respectable enough hotel, without being stuffy about it.

That suited Bowman, who considered himself an independent small businessman of sorts.

In the lobby, the green window curtains were faded, the armchairs were frayed at the edges, and the patterned rugs were threadbare. A small dining room was sparsely populated with the end of the lunchtime crowd.

A fair amount of human traffic circulated around the lobby, with knots of businessmen standing huddled together, people constantly entering and exiting. Everybody seemed in a hurry.

Going to the desk, Bowman had his saddlebags slung

over one shoulder and the carbine under his arm. He'd brought them along after getting his horse settled at the livery stable, where he'd just come from.

He asked the clerk for a north-facing room on the top floor, but there was none available. He settled for a room on the southeast corner of that floor.

"I hope it won't be too noisy for you," the clerk said. "Some folks don't like having a room overlooking Trail Street."

"Not me," Bowman said. "I like to watch the passing parade."

Reading the guest's newly signed name in the register, the clerk said, "How long will you be staying with us, Mr. Bowman?"

"About a week. That should give me enough time to complete my business."

"And what business is that, Mr. Bowman?"

Bowman eyed the clerk, finding no sign of untoward interest or curiosity. The desk clerk was just making conversation.

"I'm a speculator," Bowman said.

"Oh? What's your line?" the clerk asked.

"Iron and lead," he said. "Shooting irons and hot lead."

Somewhat nonplussed, the clerk gave him the key to Room 305. Bowman thanked him and started up the stairs.

Room 305 was a single corner room with windows facing south and west. There was a brass-framed bed, a chest of drawers with a shaving mirror mounted on top of it, a standing dark-wood wardrobe cabinet, a square-topped, thin-legged table, and an armless, straight-backed chair.

Bowman locked the door from the inside, leaving the key in the keyhole. He sat on the bed, testing the springs.

They'd seen hard use, but there was still some bounce in them.

The room was musty-smelling. That wasn't so bad, either. There were worse ways for a hotel room to smell. He opened the windows, letting the air in.

He'd wanted a room on the top floor because it presented the best vantage point, and he'd wanted a room facing north so he could keep Courthouse Square under observation.

This wasn't so bad, though. The front windows looked out on Trail Street and the south side of town. The side windows opened on Market Road and points west.

Unlike most towns in this part of the territory, Black Creek had escaped being burned during the border wars and the Civil War. Much of its original prewar layout was intact.

Trail Street was the dividing line. North of it was where most of the better-class commercial and residential areas were. To the south, buildings were shabbier, more ill kept. Rooflines sagged, uprights tilted, walls went unpainted, broken windows gaped. Below lay Rowdytown, a cluster of saloons, dirty-spoon cafés, honky-tonks, dives, gambling halls, whorehouse cribs, and the like.

Beyond the southernmost edge of the vice district, bordering it, the lower fork of Telegraph Road could be seen, the lines of poles stringing west, marking out the future course of the railroad.

Going to the side windows, Bowman glanced down into Market Road. From there, he could see the Pole Star squatting on its block-sized lot. The crowd had broken up, though a few knots of people still milled around in the street in front of the place.

Bowman studied the scene, getting the layout squared

away in his head. When he had seen his fill, he went out, locking the door from the outside. He left the windows in Room 305 open.

The inner man was crying out for food, and Bowman decided to oblige him. The hotel dining room was empty, the last diner gone, leaving not even a waiter in sight.

Crossing the lobby, Bowman went to the front entrance, pausing just inside the doorway. Studying the street scene, he spotted no signs of potential lurkers, ambushers, enemies, or suchlike sinister personages.

He went out, crossed the street, then walked east along it. The south side of the street was in shadow, the north in sunlight. He stuck to the shady side. After a few blocks, he found a likely-looking café and went in.

He ate a big lunch, wolfing it down. He went into a store and bought a couple of bottles of red whiskey, taking them with him. Smoking a cigar, he found the bath house to which the café owner had given him directions.

Soaking in a hot bath, Bowman smoked another cigar and drank red whiskey from the bottle. To the right of the galvanized, hooded steel tub in which he sat was a three-legged circular wicker table. On it were a bottle of whiskey and a hand towel, piled in a heap. Under the towel was a derringer.

A visit to a tonsorial parlor next door resulted in a haircut and a shave. Feeling clean and mean, minus one bottle of red whiskey, Bowman returned to the hotel. It was midafternoon.

Climbing the stairs seemed a lot harder this time.

It was cold in Room 305, and he closed all the windows, then opened one of the south windows a crack to let some air in. The room still smelled musty. Sitting on the edge of the bed, he opened a fresh bottle of whiskey and held it under his nose, the raw fumes burning his nostrils and bringing tears to his eyes.

He took a drink from the bottle. Clutching it by the neck, he rose and crossed to the table and chair. He moved the table so that the light from the south and west windows fell on it.

He took his gun from the holster and placed it on the table, at his right hand. He took out his derringer, cleaned, oiled, and reloaded it.

He remembered that he'd forgotton to stop by the jail to see about his money. "Hell with it, I'll take care of it later," he said.

Yawning, he eyed the bed. It looked inviting. Starting toward it, he paused and glanced at the room door. It was locked, with his key in it, but it didn't seem too secure. Anybody could just kick it in.

The chest of drawers stood nearby. Wrapping his arms around it, hugging it, Bowman wrestled it across the floor and propped its back against the door.

"Nobody'll kick it in now," he said, looking owlish. "And if there's a fire, I can always jump out the window."

He flopped down on the bed, crunching the springs. He was too tired to take off his boots, so he said the hell with it and left them on. He lay on his back, head propped up by pillows, smoking a cigar and taking frequent pulls from the whiskey bottle. His pistol lay on the bed beside him, his right hand brushing against it.

Everything was fuzzy but the gun; it was cold, hard-edged, solid. He held onto it as, floating on a whiskey-colored sea, he sank down and down.

* * *

When he awoke, the room lay in shadowed gloom. He was still more than half drunk. His hand was still wrapped around the gun butt.

If he could get his feet on the floor, that'd be half the battle. Raising them was hard, his boots weighing him down like bricks strapped to his feet. With a grunt, he swung his legs off the bed. Gravity did the rest. He was now sitting up with his feet on the floor.

One window was open only a few inches, but enough cold air had gotten in to render the room quite chilly. Bowman realized that was what had awakened him.

It was evening, dusk. The sun had set, but there was still light in the western sky. White, cool, colorless light. It didn't so much shine as slide through the window panes, giving him some light to see by.

His cigar was where he'd left it, on the night table, the tip hanging off the edge. It was cold, half smoked. His hands were cold and stiff as he fumbled for a match and lit it. He was shivering. He puffed, the orange coal and pungent smoke warming him.

When it was smoked, he felt better. He glanced at the bottle of red whiskey standing on the night table. It was mostly full. Thinking about taking a drink, he shuddered. He didn't feel that much better, not yet.

Still, he was experiencing a blazing thirst. There had been a pitcher of water on top of the chest of drawers.

That reminded him that he had to wrestle the cabinet away from the door. Thinking about it made his head hurt worse.

The water pitcher was on the small wooden table, where he must have set it before moving the cabinet. It gave him a reason for moving. He rose, lurching across the room. The water pitcher was on a tray with a glass tumbler. Picking up the pitcher in both hands, he drank from it, gulping it down, his throat working.

He opened one of the south windows and stuck his head outside, breathing deeply, filling his lungs with fresh air, clearing some of the mental cobwebs. The sky was drab white with the falling light, while a rising tide of purple-gray gloom filled the streets.

On Trail Street, in the buildings, lights shone out from behind glass window panes, turning them into yellow squares and rectangles. In Rowdytown, lights were few, dark and smoky, like banked coals.

A washing basin also sat on the table. Into it he poured some water, which he then rubbed on his face, restoring some of the feeling to it.

He stretched, working out the kinks. He paid special attention to his hands, rubbing them to quicken circulation, flexing his fingers. A working gunman's hands must be loose and supple.

Taking a deep breath, he grappled with the blocked door, hugging the chest of doors and moving it out of the way. This time, he didn't have to move it so far, for which he was grateful.

A line of light from the hall shone under the door into the room.

Breathing hard, he stood beside the west windows. In the dying light, he strapped a special holster to the inside of his left wrist. Into it he fitted the derringer, which lay flat against his forearm.

There were special spring-loaded rigs favored by gamblers and such, which could drop a derringer into a man's palm with a twist of the wrist. Bowman shunned such devices, fearing that they would go wrong at the time they were most needed. A simple wrist holster served him fine. Just ask Cotton.

He rolled down his sleeve, covering the weapon, leaving the cuff unbuttoned for easy access. With his short denim jacket worn over it, no one unaware of the derringer's presence could have guessed it was there.

He picked up his gun and slipped it into the crossbelly holster, its comforting weight nestled against him.

He went to the door, unlocked it, and opened it a crack. The corridor was empty. Leaving the door partly open so the light could get in, he closed the windows and pulled down the shades. He put on his hat, draped his coat over his left arm.

On the way out, he eyed the bottle on the night table, its mahogany-colored fluid glowing by the light shining through the open door. He thought about having a drink, decided to pass on it.

"It's a hell of a thing when you've got to take a drink to go downstairs," he said to himself. Or had he spoken aloud? He wasn't sure.

Stepping into the hall, he locked the door from the outside. He worked the key with his left hand, the coat draped over his forearm. He kept his gun hand empty, hanging loose by his side. It wasn't something he had to think about; he just did it automatically.

Bowman went downstairs into the lobby. The desk clerk was the same man who'd been on earlier.

It was dinnertime. The dining room was filled with sound and movement. Bowman went in. A beefsteak and a quart or so of black coffee later, he emerged, feeling steadier.

He picked up a half-dozen cigars at the lobby counter,

slipped all but one into an inside breast pocket, and went out.

It was night now, black night.

On Trail Street, more than a few stores and shops had closed for the day. Still, along the main stem, there was a fair amount of traffic in both directions, moving by carriage, by wagon, on horseback, and on foot.

Standing sheltered by a front pillar, out of the light fanning from the hotel entrance, Bowman got his cigar going. Moving on, he followed the boardwalk east.

The next cross street was Commerce. Pausing at the corner, he looked south, toward Rowdytown. It was quickening, with a sense of half-seen activity stirring in the semidarkness.

Turning north, he followed Commerce into the square, going toward the jail. To his left, on the boardwalk fronting the funeral parlor, Knox's assistant, Merwin, and wagoneer Cobb stood talking. Both looked up as Bowman passed.

Merwin bobbed his head, smiling. Cobb spat. Bowman nodded, not breaking stride. He went into the jail.

Mounted on top of the inside of the door was a tiny bell, which jingled as Bowman entered.

The front part of the building was an office. The walls were made of rough-surfaced dark gray stones and mortar. The central space was clear, opening on a long, dim passageway lined on both sides by metal man cages, cells.

Up front, furniture and other items were grouped to the sides. There was a big desk, a table, a couple of chairs, some lockers, and a single filing cabinet. In a corner stood a cast-iron stove, its elbow-shaped chimney pipe venting high on one of the long walls. Its belly now glowed hot and red. Perched on a stove lid was a coffee pot. A wooden box nearby was stacked with firewood.

Against one wall stood a gun rack, lined with a standing row of rifles and shotguns secured in their places by a locking chain. Opposite it, on the other side of the room, was a wall-mounted wooden signboard, papered over with wanted posters and circulars. Flanking the signboard was a framed portrait of Abe Lincoln in profile and an American flag hanging limply on a pole.

On the table were piles of bound books of wanted circulars and a half-dozen weighty law tomes, their covers dog-eared.

Facing the door at a transverse angle was a massive dark wooden desk, as rock-solid as the pedestal base of a monument.

Behind it was an equally big club chair, oversized, overstuffed, looking as if it would have been more at home in some homey front parlor.

In the chair sat Bragg, hunched over a full-course dinner laid out on his desktop. Bowman's entrance caused him to look up but not to interrupt his meal. Bragg's knife and fork kept on with their inexorable work of demolishing the food and drink before him.

Nearby sat a man with short, wavy hair and a neatly trimmed beard. Hair and beard were so black their highlights were blue. His brows were thick, rectangular, his nose broad and flat. His eyes were dark brown, black-brown, so that iris and pupil almost seemed to be one. Dark gun-bore eyes in a stiff face. He wore a badge and a gun—another of Bragg's deputies.

He sat in a wooden armchair, tilted back so that its two front legs were off the floor. The chair leaned against the wall. He was drinking coffee.

"Well, looky who's here," Bragg said between bites.

To one side of his desk was the basket that had been used to carry his dinner. Bragg's hands rested on the tabletop, fists that held the knife and fork pointing upward. The utensils looked small in his hands.

Pointing at Bowman with the fork, Bragg said, "Dick, this here's Bowman, the fellow I was telling you about. The one who got Cotton."

The deputy leaned forward, placing all four chair legs on the floor. Indicating the other with his knife, Bragg said, "Bowman, this here's Dick Dixon, one of my deputies."

Bowman and Dixon nodded to each other.

"I know what you're here for, Bowman. You want your money," Bragg said. He ate some more food. "Well, I don't have it," he said. "But I've got something almost as good. A chit on the reward, signed by the mayor."

Bragg wiped thick fingers on a red-and-white gingham napkin, a broad flag-sized square. He pawed through a stack of papers on one side of his desk, leafing through them, holding them up to the light.

"I know it's here somewhere," he said. "Here it is." He handed Bowman a piece of paper, a signed draft authorizing the reward money to be paid out to him. "Give this to Radle, the bank manager. He'll see that you get paid," Bragg said.

The document seemed in order. Bowman folded and pocketed it. "Much obliged."

"Don't thank me. It's the town's money," Bragg said. His fork speared a piece of brown potato the size of a walnut, and he popped it into his mouth. "Two hundred dollars, cash on the barrel head," he said. "How do you like them apples?"

"A month's pay," Dixon said. His voice was deep, husky.

"Maybe we're in the wrong line of work, huh? Never mind," Bragg said. "Tinsley—the man Cotton killed—was a well-liked man. Hell, I liked him myself."

"Me, too," Dixon said.

"Cotton dead marks paid in the ledger. And all without me having to get up out of my chair," Bragg said. "I ain't kicking."

Metal tinkled on the desktop as he set down the utensils. "Have a seat, Bowman. I want to talk to you for a minute."

"All right." Crossing to the table, Bowman picked up a chair and carried it back to the other side of the office. He set it down so that it was facing both lawmen. He sat down, waiting.

Resting his forearms on the desk's edge, Bragg leaned forward, causing the oversized chair to groan on its frame. "Ever heard of Harvey Kidd, Bowman?"

"I've heard the name," Bowman said mildly. "A Redleg turned outlaw, wasn't he?"

"That's right," Bragg said. "You tell it, Dick. I'll eat while you jaw."

"How much do you want me to tell?" Dixon asked.

"Give him the background."

Dixon nodded. He took a sip of coffee. "Kidd used to be one of Jim Lane's top men, running raids against the slave holders in Missouri. Only he was such a first-class thief and killer that even before the war broke out, Jim Lane kicked him out of the Redleg militia. That didn't stop Kidd. He just went into business for himself. His gang was made up of the worst scum of both sides, a real band of cutthroats. Before too long, both the North and the South had sentenced him to death. Trouble was, they had to catch him first. They never did. After the war, the gang broke up, and Kidd disappeared. A rumor started that he was wounded in a skirmish with federal troops, died of his wounds, and was buried in a lonely grave."

"Where are we going with this?" Bowman asked.

"We're coming to it," Bragg said. He stabbed the air in front of him with his fork, underlining his words. "Cotton was a member of the Kidd gang."

"So?"

"Some of the old Kidd gang have been seen in these parts lately. Even in Black Creek, in Rowdytown. Eb Oliver, Patch Hawkins, Shorty Bevins. And Cotton, of course. Sometimes alone, sometimes in combination," Bragg said. "By the time we get wind of it, they're gone."

His scalp and face were shiny, especially around his mouth, which glistened with grease. His little whale eyes blazed.

"They all started showing up once it was announced that the railroad was going to pass through town," he said. "That's when all those robberies and killings started, too. I got me an idea that the gang has reformed and that they're hiding out somewhere between here and End-of-Track." He thumped the desk with his fist again. "They know enough to stay out of Black Creek. Oh, sure, every now and then, one or two of them slip into town late at night for some whoring and drinking, and I don't hear about it until a day later, when it's too late. I'm not about to go tearing up the countryside looking for them. I'm a town marshal, paid to keep the peace in Black Creek. Outside of town, that's the county sheriff's lookout, and the federals'."

"This listening is thirsty work," Bowman said. "Okay if I get some coffee?"

"Help yourself," Bragg said expansively.

Dixon said, "There's cups on the shelf."

Bowman got a cup and poured some coffee from the pot into it. He took a sip. He shuddered, his stomach heaving. He said to Dixon, "You're a mighty man to drink this brew."

"I like it," Dixon said, his tone implying that he didn't give a damn whether Bowman liked it or not.

In the interval, Bragg had excavated more of the meat and potatoes heaped on his plate. Bowman said, "How does Cotton tie in with the Taylor crowd?"

"That's a question," Dixon said. He drank some more coffee, his attitude indicating that he'd said all he cared to for now.

"Who is Taylor?" Bowman asked. "Is he supposed to be somebody? I never heard of him."

"He thinks he's somebody," Bragg said, his little gimlet eyes hard and bright. "Calls himself a businessman, a promoter. He aims to buy up as much of the town as he can before the railroad gets here. Don't make no secret about it, neither. I did some checking on him. Last place he was in before he came here was St. Louis. He ain't no Missouri man, though. Claims he hails from somewhere in Ohio. Could be, so far as I can tell. Back in St. Lou, he was mixed up in some mighty shady financial dealings, but nothing he could go to jail for. And before you ask, there wasn't nothing tying him in with the Harvey Kidd gang before, during, or after the war. He's clean that way. About six months ago, Taylor showed up here in town, him and his wife and that fellow Gentry, his right-hand man. They all came in at the same time, came to stay. Took over the top floor of the Liberty, across the square. Along about that time, Gus Arnholt became a permanent fixture in town. Unfortunately. Gus come up from the Nations in Oklahoma, him and a gang of followers. He's an all-general no-good, him and the rest of his crew. He's got a couple of killings to his name, but nothing he can be charged for. They were all fair fights."

Bowman's eyebrows lifted.

"At least, that's what the witnesses swore to," Bragg said. "Of course, most of them were his *compadres,* and the others might have been too scared to tell what really went down. But you can't jail a man for might-have-beens. Gus's a hard case, a first-class troublemaker, a killer. It's my guess that he ain't above robbing, rustling, and horse stealing, neither. But he's smart, smart enough to rig things so he don't get caught. So far. He's been working for Taylor, as a kind of bodyguard and ramrod. So he says. It's my personal belief that Gus is doing Taylor's dirty work for him, squeezing out anybody who don't want to sell out at Taylor's price. 'Course, I can't prove nothing. After a visit from Gussie and his night riders, nobody's got the guts to swear out a complaint."

Bragg went on. "Also at the same time that Taylor set up operations in Black Creek, members of the old Kidd gang started showing up, like I said. Mostly, they operate outside of town, robbing, burning, and killing. Call it coincidence, but lots of times, the ranchers and farmers they burned out happened to be in the path of the future railroad. And who do you suppose bought up that land?"

"Taylor?" Bowman said.

"Give the man a see-gar," Bragg said. "At first, I suspected Gus was behind that, too. But he and his crowd could account for where they were at the time the raids were being committed. In fact, they were so careful about it ~~you~~ might think they knew when the raids were going to happen and had made sure to get themselves an alibi. And what few witnesses there were, those who'd survived the raids—and there ain't many, because the raiders usually killed everyone they found—the witnesses' descriptions tallied with members of the Kidd gang."

Bowman sat there, the coffee cup warm in his hand, its fluid level undiminished since the first sip he'd taken, the bitter taste still curling the edges of his tongue.

Bragg had polished off most of his meal and was now cleaning his plate with a shoe-sized chunk of bread, using it to mop up gravy. Blazing coals hissed and chuffed inside the stove. Dixon drank some more coffee, smacking his lips after each gulp. Bragg said, "For months now, I been looking for something to tie the Kidd gang to Taylor. Or Gus. I kept coming up blank—until today."

"Which is where I come in," Bowman said.

"Uh-huh." Bragg nodded ponderously. "Now, what do you suppose Dawes Cotton was doing, being sided by two of Gus Arnholt's men?"

"Why don't you ask Gus?"

" 'Cause he'd only lie to me and say that he ain't responsible for what a couple of hangers-on like Sid and Trench decide to do."

"What're you going to do about it?"

"The question is," Bragg said, "what're you going to do about it?"

"I'm not sure I follow you," Bowman said cautiously.

"When you gunned Cotton, you made yourself a passel of enemies," Bragg said, obviously relishing the idea. "His *compadres* in the Kidd gang will be gunning for you. You ain't liable to be too popular with Gus and his crowd, seein' as how you sided with Grimes when he killed two of their boys. As for Grimes, he wouldn't have been too popular in any case, even if he didn't gun nobody, on account of him being a Johnny Reb and all. Me, I'm inclined toward giving him a break, since he killed two of Gussie's crowd. Could be he's just warming up."

"Could be."

"There's already been pressure on me from some of the town council that's in Taylor's pocket," Bragg said. "They want me to run the both of you out of town. I told them where to get off. Said as long as you don't break the law, you got as much right in Black Creek as anyone else."

"Well, that's right decent of you, Marshal. I appreciate it."

"I ain't doing it for you, Bowman. I'm doing it for me. I figure that with you in town, some of the Kidd gang might come in to get you. That's when I get them. The territory's too big, with too many hiding places, for me to flush out the gang by myself, even if I was of a mind to. Which I ain't. I told you, I don't like getting out of my chair."

Bowman said, "You're using me as bait."

"Yep," Bragg said.

"Suppose I don't want to be a clay pigeon. What's to stop me from riding out, putting some distance between me and Black Creek?"

"Not a thing, not a blamed thing. Except one."

"What's that?"

"Greed," Bragg said. "You knowed what you was doing when you burned Cotton, knew who he was and how much he was worth dead or alive. Think I don't know a bounty hunter when I see one? Man, do you know what kind of a reward is posted on the Kidd gang? Cotton was small potatoes compared to some of the others. Why, there must be a couple of thousand dollars posted on Patch Hawkins alone. Oliver, Bevins, Calloway have got to be worth at least a thousand dollars each. Throw in some of the lessers, and that's another thousand right there. I'm talking about county money, state money, federal. Railroad money, bank money, express company money. I don't know why I'm telling you this. Hell, you probably know the totals better than me."

"What about Kidd himself?" Bowman asked.

"You think he's alive?"

"Nobody ever saw him dead. Where's the body? He wouldn't be the first to use the war to fake his own death."

"To tell you the truth, I've studied on the idea myself," Bragg said. "He was a slippery cuss, by all accounts. Nobody knows for sure just how old he is or what he looks like. Most of those who knew him during the war are dead, except for the gang, and they ain't talking."

"Wasn't there a sister?" Dixon asked.

"Sure enough," Bragg said. "What was her name? Elvira, Varinia, something like that, wasn't it, Dick?"

"Lavinia."

"Lavinia Kidd, that's right. She worked with him as a spy, lookout, go-between, and what-all. Fenced stolen property for him, sometimes selling it back to the person they stole it from, sometimes to whoever had the cash."

"She disappeared at the same time he did," Dixon pointed out.

"She sure did. Brother and sister both go missing at the same time, at war's end. Suspicious, ain't it? Like they planned it that way. Nobody's ever seen her again, either."

Bowman said, "Which is one more thing that makes it look like Harvey Kidd is alive."

"It's possible," Bragg said. "He's the one who could

hold the gang together. None of the others is smart enough to do the planning for them, to keep them from getting caught. But they ain't getting caught. So?"

Bowman seemed deep in thought. "Must be a big reward on him."

Bragg laughed. "See, Dick? He's hooked."

"Probably already thinking about how he's going to spend that money."

"You'll be a rich man, Bowman."

"If he lives."

"Well, yes, there's that," Bragg conceded. "But if he gets killed, the town'll set him up with a nice little grave on Boot Hill."

Bowman said, "I don't mind taking risks, if it's worth the reward."

"What I figured," Bragg said.

"But if the Kidd gang comes here looking for me, it could be pretty rough on the town, Marshal."

"I've studied on that," Bragg said. "But if things keep on the way they're going, pretty soon Taylor'll run Black Creek anyhow. And when that day comes, me and my deputies are going to be out of a job. They're young men, but me, I'm too old to have to go to work for a living. So there it is, Bowman. I've laid it all out for you. You—and your Rebel pal, Grimes—are welcome to stay as long as you like."

"He's not my pal."

"He can still stay. Gussie and his crowd are gonna want to nail his hide to the barn door. That gives them one more thing to worry about."

"While you sit back and pick up the pieces."

"Right here in this chair, that's where I'll be sitting."

Bragg sat there, looking expectantly across the desk at

Bowman. Dixon leaned back, studying a corner where ceiling met walls.

"What kind of share you figuring on for the reward money?" Bowman asked.

"Not a cent," Bragg said. "You keep it. Whoever's marshal when the railroad comes to town will be sitting pretty. So there's something in it for the both of us. What do you say, Bowman?"

Bowman leaned forward, reaching with the coffee cup, setting it down on the edge of the desk. He took out a cigar, rolled it between his fingers. He bit off the tip, anchoring the cigar in the corner of his mouth. "Cigar, Marshal?"

"Don't mind if I do."

Bowman rose, took a cigar from his pocket, handed it to Bragg. Bragg set it down to one side of the dishes and said, "I'll smoke it later, when I get done eating."

Offering one to Dixon, Bowman said, "Deputy?"

Dixon waved it away. Still looking at the ceiling, he said, "I'll stick to my own brand."

Going to the stove, Bowman picked up a pair of tongs, opened the grated door. Light from it turned his skin orange. Using the tongs, he plucked a glowing coal from the fire, holding it to the end of his cigar, puffing it.

He dropped the coal back into the fire, closed the grate, hung up the tongs, and sat down, venting clouds of smoke.

After a while, he said, "I might have to shoot some people."

"Just so long as they're the right people. That's all I ask," Bragg said. "The storm's been building for a long time, and now it looks like it's going to break."

Bowman got up to leave. "I'll be around."

"You do that."

Bowman turned, crossed to the door. Bragg called, "You might want to keep your eye on the Pole Star. Taylor's going to want revenge for Yancey being killed there."

"I was planning on dropping in there anyway," Bowman said.

"I bet," Bragg said, leering. As he looked down at his desktop, his leer melted, replaced by a frown. Turning to Dixon, he demanded, "Didn't the chef over to the Bon Ton Café pack in no dessert?"

"Sure he did."

"I don't see it, Dick."

"It's under your napkin there," Dixon said, pointing.

Bragg snatched away the crumpled red-and-white gingham napkin, revealing a plate with a pie wedge the size of a mason's trowel on it. The corners of his eyes and mouth turned upward, his face lit.

Seizing a fork, he tucked into the pie with single-minded concentration.

The audience was over.

Bowman went out, ringing the tiny bell mounted over the door.

12

The boardwalk in front of the funeral parlor was deserted when Bowman stepped out into the square. At the north end, the Liberty Hotel was all lit up, its white front shining. He went east, crossing the square.

The east side of the square was open, unblocked. Ahead lay the shore and the river. Leaving the square behind, Bowman struck out on a footpath toward the river. The ground underfoot was hard, dry. The path glided over wide, sprawling fields. There were no buildings there, just open space.

It was a clear, cold night. Low in the east, a waxing yellow-white crescent moon had risen, smearing the purple-black sky surrounding it with a bleary foxfire glow. Bowman smelled the river before he saw it. There was something rank in it, telling of slime, muck, rot.

Wind blew from the north. It was chilly at first, but after he'd been walking for a bit, he didn't mind it at all. He was alone, the only thing stirring among the wide emptiness at the river's edge.

He went over a small rise, coming to a bluff overlooking the river. A dirt road came down from the north, cutting the footpath at right angles and continuing southward, stretching across the top of the bluff. This was River Road.

Beyond, the footpath sloped down to a landing, where a wedge-shaped spit of land jutted into the river. Bulking at the water's edge was a big blocky building, a warehouse. It was dark, seemingly untended.

Bowman's eyes were used to the dark. He had no trouble picking out the path, following it to where it leveled out, running down the middle of the wedge, out to its end where there was a pier and a floating dock.

The warehouse was shuttered, silent. Whatever was in there, it wasn't worth posting a night watchman to protect it.

Bowman paused at the foot of the pier. The river was swift, rushing. Thinking about how cold it must be raised a shiver on the back of Bowman's neck. He flipped his lit cigar butt into the water, the orange coal winking out as quickly as thought.

A solitary spot, a lonesome place. Still, Bowman prowled around the area, making sure it was as deserted as it looked. Water swirled around the pilings of the dock. Bowman stood against a piling, half sheltering behind it, facing shoreward. Waiting.

Slipping around the corner of the warehouse, flitting through its shadows, a figure came into view, padding toward the dock. It passed through an open space lit by moonlight, casting an eerie elongated giant shadow across the slope.

The skulker's hat was pinned up in front to the crown, baring his face and form to the moonlight slanting down on him.

Wagoneer Cobb.

Moving in a half-crouch, Cobb set foot on the deck, turning his head this way and that, looking around.

Stepping out from behind the pillar, Bowman called

Cobb's name in a stage whisper. Cobb flinched, then came to him.

Bowman said, "Nice night for a walk."

"I'm not used to walking," Cobb said. "Makes my feet hurt. Did you have to pick a spot so far from town?"

"It's better that way. Keeps folks from knowing we're working together. Better for you—and me." Bowman looked around. "Nice and private around here."

"It's private, anyhow," Cobb grudgingly admitted.

"You can see somebody coming from a long way off," Bowman said, "like I saw you."

"Like hell you did," Cobb said heatedly.

"Let it pass."

Cobb spat. "That's the good thing about chawing tobacco. You don't have to worry about the light giving you away at night, the way your lit cigar did."

"That was to keep you from getting lost," Bowman said.

Cobb spat again, changed the subject. "That sure was lucky, your crossing paths with Cotton last night."

"Not for him," Bowman said.

"Did you know he'd be at the crossing?"

"No. But he had a pretty good idea Grimes would be passing that way."

"Why Grimes? Who's he?" Cobb asked, his voice full of genuine puzzlement.

"I was kind of hoping you could tell me," Bowman said.

"I stuck to him all day, like you told me to," Cobb said. "After he left the Pole Star, he went to the livery stable to put his horses up. Then he went to see Harper."

"Who's he?"

"Cornelius Harper, the lawyer who's handling Grimes's

bequest. He's a kind of a grand old man of Black Creek, a power in town. Been lawyering here since before the war. Most deals in town, he's got his oar in on 'em."

"Honest?" Bowman asked.

"I never heard any different, and I've been running this route for years now. 'Course, could be that he just ain't been found out yet," Cobb said. "He's got an office in the building next to the Liberty Hotel. Grimes went to see him there this afternoon."

Cobb laughed mirthlessly. "I don't think he liked what he heard, if that long face he was wearing when he came out of Harper's office means anything. He's an heir, all right. His dead uncle left him clear title to Bittersink Basin—the most worthless piece of land in these parts. It's well known in Black Creek. Nothing grows there. The water's so tainted by mineral deposits that it ain't fit for man or beast. You can't graze stock there; they just get sick and die if they ain't moved on to greener pastures. That's if they don't fall down into a sinkhole and break a leg or a neck. The basin's full of 'em, from rabbit holes that are just the right size for a horse or beef to break a leg in, all the way up to giant sinkholes big enough to swallow up a barn."

Bowman said, "It must be worth something to somebody."

"It never was yet," Cobb said. "What makes you say that?"

"Simple. Before he came into his legacy, nobody was trying to kill Grimes—nobody outside the normal order of things. He rubs people the wrong way; he's got a chip on his shoulder. So I guess there'll always be somebody looking to cut him down to size," Bowman said. "When he became an inheritor, though, he became a target. And what a target! What's Dawes Cotton to Reb Grimes?"

"When you find out, let me know," Cobb said. "If you're still alive."

"What else did Grimes do?" Bowman asked.

"Bought himself some new duds, ate lunch, drank whiskey. Took a room over to the Hafton House, a cheap hotel on Market, below Trail Street," Cobb said. "I got hungry and thirsty myself and went to eat dinner. I ain't seen Grimes since, but I doubt he'll be too hard to find. He'll be someplace getting drunk, gaming, or whoring, maybe all three. Trouble is, there's so many places for him to do it in."

"If he's looking for a fight, he won't have to look too far for one."

"That's for blamed sure," Cobb agreed. "He better watch out for Arnholt and the boys, because they're damned sure watching out for him."

"Grimes can take care of himself," Bowman said. Echoing Bragg's words, Bowman added, "And if he can't, Boot Hill is waiting."

Wind blew, damp and moisture-laden. Cobb shivered. "Cold, wet weather. Creeps into the bones. I must be getting old."

"Must be," Bowman said.

"You bastard," Cobb said, without heat. He fidgeted, shifting his weight from foot to foot, hands in his pockets. "One thing more," he said. "McCray's woman is missing."

"Nelly Curry," Bowman said.

"Her," Cobb agreed. "She never came back to the Pole Star."

"Scared she's going to get what Drummer got, maybe."

"Maybe."

"Now, where might she be hiding out?"

"Any house or saloon in Rowdytown, and believe me,

there's plenty of 'em." Cobb was thoughtful. "She might go to Stackpole."

"Rory Stackpole," Bowman said. "I heard he was operating a place in town."

"The Bucket of Blood," Cobb said. "And he wasn't just funning when he named the place that. 'Most every day, there's a shooting or stabbing in there."

"Why doesn't Bragg bust it up?" Bowman asked.

"He don't give a damn, as long as that Rowdytown element does it to each other," Cobb said. "Besides, there's bad blood between Stackpole and Gus, going way back before either of them ever came to this town. Stackpole's tough enough to buck the Taylor-Arnholt combine, which is another reason Bragg leaves him alone. If that Nelly gal is scared of Taylor, she could do worse than to tie in with Stackpole. Gus is in no hurry to try bucking Stackpole in his own place."

Bowman said, "Maybe I'll look in myself."

"Don't you be in no hurry to tangle with Stackpole, neither," Cobb said. "He ain't what he used to be—who is?— but he's got guts in his belly, not wind. Not like this new breed of no-account trash that's come up since the war."

"I'll buy him a drink."

Cobb shuffled his feet in place. "My feet are getting cold."

"Got anything else for me?" Bowman asked.

"That's all of it for now."

"Okay. We'll have to leave one a time."

"I'll go first," Cobb said. "My legs are stiffening up on me. The sooner I'm out of this cold, the better."

"On your way, then," Bowman said. "Before you go— Lawyer Harper's office is in the building next to the Liberty?"

"Yes, but he ain't going to be there now. It's late, and he's an old man."

"Like you, Cobb."

Cobb told Bowman what he could do.

"That's illegal in this county," Bowman said.

"Do it anyway," Cobb said. "Harper's part of that Liberty crowd. Eats there 'most every night, then spends an hour or two in the hotel bar. You might catch him there."

"I'll give it a try."

"If you need me, you know how to reach me," Cobb said, starting forward.

Bowman said, "I'll be in touch."

Cobb said so long, then lumbered off, following the dock to the shore. When he was on solid ground, he drifted off the path, melting into the shadows massed around the warehouse.

After Cobb was long gone, Bowman started back to town.

13

Bowman went north on River Road, turning left onto a footpath that stretched toward the north side of the square. Entering the square by the northeast corner, he crossed paths with Vestry.

The deputy was alone, carrying a shotgun under his arm, muzzle down. Bowman nodded to him and would have kept on walking, but the other motioned him to come over.

" 'Evening, Deputy."

"I've been looking for you, Mr. Bowman," Vestry said.

"That shotgun's not for me, is it?" Bowman's tone was light, easy.

"I'm on patrol, making my rounds." Vestry was straight-faced, unsmiling.

"You get much call to use that scattergun in the grounds of the Liberty Hotel?"

"A lot of suspicious characters in and out of the hotel," Vestry said seriously.

"What can I do you for, Deputy?"

"A word, Mr. Bowman."

"This official business?"

"Not unless you want it that way."

"Not if I don't have to."

They spoke low-voiced, heads together. Vestry said, "It's about that partner of yours."

"Partner? What partner?" Bowman, taken aback, tried not to show it.

"The Reb."

"Oh, you mean Grimes," Bowman said, relieved. For an instant, he'd thought that Vestry was referring to Cobb, that somehow he was aware of their alliance. It didn't suit Bowman's purposes for now for that alliance to be discovered.

"Yes, Grimes." Vestry said the name as if it left a bad taste in his mouth.

"Get this straight, Deputy—Grimes is no partner of mine," Bowman said. "I don't know how that crazy idea got started."

"Maybe because you killed a couple of men together," Vestry suggested.

"That was pure chance. You'd have done the same."

"Maybe, but we're talking about what you did."

"Listen," Bowman said, "before last night, I didn't know him from Adam. And I'd just as soon go back to being that way."

"Let's not split hairs. You know him well enough to talk to him," Vestry said.

"I'll grant you that," Bowman agreed. "I don't know that he'd listen to me, though. From what I've seen of Grimes, he's not exactly the listening type."

"If you want to do him a favor, tell him to keep away from my niece, Francine."

"Why don't you tell him yourself?" Bowman asked.

Vestry, frozen-faced, said, "If I tell him, he's going to get told hard, and in no uncertain terms. Before anyone gets hurt, I'd like to head off trouble before it starts."

"Can't say as I blame you," Bowman allowed.

"If there's two things I don't like, it's a Reb and a troublemaker, and he's both," Vestry said. "I've got no use for him, but as long as he stays out of trouble and doesn't break the law, there's not much I can do."

"Don't forget, Grimes is a Black Creek property holder now," Bowman reminded him.

"Bittersink Basin's outside the town limits. It's county property," Vestry retorted. "Owning that worthless piece of ground won't buy him a thing in this town. Or any other. Never mind about that. That's business. Francine is family. That makes it personal. I don't want him coming around her, filling her head with all kinds of fanciful notions. You know what girls are like at that age."

"Not hardly," Bowman said.

"Me neither, to tell the truth," Vestry admitted ruefully. He pushed back his hat, stroked his temples with his fingertips. He tried again. "Francine hasn't had an easy time of it, with her ma dying on her when she was a little girl, leaving her to be raised up by her pa. He meant well, but he was a drunk, and anytime he had two coins to knock together, he'd run out and spend both of them on booze. Not to speak ill of the dead, but that's just the way it was. The girl's young, romantic, with a head full of fanciful notions. To her, Grimes is a character out of a dime novel, more sinned against than sinning, a scoundrel with a heart of gold. She's too young to see him for what he really is: scum."

"Grimesy is no prize, but I wouldn't say that he's all that bad," Bowman said in mild disagreement. "Rowdy, with a chip on his shoulder. Boneheaded, pig-stubborn, full of himself—sure. But scum—no." After a pause, he amended, "Probably not. I mean, it's not like I'm vouching for him or nothing. If I had to swear to it, I'd say that Grimes is as decent as he has to be, as long as you've got the drop on him."

"That's not exactly a ringing endorsement," Vestry said. "What I want to know is, would you leave him alone with your teenage niece?"

"I wouldn't even leave him alone with my horse," Bowman declared. "Him and damned few others, if it comes to that."

"So tell him to stay away from Francine, before I have to tell him with this," Vestry said, tapping the shotgun barrels meaningfullly.

"I'll give him the word if I see him."

"Try and see him before I do," Vestry urged. "I'll be much obliged."

The interview seemed to be at an end. Bowman showed signs of being ready to move on.

"Back before the war, I used to ride shotgun on an express company coach route up around Paola way," Vestry said. "I believe I heard you say earlier today that you hailed from those parts, Mr. Bowman."

"I might have."

"Might have said it, or might have hailed from Paola?"

"Both," Bowman said. "What of it?"

"This was back in the late fifties, the border war days," Vestry said. "I remember hearing about a young fellow who used to ride with Doc Jennison's Jayhawkers, raiding the Missouri slave holders and secessionists. Now, this youngster was a wizard with the pistols, a crack shot—a dead shot. Expert in burning, looting, and horse theft, too, as a Jayhawker would be. And wouldn't you know it? His name was Bowman, too."

Bowman shrugged, bland-faced. "It's a common enough name, especially around Paola."

"So you wouldn't be him."

"Who can say? As far as I know, neither of us is

wanted for anything we might have done before the war or since."

"I believe that is the case," Vestry said, scratching his chin. "Wonder whatever happened to that fellow, anyway?"

"Seems to me, as best as I can recall, right about the time Abe Lincoln was first elected president, this youngster joined up with a detachment of Frontier Guards and went to Washington, to guard the city from Confederates trying to take over," Bowman said. "After that, he enlisted in the Union Army, and nobody's heard of him since."

"Maybe it's better that way," Vestry said.

"You share your recollections with Bragg?" Bowman asked, eyeing the other.

"I'm keeping them under my hat," Vestry said. "I'm a native Kansan. Bragg's not. He wasn't here during the border war days, doesn't know what it was like. Those were bad times—Missouri pro-slavers and border ruffians and secesh kept crossing the river, coming here and killing our people, carrying off free blacks to be sold as slaves. The army was no protection, not out here on the frontier. Something had to be done, and the Jim Lanes and Doc Jennisons and their followers did it. And if they were as bad as the Missourians, at least they were on our side. No sense in stirring up the past for things that are over and done and best forgotten. Let sleeping dogs lie, that's what I say."

Bowman shook his head. "From where I sit, the past is already stirred up, what with the old Kidd gang riding roughshod over the territory."

"Now that you mention it, it's a funny thing. First Kidd's gang showing up, and now you," Vestry said.

"Funny," Bowman echoed. "I was with Jennison. Kidd

was one of Jim Lane's Redlegs. Jayhawkers and Redlegs had as little liking for each other as they did for the Rebs."

"Ever meet Kidd?"

"Never even saw him."

"That's a problem," Vestry said. "Nobody knows what he looks like. At least, nobody living who's willing to talk. There's not even a decent sketch of him in the files."

"You talk like you think he's alive."

"Don't you?"

"I haven't studied on the matter yet."

Vestry, thoughtful, said, "Funny to think that if he is alive, he could be walking around like anybody else. Why, he might even be here in town, and you wouldn't know it. He might even be you!"

Bowman smiled with his lips closed. "How does that square with me being Jayhawker Bowman?"

"I wasn't seriously considering the possibility. I was just using it to make a point," Vestry said. "Plus, the ages don't match up. Kidd would have to be a good ten, fifteen years older than you."

"That makes you and Kidd about the same age," Bowman said. "Maybe you're him."

"That'll come as a surprise to my missus."

"Just making a point."

Now it was Vestry who showed signs of wanting to leave. "I've got to be making my rounds."

"Just wondering," Bowman said. "When's the last time you were at Bittersink Basin?"

"Why do you ask?"

"Maybe the gang's using it for a hideout. That might explain a few things, like why Cotton made a try for Grimes."

Vestry chuckled, a dry sound like a mouse rustling

around in a grain pile. "You don't know Bragg too well. Kidd's gang using the basin as a hideout? Bragg would never miss a bet like that. Not that he'd ever go up there himself. He couldn't be bothered to get out of his chair for a hard, unprofitable ride like that. That's why he's got deputies. Every few weeks, he sends a couple of us to go up there and make sure it's not a robber's roost. Well, it's not. I was there myself a couple of weeks ago. It was as clean as a hound's tooth, same way it was every time it's been looked at."

"Just a thought," Bowman said.

"Wherever the outlaws are hiding out, it's not the basin."

"Where are they hiding out?"

"I don't know that they have a hideout as such," Vestry said. "I think they've got a couple of places, lonesome patches out in the boondocks. Ranches or farms owned by friends, family, or fellow crooks—maybe all three. But that's only a guess."

"Could be," Bowman said.

"I'll be moving along on my rounds now," Vestry said. "Don't forget what I said about Grimes. Tell him to stay away from Francine if he doesn't want me coming after him with this shotgun."

"I'll tell him," Bowman promised.

"See that you do."

14

The front of the Liberty Hotel looked like a Greek temple, but it was all false front. The clusters of pillared half-columns flanking the arched entrance were purely decorative, hollow. The two-story, white wooden-frame building stood with its long sides parallel to the north side of the square. A short flight of wide, shallow stairs led up to the veranda and the high, arched entryway. Clumps of outside lanterns lit up the front of the building, so that it loomed at the top of the square like a white cliff.

Bowman went in. The lobby ceiling was treetop tall. Hanging down from the center of it on a chain was an ornate brass and crystal chandelier. The desk looked as if it were made of mahogany. Covering the floor was a burgundy carpet with gold scrollwork patternings.

The lobby chairs were boulder-sized. Bowman wondered if that was where Bragg had gotten his chair, but the style and coloring of the chairs were different. The desk clerk was tall, thin, with a thin, pale face, slicked-back black hair, and purple rings under his eyes.

Bowman went to him. "I'm looking for Harper."

The clerk yawned, unimpressed. "And who might you be?"

"I'm working with Marshal Bragg," Bowman said. Which was true enough, in a manner of speaking. Up to a point.

Now the clerk was more motivated. "I believe you'll find Mr. Harper in the smoking room, sir. Down the corridor, second door on the left."

"Thanks."

Leaning forward, the clerk said conspiratorially, "I trust it's nothing serious? Nothing that might disturb the guests or embarrass the hotel?"

"So Harper's that kind of lawyer, eh?"

"No, no, certainly not, sir. I didn't mean to create that impression," the clerk said, waving his hands in front of him as if physically dispelling the mistaken idea. "He's one of our leading citizens, a model of probity."

"That's what I thought," Bowman said. "Set your mind at rest. The marshal just wanted to get Harper's advice on a point of law." Bowman started to go, thought better of it, halted. "But don't go talking it up. I don't think Bragg or Harper would appreciate having their private business being made common property."

"You can rely on my discretion, sir."

"Well, good," Bowman said.

Crossing the lobby, he went down a long corridor. On his right, partitioned off by a wall of glass French doors, was the dining room. It was all well-dressed men and women, white tablecloths, gleaming silverware, and candlelight. Even the buzz of conversation and the clatter of knives and forks had a muted, velvety quality.

As Bowman was passing the dining room, a group of people were exiting, going down the corridor in the opposite direction.

Quite a group. There were what looked like two reasonably prosperous local businessmen and their wives, an attractive young woman in her mid-twenties, Cord Gentry, and Rufe Taylor.

They all were laughing and talking, their faces flushed and shiny from good food and drink. The businessmen and Gentry appeared unarmed; Taylor wore a holstered gun. On his arm was the attractive young woman, a brunette about half his age. Chestnut-brown hair was brushed straight back from her forehead, spilling down past the middle of her back. A midnight-blue velvet dress sheathed her supple, long-legged form.

Taylor glanced casually at Bowman, then did a take, breaking stride for an instant. He and Gentry exchanged glances. Below the shelf of an overhanging brow, Gentry's gaze was keen, bright. Lifting his shaggy eyebrows, he shrugged.

Noticing the falter, the brunette glanced at Taylor. Beaming at her, he recovered stride, proceeding with the others into the lobby. When next he glanced down the corridor, Bowman was gone.

The smoking room had something of the aura of a private club. There were wood-paneled walls, brass lamps with frosted crystal globes, thick wine-colored carpeting. At one end of the room was a polished wooden bar, manned by a large, rock-steady barman. Behind him, glass shelves crowded with bottles covered most of the back wall to chest height.

About twenty men of various ages and sizes, all well dressed, were grouped around the space, most in clusters, some singly. Cradled in high-backed, overstuffed chairs, they were smoking, drinking, and talking.

As Bowman was going in, a waiter was coming out, a

white-jacketed youth about Grimes's age, with ash-blond hair and a sharp-featured, too-wise face.

Stepping to one side, out of the path of the doorway, Bowman motioned with his head, signaling the waiter to join him. The youth followed.

Bowman held out a coin. Quick as a lizard's tongue, the other's hand flicked out, making the coin vanish. Only when it was safely pocketed did the youth ask, "What's that for?"

"Which one's Harper?" Bowman asked.

"The old white-haired party sitting by the fire," the other said, making as if to go.

"One more question," Bowman said. "Who's the good-looking woman I just saw with Rufe Taylor?"

"Mrs. Taylor," the youth said, smirking.

"That's what I was afraid of," Bowman said, sighing.

"If that's what you're looking for, mister, I know a couple of gals—"

"No, no," Bowman said. "The doctors said something like that would finish me."

Sneering, the youth went on his way out the door.

A toasty blaze seethed behind the iron mesh screen of a deep brown-and-white marbled fireplace. Seated near it, facing it, was Harper. Engulfed in the depths of a mammoth armchair, he looked like some soft, pulpy sea creature encased in a protective shell.

He sat alone, hunched over a brandy glass cradled by long-fingered, skeletal hands. His head looked too big for his pipestem neck and scrawny body. It was tilted to one side.

A feathery cap of fluffy white hair covered his scalp. His face was waxy, with wiry white eyebrows, deep-set eyes, hollow cheeks, and a white goatee. He wore a fawn-colored suit, a tan vest, and a sharply knotted, plum-colored cravat.

Harper studied the firelight through the brandy-colored depths of his glass. A shadow fell across him, causing him to look up.

Bowman stood looming to one side of him. "Mr. Harper?"

"I'm Harper, yes."

"The name's Bowman. I'm working with Marshal Bragg."

"I wouldn't brag about it," Harper deadpanned. Bowman looked at him.

"Just having my little joke," Harper said. He looked shrewd, canny. He wagged a chiding finger at Bowman. "I know who you are, Mr. Bowman. You're that bounty hunter," he said. He gestured toward a nearby chair. "Have a seat and join me."

"Don't mind if I do," Bowman said, moving the chair into position beside Harper. It was hot where Harper sat, so close to the fire. Bowman pushed his chair back, away from it.

A near imperceptible gesture by Harper summoned a barman, a stolid heavyweight in an ornate gold-and-green brocade vest, white shirt with sleeve garters, and shiny pine-green trousers.

"What's yours, Mr. Bowman?" Harper asked.

"Whiskey, straight up," Bowman said.

"I'm fine," Harper told the barman, who went away, returned with Bowman's drink on a tray, set it down on a round-topped table beside the chair, and went away again.

Bowman took a swallow. "Smooth."

Harper nodded, his nods small, tight, tentative, as if he were afraid his head would topple forward, overbalanced, unless he were careful. He sipped his brandy as if it were a hot beverage, blowing on the surface of it, taking delicate little sips and holding them in his mouth before swallowing.

He said, "To what do I owe the pleasure, Mr. Bowman?"

"Information."

"Ah," Harper said. "Getting or giving?"

"Getting," Bowman said. "I hope."

"So."

"It's about a client of yours, Jed Grimes."

Removing his hand from the glass, Harper raised a single finger. Index finger. "I am currently engaged in some dealings with young Grimes, but he is not my client. His late uncle, Obed Marsh, was my client. May I ask, what is your interest in the case?"

"I'm trying to keep Grimes alive," Bowman said. "Some people are trying to kill him. I can't help feeling it's got something to do with his inheritance."

"His inheritance," Harper echoed, rolling the phrase around in his mouth as if it were a sip of brandy. "Apparently, you've never been to Bittersink Basin, Mr. Bowman. If you had, you'd know how utterly impossible it is that anyone would ascribe the slightest degree of value to the property. Certainly, it's not worth killing over."

Leaning toward Bowman, he kept his head upright on his neck, tilting his whole upper body forward rather than bending his neck.

He said, "The true nature of Bittersink is public knowledge, so I may address it freely without fear of betraying a professional confidence. And again, young Grimes has not yet seen fit to retain me as counsel, further freeing my hands. And if, as you say, it's a matter of life and death—"

"It could be," Bowman assured him.

"—then I see no harm in sketching out the general background of the matter," Harper said. He sipped some more brandy, holding it on his tongue for a pause before swallowing.

"Obed Marsh was my friend of many years. He was also my client," Harper said. "Marsh must have sensed something in the air—the shadow of approaching fate, perhaps. Like me, he was an old man, you see. When you get old, you can feel the darkness drawing in. Not long ago, he had me draw a will for him, naming as beneficiary a sister in Texas, whom he hadn't seen for many years. A month later, he was dead."

"How did he die?" Bowman asked.

"A tragic accident. He fell down the stairs and broke his neck," Harper said. "Making inquiries, I discovered that the sister was dead, too. The only surviving member of the family, and the heir, was young Grimes. I contacted him by letter, informing him of the bequest and also informing him that in my considered opinion, the property was well-nigh worthless. That is also, may I add, the opinion of every man of judgment who's acquainted with the site. I did this to keep from creating in him a sense of expectation that he had come into any great fortune. It would be point-less and might even exact hardship, both physical and financial, to make the long trip from Texas to Black Creek on the misguided belief that he was coming into some real wealth. I doubted that he would be able to sell Bittersink, even at a loss of a few cents on the dollar. Instead, he de-cided to see for himself. Well, he's a young man. I daresay that when I was his age, I would have done the same thing and gone to see the property for myself. When he does, though, he's likely to experience a severe disappointment."

"What's wrong with it?" Bowman asked. "Seems like this is pretty good farmland around here. And with the railroad coming in, the property should be worth something."

"Bittersink Basin did not receive its name by virtue of being a salubrious garden spot," Harper said. "The Indians who used to inhabit these parts said it was cursed earth. Perhaps they weren't so far off the mark. The land is fouled. Something in the soil, some mineral element. The water is brackish, unhealthy. Nothing grows there save some weeds and thornbushes. The soil won't support a crop or a herd of livestock. The railroad coming to Black Creek will undoubtedly create much prosperity. But not even the railroad can improve Bittersink's worth by one red cent."

Harper drank some more brandy. When the glass was lowered, a reddish-brown tinge filmed his thin lips and the skin around his mouth.

"I told young Grimes as much today, when he came to see me at my office," Harper said. "I fear he may have taken it rather badly. Still, he has the consolations of youth and health, the possession of which excites in me a profound envy."

"So there's nothing about Bittersink worth fighting over?" Bowman asked.

"Or even having, as far as I'm concerned," Harper said. "If it is at the center of some murderous intrigue, as seems to be the case, I can only speculate that it's caused by some false, fatal rumor. Buried treasure or some such rubbish. Though heaven knows, there's enough places there to hide a fortune! One wouldn't even have to dig a hole. The land's honeycombed with them, absolutely rotten with sinkholes, caves, and what have you." He looked up, eyes bright. "Who knows? Perhaps some outlaws, maybe even the Kidd gang themselves, have hidden their plundered loot on the property. Wouldn't that be the final irony!"

Harper sank back in the chair's sheltering cushions. Bowman realized that he still held the glass of whiskey in his hand, where it had remained virtually untasted. He tossed it back in one gulp, setting down the empty glass.

He said, "Thanks for the drink—and the information, Mr. Harper."

"You can thank me by letting me know what develops, if anything. You see, Mr. Bowman, I like to stay well informed myself."

Bowman thanked him again and went out.

15

Bowman followed a star—the Pole Star. It drew him through the night streets of Black Creek. From the Liberty Hotel, he went south across the square, down Commerce to Trail Street, where he turned right and walked west along the north side of the street.

Nearing Market Road, he heard riders approaching, coming fast. He ducked into a dark, recessed doorway.

A trio of riders, coming abreast, tearing along the main drag. Above them, bracketed by the double row of buildings lining both sides of the street, was a yellow horned moon.

Trail Street was lit up along the center stretch and dark at both ends. The trio neared, riding hard. Hooves dug dirt, the horses coursing, the riders leaning into it. The quick, dimly lit glimpse Bowman caught of their faces as they flashed past struck no note of recognition in him.

A man caught in the middle of the street while crossing it had to jump lively to keep from being trampled. Yelping, he scrambled to the boardwalk in the nick of time, clinging to a porch's upright pillar with both arms wrapped around it.

Horses pounded past, not missing a beat. The trio raced west, following Trail Street out of town, up the lane that ran past the knolltop church and Boot Hill.

They came out of darkness into the light and flashed back into darkness, their identities unknown, their mission cryptic.

Stepping out of the doorway, Bowman continued on. He came abreast of the man who'd narrowly escaped being trampled. Knees bent, legs shaking, gaze turned in the direction where the riders had disappeared, he quavered, "Crazy damned fools! Crazy damned fools!"

The Pole Star was back in business, alive with light, motion, noise. Boards and planks were nailed up over the broken windows on the outside, while blankets covered them on the inside. Shining through the gaps were spidery lines of light, casting a ghostly web over the exterior structure and the street.

Horses were lined up at the hitching posts. There were too many horses for the posts, with the extras being tied up along the porch rails. Knots of men stood on the street, loitered on the porch. From the noise they were making, they seemed well oiled with alcohol. Off to one side, a couple of lone drunks sat slumped on the ground, propped up against the sides of the veranda.

At the front entrance, a new set of batwing swinging double doors had been put in place. The wood was new, unpainted.

Bowman went in, immediately engulfed by a mass of heat, smoke, clamor, and milling bodies.

The place was packed. To the right, at the bar, customers were lined up two and three deep. Moritz and a second bartender kept pushing a steady flow of drinks across the counter, where they were immediately snatched up by a wall of grasping hands. To the left, in the crowded seating area, there wasn't an empty table or chair to be had. The left rear section was the gaming area, where a whirling faro wheel and several card games were getting a nice play.

The clientele consisted of a wide-ranging sampling of Black Creek citizenry, or at least its male half. There were townmen, ranchers and farmers, tinhorns and hard cases, booze hounds and lechers, all whooping it up.

Threaded among them, circulating around the main floor, mingling, were about a dozen whores. Most of them looked a lot better by night than they had in broad daylight earlier that day, Bowman thought. At that, most of them were better not looked at too closely when cold sober. There were a few pretty ones, with fresh, wicked faces and firm, young bodies. Others were fading but fleshly, faces heavily painted, tight satin dresses showing plenty of bosom and haunch.

To the right of the stairs, a rugged piano built as solidly as a freight wagon stood against the wall. The piano player was a sad-faced, long-nosed, middle-aged man who, despite a raffish derby and a cigar stub clenched between his teeth, looked as if he belonged behind the counter of a dry goods store. He played a lively round of music, pounding the out-of-tune keys, milling out waves of melody.

In the center area were a couple of dancing couples— whores and their prospective customers. The men held the women close, rubbing against them. The whores had all they could do to keep their energetic if unskilled partners from stepping on their feet, causing them to cut lively capers.

Bowman, thirsty, went to the bar, plunging into the crush of like-minded individuals already massed there. Heat, whiskey, and beer fumes wafted off the throng.

Each hand that took away a drink was replaced by two more. Sharp elbows were much in play.

When Bowman reached the goal, he bought a bottle of red whiskey. He didn't bother with a glass, just got his bottle and got the hell out. The thirsty crowd parted, readily making way for one who was clearing a space at the counter, as opposed to one who was trying to fill it.

Bowman straightened his hat, which had come close to being knocked off during his advance to the bar. Out of the fray, he took up a position not far from the end of the bar, standing with his back to the wall, looking out over the booming interior.

He pulled the cork out of the bottle neck with his teeth and spat it onto the floor. He wouldn't be needing it again.

Raising the bottle to his lips, he paused, his stomach fluttering for an instant before he swallowed. Then the whiskey hit, smothering the queasiness.

Noise racketed off the walls, a garbled mix in which it was difficult to distinguish any individual voices. Suddenly, bobbing up during a fleeting lull in the din, came the sound of braying jackass laughter.

To Bowman, its author was unmistakable. "Ol' Grimesy," he said. He took another gulp of whiskey, a big one.

Craning, peering over the tops of heads, he looked for Grimes, finding him plunked down on the left side of the room, the center of a knot of revelry. Fortifying himself with another taste of whiskey, Bowman made his way toward Grimes, weaving through the crowded cluster of tables and chairs.

At a table occupied by three whores and two tinhorn hangers-on sat Grimes, holding court.

Sporting a fresh haircut and a shave, he was all duded

up in fancy new clothes and a new hat. He wore a brown velvet jacket with black trim, brocade vest, white-ruffled shirt, and ribbon tie. Strapped around his waist was Sid Shofter's elaborately tooled, silver-stitched black leather gunbelt, complete with holstered six-gun. Judging by his glittering eyes and flushed face, he'd had more than a few drinks, not counting the one gripped in his hand. The three women and two men around the table with him were in similarly riotous condition, but their eyes were sharp and watchful.

Glancing up, Grimes saw Bowman standing at the opposite end of the table. "Look who's here! If it ain't Mr. Bowman! Pull up a chair and join the party!"

All the chairs were taken. A big, rawboned brunette with a black choker collar and a red dress elbowed a burly redheaded man in a derby and green-checked suit, saying, "Get off your duff and make room for the gent, Jerry!"

Jerry's hair fell across his forehead, sheepdog style, the tips brushing his brows. It went with the hangdog expression on his face. "Why do I have to get up, Annie?"

"Because he's a paying customer," she said. An upper front tooth, made of gold, glinted when she spoke.

"Why me? Why not Mack?" Jerry asked, indicating the man seated across from him.

Mack was a youngish, round-faced man with slicked-down hair, a mustache and sideburns that seemed to have been daubed on with greasepaint, and doll-like features.

"He's never going to sprain his arm paying for a round," Jerry said. "Why not Mack?"

"Good idea. Why don't you both go?" Annie asked.

Grimes tossed a crumpled greenback at Jerry, who snatched it up as soon as it hit the table. He said, "Get us some more drinks, *amigo.*"

"Sure," Jerry said. "Sure." Pushing back his chair, he rose and went to the bar. Bowman sat down, setting the bottle on the tabletop.

"This one didn't come empty-handed," Annie said approvingly.

Gesturing expansively, Grimes said, "Meet the gang." He was flanked by two whores. Marge was round, pink, and soft. Sue was pale, petite, thin-faced, with a wide, dark-eyed, vacant look, framed by wavy brown hair falling past slim shoulders.

Indicating Bowman, Grimes said, "This ol' boy can handle himself pretty good, I don't mind telling you."

Marge said, "What else can he handle?"

"What've you got?" Grimes fired back.

"Wouldn't you like to know?"

"Maybe I'll find out."

"Maybe!" The way she said it, there wasn't any *maybe* about it.

Bowman said, "Looks like you're coming up in the world, Grimes."

Grimes swelled, preening. "Sharp-dressed man, that's me. I'm a man of means in this town, and I mean to look the part."

"You said a mouthful, honey," Marge said. She slipped an arm across his shoulder.

"And she knows all about mouthfuls," Annie said.

Bowman said, "Sid and Trench must have had plenty in their pockets."

"More'n Cotton?" Grimes said. "I doubt it."

Annie nudged Bowman's arm with her elbow. "You've both got money in your pockets. Don't be stingy. How about buying me a drink from that bottle?"

"I've been drinking straight from it," he said.

With one hand, she clutched the bottle, steadying it. With the other hand, she wiped her sleeve against the bottle mouth. "You look healthy enough. I'll take my chances."

Having a hand on the bottle was most of the battle. She slid it to her and poured a generous portion of red whiskey into her glass tumbler, filling it.

When Annie set down her glass, it was near empty. She poured herself another one. Bowman made no objection. He didn't want her to start elbowing him as she had done to Jerry.

"What the hell," Annie said. "It's a party, ain't it?"

"It's getting there," Bowman said.

Grimes said, "Where's Jerry with them drinks?"

"I don't see him," Mack said helpfully. "He must've got lost or something."

Bowman's bottle was passed around the table. They were all having a jolly time. Bowman said, "Been out to Bittersink yet?"

"It can wait," Grimes said. "From what I hear, one day more or less ain't going to make no difference anyways. I'll take a ride up there tomorrow. Hell, I've been on the trail for months. Tonight I plan to sleep in a real bed."

Marge said, "You ain't going to be doing much sleeping." She held on to him with both hands clasped around his neck. Her breasts seemed about to pop out of the top of her tight dress.

"Say, tell me," Bowman said casually. "Drummer's woman—Nelly—she turn up yet?"

"No, she hasn't," Sue said, speaking for the first time. Her voice had a breathless, quavery quality, as if vibrating with emotion. "Something's happened to her, I know it!" Her eyes showed white around the edges. She wrung her hands.

"She and Nelly were good pals," Marge said in an aside that carried the length of the table, over the din.

Annie said, "Something happened to her, all right. Her man got shot to death by the law this morning, that's what happened. Not that Drummer was any damned good anyway."

"That's not what you said when he first came here, and you were trying to get him to notice you," Marge said slyly.

"Shut up, unless you're looking to get slapped silly," Annie said. "Which in your case wouldn't take much doing, you're already silly."

Playing the peacemaker, Mack said, "Now, now, ladies, don't fight." He spoke without conviction.

"But if you do, make sure to tear plenty of clothes off of each other," Grimes said.

"If it's a show you want, you'll have to pay for it," Annie said.

"I would—gladly!"

"You're just dirty," Marge said, playfully feinting a slap at Grimes's face. She snuggled up close to him. "You can tear the clothes off my body instead."

"He don't have to," Annie said. "You're already falling out of them."

"Nothing wrong in showing off what you've got," Marge said, "when you've got it."

"And you've got it!" Grimes enthused.

Sue said imploringly, near wailing, "But what about Nelly?"

"She's all right," Marge said dismissively. "She's probably already got her hooks into some new man to take Drummer's place. A fast worker, that gal."

"But she left all her things here," Sue said.

"Which means that she'll have to come back to get them, so she's sure to turn up sooner or later," Marge said.

"Good riddance to her," Annie said. "I hope she never comes back."

"Oh, Annie, surely you don't mean that!"

"The hell I don't. There's already enough competition around here. One less Nelly means more business for the rest of us," Annie said.

"Competition? What competition?" purred Marge.

Clawlike white hands fastened on Mack's forearm, the nails digging in, Sue said, "I know I'm right, Mack! Nelly's in some kind of trouble. We've got to do something!"

"She can take care of herself," Mack said, patting her hands, which were still attached to his arm. "Would you mind letting go? You're wrinkling the sleeve."

Bowman leaned forward, moving his head closer to Sue's. "Do you have any real reason for thinking she's in danger?"

"No, I just know it," Sue said, staring into space. "It's a feeling, intuition—but I know it's true."

"She's a great one for feelings," Annie said. "The sensitive type."

"I'm losing the feeling in my arm," Mack said, prying Sue's hands loose.

Jerry returned, empty-handed. Annie said, "Hey, where's our drinks?"

Ignoring her, he said to Bowman, "Miz Lana wants to see you."

"Me? Why?" Bowman asked.

"Maybe it's your blue eyes," Annie said.

"Upstairs," Jerry said, jerking a thumb backward, in the direction of the balcony. "Tell Turk it's okay, you've been sent for."

Shrugging, Bowman rose. "Leave the bottle," Annie said. "There ain't much left in it anyhow."

"You're telling me!" Bowman said.

Grimes said, "Looks like you're moving up in the world, too."

Marge rubbed against him. "Kiss me, hon."

"Later," Grimes said.

As she leaned into him, one of her elbows slipped off the table, bringing her up short. Her right breast popped out of the top of her dress. The nipple was big, soft, and brown. "Oops," she said, pushing her breast back into the dress, taking her time about it.

When she was done, Bowman nodded to the group, said, "See you." Turning, he crossed toward the stairway.

Grimes said, "Hey, Jerry, how about them drinks?"

"Coming right up," Jerry said.

Snaking his way through the crowd, Bowman went to the stairway and climbed it. Columns of smoke floated upward, massing under the roof beams.

On the second-floor landing, at the mouth of a long corridor lined with doors on both sides, Turk sat keeping watch.

He sat backward on the chair, straddling it, arms folded on top of the back of the chair. He was bald, with a shiny cordovan-colored scalp and a thick black handlebar mustache. He was powerfully built, with sloping shoulders and a square-shaped torso. He wore a green velour vest, pale yellow-ruffled shirt, tight gray trousers. He wore a gunbelt strapped over one shoulder, the holstered gun hanging down under his left arm, butt out.

When Bowman topped the stairs, Turk stood up. Bowman said, "I've been sent for."

"I know," Turk said. Motioning with his skin-topped head to an open door off the balcony, he said, "In there."

Bowman went to it, pausing at the open doorway. Beyond lay a room done up as kind of a study. At the opposite end stood a desk, facing the door. Behind it sat Lana Crain. She seemed to be alone.

Bowman entered, crossing the threshold, halting just beyond it while he looked around the room. He reached behind himself for the door handle, intending to close the door. Not looking up from her account book, Lana Crain said, "Leave it open. I like to know what's going on outside."

He padded deeper into the room. To the left was a small fireplace, its flames banked low. It was cool in the room, almost chilly. To the right was a glass-fronted bookcase, its shelves covered with rows of handsomely bound books. Between the bookcase and the rear wall was a door connecting to an adjacent room, a door that was now closed.

The desktop was heaped with what looked like record books and ledgers, some open, others stacked in piles. Spread out before Lana Crain was an opened account book, its pages marked with columns of figures. Grouped around it were a green-shaded desk lamp, an inkwell and pen, a sheet of blotting paper. Also within reach were a crystal decanter on a round silver tray and a partly filled drinking glass.

Lana Crain's hair was pinned up at the back of her neck, accenting her fine-boned, clean-lined face. She wore almost no makeup at all. She wore a tight, dark, satiny silver-gray dress, with white puritan collar and cuffs, and a short olive-green velour jacket with black braided trim.

Bowman stood looking down at her from across the desk. He said, "Busy night."

She looked up, her pale green eyes the color of weathered copper. "There's nothing like a killing or two for bringing in business." She said it matter-of-factly, as if discussing the weather.

A pair of armchairs sat in front of her desk, facing her. Indicating them, she said, "Sit down."

Selecting the chair to his left, he moved it farther to that side, out of alignment with the open door. He sat down.

Lana Crain said, "Trusting soul!"

"I don't like to sit with my back to an open door," Bowman explained. "Gives me a chill at the back of the neck."

"Cautious, eh? That hardly seems to fit in with your line of work."

"What's my line of work?"

"In plain words, gunman," she said. Her clear-eyed gaze was level, serene.

"As long as we're speaking plainly, what do you want?" he asked.

"Maybe we can do business," Lana Crain said.

Bowman sat with his hands resting on the tops of his thighs. He turned his hands outward, showing his palms. "I'm always ready to entertain any reasonable offer."

"Good, because I've got one that you might find very entertaining."

Bowman raised an eyebrow. "Is this a matter of business or pleasure?"

"Let's not fence," she said. "The word's around town, Bowman. You're a bounty hunter. You kill for gold."

"Wrong. I sell my gun for gold," Bowman said. "The killing just seems to come with the territory."

"If it makes you feel better to look at it that way, fine. Everybody's got their reasons. I'm not judging," Lana Crain said. "I want results."

"Who do you want dead?"

She became guarded, wary. "What makes you think I want anyone dead?"

"Don't you? I can think of a few people I'd want dead if I were you, and I haven't even been in town for twenty-four hours yet," Bowman said. "But don't worry. I'm not judging."

Indicating the decanter, he said, "This talking is thirsty work. Do you mind?"

"Help yourself," she said. "To the brandy."

There was an unused glass on the round silver tray. Bowman filled it with brandy and took it back to his chair. He drank some. It was liquid fire on his tongue, trickling molten down his throat. Heat blossomed in his belly, his face.

"So that's where you've been hiding the good stuff," he said.

Lana Crain folded her hands on the desktop. "You have your drink. Now, let's get down to brass tacks. Yes, I've got enemies. I'm no fool. The railroad is coming to Black Creek, and I mean to cash in on the bonanza. So do others, greedy men who aren't content to have anybody else making money. They want it all."

"Men like, say, Rufe Taylor," Bowman said.

"He's the ringleader," she said, defiant. "There's others trying to run me out, but they take orders from him."

"And if he was dead, that'd solve a lot of your troubles . . ."

"Mine, and most of the rest of the citizens in this town," she said vehemently. "But that's their lookout. I'm not fighting for them, I'm fighting for me. Think any of them'll lift a finger to help me when the chips are down?"

"From what I saw," Bowman said, "Bragg sure braced Taylor's crowd pretty hard today."

Glass in hand, she made a wave of dismissal. "He did it for himself, not for me. Taylor's crowding him hardest of all. If Bragg shows weak, Taylor's crew'll be all over him."

Bowman went to the desk to refill his brandy glass from the decanter. This time, he didn't bother to ask permission. Lana Crain sat there tight-faced, impatient.

Back in his chair, Bowman said, "I'm going to tell you something you don't want to hear, so I figured I'd better get another glass of this good brandy while I could. Fact is, I sell my gun, but I'm not a hired killer."

"No? Bounty hunting isn't killing for pay?" Lana Crain asked.

"It's on the side of the law," Bowman said.

"Don't make me laugh," she said. "If I thought you believed that, I'd be worried."

"What makes you think I don't?"

"I've been around. I've seen your kind before. I know the breed." She took a swallow of brandy. "Because I'm the same way myself."

Letting that pass, Bowman said, "Taylor's a big man in these parts, throws a lot of weight."

"Not if he's dead and buried," Lana Crain said.

"Bloodthirsty wench, aren't you?"

"What do you want me to do, get sentimental? It's his neck or mine."

"Such a pretty neck, too," Bowman said. "It'd be a shame for the hangman to have to stretch it with a rope necktie."

"If Taylor forces me out of the Pole Star, I might as

well hang myself. I worked long and hard to get where I am, and I won't give it up without a fight."

"Fair enough," Bowman said. The brandy was warming him up, and the room didn't feel chilly anymore.

"Did you have this same talk with Drummer McCray?"

She shook her head, smiling thinly. "He was able to get himself killed without any help from me."

"That woman of his ever come back?" he asked.

"Nelly Curry? No," Lana Crain said.

"Is she dead?"

"Dead!" She sounded shocked. "Why should she be dead?"

"That's one reason why people turn up missing."

"Who'd want to kill her, and why?"

"You tell me."

"Nobody, that's who. Nelly Curry is a sweet-faced, empty-headed young tart, lazy and flighty. That's all. What happened is, she's probably so scared she hasn't stopped running yet," Lana Crain said. Her eyes narrowed. "Why the interest in Nelly? She mean something to you?"

"I don't even know her," Bowman said mildly. "But when somebody goes missing, it's worth noting. Especially when it's Drummer McCray's woman."

"Where does yesterday's newspaper go when the wind blows it away? She'll turn up. If not here, then in some other house or crib. Forget about her," Lana Crain said. "Stick to your business, Bowman. Stick to your guns, and you'll be fine. Rich, too. Being shut of Rufe Taylor would be worth quite a fair sum to me. And to you." She held up a hand, palm up. "Wait. Don't decide yet. Relax. Have another drink. Let's get to know each other better. I'm sure we can come to a mutually satisfactory arrangement."

"Who knows?" he said, shrugging. "Maybe I'll come to a different conclusion after I've slept on it."

"Don't get ahead of yourself," she snapped. Then, recovering, she smiled. "But don't fall too far behind, either."

Outside the room, clamor erupted—shouts, screams, crashing noises, pounding footsteps.

The footsteps were those of Turk, who came rushing up into view, reeling to a stop outside the open doorway.

Waving a gun around in his hand, he said, "Arnholt!"

16

Looming up behind Turk was a shadowy figure. Before he could do more than turn his head to glance over his shoulder, he was clubbed with the barrel of a gun wielded by his attacker.

Turk stiffened, an agonized expression frozen on his face. He spouted gibberish, meaningless choking noises that sounded like a machine slipping gears. The other struck him again, laying the gun barrel hard across the back of Turk's head with savage precision.

Turk fell forward through the doorway into the room, crashing face-first to the floor. Still clutched in his hand, his gun did not go off. He was motionless, inert, out cold.

Stepping over him, his spurs jingling, the attacker entered the room with leveled gun. Lana Crain and Bowman were still seated, locked in the positions they had held before the assault.

"Cozy," the intruder said, snickering. "Hope I ain't interrupting nothing."

Lana Crain said, "You must be crazy, Griff!"

Bowman recognized Griff as one of Arnholt's followers who'd been siding him earlier that day. Griff's eyebrows were peaked, and a scarred upper lip exposed a broken canine tooth, giving him a wolfish aspect. He wore a dark blue scarf and bandana. His gun covered Bowman.

"Maybe you'd like to try for that derringer of yours," Griff said, his sneering grin widening. "I heard about that trick."

Bowman said, "You've got me confused with someone else, friend."

"Wrong on both counts. I ain't confused, and I ain't your friend," Griff said. "Move wrong, even to scratch your nose, and I'll burn you down where you sit."

Lana Crain was white-faced, slit-eyed, tight-mouthed. Little thumbprint-sized smudges of color showed in her high cheekbones. She said, "Get out!"

"Uh-uh," Griff said, shaking his head. "This time, it's your turn to get out, Miz Lana. Clear out of the territory."

"What do you mean?"

"You're quits with Black Creek. Time for you to move on."

"Says who? Taylor?"

"That's what all decent, right-minded citizens are saying."

"How would you know, Griff? You don't find many of them in the Taylor crowd," Lana Crain said. "You're not as bad as some of them, and up to now, I've given you the benefit of the doubt. But I warn you—"

"You're warning me?" Griff chuckled, relishing the absurdity of her position. "I'm the one with the gun."

Behind him, a heavy tread sounded outside the door as a second man came on the scene, another of Arnholt's crew. His gun was drawn, too. He said, "It's me, Griff—Hauk."

"Come on in, I got everything under control," Griff said, glancing back over his shoulder to flash a cocky grin at Hauk.

Reaching under an open ledger, Lana Crain pulled out a gun and fired.

This was no small-caliber lady's gun; it was a full-blown, big-bore revolver. She pulled the trigger several times, her smooth, masklike face underlit by the sparking muzzle flares. In the small space, the reports were deafening.

She put three bullets into Griff, his chest and middle coming undone from the blasts. Surprised, Griff looked down at the damage. Before it could register, he was dead on his feet.

Looking even more surprised than Griff was Hauk, who gaped during the next few critical split-seconds as Griff folded to the floor.

A star feature of the cross-belly draw was that it allowed the wearer to get his gun into play speedily while on horseback or in a seated postion. Now Bowman had his gun in hand, snapping a shot at Hauk. It smashed into the door frame near Hauk's head, spraying him with wood shards and splinters.

Cursing, Hauk dodged back outside, ducking behind the wall, out of the line of fire.

Shouts came from downstairs, confused, excited.

Hauk called across the balcony to someone on the stairs. "They got Griff!"

Already in motion, Bowman catapulted from the chair, bent almost double as he rushed forward. He came in low, diving over Turk's prone form sprawled on the carpet and through the open doorway, into the hall, landing belly-down.

Now he lay half outside, half inside the door. To his left, a few paces away, stood Hauk, back flattened against the wall, gun in hand. His gun was held level at waist height, while Bowman's was pointed upward at him.

They saw each other at the same time, Bowman firing first.

Hauk lurched, blood spurting, the gun pinwheeling from his hand.

On the stairs, the top of his hat level with the landing, crouched Gus Arnholt. "Son of a bitch!" he cried, firing off some rounds in Bowman's direction.

Missing their target, they passed harmlessly above Bowman, a couple of them tagging Hauk, mortally wounded but still on his feet.

Slamming back against the wall, Hauk bounced off it and staggered forward blindly, head down, stumbling into the balustrade. It held, and Hauk jackknifed head first over the top rail, tumbling into empty air and out of sight.

A few beats later, he hit bottom with a crash, raising from the floorboards a thin puff of dust that floated lazily toward the ceiling.

Under the big ten-gallon hat, Arnholt's eyes were popping, while his mouth contracted to a tiny, puckered O shape.

"Oh, Lord!" he breathed.

Bowman's gun swung toward him. Arnholt ducked, dropping below the balcony level, but not in time to avoid having a shot drill the tall crown of his hat, lofting it into space. It soared in an arc, dropping out of sight.

Off-balance, Arnholt tripped, tumbling down the stairs. An enormous clatter ended with a thud and a groan as he rolled to a stop at the bottom of the stairs. More groans followed, peppered with curse words.

The second-floor balcony, landing, and long corridor were all empty, presenting no immediate threat.

Below, the ground floor was chaos, with the sound of tables being overturned, bottles breaking, screaming, and scattered shots.

Still lying prone on the carpeted balcony, Bowman wriggled alongside Turk. The back of Turk's hairless skull was marked by a bloody gash and a purple egg-sized bruise.

Bowman took Turk's gun out of his closed fist. He had to pull hard to get it free. Turk stirred, moaning, his eyelids fluttering, fingers clawing the carpet. Glancing back into the room, Bowman saw Lana Crain standing behind the desk, gun in hand. He said, "Get down!"

"Never mind about me," she said. "Get out there and clean up on those bastards!"

"Yes, ma'am," he said sardonically.

Shelling the empties from his gun, Bowman reloaded, something he hadn't wanted to do without having Turk's gun at hand as a backup.

Holding his gun in his right hand and Turk's in his left, he rose to a half-crouch. Not crowding the balcony rail too closely, he sidled around toward the landing and the top of the stairs.

Except for the principal players, the other occupants of the Pole Star, male and female, had already gone to cover, crouching behind overturned tables or lying flat on the floor.

Two of Arnholt's men were dragging him to safety. Each had an arm and was pulling Arnholt across the floor, Arnholt gasping and gurgling all the way. He was battered, bruised, and dazed from falling downstairs, but he hadn't yet stopped a bullet.

Another two stood at the near end of the bar, looking up. One had a snakeskin hatband and held a gun trained on Moritz and the second bartender, covering them where they stood behind the bar with their hands up. His partner saw Bowman and shouted, opening fire with two guns.

Bowman fired back. Shooting downward was tricky, and his first shots were off the mark.

The two-gun man started forward, walking toward the stairs, shooting as he came on.

"Get him, Jeff!" said one of the men dragging Arnholt across the floor.

Jeff walked the bullets up the stairs, using them to find the range. Slugs tore into the treads and risers inches below Bowman's feet.

Bowman snapped a couple of shots off at Jeff, grazing his left side, marking it with a long red streak. Unsteady, Jeff lurched sideways to the left, both guns blazing. But he was almost out of bullets. First one gun clicked empty, then the other.

Throwing himself across a tabletop, Jeff overturned it, dragging it down to the floor so that it lay on its side, then sheltering behind it while he reloaded.

Having dragged Arnholt to the sidelines, his two handlers stalled in place, each one still gripping Arnholt by an arm, watching Jeff and Bowman trade shots.

Bowman shot one of them. Crying "Ow!" the man fell back, sitting down hard, clutching his middle with both hands. He fell over on one side and lay there.

Letting go of Arnholt's arm, the other handler backed away, clawing for his holstered gun. He was more interested in backing up than in reaching.

"Don't leave me, Purdy!" Arnholt cried. Starting as if stung, writhing, he scrambled to get up. He tried to get his feet under him, but his boot soles kept slipping on the floorboards, each attempt to rise causing him to fall down and flop around on the floor.

Even so, proceeding in this way, he was able to make headway, scuttling into the huddling crowd. Bowman couldn't shoot at him for fear of hitting some innocent person—as innocent as any Pole Star habitué could get.

At the near end of the bar, the man with the snakeskin hatband sheltered behind a square-sided pillar that helped support the balcony. He stood with his back to the doorway in the wall behind him, an open door connecting to the back rooms. His attention was divided between the two bartenders and Bowman, and trying to keep from being shot.

He jerked the trigger, banging a few shots in Bowman's general vicinity, ranging wide of the mark.

Out of the doorway came Swamper, stealthily creeping up behind the man with the snakeskin hatband. One arm was raised, ready to strike, wielding a bung starter, an immense wooden mallet used to drive spiked taps through barrel staves and heads. Swamper brought the mallet down hard on the back of the other's head, pulverizing it. Pulpy red matter sprayed in a boiling mist.

Swamper threw himself flat to the floor, anticipating the bullets thrown at him by Jeff. They missed.

Moritz and the other bartender had alread ducked down under the bar.

Purdy kept on backing up toward the door. He tripped over a man lying prone on the floor, falling backward. He jumped up, dashing for the front door.

"Purdy! You yellow bastard!" Jeff shouted. "Come back here, you!"

When Purdy reached the front door, Jeff fired, hitting Purdy in the back. Purdy's arms flew up in the air. Momentum carrying him, he staggered forward out the door. Jeff fired again, and Purdy fell forward in a heap on the boardwalk.

Moritz rose, popping up, holding a gun he'd grabbed

from where it was hidden under the bar. Standing side-ways, holding his arm extended, gun in hand, he shot Jeff, squeezing shots into his shuddering form, the blasts silencing Jeff in mid-shriek.

That did it for Arnholt. He rushed toward a window in the south wall, one that had been blown out earlier that day and had been temporarily patched with a blanket on the inside and planks and boards on the outside.

Hesitating not at all, he threw himself at it headfirst. He was a big man carrying a lot of weight and moving as fast as he ever had or could.

Something had to give. Planks broke in two, others ripping loose from where they'd been nailed in place, the whole mass vomiting outward, spilling debris and Arnholt to the ground beyond.

That set off a general stampede, men and women rising from cover, rushing for the front, side, and rear exits. The press of people blocked Bowman, delaying him from reaching the window.

When he finally did reach it, Arnholt was nowhere to be seen. Outside, on the ground below the window, was a tangled blanket mixed up with a heap of broken boards.

A shadow flitted around the southeast corner of the building, into Market Road and out of reach even as Bowman was lifting his gun.

Tossing aside Turk's empty gun and keeping his own, he clambered over the windowsill, hopping down to the soft ground below. The fresh night air was cold, bracing.

He made his way to the front of the building.

The street was chaos. A big seething mass of horses and people milled about, surging and swaying. Spooked horses nipped at each other's haunches, whinnying, rear-ing, kicking, trampling. In their hurry to depart, fleeing persons were not too particular about whose horse they mounted and rode away on. Fights broke out, men yelled and cursed.

On the edges of the mass, where there was more freedom of movement, people on horseback and on foot arrowed away from the Pole Star in all directions.

No doubt the canny Arnholt had been the first to swing himself up into the saddle of the nearest mount and ride like hell—to where?

"No chance of catching Gus now," Bowman said. Easing down the hammer of his gun, he holstered the weapon.

Rustling sounded as a slight, thin form glided toward the near end of the veranda. It was Sue, calling his name in hushed whispers.

"Over here," he said.

Descending a short flight of wooden steps to the ground, she flitted toward him, hair streaming back over her slim shoulders. Putting a hand on his arm, she stepped around the corner, drawing him out of the light into the shadows.

Behind the back of the building, it was quieter. There was a garden there, now dormant for winter and oncoming spring. Wind rustled under the eaves, shaking bare trees and shrubs and tall, dry grass.

"You okay?" he asked, wincing. She had a tight grip.

"I'm not hurt, if that's what you mean," Sue said. "I have something I want to tell you."

"Say away."

"I have to ask you something first," she said. "Why do you want to find Nelly Curry?"

"I don't, not really," Bowman said. Seeing the shocked look she gave him, he said quickly, "It's not that I don't want to find her, it's that I'm not looking for her in the first place. It seemed strange that she turned up missing after Drummer was shot, that's all."

"Do you think somebody has done something to her?" Sue asked.

"Why should they? And who? What makes her so special?"

Sue's wide, dark eyes were like holes in the pale blur of her face. She nodded sagely to herself. "Nelly knows lots of things, dangerous things to know."

"Like what?" Bowman asked.

"I don't know. She wouldn't tell me," Sue said. "But I knew she had a secret, she and Drummer. I heard them arguing about it. She was scared and thought they should get out, while Drummer said that there was money to be made if they kept their nerve and didn't lose their heads. He meant if she kept her nerve and didn't lose her head. Whatever else he was, he was no coward," she said. "Not like me."

"Don't low-rate yourself. You're doing all right so far," Bowman said. "A secret worth money. What could that be?"

"I don't know," Sue said. "You want to find her now?"

Bowman shrugged. "I guess it wouldn't hurt to have a little talk with her."

"I know something that might help you find her."

"What is it?"

"Before she took up with Drummer a few years back, Nelly was with Rory Stackpole. You know him?" Sue asked.

"I know who he is."

"The way you handle a gun, I thought you might know him professionally. He's said to be very good with a gun, too."

"He was once," Bowman said. "If what I hear about his place in Rowdytown is true, he must still be pretty good."

"He and Nelly were lovers. At least, she was in love with him. I don't know how he felt about her. But since they're not together and she wound up with Drummer, I guess that tells you how he must have felt, after all. Drummer was jealous, even though it was long over and done with. He forbid her to talk about it, but when he'd get drunk and quarrel with her, he'd throw it up in her face."

"You think she might have gone to Stackpole?"

"No," Sue said. "I think she'd have come back here if she could. But if she couldn't, for whatever reason—because she was afraid—she might have gone to him."

"It's possible," Bowman said.

"Are you going to look for her there?"

"Maybe."

"Oh, please do! I have a feeling that Nelly's in terrible danger, that it's a matter of life and death," Sue said.

"I'll see what I can do," Bowman said.

"I'm sure you can help."

Disengaging the talonlike grip of her fingers, Bowman took her by the elbow, steering her toward the porch. "You'd better get inside," he said, "before somebody starts missing you. By the way," he added as a thought struck him, "what happened to Grimes? I didn't see him during the ruckus or since."

Sue said, "After you left, we all got up and went to the gambling floor. He went away with Marge, I don't know where."

"I can guess."

Sue shook her head. "They didn't go upstairs, I don't think. The last I saw of them, they were at the faro wheel.

Then the shooting started, and I didn't see anyone after that."

"None of Arnholt's crowd had a price on his head, not even Gus himself," Bowman said. "Grimes knows when to pick his fights and when to let them pass. He must be getting smart."

"I'm sorry, I don't understand," Sue said.

"It's nothing, just thinking out loud," he said. "Time for you to get moving, Sue—and me, too."

17

After reloading his gun, Bowman left the Pole Star tumult behind, heading south on foot toward Rowdytown. Some people fled the Pole Star scene; others rushed toward it to investigate the commotion. The crossroads at Market and Trail was alive with activity.

Shunning it, Bowman turned right on Franklin Street, going west to the next north-south cross street. He turned left, going south. Where the street crossed Trail Street, the square was empty, deserted. Stars and horned moon were reflected in the buildings' black windowpanes.

A few more blocks south, and the street grid abruptly ended. There was a band of open ground about fifty yards wide, beyond which lay Rowdytown.

It was a crazy-quilt patch of one- and two-story wooden-frame buildings, sheds, shacks, shanties, tents, and traveling wagons. A cluster of cribs, dives, whorehouses, gambling halls, and saloons, mixed in with a handful of flophouses, pawn shops, and one or two eateries.

Wooden buildings were made of unpainted pine with oilskin windows. At the edges of the site, there were clusters of flimsier and even more temporary structures: a clearing crowded with canvas tents, a circle of high-sided medicine-show-type wagons.

Somewhere a door slammed. A couple of unseen dogs started barking.

A lone structure stood on a wide lot. A long, one-story, shedlike wooden-frame building, it lay diagonally across the ground square, its long axis running through the southeast and northwest corners. Its front faced southeast, as if turning away from the town. A false front added an extra story, but it was all a two-dimensional façade. Painted in crude lettering across the top of the façade was the name "Bucket of Blood."

Smoky light seeped through the oilskin panes of the saloon's small, square windows.

Bowman eyed the line of horses tethered to the hitching post. None seemed familiar. It was a lineup of damned good horseflesh. Most of the animals were stolen, he was sure.

Sitting on the edge of the low front porch was a burly, dish-faced man in a shapeless farmer's hat, denim overalls, and workboots, smoking a corncob pipe. When he inhaled, the burning coal in the pipe bowl washed his face with orange light. Sitting with his hands on his thighs, he stared straight ahead, looking neither left nor right. He did not look up as Bowman went past him, entering the Bucket of Blood.

Within, the space was dim, dingy, low-ceilinged, and smoky. Beneath the layering of smoke was a foul, rank smell. The floor was covered with ankle-deep sawdust.

On the right side of the room stood a wooden slab bar supported by a pair of wooden trestles. On the left were some tables and chairs.

The rear half of the big room was partitioned off by canvas curtains hanging from a line stretching the width of the building. They were backlit by lamps that turned the screen semitransparent.

Larger-than-life shadows shifted and flowed across the screen, the silhouetted figures of men and women in various states of undress moving around back there, coming together and apart. Accompanying their contortions were the carpentry sounds of bedframes creaking, headboards hammering against walls, groans, sighs, panting breaths, strangled cries.

The front half of the building contained a cargo of villainous-looking characters—cutthroats, slatterns, and drunkards.

A man sat alone at a table facing the door. His hair was disordered, his face gaunt and hollowed, covered with several days' worth of bristling beard stubble. He was about fifty-five, outfitted in a rumpled black suit and filthy gray-white shirt.

His shoulders heaved, but no sound escaped him. He was silently sobbing. Fresh tears were squeezed from his eyes, splashing down his face, turned molten by reflected orange lamplight.

On the table before him, an empty bottle lay on its side beside an empty glass.

Grouped at nearby tables were a number of people—cardplayers, drinkers, whores—none of them taking the slightest notice of the weeper.

Behind the bar stood Rory Stackpole himself. Having seen him before in other towns at other times, Bowman recognized him. He didn't look much like his picture in the *Police Gazette*.

Ten years ago, he might still have cut an impressive figure, but since then, a once-handsome profile and athletic physique had slid into ruin.

His blowsy, jowly face was swollen, blue-veined with drink. Watery blue eyes swam milkily in puffy, baggy pouches. His widow's-peaked rooster's comb of hair was dyed jet-black with blue-black highlights. Brows and mustache were similarly colored. He was outfitted like a riverboat gambler, but his suit was frayed at the shoulders and cuffs and shiny at the elbows and knees.

Under his coat could be seen the bulge of his gun, which Bowman knew in the past to have been a special short-barreled revolver with the front sight post filed off, fitted into a holster worn high on his hip.

He stood with one arm casually circling the slim waist of a young woman who was molded up against him. She looked to be in her late teens, though she carried herself with a provocative air of experienced sexuality. Her face was sharp-featured, foxy, almost elfin, with heavy-lidded eyes and strawberry lips that curved up at the corners. Her thin, white, shiftlike dress molded to her slender, exquisitely modeled form.

Around the room, unfriendly eyes fastened on Bowman, sizing him up, appraising him as he made his way to the bar.

At the cardplayers' table, one of them threw in his hand, pushed back his chair, rose.

"Don't fold yet, Packy. I want a chance to win back my money," said a seated man.

"I'm sitting out this hand," Packy said, "and playing another. Watch this." He swaggered over to the bar, leaning in toward Bowman to shoulder him aside. Knowing what was coming, Bowman had left himself plenty of room in which to move. Sidestepping the other's lunge, Bowman came up with a gun in his hand, pressing the muzzle into Packy's big gut.

Packy's eyes bulged. Lips pulled back over his teeth as fear made what was meant to be a disarming grin into a sickly, sheepish grimace.

"Let's get this over with fast, Packy. I'm in a hurry. I've got business to attend to," Bowman said.

Packy opened his mouth to speak, but no words came out. His throat worked, vainly trying to swallow.

"Don't kill him," Stackpole said, his voice rich, resonant. "Business is bad enough without the customers being killed."

"I don't know," Bowman said. "This one seems almost too dumb to live."

Patting his young paramour on her ripely curved rear, Stackpole disengaged from her. "Pardon me, Angel." He came around the bar to the other side and said, "Don't worry about Packy. He's tamed. Aren't you, Packy?"

Packy nodded tightly, holding his neck so stiffly that it creaked when his head bobbed. He looked down from the bottoms of his eyes at the gun poking him in the middle, right above the top of his belt buckle.

Stackpole patted Packy's face, lightly slapping it a few times. "There's a good fellow."

"If you say so," Bowman said.

"I do."

Bowman eased off the gun, holstering it.

"Go sit down, Packy," Stackpole said. "And if there's another peep out of you, I'll shoot you myself. Go now."

Packy faltered, sick-looking, stiff-legged. Placing his hands on the other's shoulders, Stackpole turned him around in place, pointing him away from the bar and toward the card table.

"On your way now," he said, giving Packy a little push to get him started. Packy started forward, his movements stiff, mechanical.

When he was a few paces away, Stackpole came up behind him, giving him a tremendous kick in the seat of the pants. Packy catapulted, propelled violently across the floor.

Sweeping back his jacket to expose his holstered gun, Stackpole said, "Any objections?"

Packy shook his head no.

"And the rest of you?" Stackpole said, addressing the rest of the cardplayers.

They were silent, stiff-faced, shifty-eyed.

"Nothing to say? What I thought," Stackpole said, letting his coat slide forward, covering the gun.

Walking spraddle-legged, Packy slunk around to his empty chair, gingerly sitting down on it.

"Not a peep," Stackpole said. He went back to the bar. Leaning an elbow on it, he turned, facing Bowman. "Have a drink."

"Don't mind if I do," Bowman said.

"Set them up, Angel," Stackpole said, "and have one for yourself."

Angel set out three fired-clay cups, thick and nearly unbreakable, and filled them with whiskey. Under the more direct lamplight, Bowman saw that despite her youth, her good looks were afflicted by a ravaged quality. Blazing, dark-ringed eyes, too-white complexion, red dots of color burning on her cheeks—was she tubercular? If so, it was still in the early stages, since she didn't cough once.

Raising his cup, Stackpole said, "Down the hatch."

Holding her cup in both hands, Angel drank deep, her throat muscles working greedily. Stackpole tossed back his drink, and Bowman did likewise.

"Ah," Stackpole said, smacking wet lips. "What brings you to my humble establishment, Mr. Bowman?"

"You know my name?"

"News travels fast in a small town like this. Everybody knows everybody," Stackpole said. "Besides, you made a big splash—the man who killed Dawes Cotton."

"Friend of yours?" Bowman asked.

Stackpole chuckled. "Quite the contrary."

"And Drummer McCray?"

"I had even less use for him than I did for Cotton," Stackpole said. "But you didn't kill him. Bragg did."

"He's dead just the same," Bowman said.

"That calls for another round. Fill them up again, Angel."

Once more the cups were filled, the whiskey quaffed. "I've got some private business to talk over with you," Bowman said.

"Hmm," Stackpole said. He looked at Angel. Silently, she moved to the far end of the bar.

He and Bowman put their heads close together. Bowman said, "Nelly Curry is missing." Stackpole's expression was unchanged from its bland, buff, meaningless bonhomie. "And you thought she might have come to me?"

"Did she?"

"No," Stackpole said. "I was once very fond of Nelly, but that was long ago. Our parting was not a happy one. No, even years later, she wouldn't come to me for help."

"Not even if it was a matter of life or death?" Bowman asked.

"Is it?"

"I don't know. That's what I'm trying to find out."

"Why? What's in it for you?" Stackpole asked.

"Curiosity," Bowman said. "It's a loose end that might or might not tie into something I'm working on."

"Who'd want to hurt Nelly?"

"I don't know. I was hoping you could tell me."

"If I could, I would. I don't want her to get hurt. But I'm in the dark," Stackpole said. "You know more about it than I do."

"Well—thanks for the hospitality," Bowman said. "It's getting late. Time for me to be moving on."

"Drop by again."

"Thanks, I will."

"Anytime after noon," Stackpole said. "Angel likes to sleep late."

Angel said, "You're the one who likes to sleep late!"

Bowman turned, starting for the door. As he passed, those seated at the card table looked everywhere but at him. They'd long since stopped playing cards; the game had been stopped dead cold earlier, when Packy had been brought up short by a gun barrel poking his belly.

Bowman was a few steps short of the door when a disturbance sounded behind him as Packy stood up, knocking over his chair as he reached for his gun.

Glancing over his shoulder, Bowman drew and fired around his side, under his left arm.

Another shot sounded a half-beat behind his. Stackpole stood with drawn gun leveled at his hip, smoke wafting from the muzzle.

Slugs from two different guns drilled Packy, driving him down, dead.

Stackpole and Bowman exchanged glances, holstered their guns. Stackpole said, "That business we were just talking about, Bowman—"

"Yes."

"I'll see what I can do."

"Thanks."

Outside, the silent hayseed was still in place, sitting on the edge of the porch with his back to the front door, staring into space in the opposite direction. Only the puffing of his pipe betrayed the presence of awareness or even life.

As Bowman passed, the other looked up, removed his

pipe, and said, apropos of nothing, "Nice night if it don't rain."

"What're you smoking in that pipe?" Bowman asked.

"Heh heh," the other said, sticking the pipe back in his mouth and puffing away.

Bowman, shrugging, slipped away.

18

The crescent moon was in the western part of the night sky when Bowman returned to the Pole Star. Most of the town was locked down for the night, and the saloon was no exception. Outside, the only living soul in sight was Bowman.

The ground floor was dark, while glimmerings of light could be seen behind some of the curtained windows on the upper floor. Approaching the building, Bowman noticed that some fresh plank boards had been nailed across the southeast corner window through which Arnholt had crashed.

Too bad he hadn't broken his damned neck, Bowman said to himself.

His boot tread sounded hollow on the boards of the veranda.

When the saloon was open for business, the big front door was swung all the way back on its hinges, so that it lay flat against the inner wall. The batwinged doors were then the only barrier in place in the doorway. Now that the building was closed, the front door had been swung back in place, sealing off the entrance.

Bowman tried the door handle, rattling it, but the door was locked. He knocked on the door, hammering a panel with the bottom of his fist, making a fair amount of noise.

Stepping back, he saw light leaking through gaps where the inner blanket curtaining covered the front windows.

He pounded the door some more. After a while, from within came muffled sounds of stirrings, motion, voices.

On the other side of the door, floorboards creaked. To the right of the door, cloth rustled as a hand lifted curtain folds from the edge of the window.

"Go away," a voice said.

"It's me—Bowman."

"Mr. Bowman? Is that you?"

"Yes, it's me. Who's that?"

"Swamper."

"Let me in," Bowman said.

"It's a botheration to unlock this door," Swamper said. "Go around to the side door, and I'll let you in there."

"Which side?"

"Locust Way—that's the next street up."

"All right, I'm going there now," Bowman said. Turning, he went north to the corner of the building, turned left, and proceeded west along the north wall. The building hid the moon, leaving the area in deeper darkness.

At about the midpoint of the wall, jutting out from it at right angles like a dormer, was a three-sided oblong construction, about eight feet high and three feet wide. Under a small peaked roof, it was faced with a door, the two adjacent sides inset with head-high windows.

Light slanted and glinted behind the panes. Rattling sounded on the other side of the door as it was unbarred, unlocked, and opened. Swamper was there, holding a lamp, beckoning. Bowman entered. Swamper locked and barred the door.

Inside the door was a narrow passageway, opening into a musty storeroom crowded with boxes and crates.

The room was dark, except for the light from Swamper's lamp. It threw weird shadows on the walls and ceiling as Swamper led Bowman down a center aisle toward a doorway at the far end.

On the right, a space had been cleared. "Got something to show you," Swamper said, lifting the lamp so it shone into the space.

On the floor was a wooden pallet with a few folded horse blankets heaped on it. Sprawled on top was a huddled human form, lying on its side, face turned to the wall, legs together, knees drawn up.

"Who is it?" Bowman asked.

Placing a moccasined foot on the figure's shoulder, Swamper rolled him over so that he lay on his back with face upturned. "Grimes!" Bowman said.

Grimes's face was taut, strained, pale, blue-shadowed. His eyes were closed, his mouth gaped open. A line of drool had wet the side of his mouth and his chin. He was minus his hat, jacket, fancy gunbelt, and gun. His clothes were torn and dirty, his white-ruffled shirtfront stained and discolored.

His chest rose and fell with heavy, labored breathing. Groaning, writhing, he seemed to be suffering in the throes of a bad dream.

"Drunk." Bowman *tsk-tsk*ed. "I always say, if you can't handle your liquor, don't drink."

"He ain't drunk," Swamper said. "He's drugged. Leastways, that's what Doc Carruthers says."

"What happened?" Bowman asked.

"We didn't find him till later, in a hall behind the gambling area," Swamper said. "He was lying there, still and pale, dead to the world. Hell, I thought he was dead, that he'd caught a bullet during that big dust-up."

Swamper's face was lit with malicious glee. "And brother, that was some dust-up! I ain't seen so much excitement since the hogs et Grandmaw! Man, we sure showed that Taylor crowd what for! I even bagged one of 'em my own self, did you see it?"

"Sure did," Bowman said.

"Thought he was somebody, waving that gun around, the snotty young punk," Swamper said. "I did for him, all right and proper, and I didn't even need a gun—just tenderized his noggin with my mallet. Brains and blood was flying every which way!" He cackled. "Maybe you seen it, huh? Reckon I showed folks that I can still cut the mustard! Who's a crazy old galoot now?"

"You did a hell of a job, old-timer," Bowman said soothingly. "But what about Grimes? What happened to him?"

"Oh, right. Him," Swamper said. "Well, that's how I found him. He warn't shot—no bulletholes in him. Then I thought like you did, that he was drunk. But not even the town drunk could've slept through all the ruckus. Doc Carruthers couldn't wake him up, not with smelling salts or nothing. The doc says Grimes was drugged—somebody slipped him the old knockout drops in a drink, then robbed him. Ain't that something?"

Looking down at Grimes, Bowman shook his head. "Here I was, thinking that he was smartening up, and instead he gets taken by one of the oldest tricks in the book, shelled like a rube at his first county fair. Who did it?" he asked. "Marge? She was hanging all over him."

Swamper waved a hand in front of him. "I don't know

nothing about that! Nothing! And I ain't pointing a finger at nobody!"

"Well, I suppose it's good for him," Bowman said.

"Huh? How's that?"

"It'll help build his character."

Swamper was doubtful. "That's liable to be of slight consolation to him when he wakes up and finds he's been picked clean."

"That's the part that's character building," Bowman said. "He can't be in too bad a shape, or they wouldn't have left him here."

"Carruthers said he should come out of it sometime tomorrow. Moritz and me toted him back here, where he can sleep it off," Swamper said.

"He'll keep." Bowman tilted his head toward the door. "Let's go."

Taking the lead, Swamper shuffled forward. "Doc says that when Grimes wakes up, he's going to have himself one powerful headache."

"I can stand it," Bowman said.

On the other side of the doorway, they emerged onto the main floor of the saloon, between the piano and the end of the bar. Scattered about in the cavernous space were a few lone lamps, ovals of yellow-brown light amid mud-brown gloom.

Bowman said, "All the bodies have been taken away."

"It was some job," Swamper said. "Knox and his helper were stacking them in the wagon like cordwood. I heard 'em talking about how they're going to have to hire a couple of extra gravediggers just to get them all planted in the soil."

Upstairs, light shone on the balcony through the doorway to Lana Crain's room. She stood at the railing, looking down. Bowman didn't know how long she'd been there.

"The prodigal returns," she said. "Where have you been?"

"Out checking some of my traps and lines," Bowman said. He stood with his head tilted back, looking up at her. "Okay if I come up?"

"You know the way," she said. Turning, she went into the room.

Bowman climbed the stairs. On the second-floor landing, Turk's chair was there but not Turk. Bowman went to the end of the balcony.

The door to the study was open, the room dark. To the right was a second door, light shining behind it. Bowman rapped a knuckle against the panel.

"Come in," Lana Crain said.

Beyond the door was a small, parlorlike room. At the opposite end was another closed door. On the right, curtained windows faced east. On the left was the connecting door to the study.

In the parlor were a cherrywood table and a couple of chairs, a glass-fronted cabinet containing crockery and bric-a-brac, a sidebar with some bottles and glasses on it, and two high-backed armchairs.

Lana Crain wore a black crocheted shawl over the same outfit she'd been wearing earlier. She had a drink in her hand.

Bowman closed the door, locking it. "You never know who's going to come busting in through one of these when you leave it open."

"Where did you go?" she asked. "You disappeared and left me holding the bag."

"Considering five Taylor men were in that bag dead, I don't think Bragg raised too much of a fuss," Bowman said.

"He wants you to come in."

"Plenty of time for that in the morning."

"You're getting ahead of yourself again."

Bowman tried to look innocent. "I just meant that it's the middle of the night. Even a law dog like Bragg has got to sleep sometime. I don't think he'd appreciate me hauling him out of bed at this hour. It's time all decent folk were in their beds."

"That lets us out," Lana Crain said. She sipped some of her drink.

"What did happen when Bragg showed?"

"After he finished complaining about having to get out of his chair, he wasn't too unhappy," she said. "He told his deputies to arrest Arnholt."

"They have to catch him first," Bowman said.

"When they left, Bragg said he was going to the Liberty to have it out with Taylor."

"That won't do much. All Taylor has to do is say that Arnholt was acting on his own accord. Even if Gus is caught and talks—and that's two big ifs—it'll be his word against Taylor's. You know how far that'll get in a court of law."

"I don't care," she said. "Taylor got a bloody nose tonight. For now, that's enough."

"How's Turk?" he asked.

"He's all right. It'll take more than that to crack that thick skull of his. The doctor bandaged his head and told him to rest," Lana Crain said. "Maybe it'll knock some sense into him, teach him not to get caught unawares. Not that it was all his fault. They worked a pretty slick trick. Griff came upstairs with Flossie, one of my girls. When they were alone in the room, he tied her up and gagged her. Then Arnholt and some others started a fight downstairs. It was all a diversion, a feint. While Turk was watching them, Griff sneaked up behind him—the rest you know."

Draining the last of her drink, she crossed to the sideboard and refilled her glass from a decanter.

"Is that some of that good brandy?" Bowman asked.

"Help yourself," Lana Crain said. "You will anyway."

Joining her at the sideboard, Bowman poured himself a drink and drank.

"Ah," he said. "I like that."

"It's very expensive," she said.

"Tastes it."

"I noticed you're not shy about showing your appreciation," she said. "You know, you're supposed to sip that slowly, savoring it."

"I'm still a few belts short of the sipping stage," Bowman said, "but I'm working on it." Fixing himself another, he began making inroads on it.

Lana Crain studied him over the top of her glass. "I like the way you handled yourself tonight."

"Thanks," he said. "We aim to please, ma'am."

"Of course, you only killed two men—Hauk and Noland."

"Noland—that was his name? I was wondering."

"And you missed the big prize," she said. "Arnholt."

"He was lucky. After he fell down the stairs, I was laughing so hard that I missed my next shot," Bowman said.

"My men did for two more—Moritz for Jeff—"

"After I softened him up," Bowman pointed out.

"—and even Swamper got his man," Lana Crain said.

"I was happy for him, he was so tickled by the kill," Bowman said. "Is this your way of saying you don't want to hire me to burn down Taylor? Or are you just poor-mouthing to knock down the price?"

She shrugged prettily. "With half his men gone, he'll be easier to get. That can't but help affect the going rate."

"Now you're the one who's getting ahead of herself," Bowman said, smiling thinly. "I never said I was going to kill him."

"Don't be coy," Lana Crain said.

"Why kill him at all? You've got him on the run."

"Only for now," she said. "And not really. He's lost five men. What of it? Tomorrow he can hire five more. Or fifteen more. He can afford it. It's his money that makes him dangerous. He's not under arrest. Even if he was, he'd have that Cord Gentry on the outside, doing whatever he needs done. And he wouldn't be behind bars for long, not when he could buy his way out. Why should he worry about a town marshal when he can buy the judge? Or the town?"

"You're telling it."

"No, there's only one sure way," Lana Crain insisted. "If you want to kill the snake, you've got to cut off its head."

"Like I said before, you sure are a bloodthirsty wench," Bowman said admiringly. "Sneaky, too. That was a cute trick, hiding that gun under the ledger. Nobody could see it, and it was right to hand."

"Glad you liked it," she said.

"Or was that meant for me?" he asked.

"Maybe just to be on the safe side, until I got to know you better."

Bowman made a show of peering around the room, his gaze intent, scrutinizing.

"What are you looking for?" Lana Crain asked.

"The gun," Bowman said. "I don't see it, so I'm wondering where you've got it hidden."

"Search me," she said.

"That sounds like a plan."

He reached for her. She met him more than halfway.

19

Bowman stepped out of the Pole Star into a clear, crisp, windy morning.

A figure sat nearby on the veranda, legs dangling over the side. He sat hunched forward, elbows on knees, face buried in his hands. He was hatless and without a coat. He was Grimes.

Bowman stood over him, looking down. "Well, well, look what the cat dragged in."

Grimes looked up, the movement making him wince. He was very pale, with greenish-blue shadows under his eyes and in the hollows of his cheeks. "Mountain cat," he said woefully. "That's what dragged me in."

"You should've stayed out there."

"My head!" Grimes pressed his palms to his temples. "I'm feeling mighty low."

Bowman put his fists on his hips. "It's a good thing Francine can't see you now."

"Never mind about no Francine," Grimes said. "She ain't going to know nothing about this, less'n you tell her."

"She'll never hear it from me," Bowman said solemnly. "She'll probably hear it from her uncle, the deputy. The law was here last night, in case you hadn't heard. You probably slept through the whole thing."

"That Swamper told me about it. That cracked old

coot," Grimes said. "I wish everybody didn't have to know what a damned fool I am."

"Now you know what happens when you run around with fast women."

"Never mind about no fast women. It was Mack who cleaned me out."

"How do you know?" Bowman asked. "From what I heard, you didn't know much of anything."

"Well, I'll tell you," Grimes said. "After you left, we drank some more. I commenced to feel poorly, like I was burning up and couldn't breathe. Mack takes hold of my arm, and the next thing I know, he's leading me over by the faro wheel. I remember thinking that my head was spinning like that wheel, only faster, and like to fly off the hub. After that, I don't remember much of anything, excepting this—the last thing I remember is being flat on my back, with Mack cleaning out my pockets. When I get my hands on that honker—well!" Grimes held his hands in front of him, fingers curled as if reaching to strangle. His hands shook.

"Mack might have cleaned you, but I doubt he did it alone," Bowman said. "From the way Marge was hanging on to you for dear life, I don't think she'd have sat back and tended to her knitting while Mack made the swoop."

"She was so pretty and seemed so nice—anyhow, she sure was pretty," Grimes said. "I'm a fool!"

"And that's why you and your money were soon parted," Bowman said. "I see they got your gun, too."

"Don't you worry none about that," Grimes said grimly. "I still got my knife back at the hotel room. If it comes to that, I'll take that gun off Mack with my bare hands."

"This is no town for an unarmed man," Bowman said. "Here, I've got something for you."

Lifting his jacket flap, Bowman revealed a gun, tucked into the top of his pants. Taking it out, he handed it to Grimes.

"Where'd you get this?" Grimes asked.

"I asked Swamper if there was an extra gun I could have, and he gave me this," Bowman said. "Go on, take it."

Grimes took it. He held it in both hands, weighing it, his gaze turned inward. "Thanks."

He struggled to his feet, stiff, unsteady, off-balance. Groaning, he staggered to an upright porch beam, holding on to it. He held the gun down at his side.

After a while, the color came back into his face.

"Looks like you're going to live after all," Bowman said.

"But the way I feel, I wish I was dead!" Grimes said.

"You'll feel better after breakfast."

Grimes, looking queasy, broke into a cold sweat. His jaw and throat muscles worked. "Gah! Just thinking about food makes me sick."

"I'm buying."

"It still makes me sick, but I'll try to keep it down."

"Let's go," Bowman said. "If you think you can make it."

Grimes stepped down from the veranda into the street, starting across it, falling into stride beside Bowman. Bowman said, "Put that gun away, it looks like you're gunning for someone."

"I am—Mack."

"All the better reason to put it away. So you won't tip your hand." Bowman looked the other in the face. "Savvy?"

They went east on Franklin Street, Grimes squinting and blinking, scrunching up his face when the light hit his eyes. He walked with gaze downturned, looking at the tops of his feet. "I'm surprised that fellow didn't steal my boots, too," he said.

"He might've gotten scared when the shooting started," Bowman suggested.

"That sounded like some fracas," Grimes said, perking up. "Five men killed! I'm sorry I missed it."

"Let it be a lesson to you."

Further on, Grimes shot Bowman a dirty look. "What're you laughing about?"

"I'm not laughing," Bowman said.

"Smiling, then."

"I'm not."

"Like hell!"

"You should see yourself. You're walking like a little old man," Bowman said, laughing.

Bowman steered them to a small café on Commerce Street. About a half-hour later, they emerged, their bellies full. Bowman said, "For someone who claimed he was too sick to even think about food, you did all right for yourself. You tucked into that food pretty good."

"I'm starting to feel a little better," Grimes said. "But my head! Feels like it's being split down the middle by a railroad spike!"

"I wake up feeling like that most mornings. It's called a hangover."

"I've had hangovers, mister, and believe me, this here's the granddaddy of them all," Grimes said. Fidgety, impatient, he started sidling away. "I just thought of something. I'll see you later."

"Where are you going?" Bowman asked.

"I got to see a man about a horse," Grimes said, hurrying away. Going south on Commerce, he crossed Trail Street and kept on going.

Bowman shrugged. Just as well that Grimes had left when he had. After breakfast, Bowman liked a good smoke. He had only one cigar with him, and he hadn't cared to share it with Grimes.

"It's all mine," he said, lighting up.

The clock on the courthouse tower said that it was a quarter to eight. The bank wouldn't open for another fifteen minutes. Bowman ambled toward the jail.

Out front were Bragg, Vestry, and a third man unknown to Bowman, all mounted on horseback and preparing to ride out. Bragg said, "Some party at the Pole Star last night."

"You don't know the half of it," Bowman said, thinking of his night with Lana Crain.

"I know Taylor's got five dead men, and ol' Gussie's on the run," Bragg said. "Know what I call that?"

"What?"

"A good start," Bragg said smugly. "Things are working out just as I planned."

"What about Taylor?" Bowman asked.

"We'll get him."

"Then you don't have him."

"I got him, Bowman. He just don't know it yet," Bragg said. "But Taylor's no fool. He knows the law, same as I do, and Cord Gentry probably knows more than the both of us. I can't arrest Taylor for something Gussie did, unless I can prove that they were both in it together. For that matter, what did Arnholt do? Got drunk and shot up a whorehouse. He didn't even shoot nobody. If he goes to trial, there's a damned good chance that a jury of twelve good men and true will find him not guilty. And if he is found guilty, he probably won't spend no more than a couple of months in the county jail."

Bowman said, "He can't go to trial if he's dead."

"Funny, I was thinking the same thing myself," Bragg said. He reached into a coat pocket, pulled out a tin star, held it between thumb and forefinger. "Here," he said, tossing the badge to Bowman.

Bowman caught it. "What's this for?"

"It's yours," Bragg said. "I deputized you yesterday and forgot to give you your badge. That makes everything you've done since then all aboveboard and legal. Just in case Taylor brings in some fancy lawyers to make a big fuss over a bunch of itty-bitty legal technicalities."

"It slipped my mind, too."

"Well, now it's all fixed."

"I always say I'm on the side of the law." Bowman weighed the badge in his palm, a crude five-pointed star that looked as if it had been cut out of a piece of sheet-metal with tin strips. At that, it might have been. "Do I have to wear it?"

"Keep it in your pocket if you like."

"Good. Pinned on a man's chest, it'd make a mighty big target. Gives folks something to shoot at."

"Don't I know it!" Bragg said fervently. "We can do some more palavering later. Right now, I got to get on the trail of some horse thieves."

"Thought you didn't bother with crimes committed outside town limits," Bowman said.

"I don't, mostly," Bragg said. "You know it's got to be something big to get me out of my chair."

"Rainey here," he said, indicating the third man, "Rainey's a hand for Mr. Tully Johnson, one of the richest farmers in these parts. Late last night, some owl hoots ran off with some of Mr. Tully's prime blooded horseflesh."

"Gus, maybe?" Bowman suggested.

"Could be, but I doubt it," Bragg said. "Still, there's a chance that it is Gus, so it's got to be nailed down tight. Besides, Mr. Tully's a leading citizen and a big taxpayer. It won't hurt to remind him that the law in Black Creek's on the job night and day for him. Marshal's an elective office in this town, and don't you forget it. I don't."

Turning their horses south, Rainey, Vestry, and Bragg rode out. "Good hunting," Bowman said.

With the reward money for Cotton in his pocket, Bowman walked out of the bank with a lighter heart and a spring in his step. Angling across the square, he went to the courthouse, where the town records were kept.

The clerk, Peters, was a gnarly, red-faced man with stiff white hair and a white beard. He liked to drink coffee, and he liked to talk. He did plenty of both while responding to Bowman's request for information about Bittersink Basin.

Peters's pink pawlike hand made a dismissive gesture. "I don't have to look that up," he said. "Everybody around here knows about Bittersink. It's kind of a local joke."

"No good?" Bowman said.

Peters smiled politely. "The most useless patch of misery hereabouts."

"I had heard it described somewhat in those terms," Bowman said.

"When Obed Marsh first came in here to file claim to Bittersink, I thought he was joking," Peters said.

"You were the one who filed that claim? Fascinating. Marsh was some kind of railroad man, wasn't he?"

"Ah, Mr. Bowman, then you do know something about him."

"Just a little, what I've heard around town."

"He was a surveyer, I believe," Peters said. "You'd think that a man in that line of work, who has to take sightings and shoot elevations and map out the country-side, would be a hardheaded, practical kind of chap. Which Marsh was, hardheaded to the point of being pig-headed. Except when it came to Bittersink. I'd known him since he'd first come here to live, back in 'fifty-eight or 'fifty-nine. And in all that time, I'd never known him to indulge a folly or whim, except that once. Usually, I make a point of keeping my counsel to myself. When someone's got their mind set on owning a piece of property, there's no talking them out of it. Try, and it turns out badly. They think you're downgrading the site so you can buy it up later for yourself. The ideas people have! But that time, when Marsh wanted to file on Bittersink, I broke my own rule about keeping silent. I told him flat out that he was wasting his money, throwing it away, that Bittersink was good for nothing and would never get any better."

"And what did he say, Mr. Peters?"

"He said that he thought different and that he was bound and determined to have it," Peters said. "Strange. You had to know the man. Obed Marsh was a tight-fisted fellow who knew the value of a dollar—or a penny, for that matter. That's why it was odd, him throwing away good money on Bittersink."

"Maybe he knew something about the property no one else did," Bowman suggested.

"He certainly acted as if that were the case," Peters agreed. "But then, that was his manner on most occasions. Very fond of his own opinions, was Obed Marsh.

Most folks believe that he thought there was gold some-where on the basin. But it's been long-established fact that there's not a speck of gold in Bittersink, or anywhere else in the territory, for that matter. No silver. Not even any copper. Another rumor is that gold was buried there by outlaws. The basin is rife with caves and sinkholes, and I believe some of them were used by both sides during the war. I suppose anywhere that there's caves, there's legends of buried treasure. If a penny was ever dug up from Bittersink, though, I never heard about it. And nei-ther did anybody else from around here."

"Where is Bittersink?" Bowman asked.

Peters showed it to him on a wall map. "I understand there's a new owner, a young nephew of Marsh's."

"I believe that's the case, Mr. Peters."

"I've yet to meet him."

"I have."

"Really, Mr. Bowman? What's he like?"

"Excitable."

Peters sighed. "Ah, youth!"

20

Earlier, when parting from Bowman, Grimes had said something about having to see a man about a horse. As it turned out, he'd been telling the truth, as Bowman discovered when he went to the livery stable to get his own animal.

The stables were located a few blocks below Trail Street, east of Commerce. When last seen by Bowman, Grimes had been heading in that direction. Going to the stall where the gray was penned, Bowman noted that Buttercup was missing. Present, though, was Sid's sleek black mare.

Saddling up the gray, leading him by the reins, Bowman walked him out of the stable. The stablemaster wasn't around, but his boy was, a freckle-faced twelve-year-old kid who was busy shoveling out a pile of manure.

Bowman said, "Where's that butter-colored horse?"

Pausing in his labors, the boy leaned on the end of the shovel. "If you was thinking of buying him, mister, you're too late. The owner just bought him back a little while ago."

"Grimes bought him back?"

"Is he a Reb?"

"That's right."

"That's him," the boy said. "It was the darnedest thing. He sold a black mare to my pa and used some of the money to buy back the yellow. The black is a better horse, but I guess he needed the money. He looked like he needed it."

"Did you see which way he went?" Bowman asked.

"No, sir."

"How long ago was this?"

" 'Bout an hour and a half ago."

"Much obliged, sonny." Bowman tossed the kid a coin, which he caught.

"Thanks, mister!"

Stepping into the saddle, Bowman swung the gray out of the stable yard into the street. He went to the hotel where Grimes was staying. No butter-colored horse was in view at the hitching post or anywhere else in the vicinity.

Inside, Bowman spoke to the desk clerk, whose initial reluctance to discuss the affairs of a guest was overcome by the sight of the deputy's badge, which Bowman briefly flashed. The clerk said that about an hour ago, Grimes had come in, gone upstairs to his room, stayed there a short time, and gone out again. Gone out, not checked out. His room had been paid for in advance for a couple of days.

There was a pretty good chance that Grimes was headed for Bittersink, Bowman thought. For the moment, more interested in the property than he was in Grimes, he decided to make his way there. If he encountered Grimes there, fine; if not, he'd still have a chance to inspect the site.

Climbing back on the gray, Bowman rode west on Trail Street, out to Boot Hill and the church. Bordering the eastern edge of Boot Hill was a dirt road, Cemetery Lane, which crossed Trail Street and continued north.

Turning right on Cemetery Lane, Bowman went

north, a route that soon took him to River Road, where the shoreline curved above the town. He turned left, putting the gray on a branch that followed the river course upstream, trending north and west.

According to the map in the town clerk's office, this was the way to Bittersink.

Seeing no great need for urgency, Bowman paced the gray at a brisk trot. The midmorning sky was clear, cloudless. The air was cool, but after he'd been riding for a few minutes, he warmed up. It felt good to be out in the open, under the sky, a welcome change from the smoky saloons and dives he'd been frequenting by night.

The road tilted upward, slanting into higher ground, where the brush was sparser, the soil thinner, and rocks more plentiful. Farms became fewer and more marginal. About forty minutes later, he came to a place where the road swung wide inland, skirting a cluster of cliffs and bluffs overlooking the river, screening it from view. At the midpoint of the curve, before it started arcing back toward the riverside, the road met a dirt path, which stretched off into a row of low, humped hillocks.

Bowman turned left, taking the path, which wound its course around the base of the hills, deeper into them.

Ahead lay a low, curved ridge, part of the natural outer wall of the basin. Hanging in the air above it, from a distance, came a series of little popping sounds.

Reining the gray to a halt, Bowman dismounted. He hitched the reins to the trunk of a bush at the base of the ridge and clambered up the side, dropping prone when he was a few feet below the crest.

Crawling the rest of the way, he peered over the lip at Bittersink Basin.

The wide, shallow basin was riven by low, rocky ridges

and spurs. Its broad central region was a mud flat threaded by a few thin, trickling streams. What trees there were were bare, stunted. There was more brush than trees, with plenty of patches of thorn bushes and scrub brush clustered at the base of the rocky spurs and needles.

In the far distance, at the other end of the flat, nestled against the curved base of the basin wall, stood a log cabin. Grouped facing it was a ragged semicircle of a handful of blurred, antlike figures.

From their midst came the pop-pop-popping sounds. Little gray-white cotton balls of gunsmoke hung in the air above them. They were shooting at someone in the cabin, who was shooting back at them.

Bowman could make a pretty good guess about who that someone might be.

Scanning the scene, he spied a number of gaps in the basin wall, one of which opened to the left of the cabin and was not far from it. Descending the slope, he mounted up and rode to the left, following the curving path that circled the basin rim.

As he neared the gap, the pops sounded louder, like strings of firecrackers going off. At its mouth, he paused, shucking the carbine from its scabbard. Holding it in one hand and the reins in another, he urged the gray into the notch.

A thin trail led inward, through clumps of bush on either side, which brushed the horse's flanks and the rider's legs. Passage was slightly uncomfortable but far from impossible. Bowman was grateful for the cover, which screened him from view, allowing him to move in close.

Leaning forward over the gray's broad, muscular neck, Bowman peered through the tangled thickets. Beyond them lay empty sky, indicating that he was almost through the notch, about to emerge from the other side.

About a hundred fifty feet away, built into the base of the inner rim wall, stood a long, low wooden cabin, its long side parallel with the ridge. The structure was a partial wreck, its roof collapsed at midpoint, empty windows gaping.

Bullets tore into its brown-black log walls, tearing out fist-sized chunks. They struck with a dull thudding sound, like an iron bar being beaten against a ripe melon. Every now and then, there was a high-pitched mosquito whine, as a slug struck rock and ricocheted away.

Bowman counted three men on the flat below the cabin, covering behind boulders and fallen trees, blasting at the cabin with rifles and handguns. They were on foot, their horses tethered in a grove to the right, out of the line of fire. They poured a steady stream of lead at the cabin.

From inside, at infrequent intervals, a return shot was fired, triggering another blistering fusillade from the besiegers.

Having come as far as he dared on horseback, Bowman dismounted, hitching the gray to a tree. To approach the cabin across open ground would be suicide.

The base of the rim wall was a jumble of dry streambeds, hillocks, and mounds, trimmed with masses of undergrowth. Following them, using them for cover, Bowman figured he could circle to the right, coming close to the cabin without being seen.

Moving out, he advanced in a low half-crouch, bent almost double, carbine in hand. He came to the mouth of a dry wash, its banks higher than his head. Padding along it, soft-footed, he followed its twisty course as it curved up and then around to the right.

Lying flat on the cut's right bank, he peered over the top, through the weeds, at clearing and cabin.

About a dozen yards away, a man crouched behind a boulder, firing a rifle at the cabin.

Farther away, across the clearing, were the other two shooters, one behind a fallen tree and another behind a rocky outcropping on the slope below the cabin.

From where he lay, Bowman had an iffy shot at the rifleman, while the other two were out of his line of fire. Trees and rocks kept him from having a clear shot at the rifleman, but that might not be a problem farther up the wash.

Easing back down into the cut, Bowman followed it for another twenty or thirty feet. It twisted and turned, full of blind corners. Estimating that his position was about where he wanted to be, he crawled up the right bank and peered over the top.

The rifleman was so close that Bowman could have thrown a stone at him and hit him. The other was down on one knee, rifle at his shoulder, potting away at the cabin. His broad back faced Bowman. He wore a new hat and a rust-colored coat with fleece collar and cuffs. He was outfitted like a trail hand or a cattle drover.

That made it likely that he was one of Arnholt's men. But where was Arnholt? He wasn't one of the other two shooters.

Sighting on the rifleman's back, Bowman squeezed the trigger. The round kicked up a little cloud of dust from the man's coat when it entered his body. He fell forward, the rifle falling from his hand. Bouncing off the rock, he toppled sideways, spilling into view in the clearing.

The man nearest him, wielding two guns, stopped firing and started shooting. "Wes! Wes! You okay?"

No reply. The two-gun man yelled, "Bob! Wes's hit!"

From behind the rocky outcropping farther up the slope, Bob called, "Hit? He's dead, Charlie!"

"No, no! He ain't dead!" Charlie was frantic. "Wes! Wes! Can you hear me? It's me, Charlie! Sound off if you can hear me, Wes!"

"He's dead, you damned idjit!"

"Maybe he's only wounded, Bob!"

"Go over and see, then, if you want to get your damned fool head blown off!"

"Easy for you to say. He ain't your brother."

Taking advantage of the distraction, Grimes threw himself out an empty wooden frame on the right side of the cabin, diving through it headfirst. Hitting the ground, he rolled, covering behind the shelter of a heaped pile of loose stones.

"He's out!" Bob shouted, jerking slugs in Grimes's direction. Bullets splintered rock, spraying flinty shards. "He's out, Gus! He's making a break for it!"

Gus?

Charlie joined in, he and Bob unleashing a barrage of slugs that became keening ricochets, careening outward. "We got him pinned down on this side of the cabin, Gus!" Charlie shouted. "See if you can go around the back and get him!"

No reply.

"Gus? Gus!"

Bob called, "Quit your bellowing, Charlie!"

"Bob! I think he got Gus, too!"

"He probably ran out, the skunk!"

When calling to Gus, the others had seemed to be shouting toward the cabin's left side. Near it was a thicket of woods, but if Gus were there, Bowman couldn't see him. Circling the back of the rocky outcrop, jockeying for a better shot, Bob, all unknowing, stepped into Bowman's line of fire. Bowman squeezed the trigger, the carbine barking. Hit in the side, Bob fell backward with a cry, rolling and tumbling down the side of the hill.

When he came to a stop, he sat up, legs flat, arms at his sides, pressing the ground. Bowman shot him again.

Bob fell.

To the left of the cabin in the thicket, a commotion sounded. A voice shouted, "Yaw!"

Hoofbeats pounded. In the thicket, someone was making a break on horseback. Tree branches snapped, and a blur of motion flashed through the trees, racing downhill.

Charlie shouted, "Gus! Gus! Don't leave me!"

Bowman could guess what had happened. While Wes, Bob, and Charlie had come at the cabin from in front, Arnholt had circled around from the side, using the thicket to screen his flanking movement.

Now the odds had changed, thanks to Bowman's advent, and Arnholt wanted out. Sliding down the bank, Bowman dashed to the other side, scrambling up and over it, emerging on a rock-strewn stretch of open ground.

The space was triangular, with the point starting in the thicket, fanning out downhill, then broadening into a wide, flat wedge shape bounded by the rim wall and the wash.

Clearing the last of the trees, horse and rider burst into view, racing full tilt. A dark ten-gallon hat, wolf-fur-collared coat, and black leather chaps identifed the rider as Gus Arnholt, hell-bent on putting some distance between himself and the cabin. Standing between him and open ground was Bowman.

Both laid eyes on each other at the same time.

Arnholt howled, a wordless shriek of defiant rage. He came on, reins in one hand, gun in the other, blasting away.

Shouldering the carbine, Bowman took a bead on Arnholt's middle.

A bullet whizzed past his ear.

He squeezed the trigger, drilling Arnholt dead center.

The impossible happened.

Horse and rider came on, momentum carrying them forward, even though Arnholt was dead in the saddle, his gun silent. Hoofbeats hammered hard ground, echoing hollowly.

Suddenly, there was a cracking sound, a cataclysmic collapse. The earth gave way, swallowing man and mount.

It was uncanny. One instant, they were there, coming on, and the next, they had vanished in a cloud of noise and dust erupting from the shattered ground.

Up from a chasm in the earth a fountain of brown dust and debris came geysering.

It was so thick that Bowman could barely see a few feet in front of his face. Fine dust powdered him, covering him from head to toe. Choking, coughing, eyes smarting, he retreated from the cloud. He tied his bandana over his nose and mouth to protect them from the dust.

More earth collapsed, sending more noise and dust into the air.

Turning, he stood on top of the left bank of the cut, facing the clearing and the cabin. He blinked rapidly, trying to clear the dust from his eyes.

Charlie was on his belly, gun in hand, low-crawling alongside the fallen tree. When he reached the end of it, a stretch of open ground gaped between him and the stand of trees behind which the horses were tethered.

Grimes was nowhere in sight.

Gathering himself, Charlie got his feet under him, jumped up, and started running toward the horses.

Midway on the slope, Grimes stepped out from behind a tree. Glimpsing him in the corner of his eye, Charlie turned his face toward Grimes, swinging his gun around to meet him, all while he was still running.

Grimes fired, spinning Charlie around, knocking him down. Charlie, wounded, felt around in the weeds for his gun. Grimes walked toward him. Charlie found the gun, snatching it up with a cry.

Grimes drilled him.

"Grimes! It's me—Bowman!" Calling across the clearing, Bowman was uncomfortably reminded for an instant of how Charlie had called out in vain as his allies were cut down.

Grimes raised a hand in a half wave, half salute. "I see you."

"Any more of them?" Bowman asked.

"That's the last," Grimes said, indicating Charlie.

Once more, Grimes was wearing his battered campaign hat and Confederate gray military jacket. The Bowie knife had returned to its familiar place, hanging on the side of his belt.

Breaking his revolver, he ejected the spent cartridge casings, reloading with bullets that he pulled from his jacket pockets. Angling downhill, he paused above Bob. "Dead." Moving on to Wes, he said, "Dead. This your handiwork?"

"Him and Bob," Bowman said.

Irritated, Grimes frowned, walking toward him. "This ain't a contest."

"No? I got Gus, too."

"Too bad. I was looking forward to finishing him off myself." Looking at the dust clouds rising behind Bowman, Grimes asked, "What'd you use on him? Dynamite?"

"A bullet," Bowman said. "To tell the truth, I'm not exactly sure myself what happened. Maybe Gus had some dinah on him, or in his saddlebags, and the bullet made it go off. But that can't be. There's no smell of explosives, no smoke, only dust."

"They sneaked up on me, almost got me," Grimes said. "They would've got me, too, if not for ol' Buttercup. He started acting spooky, and I knew company was coming. I ducked into the cabin right before they opened up."

"Where's the horse?"

"Where I left him, tied up safe behind the cabin. Funny how things work out," Grimes said, musing. "I was going to sell Buttercup and keep the mare, but after I went bust, I sold the mare to build up a stake and used some of it to buy Buttercup back. Mister, that horse saved my life. I can't help feeling there was something bigger behind it, that it was fated to be."

"If you feel that way about it, you should be grateful to Mack for cleaning you out in the first place. That started the whole chain of events," Bowman pointed out.

"I'll shoot him to show him how grateful I am," Grimes said. He crossed the wash, joining Bowman on the other side. He said, "I must be weakening. I'm almost glad to see you. I don't mind telling you, them honkers were pressing me pretty hard at one point."

"Looks like I saved your bacon again," Bowman said.

"Now that you put it that way, I ain't so glad no more."

Most of the airborne dirt had settled, but thin curtains of drifting dust continued to hover over the scene.

"Damn! What hit this place, an earthquake?" Grimes asked.

Bowman said, "They don't have earthquakes in this part of the country."

"Maybe not before I got here," Grimes said. "How'd you happen to come out this way?"

"Just couldn't resist having a look at this famous piece of property of yours," Bowman said.

Where horse and rider had disappeared, there was a crack in the earth, a sinkhole about ten feet deep and fifteen feet long. Bowman moved toward it, halting well short of the edge. Grimes moved up alongside him.

The hole was more of a pit. It was wide and deep and let in plenty of light. At the bottom, sprawled on the earthen floor, half buried under a pile of dirt and rocks, lay Arnholt and the horse. The horse had died instantly from a broken neck, while Bowman's carbine had done for Arnholt before the earth gave. They looked as if they were made of earth and stone.

Grimes whistled admiringly. "Some trick. How'd you do it?"

"That's no trick; it's a sinkhole," Bowman said. "The basin is undermined with hollows and fissures. Runoff water from the hillside finds its way underground, eating it away like a worm gnawing holes in a rotten apple. All that's left is a thin crust of earth covering it. Heavy snows this winter must have made for an extra big runoff. The ground over the cave was just a thin shell. The combined weight of Gus and the horse was too much for it, and it collapsed."

"They're running out of space in Boot Hill," Grimes said. "Maybe I can sell this as a ready-made graveyard. They won't even have to dig the graves, they can just dump the bodies in the sinkholes."

Bowman said, "You might have something there."

Grimes moved closer to the edge for a better look.

"Walk soft," Bowman cautioned. "No telling how solid the ground is underfoot."

Grimes froze. "You mean, there might be another cave-in?"

"Could be."

Grimes stood hesitating, then took a baby step forward, then another, until his boot toes were inches from the edge. "Seems solid enough," he said, his voice husky. Over his shoulder, he said, "Wonder how much Gus has got on him?"

"You're welcome to try and find out," Bowman said. "All you have to do is get in the hole with him."

"I was thinking that it'd be easier to throw a rope around him and pull him up by horse," Grimes said.

"That sounds like work."

"I'm not ashamed to dirty my hands to get a dollar."

Easing closer to the edge, Bowman leaned over it for a better look. It was about a quarter to noon, with the sun nudging up against the zenith but still a few degrees short of it. Its rays shone down into the pit, illuminating all of it but the bottom, which remained a well of brown, shadowy gloom. Slowly rising dust veils outlined the slanting sunbeams. Something in the pit caught Bowman's eye. The pit walls were marbled brown and black, brown earthen walls shot through with interlacing black veins and layers.

Bowman's eyes narrowed. Intent, staring, he got down on his hands and knees, getting still closer to the edge, the better to study the black strata layering the sinkhole walls.

It was extremely enlightening.

"Changed your mind about hauling out ol' Gus?" asked Grimes, his tone sly and wheedling.

"No," Bowman said, rising and stepping back from the edge. "He's all yours."

"If I do the work, I'm keeping whatever I find."

"That's your right."

"That goes for them fellows in the clearing, too."

"All right."

"All of them, no matter who shot them," Grimes pressed.

Bowman said, "Fine."

Now openly suspicious, Grimes said, "Why so generous all of a sudden? I thought you'd be skinning me on divvying up the spoils."

"Sorry to disappoint you," Bowman said, "but I've got bigger fish to fry." Turning, he started walking along the left bank of the cut, toward the rim wall notch.

Grimes called after him, "Hey! Where you going?"

"To get my horse."

The gray was where he'd left it, unconcernedly munching on beaded green buds that jeweled the branches of the tree to which it had been tied. Mounting up, Bowman rode back toward the cabin, swinging wide around the dry wash, shunning the undermined ground.

Grimes came down the slope from the cabin, leading Buttercup by the reins. "Now where you going?" he asked.

Bowman said, "Back to town."

"Well, ain't you the high and mighty one!" Grimes sneered. "Too big to stoop down and pick some dead men's pockets, huh? I suppose you've got something cooking, something big, something that makes this look like pocket change?"

"There's one way to find out, Grimes."

"What's that."

"Come to Black Creek," Bowman said.

Turning the horse toward the notch, he urged it forward.

"And bring plenty of bullets," he added over his shoulder. He rode off.

Grimes stood there staring, wondering, watching him go. Not until Bowman had entered the gap and vanished from sight did Grimes move again. When he did, it was to scratch his head.

"Bowman's cooking up something, but what?"

21

It was about one-thirty in the afternoon when Bowman returned to town, reining in the gray on the north side of the square, in front of a three-story, narrow wooden-frame office building. To the right of it was the Liberty Hotel. Parked along the curb between the building and the hotel was a two-wheeled, one-horse, shiny black carriage that Bowman had seen before.

Coming down a path between the two buildings was the carriage's owner, Abigail Cuttle. She was erect, stiff-backed, looking straight ahead, her chin up and her nose in the air. She was carrying a wicker sewing basket by the handle. As she passed, Bowman nodded politely, said, "Miz Abigail."

She *humphed* him. "It's getting so a decent, God-fearing woman can't even walk the streets in the light of day without being accosted by a mangy saddle tramp!"

"A really decent woman wouldn't be walking the streets," Bowman said.

Her eyes bulged, her jaw dropped, her mouth gaped. "Well! I never!" Bustling by in a huff, she climbed into her carriage, gathered up the reins, and drove away, going west on Locust Way.

Shaking his head, Bowman went up the path, climbed a flight of stone stairs, and entered the building. The entry hall was empty. To one side, through an open door, the voices of two men conversing could be heard.

A wall directory noted that Cornelius Harper, Esquire, had his office on the second floor, Room 201. Bowman had some questions he wanted to ask the lawyer about Bittersink.

Climbing a flight of stairs, he found Harper's office in the front of the building. The office door was made of richly grained and textured reddish-brown wood, shinily varnished under many coats of glaze. It was closed. He knocked on it, to no result. The door handle turned under his hand, and he stepped inside.

The carpet was burgundy-colored, the drapes were brown, the walls were mustard yellow with white trim at the window frames and moldings. A desk faced the door. Behind it was a row of shaded windows opening on the square. Bulky, overstuffed pieces of furniture were arrayed around the room.

Harper was in.

He sat behind his desk, slumped forward, upper body and head resting on the desktop. His head was turned to one side. Something stiff and unnatural about his position suggested that he hadn't merely dozed off and taken a nap.

Bowman crossed to the desk. One side of Harper's face lay flat against the desktop. The upper half revealed a face frozen in death agony.

He wasn't going to be answering any questions, not about Bittersink or anything else.

A red snake of blood ran down the side of his face and neck, wriggling across the green desktop blotter. It was a relatively small amount of blood. Tracing its source, Bowman discovered a hole behind the back of Harper's ear, near the jaw hinge joint. A puncture wound, round, about the width of a pencil.

Clearly, this was the cause of death. But what kind of weapon had caused it? Not a knife but something more like an awl . . .

Recalling his thought of a moment before, Bowman took it back. Harper had answered a question after all, a most important question, that of who had killed him. The way he died, the manner of his death, pointed a finger at the killer.

Crossing lightfooted to the door, Bowman put his ear to the crack, heard nothing. He eased the door open several inches, peering outside. The landing was empty. Stepping outside, he quietly closed the door and slipped downstairs. In the ground-floor office, the same unseen speakers were still arguing, this time about tariffs and railroad freight rates.

Bowman went out, got on his horse, and rode out of the square, pacing the horse at a nice, steady walk. He went west along Locust Way. A few blocks away from the square, he increased the pace, hustling the gray along in quicktime.

He was hunting, searching for a trail. The quarry could have no more than five minutes' lead on him. Instead of threading the street grid, trying to pick up the scent, he needed a shortcut and knew where to find one. The highest point in town was Pine Knoll Church. Once the knoll had been topped by a stand of pine trees, but they had long since been cleared out to make way for the structure and grounds.

Bowman rode fast to the church, topping the knoll on which it sat. The building faced east, the knoll's height giving it a commanding view of the whole town spread out below.

A road below the knoll ran north-south. Above Trail Street, it was called Church Street. Below, bordering Boot Hill and beyond, it was called Cemetery Lane. The same road but with two different names.

No more than ten minutes had passed as Bowman sat his horse on the knolltop, scanning the landscape, when the object of his search floated into view on Church Street, going south.

Bowman backed the horse away from the edge, out of sight.

The black carriage of Abigail Cuttle slid past the knoll, continuing south across Trail Street and beyond.

The Cuttle woman was not alone but rode with a passenger beside her, a yellow-haired female who was none other than Francine.

Bowman followed them out of town.

Continuing a mile or two below Boot Hill, the lane entered an area of gentle hills, wooded valleys, and park-like meadows. It was higher, woodsier, and less cultivated than the rich bottomland bordering the river. There were many thickets of woods, few cleared fields.

Trailing the carriage, Bowman kept well behind it, hanging back as much as possible to avoid betraying his presence. The road traced a series of easy curves through gently hilly land, switching back, providing plenty of cover to screen him from view. A few miles later, the carriage turned right onto a dirt path that branched off from the road at right angles. For an eighth of a mile, the carriage climbed a gentle slope, topping out on a flat summit crowned by a clump of wooden-frame buildings.

Remembering hearing that Abigail Cuttle had a farm outside of town, Bowman guessed this was it. Turning the gray, he circled north, going around the hilltop, coming to a saddle-shaped valley. Through it ran a shallow creek, its shimmering surface struck into liquid diamond points by reflected sunlight.

He crossed the fields and rode into a thicket of woods clumped at the base of the hill. At the edge of the woods, he dismounted, leading the gray along a winding trail to a small clearing. He tied up the horse where there was an abundance of pale green shoots and emerald buds within browsing range.

Carbine in hand, he started up the side of the hill, an easy climb. At the top, he hunkered down behind a screen of bushes, peering through them at the farm. Grouped around a yard were a farmhouse, a barn, and several sheds. No one was in sight.

No dogs, it seemed. He hoped it stayed that way.

Rising from cover, crouching low, he rushed the back of the barn, the structure screening him from view of anyone in the yard or house.

The unpainted barn was gray-brown, weathered to a kind of lustrous sheen. There was the smell of hay, horses, manure, leather harnesses, wood. A plank wallboard with a silver-dollar-sized knot hole in it allowed Bowman to peer into the barn.

Opposite the rear wall where Bowman crouched was the front entrance. The big double doors gaped open, letting light and air into the structure's cavernous, vaulting gloom.

There were hay bales and stalls and a couple of horses. There was a big, hulking lump of a man in a straw hat and denim coveralls. There was a naked woman hanging by her hands from a rope tied to a rafter beam.

She hung suspended, dangling several feet above the hardpacked dirt floor. Her arms were raised above her head, loops of rope circling her bleeding wrists. Her flesh was very white, grayish white, where it could be seen between the whip marks, streaked lines of dried blood, blue and brown bruises.

She twisted slowly, the taut rope creaking. Inexorably, the rotation brought her face into view. She was unknown to Bowman. Her eyes were closed, and her mouth gaped. He couldn't tell if she were alive or dead. He looked for some rising and falling of the chest, to show she was breathing, but he couldn't tell.

Standing near the front of the barn was the man in the straw hat. He looked as if he could have been a farmhand, except for the pair of six-guns stuck in the sides of his overalls over his meaty hips.

He was busy grooming a horse, the horse that had drawn the carriage, now freed from the traces. His hands were gentle with the horse, but the horse was still uneasy, because of the woman and the blood. All the stabled horses were uneasy.

Through the open barn doors, across the yard, could be seen part of the farmhouse, coming to Bowman at an oblique angle. A door in the farmhouse opened, a man standing in the doorway.

He called across the yard. "Hey, Dobe! C'mon in!" He pronounced *Dobe* so that it sounded like *robe*.

The man in the straw hat was Dobe. He called back, "In a minute, Voss!"

Standing in the doorway, Voss said, "She wants you now!"

"I'm busy! Can't Wheezy do it?" Dobe asked.

"No!"

"All right, all right! I'm coming!" Dobe said.

"Make it fast." Voss stepped back inside the farmhouse, closing the door. Dobe, grumbling, led the horse he'd been grooming into a stall, latching the door. He spared not so much as a glance at the woman; she could have been a bale of hay for all the interest she elicited from him.

He waddled out of the barn, crossed the well-lit yard, and went into the farmhouse.

The barn was empty, except for the woman hanging at the end of a rope. Peeking through the knot hole, Bowman spied a door in the left rear wall of the barn. Making for it, he rounded the left-hand corner of the barn, suddenly coming face to face with a man striding toward him.

The other was beefy, with a face like a bottle-nosed pig's. A loose-lipped mouth hung open, stretching at the corners, sucking in air. He sounded breathless, wheezing. A lit cigarette hung down vertically from the corner of his underlip.

This must be the Wheezy that Dobe had spoken of.

Wheezy was walking with one arm extended, reaching for the side door handle. He and Bowman saw each other at the same time.

Wheezy's eyes bulged, his jaw dropping. The cigarette continued to dangle from the side of his mouth.

Bowman held the carbine, but he didn't want to give himself away by shooting until he absolutely had to. Wielding the weapon like a lance, Bowman thrust it hard into the other's middle, jamming the muzzle deep into a bulging potbelly.

The air went out of Wheezy with a whoosh. He folded up, buckling at the knees. Bowman brought the weapon up butt first, swinging it in a vicious underhand thrust to the point of the other's chin.

Wheezy dropped, but the blow hadn't quite killed

him. Bowman fixed that. He stepped on Wheezy's neck and didn't take his foot off until Wheezy was done for. In a game like this, there was no leaving things to chance. When he put a man down, Bowman had to be sure that he wouldn't be getting up again. Loose ends can so easily lead to hanging.

Heart pounding, mouth dry, Bowman stood in a half-crouch, looking around. All was as before, quiet, with no alarm having been given, no alert reaching the farmhouse. Leaning the carbine against the side of the barn, he took hold of Wheezy by the heels, dragging him toward the door. The man was heavy, an inert lump resistant to movement.

Bowman did plenty of sweating and straining, dragging Wheezy into the barn. Reaching outside, he grabbed his carbine and closed the door.

Already anxious, the horses were further upset by this fresh outrage. They sidled in the stalls, stamping, snorting.

Bowman left Wheezy's body behind some stacked hay bales. No telling when Wheezy would be missed or when Dobe would return.

Going to the post where the rope suspending the woman was tethered, Bowman drew his boot knife, sawing away at the thick strand. The labor seemed interminable, but finally, he managed to sever the strands.

Taking hold of the rope's free end in both hands, he began lowering the woman. The hempen creakings sounded loud. Playing out the rope, he succeeded in lowering her to the dirt floor.

She lay sprawled on her side in the dirt, groaning. Going down to one knee beside her, he cut the ropes free from her hands. The hands were discolored and cold from lack of circulation, and the ropes had worn bloody grooved bracelets on both slim wrists.

Her face was bruised, beaten. One eye was puffy, swollen, almost closed. Her dry, cracked lips were split. The eye that was open came into focus, gazing at him.

He said, "Nelly Curry?"

She nodded weakly.

Scooping her up in both arms, Bowman carried her to the side of the barn, laying her down on top of a pile of hay. Nearby was a water barrel. Bowman filled a dipper and took it to her.

He was on one knee beside her, an arm under the back of her head, raising it so she could drink. Holding the dipper to her mouth, he moistened her lips with water. He spilled a trickle of water into her mouth, feeding it to her slowly. Her throat worked agonizedly.

He fed her some more water. She nodded, swallowing. She raised herself to a sitting position. She held the dipper in both hands, from time to time raising it to her lips and drinking from it.

Bowman stripped off the dead man's coat and brought it to her, helping her with it. Her coordination was gone, and she couldn't fit her swollen hands through the sleeve openings by herself. Bowman had to do it for her.

The jacket didn't cover much, but it was better than nothing. She looked at him, nodded. "You . . . ?"

"Bowman's the name, Dane Bowman."

It meant nothing to her.

"I'm a friend of Sue's," he said. Not exactly true, but it worked. That was a name she recognized. "Sue sent me—to bring you back." She nodded. He said, "How many? How many inside?"

She tried to speak, her first attempt a choking croak.

After another sip or two of water, she tried again to form words. "Don't . . . don't know," she said.

He patted her hand, gave it a little squeeze. "Don't worry, I'll kill 'em all anyway."

"Kill them," Nelly Curry said. "The woman—the woman. Deadly. No chance, no chance. When you see her, shoot—shoot." She said, "She did this to me."

"Why?" Bowman asked.

"To make me talk," Nelly Curry said. "After I talked, because she liked it."

"I'll straighten her out."

"Kill her. Else she'll kill you."

Exhausted, her head sank, resting on her shoulder. Her eyes closed, pale purple-blue papery lids stretched taut over bulging orbs. They bulged still more when she opened her eyes and caught sight of Wheezy lying stretched out nearby, face upturned, blackened tongue extended.

"Poor fellow was short of breath," Bowman said.

Nelly Curry kept on staring, her gaze fastened on the face of the dead man. She wasn't so much horrified as fascinated. That worried Bowman. Picking up a pitchfork, he pitched hay off a stack until Wheezy's head and shoulders were hidden under a pile of straw.

Wiping his palms together in a hand-washing gesture, he said, "Stay here, and you'll be all right."

"Remember," Nelly Curry said. "Kill her."

Bowman hefted the carbine. "Time for me to go to work."

He went to the front of the barn, keeping undercover to avoid being seen. The open yard was in bright sunlight. The rear of the farmhouse faced it. The house was a modest one-story, white-painted, with a peaked roof.

From where he stood now, he could see the back door. It was closed. To one side of it were curtained windows that barred him from seeing inside. No eyes peeked out at him, as far as he could tell.

Stepping outside, he angled across the yard, feeling vulnerable, nakedly exposed. Muscles tensed involuntarily against the expectation of a bullet crashing into them.

On the other side of the yard, he stood to one side of the back door, back flattened against the wall. The window had thin, faded flower-print curtains, so thin he could see through them. Beyond the door lay a small, cramped kitchen, empty.

He tried the door. It was locked.

From the front of the house, voices sounded. They seemed to be the voices of two men, talking in a normal tone of voice, though he couldn't make out what they were saying.

Boards creaked, as though someone were treading upon them. After a minute, the voices stopped, and the front door banged shut.

Circling around to the front, Bowman peeked around the corner. On the front porch, in a rocking chair, sat a wiry man with a long, bony face. He wore a yellow jacket, the color of fresh-cut pine boards. His booted feet were up on the porch rail. A lever-action rifle stood within reach, leaning against an upright beam helping to support the porch roof. His hat was tilted back on his head. He sat leaning back in the chair, smoking a hand-rolled cigarette, the scent of burning tobacco thick in Bowman's nostrils. Bowman stepped into view, holding the carbine leveled at him.

"Psst!" he said, to get the other's attention.

The smoker glanced casually in Bowman's direction,

doing a take when the reality of the situation sank in. Bowman held a finger across his lips, motioning silence. The smoker raised his hands to shoulder height.

At that moment, the door opened. Dobe stepped out onto the porch. He said, "Hey, Voss, what happened to that jug—yow!"

Voss seemed faster and more competent, so Bowman moved against him first, triggering the carbine leveled on him.

Nothing happened. The weapon was jammed, no doubt from being used to bludgeon Wheezy.

In a heartbeat, Voss's face expressed emotions that ranged from the extremes of stupefied shock to disbelieving delight. Laughing, he grabbed for his rifle.

Letting go of the carbine, Bowman drew his pistol and shot Voss at point-blank range.

Voss fell back in his chair, rocking backward. On the return, rocking forward, his body toppled out of the chair.

Dobe's meaty hands grabbed for his guns, hauling them out of the side waistbands of his bib overalls.

Gunfire blasted, chopping Dobe in the middle even as his guns came level. Jerking under the impact, he backed through the doorway, falling inside with a crash.

A shriek sounded—Francine?

The front window broke as bullets fired from inside came tearing through it, shattering the glass panes, raining them onto the porch. None of the shots came near Bowman. He guessed the shooter was firing blind, using it as a diversion.

From behind the house came the sound of a door being thrown open on its hinges, crashing against a wall. He heard shrieking and sobbing cries.

Going around the back, Bowman came upon Abigail Cuttle and Francine, struggling in the yard.

It was a pretty one-sided struggle. Abigail Cuttle clutched a fistful of Francine's long blond hair, pulling it, tilting the girl's head backward. Her other hand held a gun, a big-caliber hogleg.

Seeing Bowman, she fired at him, a snap shot that came dangerously close. So closely entwined was she with Francine that he was temporarily blocked from firing a returning shot.

Changing targets, Abigail Cuttle suddenly pressed the gun muzzle against the underside of Francine's chin. Francine's eyes bulged, her face contorted with whimpering fear.

Abigail Cuttle said, "I'll kill her!"

Francine vented a choked cry.

"I'll kill you," Bowman said.

"That's a poor trade, an old woman for a sweet young thing with her whole life ahead of her," Abigail Cuttle said.

"Don't low-rate yourself," Bowman said. "You're a prize catch, Lavinia Kidd."

Her eyes narrowed, but there was a triumphant smirk on her face. Drawing herself up, she squared her shoulders, her spine stiff, her gaze fixed, intent.

"You really are a smart bastard, Bowman. When did you figure it out?" she asked.

"Not until I found Lawyer Harper," he said. "I was trying to figure out what made the wound that killed him. It wasn't a gun or a knife. Then it hit me that the hole behind the back of his ear was the right size and shape to have been made by a knitting needle. You were carrying a sewing bag when you came out of the building, but even if you weren't, I'd have made the connection. You were knitting up a storm at the crossing, the night we first met."

"You spoiled things for me then, too," Abigail Cuttle said. "If Grimes had been killed then, like he was supposed to be, there never would've been any trouble for Harper. How'd you know to be there? Some Judas on our side pass you the word?"

"It was blind chance. Fate," Bowman said. "Why'd Harper have to die? Did he get too greedy?"

"No, he got scared," Abigail Cuttle said. Her hand on the gun pressing the underside of Francine's chin was rock-steady. "After Gus's crowd got whipped at the Pole Star, Harper thought the tide was turning against us. He wanted to get out, to run. That would've been the same as an admission of guilt, and it would've shined a light back on Bittersink, and this time, someone would have discovered the truth."

"So you killed him."

"I tried to make him see reason, but he wouldn't listen," Abigail Cuttle said. "I had the knitting needle up my sleeve. I came around beside him and put my hand on his shoulder and shoved the needle into the spot behind the ear, right into his brain—such as it was. It was quick, quiet, and relatively bloodless."

"So's hanging," Bowman said.

"I won't hang," she said confidently.

"Not if I have to shoot your ass," he agreed. "If you even look like you're thinking of taking a shot at me, I'll cut loose at you."

"Then the girl dies!"

"She'll have to take her chances. Damned if I'm going

to stand here and take it while you hide behind her and take shots at me," Bowman replied.

Abigail Cuttle compressed her thin lips. A tic was flashing in the corner of one eye. "You'd do it, too, damn you."

"Why'd you grab the girl, anyhow?" Bowman asked.

"Insurance," she said. "She makes a valuable hostage. I could use her to whip her deputy uncle and Grimes into line."

"But not me."

"You're really trying to get her killed, aren't you?"

"You're holding the gun on her," he said. "Just out of curiosity, where does Nelly Curry come in?"

"She knew too much," Abigail Cuttle said. "Her lover man, Drummer, knew about the gang and talked about it to her. After he was killed, a couple of the boys found her wandering around loose and brought her here."

"Thanks," Bowman said.

"What for?" She sneered.

"For tying up a few loose ends that I was wondering about. Except for the key question: Where's Harvey?"

"Wouldn't you like to know?" she spat.

"I already do," he said.

"Talk, that's all it is. Bluster and bluff."

"Speaking of which—if you've been keeping me talking while waiting for Wheezy to come along and save the day for you, get ready for a big surprise."

"What—what do you mean?"

"Wheezy's wheezed his last," Bowman said. "Dobe and Voss, too. There's no one left to pull your chestnuts out of the fire, Miz Abby. Or Miz Lavinia, I should say." He could see her steeling herself to make her play.

"Here's what's going to happen," she said. "I'm going

into the barn, me and missy here." She gave Francine's head a good shake, making her cry out. "I'm going to ride out in the carriage, taking her with me."

"What am I supposed to be doing while all this is happening?" Bowman asked.

"Not a damned thing," she said. "When I've made my getaway, I'll let the girl go."

"Word of honor?" he said mockingly.

"You're a smart-mouthed bastard," Abigail Cuttle said. "What a luxury it would be to put a bullet into you, right in the belly. Or lower," she added.

"A luxury you can't afford," he said.

"Enough talk! Now, back off, or I'll blow the top off of missy's head here and risk taking my chances with you," she said.

Francine begged, "Please, do what she says—please!"

"You know I'll do it, Bowman." Abigail Cuttle started backing up toward the barn, forcing Francine to retreat with her.

She retreated blindly, not daring to look away for an instant from Bowman's deadly gun.

"As for picking chestnuts out of the fire," she said, "I've got news for you. The word's gone out. The gang's coming in, all of them. They'll take this town apart and burn it to the ground."

Bowman said, "You'll never see it."

"No? I'll light the first torch myself!"

Earlier, she'd been talking to distract Bowman, while all the while he'd been doing the same thing. That was because he could see beyond her, into the barn, where Nelly Curry had somehow managed to get to her feet and was now staggering forward, pitchfork in hand.

Nelly Curry didn't have much left, and it took almost

all of what she had to stagger forward on bare feet, creeping, inexorable.

At the last instant, some presentiment of danger, perhaps no more than the weight of a shadow, fell on Abigail Cuttle. Darting a quick glance over her shoulder, she was just in time to see Nelly Curry an arm's length behind her, thrusting with the pitchfork.

Taking the gun out from under Francine's chin, Abigail Cuttle started to reach back over her shoulder with it, bringing the muzzle into line with her attacker's face. Nelly Curry lunged, spearing the Cuttle woman in the back with the pitchfork's three curved, needlelike tines.

Abigail Cuttle heaved, convulsing, her back bowing forward. She let go of Francine, who fell away from her, sitting down hard on the ground, backing away crablike on hands and feet.

Nelly Curry gave the pitchfork a twist. Dropping to her knees, Abigail Cuttle fell forward, facedown into the dirt, the pitchfork sticking out of her back like a handle. Nelly Curry clutched the shaft with both hands, using it to stay on her feet.

Francine scrambled to her feet, wiping the dirt from her hands. She stood with a hand to her open mouth, looking down at Cuttle's corpse. Her face was puffy with tears and stark with near hysteria, she had a bruise on her right cheek and a split lip, but she seemed otherwise unharmed.

Nelly Curry cried out, staggering. Bowman caught her by the arm, holding her up, steadying her.

"Sent her to hell with the devil's own trident!" she said.

"She was right about one thing," Bowman said. "No hanging for her."

22

At six o'clock that night, Bragg and his deputies marched into the dining room of the Liberty Hotel. It was the height of the dinner hour, and the room was crowded with the town's big people. Occupying its usual table was the Taylor party, consisting of Rufe Taylor, his wife, Cord Gentry, and several business associates.

Looming over them, Bragg said, "Rufe Taylor, you're under arrest."

Cord Gentry looked as if he were choking on a bone stuck in his throat. Pushing back his chair, he rose, his table napkin falling to his feet. His eyes bulged, his face was purple-red.

He was taking it a lot harder than Taylor, who sat there with a flat-eyed gaze peering out of a poker face.

"What's the charge?" Gentry demanded.

"Suspicion of being Harvey Kidd," Bragg said.

Gentry literally reeled with astonishment. A beat later, he laughed into Bragg's face. "You must be mad!" he said. "That's Rufe Taylor!"

"I know who he is," Bragg said.

"Everybody does! He's a well-known public figure! Everybody knows he's not Harvey Kidd—they're two completely different people!"

"Then everybody knows something I don't."

"That's for damned sure," Gentry said, laughing bitterly.

"How do you know for sure he's not Harvey Kidd?" Bragg countered. He was as phlegmatic as a cud-chewing bovine. "Can you prove it?"

"I don't have to prove it, you big clown! Where's *your* proof?" Gentry asked.

"I'll show my hand when the time's right," Bragg said. "For now, you're coming with me, Taylor."

Taylor pushed back his chair and rose, placing his napkin on the table. Nodding to his table companions, he said, "If you'll be so good as to excuse me—"

His wife burst into tears. The other guests sat there frozen-faced, staring, numb. Gentry, on the verge of a major explosion, was restrained by a gesture from Taylor. He said, "It's all right, Cord. Best to do what the marshal says."

"That's right," Bragg said.

"But it's all so transparent, so patently outrageous!" Gentry was sputtering. "It's flagrantly unconstitutional! It's—"

"We'll get it straightened out. I assure you all," Taylor said, addressing the guests, "and especially you, my dear"—this said to his sobbing wife—"that this is all a ridiculous misunderstanding, a grotesque farce. Tomorrow, we'll all have a good laugh over it."

"The whole territory will be laughing," Gentry said. "Laughing at you, Bragg, for making such a horse's ass out of yourself. By the time I get through with you, you'll look like the biggest damned fool in all creation. Never mind that. You've already made yourself look like the biggest damned fool in all creation. You can't get away with this, Bragg. It's too raw—jailing your political enemies on trumped-up charges."

"Trumped-up, hell," Bragg demurred. "I got a couple people coming down from Lawrence who knew Harvey Kidd way back when. They'll say whether or not Taylor is Kidd, and I'm betting they'll say aye."

"You're betting your badge," Gentry said.

Bragg blinked, his expression mild. "Let's go, men."

"You're finished in law enforcement," Gentry said. "By tomorrow, no jail in the territory would hire you to clean out the spittoons. You're the one who's going to jail, Bragg!"

Vestry and Dixon fell in beside Taylor, flanking him. Bragg turned, started out of the dining room, the others falling in behind him, following him out of the hotel and down the square to the jail, where Taylor was locked up in a cell.

Around midnight, a ruckus broke out at the jail. Shots, shouts, galloping riders, flashes of light, more shots. Chaos.

When the shooting stopped, people poured into the square to see what had happened.

Somebody shouted, "A gang of masked men just busted Rufe Taylor out of jail!"

Incredible as it seemed, the story was soon verified by Vestry—Bragg being so mad he could barely speak. Bailey had been the only lawman on duty in the jail, the others being out on patrol. Slipping inside, a masked desperado got the drop on Bailey, locking him in his own jail cell, freeing Taylor from his, and taking him away.

The crowd buzzed, one citizen solemnly observing, "Sloppy. Very sloppy. It looks bad for Bragg."

"Bragg?" somebody else said. "What about Rufe Taylor? This sure makes it look like he really is Harvey Kidd!"

The gawkers broke up soon after, as a grimly determined Bragg and his men saddled up to give chase to the fugitives. Fearing that they might be asked to join a posse, the citizens quickly dispersed, melting away to their homes, leaving the square empty as Bragg and company rode out in hot pursuit.

An hour later, after the hubbub had long been quieted, the deserted square rang with the sound of approaching hoofbeats.

Reining to a halt in front of the Liberty Hotel was a lone rider on a steel-gray horse. A bandana covered his face below the eyes.

Emptying a six-gun in the air, he cried, "Gentry! Cord Gentry!"

Lights shone behind the curtained windows of Gentry's room. Shadows flitted across the shades, looming monstrously for an instant, before the room went dark. A few beats later, there was the sound of a window being raised. Not showing himself, Gentry cried, "Who's there? What do you want?"

"Money!" the rider said. "We've got Taylor!"

"What?"

"He didn't break jail, we busted him out! If you want him, bring ten thousand dollars to Boot Hill at sunup tomorrow!"

"Ten thousand! You're insane!"

"Ten thousand dollars at Boot Hill at sunrise tomorrow!"

"I can't get that kind of money."

"Ten thousand, or he goes back to the law! You know that'll cost you a lot more than ten thousand!"

Gentry pleaded, "Give me some time to raise the money, at least. The bank won't even have opened by that time."

"Ten thousand by sunrise, or back he goes to the law!"

Some curious parties from inside the hotel came out onto the front porch to see what was happening. The rider fired some shots in their direction, narrowly missing them, sending them scurrying inside.

Putting heels to the gray, he raced from the scene, vanishing into darkness.

23

At break of day, on Boot Hill under a bare tree, four men were gathered, all facing east. Cold, gray predawn light filled the bowl of sky. On land, shadows were still thick, dense. "It'll be dawn soon," Bowman said.

"Good," Grimes said. "I'm tired of waiting out here and freezing my ass off."

Waving around a silver flask, Rory Stackpole said, "Have some of this. It'll warm you up." The flask was passed to Grimes, who wiped its mouth on his sleeve and took a long pull, tilting the flask to vertical. He gave it back to Stackpole.

Stackpole upended it. Barely a drop came out. "What the hell?" he said.

"There was only a swallow in there anyhow," Grimes said.

"For a camel, maybe," Stackpole said.

They were grouped under a gnarled bare tree, its twisted limbs branching into a spiky overhead canopy. One such limb jutted at right angles from the trunk, extending horizontally about eight feet above the ground.

Thrown over the limb was a rope. Secured to the tree trunk at one end, the rope was thrown over the branch, coming down the other side, its opposite end terminating in a hangman's noose, which was snugly fitted around the neck of Rufe Taylor.

Hands tied behind his back, mouth gagged, he sat astride a horse whose lead rope was tied to a nearby wooden cross grave marker.

His face was swollen, red, only part of which could be laid to the noose. The rest was the product of fear, maddened frustration, rage. His eyes were popping, froglike. Finger-thick veins stood out on his temples.

The tree stood in the southwest corner, at the edge of the gravesites. Behind it, the ground sloped up into a hill. Nearby were a couple of freshly dug graves, with cone-shaped mounds of moist, dark earth heaped up to one side of them.

A wind sprang up. Grimes said, "Lonesome place."

"Don't worry," Bowman said. "Company's coming."

"You reckon? Who'd want to pay ten thousand for his tired ass?" Grimes said, indicating Taylor. Glaring down at him, Taylor seethed with eyeball-rolling paroxysms of hate.

Bowman said, "They won't pay. They'll try to kill us and take Taylor."

Grimes circled Taylor, looking up at him. "Bet you never expected to get this close to a rope." Behind the gag, Taylor unleashed a string of muttered obscenities.

Bowman said, "Look."

Riders appeared on Trail Street, racing west through town, coming fast. Leaving behind the town, the riders neared.

Stackpole said, "I count eight."

Bowman nodded. "This is no bunch of rowdy cowboys, like Gus's crew. These are some bad *hombres*. But we'll make angels out of them."

Nearing the bottom of the hill, the riders slowed, circling the eastern base of it, facing the group under the tree on the cemetery hillside. Their advance was blocked by the iron spear fence bordering the grounds, but the obstacle was only temporary.

Two of the riders loosed their lariats, roping fenceposts at critical points along the barrier. Backing their horses, they pulled down broad sections of fence, leveling a twenty-foot gap in the wall.

Through it they came, fanning out, slower now, walking their horses, making their way toward the hanging tree and those beneath it. Riding over graves, trampling them, knocking down markers and crosses.

"Some bunch!" Bowman said half admiringly. "There's Patch Hawkins. Leonard Fry, Bill McCullough. Shorty Bevins. Pardee. The other two I don't know."

"I can tell you," Stackpole said. "The kid with the glasses is Pinky Cravat, and the big oafish one is Earl Coldwell."

"Never heard of them," Grimes said disparagingly.

"That makes it even," Stackpole said, chuckling. "They never heard of you either, sonny."

"They ain't never going to forget me, I'll tell you that." Glancing sideways at him, Grimes said, "Who you calling sonny?"

"Not now," Bowman said.

Coming to a halt, the line of riders formed in a semi-circle facing the tree.

Patch Hawkins, Kidd's lieutenant, had gained his name from the black eyepatch he wore over one eye. It made him look piratical—a land pirate on horseback. Leonard Fry wore a derby hat and chewed on a lit cigar stub in the corner of his mouth. A square-faced, strapping hearty,

Bill McCullough looked like the keelboat man he'd once been. Shorty Bevins was a little dynamo, his massive shoulders and torso giving the illusion that he was almost as wide as he was tall.

A beardless youth with round wire-rim glasses, Pinky Cravat could have passed for a college student. Earl Coldwell had close-set, beady eyes and a lopsided grin in a potato face. A burly, ginger-bearded man in a bottle-green suit and pants with checked vest was Pardee.

Every man a robber, marauder, killer many times over.

At the center of the group was their leader, Harvey Kidd.

Grimes frowned, puzzled. Out of the corner of his mouth, he said, "Hey! What's Gentry doing with them?"

"Don't you get it?" Stackpole snorted. "Gentry is Harvey Kidd!"

Gentry laughed. "Ten thousand dollars. Ten thousand!" He stopped laughing. "Ten thousand bullets is what you'll get."

Bowman said, "I'm sure your partner Taylor is none too comfortable with that rope around his neck."

"On him it looks natural," Gentry said. "Rufe was born to hang."

"Let's make the swap. Did you bring the money?"

"Ever since you hit town, Bowman, I've been watching you, trying to figure out what you were up to. Now it all makes sense," Gentry said. "You planned on holding me up for ten thousand dollars. Me, Harvey Kidd! And you even got Rory Stackpole to side you. Too bad he's twenty years past his prime."

"You'll find out," Stackpole said.

"You should have stuck to your rathole instead of crawling out of the bottle to buck me," Gentry said.

"You shouldn't have put a hurting on Nelly Curry. She's a friend of mine."

"You'll soon be with her, Stackpole."

Bowman said, "He will, but not in the way you mean, Harvey. You don't mind if I call you Harvey, do you? I've been hearing about you for so long that I feel like I know you."

"Funny how things work out," Gentry said. "Two fine sons of Kansas like us at each other's throats."

"It's the way of the world, I guess," Bowman said. "Well. The money?"

Gentry laughed. "Well, what do you know? I plumb forgot it." Others of his gang laughed too, mean, knowing laughs.

Taylor set off a renewed round of squawking through his gag. "Hold your horses, Rufe," Gentry said. "You'll come through this fine."

"Are you saying we don't have a deal, Harvey?" Bowman asked.

Gentry shook his head in disbelief. "The trouble with fellows like you is that you get too fancy, too fancy by half."

"How so?"

"Even if Rufe hangs, he won't die right away. It takes a couple of minutes to die by strangulation. Before that, I'll cut him down from that rope."

"Huh!" Grimes said, fists on hips. "And while you're cutting that rope, what do you think we'll be doing?"

"Nothing," Gentry said. "You'll be dead."

Bowman said, "Afraid I've got some bad news for you, Harvey. Abigail—or should I say Lavinia?—she's riding that hellbound train."

Gentry's face darkened, his smile dissolving. "That's a lie."

"She's dead, and Nelly Curry's alive," Bowman said. "That's how I knew Taylor wasn't Kidd and that you are, because Nelly told me. As for your sister, Abigail-Lavinia . . . well, at least she didn't hang."

The storm was about to break.

Gentry said, "You should've stayed out of my business, Bowman."

"You should've stayed dead after the war, Harvey. We'll fix that."

"How? With your three guns to our eight? You out-smarted yourself, tricking Bragg and his deputies out of town to chase you up and down the countryside, when you were hiding here all along. Now there's no one to save you," Gentry said.

"Not exactly," Bowman said. "I'll give you one last chance."

"You'll give me one last chance?"

"Throw down your guns, and I'll let you live. You have my word on it."

Gentry scoffed. "We'll throw down, all right."

Over his shoulder, Bowman said loudly, "Anytime, men!"

"That is sad," Gentry said pityingly, "trying to pull a schoolboy trick like that. It'll be a mercy to put you out of my misery."

To one side, a pair of freshly dug graves yielded up their contents.

One held Cobb, another Swamper. Cobb was armed with a pair of sawed-off, double-barreled shotguns, one in each hand, wielding them like pistols. Swamper was armed with a conventional double-barreled shotgun.

Across Trail Street, racing out from behind the church where they'd been hiding, came Bragg and deputies

Vestry, Dixon, and Bailey, with rifles shouldered and guns level.

One of Kidd's gang screamed, "It's a trap!" All at once, everybody started shooting.

His horse rearing, Gentry traded shots with Bowman. He missed. Bowman didn't. His shot hit Gentry square in the torso, striking with the meaty thump of lead burying itself in flesh.

Cobb and Swamper cut loose with their scatterguns, unloading directly into the milling mob of outlaws. The results were horrendous.

A buckshot pellet exploded Patch Hawkins's good eye. Another blast tore into Leonard Fry, blowing his derby skyward and shredding his side. Fry stayed on horseback, wrestling an oversized gun from the holster under his arm, swinging it around, firing.

Standing like a duelist, facing sideways with gun hand fully extended, Stackpole shot Fry off his horse.

The uproar spooked the horse under Taylor, causing it to break loose and run away. He dropped, the noose tightening. His body swung pendulumlike, legs working.

Bragg and his deputies opened fire, laying down a withering stream of lead that sieved the mounted outlaws. It was more like a firing squad than a gunfight. Caught in a murderous crossfire, the Kidd gang didn't know what to do first, except die.

At the graveyard on Boot Hill, a storm raged—a gunstorm.

The booming racket of shotguns and six-guns echoed off the hills. Clouds of gunsmoke fogged parts of the site. Spear points of flame leaped from gun muzzles.

Working his gun until the barrel was red-hot, Grimes said, "This ain't no fight—it's a massacre!"

"It's better that way," Bowman said.

The disturbance quelled, the noise quieted, the racketing clamor of gunfire died down to a few scattered shots.

To a man, the Kidd gang had been slain or mortally wounded, their bodies sprawled around the graveyard.

The sun cleared the horizon, sparkling, turning the morning mists all pearly and rosily glowing. In the west, in a cloudless sky, the moon was a ghostly pale crescent.

"Nice morning," Bowman said. "It's going to be a good day."

24

Now that the shooting had stopped, awed townsfolk began making their way toward the scene of the showdown on Boot Hill.

One of the first was Francine. Seeing Grimes, she hurried to him and threw herself into his arms. She was laughing and crying at the same time. "You're alive!"

"Sure am," he said, and proceeded to prove it, hugging and kissing her.

After a long clinch, they came up for air. Francine clung to Grimes, looking up at him with lovelight shining in her eyes. He looked at her the same way.

"I reckon they found time for romance somewhere along the way," Bowman said to himself, grinning.

Grimes's dewy-eyed bliss was somewhat shattered by the sight of Bowman standing nearby. He said, "You don't give a fellow much privacy."

"I've got something to tell you, Grimes, and this looks like the right time for it, while you've got your arms around a pretty girl," Bowman said.

Grimes said, "Tell it."

"Let's go over by the church, get Francine away from all these bodies," he said. "Not to mention her uncle, who's got no great love for you."

The trio left Boot Hill, crossing Trail Street and climbing a flight of wooden stairs to the knolltop and the church that crowned it. Francine and Grimes were arm in arm, gazing adoringly at each other.

Bowman put a hand on Grimes's shoulder. "Brace yourself for what I'm going to tell you, Grimes."

Grimes set his jaw, defiant. "Whatever it is, I can stand it."

"You're rich," Bowman said.

"Huh?"

"You're a rich man. Or at least, you're going to be."

Grimes nodded. "I reckon my share of the reward on those outlaws ought to come out to some considerable amount."

"Not after it's all been shared out among us, Stackpole, Swamper, Cobb, and Bragg and his deputies."

Fighting his dismay, Grimes said, "Thought you said I was going to be rich."

"You are," Bowman said. "The reason is also the reason Gentry and Taylor wanted you dead."

"Why?" Grimes asked.

"I suspected it early on, but it wasn't until yesterday, out at Bittersink, that I knew the answer," Bowman said. "It was in the hole with Gus."

Grimes's eyes widened. Francine said, "Jed, honey, you're squeezing my hand so hard that it hurts."

"I'm sorry, darling." Almost choking, he gasped. "Bowman—is it—is it gold?"

"No."

Grimes's face fell.

"Not in the sense you mean," Bowman added. "But it's wealth all the same, real wealth."

"What is it? Silver? Buried treasure? What?" Grimes asked, nearly frantic.

"Coal," Bowman said.

"Huh? What's that you say?"

"Coal. That's what it was all about," Bowman said. "It all goes back to your uncle, Obed Marsh. He was a surveyor and a geologist. That's someone who's an expert in rocks and minerals," he added.

"I know what it is!" Grimes snapped.

"You looked confused," Bowman said.

Grimes said, "That's what comes of trying to figure you out. You're a slippery cuss, the slipperiest I ever did see."

Bowman continued, "Back before the war, Marsh was part of a government survey team, one of a number of teams looking for the best route for a transcontinental railroad. His team was surveying these parts. Most likely, it was the water gave him his first clue. Black Creek river water, with that distinctive smoky taste. Not harmful but sharp enough so that most folks prefer to get their water from wells that don't have the taste. That taste comes from coal tars. They make Black Creek black, giving it its special color and sharp taste. Somewhere upstream, the watercourse runs across a massive underground coal deposit. Tracing it to its source, Marsh located the site of the coal deposit in the north ridge of Bittersink. Underneath its covering of soil and brush, most of the rim wall must be a lode of solid coal. That's why he bought the property. Marsh was a visionary in his way. He knew that railroads eat coal. War or no war, eventually the road would come this way. Coal fields are mighty scarce in these parts.

"Marsh settled here and waited for the coming of the railroad, to make his fortune. The one thing he didn't count on was Kidd and Taylor. Near war's end, Harvey Kidd and his sister and partner in crime, Lavinia, both disappeared. He didn't break up the gang; he just disbanded them for a while, telling them to lie low until he gave the word for them to gather and start up operations again. In the meantime, Kidd became Cord Gentry, while sister Lavinia became—that's right—Abigail Cuttle. Somewhere along the way, Kidd teamed up with Taylor, probably in St. Louis, where Taylor was cutting up some pretty fancy financial capers. Knowing that the railroad was coming, they cooked up a plan to get rich off it. The plan was to take over the town all legal-like and own it when the railroad came in. Black Creek was sure to boom, and they'd have all the prime property.

"Taylor was the money man, while Kidd—Gentry—got the dirty work done. That's where the gang came in. If somebody didn't want to sell out their ownings, the gang would run them out or just plain kill them. Then Taylor would buy the property legally and hold title to it. Abigail Cuttle—Lavinia Kidd—served the same role that she had during the war, working as spy, go-between, and what have you. She passed Kidd's orders to the gang. All her volunteer work was a blind for her to run back and forth across the territory, passing messages between the outlaws. That's why she offered to ferry you back from Zenith, Francine. While there, she passed Cotton his orders, which were to intercept you at the crossing, Grimes, and kill you."

"But how'd she know I was going to be there?" Grimes asked.

"Harper told her," Bowman said. "Lawyer Harper, the agent for your late uncle's estate. He was in touch with you by letter, knew when and by which way you were coming to Black Creek. Harper is the key that ties it all together. He was Obed Marsh's lawyer and friend. Somewhere

Marsh must've let slip some of the truth about Bittersink to Harper, enough to give him a pretty fair idea of what it was really worth. Harper told Taylor, and the two of them put their heads together to see how they could get their hooks into the property.

"Marsh got wind that something was in the air. He made out his last will and testament, leaving Bittersink to his sole surviving relative—you, Grimes. He died soon after, in what was supposed to be an accident. My guess is that it's more likely that Kidd had him killed and made it look like an accident. That left you, Grimes. If you died, the property'd go up for sale, and the schemers could have picked it up for a song. So, they tried to fix it so you would die."

"Only I ain't dead, and they are," Grimes said. "Alive—and rich!"

"You were a problem, Grimes. So was Nelly Curry," Bowman said. "Drummer McCray was an outlaw and a killer. He moved in the same circles as the Kidd gang. Somehow he learned that Harvey Kidd and Cord Gentry were the same person. That marked him for death, too. Nelly told me that Drummer killed Harl Yancey not out of jealousy but because he thought Yancey was an assassin, sent by Kidd to kill him. As it worked out, it was Bragg who killed McCray, all in the line of duty. That took care of Drummer, but there was still Nelly. He liked to talk, and he'd told her enough of what he knew to scare her half to death. When he got killed, she ran—right into some of Arnholt's men, who were out looking for her.

"Gussie's crew getting cleaned up on at the Pole Star last night was the last straw for Harper. He was scared and wanted to run. Sister Kidd did for him, jamming a knitting needle into his brain. I happened along at that time, wanting to ask Harper some questions. I saw her leaving his office and put two and two together. After she left Harper, she went to Vestry's house, where Francine is staying. She told Francine and her aunt some cock-and-bull story about Vestry wanting to get Francine out of town, in case Gus or some of his boys tried to make a grab for her. She took Francine out to the farm, but by then I was on the trail."

Grimes said, "What was all that business about Taylor being Kidd?"

"That was a trick to draw out the Kidd gang," Bowman said. "The hardest thing about bagging the gang was to get them all in one place. I knew Gentry was Kidd—Nelly Curry had already told me, out at the farm. But I wanted the whole gang. I talked Bragg into going along with me, especially when I mentioned splitting up all that reward money. Bragg arrested Taylor. Gentry-Kidd couldn't afford to throw him away, because Taylor was the key to all of their financial schemes for taking over the town. Kidd sent word for the gang to come in. They'd free Taylor and kill everybody who knew too much about their dealings. Bragg and I staged Taylor's jailbreak, then he and his deputies rode out of town, as if in hot pursuit. They rode out a little way, doubling back for the finish. I told Gentry to bring the money to Boot Hill to buy back Taylor. He brought the gang instead."

"Say, what happened to Taylor, anyway?" Grimes said. "Last I saw of him, he was hanging from that rope."

"He still is. Seems that in all that confusion, nobody thought to cut him down," Bowman said. "I guess Kidd was right about Taylor—he was born to hang."

Grimes frowned fiercely, a sign that he was thinking hard. Absently, he scratched his chin whiskers. "When did you learn that Bittersink was a big coalfield?"

"Today, when I looked in the hole."

"You knew, and you didn't tell me?!"

"I didn't want to affect your fighting spirit, Grimes. A man who's got nothing to lose will fight like hell. A man who's got something to lose, a man of property, isn't so eager to mix it up. He's more likely to play it safe."

Grimes was burning. "You used me! Why, you dirty—"

"Ah-ah, there's a lady present," Bowman said.

Francine clung to Grimes, hugging him, pinning his arms to his sides so he couldn't get to his gun too easily. Once her arms were around him, he stopped struggling and started swallowing hard. She said, "After all, Jed, he saved my life."

"And yours, too, Grimes," Bowman pointed out.

Francine leaned into Grimes, causing him to break a sweat. "Jed . . ." She was starting to honey-talk him.

He began, "Now, Francine—" but his voice cracked, and he ran out of breath.

"Jed, honey, you know you're so much nicer when you're being nice," she said. "So cute and sweet . . ."

"Now that you're on your way to being a man of property," Bowman said, "Deputy Vestry's sure to look on you with a lot more favor, Grimes. You're shaping up as prime in-law material."

"In-law? Who said anything about getting married?" Grimes roared.

Francine let go of him, her face clouding. "Well, I like that! After all your billing and cooing and turtle-doving, and calling me your sweet thing!"

"You are my sweet thing," he insisted.

"You've got a funny way of showing it," she said, fuming.

"You just watch me," Grimes said. "I mean—heck—oh, hell, why not? Let's get married!"

"Is that a proposal?" Francine asked.

"Yes, dang it, it's a proposal! Will you marry me?"

"Oh, Jed, honey! Yes!" she squealed with delight. "Yes!"

They embraced. Going around to the back of the church, Bowman unhitched the gray, leading it around front by the reins.

Grimes stood with his arm around Francine's waist. He said, "Who are you, Bowman? I mean, where do you fit in all this?"

"Well, I'll tell you," Bowman said. "The gang was hitting the railroad, so the railroad hired somebody to hit back hard."

"A railroad gun! I might have knowed it!"

"How else do you think I could've talked a hardhead like Bragg into going along with my plans?" Bowman asked. "I told him that if he didn't play along, the next man the railroad sent might not be a peaceful, easygoing fellow like me. That convinced him."

He stepped up into the saddle. "A word of advice," he said. "Enjoy the peace and quiet while you can. When the railroad gets here, things are liable to get exciting!"

Urging the gray forward, he started downhill. At the crossroads of Trail Street and Cemetery Lane, he looked back over his shoulder. Grimes and Francine were kissing again.

"Better get married soon!" Bowman said. He rode on.

Holding Francine in his arms, Grimes said, "Oh, well, I guess he's not such a bad fellow at that—for a damned Yankee."

Bowman rode, not far. Like an iron filing drawn to magnetic north, he followed a course for the Pole Star, where Lana Crain was waiting.

"The prodigal returns," she said.

He reached for her. She met him more than halfway.

ROUND 'EM UP!

CAMERON JUDD

The Carrigan Brothers Series

Shootout in Dodge City
0-7434-5708-0

Revenge on Shadow Trail
0-7434-5709-9

COTTON SMITH

The Texas Ranger Series

The Thirteenth Bullet
0-7434-7568-2

GARY SVEE

Spur Award-winning Author

The Peacemaker's Vengeance
0-7434-6346-3

Spirit Wolf
0-7434-6352-8

Showdown at Buffalo Jump
0-7434-6351-X

Sanctuary
0-7434-6350-1

Visit
❖ **Pocket Books** ❖
online at

....

www.SimonSays.com

....

Keep up on the latest new
releases from your favorite
authors, as well as author
appearances, news, chats,
special offers and more.

SIMON & SCHUSTER
A VIACOM COMPANY
www.SimonSays.com

Pocket
Books

2381-01

'From the relaxed, reflective Roman episodes, to the remustering of the regiment, to the journey to India, the training of the inexperienced troopers, the march into the jungle and the final bloody engagement – the book picks up a pace that mirrors exactly a cavalry charge, from walk, to trot and, finally, to charge . . . Hervey continues to grow in stature as an engaging and credible character, while Mallinson himself continues to delight in the minutiae and arcaneness of military life' *Observer*

'Mallinson is a good historian. He gives his people a well-researched hinterland. He knows what it is like to command and to serve. He is as good on the details – and it is detail we historical novel buffs like – of the workings of a cavalry regiment in 1820 as ever Patrick O'Brian was on the workings of an 1820 warship' *Spectator*

'Oozing action, *A Call to Arms* is a military tale of epic proportions that will leave fans counting the days to the next adventure' *Ireland on Sunday*

'With each book, Hervey himself is becoming a more complex and interesting character . . . Mallinson writes of his inner questionings with subtlety and sympathy. This series grows in stature with each book' *Evening Standard*

'Mallinson has lost none of his vigour for writing intense prose; whereas lesser authors might go off the boil slightly four novels into a series, Mallinson patently agonizes over his descriptions, gets the balance right on just how much cavalry information to slip in, and masterfully dovetails historical events to create an excellent balance' *Good Book Guide*

A REGIMENTAL AFFAIR

'Mallinson deals with the historical and military minutiae with his customary panache . . . It is his consummate ability to incorporate the social details and niceties of the times that marks his novels out from the common herd of big boys' books of big boys doing jolly brave things . . . *A Regimental Affair* confirms his undoubted talents and marks him as the heir to Patrick O'Brian and C. S. Forester' *Observer*

'An assured and capable work that proves Hervey is worthy of a long series of novels . . . a fine read . . . Mallinson is superbly well qualified to relate the tribulations of the (fictional) 6th Light Dragoons as they undertake duties "in aid of the civil power" in Britain and Canada in 1817' *The Times*

'A riveting tale of heroism, derring-do and enormous resource in the face of overwhelming adversity. Season the whole with a generous sprinkling of riding expertise and military history – the author is an acknowledged master of both – and the book is another prime example of the unputdownable historical novel. In the lexicon of fictional military and naval heroes, Matthew Hervey has now joined Bernard Cornwell's Sharpe and Patrick O'Brian's Jack Aubrey as a creation of superlative skills and character' *Birmingham Post*

'Hervey is the epitome of a sometime deputy head boy. He loves his wife, cares about his men, and does his duty without racking up an excess mess bill. Can such a faultless character sustain a reader's interest? When he is the work of Allan Mallinson, then the answer must surely be yes' *Spectator*

'Mallinson writes well and effortlessly across fields of conflict which cover a vast panorama from chasing smugglers in Brighton to Luddite violence in the English Midlands and ending finally and disastrously with a border conflict in the snows of Canada'
The Historical Novels Review

'Many fascinating strands woven into this beautifully written saga endorse the author's mastery of narrative and of deep historical and military erudition. Sympathy, style and control mark the polished horseman; these talents are surely applicable to this talented writer'
Country Life

THE NIZAM'S DAUGHTERS

'A marvellous read, paced like a well-balanced symphony. There are allegro movements full of surprises and excitement in which Hervey is the resourceful man of action ... Interspersed are thoughtful, andante passages in which Hervey explores the unfamiliar and perplexing worlds he encounters ... This is more than a ripping yarn ... I look forward enormously to hearing more of Hervey's exploits; he is as fascinating on horseback as Jack Aubrey is on the quarterdeck'
The Times

'Mallinson writes with style, verve and the lucidity one would expect from a talented officer of l'arme blanche ... His breadth of knowledge is deeply impressive ... Kick on, Captain Hervey, we cannot wait for more' *Country Life*

'An exciting, fast-moving story, full of bloody hacking with sabre and tulwar, which can at the same time be reflective and thoughtful about its setting and situation' *Evening Standard*

'An epic adventure . . . a book with a texture as rich as cut velvet, and a storyline as detailed as a Bruges tapestry. Patrick O'Brian may no longer be with us. But Mallinson has obviously taken up the historical baton' *Birmingham Post*

A CLOSE RUN THING

'An astonishingly impressive début . . . convincingly drawn, perfectly paced and expertly written . . . A joy to read' Antony Beevor

'Cracking tale of love and heroism in the Napoleonic Wars . . . I have never read a more enthralling account of a battle . . . This is the first in a series of Matthew Hervey adventures. The next can't come soon enough for me' *Daily Mail*

'O'Brian's equal in accurate knowledge of the equipment, methods, weapons and conditions of serve of the fighting men of whom he writes . . . An imaginative feat of high order' *Country Life*

'Now at last a highly literate, deeply read cavalry officer of high rank shows one the nature of horse-born warfare in those times . . . *A Close Run Thing* is very much to be welcomed' Patrick O'Brian

'Fast-moving, exciting, and above all, accurate. The author combines the experience of a serving cavalry officer with the knowledge of a military historian, blending the two into a colourful historical tale' *Army Quarterly & Defence Journal*

Also by Allan Mallinson

A Close Run Thing
*The Nizam's Daughters**
A Regimental Affair
A Call to Arms
Rumours of War

*Published outside the UK under the title *Honorable Company*

THE SABRE'S EDGE

ALLAN MALLINSON

BANTAM BOOKS

LONDON • NEW YORK • TORONTO • SYDNEY • AUCKLAND

THE SABRE'S EDGE
A BANTAM BOOK : 0 553 81662 4

Originally published in Great Britain by Bantam Press,
a division of Transworld Publishers

PRINTING HISTORY
Bantam Press edition published 2003
Bantam edition published 2004

1 3 5 7 9 10 8 6 4 2

Set in 11½/13pt Times New Roman
by Falcon Oast Graphic Art Ltd

Bantam Books are published by Transworld Publishers,
61–63 Uxbridge Road, London W5 5SA,
a division of The Random House Group Ltd,
in Australia by Random House Australia (Pty) Ltd,
20 Alfred Street, Milsons Point, Sydney, NSW 2061, Australia,
in New Zealand by Random House New Zealand Ltd,
18 Poland Road, Glenfield, Auckland 10, New Zealand
and in South Africa by Random House (Pty) Ltd,
Endulini, 5a Jubilee Road, Parktown 2193, South Africa.

Printed and bound in Great Britain by
Cox & Wyman Ltd, Reading, Berkshire.

Papers used by Transworld Publishers are natural, recyclable products
made from wood grown in sustainable forests. The manufacturing processes
conform to the environmental regulations of the country of origin.

To

Skinner's Horse

raised 23 February 1803

Brass g
BHUR
January

FOREWORD

In his enigmatic memoir *Bengal Lancer*, Francis Yeats-Brown recounts how the Honourable East India Company received its licence to trade in Bengal. The Mughal overlord, the Emperor Shah Jehan, who built the Taj Mahal, had a daughter, Jehanara – 'modest and beautiful'. One day Jehanara's maid upset an oil lamp in the palace, and in trying to save her the princess scorched herself about the face and hands. Shah Jehan, distraught, sent word for the best physicians in the empire to come to Agra. One Gabriel Broughton, surgeon of the Company's factory at Surat, arrived quickly and, though hampered by the etiquette of purdah (he was only allowed to feel his patient's pulse from behind a curtain), he not only healed Jehanara but also saved her legendary beauty. As reward, he would take nothing for himself, but asked that a charter be given to the Company to trade in Bengal. 'These are the threads of *karma* that go to the making of ant-heaps and Empires,' writes Yeats-Brown: 'a clumsy slave girl, a kind princess, and an altruistic doctor who asked for the charter on which the British built Calcutta.'

When the Mughal hegemony began to weaken, in the middle of the eighteenth century, Bengal broke away from Delhi's rule, along with Sind, Oudh and Gujerat, and the Company found itself increasingly drawn into the power politics of the successors to the empire. Fortunately there were Robert Clive, Warren Hastings and a great many others of their kind to advance British interests, and by the third decade of the next century John Company was the predominant power in the whole of India.

But there were always challengers, within and without, and the sepoys of the armies of the presidencies of Bombay, Madras and – above all – Bengal, together with the handful of British (King's) regiments for which the Company paid, found themselves from time to time campaigning hard. However, in India the climate and disease claimed many more lives than did the tulwar, the jezail or the jingal – in the war that begins my story, nineteen men out of the legions of twenties who died.

But dead men's boots meant promotion for the lucky ones who survived. That was the soldier's silver lining in the clouds of war ... In addition to those I have thanked in previous books, and in whose debt I remain, I would add this time Major Patrick Beresford, regimental secretary of the King's Royal Hussars (and their Winchester museum's curator), Sally Brown of the British Library, Liza Verity of the National Maritime Museum and Christopher Calkins of the Petersburg National Battlefield. I must likewise acknowledge my debt over some years now to Dr Anne-Mary Hills, whose long study of Nelson's pathology, and of his navy's medicine, she has unstintingly shared with me. My thanks are also due to Dr Michael Crumplin, surgeon, whose knowledge of surgical practice in Wellington's army is, I suspect, unrivalled. I am, as ever, full of appreciation for Chris Collingwood, whose cover illustrations show a deep knowledge of the minutiae of uniforms and equipment, and whose skill in composition and drawing so vividly sets the scene for my cavalry tales.

On the reverse of the jacket of this, the fifth of Matthew Hervey's adventures, there are two sowars in the distinctive yellow kurtas of Skinner's Horse, better known to the world, perhaps, as the 1st Bengal Lancers. This glorious regiment was raised on 23 February 1803, and this year therefore celebrate their bicentenary. To them, in admiration, I dedicate *The Sabre's Edge*.

And Israel smote him with the edge of the sword, and possessed his land from Arnon unto Jabbok, even unto the children of Ammon; for the border of the children of Ammon was strong.

The Fourth Book of *Moses*,
called *Numbers*

THE BAY OF BENGAL
1823

'The Commander-in-Chief can hardly persuade himself, that if we place our frontier in even a tolerable state of defence, any very serious attempt will be made by the Burmans to pass it: but should he be mistaken in this opinion, he is inclined to hope that our military operations on the eastern frontier will be confined to their expulsion from our territories, and to the re-establishment of those states along our line of frontier which have been overrun and conquered by the Burmese. Any military attempt beyond this, upon the internal dominions of the King of Ava, he is inclined to deprecate; as instead of armies, fortresses, and cities, he is led to believe we should find nothing but jungle, pestilence and famine.'

The Adjutant-General of the Presidency's Army, to the Government of Bengal, 24 November 1823

PART ONE

JUNGLE, PESTILENCE AND FAMINE

CHAPTER ONE

THE WOODEN WALLS

The Rangoon River, noon, 11 May 1824

'Sile-e-ence!'

The gun-deck of His Majesty's Ship *Liffey* at once fell still. The big fourth rate had furled sail, dropped anchor and beat to quarters, and her first lieutenant would have the gun crews silent to hear the captain's next order.

Astern of *Liffey* were the sloops of war *Larne*, *Slaney* and *Sophie*, their guns likewise run out and trained ashore. And astern of these, with great pyramids of white sail still set, was the rest of the British flotilla – close on a hundred men-of-war and transports, sailing slowly with the tide up the broad, brown Rangoon river.

The stockades at the water's edge were silent too. Like the gun crews aboard the warships, the Burman soldiers crouched behind their wooden walls, but teak-built walls, not oak. With their spears and ancient muskets, they had no doubt that the white-faced barbarians would pay for their effrontery in sailing up the river without acknowledging the supreme authority of King Bagyidaw, Lord of the White and All Other Elephants.

On *Liffey*'s quarterdeck, Commodore Laughton Peto turned to Major-General Sir Archibald Campbell, general officer commanding the Burmese Expeditionary Force. 'Well, Sir Archibald?'

'They have had their time, Peto.'

But the commodore required a more emphatic order. Firing first on an almost defenceless town was not a decision to be entered lightly. 'You wish me to commence firing, sir?'

Before the general could reply, the shore battery erupted in smoke and flame. Two or three heavy shot whistled harmlessly through *Liffey*'s rigging.

The general was obliged, but amazed. His flotilla had violated the sacred waters of the Kingdom of Ava: but in such force that could not be resisted. He, Sir Archibald Campbell KCB, veteran of the Peninsula, had offered suitable terms of surrender. By all the usages of war the Burmans should have accepted at once.

'Presumption, and folly,' he declared, snapping closed his telescope. 'Commence firing!'

Peto nodded to his first lieutenant. 'Commence firing.'

The lieutenant raised a speaking trumpet to his lips. 'Fire!'

Hervey started. The roar of cannon was like nothing since Waterloo – fourteen twenty-four-pounders firing as one, nearly the weight of shot that the whole of the horse artillery could dispose that day along the ridge of Mont St-Jean. He gripped the taffrail as if he would be shaken off his feet. But before the smoke rolled back over the quarterdeck, he just managed to glimpse the destruction that the broadside had wrought – the guns in the shore battery toppled and the great teak doors of the stockade beaten down.

There was another broadside, this time from *Larne*, and even closer to the bank. Not as heavy as *Liffey*'s, but almost as destructive, it battered down yet more of the stockade, the nine-pound shot from the guns on her upper deck firing high and sending showers of bricks and tiles from the buildings within. Hervey did not think the business could take much longer.

Now *Slaney*'s and *Sophie*'s guns were bearing on the

walls, and soon too were those of the East Indiamen-of-war astern of them, so that there was a drumroll of fire as the crews worked their pieces like demons.

No, the Burmans could not take a pounding like this for much longer. No one could.

Campbell agreed. He turned to the little knot of staff officers behind him. 'How our work might have been easier in Spain, eh, gentlemen, had we been able to sail our artillery about so!'

And had the enemy been so obliging as to call a pile of logs a fortress, said Hervey to himself.

Major Seagrass, the general's military secretary, turned to his temporary assistant. 'Where are these war boats of yours, Hervey?'

Hervey nodded. He had warned of them, albeit from limited experience, and the flotilla was taking particular precautions against surprise. 'It seems our luck is great indeed. And the Burmans', too, for those boys yonder are bruising for a fusillade.' He indicated the lines of red at the gunwales of the transports, private men and sepoys alike in their thick serge, muskets trained ready to repel the war boats. The attack would be a swift, swarming affair if it did come.

The general judged it the moment. 'Signal the landing!'

A midshipman had the signal-flag run up in a matter of seconds. There was cheering from the transports, audible enough even with the crashing broadsides. Soon boats were being swung out and lowered, or hauled alongside by their tow lines, and redcoats began descending to them.

As they began pulling for the bank, fire erupted once more from the battery. *Liffey* answered at once, and there was no more firing from the stockade.

The landing parties scrambled from the boats and raced for the breaches. They exchanged not a shot, and soon there was more cheering as the Union flag rose above the shore battery. Campbell saw his success, called off the bombardment and ordered the rest of his force to follow. In half an hour two brigades were ashore, with still not a musket discharged by either side. Later the general would learn that not a man of his had been so much as grazed, and he would remark again on the address with which battle could be made with artillery such as he had.

He turned now to the little group of officers on *Liffey*'s quarterdeck. 'Well,' he said, with a most satisfied smile, his thick red side-whiskers glistening with sweat in the clammy heat of the season before the monsoon. 'Let's be about it. We have a great need of beef and water, and it is there ashore for the taking. My boat, please, Commodore Peto!'

Captain Matthew Hervey had watched many an infantry action in his dozen and more years' service, but always from the saddle. The quarterdeck of one of His Majesty's ships was undoubtedly a more elevated vantage point, and perhaps preferable in that respect, but it was no less frustrating a place for an officer to be when there was hot work to be done with the enemy. But then the only reason he was able to observe the action at all was that he had a friend at court – or, more exactly, on the supreme council of the presidency of Bengal – who had arranged that he join the expedition on General Campbell's staff, the general being clearly of a mind that there was no place for cavalry on this campaign. Indeed, the general had planned his operations certain that everything would be accomplished by his infantry – King's and Company's – with the sole support of the guns of the Royal Navy, and without any transport but that which floated, or supply other than obtained locally. It was, by any reckoning, an admirably economical expedition.

Hervey's regiment, His Majesty's 6th Light Dragoons, had been scattered about Bengal on countless trifling errands these past three years, frustrating to officers and men alike. They had hoped to be employed against this impertinent King of Ava, who threatened the Honourable

Company's domain, insulted the Crown and boasted of his invincibility, but it seemed that nowhere on the eastern frontier were their services required. Especially not in this *coup de force*, by which it was calculated that the Burman king would at once capitulate. No, their value to the Company – which, after all, paid the Crown handsomely for their services in India – lay in their ability to be fast about Hindoostan in the event of trouble. The commander-in-chief would not easily be persuaded, therefore, to tie down a single troop of King's cavalry that constituted his meagre reserve. And so, with the prospect of further months of tedium before him, any diversion had seemed attractive to Hervey – even as assistant to an officer who himself had little to do. But it had truly been an unexpected delight to learn that his revered friend Peto had the naval command.

Not that in other terms Hervey had been ill content with the years since Chittagong. Chittagong had been an affair, indeed, of real cavalry daring, if through country wholly unsuited to the arm. 'And we shall shock them': that had been his intention. And how they *had*, cavalry and guns appearing from the forest like chinthes, routing the Burman invaders and burning their war boats. Yes, he had hazarded all, and the Sixth's reputation in Calcutta had been made. And he had watched his troop's star continue to rise afterwards. He had taken real pleasure in advancing several of his men, though he had had occasion more often to shed a tear when the fever or some such had claimed one of them (the regiment's corner of the cemetery in the Calcutta lines now held the bones of more dragoons than any single troop could muster). Above all, however, the regiment was at ease with itself. That was their colonel's doing. Sir Ivo Lankester may have been an extract, but he had his late brother's blood in his veins, and never did the Sixth have a finer officer than Sir Edward Lankester until they had had to bury him at Waterloo. And the regiment was no less handy for being at ease, for Sir Ivo managed somehow to have the best of them, always, without recourse to any more rebuke than he might for an inattentive hound. It was said that he had only to look pained for the hardest of sweats to feel shame, and only to smile for the same to believe they were as good as chosen men. He had returned to England for his long leave two months before, and he had done so with utter confidence: the major, Eustace Joynson, for whom sick headaches and endless returns had been the miserable order of the day under the previous colonel, was now modestly self-assured. Sir Ivo knew that Joynson would always err on the side of kindness, and that since the troop captains and lieutenants, and the non-commissioned officers, were all sound enough, a right judgement would be reached in those things that mattered most. One of those judgements had, indeed, been to permit Hervey his attachment to the general's staff.

Despite having almost nothing to do, Hervey had from the outset found the appointment fascinating, for it allowed him a seat at the general's conferences, albeit in an entirely attendant capacity. He had thus been privy to the plan of campaign throughout almost its entire evolution. It was, like all good plans, in essence simple. The Governor-General, Lord Amherst, was of the opinion that it would be necessary only to occupy Rangoon, the country's great trading port, for the King of Ava to lose courage and ask for terms, and that the Burman people, in their condition of effective slavery to King Bagyidaw, would welcome the British as liberators. Thereafter it would be an easy enough business to sail the four hundred miles or so up the Irawadi to Ava itself and take it – opposed or otherwise. Even the timing was propitious, for the rainy season was soon to begin, and the river would thereby be navigable to Commodore Peto's flotilla. Furthermore, since this was to be a maritime, indeed a riverain, expedition, there would be no need to embark the transport required to maintain the army. It was altogether a very thrifty way of making war, and General

Campbell was justly pleased with the speedy accomplishment of the first part of his design. Pleased and relieved, for he had provisioned his force only for the crossing of the Bay of Bengal, and there had been delays. Now he had the better part of eleven thousand mouths to feed, and the sooner they were ashore the sooner they could begin buying beef – and water.

Hervey beckoned to his coverman to get into the cutter before him. Besides the sailors at the oars, they were the only occupants of the general's two boats not wearing red. They settled towards the bow and Hervey took off his shako, then mopped his forehead and fastened closed the front of his tunic. 'Did you see anything of the cannonade?'

'No sir,' said Lance-Corporal Wainwright, grimacing. 'I was helping bring shot. My ears are still ringing.'

'Mine too,' said Hervey, looking at his watch. It was not yet one o'clock.

'Pull!' called the midshipman, and a dozen oars began ploughing the flat brown water of the Rangoon river.

In not many minutes they were grounding on the shallow slope of the bank in front of what remained of the great teak gates of the stockade – no need even for wet feet. Tidy files of redcoats, King's and Company's alike, marched ahead of them with sloped arms as if at a field day. Hervey jumped from the boat wondering if his misgivings had been wholly unfounded after all. Eyre Somervile's misgivings, rather, for it had been his friend at court who had voiced them first. His own doubts could be only those concerning the military arrangements, although in truth these he found worrying enough.

Somervile had been convinced that the greatest peril lay in King Bagyidaw's self-delusion. The third in council of the Bengal presidency had his own sources of information in Ava, which told him that the king was surrounded by sycophants and believed all their blandishments about the

25

invincibility of the Burman soldier. Indeed, Somervile had learned that the king had not even been told of Hervey's spoiling raid at the headwaters of the Chittagong river three years before; that, instead, the king believed it had been the hand of Nature that had laid a torch to his boats, for no barbarian could set foot on Avan soil without the authority of the Lord of the White and All Other Elephants. And anyway, did not he, Bagyidaw, have the greatest of generals – Maha Bundula – to pit against an impertinent invader?

Eyre Somervile was therefore of the decided opinion that the fall of Rangoon would merely presage a long and arduous campaign. And he was by no means convinced, either, that the Burman people would welcome the invader as a liberator. Why, indeed, should they, if they too believed that Maha Bundula would throw him back into the Bay of Bengal whence he had come? And if that were to happen, death would follow automatically for anyone who had in the least part aided the invader. Eyre Somervile, after years of study, and years of practical business, did not believe for one minute that a single Burman would risk his neck in the Company's cause.

But this landing at Rangoon was so easy, the resistance so lacking in spirit, that perhaps, thought Hervey, Somervile had given too much credence to his admittedly well-placed agents. There were things he must see for himself, and quickly. 'If you have no direct need of me, sir,' he said to his principal, as matter-of-fact as he could, 'I should like to make a reconnaissance of the town.'

'Of course, Hervey, of course,' replied Major Seagrass, distracted. General Campbell's military secretary had somehow contrived to be the only member of the staff to get his feet wet, and was trying to rid his boots of water. 'There'll be scarce enough for one of us to do till the headquarters are open.'

Hervey had used the military term to describe his intended survey of the town, and it was certainly the case that he had a military purpose to his perambulation, but in truth he was just as curious to see the sights of the fabled seaport of the Burmans. By all accounts some of its temples were singular. 'Very well, then, sir. I shall report back by sunset at the latest.' He saluted and made away before Seagrass could have second thoughts.

Corporal Wainwright unclipped his carbine and took a cartridge from his crossbelt pouch. He bit off the end, tapped a little powder into the priming pan, then poured the remainder down the barrel, dropped in the ball from between his teeth and rammed it home with the swivel rod.

Hervey noted with satisfaction that it was done in mere seconds.

'Just in case, sir,' said Wainwright, feeling it necessary to explain the precaution even with so many redcoats abroad.

Hervey smiled grimly. 'Don't be too sure that you'll draw the charge, Corporal Wainwright. The Burmans may have fled, but I doubt they'll count themselves beaten.'

There were so many infantrymen about the streets, however. Even if the Burmans counter-attacked, Hervey thought they must be repulsed before they could get a footing on the stockades. But in fleeing before the bombardment, they had made a good job of leaving little for the comfort of the invader. House after house was empty of portables, the heavier furniture was broken up, and Hervey was further disquietened by the evident system with which it had been accomplished. It spoke of a discipline that might be turned to good effect against an invader. It was evidence, certainly, that Calcutta's assumption of cooperation was wholly ill-conceived. As he made his way past groups of infantrymen waiting for the serjeants to allocate a billet (at least they would have a roof over their heads when the rains came), Hervey began to fear the worst – that the rice stores and granaries had been emptied too, and the cattle driven into the jungle.

He tramped the town for an hour. It proved an unlovely place, with few buildings of any solidity and aspect, even the official ones. In the wake of the redcoats he saw not a house whose doors or windows remained barred, but neither did he see a man with anything more valuable in his hands than an iron cooking pot or a pan. Here and there a Buddhist shrine would impress, as much by the gilded contrast with its surroundings as by any true merit, and from time to time he would catch sight of the soaring pagoda of Shwedagon a league or so to the north, rising above the squat meanness like St Paul's above the rookeries of the City.

'I would lay odds that yonder place will be a regular hornet's nest,' said Hervey to Wainwright as they climbed a wall to get a better view. 'I'll warrant that's where they've bolted with the treasury.'

There was shooting still, sporadic shots from the redcoats searching the streets. But it did not trouble him. He knew they were aimed not at the enemy but at obstinate locks. It had been the same every time they had captured a place in Spain. It took a while, always, for the officers to regain order – hot blood, the exhilaration of being alive after the fight, the prospect of a bit of gold, the certainty of finding something to slake a thirst. That was all it was, but it could be brute enough when it ran unchecked for too long. At least he would not see the worst of it today, for there had been no fighting to hot the blood, no long march beforehand. Only the wretched, clammy heat of the day.

They pressed on. Several much smaller pagodas bore the signs of the infantry's passing.

'Ah, this looks worthier,' said Hervey, stopping at one of them. 'As resplendent, I'd say, as any of the shrines around Calcutta. Except, of course, it's all sham.' He prodded at the gold leaf with his sabre. 'In Calcutta it would be marble instead of this teak, and the inlay wouldn't be glass. Evidently our red-coated friends thought little of it.'

The pillaging seemed to have consisted in dashing all the

28

lattices to the floor and then being disappointed to find that the imagined rubies and emeralds became so many cheap shards. Hervey sighed to himself. He'd seen a lot worse – the Prussians, for one (after Waterloo they had been thoroughly wanton in their destruction). But knocking down even gaudy pagodas was hardly the way to win the hearts of the Burman people, let alone their active support. And support was what General Campbell's plan of campaign depended on. He just hoped the officers would have their men in hand soon.

'But solid enough, sir,' said Wainwright, having made his own assessment of the structure. He pointed to the roof. 'Look at that.' An iron shot from one of the broadsides was embedded in a joist. It had not fully penetrated but had somehow caused the wood to splinter on the inside. Hervey had heard Peto speak of the especial danger in teak-built men-of-war. Unlike oak, Peto said, a teak splinter invariably meant a septic wound. He had been most insistent on it, most insistent that while the Indies might be a place of sickness for the soldier, the sailor faced his trials too.

Many would be the trials in this campaign, right enough. Hervey sheathed his sabre and took off his shako. 'You know, Corporal Wainwright, it is one thing to enter the roads of a seaport and bombard the town – many a captain's done that. But it's quite another to sail upstream for all of five hundred miles when the degree of resistance is uncertain.'

Corporal Wainwright had been a dragoon for nearly five years and had worn a chevron for two of them. Hervey held him in particular regard, not least because he was recruited from his own town, but more so because of his thorough-going decency and unwavering sense of duty. He reminded him of Serjeant Strange, yet without that fine NCO's somewhat chilly piety. Hervey had made him his covering corporal at the first opportunity.

'Well, it couldn't be less resistance than here, sir.'

It was true that the defenders of Rangoon had been

scarcely worth the name so far, but was the town defensible against so powerful a cannonade as that which Peto's ships had delivered at point-blank range? Hervey sat down on the pagoda steps and loosened his collar. 'But what does the disappearance of every living soul, and all their chattels and livestock, bode?'

Corporal Wainwright had not been on campaign. He had tramped through the jungle three years before with Hervey's troop to fire the Burman war boats, but that was a mere raid, scarcely comparable in military organization with the scale of this expedition. This indeed was war. Nevertheless, he could make a fair estimate. 'One way or another, sir, we're going to be here longer than we thought.'

Hervey nodded. He knew from Peninsula days that General Campbell could make battle, but he had no idea if he could make war. What he had seen so far – not least the delays even in getting to Rangoon – was not auspicious. 'Well, Corporal Wainwright,' he said, taking a draw on his canteen. 'I think that it is a show of resistance and we might expect more. I think the battalions had better get this place into a state of defence quickly, lest the Burmans counter-attack. Our men-of-war wouldn't be able to support them. It may well be why the Burmans abandoned the town.'

As if in response to Hervey's assessment, redcoats of His Majesty's 38th Foot now came doubling past. Except that things weren't quite right.

Hervey sprang up. 'Come on, Corporal Wainwright. There's the glint of gold in those eyes.'

More men rushed by, without NCOs, almost knocking Wainwright to the ground.

'Or liquor, sir.'

'Either way it'll be trouble.'

They drew their sabres. Wainwright lashed out with the flat of his to check the barging of another gaggle, this time from the Thirteenth. 'Hold hard! Don't you see the officer?' he bawled.

They took off after the Thirty-eighth, Hervey cursing.

The narrow ways between the houses were soon choked with men, some without their muskets. Then it was impossible to go any further. Wainwright clambered onto the roof of one of the more solid-looking houses to try to see ahead. He was down again as quickly, bringing a shower of tiles with him and a foul string of abuse from the infantrymen below. 'Drink, sir. They're tossing bottles of it out of a warehouse. There must be two hundred men there, at least.'

'Well, we can't do anything of ourselves. Where are their NCOs?' Hervey turned and began pushing his way past men still homing on the irregular issue. 'Always the same,' he snarled, using his own sabre freely to force his way through. 'And these not even Irish!'

Down one of the side streets they found a picket of the Forty-first in good order. The corporal came to attention.

'Where is your officer?' asked Hervey, raising his sword to acknowledge.

'The colonel is only just in there, sir,' replied the man in a pronounced Welsh accent, indicating an official-looking building with a high-canted roof. 'The picket officer 'as just been round, sir.'

Hervey nodded and sheathed his sword, then made for the battalion's headquarters.

The Forty-first's colours were hanging from a window, with a sentry close to. 'I am Captain Hervey, of General Campbell's staff. I should like to speak to your colonel.' Hervey touched his shako in reply to the private man's butt salute.

'Sir!' The sentry turned and went inside.

Hervey shook his head. Between the Forty-first and the Thirty-eighth, and for that matter the Thirteenth, there was nothing to choose as a rule. They were all steady on parade: he had seen it with his own eyes in Calcutta. But once the NCOs had lost their hold—

The adjutant came out, hatless. 'Captain Hervey!' He

made a small, brisk bow. 'The colonel is with the brigade-major. May I assist you?'

'There's a riot towards the north gates,' began Hervey, indicating the general direction. 'The Thirteenth and the Thirty-eighth, two companies and more arriving, and no sign of their officers. They've found a drink store.'

The adjutant did not hesitate. 'Serjeant-major!'

Out came the shortest regimental serjeant-major Hervey had ever seen, shorter even than Private Johnson. 'Yessah!'

'There's a riot of the other two battalions. Summon the picket.'

'Sah!'

'I'll have the reserve company under arms at once, Captain Hervey. But the picket – a stitch in time.'

Hervey was not certain he understood. 'I don't think a picket will be—'

The RSM reappeared. His eyes blazed as he struck the palm of his hand with the silver knob of his cane. 'Right, sah!'

The picket – a dozen men – were already falling in.

The RSM was impatient for the off. Twenty years in a red coat told him that indiscipline was contagious, and he was not about to have his Welshmen tempted from military virtue by intemperate roughs from other regiments. 'Follow me, Corporal Jones. Double march!'

Hervey had no choice but to take the lead.

A curious sight they made, a captain and a lance-corporal of light dragoons doubling through the alleyways of Rangoon with a dozen red-coated infantrymen in file behind them, muskets at the high port and the diminutive RSM at their head. But the stitch was not in time enough to prevent the drink from doing its worst. When they reached the warehouse there was hardly a man on his feet, and those that were staggered hatless and without their muskets.

'Lord, deliver us,' said the RSM, holding up his cane to halt the picket. 'What in the name of God have they got inside them?' He seized a canteen from the hand of one of the capering privates and sniffed it. 'Brandy!' He poured what little remained to the ground.

The Thirteenth's private objected very foully. Corporal Jones stepped forward and felled him with a butt stroke to the chest.

'Stand up, you men!' bellowed the RSM, jabbing his cane here and there. 'Officer present!'

They were too far gone. They neither knew nor cared about their delinquency. 'Right!' growled the RSM. 'If that's the way it is to be. Picket, fix bayonets!'

Hervey had a moment's doubt, but there seemed no alternative. More men were appearing with every minute, all in search of their 'dues'.

The RSM began pushing through the mob of redcoats, shouting orders, cursing, lashing out with his cane, while to his left and right a single file of bayonets marched ready to do the worst if anyone should resist with more than abuse. Hervey, and Corporal Wainwright with his sabre drawn, followed as best they could.

They reached the source of the intoxication for the cost of a mere three further men succumbing to the musket's butt. The point of the bayonet had only been threatened, and the RSM had still not drawn his sword. Hervey marvelled at the man's self-possession and resolve. By his reckoning there were the best part of three hundred soldiers about the streets in abject disorder, yet the RSM seemed no more perturbed than if he were stepping between two brawlers in a barrack room. 'Right, Corporal Jones, two men on the doors, then get inside and clear them out!'

'Sir!' shouted the corporal, turning to look at the picket. 'Morgan and Jones-Seven-seven – on the doors. The rest of you, inside with me!'

'Of all the things them Burmans took, sir, and they have to leave brandy behind!' said the RSM, rapping his hand again with the cane.

Hervey shook his head. 'I shouldn't be surprised if they left it for the purpose, sar'nt-major. It's halted more men than their muskets have.'

'That is true, sir. A European merchant, do you suppose?'

'Probably. He's doubtless taken to the jungle with the rest of them. I hope he had more sense than to try to guard his stock.'

It took fifteen minutes to secure the warehouse, and another thirty to have the comatose occupants carried out, the RSM pressing disappointed new arrivals to the task. Only then did officers and NCOs from the offending regiments begin arriving. It seemed that this was not the only brandy warehouse, though Hervey was past caring what had detained them. One of the lieutenants told him plaintively that liquor had gone about the ranks faster than he'd ever seen. Hervey could believe it. It was no excuse, but it happened when the taut discipline of going into action was suddenly let down, when NCOs, their eyes on other things for the moment, lost their firm grip of the ranks. It was no more than a horse let off the bit surprising its rider with a nap. Except here it was getting on for a whole battalion off the bit.

Hervey saw smoke rising above the rooftops beyond the warehouse. He thought the redcoats better left to their own, and set off instead with Corporal Wainwright to investigate the source.

They felt the heat even before they saw the flames. Hervey, now alarmed, began running to see what had taken hold. Almost every building he'd seen was made of wood, and the streets were so narrow there would be nothing to check the spread of the fire. A few sepoys were doing their ineffectual best, but there was yet no organized attempt.

'Shall I get the RSM again, sir?' asked Wainwright, seeing the sepoys willing but without means.

Hervey saw a havildar, and then a lieutenant. 'No, I think the native battalion will have to cope. Better return to

General Campbell's headquarters and report. I'll warrant he'll have no notion how perilous things are in this part of the town.'

It took a long time to reach headquarters. The streets and alleyways were a press of men, some fully under discipline, some imperfectly, some not at all. Smoke kept barring progress, and from time to time flames, for the fire was spreading aloft and others had been started as carelessly as the first. When Hervey finally arrived at his destination, the customs house close by the main gates, and begged leave to report, he found the general in a deal of agitation and his face the colour of his red side-whiskers.

'What in God's name is going on?' Campbell spluttered, staring at the smoke now filling the sky over the northern part of the city. 'What are the brigadiers about?'

Hervey told him as much as he knew.

The general looked fit to burst.

However, his staff colonel appeared with news that relief was at hand. 'Sir, I have just learned that Commodore Peto, seeing the fires, has ordered ashore as many of his and the other ships' men as possible to our assistance.'

Hervey allowed himself a smile at the thought of the choice words with which Peto would have given his opinion of affairs on land. But it was Peto through and through – as prompt to take action as any man in the service.

General Campbell turned to his colonel. 'Get me the brigadiers,' he rasped. 'By the sound of things we stand close to being burnt out, and the Burmans could put half the brigades to the sword if they'd a mind!'

Not for the first time did Hervey find himself making unfavourable comparisons between the wooden world and the ranks of red. And he had no doubt that Peto was at this very moment doing likewise.

CHAPTER TWO
AGAINST THE TIDE

That evening

Flowerdew poured two glasses of Madeira. He offered the silver tray first to Hervey and then to his captain before Peto dismissed him with his customary nod.

'Well, a damned sorry start to a campaign!' said the commodore when his steward had gone. 'Half the men ashore drunk and incapable of standing to their posts, and all the signs of a country as hostile as any other that's invaded.'

'Hardly *half* the men, Peto!'

'I grant you the native troops may be in good order, but I've a thousand hands and marines ashore doing others' duty. There'll be no relief for those in the guard boats tonight.'

'It's certainly dark enough for the Burmans to get alongside,' agreed Hervey.

'It's not the war boats that trouble me but fire boats. The tide's still running out. They could run them down all too easily, and it'll be the best part of tomorrow before we have the boom finished.'

Hervey grimaced. There was no doubting the havoc that fire boats would wreak, for a topman could very nearly climb from ship to ship. 'The general's sent pickets for a mile upstream. They ought to be able to raise the alarm, at least.'

Peto took another sip of his Madeira. 'We must believe it. But I am already uneasy about what Campbell intends next. I assume the native provision will remain elusive but that he will march on Ava nevertheless. In which case how does he expect me to supply him, with both banks of the river in hostile hands? How may I risk a merchantman up or down without escorts? And I have not the ships.'

Hervey thought Peto uncommonly downcast. After all, here was the man who, but six or seven years ago, had sailed the frigate *Nisus* up the Godavari until there was nothing beneath her keel, and had then dismounted her guns and sent them in boats to the aid of his friend. 'You have the ships to force the river to Ava, though, have you not?'

'Four hundred miles, Hervey; four hundred! And I have but one steamer. Just imagine it.'

Hervey could. Memories of the Peninsula had not faded with the years. 'I don't suppose it would be any easier to stretch a line of communication here than the French found in Spain. And there, at least to begin with, the people supported them.'

Peto nodded. 'There should have been warning enough in what was learned these twenty years past in Holland. Folly to embark on an expedition in the hope of a country turning its coat.'

'But now we are come, I don't see that the general has any choice but to go to Ava.'

Peto refilled their glasses and shook his head. 'Nor I. But as soon as the Burmans learn what we're about, they're bound to bring back every last man from Arakan and Assam. There'd be the very devil of a job fighting through them all. Campbell's only course is to make lightning work of the advance. Do you see any prospect of that?'

Hervey frowned. 'It has been an inauspicious beginning, let us say. But in fairness, these are early days.'

37

'We wasted enough of them at Andaman looking for beef and water. I've never heard of an army that marched without provisions before.'

'You know,' began Hervey, measuring what he had to say as if not completely certain of it himself, 'Eyre Somervile told me the commander-in-chief and the Governor-General had disagreed very profoundly over the campaign.'

'I had not heard, but then why should I? I've met with Paget only once, and that was to present my compliments. The Governor-General I have never set eyes on.'

Hervey looked surprised. This was their first opportunity for intimacy since the expedition had got under way, and he had imagined Peto might have had at least some say in events. 'It seems the reason for our expecting the populace to rise is that Lord Amherst had intelligence from Ava to the effect that King Bagyidaw would at once lose heart if we took Rangoon. It would appear that Bagyidaw knows all too well that his officials so oppress the people they would see us as come to lift their yoke, so to speak.'

'Perhaps they believe their yoke is easy compared with what a foreigner might bring on them. What was Paget's opinion?'

'General Paget was convinced that operations should be directed principally towards securing Chittagong. He believed the Burmans were best punished then by striking from the sea.'

'It doesn't seem to amount to any great difference as far as we are concerned at this moment.' There was a distinct note of disdain in Peto's voice. 'I do despair of our great men at times. They show so little propensity to think a matter through. They seem always to think it somehow sufficient for the navy to put ashore redcoats, and that by that very act there will be fearful trembling at the heart of the enemy's enterprise. I blame Pitt – he was forever breaking windows with guineas.'

Hervey merely raised his eyebrows (Peto knew his mind

in these matters without need of words). 'I should say that it is, too, Somervile's opinion. And he, I think, sees the whole very well.'

Peto shook his head despairingly. 'So it seems we have embarked on a strategy which may already be turning turtle.' He rose to fetch a chart from the table, then sat down again and began peering at it. 'We descend upon Ava from the sea, so to speak, because we cannot do so from land. And we bring no provisions or transport with us because, consequent on the taking of Rangoon, the populace will not only desist from interfering with our progress upstream but supply us with all our material needs as my ships take the army to gain its object.'

Hervey raised his eyebrows again. The course of Peto's logic was evident.

'Rangoon is burned and the populace driven off, and the Irawadi will need clearing with the bayonet to enable my ships to reach Ava. I count that a major reverse in design.'

Hervey could only nod.

'And of course, to give us every facility in the venture, the expedition is timed so that the rains which begin any day will swell the Irawadi to enable my ships to make easy progress.' Peto laid down the map, shaking his head and looking as sad as he was angry. 'You and I know those same rains will fix the army here in Rangoon. The country'll be turned to swamp. I'll warrant even Amherst would want to rethink his stratagem if he were to think through these little matters.' He smiled, but wryly. 'I concede, however, that these are early days still!'

Hervey found himself in an unusual position: he was a mere observer of events. However, all his instincts demanded still that he took his commander's view. And that required that he forgo too much criticism and look for advantage instead. 'Let us see what the day brings. Rain will at least make the country equally impassable to the Burmans.'

'You must hope so,' said Peto. He sipped his Madeira in a way that spoke to Hervey of the chalk-and-cheese difference in their fighting milieus. 'But I shall want the general to take the offensive upstream tomorrow, for we have to have all the Burman boats burned within a league. I cannot sit here beyond another day. You may take that message ashore with you, if you will.'

'It might be best if you were to impress it upon Campbell in person.'

Peto shook his head again. 'No. I'll not go ashore when there's the threat of fire boats. I'll see him early in the morning and we can agree on what support I can lend him. I take it he'll want the rest of the divisions landed?'

'I'm sure of it.' Hervey made to rise.

Peto rose with him and clapped a hand on his arm. 'I'm sorry you will not stay longer. It is very good to see you, though I could wish for better circumstances.'

Hervey smiled. 'Ours are not professions that would prosper in better circumstances!'

'Indeed, no. And I had at one time thought I should never get a command again once Bonaparte was put in his box.'

'Should we not still be saying "God rest his soul" then?'

Peto returned the smile. 'Perhaps. It will be an unquiet one otherwise, for sure.'

'Thank you for my dinner. I have a premonition of its being the last of any substance or quality for some time.'

'Not if you can find reason to come aboard *my* ship, I assure you!'

Flowerdew brought Hervey his cape.

'By the way,' said Peto, his smile turning wry again. 'I did not say how very active and smart your corporal seems. A considerable improvement on your Private Johnson.'

Hervey remembered the first time his groom had presented himself to Peto's ship, almost ten years ago. No one would have declared him a model of military bearing. 'I could not bring the two of them, and Johnson's place is properly with the chargers. But I suspect I shall miss his resource.'

Peto came on deck just before dawn. The officer of the watch touched his hat but said nothing. It was not his place to extend even a greeting without invitation, and had he been sure of which side the commodore wished to stand, he would have quitted his place at once to take the other. Peto looked quickly about, searched the heavens to see what they revealed of the coming rains, then went to the starboard rail. There was the faintest glow in the sky above the jungle. The sight was not new to him, but he was fascinated still. In another ten minutes the sun would rise, and the creatures of the earth would begin the drama of another day, unseen – unseen but noisy. And here in the Indies there was no leisurely beginning, as in temperate parts; no lengthy over-ture in which to settle to the change to come. It was night, and then it was day, at full throat. Peto watched, wondering. He thought for a moment of the sunrise in his native Norfolk, of the times as a boy he had slipped out of his father's vicarage to run the mile or so to watch the sun come up over the grey waters of the North Sea. He had been so many years in His Majesty's navy; could he ever imagine himself on land again? He shivered, though the air was warm enough. It was not the thought of the land itself so much as the want of companionship there, for his family were few and he had never taken a wife. Indeed, he had scarcely been in the habit of speaking to a woman beyond what was necessary for courtesy – except perhaps Hervey's sister.

He had spoken of Elizabeth with Hervey at dinner. Not much, for their preoccupations had been the here and now, but he had praised her, calling her a woman of spirit and dis-cernment; to which Hervey had replied that she was greatly more than that, worthy though the description was. She had devoted herself wholly to familial duties, not least indeed the care of her own niece, her brother's child. She made sacrifices that were humbling to contemplate.

And Peto had been moved to hear it, as well as, in truth, disheartened by the degree of nobility it spoke of.

He looked over his shoulder towards the stockaded town. It was dark now where last night it had been ablaze. Fires by night always looked worse than they were. He turned to the officer of the watch. 'Has there been gunfire at all?'

He asked so abruptly that the lieutenant half stammered his answer. 'None that I have heard these past two hours, sir. And there was none reported on my relieving Mr Afflick.'

Peto made no reply, merely turning back to watch the eastern sky. So Hervey had had a peaceful night too. Maybe these *were* early days after all. Maybe the populace had taken to the forest in fear for their lives, and would return as soon as the invaders showed themselves benevolent. Maybe the Burman soldiers had no fight in them when it came to facing regular troops. Maybe they had fled the ranks. Peto sighed. There were altogether too many 'maybes'.

Hervey too was awake. In the early hours, General Campbell had given orders for the 89th Foot to be landed and to make ready for a sortie from the stockades at first light. The general had not been idle. He had applied his mind to the situation his brigadiers had reported, and had become convinced that the Shwedagon pagoda was the rallying point for the Burman 'defenders'. Major Seagrass had not objected when Hervey had asked if he might accompany the Eighty-ninth, and so he now stood, with Corporal Wainwright, next to the two ensigns carrying the regiment's cased colours, waiting for the gates at the northern end of the stockade to be swung open. He was not greatly apprehensive, for like the Eighty-ninth he was only too glad to be unconfined at last. On the other hand he was at a loss to know why the general had not ordered a reconnaissance during the night. It was but normal practice after all. Someone had said the reason was that the fires would have lit up anyone moving outside the stockade. But the flames had been doused by three o'clock, and the pagoda was little more than a league distant.

The commanding officer's orders had been straightforward. The battalion would advance in column of route by companies, the light leading, and in double time for the first mile or until contact with the enemy was made (in the cool of the dawn doubling would be no hardship). On meeting the enemy's pickets, the light company would deploy to skirmish and the others in column of companies would take the position with the bayonet.

The men looked eager, even on a breakfast of biscuit and rum. Corporal Wainwright had spoken to several of them as they formed up: it seemed there were many Irish, that some had fought on the Niagara frontier a decade before, but for the most part the battalion had not been shot over.

'I have never marched in a regular advance by infantry,' said Hervey, looking about him at the novel order.

'I don't think I care for it much in truth, sir,' replied Corporal Wainwright, unclipping the carbine from his crossbelt. 'You can't see anything in these ranks, just the man in front.'

It was true, although in the dark there was little enough to see beyond the man in front. 'Yes,' said Hervey, drawing on his gloves. 'From a horse there's a good view of things. And a troop of them now would be worth their while. That is for sure.'

The great gates at last swung open. Commanding voices front and rear animated the ranks. 'Company, atte-e-nshun!'

'Trail arms!'

Hervey took up his sabre scabbard.

'Company will advance. By the front, double march!'

The battalion company in front set off as one – an impressive feat, thought Hervey, since breaking off at the trot was always a ragged affair with cavalry.

'Colour party, double march!' barked the senior ensign.

The two ensigns and their serjeant-escorts took off in step with Number One Company, colours now uncased and at the slope, the commanding officer and serjeant-major to a flank, and Hervey and Wainwright to the rear.

Hervey found it surprisingly easy to keep time. Serjeants called out continuously and with such authority that to break step would have required a marked will. He had not marched to a serjeant's command since joining the depot troop as a new-minted cornet straight from school. There was something of a comfort in it: no need at all to think. But that was the purpose of drill, was it not, to make a man act as if he were a machine, oblivious to all else? And Hervey for one was pleased to be relieved of the need to think too much this morning. He had slept little. There had been a continual coming and going at General Campbell's head-quarters during the night, and at one stage there had been a general alarm, with reports that Burman soldiers were observed creeping up on the stockade from the west. But it had proved false. And then there had been another alarm when one of the bamboo cottages near the headquarters had burst into flame, for no reason that the sentries could see. It had been past four o'clock, by his reckoning, when he had at last fallen into a good sleep, only to be woken by Corporal Wainwright at five with tea and a bowl of hot shaving water – exactly as Private Johnson had instructed.

After five minutes the companies changed to quick time, and sloped arms – prudently, thought Hervey, for the eastern sky was now lightening. He had walked these paths before, so to speak: the affair at the river, three years ago. How determined he had been to time the moment of the attack perfectly with the appearance of the sun above the jungle canopy. Almost a ritual, it had been, like the sun rising at the stone circle on the great plain at home in Wiltshire.

It was curious how marching freed the mind to wander. How many hours more would they have to wait in Wiltshire before this same sun rose on them? And how did it rise on his daughter? Did it fall directly on her, or did it light her room only indirectly? Did she wake to see it? Did she fear the dark when it was gone? How strange not to know the answers to such simple questions. But it had been five years, almost, since last he had seen her. Her first letter he carried in the pouch of his crossbelt, along with Henrietta's likeness, though he had taken neither from their oilskin in a year.

The sky was heavier than that day at the river. There was rain to come; they all knew it. But when? He looked back towards the town. A pall of smoke hung over the greater part of it, and, mean as the place was, he thought it as sorry a sight as at Badajoz or Vittoria, or any other of the Spanish towns that had fallen prey to the revels of the drunken soldiery in their celebration of victory. The Duke of Wellington had cursed the army often enough – the Sixth not excepted – for being too drunk to follow up victory. And usually the men had resented it; officers too. They had had to make long, wearying marches; they had had to fight desperately; they had lost friends; they thought they had earned their rowdy ease.

Not since Waterloo had Hervey been surrounded by so many redcoats, and even that day he was first amidst his own regiment (and at the very end in their van). It felt different from being in ranks of blue. Yet their common bond was discipline, the prime requirement of an army, for without it no other quality was guaranteed. Could it really be the lash that guaranteed these men's good order? Were the Eighty-ninth, and for that matter every other battalion of infantry of the Line, so different from his own?

The Sixth abhorred the lash. They had abhorred it since before he had joined. They took it as a point of pride that a dragoon was animated by something more noble than fear of a flogging. But the duke had always supported the lash, and his judgement had been long in the forming, and tested

45

in the worst circumstances. He held that without it all the lesser punishments could not have effect. 'Who would bear to be billed up but for the fear of a stronger punishment?' Hervey had once heard him say. 'He would knock down the sentry and walk out!' And had he not heard many a man in the old light division say that Crauford had flogged them through the mountains to Vigo, and that had he not done so they would never have got there? But how far would men acknowledge that the lash kept them alive when the going became desperate? And did General Campbell have the determination to see the expedition through to Ava, as 'Black Bob' Crauford had seen the retreat through Galicia?

'Company will break into double time; double march!'

In another five minutes there was but a half-mile to go, and it was light enough to make out Shwedagon's soaring dome. Hervey thought it unlikely that the Burmans would have abandoned it unless they had no intention at all of fighting.

'It's like piss-proud Pat of a Sunday morning,' came a voice from the ranks behind.

A welter of reproach followed from an NCO.

'D'ye think there'll be much gold, Serjeant?' came another voice.

'Stick to the drink, Mick. You won't have to carry it as far!'

'He can't hold on to either for long!' came yet another voice from the ranks.

Hervey smiled. The banter was not so very different from the Sixth's, though he did not doubt the capacity for riot in the Eighty-ninth's wild Irish ranks. It was as well that its NCOs brooked no disorder.

There was a shot. Then half a dozen others. A couple of hundred yards ahead? It was difficult to tell. Hervey felt the momentum check just a fraction. Then came the shouting – *quick time!* – and the companies breaking from the double march. Serjeants barked out the step – left, right, left, right;

pick it *up*! The ensigns raised the colours. The commanding officer took off for the front of the column. Runners began coming and going. The thrill of action flashed through the ranks like a quickmatch. It would have been the same in the Sixth, thought Hervey – but perhaps more so here, for the ranks were tighter-packed, the men shoulder to shoulder rather than knee to knee.

'Skirmishers out!'

He heard the order ripple along the column. And then a bugle. He didn't recognize the call, supposing it must be for the light company. If *they* were deploying, it couldn't be many minutes before the battalion companies did the same.

'Number One Company, *halt*! Company will incline left; left *incline*! Company will form right, at the halt; right *form*!'

It took less than a minute for Number One Company to change from column of route to face front in two ranks, and with no more seeming effort than if they had been on parade. And this in spite of the semi-darkness and the broken ground.

'With ball cartridge, load!'

The best part of a hundred men reached as one into black leather pouches to take out a greased paper cartridge. They bit off the end, poured a little of the powder into the pan of the musket-lock, closed it, emptied the remainder down the barrel, spat in the one-ounce ball of iron, pushed in the paper tube and rammed it home with a clattering noise like a mill full of flying shuttles. Then up came the East India-pattern muskets to the port. Even after so many years Hervey found himself awed by the drill. Rough men, these; unlettered for the most part, the sweepings of the gutters. Yet they worked like the well-turned mechanism of a fine watch. He could feel the swagger in the drill, the pride and confidence in what each man was about, as if he were saying there was no one better at this – no company better, no battalion better; and certainly no army. The 89th Foot, well

47

to the left of the Line, had no royal lace to distinguish the regiment, only green facings like many another; but the 89th (Prince of Wales' Irish) counted themselves second to none, and neither Burman nor monsoon would stop them getting to Ava if that was the general's command. It would have been the same too had the battalion been the 90th Foot, or the 91st. Indeed it would have mattered not what number was worn on the pewter buttons or the blackened 'trotters' – except to the men who wore them. Hervey smiled to himself: the drill would be the same anywhere along the Line, and the spirit no less so.

'Company will fix bayonets; fix . . . *bayonets*!'

More clattering, then sudden silence.

''Shun!'

Number One Company stood stiffly at attention. No man dared move a muscle lest it bring the withering rebuke of an NCO. It was a moment that could not long hold. Neither was it meant to; it was just the captain's final check before the off that he had his men in hand, as a dragoon might bring his horse up sharp onto the bit before pressing him forward to a gallop.

'Company, should-e-e-r *arms*!'

The line seemed to sway, eager to be on with it, though not a foot moved.

'Po-o-rt *arms*! By the right, quick march!'

It would be full light in not many minutes. Hervey strained to see their objective as they struck off, but too many shakos stood in his way. There had been no more firing. It didn't surprise him: the shots came from the outposts, for sure. They'd done their job: raise the alarm, then fall back. He wondered how many cannon the Burmans had, and how close they'd let the battalion come before putting the slow matches to the touch-holes. But he didn't suppose there was a man afraid, nor even for a moment anxious. As soon as the Burmans fired, the battalion would give them a volley and be in on them with the bayonet before they could reload. A ball might take a head off, and grape might tear through flesh and bone, but there was nothing anyone could do about it, so there was no point in having a care of it.

But there was no thunder of cannon, nor rattle of musketry. Only the sudden command, 'At the double!' And then they were running again, faster this time, not quite charging speed he imagined, but definitely faster. Still he could not see where they were doubling to, only the dome of the pagoda itself a couple of hundred yards away. In no time they had closed the distance without another shot, and officers and NCOs were shouting orders for sections and half-sections to follow. Up the steps to the pagoda itself, or to either side of its balustrades, or to beat out the cover to right or left, or to search the shrines that lined the great maidan at the bottom of the steps. They went at it like harriers into kale.

Hervey saw relief and disappointment in equal measure in the faces around him. The Prince of Wales' Irish did not load with ball cartridge here except to discharge it at a live target; they had discharged shot enough at practice ones these several past years. But at least there were not the screams of fallen comrades to heed. Could there be such contradictory feelings in any other craft? For his part, Hervey had no particular desire to blood his sabre again, nor to discharge the pistol that was lodged in his belt. His only thought was what this peculiar absence of resistance portended.

He came upon the commanding officer, a man not much older than he, who wore an expression of both determination and perplexity.

'What in God's name is going on, Hervey?'

They had first met at Vittoria, a dozen years before, when each man's sword had been red, for there had been no doubt what they were meant to be doing *that* day. 'I cannot say, Colonel. But there seem to be only two possibilities.'

'Indeed,' sighed the Eighty-ninth's man, ramming home

his sword in its scabbard. 'And I wonder how long we shall have to wait to discover which it's to be. There's a degree of confusion so far that I haven't seen since Corunna.'

The captain of the light company came up and asked for orders, to which the colonel replied that his men should beat towards the jungle's edge.

It was exactly as Hervey would have done. 'I fancy the answer will only be found in there, sir,' he said as the captain made off. 'I think sooner or later the general shall have to send patrols some way into the forest to see if the Burmans make a stand or no.'

'Ay,' sighed the colonel. 'And it won't be easy. But first Campbell had better strike upstream, for if the Burmans mount any sort of attack along the river we'll be at sixes and sevens. And fire boats'll be giving yonder commodore a deal to think about, too, I'll warrant.'

'Sir,' was all Hervey thought it necessary to say, for they were but Commodore Peto's own strictures of the night before.

'Well, this place has the makings of a decent billet, at least,' said the colonel, beckoning over his adjutant. 'Come, Merrick. Let us have a look inside that pagoda before Alltoft's men do it any great injury.'

Hervey smiled again. Here was the dry humour of one who sat permanently atop a powder keg, an officer whose easy victory might yet turn to ruin at the hands of the same men who had delivered him the prize. And Shwedagon was a place where riot even on a small scale would not do – a religious site of prominence, of some grandeur indeed. The general would certainly want to see it in one piece. No doubt the colonel was half disbelieving in his good fortune in not having had the battalion ashore when the brandy was flowing. Hervey wondered how the Eighty-ninth's discipline would hold now they were no longer in close order. How active were the subalterns? How true were the corporals? Once, in Spain, he had seen an entire company fire its muskets at the windows of an empty palace rather -

than draw the charges; the smashing of every pane seemed to give satisfaction to men denied a shot at the French. And gilded carvings and finials were an awfully tempting target.

Now there was more shouting. 'Pres-e-e-ent *arms*!'

Hervey looked about to see what the sudden fuss was, and saw General Campbell coming up with Colonel Macbean, commander of the Madras brigade.

The general looked pleased. And well he might, thought Hervey. Yesterday had been one of mixed honours, at best, and this morning's work was a model of method and celerity by comparison.

General Campbell raised his hat to the saluting muskets. 'The guns will be up with you within the hour, Ireson,' he said, eyes twinkling, his red whiskers as bright as his coat. 'This without doubt is the key to Rangoon. Hold on to the pagoda, Ireson, and any attack on the town must falter.'

'Very good, General,' said Colonel Ireson, sounding matter-of-fact.

The colonel's luck was indeed great, thought Hervey. What any man would do to be in a position of the first importance, though he wondered why the Burmans must attack from the north through Shwedagon. But he had not seen a good map and he supposed the general had.

The general had certainly not seen *him* until that moment. 'Ah, Hervey! What brings you here?'

'Major Seagrass had no need of me, General.'

'And you had a mind to see how infantry work! Well you might, sir; well you might. I imagine this campaign shall go down as the first to be made without benefit of cavalry!'

Hervey checked himself. 'Indeed, sir?' The general's novelty knew no bounds. It was already a most singular campaign having no transport or supply.

'Yes indeed. Audacity and the bayonet, Hervey. That is what this campaign is about.'

The general slapped his neck, but the mosquito evaded his hand. It would be the first of many to do so.

51

An hour later it was raining. The rain fell not in drops, or even in torrents, but as a single sheet of water, so that it was impossible to see more than a dozen yards, and only then with a great distortion. Hervey did not think he had seen anything like it. Neither was it how the monsoon was supposed to begin. But for once the poor redcoats, the infantrymen of the Line and the sepoys, on whom alternately rain fell and fierce sun beat, were dry, for the shrines that surrounded the pagoda of Schwedagon afforded cover for all. Cooking fires blazed inside – teak burned very satisfactorily – and there was skilly and tea in every belly before the hands of Hervey's watch showed nine. Sharing a canteen with the men in whose billet he had taken cover might have seemed an unlikely pleasure for him, but it was almost like being in the Peninsula again. He stood a little apart, with Corporal Wainwright, trying to make out the language of their gestures and method – as strange to him at times as the accents in which they spoke. As flesh and blood they could not, in truth, be so very different from the Sixth, but they were men who drilled as a body, whose military utility was solely as part of that body. They marched as a body, took aim as a body and they fired in volleys. They did exactly as they were told, when they were told. He could certainly admire them for it. He had seen enough red-breasted lines stand rock-like in the face of Bonaparte's columns, and he had seen those lines go forward with the same unshakeable resolve. His dragoons were different. At his best, each was his own man, who used sabre and carbine as he himself judged fit, yet who knew how to combine with others to multiply the effect. Was a man better suited to the one method drawn to the bringers of a particular regiment by some unknown process perhaps? Or was it only drill that made them different? Hervey wondered.

It could not be other than drill, surely, for the recruiting process was haphazard to say the least. He had only to look at Corporal Wainwright to be reminded of quite how haphazard. Wainwright would not have been in uniform at all had not he, Hervey, and Serjeant Collins gone that day to Warminster Common to search for the odd lad who had sunk to where he could sink no further – who was more likely than a husbandman or mechanical to be tempted by the King's shilling. It could only be the process of drill that made a soldier what he was; the drill and how it was imparted. And on this latter the difference was plain enough to him, for he had already noted how awkward these men seemed at being spoken to directly, addressing their remarks in return to Corporal Wainwright. No doubt it was necessary in drilling men to volley and manoeuvre as one body, but it must be deuced awkward never being able to speak directly to a man.

By the time the downpour had eased, a full hour later, Hervey had concluded that of the seven private men, five of whom were from Dublin and thereabouts, four might take to being dragoons with very little effort – supposing, of course, they showed a modicum of aptitude for the saddle – and that of the other three, two were inveterate 'machine men', happy only when their every action was preceded by a word of command from the corporal, while the other was quite probably unsuited even to his present position, so sullen was he that Hervey imagined the serjeant's pike a regular prompter. However, much as he admired the Eighty-ninth's drill that morning, and the relish with which they had gone to the expected fight, he would admit to missing E Troop with its cheery, sometimes outspoken, dragoons. Whatever General Campbell might say now about the utility of cavalry, Hervey was certain he would feel the want of them before the month was out.

As the rain had become little more than a drizzle, he stood up and went to the door of their shelter. He could now see the river again. Pulling upstream were a dozen boats filled with marines and men from the Calcutta brigade, not yet 'blooded' in this curious inaction. He had helped write their orders the night before: they were off to do what he and his dragoons could have done in a fraction of the time and with far less effort. If only those who had conceived this adventure had allowed the possibility of action over land rather than solely from water! He had heard it said in Calcutta that horses could not pass over such terrain. How could anyone doubt that, where a man could go in this country, there for the most part could a horse? Nor, indeed, that when the monsoon turned the country to nothing but swamp there would be no passage for beast *or* man.

Hervey thought of hailing the boats. It would be diverting to join them, for there was nothing to do here but watch the Eighty-ninth put the place in a state of defence. But he reluctantly concluded that it was time he reported himself back to Campbell's military secretary. He was sure there would be nothing for him to do – nothing, at least, of the slightest consequence – but if he exhausted Major Seagrass's indulgence too soon it would be so much the harder to get leave for when the infantry made a determined foray. He slapped his neck with left and right hand in rapid succession, but too late to prevent the bites, and he cursed. It was worse than the fleas in the lousiest billets in Spain.

CHAPTER THREE

THE POINT OF THE BAYONET

Four days later

Hervey slipped into the room where Major-General Sir Archibald Campbell was about to hold his council. It was not very large – enough for a couple of dozen people – and the lamps and candles were making the otherwise coolest time of the day hot. Hervey wondered what could be the imperative for calling the conference three hours before dawn. He supposed he would have heard of any alarm, so the general must have intelligence new come by; or else he had resolved on something that he had been privately turning over for days.

The two brigadiers rose as the general entered, and with them the dozen or so officers on the headquarters staff. Sir Archibald Campbell nodded – all sat – and then he nodded once more, to his quartermaster-general, who pulled loose the knot that held furled a sheet on the wall. Down rolled a hand-drawn sketch of the stockaded port and the Rangoon river to the extent of some two leagues to the north. At the furthest point of the river, on the eastern bank, there was a red circle.

'Gentlemen,' began the general briskly, seizing the bayonet on the table beside the wall and tapping the map with it. 'In the five and one-half days since we hove to in the river yonder' (he inclined his head to indicate the direction), 'our circumstances have changed so decidedly that I am obliged to conceive a wholly new plan of campaign.'

Hervey, as every man in the room, was all attention. He was hardly surprised to hear the assessment, only that it had been the best part of a week in the making. And he was as much relieved as he was surprised to hear it stated so candidly. There had never been any doubting Major-General Sir Archibald Campbell as a fighting officer. Word was that he had been given the exacting command of a Portuguese brigade in the Peninsula because of his impressive physique and offensive spirit, and because the duke himself knew at first hand of his youthful exploits in Mysore. But fearless and spirited fighting was one thing; the design of a campaign – the decision *how* to fight – was quite another. And the design of a campaign was not something to which General Campbell had had any apprenticeship.

'Or perhaps, gentlemen, I should say that it is necessary to recognize that our circumstances are not as were earlier imagined. It is evident that the Burman people are either too afeard to rally to us, or have no heart to do so. We are therefore in want of supplies from Calcutta, and any expedition to Ava will be through hostile territory. Indeed, it will need to be *supplied* through hostile territory.'

Every man in Rangoon must be of the same opinion, thought Hervey. Indeed, Peto had told him yesterday that the sloops he had sent to reconnoitre the mouths of the Irawadi had reported the channels running close in to numerous forts. But at least now they might proceed openly on the presumption of Burman hostility. They might even be allowed to butcher the few cattle that remained. Immunity from the slaughterman's axe had been one thing five days ago, but there was scant reason now to let the troops starve so that sacred cattle could live.

'It is also evident,' continued General Campbell, his voice slowing a little as if to emphasize the importance of

56

what was to follow, 'that the enemy have built themselves stockaded forts upriver, and that thence they are in a position to assail us at will, by land and, what is more, by river, and not least is the renewed threat of fire boats.'

Hervey wondered which might be the general's inference, for there were two that he and Peto had drawn. Would he require to hold Rangoon as a base for operations against the interior, or did he intend to abandon the port since its capture was evidently not the calamity the Governor-General had anticipated? Although, in fairness, there had scarcely been time for the news to shake Ava.

The general brandished the bayonet again. 'And so, gentlemen, our first object is to destroy the Burman capacity for the offensive.'

The declaration of the objective and the jabbing of the bayonet had an immediate effect. There was such a hubbub that the sentry posted outside peered round the door.

The general raised his other hand, and there was silence again. 'Today, therefore, we make a beginning. Colonel McCreagh, you will seize the stockaded village of Kemmendine, *here*.' He stabbed at the red circle on the map. 'And I wish the assault to be given to my own regiment, the Thirty-eighth.'

Colonel McCreagh simply nodded. There was no need of questions: it would be boat work and the bayonet.

'Colonel Macbean, I wish the Madras brigade to ascertain where to the west of Rangoon the enemy are encamped, and what their intentions are.' The general pointed vaguely at the left of the map, where the forest was represented by pictures of trees of very English appearance.

Hervey hoped that no one imagined it would be like taking a walk in an English park. He had memories enough of the jungle, and he counted that he had been very lucky in his adventures.

'Very well, General,' replied Colonel Macbean. There was no need of questions in this either, for the colonel saw it much like searching for the needle in the bottle of hay.

'And now the matter of supply.'

The general's voice did not falter, but Hervey thought he detected a note less assured. It beggared belief that within hours of the start of England's first war since Waterloo (as Campbell had grandly announced it to his officers in Calcutta), the regiments had been placed on half rations and sentries set to guard the water butts. In the decade since that battle had every hard-learned lesson been forgotten?

'Gentlemen, as I speak, the Royal Navy is taking in hand the unsatisfactory state of affairs in which we find ourselves. They shall provision the expedition direct from Bengal.'

There was much nodding of heads, and murmurs of 'Hear, hear'. Hervey smiled to himself. The navy would have to keep them alive in the old way. It were better, without doubt, that the extended 'exterior lines' were afloat rather than on land – even on a river whose banks were not free of the enemy – but he couldn't help wondering if it would end in the old way, like Walcheren and Corunna.

There followed detail that would much occupy the staff in the days to come, and then the general stood up again. 'I shall have a word in private with the brigadiers,' he said, laying the bayonet at rest on the table. 'For the remainder, you may dismiss to your duties ... except for Captain Hervey, if you please.'

Major Seagrass eyed his deputy curiously. And well he might, thought Hervey, for he himself could not imagine why the general had singled him out. Poor Seagrass: he was not enjoying this expedition one bit, and now he was looking in distinctly poor spirits – an ague coming on, perhaps?

When the room was empty but for those bidden to stay, which also included the general's chief of staff, the quarter-master-general, Hervey stepped forward and stood at attention.

'Take a seat, Hervey,' said General Campbell, evidently

finding the room rather too close and opening the collar of his jacket.

Hervey found himself admiring the tartan lining of the lapels, evidently the general's own, for it was well known that he had commanded an English regiment. There was no doubting it: Campbell had the crack. In battle, men followed officers like him.

'Captain Hervey?'

'General?'

'You appeared distracted.'

'My regrets, sir.'

The general frowned, but benignly. 'Gentlemen, Captain Hervey is the only man in the division to have any experience of fighting the Burmans. You may find his counsel of assistance, therefore.'

Hervey stood up.

'No, no; sit at ease, Hervey. Give the brigadiers time to reflect. But in any case, you shall place yourself at their disposal as they contemplate their plans.'

'Very good, General.' He turned to the brigadiers. 'At your service, gentlemen.'

Neither McCreagh nor Macbean looked to him as though they would be eager to engage that experience.

'Is there anything you would say here and now?' asked the general.

Hervey wished he had a few minutes to marshal his thoughts. Before Waterloo, by a happy accident of the chase, he had found himself riding beside the Duke of Wellington, who had asked him what he thought Bonaparte's design would be. There had been no alternative but to answer at once and he had done so, to the duke's approbation. But that was with the carefree confidence of youth – and the assurance that the duke was merely sporting with him. 'Sir, my experience of the Burmans is very limited, and I am not sure what general principles may be drawn from it. I should say that they are not fighters as good as the Sirmooris or Rajpoots. They can be deadly enough when at close quarters, but I observed they were reluctant to close with us. I judge, however, that they would be ferocious adversaries in the way of the Spanish *guerrilleros*. And I know, by accounts I have a regard for, that they are most active in stockading and entrenching.'

'This much reluctance to close we have witnessed already, I should say,' said the general, looking at the brigadiers.

They nodded.

Hervey nodded too. 'But I say again, sir, they have a reputation in developing an assault, akin to how we would go about a siege. They are prodigious builders of these stockades, and they dig holes in which their men conceal themselves very cunningly. They can advance upon a position very surely.'

'Is this how we shall find them in the jungle?' asked Colonel Macbean.

'I cannot say for certain, Colonel, but I would suppose that would be their practice. And if you should find them so, then it would indicate they are intent on fighting.'

The nodding of heads said the logic was sound.

Hervey felt encouraged to develop his appreciation further. 'But I must add,' he began, and with a distinct note of caution, 'I believe the Burman may be in want above all of generalship. There is, perhaps, no telling how much better would their fighting men be if led well. And they do have one general, at least, of repute—'

'Maha Bundula,' said General Campbell.

Hervey nodded. It was the first time the general had given any intimation of prior knowledge. 'Just so, sir.'

'He is by all accounts in Assam,' said the quartermaster-general.

Hervey was encouraged. Here indeed was evidence that the expedition was not entirely blind to the significance of what the enemy might do.

'Then we must hope he is tempted here,' said Campbell, most emphatically. 'The defeat of their best general would indeed be the likeliest way to bring about a surrender.'

Hervey raised his eyebrows before he could stop himself. Why Campbell supposed he was the superior of Maha Bundula he could not imagine, especially with the evidence of the past two weeks before them. Yet he could still admire the gallant confidence. It might yet get them to Ava. But he greatly feared the cost.

'Is there anything else, Hervey?'

'No, sir. I shall try to recall those details which might be of help, and communicate them directly with the brigadiers.'

'Very well, gentlemen,' concluded the general, picking up the bayonet once more. 'Let's be about it. But make no mistake. We shall be sitting out the best part of the rainy season here, and it will be far from pleasant.'

In his quarters, a well-made brick affair which had been the rice store of the *myosá* – the 'town-eater' – the official whose duty it was to extort the most revenue he could from the citizens of Rangoon, Hervey sat down to a breakfast of biscuit and coffee. At least here, though, he was free of the plague of mosquitoes. And plague they had become. He had bought a good quantity of oil of citronella in Calcutta, which he burned in the lamps on the table and by his bed, and no mosquito seemed inclined to linger. But he knew now he would have to calculate very carefully the rate at which he could use it. 'Far from pleasant,' the general had said. They were, to all intents and purposes, besieged in Rangoon, if not exactly by the Burmans – yet – then certainly by the monsoon. How long would it be before the siege was lifted, or they themselves broke it? The rains would continue until the end of September, and during that time there would be nothing to stop Burman reinforcements coming south by river. Meanwhile, the sick rate in Rangoon

– even once the Royal Navy had begun provisioning them – would rise, for the air would soon be corrupted by swamp and stagnant water.

He had written at length to Eyre Somervile the evening before, and now he would have to write a postscript. He calculated that operations could not begin in earnest before October at the earliest, for until they were able to clear the forts the flotilla could not navigate the Irawadi. And so the Burmans would attack first, being in the position of greater strength. The only thing Campbell could do was keep making spoiling attacks to disrupt the preparations. But they would be costly. Hervey was certain nothing would be decided before November. The citronella would be long used up, but by then it would be the least of his cares.

Corporal Wainwright came in. 'I'm sorry I could find nothing better than biscuit, sir,' he said, tucking his shako under his arm.

'I doubt even Johnson could find better,' said Hervey, frowning and motioning to the other chair. 'And *he* would not scruple to forage in the general's own kitchen!'

'I heard the Eighty-ninth had beef last night, sir.'

'Indeed?'

'A regular ox-roast I heard it was.'

Hervey was sure there had been no rescinding order. 'Corporal Wainwright, I cannot imagine the officers would allow—'

'All the officers were dining together – a regimental day, or something.'

Hervey smiled. 'But not on beef.'

'I should imagine not, sir.'

'Mm. Well, if you have half a chance of buying any then take it. I'd be pleased to part with a fair few rupees for a plate of something other than maggoty biscuit.'

'Sir.' Wainwright tried not to smile; they had been under pain of the lash not so much as to lay hands on a beast up until now. 'The word is we're to go after them, by the way, sir – the Burmans.'

'And it is right, which is why you found me already about at reveille. I was copying orders for two hours.' He pushed away the remains of the biscuit porridge. 'The Madras brigade's to beat into the jungle to find where they have gone. The other brigade's to attack upstream and clear the stockades.'

Wainwright looked pleased. 'Do we go with them, sir?'

'We do, I hope. I shall want you to go to the Thirty-eighth and find out when they are to begin. They have orders to take a stockade about two leagues north. I intend going with them, but I'll first have to ask leave of Major Seagrass.'

In the event, the interview with the military secretary proved an unusual exchange. By nine o'clock it was raining again, a steady downpour of the type that cruelly tested the builder's art. The *myosá* had built his rice store well, and Hervey remained dry while others in more exalted positions found themselves dodging leaks and inundations. Major Seagrass was abed complaining of cramps and a sore head when Hervey reported to him. His quarters were almost adjacent to the general's, but water dripped with the regularity of a ticking clock onto the floor near his head, and mosquitoes hovered like wasps about a fallen plum on an English summer's day.

Hervey assumed at once that Seagrass's indisposition would rule out his own hopes of slipping away from the headquarters to join the Thirty-eighth, but he was surprised to find instead that the major did not in the least object – although his manner of reasoning was startling. 'Go on, Hervey,' he moaned, hardly opening his eyes. 'You may as well be killed in the cannon's mouth as sickening and dying in this place!'

Hervey was appalled at the self-pity. Could a man sicken quite so quickly? He looked down at the plump outline of the military secretary concealed beneath the grey blanket, and he sighed. How was it that men were appointed to commands and to the staff who were so manifestly incapable? There was another way of looking at it, of course; and perhaps he ought not to be quite so contemptuous of Seagrass's words, for the major knew as well as he that sickening was not a soldier's business. Perhaps he was only lamenting his disability. In any case, Hervey himself had no intention of either sickening or succumbing to the cannon's roar. He took his leave, summoned Major Seagrass's servant to his quarters and sent him back with a phial of citronella.

Hervey cursed himself and everything as he hastened to buckle on his sword and bind his pistols with oilskin. It was barely an hour since reveille, but the Thirty-eighth had been quicker off the mark than he fancied even his own troop would have been. *Liffey*'s boats were already on the water and pulling through the deluge as if it were nothing but a spring shower. He ought to have known it, he muttered, fastening closed his lapels: men who had been cooped up for so long would be off at their quarry like hounds on to a hare.

The door flew open. 'Sir, the Thirty-eighth—'

'Yes, Corporal Wainwright. I've just seen for myself. Are you ready?'

'Ay, sir.'

They ran all the way to the river, slipping and sliding in the mud, drenched within a couple of minutes. Corporal Wainwright began hailing the boats. There was no one else about in that rain, so their object must have been plain enough, and it was not long before a cutter began pulling towards them.

The boats were packed with the Thirty-eighth's biggest men, the grenadier company, and there was scarcely space for one more, let alone two. But the grenadiers looked happy enough that an officer in another uniform – from the staff indeed – thought their enterprise worthy.

The grenadier captain was welcoming. 'It would not do for a dragoon to be overtaken by foot,' he said, smiling and holding out his hand. 'I am Richard Birch, sir.'

'Matthew Hervey, sir. And very pleased to join your ranks, though I fear my coat a little conspicuous in so much red.'

'I should worry not, Captain Hervey, for I have no doubt we shall all look the same within minutes of scrambling ashore.'

Seeing the colour of the grenadiers' belts, Hervey could only smile ruefully; the white pipeclay had run off onto their jackets and trousers, and even the red dye was not holding fast. 'I freely confess that your alacrity took me by surprise, though. It was but a few hours ago that the general gave the brigadier his orders.'

Captain Birch smiled. 'The colonel has had a company under arms since we landed. It was my good fortune that it was the grenadiers' turn for duty today.'

Hervey nodded. Even so, he thought, it was smart work.

'The rest of the battalion will follow. Our intention is to test the strength of the stockade and to try to take it by surprise.' Captain Birch had to raise his voice against the beating rain and the sailors' oar work, and his resolve seemed all the stronger thereby.

Hervey had no doubt that Birch's company would carry all but the most determined resistance before them – if they could make headway enough to reach their objective: so strong was the current that the sailors were red in the face despite the cooling drench. If ever they had need of the steamship to give them a tow it was now, but Commodore Peto had said he would not risk *Diana* until he was sure the banks were clear of cannon, and the river of fire boats.

Captain Birch's little flotilla was not without resource, however. The naval officer in command, one of *Liffey*'s lieutenants, had as good an eye for water as Hervey prided himself he had for ground. As they reached the point of the big bend that hid Rangoon from further observation upstream (and, as Hervey observed, vice versa), and where the oars could shift no more water in that swollen flow, he signalled for the boats to turn full about and for hands to pull hard for the slack water by the left bank.

It was done in less than a minute, and very neatly thought Hervey – quicker, for sure, than trying to row broadside across the stream, as *he* would have attempted. The crews now put the boats about again and struck off with a will, for there was an obvious danger in going for the slacker water – too close to the bank, easy prey to musketry no matter how ill-aimed.

It was a tense quarter of an hour before the lieutenant was able to lead the boats to the middle of the river again, but there was no sign of life on either bank except for a solitary zebu that watched them pass, mournful-looking.

'Can we make room in the boat for him on the way back, Corporal?' came a voice from the bows.

Captain Birch replied. 'It will be yours if we take the stockade!'

There were cheers. Hervey smiled to himself. A beef dinner – not a promise that would excite men ordinarily to great feats of arms. But such was the miserable fare to which the expedition had been reduced that a pile of gold was worth nothing compared with boiled meat. He turned his cloak collar up once more against the rain.

'Pull hard now, lads; pull hard!' Though the lieutenant's voice carried easily to the other three boats, there was just something in his tone that *coaxed* the extra from his sailors rather than commanded it. It promised them something if they did pull hard rather than threaten if they did not. In truth, they needed little encouragement. Months confined, cruising the Bay of Bengal, and now the prospect of action. It would take more than the monsoon and the Rangoon river in spate to damp their ardour.

After half an hour's pulling hard, the boats swung closer

to the right bank to clear a thick knot of mangrove that reached into the river like a giant's arm. And then their first sight of the enemy, or rather his work – a hundred yards distant on the opposite bank.

'Still a mile to go by my reckoning, at least,' said Captain Birch. 'An outpost do you think?'

Hervey had no more prior intelligence than Birch. 'I think it best to work on that assumption. It's not a thing to have at your backs as you go for Kemmendine – or, for that matter, in front of you as you come back.'

'My view precisely.' Birch cupped his hands to be heard above the fall of water. 'Mr Wilkinson!'

The lieutenant brought his boat within easier hailing distance, and without once losing the stroke.

'I want to put half the company ashore to assault yonder fort,' called Birch, gesturing with his pistol. 'The rest I would have Mr Ash work upstream to assault the Kemmendine stockade. We can go at it from two sides at once. But maintain a contact.'

Both officers signalled their understanding, and put their boats for the bank.

Out scrambled the grenadiers like ants swarming from a nest, with Hervey and Wainwright almost knocked over in the rush. There were no orders, no forming-up, just a head-long rush with the bayonet.

Shots rang out from the fort. At a hundred yards the musketry was well wide, though one ball sent a man's shako flying.

It continued as grenadiers splashed through the sodden padi, and still no nearer the mark. Hervey could hear the whizz of balls high above, or see the odd one spatter in front. He was surprised the Burmans stood their ground at all, for they could neither volley nor snipe.

Now they were under the bamboo walls, breathless. 'Up, up, get *up*!' shouted the corporals as grenadiers clambered onto each other's shoulders: the Burmans were only ten feet above them, and the redcoats wanted but a fingerhold to claim first blood.

But the Burmans wouldn't wait for them to gain the top. They leapt from the parapet and ran for the gate for all they were worth. The stockade was no longer a fort but a pen.

Over the parapet came the Thirty-eighth, wild-eyed and baying like hounds on to their fox.

The gate wouldn't open, and then not wide enough. And then the press of Burmans was so great that it jammed closed again, trapping three dozen of them, perhaps four.

Hervey picked himself up after half tumbling from the wall.

The grenadiers' yelling was truly terrible. The Burmans turned to receive them on their spears, but they had never faced English bayonets before.

The ferocity astonished even Hervey. Two dozen of them fell to the point of steel in a handful of seconds, a single man sometimes to three and more bayonets. The rest would have fallen the same had not the gates been suddenly wrenched from their hinges, terror-stricken Burmans throwing down spear and musket and fleeing through the ooze in bare feet twice as fast as boots could follow. They were lucky that the rain kept lead from following, too.

Hervey looked at the heap of dead, a sight he was spared as a rule since the horse took him and his dragoons on from their slaughter. The Burman soldier looked the same in death as any other: untidy, unsuccessful. He felt nothing for them. Had they stayed at their posts and fought they might at least have repulsed the first headlong attack. Was that not what they were paid to do? Perhaps Calcutta was right: perhaps there *was* no fight in the Burman army.

'Good work this, eh, Hervey?' called Captain Birch from outside the gates. He bent to wipe his sword on a Burman coat.

'Very good work indeed. But I wonder they were not more determined. You might have lost a fair few men had they stood their ground.'

'Perhaps,' said Birch, returning his sword. 'But in this rain they would not have been able to reload, and we'd have pushed them from that wall in no time. See the size of these men compared with mine.'

Hervey did. The grenadiers were picked men. It had been many years since the biggest soldiers in a battalion had been mustered together to throw the grenade, but the custom of putting the biggest men in the same company remained – quite evidently so in the Thirty-eighth. He nodded. 'But I doubt we shall be so fortunate every time. I can but admire the ardour of your men, though,' he added quickly, not wanting to belittle it in the slightest.

Captain Birch turned to his ensign. 'Have them form up in column of route, if you please.' And then to Hervey. 'Shall you come with us?'

'Indeed I shall.'

'Good. We all know of your exploits in Chittagong.'

Hervey was gratified, if surprised. He made no reply.

He did not speak for the best part of one full hour. They marched the while, first through mud so gummy that it pulled boots from feet at every step, and then through forest that from the outside looked deceptively like an English wood.

'No, no; it's too much,' said Captain Birch, coming to a standstill in the middle of a particularly dense tangle of *byaik*.

'I've never seen thicker,' agreed Hervey.

'We'd better make for the river and re-embark. We've lost enough time – and surprise, too.'

Hervey could but agree again. 'The shots may not have carried that far in this rain, but the runaways will have. They're bound to know a way through this.'

Captain Birch cursed.

Hervey sympathized. An approach march through difficult country for an attack from an unexpected direction was an admirable undertaking, much to be preferred to a frontal assault from the direction they were expected. But, as he had heard say often enough, the business of war was merely the art of the possible, and passage of this verdure was not possible in the time they had.

'At least this rain's to our advantage,' said Birch, signalling the change of march with his hand to those behind.

Hervey smiled. Here was an infantryman who knew his job: a man who preferred a soaking to the skin in order that it might soak the powder of his enemy too.

'Pull hard again, my lads; pull hard!' called *Liffey*'s lieutenant as they struck off.

'I'm grateful to you, sir,' said Captain Birch, who had decided to place himself in his barge as they re-embarked. The rain had not eased in the slightest; he turned up the collar of his cloak again. 'You kept a good contact. Did you see aught of the fugitives bolting the stockade?'

'We did indeed, sir! Your lieutenant was all for putting ashore to give chase, but they sped so there was little chance of taking any. I fancy they're hiding in that wilderness and won't come out for a week.'

'And *I* fancy they're already half-way to Kemmendine to raise the alarm. What say you, Hervey?'

Hervey was trying to secure the bib of his jacket, having pulled off a couple of buttons while scrambling into the cutter. 'We must pray they're not like the Thirty-eighth, Birch, but proceed as if they are.'

'Well said. And very wise. I think we'd better take their measure this next time before hurling ourselves at the walls. Anyway, we're number enough to give them a fright.'

Hervey was relieved. It saved him the trouble of telling a

man his job. A bayonet rush may have overawed the stockade, but Kemmendine would be different. A show of discipline and steady bearing, and all in red, might do better. It would at least preserve a good many of them, for he could not quite believe that Kemmendine had as little fight in it as the place they'd just sent packing. 'And we shall shock them!'

'Ay, indeed, Hervey. Naught shall make us rue!'

'I recall when last I said that, just as we were about to attack a Burman camp. We thought ourselves very bold.'

'You were.'

'It was a comfortable affair compared with this.'

'You would count yourself happier in the saddle, I suppose?'

Hervey smiled. 'Does it seem ill that I would?'

'Not at all. The cobbler is better at his last. I wonder you've exchanged a dry billet at all for this.'

Hervey clapped a hand on Birch's shoulder. 'Oh, don't mistake me; I would not miss this for all the tea in China, even if I mayn't be dry-shod.'

Birch offered him his brandy flask.

'What is your intention then?' asked Hervey, taking a most restorative swig.

'It is not easy to say without seeing the object, but I shall land out of musketry range and then advance with skirmishers. I think the navy might feint beyond. You never know: we might yet bolt them as we did before.'

'It will be a famous business if you do,' said Hervey, taking another draw on the flask. 'That and to put a torch to the place.'

The reason they were making now for Kemmendine was Peto's fear of fire boats, for it was no hindrance to progress if the general struck for the Irawadi. That said, if Campbell could not proceed for a month or so – and in this weather Hervey thought it nigh impossible – then it would not do to have the village become a fortress from which Maha

Bundula's men might sortie. The general himself believed that the same weather would also hold up the Burmans, but Hervey had reasoned that they would be moving on interior lines and might therefore do so much swifter. And he knew enough of Maha Bundula's reputation to know that he would march where others could not. Captain Birch's work today might well be an affair on which the expedition turned. He had better let him know it.

How those sailors pulled on the oars! Hervey marvelled at their skill and strength – like the free hands that propelled the triremes of ancient Greece faster than could the galley-slaves of their enemies. The rain had stopped, quite suddenly, revealing how warm was the morning – and how soon could the mosquitoes set about them again, so that in a little while both red- and bluejacket alike would have welcomed back the rain in whatever measure. And, of course, the rain dispersed the miasma, the mist that brought the fevers. Hervey, having lowered his collar and unfastened his cloak, quickly reversed the decision with the first bites at his neck. He was lucky to have his hands free for it, unlike the oarsmen.

'There's the place,' exclaimed Captain Birch suddenly, double-checking his map. 'It's good and flat, and Kemmendine just around the bend ahead. We land there.'

Hervey searched with his telescope. It was an excellent place to disembark. Boats could beach and the grenadiers jump to dry land, if that description was at all apt. ' 'Ware pickets, though, Birch. It's altogether too likely a place.'

'It may be so, Hervey, but we're beggars in choice.' He hailed his ensign in the boat alongside. 'Secure a footing, Kerr!'

Ensign Kerr, looking half the years of any man in his boat, saluted and put the cutter at once for the shoal.

'Pull!' bellowed the mate: he would have it run well up the bank.

Out scrambled the grenadiers as the boat stuck fast, a full ten feet of keel out of the water. At once a fusillade opened on them.

Musket balls struck the clinker side. A grenadier crumpled clutching his stomach. One dropped to his knees, his hip shot away. Another fell backwards into the water with a ball in his throat.

'Lie down!' shouted Ensign Kerr.

They did so willingly, even in so much mud, while Kerr himself stood brazenly looking for the source of the musketry.

Another volley. White smoke billowed from a thicket not a hundred yards away.

Bad soldiers, tutted Kerr. No target for the volley and all to lose by giving away the position. The bayonet should dislodge them easy enough!

But no – his eyes deceived him. It was no haphazard cover in which the musketeers hid, but bamboo walls as before, only this time most artfully, *cunningly*, concealed. He looked up and down the bank. There was no other place to land to advantage.

'Stand up, men!'

As soon as fire was opened, Captain Birch had signalled for the other boats to row for the bank, covered from view by abundant mangrove. 'We'll just have to hack through,' he called to Hervey, gesturing at the tangle that overhung the river.

Both were now standing in the stern trying to get a clearer picture of Kerr's skirmish.

'Not two dozen muskets by the sound of it,' said Hervey. 'Your man might yet do it on his own.'

That indeed was Ensign Kerr's intention. 'Fix bayonets! On guard!'

He would waste no time trying to load – certainly not to have so many of them misfire with damp powder. And the clattering of bayonets locking home was a fine sound!

'Advance!'

Captain Birch gasped at the audacity. 'Make after them!' he bellowed. 'Pull hard!'

They fairly raced through the slack water of the bank, but there wasn't the same room to get the boats run up the shoal.

'Out! Out!' roared Birch, leaping from the stern into water knee-deep, followed by Hervey and Corporal Wainwright.

The silting was so bad it took the greatest effort to make the five yards to the bank. 'All right, sir?' asked Wainwright as they crawled out.

'Ay, just,' said Hervey, sliding back a second time before getting to grips with a firm-rooted clump of rushes to pull himself free of the silt. 'I'd forgotten how much easier it is on four legs.'

Captain Birch was only a stride ahead of them, and Ensign Kerr's picket was half-way to the stockade. 'Come on you grenadiers, form line!' he bellowed.

But his voice could barely be heard above those of the NCOs, all of whom had the same idea.

'Right *marker*!' a corporal was screaming, his hand raised.

A line started to take shape, in double rank – if not as on parade, then no very great distance from it.

Birch doubled to the front and centre. He would have regularity. 'Company will fix bayonets. Fix . . . *bayonets*!'

Hervey, coming up beside him, drew his sabre.

Behind him came the rattle of a full five dozen blades being rammed home.

'Company, on guard!'

Up came the muskets, bayonets thrust out to impale the luckless souls who stood in their way.

'Company will advance, by the centre, quick *march*!'

The stockade had fallen silent. The going was heavy but Ensign Kerr's dozen grenadiers had kept admirable dressing. They had but twenty yards to go.

Kerr raised his sword. 'Double march!'

A ragged volley greeted them. A ball struck the hilt of Kerr's sword, knocking it from his hand. Another struck him in the groin so that he staggered left and right, then fell to his knees, his mouth open.

The line wavered.

The serjeant, his face a picture of horror, shouted for them to keep going as he rushed to the ensign.

'No, no. That's not the way,' groaned Captain Birch, seeing plainly the loss of momentum. He pointed his sword at the fort. 'Company, *double march*!'

It was not what he'd wanted to do – not to blow them all by doubling through this mud. They'd need every bit of breath to scale the walls. But he couldn't have the picket faltering.

Hervey saw it too. These Burmans were a deal more resolute than the others. If they could volley as fast as British infantry they had less than half a minute to get to the lee of the stockade.

It was as well the defenders were more resolute than capable, for the mud clung to the grenadiers' feet as if demons were trying to pull them into hell. Never did Hervey think himself so powerless.

He could scarcely get his breath as they made the walls. The others looked no better, and some much worse. Furious musketry from above felled two corporals and enveloped the walls in smoke. A ball struck a grenadier full in the mouth. He ran back towards the river squealing like a stuck pig until another ball sent him sprawling in the mud, choking his way to a merciful death.

Hervey crouched watching as two grenadiers holding a musket between them put their shoulders to the wall.

A third, a big Irishman, jumped onto it. 'By Jasus I'll not spare one of them!' he cursed as they heaved him up full stretch.

Hervey could only marvel at their strength – and then at

the Irishman's raw fight as he withstood the rain of blows to his head and hands. He got a footing on the parapet and at once the defenders shrank back, but another rushed him with a spear, and the point sank deep in his chest. The Irishman seized the man's head with both hands and they fell to the ground as one.

Hervey drew his pistol to despatch the executioner, but the grenadiers beat him to it.

There was no shortage of volunteers for the escalade. The lieutenant himself, not long out of his teens, was now hauling himself up, his sword in his mouth like a pirate boarding a prize.

Where were the ladders, wondered Hervey? Why were they going against stockades without so much as a grapple and line?

'Will you be going, sir?' called another of the grenadiers, as if they were asking if he intended taking a walk.

'Me first, sir,' said Corporal Wainwright, his foot on the musket in an instant.

Up it went before Hervey could protest. Wainwright, a jockey-weight compared with the grenadiers, was almost flung over the parapet.

He rolled forward in a neat somersault and sprang to his feet facing the way he had come, sabre already in hand. A clumsy lunge from a spearman was met by a parry and then a terrible slice which parted the spear, and the hand gripping it, from its wielder. Another two spearmen backed away at once. 'Clear, sir!' he called.

Hervey clambered up the same way seconds later, by which time Wainwright had accounted for the reluctant supports. He looked at his covering-corporal's handiwork, and nodded: he could not have done it neater himself – perhaps not even as neat.

Left and right, all along the parapet, there were grenadiers duelling with Burmans. Theirs was not so neat work – the jabbing bayonet, the boot, the butt end. There were few shots, a pistol here or there. It was the brute strength of beef-fed redcoats and good steel that were carrying the day, although the grenadiers had had precious little beef this month.

The parapet was now treacherous, running as much with blood as rain. Hervey nearly lost his footing as he made for a down-ladder.

Wainwright was first to the ground, sabre up challenging any who would contest his entry. But there were none that would. Those who could get away from the parapet were making for the back of the stockade, some of them crawling with fearful wounds and a trail of blood. The grenadiers pouring over the wall were looking for retribution, and these men now obliged them. With each point driven into Burman flesh they avenged their comrades – a very personal slaughter, this. Hervey was only glad of the anger that could whip men up to escalade high walls with no other where-withal than the determination to do so. Ferocious, savage; not a pretty sight, but the proper way, no question. And then get the men back in hand so that blind rage did not lead them to their own destruction. Where *was* Captain Birch?

Hervey soon learned. The serjeant-major was a colossus even among the giants of the grenadier company, and Captain Birch lay across his shoulder like a rag doll. 'Have you seen Mr Napier, sir?' he asked, coolly, seeing the fight was all but over.

'No, Sar'nt-major, I haven't,' replied Hervey, dismayed at the lifeless form of the company commander. 'Is the captain dead?'

'Sir. He took a ball in the throat just as he was broaching the wall.'

'Very well, Sar'nt-major. Will you have his orderly attend him, and come with me if you please. We must put the stockade in a state of defence at once.' Hervey did not imagine a counter-attack was likely, but that did not remove his obligation to take measures to repel one.

'Ay, sir. But let me just lay the captain aside decently first.'

Hervey hurried to the back of the stockade. 'Close the gates!' he shouted to two grenadiers.

They seemed uncomprehending.

He cursed, saw a corporal, gave him the same instruction, and at once the gates were pushed shut.

Up came the serjeant-major again. 'Set them shakos straight!' he bellowed at two men on the parapet.

Hervey could hear Armstrong in that command. It was remarkable how quickly a wound began healing in a regiment: that need to carry on, the notion of next-for-duty, and all. Where *was* the lieutenant?

Lieutenant Napier had given chase. He now returned with a look of thunder. He saw Hervey and shook his head. 'They've bolted, damn them. They beat us to the jungle by a minute, no more, but it's so thick—'

'I'm afraid Captain Birch is killed,' said Hervey.

Napier's thunder was stilled. He had already seen the ensign's death with his own eyes. He looked about the stockade and saw redcoats lying wounded; he knew there were more outside. 'How many, Sar'nt-major?'

'We can muster fifty sir, thereabout.'

That was a lot for the surgeon, or for the chaplain to say words over; a heavy butcher's bill indeed. The lieutenant set his teeth. 'See if we can torch this place, Sar'nt-major. Then we get our wounded back to the boats, and the dead too, and then press on for Kemmendine.' He checked himself, turning to Hervey. 'If you approve, sir.'

'Carry on, Mr Napier,' said Hervey grimly.

The lieutenant nodded.

The serjeant-major saluted. 'Serjeant Craggs, bearers! Serjeant Walker, find everything you can that will light – Burmans included!'

Hervey took the lieutenant to one side. 'Do you judge that you will be in a position to take Kemmendine?'

he asked, the doubt more than apparent in his voice.

The lieutenant looked as if the question had never crossed his mind. 'Those are our orders, sir.'

'But I asked you if you considered that you had the strength to execute them.'

Still the lieutenant was incomprehending. 'The Thirty-eighth do not balk at trials, sir, however great.'

Hervey was becoming irritated. 'I do not doubt it. But to expend more life in a *hopeless* venture is base. More than that, however, it would be hazardous for the expedition as a whole. If you fail to take Kemmendine then the enemy will be emboldened. The essential thing while we stand on the defensive at Rangoon is not to have a setback in combat with them.'

'That is as may be, sir, but the Thirty-eighth were given orders to—'

'And *I* am now giving you an order to remain here until the rest of your battalion arrives!'

The lieutenant visibly braced himself. 'Very well, sir, but I must ask for the order in writing.'

'You may have it in any form you wish, Mr Napier. But I counsel you not to protest too much in front of your troops. They have fought bravely and it is no dishonour to them that they retire now.'

Corporal Wainwright listened intently to the exchange. He had seen his captain, sword in hand, display enough courage for a dozen men; yet countermanding a general's orders must require a different courage from the everyday kind. He wondered at it, took careful note, and hoped fervently that his captain was right as well as brave.

CHAPTER FOUR
THE SORTIE

Two days later

Hervey picked up a pencil. Pen and ink was no good. The paper was damp and the ink spread, so that even his carefully formed letters became indistinct in a matter of seconds. Damp paper, damp powder, damp biscuit – mouldy, even – on which they now subsisted, damp leather inside which men's feet chafed, the sores then suppurating: it was as inauspicious a beginning to a campaign as ever he had known. Indeed, it was more than inauspicious: it was ignominy in the making. Four hundred miles still to their object – Ava – and here they struggled through the delta's mud to attack stockades with only bayonets and the breasts of brave men. Hervey was ashamed, and not a little angry.

Rangoon,
17 May 1824

My dear Somervile,
I am very afraid that your strictures regarding the
assumptions on which this war is prosecuted appear
already to have been most sadly prescient. We made a
landing here but one week ago against opposition unworthy

of mention, but the populace has not risen in our support. Indeed, the native people are nowhere to be seen, and with them, we may suppose, are all the provisions and transport upon which the supply of the army was to be found. There are some cattle hereabout, but the order that they be unmolested remains, and therefore our soldiers starve that the sacred cows might live. The rains have come – in such torrents as I could scarce describe – and the river is now swollen in the manner required, but Peto's flotilla is unable to make progress until the supply is ordered and the gun forts all about – of which nothing was known hitherto – are reduced.

Two days ago I attended the Grenadier Company of the 38th, which is Campbell's own regiment, in two most gallant attacks upon stockades upstream of here. Their Captain was killed, and the ensign too, and they lost one in three of the Company, but they were all for assaulting a third and stronger fort until I ordered them to await reinforcement by the battalion companies, which, in the event, did not show because of some alarm here. The fighting spirit of the men is admirable, but I have a fear that it will be frittered away in ill conceived assaults – the Company had not even ladders for the escalade – and, perhaps the more so, by sickness, which is already rife.

Major Seagrass is dead of a fever, and I am thereby now General Campbell's military secretary. There is little for me to do, however, and yesterday when I gave my opinion of the parlous state into which we were lapsing (my cause was in respect of the mounting sick lists), Campbell became so angered that I am still unaware if it were on account of his despair at our situation or with my candour, though in this connection I must say that I do not believe he has a true grasp of our peril. I see none of the energy for which he had reputation in Spain, nor any faithful imagination of the scale of the undertaking. I pray most fervently that I am wrong in this assessment, but . . .

There was the sound of spurs outside and then a knock. The door opened and into Hervey's quarters stepped one of General Campbell's ADCs, well-scrubbed, hat under arm and sword hitched high on his belt. 'Sir, the general would speak with you; at once, if you please, sir.'

'Very well,' said Hervey, rising. 'Do you know in what connection?'

'I am afraid I do not, sir. The general has spent much of the morning in conference with his brigadiers.'

Hervey placed the letter to Somervile in the pocket of his writing case, gathered up his sword and shako, and left his quarters certain that he was to hear another paragraph of sorry testimony for inclusion in the letter.

The general's door was open. Hervey knocked and stood to attention.

'Come in, Captain Hervey; come in.'

General Campbell looked tired. Or was it worry? Hervey had received no word from him after handing the quarter-master-general a report on the Thirty-eighth's endeavours. He was unsure even if he had read it, for there had been nothing but routine orders from Campbell's office in days. Neither had there been any sort of conference; Peto had fumed about it when they had dined together the evening before. 'Good morning, General,' said Hervey, a shade warily.

'Sit down, sit down.'

It was curious, thought Hervey, how the general repeated his bidding. He did it not infrequently, of late especially. Was it a mere affliction of the nerves, like blinking or twitching, or did it reveal an uncertainty? Since the general could not doubt that any order would be obeyed, it could only be that he tried to overcome his reluctance to give the order by repeating it for his own hearing. Yet in such small matters as entering a room and taking a chair, what could there be by way of difficulty? Except, perhaps, that the general intended saying something disagreeable.

Surely not? Surely a major-general would not rebuke a captain direct when there were others to whom he might so easily delegate the unpleasant task. Hervey took off his shako and sat in a rush-seat chair in front of the general's writing table.

'I did not say that I approved of your conduct the other day – on the river, I mean.'

Hervey was perplexed. The fact was indisputable, but the words suggested one thing and the manner of their delivery another. Was this a statement of disapproval or not? The general did indeed seem weary. 'No, sir.'

'I *did* approve, most decidedly. We can have no frittering-away of our troops, especially not our best ones. We shall need every man.'

Hervey nodded. He would once have said 'Thank you' to a sign of approval, but now he saw no occasion for thanks.

'I have intelligence that Kemmendine shall be the base from which the Burmans will launch their attacks on us. It is in all likelihood in a strong state of fortification already.'

Hervey nodded again, wondering what these remarks portended.

'Your observations on the Burman manner of fighting would appear most apt. It would seem they are advancing on us by degrees through the jungle, digging and throwing up their damned stockades with each day.'

Hervey frowned. 'That is exactly the manner in which I understand them to fight, General. But I must say that it is not by my observation as much as by study of what others have written before.'

The general waved a hand dismissively. 'Yes, yes, but it was you who wrote the memorandum. *That* is what I meant. And now you've been inside one of these damned bamboo forts of theirs, you'll have other notions of how to deal with them, no doubt.'

Hervey was about to say that he considered any attack without artillery to be iniquitous, when the general pronounced his intention to deal with the encroaching threat. 'I shall attack at once – tomorrow. I shall take them utterly by surprise.'

Hervey, certainly, was surprised. Indeed, he was as intrigued by the notion as he was by the general's purpose in summoning him.

'You think ill of my design, then, Captain Hervey?'

Hervey would once have been flattered by such an enquiry. Now he felt only anger for the reply he would have to make, for it hardly seemed a design at all – more a statement of hope. 'I should not advise it, sir.'

The general looked taken aback; whether by the sentiment or by its plain expression, Hervey could not tell. Nor, indeed, was he in the slightest degree concerned.

The general frowned. 'How so?'

Again, Hervey would once have measured his words; now he paused but a moment. 'The jungle is the Burman's habitude, General. It is where they would choose to fight us. To fight them there we should have an approach through very trappy growth, and could scarce keep formation. Or, if we were in column, it would be the very devil to deploy, especially if there were skirmishers concealed. And in all this it would seem to me utterly impossible to achieve the slightest degree of surprise.'

General Campbell looked astonished. 'That is not the opinion of my brigadiers.'

'They must answer for themselves, General,' replied Hervey confidently. 'With respect, sir, you asked me for my opinion.'

The general made no reply for the moment. He might at other times have been angry, but now he was thoroughly baffled. He might be new-come to India, but he had fought here long ago, and in Mysore, and it was 'the India rule' that a prompt attack confounded the enemy. Was that not, indeed, the duke's own tactic at Assaye? It had certainly been their method at Seringapatam. 'Then what would be your course?'

Hervey imagined the answer was obvious. He managed nevertheless to hide his dismay. 'Let them expend their effort in coming to us. Fight them in the open, or at the forest's edge, not when they're behind their walls. We might borrow some of the navy's artillery, too.'

'I don't care for the notion of waiting,' replied Campbell, shaking his head very decidedly.

'I am not suggesting we sit idly, sir. There is much to be done by way of outposts and patrols, and harassing. The thing is this: the Burmans must come to us if they are to seek any decision. They have no alternative. In which case we can make their work devilish unpleasant.'

The general sighed, loud and rather peevishly, then lapsed into silence.

After what seemed an age, Hervey judged his attendance no longer required. He replaced his shako, saluted and left for his quarters without a word.

He was not long there when the same ADC announced that General Campbell would see him again. Hervey put down the pencil once more and returned to the headquarter office, unsure this time whether he would hear testimony for inclusion in his letter of denunciation, or another outburst of anger (Campbell was hardly likely to reproach him for not seeking formal permission to dismiss?).

In truth, he did not much care what was the reason. Indeed, there was almost an air of truculence about Captain Hervey as he opened the general's door.

'You make a lot of sense, Hervey,' said Campbell, briskly. 'A lot of sense. I have decided to attack the Burmans when they reach the forest edge. But I shall not sit idly until then. We must have very active outpost work – patrols and the like – day and night. Put the Burmans on edge, deny 'em sleep. And I've decided to lead an attack myself on one of these stockades. Tomorrow. Can't abide sitting here another minute!'

Hervey was cheered; also gratified by the general's

confidences, if uncertain as to their cause. 'Shall you want me to accompany you, sir?'

Campbell looked rather surprised. 'If you would like to, yes. But don't trouble yourself if there are other duties to be about.'

Hervey took his leave, formally this time. He returned to his quarters and resumed his letter-writing mystified in no small degree by the affair.

At long length he finished the deposition, with its post-script on the general's new intentions, and signed it wearily. He laid down his pencil, then he picked it up again, adding after his signature, 'We must, however, allow that the general is a gallant man.'

In the afternoon, there being no duties to detain him, Hervey went aboard *Liffey* to dine.

Peto's mood had changed; he was no longer merely exasperated. Flowerdew had to give him wide berth as he circled with the decanter, the commodore's gesticulations becoming more and more extravagant. 'Half my ships ply to Calcutta like packets, now, and the rest all but careened here. And the crews sicken: Marryat hasn't an officer or warrant officer fit for duty, and he's had ten men die already. I'm sending *Larne* to sea for better air. In a month I'll have no ships in fighting trim at this rate.' He waved the decanter away, and then waved it back again. 'Dammee, this is no longer just a business of the Company's sovereignty. The honour of the Service is at stake!'

Hervey sipped at his glass of hock, chilled very tolerably by its immersion for several days in the river. He could understand his friend's dismay, for this was His Majesty's navy's first trial since— 'But the two are in consonance, surely? Ava is the object, is it not?'

Peto subsided but frowned severely. 'Only up to a point, Hervey. The Company will have safeguarded its position by defeating the Burmans' design. All they have to do is stop his offensives in Arakan and force a treaty. You know full well it was the commander-in-chief's opinion that we should have stood solely on the defensive. Whereas the Royal Navy shot its way into Rangoon and cannot now move but out the way it came!'

'Ay, but unless Bagyidaw is deposed there'll be no end of alarms,' countered Hervey, shaking his head and reflecting the commodore's frown. 'Someone shall have to go to Ava. Of that there's no doubt.'

Peto beckoned his steward to serve their dinner. 'And what if he should delay so long as to be then unable to clear the Irawadi? It would be *my* ships that are seen to turn.'

Hervey blanched. 'Are you suggesting we abandon it? How will that serve the honour of the navy?'

'I am suggesting no such thing. I am suggesting that the commander-in-chief will break off the campaign here when the attacks on the borders of the Company's territory have been repulsed. And we shall have to steal away from this place without a shot – like thieves in the night.'

Hervey looked doubtful. 'That is if the Governor-General is of the same mind as the commander-in-chief.'

Peto huffed. 'Amherst has the mind of a nincompoop, as we have ample evidence.'

'What would be *your* design?'

'To reduce the garrison here to what is required only to repulse an attack. What would that be? A brigade? No more, surely? And then to take off the remainder at once to force the Irawadi. Rangoon will draw in the Burmans from far and wide, and that we should take advantage of. But there's no profit in sitting here the while with so many, and all my ships tied up supporting them. And for that matter, every day our numbers dwindling.'

'I grant you we might force the Irawadi. But without the strength to garrison it, the lines of communication would be at the Burmans' mercy. This general, Maha Bundula – he would see it at once.'

Peto looked put out. 'I thought you might have allowed that I would see the same!'

Hervey frowned. 'I don't comprehend, Peto.'

'All these transports and escorts now plying back and forth across the Bay of Bengal: all they're doing is feeding the garrison here. Cut the garrison by two-thirds and there'd be no need of external supply. I could land half my own stores. It would see them through any siege. And the ships released thereby could keep open the Irawadi.'

Hervey pondered the notion as Flowerdew laid a plate of fish on the table. 'Have you shared this opinion with the general?'

'I have sent him a memorandum, just before you came.'

Hervey wondered how it would be received. The fall of Ava was not essential to the general's reputation. All that was necessary was for him to hold Rangoon. It was not his fault that the Burmans hadn't flocked to his support. If the commander-in-chief wished him to take Ava against such opposition, then he would have to supply him with the means to do so. And yet, the taking of Ava in such very trying circumstances – against the odds – would surely be his making? 'He intends awaiting a general attack for a week or so. He will certainly want the support of your guns. And tomorrow he is going to lead an assault on one of the stockades.'

'And do you go with him?'

'Yes. He intends that I should write the despatch.'

'I've a mind to come with you, but I've called my captains aboard.'

Hervey smiled. 'There'll be more opportunities, I assure you. The general is determined to have the garrison as active as possible while he waits.'

Peto helped his guest to a fair portion of fish. 'Bekti. The best you'll ever taste. Caught this morning and brought upriver by *Diana*. What a boon she is.'

Hervey had seen steam on water before, first in a boat no

bigger than *Liffey*'s cutter on the Blackwater river in Ireland, and then the barge that had towed their transports steadily upstream on the St Lawrence, six winters ago. But nothing like *Diana*. *Diana* was a gunship, her ports painted Nelson-style, and her smokestack half as high as *Liffey*'s mainmast. 'The baby figure of things to come, do you think?'

'Of some things, perhaps. But *Diana* could never stand off in a fight. A twelve-pounder would smash her paddles to pieces. I can't risk her in the van too long if the river narrows and the forts get her range.'

Hervey tried his fish. 'I don't know whether it's because I've not had a spoonful of anything half-decent in a week, but this I agree is uncommonly good.'

Peto looked pleased. He drained his glass and let Flowerdew refill it. Then he leaned back in his chair. 'Let us speak of agreeable things for a time. I never told you my news, did I? It is signed and sealed and I had a note of it only yesterday.'

Hervey indulged his friend by laying down his fork and sitting back to receive the evidently happy intelligence.

'I have bought an estate near my father's living.'

'An estate, indeed,' said Hervey, as impressed as he was surprised.

'Nothing on any grand scale. And the house shall need attention. But it has a good park, and is but a short drive from the sea.'

Hervey wondered why a man who so much disdained being ashore should take such a course. 'Do you plan going on half pay?'

'It will come to it, Hervey; it will come to it. I have a tidy sum invested in Berry's cellars, and another in two-per-cents, but I have a notion of something a shade more . . . substantial.'

Hervey smiled. 'Then you are not contemplating matrimony?'

Peto raised his glass and took a very urbane sip. 'A man in his right mind who *contemplates* matrimony will never embark upon it, Hervey. In any case, a house has no need of a mistress – only a keeper.'

Hervey said nothing.

Peto realized the import. 'Oh, my dear fellow: I am so dreadfully sorry. I—'

Hervey smiled and shook his head. 'Think nothing of it. I'll take another glass of your hock, and drink to your arrangements in Norfolk.'

Peto cursed himself for being the fool.

Corporal Wainwright came to Hervey's quarters before first light with a canteen of tea, and returned shortly afterwards with hot water. Their exchanges were few.

'It's raining, sir.'

Hervey wondered at the need of this news, supposing that the hammering on the roof was the same that had been for the last fortnight.

'And the guard says it's been raining all night, sir.'

This much was perhaps of some moment, since the going would clearly be of the heaviest, perhaps even preventing the general from taking the field piece. Hervey sighed to himself at the thought of another affair of the bayonet. The wretched infantry – no better served now by the Board of Ordnance than if they had been with Marlborough a century past. For ten years – more – he, Hervey, had had a carbine that would fire in the worst of weather, yet the Ordnance showed not the least sign of interest. The notion of a percussion cap when a piece of flint would do seemed to the board an affront to economy. And little wonder if its members were as fat-headed as Campbell.

Hervey sighed again as he drank the sweet tea in satisfying gulps. Perseverance – that was the soldier's virtue. It was both duty and consolation. 'Corporal Wainwright, I give you leave to remain here and keep things dry.'

'And I decline it, sir, if you please. Thanking you for the consideration, that is, sir.'

Hervey smiled. 'It was not entirely for your welfare, Corporal Wainwright. I had a thought to my own comfort on return!'

'I'll engage one of the sepoys, sir.'

Hervey smiled again as he rose to his toilet. 'It's not what I said it would be, Corporal Wainwright, is it? Hardly the dashing campaign, with gold to fill the pockets.'

Corporal Wainwright pulled the thatch from Hervey's boots and began to rub up the blacking while Hervey began lathering his shaving brush. 'I don't hold with stealing, sir, and it seems to me, from what I've heard, that that's all it amounts to half the time. Prize money's a different thing. But plundering a place is no better than thieving.'

'Your sensibility does you credit, Corporal Wainwright. The duke himself would applaud it.' Hervey spoke his words carefully, but only because he had regard to the razor's edge.

'Pistols sir? I'm taking mine.'

'I suppose so. It is conceivable the rain will cease.'

'What I should like to know, sir, is how rain stays up in the sky before it begins to fall.'

Hervey held the razor still. 'You know, I have never given it a thought. Nor, indeed, do I recall anyone else doing so. I suppose there is an answer.' He resumed his shaving.

'I'll bind the oilskin extra-tight, sir. Wherever this rain's coming from, there doesn't look to be any shortage.'

In a few minutes more, Hervey was finished. He dressed quickly, thinking the while of the rain question. 'The rain is in the clouds. That much is obvious.'

Yet that was only a very partial answer (consistent with his knowledge of natural history). The rain outside descended as a solid sheet of water – the noise on the roof was, if anything, louder than when he woke – yet how did it rise to the height of the clouds in the first place, and then stay aloft?

'Steam. Steam *rises*,' he said, pulling on his boots. 'That *Diana* works that way, I think.'

Corporal Wainwright said nothing, content instead to listen to the emerging theory.

'A great deal of this rain must have begun as steam.'

But then why should it now fall as rain? And where did all the steam come from in the first instance?

'For the rest I must ask Commodore Peto. The weather is his business. For us it is just weather, I fear.' He fastened closed his tunic. It had become a poor affair with a daily soaking this past month.

Wainwright took away the bowl of water.

Hervey looked out, observed the downpour and put off his visit to the latrines until after breakfast.

He sat down at his desk-cum-table still turning over the rain question in his mind. Peto would surely know a great deal more – all there was to know, probably. But what opportunity he would have to pose his query in the coming weeks, he couldn't tell. The commodore had declared he would be taking *Liffey* and two of the brigs out to blow good sea air through her decks and give the hands practice with canvas again.

Wainwright was soon back with Hervey's breakfast – excellent coffee (he had been careful to lay in a store of that before leaving Calcutta) and a very indifferent gruel. Hervey thanked his luck for the supper of bekti the night before, and for the lump of salt pork that Peto had pressed on him to bring ashore. It would be their ration today, for the salt beef had now gone, and it was biscuit only again.

In half an hour the bugle summoned him – 'general parade'. He put on his shako, fastened his swordbelt and drew on his gloves. He looked at the pistols, wondering. He picked up both and pushed them into his belt: if the rain did stop, he'd feel undressed without them. He wished he'd brought his carbine, but it had seemed the last thing he would need when he joined the general's staff in Calcutta.

The sortie paraded outside the north gate. They were six companies, three British and three native, together with two field pieces – a six-pounder and a howitzer – some five hundred men in all, and another fifty dhoolie-bearers. They gave an impression of unity by their red coats, except for the artillerymen, who wore blue, but close to they were rather more disparate than a Calcutta inspecting officer would have been used to. It was but a fortnight since the landing, and already some of the troops had a ragged appearance which spoke of their exertions and the flimsiness of their uniforms, as well as the lack of supply. For the most part, the trousers were white, summer pattern, but heavily patched, and the sepoy companies had abandoned their boots. Some of the officers wore forage caps. The general, indeed, wore one. Hervey would have been appalled had he not witnessed all that had gone before: an officer of the Sixth never wore a forage cap but in the lines. That it should have come to this in one month beggared belief.

There was no doubting the effect as a whole, however. In close order, and from a distance, these men looked like a solid red wall. They would stand, come what may. And their muskets – they would know how to handle them, for sure. Five rounds in the minute at their best – how could the Burmans match or bear it? The trouble was, the best volleying was only possible with dry powder.

General Campbell was rapt in conversation with the sortie's lieutenant-colonel, a short, stocky man whose voice was said to be the loudest in the expedition. Hervey studied the general carefully. He had not fully appreciated his height before, for he seemed now to stand taller than any man on parade. Without doubt, Sir Archibald Campbell had the crack and physique to convince a subordinate of his competence; Hervey pushed all his doubting thoughts to the back of his mind.

Would Campbell address the sortie? The rain hammered so loud it would be pointless but for a few men in the front rank. So they would just turn into column of route and

93

march off down the track into the forest. Poor infantry – trudge, trudge, trudge, a mouthful of black powder biting the cartridge, a minute of rushing blood in a bayonet charge, and then . . .

Then it was the same for all of them – kill or be killed. The soldier's life was nearest Nature – lowly, nasty, brutish, and all too frequently short.

It was, of course, why they made comrades of one another so quickly. Everyone knew that. Hervey had seen it in his first week at the depot squadron, and he supposed it was why, perhaps, decent society could sometimes hail the soldier, for all his licentiousness. The quality certainly liked an officer in his regimentals. He wondered if they ever imagined them as they appeared this morning, however – sodden, tattered, grubby. Or what they looked like when rent with grape, ball, or the point of iron and steel.

It was strange he should think now of Henrietta. Now, when things stood at their most brutish. But Henrietta had had a good imagination of the truth, for all her feigning otherwise. Not so Lady Katherine Greville. Hervey did not suppose *she* had ever thought of it, let alone was capable of imagining it. Regimentals were not for this. They were for the delighting of her and those like her – a mark of potency rather than aught else. He did not suppose it, indeed; he knew it. Her letters told him as explicitly as she had implied the day they had ridden together in Hyde Park. That was four, nearly five years ago, and still she wrote. He wrote too, not exactly by return, but with sufficient despatch to keep the correspondence lively. It flattered him. She might have her pick of officers in London – and no doubt did – and yet she penned him letters. He smiled to himself, now, at her questions. Did he wish to be an ADC? Did he wish for an appointment at the Horse Guards? If he would not return soon to London, did he wish a place on the commander-in-chief's staff, or even the Governor-General's? There was not much, it seemed, that Lieutenant-General Sir Peregrine

94

Greville could not arrange if his wife were to ask him.

'Sir?'

Hervey turned.

'I asked if you still don't want your cape, sir,' said Corporal Wainwright, water running down his shako oilskin as if it were an ornamental fountain. 'I can fetch it quick enough.'

Hervey shook his head. 'No. I think we're beyond all help in rain like this. It'll be sodden in minutes and then a dead weight. Why don't you take yours though?'

'No, sir. It'll be just as sodden. And I'd as soon kick off these boots.' He smiled.

Hervey smiled back. Corporal Wainwright had been wearing shoes when first he had seen him on Warminster Common, though the rest of the inhabitants of that sink had been barefoot. 'Easier going in the approach, I grant you, but just wait till you get a bamboo splinter!'

Words of command now rippled through the ranks, like dominoes toppling. Back up to attention came the companies; they shouldered arms, moved to the right in column of route, then struck off to the dull thud of soggy-skinned drums and watery fifes – a cheery enough display for the general, thought Hervey, even if the sepoys did look distinctly ill-used to marching in torrents of rain. The King's men, he didn't doubt, would have marched in many times worse, and some of them in the Peninsula, where the rain could fall as a stinging hail of ice rather than as a warm drench. Poor, wretched infantry – the regiments of foot – and their feet often as not cold and wet. The cavalryman knew privation, and worked the harder for having a horse to look after as well as himself, but his feet bore nothing like the punishment of the infantryman's.

'Nice tune, sir,' chirped Corporal Wainwright as he picked up the step.

'Yes,' said Hervey, in a vague way.

'Don't you recognize it, sir?'

'No?' Corporal Wainwright obviously thought it of significance.

'The rain it fell for forty days!'

'Of course,' he said, smiling – black humour, the soldier's privilege. 'But I'm afraid the drum-major is excessively an optimist. The rains will be an affair of months, I fear.'

They were not set off more than half an hour, and only a short distance into the jungle, when the first shots were fired. In this rain they defied belief. Hervey could not conceive how any powder might be dry enough, especially in Burman hands.

There was at once a great cheer and the leading men went at the pickets with the bayonet. It was over in a minute. Hervey saw nothing.

The column halted and the general pushed his way to the front, Hervey with him. They found a half-finished stockade built directly across the track and extending the length of a cricket pitch each side into the forest, empty of all but redcoats, and half a dozen Burman musketeers too slow on their feet. General Campbell peered at the bodies, as if they might reveal something of the campaign before him. 'Pull the place down!' he snapped. 'Press on, Colonel Keen!'

They left a sepoy company to the work, and the column trudged on into jungle made increasingly dark by the heavy skies. In another half-hour they passed three more stockades just as hastily abandoned, and then not a sign of the enemy in five miles of swamp and thicket until the artillerymen were too exhausted to pull their guns any further.

'In God's name get the sepoys to the ropes!' cursed the general.

Hervey despaired. He had taken gallopers into the jungle – two-pounders dismantled, and carried by pack-horses. But guns like these . . . it would not serve. 'Sir, I believe the effort may not be worth it. And when it comes to withdrawing, we could never afford to abandon them.'

'I agree, General,' said Colonel Keen.

Campbell looked vexed. He wanted to blow in a stockade and tell the Burmans there was nowhere safe for them. But he had brought the wrong guns and he knew it. The Madras artillery's commander had told him so last night. 'Very well. The sepoy company will remain guarding them until we return.'

There were no packhorses, of course. Not one. Indeed, there was not a single animal in the entire expeditionary force. But this was to be an entirely novel campaign, one that did not observe the normal usages of war. Hervey seethed. Who *were* these officers who would undertake a campaign without a few ready horses?

The next two miles were done much quicker without the guns. They did not find the enemy, however, nor any sign of him, and in an hour the column emerged from the forest into green padi fields six inches deep in water.

Colonel Keen halted the column to allow the general to come forward.

'What do you make of it, Colonel?' asked Campbell, sounding confident still.

The colonel had the advantage of two minutes' survey through his telescope, but even so there was not much he could tell him. 'I feel the want of a map very sorely, General. I suppose yonder village is fortified, or at least has some hasty stockading erected, for they must have known of our approach these several hours.'

General Campbell now surveyed the ground for himself.

The village lay half a mile ahead astride the track by which they had come. Without a map it was impossible to tell if it ran through the village and beyond, in which case the village commanded further advance, or whether it ended there. Colonel Keen thought the question apposite since, he reasoned, the Burmans would be bound to defend the former whereas they would probably have abandoned the latter.

The general nodded to the logic, but either way he would have the place. 'And if I find so much as a loophole in yonder buildings I'll raze the entire village.'

Colonel Keen folded his telescope. 'Column of companies, I think, General?'

'If you please.'

The colonel turned to his adjutant. 'Column of companies if you please, Mr Broderick.'

While this evolution was taking place, which required the sortie to advance a good hundred yards to make manoeuvre room, and for the companies to extend left and right for about fifty into the padi, Hervey climbed to the lower branch of a sal tree and began his own survey. To the right of the village, perhaps a little closer than to the forest's edge, was water – one of the delta's many creeks, he supposed. To the left, and beyond, the same distance, was jungle. He strained to make out something of the village, but the cloud and the rain made it impossible to tell whether there was any stockading. There was certainly no sign of life. He looked at his watch: a little past midday. They could not advance much further without spending the night in the forest. And there were the guns to think of.

The companies struck off at a good pace, splashing through the muddy rice as if skylarking on a beach. Hervey climbed down and pushed his way along the track to where the general marched with the Thirty-eighth's lieutenant-colonel, just to the rear of the leading company. He fell in behind the adjutant, counting himself lucky to have his feet out of the padi. It was only then that he observed how effective was a general's cocked hat in a downpour. Campbell had his pulled over his ears, and water ran down the points 'fore and aft' clear of both face and neck. Strange, the things one noticed at times such as these, he mused.

'View halloo!'

Hervey woke instantly. Where? What? He couldn't see beyond the shakos of the company in front.

'Skirmishers out!' he heard the lieutenant-colonel order.

Men from the light company began doubling past on both flanks to form a skirmishing line. How would they load in this weather?

'Smart work!' said the general.

Hervey could now see the Burmans forming up on either side of the village – with officers on horseback. He prayed there would be no cavalry, however inexpert. They would have the advantage, for sure, even in this going.

'Curse this padi!' It was taking forever to make headway. Hervey glanced left and right: the lines were uneven, and they were having to mark time in the middle, the men on the flanks up to their knees in water, mud sucking at every stride. He thought it bordered on the reckless. If there were cavalry behind the village they could be onto flanks in an instant. He began unbinding one of his pistols, but he had little expectation of its serviceability. He cursed again. A pistol which misfired, perforce at short range, was worse than useless. He began rebinding. He would trust to the sabre, as the infantry would trust to the bayonet.

At a hundred paces musketry broke out from in front of the village, left and right. Hervey could scarce believe it. Just as at Kemmendine the Burmans had concealed their stockades in *byaik* little more than shoulder high, *and* kept their powder dry. But again they'd fired too soon and not a ball struck home.

The skirmishers held their fire: theirs was to discourage any who would stand in the open.

Coolly, as if at a field day, the general took in the business before him. 'One company, if you please, Colonel,' he said, matter-of-fact. 'Remainder to stand fast in reserve lest those there begin to advance.' He pointed at the Burmans drawn up either side of the village.

It was promptly done. Eight dozen bayonets in two ranks inclined right and quickened almost to double time, Campbell following.

Hervey was hard-pressed to keep pace.

The musketry increased, but it was ragged and had no more effect than before.

The ground now fell away – three feet, perhaps more. Down the slope to the bamboo walls ran the company – eight-foot walls, not five.

There were shots from the left – hopelessly too far again – as Hervey and the general raced to catch them up. He couldn't understand how the Burman fire discipline could be so poor when their other skills were so admirable.

The general glanced left, marked the smoke, then drew his sword and sprinted the last dozen yards to the fort.

The Thirty-eighth were already atop the walls. Hervey glimpsed the bayonets at work – bloody, vengeful work.

The general climbed on a corporal's shoulders and heaved himself up. Hervey and the ADCs followed as best they could. Hervey lost his footing on the wet bamboo several times until Corporal Wainwright leaned out and got hold of his crossbelt.

But it was over by the time they were up. Five minutes' work, at most, to turn the fort into a slaughterhouse as bad as he'd seen. There were dozens of dead piled against the gates, and as many more scattered about the stockade in ones and twos where they had stood and fought or cowered and craved mercy, both in vain.

General Campbell, sword still drawn, but unbloody, at once ordered out the company to assault the second stockade. Hervey, standing on the parapet, glanced back at the other three companies formed up ready, their colonel in front, and wondered at the general's impetuosity. Was it that he was happy at last, knowing exactly what he was about – the simple certainty of fighting, and with his old corps? He might almost be seeking a glorious death. He made work for his covermen, for sure.

'Two ranks! Get fell in!' The serjeant-major blew his whistle fiercely and waved his sword. 'That was nothing! Look sharp, damn you!'

The voice of the Black Country made Hervey think of Ezra Barrow: dragoon to captain – what would *he* make of it? He would not have volunteered for it, that was certain. 'Never volunteer for anything' was a maxim Barrow had long lived by. And it had evidently served him well. Hervey might almost envy him at this moment, undoubtedly taking his pleasure in an afternoon's repose.

At last the company was fell in to the serjeant-major's satisfaction. They were scarcely depleted, for all the ferocity of the first assault, though every man was as gory as a surgeon's mate. No matter, the rain would wash them clean. But by their look, Hervey wondered if it was what they would want.

The general now threw over all restraint and placed himself in front of the line. He waved his sword at the objective, two hundred yards ahead. 'Once more, the Thirty-eighth! Let 'em have *Brummagem*!'

There was a great cheer.

Poor Colonel Keen, sighed Hervey. The general was a captain again and nothing would stop him.

He took post on the right of the front rank, along with the ADCs, with Corporal Wainwright beside him. It would be the closest he had come to a bayonet charge – just as he'd wanted. He could already feel the strength of a line of well-drilled men elbow to elbow, 'the touch of cloth', even blue with red. If only the enemy were not behind a palisade! But no, he needn't worry: the bamboo walls would delay them, not stop them, surely? These men's blood was hotted: they would take the place by escalade again, and the Burmans would once more rue their lot.

* * *

But the second stockade was not as easy as the first. The walls were no higher, and the defenders no greater, but the Burmans held their fire and then stuck at it just that bit longer. The first volley came at about seventy yards – some lucky hits, enough to shock – then another at fifty which felled several men including a serjeant.

'Charge!'

The general's voice was louder than the rain and the firing combined, and the cheering louder still as the right-flank company of His Majesty's 38th Foot, under their erstwhile colonel, ran slipping and sliding to the wooden walls.

This time the defenders would not be bolted. They held their ground and kept up a steady fire even as the first redcoats were scrambling up the palisade.

The second rank began desperately unwrapping their flintlocks to engage them. Few managed to fire.

The Burmans had the advantage and the will this time, and the fallen red coats began to show.

But little by little – it seemed an age yet could not have been more than minutes – red began to preponderate atop the palisade. It defied reason, for they could not be gaining it by fire. Hervey himself had fired both his pistols, and the rounds were wide. No, it was not fire that let the redcoats escalade the fort.

He got a shoulder again from a thickset private – 'Yow mun gow, sir; me leg's shot through.' This time he reached the parapet while there was still fighting. 'Where's the general?'

'I can't see 'im, sir,' said Wainwright, looking either side of the wall.

'Christ!' It wasn't his business to guard him, but—

An ear-splitting roar and the whizz of shrapnel – smoke rolled across the stockade floor and hid all for an instant.

Hervey leapt from the parapet and dashed for the gun. A dozen redcoats beat him by a mile. A dozen more lay full of iron.

He saw his man though, spear couched, hesitant but standing his ground. Up went the sabre as he ran in, Wainwright with him.

He didn't feel the ball strike. He only saw the lights dancing in the sky as he fell. And then the shadow of Corporal Wainwright over him, saying something he couldn't hear.

CHAPTER FIVE

THE SURGEON'S BLADE

That evening

The sight of a horse, even a lone horse, made the sentries at Rangoon's gates rush to their posts, and the inlying picket stand to. A horse was at best the bearer of a Burman who wished to treaty; at worst it bore the forerunner of a Burman army.

'Shall I take a shot at 'im, sir?' called the picket-corporal to his officer.

The lieutenant strained to make out the target. Two hundred yards: he could not determine who sat astride, and he was as certain that his corporal, for all his reputation as a hawk eye, could strike neither horse nor rider at that range with a common musket. And with the extra windage of the French balls they'd been issued with he'd have no more chance at half the range. He looked for reassurance towards the field piece in the mouth of the gate – the gunners were already ramming home shell. 'No. Let him come on some more.'

The guard company now stood to, hastily, dressing in two ranks.

Their captain scaled the ladder to the palisade to see for himself. He raised his telescope; a hundred yards the rider had closed to.

The lieutenant rued his own want of so useful an instrument.

'*Two* men, Torrance – one leading. They're not wearing red, but they're not niggers either.' He turned and hailed his ensign. 'Out, Wilks, and give a hand!'

They brought Hervey to the surgeon in a dhoolie. Corporal Wainwright, every muscle weary, stayed with him despite the serjeant's entreaties to fall out and take his ease. The horse, exhausted too, and lame, was led away by a corporal – fresh meat at last, joked the men.

The hospital occupied the town-eater's collecting house – and every building around it, now. Men lay everywhere, barely tended. The place stank worse than Calcutta when the Hooghly was on the turn.

'Out you go, Corporal,' said the surgeon. He had come at once, tired and red-smeared from his ministrations with the bleeding stick.

'I'd rather stay, if you don't mind, sir.'

'I *do* mind. You're no use to me in here.'

Hervey lay unconscious. The assistants were already cutting away the left sleeve of his coat. Corporal Wainwright did not move.

'Oh very well,' grumbled the surgeon. 'But be out of my way. You both reek of rum.'

Corporal Wainwright stepped back, allowing the surgeon and his assistants full play at the table. One of them held a lantern up close to Hervey's shoulder.

'Too late,' said the surgeon.

Corporal Wainwright's jaw dropped.

'It'll have to come off. It looks like a ball in there. The shoulder will be a deal too smashed, and putrefaction too far advanced.' He sounded as tired as he was certain.

'Sir, with respect, sir,' pleaded Wainwright, stepping forward. 'Captain Hervey couldn't draw his sword and hold the reins with but one arm.'

The surgeon spun round. 'Damn your impudence, Corporal! I've a mind to have the guard throw you out! Another word and I'll have that stripe from your arm.' He turned back to his assistants. 'The saw, please!'

Corporal Wainwright did not flinch. 'Sir, you *must* try and save Captain Hervey's arm!'

The surgeon went purple. 'Throw 'im out!'

Corporal Wainwright drew his sword and pulled the pistol from his belt. The assistants fell back. 'I'll take the captain with me then, sir.'

'You damned fool,' spluttered the surgeon. 'This is gross insubordination – *worse*. The arm's got to be amputated, and quickly, otherwise it will gangrenate.'

Wainwright sheathed his sword.

'Sensible fellow,' said the surgeon, nodding. 'Now why not wait outside?'

Wainwright levelled the pistol again.

No one moved a muscle.

He stepped forward, crouched slightly, beckoned an assistant to help, and took Hervey over his shoulder. He stood full upright in one movement, with a strength that awed the watchers, and walked out of the hospital.

He walked past orderlies too alarmed by the fierce eyes and the pistol to stop him. Indeed, so compelling was Wainwright's bearing that soon there were sepoys supporting him.

At the river he found more allies, this time in blue. 'It's Captain Hervey, sir,' he called to one of *Liffey*'s officers in an approaching gig.

Liffey's officer of the watch had also been observing from the quarterdeck. 'Fetch the captain,' he snapped at a midshipman. 'And the surgeon. I think it's Hervey.'

Peto came at once with Surgeon Ritchie, both of them fresh-scrubbed and dressed for dinner. 'Hervey, you say?' The edge to the tone was obvious. Peto leaned well out as the boat bore alongside.

106

'I believe so, sir,' said the lieutenant. 'And his—'

'Great heavens,' exclaimed Peto, springing back from the rail. 'Mr Ritchie, your best work; your best work please!' He rushed to the gangway. 'Two marines – leave your muskets!'

The sentries at the foot of the companionways grounded arms and followed the captain down.

'Sir, Captain Hervey's shot, sir, in the shoulder,' said Corporal Wainwright, as Peto bounded down the gangway. 'The army surgeon wanted to take his arm off, sir.'

Peto pulled back the cloak to see for himself. He grimaced when he saw how much blood there was. The whole of the buff bib was red-brown. 'A hammock, there!' he shouted to the lieutenant, who had already anticipated the need.

Another marine scuttled down the gangway with it.

'Bear him up gently, men,' said Peto, more a plea than an order. 'Gently as you can.'

Seamen and marines began lifting him into the hammock.

'My cabin, if you please, Ritchie,' he called to the surgeon.

Surgeon Ritchie raised his hand to acknowledge and sent the loblolly boys sprinting to the cockpit for his instruments and the medical chest.

The marines, red in the face and sweating like pigs, bore Hervey up gently. Two more came to the job as they reached the main deck.

'I'll have your table, if you will, sir,' said the surgeon, as Peto came back on deck.

'Ay, of course, of course,' replied Peto absently. He pushed past, calling for his steward. Together they began clearing the table of its silver and fine china.

'Save the tablecloth, sir, if you please,' called the surgeon. 'Sit Captain Hervey upright,' he said to the marines. 'Support him with the cloth until I know what we're about.'

Back came his assistants.

'Lay it all out here and give me the sharpest knife!'

107

Corporal Wainwright's stomach heaved. 'Sir, I—'

'One way or another the coat will have to come off, Corporal,' said Ritchie, moving candles closer.

Corporal Wainwright's relief was palpable.

'A bowl of hot water and some brandy, if you will, Flowerdew.'

To anyone who observed the preliminaries of the two surgeons – the army's and *Liffey*'s – the reason for the crew's high opinion of theirs would have been clear. Whereas, ashore, the man had worked in Stygian gloom, though there was no obvious cause to, and his prognosis was made after the most cursory of visual examinations, Surgeon Ritchie made full use of the evening sunlight that streamed through the stern windows – and his magnifying glass.

His prognosis, however, tended to the same. 'Not good, I'm afraid. Lint, please.'

An assistant rummaged in a haversack.

'*Clean* lint. Let's not have any more stink than needs be.'

Hervey opened his eyes.

'Capital, my dear friend!' said a delighted Peto. 'You're in good hands, now.'

Hervey appeared not to register where he was or even who was there.

'An ill-timed recovery, I'm afraid, my dear sir,' muttered the surgeon, pouring brandy on the lint and wiping away some of the blood caked about the wound.

Hervey's head rolled.

Peto peered over the surgeon's shoulder at Hervey's. 'He reeks of rum, Ritchie,' he said, shaking his head. 'Little wonder he nods.'

Ritchie threw the lint to the floor.

'Hold hard there, my old friend!' Peto called, as if to a deaf man, which, to all intents and purposes, Hervey was.

'How much rum has he drunk, Corporal?' asked Ritchie.

'Only a very little, sir,' replied Wainwright, standing to

attention by a bulkhead. 'I poured the most of it into Captain Hervey's shoulder, sir.'

Ritchie turned and looked at him before more rubbing with new lint. 'And why, pray, did you do that?'

'I know Lord Nelson's body was preserved in brandy, sir. I thought it could help Captain Hervey.'

'You did, did you? Well, it can't have done too much harm, though it might have been better had you poured it all down his throat.' He took off his coat and pulled up his shirtsleeves. 'A digital examination, then, now the wound's exposed proper.'

Peto screwed up his eyes, the better to see the work, although it anticipated the flinch too.

Ritchie inserted a finger – the right index – with the utmost care, but the pain was so great that Hervey let out a cry and at once passed out.

'Good,' said Ritchie. 'Much the best way,' as he continued probing.

Peto grimaced, but more in anticipation of what Ritchie might say. Wainwright stood stock-still, at attention. He could do no more now than trust.

'There's been prodigious bleeding,' said Ritchie after a while. 'But no disruption of the glenoid cavity. No bone splinters either. And I believe I may feel the ball.' He withdrew his finger and wiped it on some lint, taking good care to observe Hervey's breathing as he did so.

The marines shifted their weight a little.

'Keep him proper upright, and hold his head back, one of you,' said Ritchie, wiping the sweat from his brow with his left arm. 'Probe-point bistoury, please, Magan.'

One of the assistants handed him the curved knife.

'Corporal, be aware that I might be doing your captain no favour in this. I may remove the ball, but if the shoulder is more damaged than I surmise it would be better that I disarticulate the limb now.'

Corporal Wainwright nodded. 'Sir.'

'Stand easy, man,' said Peto, kindly.

'But first there'll be more blood,' warned Ritchie, wiping his forehead again. 'Turn him round a wee bit more to the light.'

The marines turned him carefully with the linen sling.

'First I have to enlarge the wound.' He dipped the bistoury in the hot water. 'Curious thing how the patient afterwards says he felt the cold blade. Nelson did. Might as well make things as comfortable as possible.' He wiped the bistoury on his sleeve then deftly elongated the wound two ways, pulling the flesh apart either side with the thumb and finger of his left hand while he probed for the ball with the knifepoint.

Blood began to run copiously again. The assistants dabbed at it with lint.

'Forceps.'

Magan handed them to him and took the bistoury. Ritchie, as he had done with the knife, warmed the bullet-extracting forceps before putting them to the flesh.

Peto began silently to pray, although he was not a praying man. Wainwright *was* a praying man; he had scarcely ceased praying since first lifting Hervey into the saddle.

'Hold him hard. I don't want a struggle,' growled Ritchie as he pulled aside the flesh again and inserted the forceps.

But Hervey was in too deep a syncope to know how the instrument probed.

In the end it was done quickly. Out came forceps and ball in less than a minute. Ritchie examined the missile for signs of having struck bone. Then, satisfied, he tossed it to Corporal Wainwright. 'Your captain may want to see the intruder.'

'Sir. Will that mean he'll be well now, sir?'

Ritchie was already back to work with magnifying glass and the smaller forceps. 'I dare say so.' He tutted, picking out particles of blue serge from the wound. 'Lord, but this cloth's bitty. More light, there! A candle or two.'

It was Peto who obliged him quickest.

'But no braid, though, it seems,' said Ritchie in a tone of some relief, and peering even closer. 'Well, he's as good a chance as any. I'll suture now, Magan. Keep him steady, my lads. Good work.'

'And then to my cot,' said Peto, nodding with the greatest appearance of approval. 'Well done, Mr Ritchie. Well done, sir!'

'I could do no better, Captain. But your praise may be premature. It will be two weeks, perhaps three, before we see the laudable pus – the exuviae of the sickness. Only then can we say the arm is saved. What he needs now is to rest, and to be still. I'll bleed him tomorrow.'

PART TWO

HOME TRUTHS

CHAPTER SIX

CAMP FOLLOWERS

Calcutta, four months later

The girl ran a finger down the neat line of the scar. Hervey felt no pain. Quite the opposite, for her touch was always delicate and accompanied by the gentlest of kisses. He sighed with the pleasure of their intimacy. 'You had better go, Neeta. Manu will be here shortly, and you know how you dislike him.'

The girl hissed. 'I do not know why you keep him as your bearer when you have so good a servant as Mr Johnson!'

Hervey smiled. 'Manu is a good bearer too. And he does Johnson's bidding willingly.'

The girl rose from the bed, tied a lungi about her, then sat at Hervey's dressing table and took one of his brushes to her long black hair, as Henrietta used to do.

What a solace she was – companion these past two years, and nurse these last two months. Yet how dismayed he had been when first she had come to Calcutta looking for him. Chittagong had seemed so far behind. He rose, put on his dressing gown, then took her shoulders, watching in the mirror as she brushed – so very like Henrietta, and yet in appearance so different. It was all very safe, therefore. But he broke the rules. A bibi did not visit; she was but a 'sleeping-dictionary'. He kissed the top of her head, then went outside.

It was a quiet afternoon in the lines, even allowing for the usual retreat to the shade and the punkah, although the worst of the south-west monsoon's clammy heat was long past. There were a few mounted men about the cantonment, but no hawkers, no rumble of wheels. The Company was at war with Ava, but the war was so far distant that the seat of government was undisturbed.

It had no right to be. Hervey had seen the effects of that detachment, men dying for want of the staples of war. And if the Calcutta quality, and the clerks and the merchants, really knew how badly went things they would be busy burying their silver and taking passage home. Not that the war would ever come to this. Ava might boast of marching into Bengal, and her great general, Maha Bundula, might lead the army, but the Burmans could never prevail against redcoats. In the end, he believed there was no one who could, for however ill he was served, a redcoat – a *King's* redcoat – fought with the ferocious conviction of his own superiority. That was why so many of them died: they did not accept defeat, because redcoats were never defeated. Too many people had traded on that simple notion in years past. They did so now with the army in the east.

Hervey wondered how many of those good companions he had known in Rangoon had since been stilled by the enemy's shot or the fever. He scarcely dared think of how Peto was faring, for he knew that gallant man would be everywhere his sailors faced danger, be it the enemy or the country. There would be so many widows' letters, or to other kin. And none of them would say that such and such a good servant of the King had died because other servants of the King had been careless of his life. But, in the end, the merchants of the Honourable Company would not need to bury their silver. The Burmans were no martial race. Their armies had been formed neither by the British, the Moghuls nor the French. Indeed, by what right did they begin a fight they could not win?

But it would be some time. Yesterday, Eyre Somervile had come, as he had every day since Hervey's return weak with fever, and the news from the east had been as dispiriting as might have been. General Campbell's force had fewer than three thousand effectives, and the flotilla was in a poor way too, with whole crews laid low by remittent fevers – even the bigger ships (*Larne* was so incapacitated she had had to be replaced by *Arachne*). There had been some successes, but Campbell was besieged still, by Nature and the Burmans. And now there was speculation that Maha Bundula himself, at the head of his army of Arakan, twice the strength of anything Campbell could muster, might soon be marching through the Irawadi's delta.

Well, he must put it all out of his mind. Today he was to dine with Somervile and Emma for the first time since leaving for Rangoon; Ledley, the regimental surgeon, had at last pronounced him fit (Hervey had pronounced himself fit more than a week ago). It was near six o'clock and his bearer would soon be here to supervise the team of bhistis who filled his bath with hot water. The surgeon had been most explicit in his warning against any chill, for he was advised that the fever was born of the malaria of the Rangoon marshes and could recur at any time, perhaps even in severer form.

Hervey took care to put on a good lawn shirt when he had bathed, and a linen coat, for as soon as the sun set he would otherwise feel the cool of the evening keenly. He took up his brushes and smiled as he picked the strands of black hair from them. One evening soon he would dine with his bibi here – whatever the rules said. But she dared not return this evening. He would go instead to her at the bibi khana beyond the civil lines towards the Chitpore road, where the rich Bengali merchants lived. It was a comfortable and private place. He liked it there. He was pleased he kept her properly.

Emma Somervile greeted him with a kiss to the lips. 'I never doubted you would be restored,' she said, smiling. 'But it has been many weeks, and you looked so fevered when last we visited.'

Hervey took a glass of champagne from the khitmagar and sat, as she bade him, beside her.

'Eyre will be here presently. There is an express boy come.'

'He is much occupied, I think. It must be the hardest thing to be so at odds with the Governor-General.'

Emma raised an eyebrow. 'It wears him more than I could have imagined. Oh, I do not mean the disagreements themselves, but the dismay at seeing so much going wrong when he had counselled against it from the start. And still Lord Amherst is not inclined to listen.'

Hervey frowned. 'There's a certain sort of man who would rather exhaust all his stock than admit to a wrong course and take a new one at half the cost. I fear there's many a grave that will be testimony to our Governor-General's obduracy. I'm only glad there are men such as Eyre who will expose the folly of it.'

Moments later Eyre Somervile entered the room with a look half triumphant and half exasperated. He dispensed with formal greetings. '*This* is just as I had expected – *worse*.' He waved a letter at them. 'Maha Bundula is now in Ava. Bagyidaw's recalled Prince Tharrawaddy and Bundula is to have command of the army they've been assembling these past three months.'

'Do you have any notion how large?' asked Hervey.

'Thirty thousand – over and above the same number back from Arakan.' Somervile consulted the letter again. 'Also, three hundred jingals, the Cassay Horse from Manipur – about a thousand of them – artillery on elephant-back . . .'

'What is a jingal?' asked Emma.

'A gun,' replied Hervey, turning to her. 'Very light – the

ball weighs less than a pound – but they tote them any-where. And very destructive they are too.'

'Campbell will be thrown out of Rangoon in very short order indeed,' added her husband.

'How do you come by the intelligence, Eyre?'

Somervile seemed rapt in thought.

'Eyre?'

'I'm sorry, my dear. I was thinking how much time we had, for the report says that Bundula boasted to Tharrawaddy he would feast in Rangoon in eight days. He could not, of course – not from the time of making the boast. The distance is too great in the best of weather. I suspect he meant eight days after once besieging the place.'

Emma stayed her questions for the time being.

Hervey looked uncertain. 'Unless, that is, Bundula were to engage Campbell piecemeal.'

'That is against the best precepts, is it not?'

'As a rule, but there would be advantage in bringing pressure to bear gently on Rangoon, for Campbell's so weakened that he might seek terms—'

Emma looked shocked. 'Do you mean to say that General Campbell could surrender?'

Hervey shook his head. 'I think it the last thing he would do. But Maha Bundula might not. The Burmans do not have a very high opinion of the Company.'

'Well,' said Somervile, making to turn. 'I must send to the commander-in-chief and to Amherst. They will surely now wish to reinforce Campbell's garrison. That, or order its withdrawal. You will excuse me for the moment.'

Hervey sat down again, taking a second glass of champagne.

'Do *you* know the source of his intelligence, Matthew?' asked Emma. 'Is it the same as before?'

'I imagine so,' he replied, cautiously. Somervile's best intelligence had come thence, and he knew of no other capable of yielding such precise and valuable information.

Not the girl herself – she had merely been the cause for the boundless gratitude of a father whose abducted daughter had been returned unsullied, an unexpected prize from Hervey's action against the war boats on the Chittagong three years before. But Somervile had played up Hervey's chivalry in the jungled hill tracts to great purpose – like Rama and Sita, he had described her rescue. Indeed, he considered himself to be an intriguer of the first water on account of it. And so a favourite of King Bagyidaw's had become a most willing collaborator with the Company. 'And very good intelligence it is, too. Though I fear that neither Campbell nor the commander-in-chief can make the best of it.'

'How do you mean?'

'I don't know what plans Paget has in hand to reinforce Rangoon, but if there are none it is almost certainly too late to do so. And what will Campbell do when he learns that an army twenty times his strength is bearing down on him? He has the flotilla's guns, of course, but they might not be in a position to intervene decisively. If he is so reduced in numbers through sickness as we hear, then he would be best advised to quit the place, to use the ships to take off his force before it is utterly destroyed.'

'He is not likely to do that, surely? You yourself said as much.'

'I said he would not surrender. But he was with Moore at Corunna. And so was Paget for that matter. He has seen good precedent, therefore.'

Emma suddenly looked worried. 'Matthew, what if the intelligence is false?'

Hervey raised his eyebrows, and nodded. 'Just so. It is highly favourable to the Burmans, that is for sure. And for that reason it must be regarded circumspectly. Campbell's quitting Rangoon on a false report would be a most sorry business indeed.'

'You will warn Eyre of this, Matthew?'

'He will not need my warning, but, yes, I will speak my mind.'

Emma was relieved. She had felt the perturbation of the past year very keenly. Lord Amherst had set his face very decidedly against her husband's opinion. Somervile was a relatively junior member of the presidency council, although he was the acknowledged authority on the country powers and their neighbours. But he was an interventionist. Or rather, he advocated military action to obtain conditions favourable to the Company; the action itself – as in the case of Ava – did not have to take the form of an offensive. And so he found himself frequently in contention with the Governor-General, who thought him contrary, one minute seeming to urge boldness in meddling in native affairs, and in the next seeming to recoil from it. Somervile confided much in his wife, but she knew he did not tell all. That was too often apparent in his countenance and disposition.

'What about the regiment, Matthew,' said Emma abruptly, if brightly. 'I've not seen much of them since Sir Ivo left for England.'

Hervey was pleased to oblige her, for although he could not give the best of reports, or the fullest, he would rather be speaking of the regiment now than contemplating the mournful situation in Rangoon. 'I think they are well. But there's little for them to do save guards and drill, says Serjeant-Major Armstrong. And I'm not sure Eustace Joynson is happy with the regiment's reins entirely in his hands.'

'How long shall he have them?'

'A full twelve months, less the two already gone.'

'I do wish it were not so long. We are in need of society here, and Lady Lankester will be a welcome increase. Do you know anything of her?'

'Her people are from Hertfordshire, Lankester's seat. Her father is Sir Delaval Rumsey. I have not met her but it is said she is a very handsome woman.'

'I knew Sir Delaval at one time,' said Emma, just as brightly as before. 'Rather, I knew Lady Rumsey. She was a kindly woman, and herself quite a beauty, and a wit too.'

'Then we should all be content. Did I say that poor Joynson is having trouble with his daughter again?'

'Indeed?'

'According to my lieutenant. Seems she's been a deal too wayward since first we arrived. The attentions of so many officers have sorely tested her senses, it would seem. I'm sure Joynson would wish you would take her in hand.'

Emma raised her eyebrows. 'I should not say it, but I have observed many times how it is the plainer girls whose senses are the least apt for testing.'

Hervey frowned again, but more playfully. 'Frances Joynson is not so *very* plain, Emma.'

Emma frowned, but more determinedly. 'I rather fancy that that is an acclimated opinion, Matthew.'

Hervey thought it indelicate, and unsafe, to proceed.

'In any case, her reputation has not been remarked on in the drawing rooms yet, so her behaviour cannot be so very bad.' Emma sipped at her champagne. 'Your name has been spoken of, however, Matthew.'

'Oh yes?' He intended to sound only the merest degree interested . . . curious.

'Lately, at the general's.'

Hervey simply raised an eyebrow and took another sip at his champagne.

'I fancy by the time Sir Ivo's bride is brought here it will be the talk of *every* drawing room.'

Hervey put his glass down, scarcely troubling now to hide his real sentiments. 'Emma, what is the matter with Calcutta? In Madras—'

'She visits, Matthew. That is what is the matter. And do not be angry with me because I tell you.'

He sighed. 'I am not angry with you, Emma. When I first

came to India, almost ten years ago, things were . . . I am just astonished at so much canting.'

Emma would not be drawn. 'And another thing, Matthew. You have refused all society with Bishop Heber.'

Hervey frowned impatiently and held out his glass to the khitmagar. 'Please do not think I include Heber in my strictures, Emma. He is a good man from all I hear. But I do not feel the need of a bishop's society.'

'He only presses his claim on your acquaintance because your Mr Keble wrote to him.'

'Mr Keble presumes a deal too much.'

'Oh, Matthew!'

She touched a nerve, but he was not minded to give in. 'I sometimes think that Mr Keble believes the prospect from his parsonage window is the only one in the world.'

She frowned again. 'And you have seen so much more of the world!'

'Yes; I have.'

Emma sighed deeply. Had she not known him better it might have been a sigh of despair. Instead it was the mildly rebuking but tolerant sigh that his sister might have breathed. 'Then I should be careful not to see excess of it, Matthew.'

Eyre Somervile returned, to Hervey's relief. 'Well, it is done. I have sent my opinion to both Amherst and Paget. Doubtless they'll think it unreliable. But nothing I've sent them to date has been other than borne out by events. Paget's no fool. He may be a little too ready to defer to Amherst, but he's no fool.'

'You are perfectly certain of your intelligence?' Hervey held his gaze until an answer came.

Somervile inclined his head very slightly. 'There is, of course, the possibility that it was sent to me with but one object. In which case I might well precipitate an evacuation of Rangoon for no reason. That is what you allude to, I imagine? This I have laid out in my memoranda to Amherst and Paget. The veracity of the report is unknowable, unless some corroboration is received, but the *possibility* of it is certain, and in consequence the peril of Campbell's force. One way or another, it is imperative to act. *That* is the material point.'

Hervey glanced at Emma, and smiled. 'Somervile, for once I do not fret at not marching towards the sound of the guns. I fear it will be a wretched business either way. Campbell is a brave man, but I give it as my opinion that he has no place in command of a campaign such as this. And I for one am done with such men.'

Emma looked startled, but her husband had heard this opinion often enough these past two months. 'My dear,' he said, half smiling and taking a glass from the khitmagar. 'You must know that we have a dinner companion of very refractory military disposition. I do have a notion that he believes all between him and the Duke of Wellington to be but deadwood.'

Hervey frowned. But as things stood, he felt little inclination to deny it.

'Come, let us eat, then,' said Somervile, content in the knowledge that there was no more a man in his position could do for the moment. 'I would hear of how things are with the regiment.'

Emma rose.

Hervey followed, though not so nimbly as once he might. 'Does it matter very much how things are? Whatever course Campbell chooses, there's no place for cavalry in it.'

'Hah!' Somervile stepped aside to let Emma lead them to the dining room. 'You make the same mistake as those in council who seem capable of looking in only one direction at a time. In India, Hervey, as you must surely know, one must be Janus-like with regard to whence the next blow shall come. Let me tell you what has been happening among the country powers while our eyes have been diverted eastwards . . .'

* * *

Next morning, Hervey rode out for the first time since returning to Calcutta. Private Johnson had brought Gilbert to his bungalow just before dawn, as Hervey took his *chota hazree* – sweet tea and figs. He had never, as a rule, taken anything but tea before morning exercise, even in the cold season, but he had felt weaker than he supposed he would on rising. He cursed the time it was taking for him to regain his full strength. The shoulder had, to all appearances, knitted together well enough, but the fever had left him like a woman in the first gravid months – dizzy, puking, listless. It had come and gone, and each time seemed worse, but in the last weeks he had felt himself recovering his proper spirits with each day. It was just the mornings, now, that reminded him there was still a course to run.

'Is tha sure tha's all right, sir?' enquired Johnson, watching him, curious.

Gilbert's manners were not as he would have wanted, and Hervey seemed unable to stop the jogging.

'To tell the truth, Johnson, I'd as soon be listening to one of the chaplain's sermons.'

'*That* bad, sir.'

'Perhaps not. But it can't go on.' He tried once more to sit easy, to persuade the gelding to get off its toes, but it made no difference. 'What have you been doing with him all these months?'

'Swap 'orses, sir?'

'Don't be impertinent.'

Johnson smiled. Ten years they had been together now – more, almost eleven – longer than any officer and groom in the Sixth, or in memory indeed. He had no pleasure in his captain's infirmity, but he could at least take satisfaction in the tables being turned just a little. ''As tha 'eard t'RSM's to be wed?'

The dodge worked. Hervey looked astonished. 'You would as well persuade me that the sar'nt-major is to take

125

the cloth.' He flicked his long schooling whip at Gilbert's quarters in mounting exasperation.

There was little reason why he should believe it. Mr Lincoln had been regimental serjeant-major for fifteen years. It was generally imagined that he was the senior in the whole of the cavalry. Why should he suddenly feel the need of a wife? Except that Johnson's canteen intelligence was almost invariably accurate . . .

'I'd put any money on it, sir.'

'Who is she?' demanded Hervey, sounding almost vexed.

'Widder o' one o' t'Footy's quartermasters.'

Hervey, for all his nausea and discomposure, managed an approving smile. 'She must be a redoubtable woman. How is it known? Has there been any announcement?'

Johnson became circumspect; there were canteen confidences to safeguard. 'Mr Lincoln saw Major Joynson yesterday an' asked 'is leave to marry.'

Hervey smiled again. A clerk with an ear to the door, and a thirst to be quenched by selling tattle in the wet canteen. Things hadn't changed. Not that Johnson would have paid for his information. Hervey had learned long ago that Johnson received word from many a source because the canteen attributed to him considerable powers of prophecy and intercession. 'What a tamasha that will be, then. And colonel and RSM wed in the same year.' Then he frowned. 'Oh, I do hope this doesn't mean Mr Lincoln intends his discharge.'

It was a curious thing, and Hervey knew as well as the next man, and better than most, that 'new blood' was as necessary in the officers and senior ranks of a cavalry regiment as it was in its horses. And yet with Mr Lincoln it was different. It was scarcely conceivable that there could be any want in the performance of his duties, and his grey hairs served only to add distinction to his appearance. In any case, the RSM would yield to no one in the jumping lane at the end of a field day. To many, indeed, Mr Lincoln *was* the regiment. No one in the Sixth had served longer, though his actual record of service, with its attestation date, had been conveniently lost years ago.

'I bet that's not what Serjeant-Major Deedes thinks,' said Johnson, screwing up his face.

That was the problem. There could only be the one crown, and for as long as the admirable Lincoln wore it above his stripes no other could. Deedes was next in seniority, and had been for five years or more, and behind him were others wondering if the crown would ever be theirs to wear before they were obliged to leave the colours. One of those, indeed, was Armstrong. Hervey had never given it much thought before. Could he imagine Geordie Armstrong filling Lincoln's boots? It was pointless his making any comparison, for so different were the two men. Except, perhaps, that Armstrong's formation had been at Lincoln's hands as much as anyone's.

There was, of course, one man who would by now have been the acknowledged heir. Serjeant Strange could have worn the crown, a worthy successor in every respect, except that by now another regiment might have made a claim on him, or even a field commission might have come his way. It was nigh on ten years ago, in a corner of the battlefield at Waterloo, that Strange had demonstrated his singular worth – and had lost his life doing so. Hervey still thought about that day, and his own part in Strange's fall. He asked himself the same questions, and the answers were always as uncertain.

'Still, dead men's boots are a sight easier to come by 'ere than at 'ome,' chirped Johnson. He did not actually nod to the garrison cemetery, and its growing regimental plot, but the timing of their passing could not have been more apt.

'For heaven's sake, Johnson, have a little compassion!'

Johnson mistook Hervey's meaning. 'Sorry sir, I didn't mean as I thought *tha* were—'

'Oh, thank you. You'll be sure to let me know when the canteen shortens the odds on *my* getting to the end of this posting, won't you?'

Johnson looked only very slightly abashed.

'Come then,' said Hervey, sighing. 'Let's shorten the reins instead and see what we can do.'

Gilbert broke into a trot a fraction before the aids applied, leaving Hervey to curse his own lack of handiness as well as his horse's. It was going to be a long business, this getting back to condition.

When they returned to the bungalow the best part of an hour later, for he had wanted to ride right out of the lines onto the plain, Hervey slid from the saddle in better spirits and health, and said that he would attend morning stables. Then he went inside for *hazree* and an hour with his pen. There was correspondence long overdue and he meant to make a start today, just as he intended taking back the charge of his troop.

On his desk were five letters. Two were from Horningsham, one from Elizabeth, the other from his father. They had been written a fortnight apart but had arrived together. That from his father contained the same warm paternal sentiment as that sent to Shrewsbury when first he had gone up, on his fourteenth birthday. Indeed, it was in essence the same letter, except for a line or two on diocesan affairs (which hitherto Archdeacon Hervey had rarely mentioned) and the news that his monograph on Archbishop Laud was at last nearing completion.

The letter from Elizabeth was not greatly longer but contained altogether more information – about the village, their part of Wiltshire, the country as a whole (garnered, she admitted, from the newspapers), about their parents and relatives, and last, but at greatest length, about his daughter. Georgiana was six months older than when Elizabeth had last written, and it seemed she was a favourite at both

Longleat and the vicarage. She showed all the signs of a fine intelligence, was able to read, and she could sit a pony well. She laughed a great deal. It was a letter to reassure an absent father that he should have no concerns for the well-being of his child. And yet this agreeable report had the effect of making Hervey want to be with his daughter as keenly as would an unhappy one, for Georgiana was Henrietta's offspring.

He laid the letter to one side. It would be as difficult to begin a reply to his sister's as to his father's, if for wholly different reasons. He picked up the third, from John Keble. He imagined it written with that same prospect before the writer against which he had inveighed the evening before at the Somerviles. It was a letter composed in a Gloucestershire curate's house, an untroubled place where dreams could be dreamed, a letter full of rebuttals of this divine and that, with a lengthy description of the work he was jointly embarked on with Hervey's father – a charge to the clergy of the archdeaconry of Sarum. There was the startling revelation that Keble had been asked if he would go to the West Indies, as archdeacon of Barbados no less; and the wholly unsurprising addendum that he had declined. The letter concluded with an evidently pained enquiry into whether or not Hervey had yet had occasion to discourse with Bishop Heber, it being more than a year since that prelate had been enthroned. It was, indeed, so worthy a letter that Hervey felt it required a peculiar state of grace before any response could be attempted. He laid it down and picked up the fourth.

He already knew its contents. Yet even as he began rereading a third or fourth time, it had its effect. The hand was the freest of the four, the sentiment likewise. What it was to have a female of the likes of Lady Katherine Greville bestowing her time on him. How diverting seemed the gossip that had formerly repulsed him so. How fondly, now, he remembered their brief company, and her uninhibited pleasure in it – and how lame his own response had been.

But it had been different then – too close to events, his mind encumbered by all sorts of notions and doubts. Things were not the same now. India, for all her heat, had moistened that dried-up interior of his. First she had given him back his very being as a soldier. It did not matter that in reality the affair of the headwaters of the Karnaphuli had been un-honoured by Calcutta, or that the campaign he had so recently left in a dhoolie was the re-creation of that muddle in the Low Countries a quarter of a century before. India was a stage on which the soldier could expound his art, learn stratagems and devices unheard of at home, and above all might have that most prized thing – the true exercise of command. Yes, Hervey was angry with Major-General Sir Archibald Campbell and the campaign in Ava; but it and the other diversions of this singular country made him feel as alive as ever he could remember.

He took a sheet of paper from the drawer and picked up his pen. Perhaps as little as a year ago he would have begun his replies in the strict order of filial duty, then sibling love, then respectfulness for the cloth, and then . . . But this morning he began, 'Dear Lady Katherine'. An hour or so later, having written rather more than usual to this wife of an absentee husband, and likewise having returned her teasing and toying in fuller measure, he put on cantonment dress – the looser-fitting cotton jacket that the Sixth had adopted soon after arriving, with light cotton overalls and forage cap – and walked to the regimental headquarters to report himself back at duty.

Major Joynson heard him through the open door of his office and came at once into the adjutant's room to add his salutation. 'And a word with you as soon as you are done here,' he added, in a manner that Hervey could not quite determine as encouraging or otherwise.

He wanted to appear neither apprehensive nor indifferent, and so after ten minutes with the adjutant, in which he was apprised of the comings and goings of his troop, and its

130

defaulters, Hervey signed the orders book and then repaired to the major's office.

Since the death of his wife, an invalid to laudanum, and the military demise of Lord Towcester, Eustace Joynson had grown steadily in stature and affection in the regiment. His reputation for painstaking administration had always been high, but the demands made on him by his late wife had sapped his vigour, and Towcester's martinet command had all but eviscerated him. Now, the sick headaches that had removed him from duty with monotonous regularity had all but gone, and he enjoyed many a mess night where before he had found them a sore trial. However, he did not feel himself entirely a match for the decision before him now. And there were none, perhaps, who would blame him, for the decision was one of the utmost importance to every man in the Sixth.

'Hervey, close the door and take a seat. Have you had coffee? Would you like a little Madeira? No? Perhaps a shade early. I never do, not before eleven. Have you heard that Mr Lincoln's to marry?'

Hervey sat in a tub-chair that creaked with the slightest move of a muscle. 'I have. Joyous news.'

'You think so? Possibly, I suppose . . . yes.'

'Is there some objection to the lady?'

'Oh no. No, indeed not. She is a very respectable woman; very highly regarded by the light infantry's colonel. Lincoln's calling on him this very morning.'

'Then why do you sound uncertain?'

'Because Marsh is to send in his papers. Says he wants to spend his declining days in Ipswich rather than be quarter-master here.'

'Singular!'

Joynson smiled. 'A man who prefers Ipswich to Calcutta might rightly be said to have begun his decline already. I could not say that even the worst of the stink here would drive me to such a decision.'

Hervey nodded, returning the smile, a sort of mock grimace. 'Ipswich. Indeed no.'

'But you will imagine that there must be a replacement quartermaster.'

'And a replacement for the replacement.'

'Exactly so. I am excessively pleased that Lincoln shall join us at last in the mess. Indeed, it is long overdue. But the pleasure is dulled by the thought of having to determine his own succession.'

The word was well chosen. Lincoln's had been a long reign by any standard. Hervey wondered what the RSM himself thought of relinquishing the crown. 'It should be Deedes, by rights. Is there any serious objection? It has always been seniority tempered by rejection.'

Joynson took off his glasses and polished them with a silk cloth. 'I've been disappointed with Deedes these past twelve months. There's a want of vigour. I dare say that he'll make no mistakes, but if we're to have him for any time then I fear he'll begin to drop the bit. Rose thinks so too.'

Hervey raised an eyebrow. 'Deuced tricky superseding Deedes. He'll fall right away and become a malcontent, no doubt. And the rest of his mess will be ill at ease if they perceive no very good reason for it. Who is next in seniority? Harrison?'

'Telfer.'

'Oh dear.'

'Precisely. Who would *you* want?'

'Hairsine.'

'Exactly.'

Hervey frowned. 'They've all been too long in the rank, even Hairsine. In that respect the war brought them on too quickly. I can remember Hairsine the night we had word of the surrender, at Toulouse. He was orderly serjeant-major. It was *ten years* ago.'

'Deedes's time will be up in a couple of years in the normal course of things. And Harrison's not much later. I suppose we could take a chance on him, and Hairsine could bide his time a while longer.'

'There'll be more talk of dead men's boots. But it wouldn't do any more harm, I suppose. What would Sir Ivo want to do?'

'Strange to say, we never spoke of it. Marsh looked the last man to give up so cosy a billet as quartermaster.'

Hervey supposed it an apt description of quartermaster in a station such as Calcutta. 'Can he not be persuaded to remain in post a little longer?'

Joynson shook his head. 'He's determined to leave by October – to have the spring in Ipswich, he says. And in any case, all we should have is six months of jockeying and wagering and heaven knows what else. All very unedifying. No, it's a decision I shall have to take myself, and be content with the notion that it will not be possible to make the right one.'

Hervey smiled again. Joynson knew his pack. The only decision that had the remotest possibility of being acknowledged the right one was that made by the commanding officer himself. The major might carry the horn this season, but he was not the master. 'Anything else?'

Joynson hesitated. 'Are you sure you won't have some Madeira?'

'Thank you, no. In truth, I think my gut ought still to be listed sick at present.'

'I list mine sick one week in every month, and feel the better for it. Coffee then?'

'Yes, coffee.'

Joynson called for his bearer to bring two cups. 'What do you make of Barrow?'

It seemed a strange turn in the conversation. Hervey looked wary.

'If he has any he could call a friend it would be you, I think,' said Joynson, polishing his glasses again.

'I think it would be fairer to the three of us if you first

133

said why you asked, sir,' replied Hervey. 'Especially since I have been absent for the best part of the year.' And he always tried that much harder with Barrow, for Barrow was an officer from the ranks – the ranks of another regiment, indeed – and Hervey had not cared for him to begin with. Not that Barrow had seemed to want to help himself in terms of popularity with his new-found fellow officers.

Joynson nodded. 'You're right. It may come to nothing. Let's hope so. But I've had word – it doesn't matter where from; it's not the regiment – that he's on the take with his remount fund.'

Hervey smiled. 'I saw some of his remounts this morning. How he's managed to find that quality *and* take a backhand glass I can't imagine!'

'I thought that too only yesterday when his troop paraded for escort. However, the accusation comes from one of the dealers, it seems.'

'What are you going to do?'

'I don't know. I was only apprised of it yesterday. The next board of officers isn't for another six months. I can't very well roist his accounts about meanwhile without good cause. We can't jump to every bazaar-wallah who complains of *backshee*. I'm inclined to have the dealer arrested if he won't make a proper deposition.'

'What do you want me to do?'

Joynson looked uncertain. 'Could you think it of Barrow?'

'Why should I think it any more or any less of Barrow than of the others?'

'You know very well why.'

'So Barrow's coming from the ranks puts him more in the way of temptation?'

'Don't sport with me, Hervey. If it were Hugh Rose we'd never hear the charge out.'

Hervey frowned. 'I think that if we are making private means the touchstone then we would be obliged to enquire whether Rose's fortune had disappeared.'

'You are not being of much assistance.'

The bearer brought their coffee. Hervey took his and began stirring the strong black liquid. 'I'll keep an ear cocked,' he said when the man had gone.

'Thank you.' The major took his coffee and heaped sugar into the cup.

Hervey thought he would try to end the line of questioning. 'How is Frances? I haven't seen her in months.' He meant it not unkindly. No regimental officer could be an island when it came to domestic troubles, and it was as well to know if there were any vexations in that respect.

Joynson sighed, heavily. 'I have been on the point of speaking to the colonel of the Thirteenth, and several of the Company's, many times these past six months. I feel they have as much responsibility in allowing her to expose herself in so frequent a way. I am very happy that she has such diversions as these levees and balls, but . . .'

Hervey nodded.

'She sorely misses a mother. She always has.'

Hervey felt the footsteps over his grave.

'Are you quite well, Hervey?' asked Joynson, narrowing his eyes.

'Of course, sir. Perfectly well. Very well indeed.'

Poor Joynson. His nickname had been 'Daddy' for the short time he had had a troop in the Peninsula. He had his weaknesses, and he knew them, but in intention he had served his country as well as anyone, and he had a true attachment to his regiment. Hervey thought it most unjust that his standing should be risked by a silly daughter.

'I think it would be ill to deny her any society properly ordered. Perhaps she might attach herself to some matron here?' It was as well as he could manage, for he had little enough experience to draw on.

They sat awhile, talking of how things were going in the east, and of what the regiment might do in the autumn by way of field days. At length Hervey rose to take his leave so as to catch his troop at morning stables.

'Very well, Hervey,' said Joynson, a little brighter. 'It's good to have you back again. Come and dine with us soon.'

'I should like that, sir. Thank you.' He put on his forage cap, saluted, then left the regimental headquarters pondering the peculiar trust that Joynson had shown. He liked the intimacy of the personal confidences, even if they had momentarily reminded him of his own situation. And in respect of the succession of serjeant-majors, it was good to be assured periodically of one's own stake in the regiment.

E Troop's stables stood at the end of the single line of back-to-back standing stalls that stretched for three hundred yards beyond the regimental maidan. They were brick-built and whitewashed, with a good thatch and khus-khus tatties that extended from the joists to about the chest height of a dragoon. In the summer, therefore, the troop-horses stood in shade, and the doused tatties and punkahs provided some relief in the otherwise still, oven-hot air, while in the monsoon season and the winter the animals were protected from rain and wind, be it hot or cold. At the end of each troop block was the stabling for the officers' chargers, six loose boxes in line with a separate store for saddlery and tackling.

At nine o'clock of a morning at this time of year, early October, the lines were all activity. The rains were receding, and the regiment had begun its cool-weather routine. Horses had been fed two hours before and the dragoons had breakfasted. It was a hearty meal, a dragoon's breakfast, just right for a morning's work: half a pound of bread, the same of beef, and plenty of coffee. Hervey wondered if he would be able to keep such a meal down ever again. But a dragoon needed his beef for such a morning – the fetching and carrying, the brushing and strapping, for there was only so much the native grass-cutters were allowed to do. The men clattered about the brick-laid floor in their clogs and stable dress like workers in a cotton mill, but ten times as lively. At nine-thirty the trumpeter would sound 'boot and saddle', and the serjeants would check every last buckle and strap. And many a hapless dragoon who had thought the shine on his leather more than adequate as he polished by lamplight would find that the Indian sun was a merciless revealer of insufficiency. And then he might think for a moment, but only a moment, that he might prefer other employment.

For the time being, however, they were still at work with brush and curry-comb. It was just that bit easier while horses had their summer coats, but there was sweat on every dragoon's brow nevertheless. It was not a time for shouted commands, rather of careful observance of standing orders and the accumulated experience of the corporals. Above all it was not a time for officers. It was the serjeant-major's hour. It was he, and his trusted NCOs, who turned out the troop to perfection – both horses and men. Then the officers led them in the practice of war, real or imagined. And the serjeant-major did not expect supervision.

Hervey's appearance in the lines this morning was therefore doubly unusual. He had not even sent word to Myles Vanneck, his lieutenant, that he was reporting himself fit for duty, and there was at once a buzz as the news passed from stall to stall. The dragoons nearest the end stood to attention as others gawped or tried to steal a look. Hervey felt as if he were some ghost. 'Carry on, Harkness,' he said, nodding and smiling as he began walking the line of stalls.

Private Harkness, the broadest of shoulders making his trooper look short-backed, returned the smile confidently.

Another dragoon came to attention as Hervey reached his stall.

'Carry on, Hicks. How is your leg now?'

Private Hicks turned red. His leg had been mended for all of three years, but still his nickname in the troop was Giles, 'the cripple'. 'Very good, sir, thank you, sir.'

The next man had neither brush nor comb in his hand, and he therefore saluted.

Hervey smiled again. Beneath the watering cap were thick black curls, unmistakable. 'Good morning, French. What is the news from Wales?'

'Agreeable, I think, sir. My father has taken another living, and my brother is to be ordained too.' The voice was not perhaps so differently cast from the other recruits' as first it had seemed on joining; but it was still the voice of a man of some education.

The ringing of spurs made Hervey turn.

'Good morning, sor!'

Hervey smiled the more – an indulgent sort of smile. 'Corporal McCarthy!'

'It's good to see you on your feet again, sor. And back in time for all the drill, too.'

'Indeed, indeed.' Yes, he had timed his return well – as if he had had any say in it.

'Go and fetch the sar'nt-major, Rudd,' said McCarthy, addressing the next stall.

Hervey looked across keenly; he had not noticed Private Rudd, and he watched with satisfaction as he doubled away, for he had saved the boy from a cloying mother and the dubious occupation of milliner. Rudd ought to be corporal soon: if only there were more *places*.

He carried on down the line, Corporal McCarthy by his side. 'How is your section then, on the whole?'

'Well, sor; *very* well. Not a horse lame nor a man sick.'

Hervey nodded appreciatively. It was as well at the beginning of what they called here the unhealthy season.

Next he stopped by Private Needham's stall. Needham's hair almost covered the stub of his right ear, but the old wound was vivid enough. Hervey recalled the bloody sight when the Burman tulwar had sliced the flesh away. Needham stood to attention now with brush and comb clasped in each hand by his side, as fit as the day Hervey had enlisted him on Warminster Common, but he did not smile.

'Good morning, Needham. How is your mare?'

Hervey chose well. Needham and his mare were ever closer by the day. 'She's doing a treat, sir. She won best turnout last week.'

'A credit to you,' said Hervey, nodding approval. And he would say no more for the time being, for they had buried Needham's best friend, Private Spreadbury, barely a week ago, and there were now but two of the original 'Warminster pals' left.

How well the pals had served him, thought Hervey. That day, five years ago, when he had defied all his instincts and gone to Warminster Common to look for recruits – it had repaid his efforts no end. Indeed, would he be alive this day had he not done so? For Wainwright was first of the pals. He smiled at the thought of what the King's shilling could buy – and what the King's uniform could do for a man in return. He hoped he would live long enough to see four chevrons on Wainwright's sleeve.

'Good morning, Captain Hervey sir!'

The voice filled the stables. There was no need for Hervey to turn to see whose it was. 'Good morning, Sar'nt-Major!' he replied, as cheerily as he had been hailed.

'Not a horse off the road, sir, nor a man neither.'

Troop Serjeant-Major Armstrong, collier-turned-cavalryman – the only horse he had seen before enlisting was pulling a coal tub; but what a source of strength, always, was that voice of the Tyne. Hervey's thoughts were at once of Sahagun, Corunna, Albuhera, and a dozen other places where Armstrong's voice had done its work: cursing, checking, cajoling. To his mind, Armstrong *was* the Sixth, as much as was Lincoln (and, God rest his soul, as Strange had been). Without him the regiment could surely never be the same – or as good?

'Corporal McCarthy tells me so. Very good husbandry,

139

Sar'nt-Major.' It was, perhaps, fortunate that Hervey was enquiring this day and not a week before. That the last man sick, poor Spreadbury, had died was not something to be reflected in the day's parade state. In their five or so years in Calcutta E Troop had lost eighteen men to the agues and fevers that plagued the cantonments every season. And before he had left for Rangoon the sick rate had been three men in ten. The other troops had fared no better, but that was little consolation to mess mates – nor to Hervey and Armstrong whose concern it was to maintain a decent muster. But no men sick this morning – not a bad way to begin command again.

'The vet'in'ry's round the other side, sir, if you want me to tell him you're here. Just doing his rounds, that is. No problems.'

'Just say not to leave before I'm able to have a word.'

Armstrong nodded to Rudd, who cut away smartly.

They advanced another stall. 'A new face, I perceive.'

The dragoon stood at attention, as Needham before him, with brush and curry-comb in either hand. But his look was a touch anxious rather than melancholy.

'Private Toyne, sir,' said Armstrong. 'Joined last month.'

Hervey looked him up and down – a well-made youth, fresh-faced and clean. 'Where are you from, Toyne?'

'Appleby, sir,' in a voice not unlike the serjeant-major's.

But Hervey was none the wiser.

'Westmorland, sir,' explained Armstrong. Long years had taught him that officers spoke of counties, not places.

Hervey knew there were hills in Westmorland, but that was about all. 'What brought you to the Sixth then?'

'My cousin is in the Fifty-fifth, sir, and 'e took me to enlist. But I said I wanted to work with 'orses, and so the Fifty-fifth let me change.'

'Did they, indeed? That was very generous of them.' And most unusual, too. No doubt the recruiting serjeant had sworn blind that the Fifty-fifth were mounted on the best bloods – and more besides if it would secure another man.

'Well, sir, I had to pay a bit of money.'

'A recruit *buying* into the cavalry. Now there's a thing!'

Toyne would not understand the humour just yet, but Armstrong smiled pityingly. 'There's not much for company but sheep up there, sir. He's made a good start, though. Sits well.'

Hervey nodded to show his appreciation. 'You worked with horses in Appleby then?'

'Yes sir. I used to help with the fair, sir.'

'Fair?'

'Yes sir. There's an 'orse fair twice a year. People comes from all over to buy.'

Hervey nodded again. 'Well, I'm pleased to have you in my troop. Carry on.'

Toyne turned as red as Hicks had done.

'A good 'un,' said Armstrong, voice lowered, as they stepped off. 'A real liking for horses. He'll make a good groom in his turn.'

Hervey took note. It was difficult not to when a man had parted with money in order to be with horses.

At the other stalls it was reunion rather than introduction – and sometimes banter. Hervey, his spirits already lifted, was content, for here were a confident troop, who thought themselves a cut above the others since the affair at the river three years before. None of the other troops had so much as chased a dacoit, let alone bloodied a sabre, and a man who had not cut or thrust – or even fired carbine or pistol in anger – could hardly think himself a proper dragoon. For sure, it was the veterans of Waterloo who were honoured above all others in the wet canteen. Not with exaggerated reverence, but with the nodding respect that they had seen something never to be seen again, and were therefore possessed of certain insights and certain rights. And sometimes an E Troop man who had overreached himself in the canteen on the business of fighting would be brought up sharply by a Waterloo hand and reminded that the affair at the river, sharp though it had been, could never compare with that day in June. But an E Troop man stood in the veterans' respect nevertheless.

It was no longer true perhaps that the army divided into two parts – those who had been at Waterloo and those who had not – but the army was just as divided in its opinion of the future. It was true, certainly, that no officer believed in his heart there would be a battle the like of Waterloo again; never so many men in the field at once, never so great a number of guns. And – worst of all for those of Hervey's calling – never again so many cavalry manoeuvring to decisive effect. No, not even in India. What, therefore, would be their fate? Was it to be as mere spectators, from afar even, as in Burma – a pretty corps of escorts, in uniforms more and more elaborate and less and less serviceable? Or would they just become a corps of skirmishers, little better than Pandours and Croats?

Hervey had his opinions. They were formed in the Peninsula, confirmed at Waterloo and proven often enough these past three years. Perhaps he would write of them – write a book – as Peto had suggested. Many would sneer at his doing so of course, but he didn't care; not any longer.

'Good morning, Captain Hervey,' said the veterinary surgeon.

'Ah, David – good morning.'

David Sledge was the only officer habitually called by his Christian name, from colonel to cornet. The veterinary surgeon stood in a curious position regarding rank and seniority, and the Sixth had come to an admirable working arrangement.

'You wanted to see me?'

'No, not especially. Only to say that I am returned to duty. I gather I have a fit troop?'

Armstrong took his leave. There were things he would

attend to with Serjeant Collins: 'Them gram-grinders, sir. Still not sized off.'

Hervey nodded, then turned to Sledge again. 'It says a good deal for Armstrong, that parade state.'

'Yes, very satisfactory,' said Sledge, checking his pocket-book. 'Not a cough nor a warm leg in the stables these past six weeks. And I take my hat off to Brennan too.'

Hervey had long been convinced that E Troop had the best farrier. And so much steadier was Brennan these days with a fellow countryman in McCarthy to share tobacco and grog with (and a fellow with stripes to boot). 'I shall tell him. But he's had light work in respect of numbers, I see – a good dozen short. Do you know what are the remount arrangements?'

The purchase of remounts was not the business of the veterinary surgeon, but he had an obvious interest. 'Nothing's coming from the Company studs this year, apparently, so it's all down to dealers. When you're ready to look I'll come with you if you'd like. We've kept the lines free of infection all year and I shouldn't want anything brought in on approval.'

Hervey smiled. 'David, I should value your opinion on more than just the animal's health. But not for a day or so, I think – unless you say others will be looking too. I'll ask the RM as well.'

Sledge looked pained. 'Broad's not been in best sorts of late. Ledley's had to dose him a good deal.'

'Fever?'

Sledge still looked pained. 'N-o-o.'

'Well, I hope whatever is the cause he will not be in-disposed long. I've seen no better man with remounts.'

'I shall be seeing him later. I will pass on your regard.'

Hervey scowled. 'Come, David; you are not telling me all.'

Sledge looked relieved. 'To be explicit, it's a case for mercury and nitrate.'

'Oh God,' groaned Hervey. 'But what of *Annie* Broad? Has she gone home or something?'

Sledge raised his eyebrows. 'I should ask Rose.'

'What?'

'Been drawing his yard there, it seems. Better not speak of it here.'

Hervey shook his head slowly. 'Is it much talked about?'

'What – the mercury or Rose?'

'Both.'

'Neither generally, but the mercury's out in the ranks, I think. The Rose business Broad himself told me. But not here, Hervey. Can you come to my dispense later?'

Hervey finished his tour of the horse lines alone, then went to the troop office, where he found Myles Vanneck and his new cornet, Green.

'Good morning, Hervey!' said Vanneck, and with evident pleasure – even though his captain's return meant he would no longer have charge of things.

Hervey had found it easy leaving the troop in his lieutenant's hands. It was, after all, what was intended by the name of that rank. But in Myles Vanneck he had especial trust, as much as he had known in Seton Canning, even. Vanneck had been with the Sixth scarcely five years, but he had taken to command with the greatest of ease – the same ease, indeed, as that of his elder brother in the Eighteenth, whom Hervey had known in the Peninsula. And Vanneck had been lucky, too, for the means to buy a lieutenancy when the time came had been but a trifle to him at 'India rates', though when it was his turn for a captaincy the regiment would, for sure, be back in England and he would thereby have to pay well over price. Not that that should present the Honourable Myles Vanneck with too much difficulty, however: Lord Huntingfield's sons did not go in want of anything. And it was one of the reasons that Hervey so liked him, for he could easily have bought into a home regiment and enjoyed the pleasures of London or Brighton rather than the dust and heat, and the doubtful society of Calcutta. And, of course, the young *Cornet* Vanneck had comported himself so admirably in the affair of the river. Blue blood, and not afraid to shed it – it was hardly surprising the men regarded him.

Hervey smiled and took off his cap.

'This is Cornet Green.'

Hervey held out his hand, which the cornet took a shade hesitantly.

'How d'you do, sir,' said Green.

The cavalryman's *coup d'œil* was not always faithful when it came to the man rather than the situation. That much Hervey would freely acknowledge. But Green was not of the usual stamp: that much was impossible not to observe. He looked ungainly, a touch heavy-limbed to be a man at home in the saddle. And his features were a deal less fine than the subalterns prided themselves on. In the few words of his salutation he revealed that he came from the north of England (although that in itself said nothing, for the proud and independent gentry of the northern counties had provided many a son to the regiment during the war). But there was just something . . . *No*, thought Hervey; here indeed was a queer card.

'When did you come?' he asked, with deliberate kindness.

'Three months ago, sir.'

'Did you come via the depot?'

'No, sir.'

Nothing more volunteered than the precise answer – this was going to be heavy.

Vanneck sought to help. 'He has bought two fine chargers, I might say. One of them was that bay of Williams's in the bodyguard.'

Hervey nodded. 'I much approve. I had a mind to buy him myself if ever he came up.'

'Thank you, sir.'

Green's hair was sticking up by his right temple, like a duck's tuft. Hervey found himself staring at it.

Vanneck kept trying. 'Green was just about to go to the adjutant. He's picket-officer today.'

'So I see,' said Hervey, glancing at the cornet's review order.

Green's tunic, and all, looked in themselves immaculate, but even Mr Gieve's best efforts could not make a military coat hang well on a dumpling.

'Very good, Green,' said Hervey, trying hard not to sound dismayed. 'We'll speak at length tomorrow when your duties are done.'

Cornet Green coloured a little, put on his shako (askew, but Hervey thought best to say nothing – the adjutant would correct it soon enough), saluted and took his leave.

When he had gone, Hervey sat down and looked at Vanneck quizzically.

Vanneck sighed. 'I know. But he means well. The others have given him quite a rousting, though. His nickname's "grocer".'

'Green—, I suppose?'

Vanneck nodded. 'That, and his father's a tea merchant, in Lincolnshire.' He paused, then added, 'In Stamford,' as if that fact might be of some use.

Hervey smiled ruefully. 'Evidently they drink a lot of tea in Stamford if he can afford Williams's bay.'

'Oh, he's not short of money. On the contrary. The trouble is his ambition is rather in advance of his capability. He's yet to pass out of riding school.'

'Indeed?'

'I did tell him that he might buy a more tractable charger to begin with, but he seemed keen to make a splash.'

'Poor fellow.'

'Yes. And the RM's been sick the while, so the rough-riders have had their fun with him, I'm afraid.'

Hervey laid his cap and whip on the table. 'Can't you help at all, Myles?'

'I'm doing just that, Hervey. I take him out beyond the syces' huts late of an afternoon, where there's no one to see. But I'm not sure he has the hands or legs for it, and I'm pretty sure he hasn't the head.'

'Oh dear. And the drill season about to start.'

'Quite. I'm afraid the dragoons have a poor opinion of him already. He's too stiff about the place.'

'It's hardly surprising from what you tell me. But there have been stiff-necks before; he can overcome that in time. You will keep at him, Myles?'

Vanneck sighed. 'Yes, Hervey. Of course I will. But the others have no such duty as they see it. The trouble is, he has no conversation – and seemingly no interests. At mess the other night even the chaplain gave up on him, and then he fell off his chair quite stupefied.'

'The chaplain?'

'No, Green.'

Hervey smiled again. 'Well, there at least is sign of a kindred spirit, is there not?'

Vanneck smiled too. 'You would think so, but to hear them you'd imagine the cornets had become temperance Methodists.'

'Seems a hopeless case then.'

But Vanneck's sense of propriety took hold again. 'There must have been worse, Hervey. It's perhaps because there's scarce been anything to do these last few months but bear the heat and the rain.'

It was a decent response, and Hervey would not gainsay it, though in truth he could not think of another officer who had made so unpromising a beginning. 'How has Armstrong been, by the way?'

'It would be impossible to praise him excessively.'

'That's as I supposed. How is his family?'

'All well, I understand. Mrs Armstrong is schoolmistress

147

again. There's an ayah for the three babies.'

Hervey faltered – just an instant – at being reminded there were now three. '*Big* babies, two of them.'

'Yes. They brought the eldest to stables the other evening.'

Hervey made an effort to collect himself. 'Now, we must speak of the state of the troop. I think I had better look at the order books of late, and then perhaps the acquittance rolls.'

But first he would need to see the muster, and Vanneck looked pained as he opened it at the first page, for it seemed there were as many names struck through with red as not.

Hervey stared at it forlornly. He had shaken the hand of every man on attesting. These had been *his* dragoons. The red pen strokes looked every bit as bloody as the sabre's, and not a fraction as glorious.

CHAPTER SEVEN
FAMILY MATTERS

Three days later

Hervey's little Marwari stood motionless, head down to her knees, the fever so great that her neck and flanks ran with sweat as if she had just galloped a mile.

'What do you think, David?'

The veterinary surgeon shook his head as he felt the mare's chest and belly. 'A most violent swelling – malignant, certainly. When did it first come to notice?'

Private Johnson answered. 'Last night, sir, when I came after watch-setting. She'd broken out a bit on 'er neck, an' she'd left 'er feed.'

'What exercise had she had?'

'An hour in the mornin', sir, in hand.'

Sledge stepped back to look at the mare again. 'By common practice I should draw at least two quarts of blood, but I hold with it less and less.' He shook his head. 'If the blood's poisoned it will have some beneficial effect, but otherwise we'll only weaken an already weak animal, and I think she's going to need her strength.'

'I'm content to follow your advice,' said Hervey, sounding mystified. 'I've not seen a horse looking as she. What do you suppose it is?'

Sledge's brow furrowed more. 'The inflammation – quite

possibly it is tumorous. Too early to say, though. It might be a case of the feltoric. I think we had better purge her.'

Hervey nodded, and turned to his groom. 'Johnson?'

'Ay, sir.'

'I can make up the purgative myself if you want,' said Sledge, putting his coat back on.

'We can do that well enough, can't we, Johnson?'

'Sir.'

Sledge turned to Hervey's groom. 'A full quart of hot gruel with four ounces of electuary of senna and double of castor oil. Put in a measure of Glauber's salts, too.'

'Right sir.'

'You shall have to watch her carefully, Johnson. I must know if there's any material change. And the swelled part must be rubbed twice daily with the blistering oils. Come to the dispense and I'll have my assistant give you a good measure.'

'Right sir.'

'And I'll make a fever ball. She may take it at evening stables.'

Johnson nodded again, writing carefully in his notebook.

'Give her only warm water, in small quantities, mind, and the same with mashes. Three or four times in the day. She might be tempted. But she will require every attention.'

'Of course, sir.'

'Good man.'

They left Johnson to begin his ministrations, and walked back along the troop lines. 'You don't think we need move her?' asked Hervey.

Sledge shook his head. 'I see nothing she might transmit. Best keep her be.'

Hervey said nothing.

They walked a few more steps. 'You'll have heard about the RM last night?'

'No.' The rising cadence suggested Hervey was now alerted, however.

'Blind drunk and put to bed by the picket.'

He was not surprised he hadn't heard. It might be a shade embarrassing for the riding master this morning, but hardly of great moment. 'And?'

'He was ranting against Rose.'

'*Oh.*'

'Yes.'

Hervey thought for a moment. 'How did you come to hear of it?'

'I saw it. I was called out to the colic in B Troop. Broad could be heard the other side of the lines.'

'Then it is known about officially.'

'I don't know for sure, but I think not. I told the picket-corporal to say nothing.'

That was a bold thing to have done for an officer who held no powers of command, thought Hervey. And humane, too. 'Who was it?'

'Someone from A Troop. I forget his name. Did you speak of Broad and Rose with Joynson, by the way?'

When, three days ago, Sledge had told Hervey all he knew, they had talked about it long. And in the end they had decided that Hervey would speak confidentially with the commanding officer. But now he shook his head. 'I had thought to speak first with Rose, as soon as he comes back from his shooting. I think I'd better apprise Joynson now, though. It's not right that we don't warn him if it's come to this.'

'Rather a fine mess in the making, I'd say.'

'Well, it wouldn't be the first time.'

'Hervey, you seem remarkably phlegmatical.'

'You misjudge me if you think I approve. Rose has not acted like a gentleman. There's scarce more to say, is there?'

'Not acted like a gentleman? I doubt Rose would see it that way, since he'd not recognize Broad as one. Just like a bit of foolery with a housemaid, really.'

'Don't be too hard, David. It seems ten times worse here

151

than if we were in Hounslow. And Mrs Broad's a deuced handsome woman.'

Sledge held his peace. Instead he stopped at one of the stalls to look over the new grey that Hervey had bought for his trumpeter. 'The talk in the wet canteen, by the way, is of money changing hands between Barrow and Nirmal Sen.'

Hervey sighed. *Two* of the troop-leaders on the primrose path, and for all to see. He felt sorry for the major. 'Ay, Johnson told me last night. How do these things get abroad? It could hardly have come from Nirmal Sen. He can't very well own to bribing a Company official.'

'So you suppose the talk is accurate?'

'I suppose no such thing. You must not let on, but the major spoke to me of it three days ago. I told him there was no more reason to presume Barrow capable of it than anyone else.'

Sledge stood up having run a hand down each of the grey's legs. 'Very noble. Do you suppose any would agree with you?'

Hervey looked surprised.

'If it were me or Ledley or the paymaster it would be the same,' said Sledge.

'Oh, come. That is a calumny on the regiment. It might have been Towcester's view but that's of the past.'

Sledge raised his eyebrows as if unconvinced. 'I think you chose well, this grey,' he said, nodding to the trumpeter's new pride. 'I think it safe to pay the balance.'

'Even to Nirmal Sen?'

'There's no question but that he's supplying good horses.'

Hervey smiled in a resigned way. 'Shall you come to evening stables?'

'Of course.'

'And shall you dine? I intend doing.'

'Then so shall I.'

* * *

Hervey drained his coffee cup and placed it on the major's desk. 'And that is the long and the short of it.'

Major Joynson had taken off his spectacles and begun to polish them. It had become so much his idiosyncrasy that Hervey found himself wondering at what point the polishing would begin, and the length of time and vigorousness of the polishing, for this tended to indicate the process of cogitation and the degree of difficulty presented by the solution. This morning the polishing had been slow and methodical, suggesting that the case of Rose and Broad was not to be treated with summary, and perhaps condign, justice. 'How much of it do you suppose is generally known?'

Hervey raised both eyebrows.

'Yes. You're right,' said Joynson wearily.

'And if it's not known about already then it can be but a matter of time. Broad is a sick man, his wife is unfaithful, and with a brother officer. These things can hardly conduce to tranquillity.'

Still Joynson polished. 'What would you do were you me?'

'What *could* I do? Would I have any option but to require Rose to leave?'

Major Joynson had not hoped for a reply in the interrogative. Nevertheless it gave him an opportunity to exhaust all hope of alternatives. 'Would he have to leave the regiment? Sell out, I mean. Or might he go elsewhere for a time? Somewhere else in India, even. The staff?'

Hervey paused to consider. 'If Broad had been other than riding master or another from the ranks, and had Rose intended marriage with Mrs Broad, then I suppose it might just have been arranged. But very evidently these are not the conditions.'

'And so Rose must sell out?'

Hervey was becoming exasperated at the major's unwillingness to draw the remaining conclusion. 'Neither you nor I make the rules, sir.'

The major sighed. 'If only we were ordered on campaign.'

'There is that, I grant you,' said Hervey. 'But very evidently that is not a condition on which we can count either.'

'I suppose, then, that first I must have Broad before me and ask what he wishes to be done. Or perhaps first I should see Rose?'

Hervey sighed to himself. 'Really, sir, I think it makes no difference whatever. You shall have to see both of them.'

'And Mrs Broad shall have to leave the cantonment at once.'

Hervey hesitated. 'I think she must. But do let us be kind.'

'Yes, yes,' said the major, suddenly increasing the speed of his polishing. 'Oh dear. Poor woman, poor woman. These things in my experience are never quite as the Commandments suggest.'

Hervey was not sure of the major's point, but he judged it of no matter. 'And as for the tattle about Barrow, I'm afraid I can add nothing but that David Sledge has told me it is the talk of the wet canteen. Indeed, I had heard so myself.'

Major Joynson stopped his polishing and replaced his spectacles. 'Very well. I shall summon Nirmal Sen. We had better lance this sore in the same way.'

Hervey got up and took his cap.

The major took off his glasses and unaccountably began polishing again. 'Oh, and Hervey, I am very gratified by your counsel. As you say, neither you nor I make the rules.'

'No, sir.'

'And in that connection I would urge you most earnestly to look to your own arrangements regarding . . . regarding your arrangements. There has been talk, I hear . . . in the drawing rooms.'

That night in the mess there were few officers, and Hervey, more tired than he had supposed after his first full day in uniform, had not been greatly inclined to join them. However, he had been absent from the table for so long that he thought it a positive duty to dine. He had arrived not many minutes before the khansamah announced dinner and found himself at once the senior.

It was the Sixth's custom for the most junior dining officer to sit on the senior's left, with any guest of the mess on the other hand. It was usually an agreeable position to find oneself in, for both senior and junior, but this evening Hervey found that it promised otherwise, for the junior was Cornet Green and the senior of the two guests was the bishop's chaplain, there at the invitation of Seton Canning with whom he had been at school.

'Reverend sir,' said Hervey as they stood by their chairs. 'Would you say grace?'

'Benedic Domine . . .' began the bishop's chaplain solemnly, and continued at some length.

'Per Jesum Christum Dominum Nostrum. Amen,' answered the table, as best they could, when at last he was finished. Strickland made the sign of the cross – evidence, indeed, of Sir Ivo's benevolent dominion. Poor Strickland had almost been forced onto half pay by Lord Towcester's malignance in matters of religion.

Hervey turned to his right as they sat, to begin what he feared must be an unedifying conversation. He had formed no very high opinion of the Bishop of Calcutta, and he supposed his chaplain to be of the same stamp. But from the other side of the table the senior lieutenant addressed him on behalf of the subalterns. 'We were deliberating, sir, on the efficacy of the sabre's point as against the edge, and wondered what was your opinion in the matter.'

Hervey was taken aback somewhat. Indeed, he suspected a prank. It had never been the Sixth's custom to speak of matters of this sort, and Oliver Finucane had certainly shown no previous zeal. He glanced at the other subalterns, each of them showing quite extraordinary attention (except Vanneck, whose eyes were lowered), and wondered what transformation there might have been in the months of his absence. 'I am not rightly sure it is a proper subject to discuss in front of a guest such as Mr Stephenson,' he replied, with a note that implied he would somehow welcome clarification.

'Oh, do not desist for my part,' implored the chaplain. 'These are matters of very evident moment to gentlemen of your calling.'

Hervey would rather have received a less enthusiastic endorsement of the subject, which now commanded the attention of the whole table, and which the serving of soup did nothing to abate. 'It is not reducible to an absolute position. It depends on the nature of the engagement. And opinion would also vary depending whether we spoke of the old- or the new-pattern sabre.'

'But it is so, is it not,' continued Finucane, 'that but three or four inches of the point only is generally sufficient to despatch an adversary, whereas a cut will wound him only – albeit perhaps grievously.'

'True, but if you close with your adversary at speed – which is to what cavalry ought to aim – then it is not easy to draw back the blade after the thrust home. I have known of swords being struck from the hand, or breaking, with the hilt striking a man's breast after the blade had run through his body—'

Hervey did not see Cornet Green's face drain rapidly of its colour – only that he suddenly sprang up with hand clasped to mouth and rushed from the room.

There was much laughter.

Hervey now saw what was the game, and was in two minds about being used in the subalterns' rag. But he could not find it in him to show it. 'Something I said?' he asked, with an expression of forced solemnity.

Seton Canning shook his head in mock despair. Vanneck

continued to look down, and the others stifled their sniggers as best they could.

The rest of dinner was a wearying affair, for the chaplain's conversation proved as uninteresting as it was wholesome. He seemed entirely in innocence of what had passed, so that there was little profit in Hervey's trying to explain it, and instead there followed a tedious dialogue on the state of the various missions to Hindoostan. Afterwards, when the port had circulated twice, Hervey led the party back to the ante-room, where a game of primero was got up. He himself stood aloof from it taking his brandy and soda – the married officer's 'nightcap', the sweetener of libatory breath.

Seton Canning came up. 'I fear you've had not so diverting an evening. Stephenson can be earnest, but he's a good man, and he can still thrash me at fives.'

Hervey smiled. 'He must have thought me very dull. I fear I had little by way of conversation. I confess my mind was otherwise engaged.'

'Agreeably, I hope.'

'As it happens, no.'

Harry Seton Canning had joined the Sixth just before Waterloo and had been cornet during the battle when Hervey found himself in command of a troop. Canning had, indeed, brought the troop out of the charge against the French lancers, to the acclaim of many an old hand. But until late he had been Hervey's subordinate, and the two had never become quite as close as officers might who had shared so much. Today, however, they were equals in rank just as they were equals in society. 'Disagreeably on account of Barrow, perhaps?'

Hervey looked surprised at the mention, though he knew it was unreasonable to be. 'As a matter of fact, yes. And other things.'

'What is your opinion?'

'I don't have one, for at present there are no facts as I discern.'

'But are you inclined to think it the smoke and the fire?'

Hervey frowned. 'Harry, I have said; I am not inclined to think anything without facts.'

'But what's to be done about Barrow? There can't be this talk for long. It's not good for any of us.'

'Joynson's to have it out with Nirmal Sen. I think there might have to be a board of officers.'

Seton Canning frowned. 'That would be tricky, in the circumstances.'

'What circumstances are these, exactly, Harry?'

'You know perfectly well. Barrow has never been popular. He's always kept himself to himself. And . . .'

'And what?'

'Well, with this other business . . . Rose, I mean.'

Hervey sighed. There was no doubting that the Rose business would divide opinion in the mess, and a divided mess was not a good place from which to assemble a board of officers. 'Then it would be better to have a board of officers from another regiment. An unhappy day that will be.' He put his empty glass on the khitmagar's tray, declining more. 'I beg you will excuse me, Harry. I want to see my mare before retiring. She's running a high fever. I had thought to see David Sledge at mess this evening, but . . .'

'Yes, of course,' said Seton Canning, taking another glass of port. 'I hope I shall not be long detained myself. Where do you suppose your new cornet is, by the way?' he added, with a wry smile.

David Sledge wore a long smock like a shepherd's, and he was looking grave. 'I'm sorry not to have dined, but Johnson sent word soon after evening stables. He feared she was about to have a seizure. I've been with her since. I thought it best not to trouble you until after mess. I'm afraid I see no alternative to opening up the tumour. She's deteriorated so quickly I wouldn't lay odds on her seeing the morning.'

Hervey simply nodded: there was evidently no alternative to the knife.

The trouble was that Sledge knew little more than Hervey in the matter. He had his manuals for reference, but he had seen nothing the like of these symptoms. 'I must warn you it's a desperate remedy. The blood's in so bad a state it renders it difficult to bring the wounds to a good digestion, and if this is not effected, there'll be a gangrene and mortification.'

Hervey understood. 'Where is Johnson, by the way?'

'I sent him for brandy. I find it has admirable cleansing properties, better than water for digesting dirt and blood. And it will preserve the flesh, too.'

Hervey smiled to himself. How alike seemed the methods of a good surgeon and a veterinarian.

Sledge opened his valise and laid out the tools of his trade on the manger – lancet, probe, scalpels, forceps, clamps, a cautery and two needles with gut already threaded. And a great quantity of lint, and a large bottle of green liquid.

Johnson returned soon afterwards with two flasks of arrack. Sledge took one of them, poured a good measure onto a handful of lint and began swabbing the mare's swollen breast. 'A bit more light, please, Johnson. And then this, if you will.' He handed him the cautery.

Johnson shifted the oil lamps closer, then set about lighting the cautery stove.

Sledge crouched looking at the swelling for some time, touching occasionally to feel for a vein. Then he picked up the lancet. 'Very well, let's try to expunge the malignance.'

He made five incisions in all, using the scalpel to elongate the lancet's work. After each one he expressed a quantity of fluid and blood, wiping the wound gently with arrack before studying it closely with his magnifying glass.

Throughout, the mare remained perfectly still. Her

resignation warmed Hervey to her the more. He leaned forward as far as he could to see at close hand the veterinarian's art. 'What do you think, David?'

'I'm tempted to make more incisions. From each there's come a good deal of corruption. But there's a greater risk of mortification each time. No, I think I'll cauterize now, and sew up the two longer incisions. Johnson—'

Johnson handed him the cautery. 'I thought there'd be more blood, sir.'

'Yes, I think I did too. It seems that bad blood was likely not the cause of the inflammation. It was as well we didn't bleed her this morning.'

Johnson's admiration for Sledge these days was as great as it had been for his predecessor, Selden. Selden had elevated the Sixth's veterinary method from farriers' lore to science, and Sledge had confirmed the regiment in that practice.

'I wish she would take a little feed, though. Nothing at all, you say, Johnson?'

'Not a thing since yesterday, sir.'

'And the purgative?'

'Not 'ad a lot of effect, sir.'

'Mm.'

When he had done with cautery and needle, and had dressed the wounds with the green digestive ointment, Sledge turned to Hervey. 'Colic is the immediate concern. I worry about her gut twisting if she's eating nothing. A watch on her all night, and call me at once at any sign of distress.'

Hervey nodded. 'Thank you, David.'

'Ay, sir. Thank you,' added Johnson, moving the lamps back to safety.

Sledge nodded, wiped his instruments clean with lint and arrack, put them in his valise and bid them both goodnight.

'I'll bed down 'ere, then, sir,' said Johnson when he was gone.

'Thank you, yes. I have some matters to attend to

first, and then I'll come in the early hours and relieve you.'

'I'd rather tha didn't, sir. I wouldn't want it said I couldn't stag for a night.'

Hervey smiled. 'Very well. I'll come before muster, though. And if you have to send for Mr Sledge then send for me too.'

'Right, sir. 'E's good, Mr Sledge.'

'He is,' said Hervey, gently pulling the mare's ear. 'And as good a man too when *not* wielding a knife.'

There was a light in the bungalow next to his when, an hour after midnight, Hervey walked the cantonment road. He paused for a moment, then turned down the path to the door. The chowkidar, squatting on his haunches at the foot of the verandah steps, stood and made the exaggerated salute which native servants thought correct in acknowledging the soldier-sahibs.

'Good evening, chowkidar. Is the sahib returned home?' said Hervey in confident Bengali.

The chowkidar nodded his head vigorously, gesturing with his night stick towards the door.

Hervey ascended the three steps to the verandah and pulled at the bell rope.

The bearer came quickly, saluting as high as the chowkidar, and admitted him at once. 'Captain Barrow-sahib, Captain Hervey-sahib is come,' he called as he closed the mosquito door.

Barrow appeared in his shirtsleeves, glass in hand. 'What are you doing up and about at this time, Hervey? You're not captain of the week.'

Hervey smiled as best he could. 'I've been with Sledge. He had to cut up my mare.'

'Oh? What's her problem?' The voice of Birmingham was always that much more pronounced when Barrow had had a drink or two.

'The feltoric, he thinks.'

161

'Lord. Will you have a peg?'

'Yes; thank you – brandy.' Hervey hoped it would wash away the dispirits as effectively as it had the blood.

'Brandy-pani for Captain Hervey, Ranga.'

The bearer produced glass, decanter and bottle as Hervey settled himself into a chair, and began to pour.

'No, Ranga: chota brandy,' Hervey protested, although his instinct was to take a very large measure indeed.

'A good evening at mess, was it?'

'Yes, though we were few. Only Seton Canning of the captains.'

'I'm not long back from Calcutta – one of the Shitpoor road wallahs. Quite a tamasha, it was. Fine wine – hock and best burgundy. And women.'

Hervey nodded non-committally.

Barrow smiled. 'Or boys, for that matter, I suspect. You know these Bengalis.'

Hervey had been to tamashas at the merchants' houses, in the early days. They were lavish affairs, and the generosity of the hosts could indeed be great. Some of the merchants were undoubtedly men of culture and sensibility – and, he supposed, of honour – who merely enjoyed the company of the sahibs. But all the sahibs knew that the entertainment was in some expectation of pecuniary benefit. Barrow made no secret of his enjoying the hospitality, however much the 'proper' officers might disdain it. He was never entirely at home in the mess, and it was hardly surprising that he found his situation as guest of honour in a merchant's house so agreeable. In any case, it gave Hervey his pretext. 'Whose tamasha was it?'

'The man I bought my last lot of remounts from. And good they were too.'

'Nirmal Sen, is that?'

'You know 'im?'

Hervey thought it unworthy of their long acquaintance to dissemble. 'Barrow, I'm sorry to put this to you thus, but tomorrow Joynson will call Nirmal Sen to orderly room and question him about rumours of you and him dealing ... improperly.'

Barrow looked stunned.

'I'm sorry. It seems the rumours are abroad so much that Joynson feels he has no alternative but to act ... formally. I understand he will ask to speak with you first in case—'

'In case what?'

'In case, I imagine, that you wish first to say anything.'

Barrow drained his glass. 'And what might there be to say?'

Hervey saw a face he had never before seen. Barrow had looked death in the eye, and defiantly, many a time, yet now he had the look of a fearful man. The eyes spoke of losing all, not simply life. And for the first time Hervey imagined him guilty. What a wreckage he had wrought in but a few seconds. 'I don't know, Ezra. I truly don't.'

'Do you think me capable of a corrupt thing, Hervey? You know me better than most, and longer.'

What was the point in expounding on the doctrine of original sin at such a time? Loyalty demanded that Hervey support him now. 'To me it is inconceivable.'

Barrow stared at him, as if trying to judge his sincerity. 'And what do you suppose the others would answer – Rose and Seton Canning, and Strickland?'

'I cannot say.' He knew it to be false, at least in the one case. 'Why should they answer different from me?'

'You know why, Hervey. You know very well why.'

Barrow's bearer returned to refill their glasses. Hervey wanted no more, but it was not possible to refuse at such a moment.

Barrow drained his new glass at once and held it out again. 'Burra peg, Ranga. And leave the bottle and be off. And tomorrow morning, my best dress.'

'Acha, sahib.' He left, looking anxious.

'*He* knows summat's up,' said Barrow, scarcely waiting

163

for him to leave the room. 'Probably did before you said a word. Before you came, even. Whole cantonment's probably jawing me dead: "Ezra Barrow, on the *picaro*. What d'ye expect from one as is no better than us?" – or *them* if it's Rose an' 'is like!'

'There's no cause to think that way.'

'Isn't there! Isn't there indeed! Hervey, you think me a fool. I wasn't wanted when Lord George brought me in, but I never flinched from doing what was right on account of popularity.'

'That might go for many a man brought in. But there aren't that many that get field promotion. What does that speak for the regard in which those who mattered held you – *hold* you, indeed?'

'Hervey, you've no idea what it's like to be despised from above *and* below.'

For all their years in arms together, Hervey had no wish to debate with a man in his cups. If he had made a mistake in coming here in the first place, there was little to be gained by staying. And if he had not, then Barrow needed not brandy and commiseration but sleep and a clear head to hold up high in the morning. He stood up. 'Forgive me, Barrow. It's been a long day.'

'Ay, that it has. Home then to your bibi, Captain Hervey. The colonel wouldn't like it, you being a proper officer and all, but it's nothing like the sin of being a ranker.'

Hervey picked up his forage cap. 'Good night, Barrow. I'll come tomorrow morning.'

An hour later, as Hervey lay beside his bibi in the moments before sleep, there was a shot. He knew its cause at once. And the stab in his gut was as if the ball had struck him too.

CHAPTER EIGHT
HALLOWED GROUND

Three days later

The coroner was disobliging. Although Joynson and Hervey had gone to considerable trouble to sow doubt in the minds of the jury, that upright officer of the court had summed up in such a manner as to make that doubt seem unreasonable. Under oath, Hervey had been unable to give any indication that Barrow had wanted to clean his pistols at that time of night, and so the suggestion that he might have could be but speculation. And why, indeed, just the one pistol? It was the greatest pity that the inquest was not held under military jurisdiction. Accident or misadventure was not the probable cause, the jury decided, but death by the officer's own hand.

The verdict presented Joynson with several problems, the most pressing of which was Barrow's funeral and interment. The chaplain, who had turned a blind eye to the rubrics when Private Sisken had hanged himself aboard ship during the regiment's passage east, found himself in some difficulty on this occasion, for the circumstances were known to the entire city, and episcopal supervision was very much closer at hand. However, when it had become known in the canteens that Barrow could not be buried in the consecrated ground that was the regiment's corner of the cantonment cemetery, a deputation had come to the RSM – NCOs and sweats mainly, but not exclusively, from Barrow's troop – to request in no uncertain terms that the captain be laid to rest 'alongside the other poor souls who've succumbed to this place'. Accordingly, and on the recommendation of the RSM, Joynson had summoned the chaplain, adding materially to his troubles by insisting it be done.

The chaplain was tolerated, respected even, to an unusual degree in the Sixth. It was well remembered that he had stood up to Lord Towcester in the matter of Private Hopwood's flogging, so far as he had been able, which was in truth not very far. And there had been Private Sisken's committal at sea, when all who heard his address had been much moved. Indeed, there had been many occasions since when the chaplain's funerary eloquence had been displayed – altogether too many occasions for so small a regiment. But in Barrow's case, the chaplain's solution was, the officers all agreed, worthy of a Jesuit. An hour before the funeral he conducted a ceremony of deconsecration, limited to the ground that had been prepared to receive the coffin, and had then read over Barrow's mortal remains, in the usual way, 'in the sure and certain hope' and all the other ringing phrases that somehow gave succour to usually godless men who stood in ranks fearful that the next time might be theirs.

There was no carouse afterwards, though. The canteen was a dull place that evening, and few officers were at mess. Hervey himself did not dine, an omission that made him feel uncomfortable, for he had berated poor Green for not having the pluck to return to the mess the night he had parted with the contents of his stomach. No one had so much as suggested it was unfortunate that he had called on Barrow that evening, for there was a supposition that the outcome was preordained. And, indeed, Barrow's act had spared the major and those about him the shame of an investigation. Above all, it had spared the regiment the dread board of officers from outside. Barrow's guilt was presumed by the very fact of his noble action, yet Hervey felt his own hand in the business, and he did not rest easy.

Joynson had asked him to be president of the board of adjustment, which would make an inventory of Barrow's possessions so that those of a personal nature might be sent to his next of kin – when that detail was discovered – and all else sold at regimental auction, as was customary. This Hervey had now done, by himself, and at the expense of dinner in the mess, for it had occupied the entire evening after stables. But that was no matter: it afforded him an alibi.

It had been a thoroughly melancholy job. So much more than he had imagined. Whatever his pleasures on the Chitpore road, Barrow's habits had been sober and moderate, his practice soldierly and prudent. His possessions were few and utilitarian; nothing out of the ordinary, and if he had gained pecuniary advantage in his dealings with Nirmal Sen there was no evidence of its enjoyment here. Barrow's papers were no more elaborate than his other possessions, but there was one letter that indicated to where Joynson might write his condolences – and, indeed, the trouble he would have composing them. The superscription, in a spidery hand, read 'The Almshouses, Yardley', and the signature 'Your ever proud father'.

When he had finished, close to midnight, Hervey bade the bearer secure the bungalow, and left trusting him to the job. What opportunity of thieving could there be, indeed, if he had a list of everything? Anyway, Ranga looked sad, and it could not have been for his own situation, for he had already been offered another. It pleased Hervey to think there was other than a father who had some attachment to Barrow, for although he himself had slowly come to respect the man's capability as a soldier, he had never been able to count him a boon companion.

He walked slowly to his own bungalow. It was a cold night for all that it was not long since the monsoon. The stars were as bright as in the Peninsula – those long, bitter-chill nights when he had learned so much about the heavens. And the air was sweet, perhaps with incense or spices; he could not tell. A barn owl hooted. It seemed strange to think that Ezra Barrow was no longer on this earth when all else remained the same. But things had changed. Tonight would be the last time he enjoyed the companionship of his bibi here. Tomorrow he would set her up in a little haveli outside the cantonments, like so many others. And it really would not be the same.

Next day, the Sixth busied themselves more than usual. Things had to be brought back to good order, and quickly, and nothing helped so much as activity, especially when it was compelled by an RSM of Mr Lincoln's mettle. There were inspections all morning and drill all afternoon. And at colonel's rounds of evening stables, the major, though it was never his bent, made a very passable attempt at what the regiment knew as *jaldi*. At any rate, he managed to roust about the more timid.

At midday, the adjutant had conducted the auction of Barrow's effects. Usually, when a widow was known to the officers, or else the family, it was an occasion for generous over-bidding to provide a gratuity that a grateful government could not find itself able to disburse. In Barrow's case there had always been mixed feelings, although in the end there was a grim admiration for his ultimate gesture of honour. The major, it was agreed, excelled himself, opening the auction by telling the assembled bidders to where the money would be sent, declaring that 'a man is more than his worst error' and that Captain Ezra Barrow had served his king for over thirty years and the Sixth for more than fifteen. At the end of the proceedings, the adjutant announced that the sum of £857 would be sent to Mr Joshua Barrow of the Almshouses, Yardley, near Birmingham. It was a handsome figure, and, in the curious way of these things, it did something to restore the pride of those assembled, for in the last resort they had not let down their erstwhile comrade; and loyalty was nothing if it was easy. Barrow had certainly paid a heavy price himself: a penny-worth of powder had blown away three thousand pounds, at the very least, for on death the value of his commission reverted to the Crown.

That evening Hervey dined with the Somerviles. He was especially glad to do so, for as well as having the ugly circumstances of the past days to put behind him, he had not seen his friends in more than a week. He arrived a little late, however, having gone by way of the horse lines to reassure himself of the progress of his mare. Within a day of the veterinarian's surgery, the little Marwari had begun to eat – at first warm mashes, and now hard feed. The wounds had remained clean, the inflammation was gone, and so was the fever. In so short a time, Hervey thought it a veritable miracle, and he was extolling David Sledge's skill for a full quarter of an hour after arriving at No. 3, Fort William.

'And what so particularly commends him,' he concluded, now well into his second glass of champagne, 'is his devotion to his own greater understanding. His rooms are piled with treatises and papers.'

Somervile was happy to indulge him, and for practical reasons. At the onset of the unhealthy season, confidence in any practitioner, even veterinary, was reassuring. 'Calcutta is as full of quacks as anywhere – fuller, probably. I shall ask him to dine with us,' he said. 'Would it be entirely proper to ask him to look at my stable?'

'I don't see why not. He's not greatly engaged at present, I'm pleased to say.'

Somervile nodded, indicating that the matter was decided.

A khitmagar made to top up Hervey's glass, but he declined. 'Is Emma to join us?'

'Yes, very shortly. I'm sorry to say she has been sick these last few days.'

Hervey supposed that few husbands in Calcutta could be as direct as Somervile. 'I hope nothing—'

'No, no. I shouldn't think so. Calcutta's just a deuced sight unhealthier place than Madras, but Emma has a native constitution. I shouldn't distress yourself.'

He would try not to, difficult though that was with notice of even the slightest illness.

Somervile seemed keen to change the subject. 'I have some intelligence that will interest you.'

'I dare not hope it is of Peto?' replied Hervey, sounding a shade despondent. 'His last letter was a disheartening affair. Said he might as well be commanding a guardship.'

'I regret not. Not even of the war, indeed, for that generally proceeds ill, although there are to be reinforcements – and in good measure – for Rangoon. Campbell ought soon to take the offensive.'

Hervey snorted. 'That was, of course, his purpose in going to Rangoon in the first place!'

Somervile merely raised his eyebrows. 'Well, I am glad to say that my intelligence has at least provided Campbell with the means to do his job. No, the news I was referring to is that Combermere is to replace Paget.'

Hervey sat up. A new commander-in-chief would at any time be ripe news, but now, and the name Combermere – it was the ripest. 'Is this the Governor-General's doing? It would be ill indeed if Paget is to take the blame for things in Ava!'

'Oh no, there's no suggestion of Paget's being relieved. His tenure in command is routinely ended. Indeed, the change – if our intelligence is correct – will not be until next year. But Combermere is a friend of yours, is he not?'

Hervey smiled. 'I could hardly claim that. We have met on occasions, and he has a good memory.'

Somervile smiled broader. 'Then you shall have to meet

170

on more occasions, and place yourself at the *forefront* of his memory!'

Hervey smiled again. But that, indeed, was how it was done. He'd seen it time and again. Perhaps if he had not been so keen to leave the Duke of Wellington's staff he would by now be well placed for advancement instead of, in truth, having marked time a full ten years. And – he hardly dared admit it – with things as they were in the Sixth, what future was there at regimental duty? In Calcutta nothing happened other than death by Nature's hand (or one's own, for every regiment had its Barrow). 'We must see.'

Emma Somervile came in. She looked well enough, thought Hervey, but the rouge did not entirely mask her pallor. She sat next to her husband on a high-backed settee and placed her hand on his. 'And how are you, in the circumstances, Matthew?'

Hervey returned her smile. 'In the circumstances, well, I believe. I am troubled to learn you are not in the best of sorts, however.'

Emma frowned. 'Oh, these things . . . but tell me, what else have you been speaking of?'

'I was telling him the news of Lord Combermere's being appointed to commander-in-chief, my dear.'

Emma brightened again. 'Yes, *good* news for you, Matthew, is it not? Tell me of him.'

'He was at the best of schools.' Hervey smiled just a little wryly.

She at once understood, and turned to her husband with mock solemnity.

'A very long time in advance of me, my dear. And I do not recall his name in academic honours.'

'He was a great man for campaigning,' added Hervey. 'Since the Peninsula, though, he has not been at field duty. There again, neither, indeed, has anyone other than here in India. I confess I don't know how things are in Ireland. He's commander-in-chief there.'

'So I understand too,' said Somervile. 'Well, he is going to need a very fine head upon those fine military shoulders of his to ravel up the mess in Ava. And believe me, there's trouble brewing in Hindoostan too. Every week that we flounder in Rangoon – and Arakan for that matter, since it seems little better there – the malcontents among the country powers grow more impudent. But Amherst won't see it.' He glanced at Emma and shook his head a shade wearily. 'Oh yes, be in no doubt: if Combermere takes the reins here he'll be pitched into the middle of trouble – east *and* west.'

'Shall we go and dine?' said Emma, looking a little anxious, and making to stand. 'Ghulam says we may.'

Somervile was on his feet at once with a hand to Emma's elbow, but she rose unaided.

'I really am in fine health, Eyre,' she insisted, using her fan just a touch. 'I should have returned a little earlier from the assembly, that is all.'

The dining room minded Hervey of home, for whereas the mess and his bungalow were handsome enough, they were wood-built, and the houses at Fort William were stone. And there was a solidity about the place that spoke more of the permanence of the Honourable Company than could the military lines, whose occupants were after all mere birds of passage. The furniture and fittings were mahogany, teak and brass rather than the quartermaster's pine, cane and pewter. And the family portraits, here and not at some English seat, said that the Someviles were India people – native almost, as Eyre Somervile himself had once said. Emma had been to England, as she always called it, not 'home', but once in the dozen and more years since she had first joined her brother in Madras. Her husband had not been even once.

'How is your groom?' she asked, as a khitmagar began to serve them soup. 'And that corporal of yours – the one who brought you to the ship?'

'Wainwright, you mean.' Hervey's face at once registered intense pride. 'Without whom I should not be enjoying your hospitality now. I'm pleased to say he has been advanced to the head of the seniority roll. He may be corporal, full, before the year's out.'

'Bound to be, at this time of year,' said Somervile without looking up from his soup.

Hervey smiled disconcertedly. 'There are other ways, Somervile.'

Somervile continued to give all his ocular attention to his soup. 'Men putting bullets in their brains, you mean?'

'Eyre!'

Somervile at last looked up. Emma's scold was not to be ignored.

'What I meant,' said Hervey, not in the least perturbed, 'is that serjeants leave or are promoted, making vacancies below. Nothing more.'

'I'm glad to hear it,' said Somervile, as if it were well known to be otherwise. 'And when do you suppose it will be the same for officers?'

'In essentials it is,' replied Hervey, sounding cautious.

'Humph! You and I know it's a case of money and little more. How much would a majority cost you?'

Hervey looked rueful. 'Another thousand at least. If we were posted home probably twice as much.'

Somervile smiled. 'Then your toasts should be to a short war but a bloody one.'

'Eyre, I really think this a most unedifying line,' Emma protested.

But Hervey was now smiling. 'No, Emma: that was the toast in the Peninsula. Grim, perhaps, but that is the soldier's way with his humour.' He turned back to Somervile. 'We shouldn't forget the brevet. They're a good deal easier to come by here than in England. There were a fair number in Rangoon, as I recall.'

'What is a brevet?' asked Emma.

173

'Promotion in the army as a whole, but not in the regiment as such. It's all very well if you want a life on the staff.'

The khitmagars began clearing away the soup, breaking the line of conversation for the moment.

'But how are things otherwise, Matthew?' asked Emma, as the khansamah poured a little claret for her husband to taste. 'We have so missed our visits to the regiment. The officers are well?'

Somervile nodded; a good vintage, predating even Bonaparte.

Hervey inclined his head, as if to say the reply would not be straightforward. 'For the most part I suppose things are pretty good.'

'Oh? No more than "pretty good"? That sounds ill to me.' Emma knew him better than he sometimes remembered.

Hervey braced himself. 'To tell the truth, I fear we shall have another to-do. Hugh Rose . . .'

'Yes?'

'Rose has been dallying with the riding master's wife, and I fear Joynson must have him quit the place.'

Emma raised her eyebrows. 'That is sad, for all. His company is always much sought after.'

'If I were Joynson I'd be looking for some way to keep him,' her husband declared. 'Rose is a good officer from what I see.'

'Indeed he is,' said Hervey, helping himself to a fair portion of beef from the khitmagar's salver. 'And I'll warrant he'd be the hero of any battle. But you know very well what is the principle that Joynson has to abide by.'

Somervile had drained his glass even before the beef came to him, and he now heaped double rations onto his plate. 'Ay, I know well enough. But I'm also of a mind that Joynson's going to need good men about him, and sooner than he supposes.'

* * *

Next morning, after exercise, Hervey was called to regimental headquarters. There he found the major in even lower spirits than before. The Barrow affair had been one thing, but Rose and the riding master – and, for that matter the succession of RSMs – was quite another. Whereas with Barrow the course of action was clear (and he trusted he had dealt deftly with it), his other trials required much thought before action. And much thought in these matters lowered the spirits.

'But you declared that Rose would have to leave when last we spoke,' said Hervey, shaking his head. He had no special wish to see Rose go; he shared Somervile's pragmatic view that if the war clouds had actually been gathering something could be done. But manifestly this was not the case.

'Circumstances have changed, Hervey. I'm not sure that I wish to have the captains' ranks so thinned. It will be deuced unsettling.' Joynson took off his spectacles and pulled the silk square from his sleeve.

'Yes, I can see that. But—'

'Rose has asked for leave, and I'm inclined to grant it. Broad must go somewhere a bit healthier for a month or so, too.'

Hervey wondered what was the imperative for Joynson's change of mind, though the major was ever a cautious man. 'In my view, sir, it will merely put off the moment for action – might make it more difficult, indeed. But that is a judgement, and I of course respect yours.'

'That's gratifying at least,' replied Joynson, polishing and frowning. 'And I've settled on Deedes for RSM, though I expect I'll live to regret it.'

Hervey sighed.

'You would have jumped both and taken Hairsine.'

'Yes. That way, at least, you'd be assured of a good RSM. The other consequences you would just have to deal with.'

'Don't imagine I didn't think hard on that solution, but with things as they are I am certain it is better to have as few causes for immediate discord as possible. Incidentally, I have asked Sledge to conduct an enquiry into the Barrow business. I don't regard the matter closed with the universal supposition of his guilt.'

Hervey was surprised. He smiled and nodded.

'I'm glad you're pleased, for I've unwelcome news for you. Assheton-Smith shall have B Troop. I should very much like Vanneck to replace him.'

Hervey's face fell. 'Not Vanneck, not now. Not with that idiot boy as my cornet!'

'I have first to think of the regiment, and Vanneck would make the better adjutant than any other.'

Hervey cast about for the obvious alternative, but soon realized that Joynson's assertion was unchallengeable. 'Shall there be a replacement for Vanneck? I really can't—'

'Assheton-Smith's lieutenancy will be for the buying. I imagine Perry will have it.'

Hervey sighed again. Perry had the makings, for sure, but he'd seen nothing more than a couple of seasons' drill.

'I haven't finished, Hervey. Though this should not be unwelcome news. I want you to take your troop to Dehli for a month or so.'

Hervey was indeed brightened. 'Dehli? Why?'

'This morning I received word from the brigadier that a troop was to be sent within the week as escort to the resident. I have no other details of the assignment as yet.'

'It is by *no* means unwelcome news – not at all. Though it would be a deal more welcome if I had Vanneck with me and not Green. But are you sure you would not want me to be here . . . in the circumstances?'

'I should prefer that Skinner's Horse did the Dehli duty, but the Governor-General was apparently quite explicit on the matter – *King*'s troops. On the whole I think it right that it should be you. It would seem strange otherwise. You are next senior to Strickland, and his leave is more overdue than anyone's.'

It was true. Not even Strickland could be expected to give up home leave for a month in Dehli. 'Then I suppose I had better make ready at once. Am I at liberty to speak to the engineer?'

'I see no reason why not.'

'Is that all, sir?'

'Yes, Hervey. That is all. Unless . . .'

'Unless what?'

'Would you dine with us this evening?'

'Of course, Joynson. I should be delighted.'

There was even more satisfaction in the major's smile, however (and, had Hervey known it, relief). 'Shall we say seven?'

Hervey nodded, replaced his cap, and took his leave.

There were any number of things he would rather do, especially with only a few nights remaining in Calcutta, for he knew perfectly well why he was bidden to the major's table. But how he might be expected to exert any benign influence in Frances Joynson's direction he could not think. Regimental duty was a queer thing at times.

Only later did Hervey realize that in going at once to Dehli he would miss the RSM's wedding, and it displeased him. It was not just that it was already being spoken of as the best tamasha in Bengal, undoubtedly to be the most notable event in the living memory of the serjeants' mess, rather it was an instinct that he should just be there. He decided at once that he would leave Armstrong behind until after the nuptials, for to do otherwise would have been a deprivation to both his serjeant-major and the RSM – and, indeed, to Caithlin Armstrong, for Lincoln had become a regular guest at their table since their return to the regiment. Armstrong greeted the news exactly like a serjeant-major who knew where his duty lay. 'An' it'll do Collins the power of good to wear a fourth stripe for a while,' he added for good measure.

Myles Vanneck was not so pleased. He had no desire to

leave the nominal administrative duties of troop-lieutenant for the weighty ones of adjutant, and he certainly had no need of the modest increase in pay. The adjutant of a cavalry regiment, by long custom, came from the ranks. Often he came from another regiment, as Barrow had done. Assheton-Smith had been the first gentleman-adjutant, as his fellows had soon dubbed him in mock reference to the hyphen in his name (the first not counting Dauntsey, that is, which none of the officers did). The trouble was, he had done so fine a job that it was natural for Joynson to wish to replace him with another of his like. And indeed, Joynson also held the novel notion that an officer might be the better troop-captain – and ultimately even colonel – for having seen the workings of the orderly room. Come what may, all Vanneck's protests were to no avail. By the end of the morning he had handed the various ledgers to Cornet Arthur Perry and taken his seat in regimental headquarters.

Meanwhile, Hervey had been at the garrison engineer's searching for the requisite maps and dak instructions. As the crow flew, Dehli lay in excess of seven hundred miles, and by the dak route nearly eight. With the marching norm for cavalry being twelve leagues a day, it would be a journey of three weeks, and an occasion for sport and other pleasant diversions which could scarcely have come at a better time. He was half disappointed, therefore, when that evening at dinner Joynson declared it his opinion that he should stay for the wedding. 'Give Perry his head a bit,' said the major, with unusual zest. 'They get precious little chance otherwise. You and Armstrong'll be able to catch 'em up in a few days. You should *both* be there.'

Joynson's dispensation gave Hervey much cause for pleasure, but it was only next day that he began to learn of the import of his mission. He rode over to the Somerviles in the middle of the afternoon for just that purpose, feeling sure that he would learn more useful intelligence there than the commander-in-chief's office was likely to divulge.

Emma was not at home, but her husband was, and deeply engrossed in his book room having come immediately from the council's luncheon table (only the writers and junior officials returned to their offices of an afternoon). He looked up absently as the khansamah announced his visitor. 'Oh, Hervey: you are come very early today. Is there another to-do?'

'Not at all. I'm for Dehli with my troop for a month or so.'

Somervile was transformed in an instant, at once all attention. 'Indeed! I had notice yesterday that Ochterlony had asked for an escort, but I hadn't supposed a decision would be reached so quickly. Indeed I'm surprised: Ochterlony doesn't enjoy the confidence he used to have. Sit you down. Tea, sherbet? Ghulam!'

'Tea, thank you. And some limewater if you have it.'

'*Ji, sahib?*'

'*Bhat, nimbu pani, Ghulam.*'

'*Ji, sahib.*'

'That is the reason I came here, to discover what I could about the assignment. Joynson knows nothing yet.'

'Sit down, sit down,' Somervile insisted, even more attentive. 'There's trouble brewing in that direction.'

Hervey's ears pricked up. He had not supposed the escort wholly ceremonial, but . . .

'Ochterlony's an old man – "Loony Ochter" they're calling him, and not entirely in affection. You must have heard?'

'No, I have not. I know of him of course – everybody does.' There could be no one who needed reminding of his reputation – Major-General Sir David Ochterlony, victor of the Ghoorka war a decade ago.

'Ay, well, he's an old man, as I said. I think Amherst believes him a fool. But I'll say this too: he's one of the few men with any true understanding of the country. He knows

179

when to fight and when to parley. And how to fight, for that matter – but that's not my principal concern.'

Ghulam returned with a khitmagar bearing limewater. Another followed with tea a few minutes later. Somervile waited for them to leave before resuming, and in a voice deliberately lowered.

'I'd wager any amount that what lies behind this is Bhurtpore. There's an unholy tussle for yonder throne coming. The old rajah's not long for this world by all accounts.'

Hervey looked unenlightened. 'And this is the Company's business?'

'It may well become so. You have to be especially careful with sleeping dogs in India. And Ochterlony's backed the rightful heir, the son – invested him with a *khelat*, or some such. Doubtless the old fox wants to parade the escort as a promise of troops from Calcutta if things go against the claim. And you know why Bhurtpore would have the doocots aflutter here, don't you?'

'We are speaking of the same Bhurtpore, the fortress that Lord Lake failed to take?'

Somervile smiled, but pained. 'The same. Our only defeat in two centuries. When first I came out from England there was still the taunt, "Go take Bhurtpore!" And the truth may well be that we could no more do so now than we could then.'

CHAPTER NINE

A GREAT TAMASHA

Two weeks later

Mr Lincoln further added to regimental lore when the major asked if he would like to be wed as a quartermaster rather than as serjeant-major. He had replied, with absolute decorum went the story, that he would prefer to take the biggest fence first.

The wedding day had been postponed a fortnight on account of Barrow's death. A fortnight's mourning in India was a long time by all but the most fastidious standards, for death was so commonplace and sudden that it was neither especially appropriate nor practical to observe the passing of one man, or woman, many days after the committal of their mortal remains. The bereaved or the orphaned went home to England, or else the former began life anew, and as often as not remarried in a short time with someone in their own circumstances. Alternatively a widow might accept a proposal from one of the many all-too-eager bachelor-writers, while a widower might make one to 'a new-arrived angel' from England – a member of what later wags would know as 'the fishing fleet'.

The arrangements for the RSM's wedding were overseen by Mr Lincoln himself. There were to be upwards of four hundred guests – all the officers and non-commissioned officers of the regiment, together with a good number of the latter from the other regiments of the garrison, and a surprising number of civilians. *And* the commander-in-chief, for such was Lincoln's reputation in Calcutta.

The marriage service would take place in the garrison church, which, with its double galleries, had just enough space for all of the guests and the regimental band. Its decoration was the only arrangement that Lincoln left entirely in others' hands, for the future Mrs Lincoln was a staunch member of the congregation. On the day itself, she and other members of her Dorcas circle came early, before watering parade, with great boughs of greenery and bunches of vivid orchids in the regiment's colours.

Meanwhile, the regimental quartermaster-serjeant and his working parties were labouring in the garrison gymnasium to work a similar, if secular, transformation – to prepare for what the future Mrs Lincoln delicately referred to as the wedding breakfast, but which all in the Sixth called the tamasha. The RSM came at midday to inspect the work, said not a word as he walked the 'assembly room', as it had become, then astonished the quartermaster-serjeant by saying simply, 'Thank you, Harold' – the first time he had ever addressed him by his Christian name (indeed, the quartermaster-serjeant was astonished to discover that Lincoln even knew it).

At four o'clock, the worst of the heat being past, the first arrivals at the church heard the band strike up its programme of music. The RSM confessed to having an untutored ear, but he had nevertheless scrutinized the programme, striking out the overture to *The Marriage of Figaro* (being uncertain of its propriety) and 'Blow, blow, thou winter wind' (being certain of its ambiguity), and approving more Haydn and Piccini instead.

At twenty past the hour exactly, Mr Lincoln marched up the aisle, eyes front, spurs ringing, as if on parade. He wore review order, shako under his right arm, sword scabbard grasped in his left, leather and metal shining as no one had quite seen either element shine before. Beside him (in truth, half a pace to the rear, for the man could not bring himself to draw level even on such an occasion), was his supporter, Deedes, the senior troop serjeant-major and next RSM. On his left, the same half-pace behind, was his long-serving orderly, who now took from him his shako and gloves and handed him the service sheet. Lincoln made a sharp bow of the head to Sir Edward Paget, the commander-in-chief, and to Joynson sitting in the row behind, and took his place at the end of the front pew. The band then struck up 'Treue Husar'. Herr Hamper had not included it in his submission, for Lincoln would never have approved, but it was a favourite of the Sixth's, and the best part of the congregation believed it exactly apt. The murmur of approval at the end caused the bandmaster to repeat it.

At two minutes to half-past the hour, Herr Hamper and the band embarked on the final 'overture' – *Alceste*, which seemed to compose the congregation perfectly, as indeed the RSM had intended when he chose the piece 'for its dignity and bearing'. The bandmaster particularly approved of the choice because it could be repeated without an obvious break in case of the customary delay in the arrival of the bride.

The future Mrs Lincoln was, however, a soldier's daughter and a soldier's widow, and she had no intention of being, as she put it, 'late on parade'. At exactly the half-hour, Herr Hamper was startled by the signal to curtail the Handel and launch at once into 'Sweet lass of Richmond Hill', to which the bride would process to the chancel. It had been an express choice, for the future Mrs Lincoln hailed from Putney, where her father had been a waterman before enlisting in the artillery train, but Putney was close enough to Richmond to make the choice of music fitting. And in any case, though few knew it, her mother had kept the cows in Richmond Park – together, indeed, with Beau Brummell's mother, as she was proud to relate. She walked up the aisle on the arm of the light infantry's commanding officer, in a blue dress trimmed with yellow and white, which at once won the approval of all in the bridegroom's camp.

'Dearly belovèd,' began the chaplain, managing somehow to overcome the inappropriateness of the salutation, and commanding a respectful silence. 'We are gathered together in the sight of Almighty God . . .'

And so the old, familiar words began to come, like a warm breeze bringing the scent of happy memories. Hervey let them drift over him, savouring a phrase here and there, and with no regrets.

When it came to the homily, seeing the commander-in-chief sitting attentively not more than a few feet before him, the chaplain's nerve almost failed him. But in glancing at the RSM he was suddenly more afraid of his opinion than the general's, and he managed somehow to fill his lungs with sufficient air. In truth, he need have had no worry, for he had composed what all would agree was a very proper address, by no means too long, at once respectful yet sound in its teaching, combining as it did appropriate adulation for the RSM and all his works, the recognition that in Mrs Lincoln the regiment had gained, in his words (or rather those borrowed from Scripture), 'a pearl of rare price', and last but by no means least God's rightful due in this blessed state of affairs. None of the parties, on earth or in heaven, could have been in the least disappointed.

There followed more singing – Toplady served the mood of temporary exile extraordinarily well – and the signing of the register, on only the second page.

And then, as it were, came the command *stand at ease* (if not quite *stand easy*) as Mr and Mrs Lincoln began their march down the aisle to the band's lusty rendition of 'Young May moon', the regimental quick march. Here and there a brave serjeant clapped a hand on Lincoln's shoulder, wishing him well and 'God bless, sir!'

The troop serjeant-majors had already slipped out of the church to form the guard of honour, sabres in salute at the carry, smiles broad and eyes twinkling. Mr Lincoln took it all in – not least the shine on the leather and the buttons, judging with special satisfaction that Armstrong was better turned out even than Hairsine. Lincoln had never shown a moment's emotion in living memory, and he was not about to do so now, but he could never have imagined such a day, his last as RSM, and he would miss not a detail of it.

Bride and groom left for the gymnasium in a calèche which one of the nabobs had put at their disposal, a gesture that said as much for the RSM's personal standing in Calcutta as the regiment's, and which those from outside the Sixth could not fail to note. The carriage was bedecked with ribbons – blue, yellow and white – with two dragoons posted behind, and driven by the rough-rider serjeant high on the box. It was a turnout fit for Lord Amherst himself, yet none was inclined to think it in the merest degree inflated for Mr Lincoln.

Especially not the private men, who, unknown to the RSM, had lined the road from church to gymnasium in their watering order, having come straight from stables. The cheering could be heard all about the garrison. It broke the rules, of course. Cheering superiors was not approved of. The Duke of Wellington himself had forbidden it – 'for if once you permit them to cheer they may do the opposite when circumstances are not so favourable'. But it was the RSM's last day, and no regulation could adequately apply to that.

In the gymnasium, where the sutler's little army of khitmagars were turned out in their best white, Mr and Mrs Lincoln took post to welcome their guests. On the platform at the other end of the hall, which served usually as a boxing booth, bandsmen were taking their places. The band-serjeant would direct them this time, and the music would be altogether merrier, with the regimental glee club joining them later with glees written for the occasion. The huge punkahs hanging the length of the gymnasium's high ceiling, and strung specially, now began to swing, the punkah-wallahs in the gallery heaving for all they were worth, like ringers first pulling up the bells of a Sunday morning.

The sight which would command greatest admiration, however, was that evidence of the sutler's craft (and the RSM's generosity) which lay on trestles the entire length of one wall. Here was a collation worthy of St James's – sides of beef, mutton, fowls of all kind, fish lying on ice, lentils, rice, pickles and sauces. And on tables down the middle of the hall was the means to quench the thirst of the four hundred: six whole hogsheads of Allsop's pale ale, decanters of Madeira for the officers and their ladies and any others who preferred it, and for those whose taste was neither for beer nor strong wine, punchbowls of *lol shrob*.

When the speeches came they were brisk and brief, the RSM's especially. Mr Lincoln was ever a man of few words. From the band platform he made his thanks to all, paying handsome respects to his wife and her maids, and called for three cheers for the regiment. Serjeant-Major Deedes spoke next. It was considered the form to make some jesting remarks about the bridegroom, revealing past indiscretions perhaps, or some embarrassing aspect of his life off parade. Both Deedes's research and nerve had failed him, however, and he contented himself – and, he hoped, all who heard – with a harmless story of how once, in the middle of a battle in Spain, Lincoln had ridden up to a British and a French officer locked in furious combat and ordered them to stop at once: 'for it is very unseemly, gentlemen!'

There was great laughter and cheering all about the hall, but in truth, any words delivered with a smile would have served this day.

'Ay, it's a fact I did,' declared Lincoln, permitting himself to be a heckler just for once. 'But I made the French officer give up his sword to me there and then!'

There was even greater cheering.

And then Deedes braced himself for the final jest. 'Mrs Lincoln, ma'am. I'm sure I am permitted to say that you are most welcome in the regiment. And doubly so, for tonight you retire with a serjeant-major and tomorrow you awake with an officer beside you instead!'

There was now rumbustious, earthy cheering.

'That will touch a raw nerve or two,' said David Sledge to Hervey as they stood together by one of the hogsheads.

'The Broad-minded, you mean?'

Sledge grimaced in mock disapproval. 'I reckon Rose has had a very close shave. A funeral and a wedding to distract attention – I call it very lucky indeed.'

'Well, I for one would not welcome being Paget's quill-driver.'

'Maybe not, Hervey. But then you would not have bedded another man's wife in the first place.'

Hervey blanched. 'David, you take it a little too personally. And there's something in Scripture, is there not, about casting the first stone?'

Sledge was a son of the manse, however, and knew his Scripture rather better than Hervey recalled his. 'That was speaking of punishment, not judgement. Anyway, it's not the same, is it, if the lady's not a lady – not a *real* officer's wife?' He took a long draw on his pot of ale.

'Oh, David, that's unfair. Joynson has the very devil of a job at present.'

'Ay, well, that's as maybe. But a horse that's once kicked over the traces is best shot from the team.'

Hervey was saved by the commander-in-chief. Just when it seemed the speeches and toasts were done, the general ascended the platform.

There were murmurs of surprise, and then silence.

'You tell 'im, sir!' came a voice from the back of the hall, followed by more laughter, and a certain anxiety on

Joynson's part that the hogsheads might be emptying too quickly for comfort.

'Mr and Mrs Lincoln, it is an honour to be here,' began Sir Edward Paget in a voice at once commanding and warm. 'Mrs Lincoln would not know that I first met her husband more than fifteen years ago, in Spain. Indeed, it was on a very dark night and it was at a place called Corunna.'

The proverbial pin could now have been dropped. Corunna was a distant memory to just a very few of the bluecoats, but it was second only to Waterloo in the consciousness of the Sixth.

'I, a general officer, was in command of the reserve during that battle, and I and my staff had become lost. I will say no more, but had it not been for the address of a certain serjeant-major the French would have had me in their bag that night.'

There was much approval about the hall, if muted still. This was news indeed.

'As it was' – Sir Edward broke into a broad smile – 'they had me but two years later, I'm sorry to say, else it might have been me and not my brother with you at Waterloo!'

'Yer wouldn't be standing as steady then, sir!' came the voice of another wit from the back of the hall.

And there was cautious laughter about the room from those who understood the reference to Lord Uxbridge's missing leg (while Paget had lost an arm).

'It sounds as though *you're* not standing all that steady either!' returned Sir Edward.

There were hoots of laughter now. There was nothing more entertaining than the heckled putting down the heckler.

'But let me not suspend the celebrations any longer. Except to wish the bride and groom the best of good fortune, and to say that I half think I could send the Sixth east and be finished with the Burmans at once!'

There was now loud and sustained cheering from all

quarters. Sir Edward played to the gallery, but he did so perfectly.

Eyre Somervile shook his head. 'A most curious animal, the soldier.'

Emma smiled. They stood apart from the regimentals, and she was enjoying this intimacy. 'In what way, my dear?'

'He is happier to be thought of as a number in a line, just so long as the line is his own, and with others who belong to it. You saw. There cannot be more than a few dozen who were at Corunna, and yet they all think of it as *their* honour, as though they had all been there, indeed.'

Emma nodded. 'A very proper pride, the sort that comes *not* before a fall.'

'And in men who might otherwise be outside all society.'

'Oh, indeed. They sang well in church, but I have no illusions.'

Her husband took another glass of Madeira. 'And I have observed how they are with their officers, some of whom are as stupid as half those in parliament, yet the little that is good in them is somehow magnified by the connection. And these men' – he nodded to the dozens of chevrons about the place – 'would no doubt be hurling bricks at magistrates were they not in regimentals. Yet here they all are, as if the same family. And those we saw on the road here without chevrons just biding their time until *they're* allowed a bit further under the blanket. I tell you, it's a system that defies reckoning. I've mocked its little absurdities often enough, but I half believe the Company could go anywhere with men like this.'

Emma sighed. 'I hope, therefore, that the Company will remain in ignorance of its treasure.'

Somervile touched her arm, for him a public gesture of unusual warmth.

'Good afternoon Mr Somervile, sir. Good afternoon, ma'am.' Armstrong's greeting recalled the two of them.

'Good afternoon, Serjeant-Major – and Mrs Armstrong,' replied Somervile, with a look of genuine pleasure.

Emma smiled as wide. 'Oh, please, don't on my account,' she said to Caithlin as she curtsied. Emma's Indian maids might bow gracefully, but they never curtsied, and, in any case, she could never think of Caithlin Armstrong as of inferior status. 'Especially, my dear, not in your condition.'

Caithlin and her husband glanced with customary pride at the swelling beneath her dress.

'I should say in *our* condition,' added Emma, with the same look of pride.

'Oh, Mrs Somervile,' exclaimed Caithlin, her melodious Cork never stronger. 'How happy I am for you! Is that why Miss Joynson is to be your companion, then, ma'am?'

No fact remained in the possession of but two people in Calcutta for more than a day. 'It is,' said Emma, agreeably. She could not very well add 'ostensibly', although indeed she might. Hervey's suggestion of taking in Frances Joynson for a while had come at a propitious time, though Emma certainly felt in no need of a companion.

Somervile himself was looking rather embarrassed, especially since Armstrong was smiling in a manly, confidential sort of way. There were affairs, indeed, that transcended all barriers. That did not trouble him in the slightest – Somervile was more impatient of the confines of rank than most men – but 'country matters', as he was still wont to call them, he was not at home with.

'What is the news from the east, sir?' asked Armstrong, thinking to save further talk of domestic affairs.

Somervile shook his head. 'Not good, I'm afraid, Serjeant-Major. The business is taking longer than was imagined.' He did not say by whom imagined, nor that there were some who never imagined it otherwise – the commander-in-chief, for one. 'And I fear that our embarrassment there will encourage others to . . .' (he noticed both wives listening intently) 'to . . . become rather impudent.'

Armstrong nodded. 'Well, sir, I for one shall be making in the opposite direction tomorrow with Captain Hervey. And pleased of it, too. I've no partiality for fighting with trees everywhere you turn. That Burma is no place for cavalry.'

The band had struck up a lively jig, and the commander-in-chief had rejoined the major. 'A capital display, Joynson; capital. My compliments to you. But I fear I must return to my desk. The despatches from Rangoon this morning were not at all felicitous.'

'But you still do not think the Sixth will be needed, Sir Edward?'

'No, I think not. If Campbell can break himself out of Rangoon then all should be well, even if takes some weeks more – months, even. And break out he's bound to do at some stage. But the country isn't suitable to develop cavalry operations. I've sent him reinforcements, and if need be, for escorts and the like, I'll send one of the Madras light horse.'

Paget began taking his leave, shaking hands with Mr and Mrs Lincoln, and several others besides, his smile in contrast with the earnestness of his manner with Joynson. As they reached the door he turned again to Joynson, and his former look returned. 'Things are by no means settled among the country powers hereabouts, and our difficulties in the east will only encourage them. I want a handy force here in Bengal if trouble ensues. I have to be able to count on King's cavalry. You'll have the Sixth in best condition, Eustace?'

'I'm sure we understand that, General.'

Sir Edward nodded. 'Hervey will soon be at Dehli, I should imagine?'

'The troop left on Tuesday. Hervey goes tomorrow.'

Sir Edward nodded again. 'A good choice, Hervey. Ochterlony will like him.'

Joynson raised an eyebrow. 'And what's equally to the point, General, Hervey will like Ochterlony!'

Sir Edward smiled. 'Oh, yes, indeed. That is equally important!'

CHAPTER TEN

THE RESIDENT

Dehli, three weeks later

Sir David Ochterlony, the Honourable East India Company's political resident at the court of Shah Mohammed Akbar Rhize Badshah, the Great Mughal, was sixty-six years old. He had entered the Bengal army when he was not yet twenty and had spent his entire service in Hindoostan. He had fought the French, the Marathas and the Nipális, and each time he had added garlands to his reputation as both a soldier and a diplomatist. He had been a major-general since 1814 and resident since 1803. His name was held in the highest esteem – venerated, even – throughout India, although it was the opinion of some members of the Bengal council, and Lord Amherst himself, that his retirement was overdue. Indeed, if any man gave the lie to the oft-heard native lament that a grey hair on the head of a European was never to be seen in India, it was Ochterlony – although, ironically, he had been born and bred in America.

Hervey reported to the residency towards the end of the afternoon, within an hour of entering the great old Mughal capital, but already he had formed the strongest impression of decay and ruin in Dehli – of desolation, even. The city walls, half of stone, half of brick, were in poor repair, tombs and mausoleums were everywhere in dilapidation, grass grew long all about. In places there was a smell of corruption as bad as in Calcutta, and his guide told him there was not a house from where the jackal's cry could not be heard of a night. The centuries of depredations, the sackings and the looting, the sieges and the slaughter had brought the once sumptuous imperial city to little more than a tract of dreary and disconsolate tombs.

'Sahib, here nothing lasts,' said Hervey's guide. 'There is much tribulation and little joy. In years past, the living thought only of reposing after death in splendid sepulchres, and their descendants have thought only of destroying what was intended for eternity.'

And Hervey had half shivered in the chill of that judgement.

But the guide had not been melancholy. He had spoken with the indifferent acceptance of fate that was the mark of his religion. And indeed there was cheer in his judgement, for he told Hervey that things would have been immeasurably worse without Sir David Ochterlony. 'Ochterlony-sahib is greatest man in all of empire after Great Mughal himself, sahib.'

Hervey considered himself well used by now to native blandishments, whether from gholam or pandit. Perhaps, though, in the living memory of Hindoostan – and certainly that of his guide – Sir David Ochterlony had a reasonable claim to greatness. It had been he who had kept Jashwant Rao, the Holkar of Indore, the most powerful of the Maratha chiefs, at bay two decades before, while the Wellesleys made war on the Scindia and the Bhonsla. Greatness, indeed, did not seem too inapt a word as Hervey now contemplated the residency, a classical *palazzo* on Chandnee chouk near the Lahore gate. It spoke of a confident power, for it had nothing to do with the art of the empire of Tamerlane, only that of the Honourable Company.

As he rode up to its gates, the quarter-guard turned out

and presented arms. The havildar saluted and stood his ground, so Hervey dismounted and obliged him by inspecting his men – smart Bengali *sipahis*, red-breasted, bare-legged, straps and pouches whitened, muskets burnished. Then a young ensign, very fair-skinned, came. He wore a frock coat and forage hat, as if on picket duty at St James's, and he saluted as sharply, introducing himself and then conducting Hervey to Sir David Ochterlony's quarters. It was, truly, just as if he were arriving at the Horse Guards again.

For weeks Hervey had wondered what he would find at the residency, so many had been the stories. But all he knew for certain was that Sir David was an elderly major-general, and so he composed himself accordingly: the usual military formalities, the stuff of any general headquarters – a brief interview, the presentation of compliments, and so on and so on. But instead of being bidden to wait in an ante-room and then being announced at the door of the resident's office, as he would have expected, the ensign showed him at once into a sitting room furnished in the Mughal style with cushions and divans about the floor, in the middle of which sat a barefoot major-general in a bamboo armchair, wearing a florid silk dressing gown, with a hookah to his mouth.

Hervey rallied quickly enough. 'Good afternoon, Sir David. I am Captain Hervey of the Sixth Light Dragoons.' He had considered the mode of address carefully, concluding that as Sir David Ochterlony was the political resident it was more appropriate to address him by that style rather than as 'General'.

Sir David did not reply at once, nodding as if in a dream.

Hervey stood at attention but removed his cap, uncertain how the interview would proceed. Without doubt, there was here before him what in Calcutta they called a 'mofussil eccentric', one who had been overlong in native India. Any reference to military rank seemed incongruous, and the display of military normality that had attended his arrival only served to make the situation seem more absurd. It was not entirely true to say that his heart sank, but it was not nearly so light as when he had begun his assignment. 'I have the honour to report for duty, three officers and fifty-three dragoons at your service, sir.'

Sir David took the pipe from his mouth and beckoned a khitmagar to bring a chair. 'And a pipe,' he called after him in Urdu, or something very like it, for Hervey grasped its meaning.

'No, thank you, sir. I am, in truth, rather parched.'

'My dear boy, my dear boy!' Sir David took the pipe from his mouth again and bellowed, '*Quai hai!* Sherbet for Captain Hervey-sahib!'

Hervey took his seat and waited to be spoken to, doubts crowding in apace.

The silence continued. Sir David, pipe to his mouth once more, was content to sit and contemplate the new arrival.

At length he seemed satisfied. He took the pipe from his mouth and nodded. 'How are things in Calcutta?'

It was a not unreasonable question, except that Hervey had scarcely moved beyond the confines of the garrison save to the Someviles' house at Fort William since coming from Rangoon. He trusted that the resident had no more appetite for drawing-room gossip than he. 'In as far as I can say, Sir David, the war with Ava goes badly. There is news, or rumour perhaps would be the better description, that Lord Combermere shall succeed Sir Edward Paget next year. Beyond that I fear there is little I know.'

Sir David's expression of surprise was very pronounced. 'Calcutta has become an exceedingly dull place these late years if that is the extent of your intelligence!'

Hervey sighed inwardly; this was very like keeping company with an ageing parent. He would have to try hard not to become by turns impatient or indulgent. 'In truth, Sir David, I have been laid low these past months, and confined largely to the military lines.'

Sir David looked vexed. 'Laid low? Laid low with what?'

Hervey forced himself to remember that he was speaking to the hero of Nipál. 'I received a ball in my shoulder at Rangoon, Sir David, and thereafter contracted the fever.'

Sir David's mien changed at once. 'Rangoon? Tell me of it.'

It was like the stirring of a sleepy old lion – at first the mere twitch of an eyelid, a flick of the tail, until by degrees the huge beast was on all fours and circling with intermittent grunts and snarls. Hervey spared him nothing. At the end of his account the resident shook his head and sighed. 'That won't do; it won't do at all!'

'I wonder, sir, if I may have more sherbet?'

Sir David scolded the khitmagar for his inattention, as a lion might swipe at an errant cub. 'You will stay to dinner, Hervey, and lodge here. You will no doubt wish to see your troop properly billeted, but your lieutenant may easily exercise command.'

Sir David, for all his eccentric attire, had by now acquired a wholly commanding bearing. Hervey saw no point in protesting. It threw onto Perry an undue burden of society with Green, but that was the way of it: he was captain and he had other concerns. 'I am very obliged, Sir David. But I had better send for my small kit. I have nothing but . . .'

'Oh, we shall not dress,' said Sir David, airily. 'Not in this month. I'll have the khansamah bring you a robe.' He looked at him intently. 'And at dinner I shall tell you of where *our* troubles may lie in the months ahead.'

Hervey bathed and then lay down on the narrow divan in his otherwise ample quarters. All about was marble, like the palace at Chintalpore, but whereas at the Rajah of Chintal's seat the air was full of intrigue and menace, here it was peace, although in the resident's words there was a promise of action. He began looking forward to his commission once more. Dereliction there might be – in so many ways Dehli reminded him of Rome – but he sensed it could fascinate. In any case, it was good to be away from the Calcutta garrison, a station full of left-behinds while hounds were hard at work elsewhere.

Hervey closed his eyes. There was not a sound but for a hoopoe and its mate in the garden beyond his shuttered window. They brought to mind Chintalpore again. How long ago it seemed. Was it seven, eight years? He remembered telling the rajah how he wished one day to entertain him in England. Had he really imagined that he might? Or was it that everything was lived so intensely in India? Could he go back there? It would be easy enough – one of the Calcutta coasters down to the Godavari, thence by budgerow as far as he might up that disobliging river, and on to Chintalpore. Godaji Rao Sundur, Rajah of Chintalpore – Hervey was, after all, one of his *jagirdars*, and his jagir returned a respectable income each year, not all of which was covenanted to the widows of those desperate days' fighting the nizam's guns and the Pindarees. Would the raj kumari be purged of her crimes? Would her father have recalled her from deep in the forest of the Gonds? Or did she scheme and plot still – so reckless a daughter of so sensible a man? Did he really want to see her again? In one respect at least he had no doubt, for even as he lay, her allure had its effect.

At seven, the sun on the horizon and the heat of the after-noon given way to a balmy dusk, Hervey put on the green robe that the bearer had brought him and joined Sir David Ochterlony in his Mughal courtyard. With the resident was a tall, well-made native man, clean-shaven, with sleek hair drawn back and held with a clip. He wore a loose-fitting kurta, white trousers and embroidered slippers, and he spoke freely and easily.

'Hervey, this is Jaswant Sing, my master of horse. And this,' said Sir David, turning to the man, 'is Captain Hervey of His Majesty's Sixth Light Dragoons, who, as of this after-noon, is captain of my escort.'

They both bowed.

'What are your horses, Captain Hervey?' asked Jaswant Sing, with a warm aspect.

'Marwaris, for the most part.'

Jaswant Sing inclined his head in a way that signified approval. 'And you yourself ride the Marwari?'

'I have a charger brought with me from England, but my second is a Marwari, though she is not with me for the present, having been sick.'

'And the Marwari pleases you, Captain Hervey?'

'Oh yes. Yes indeed. I have never seen a better doer' (Hervey checked himself), 'that is, I have never seen a horse that subsisted on so little, and is yet so handy and obliging.' It was too early to volunteer information about the Marwari's endurance in his jungle raid, however.

'The Marwari is from Rajpootana, Captain Hervey, which is my home. If your duties are allowing, I should be very pleased to show you the breeding horses there.'

'If my duties were to allow it, Jaswant Sing-sahib, I should like that very much.' He would leave it at that, for he did not imagine Sir David would be inclined to spare him too soon, if at all.

Sir David was attentive, however. 'One of Rajpootana's neighbours gives me considerable cause for worry, Hervey. I am frankly fearful of a struggle over the succession in Bhurtpore.'

Hervey was surprised by such frankness in their present company.

'You will not know of it, I dare say?'

'I know but a very little, Sir David.'

'Nothing much troubles Fort William but the war with Ava, I suppose. Well, the Rajah of Bhurtpore, Baldeo Sing, has long honoured the treaty of friendship with the Company. He is now becoming frail, and his son Balwant is but a boy, and the rajah is fearful that his nephew Durjan Sal has designs on the succession. The old rajah asked that I invest the boy with a *khelat* – a sort of honorary dress – as a sign of our recognition of his rightful claim, and this I did in the early part of the year.'

Sir David beckoned his khansamah and told him that he wished to eat at once.

Hervey decided he would not wait on Sir David's pace. 'And I presume therefore, sir, that you have intelligence that this action has not entirely dissuaded Durjan Sal from his designs?'

'Just so, Hervey,' replied the resident, in an approving tone. 'And everything that we know of him says he is without scruple.'

'Jhauts,' said Jaswant Sing, shaking his head. 'They are stubborn beggars.'

Sir David nodded. 'But when they're not being stubborn, Hervey, they're the most courageous men. In our service they would make fine *sipahis*. I had a mind to visit the rajah now that the cooler season will soon be upon us, for I was not able to invest the *khelat* in person. I judged it appropriate to go with an escort of King's cavalry rather than native, for Durjan Sal would no doubt believe it possible to buy off any native troops, and it would be well to remind him that not all of the Company's forces are engaged with the King of Ava.'

'You mean as a portent, Sir David? I have but fifty dragoons.'

'Yes, just so. Now, let us eat.'

Two weeks passed, during which Hervey saw little of Sir David but much of Jaswant Sing. The resident was sick for several days – he ascribed it to the change of season – and then when he was recovered enough to attend to his papers, was much occupied with the estimates which were overdue for submission to Calcutta. So Hervey found time aplenty to learn the Rajpoot way of horsemanship, and his neglect of the troop – or rather his delegation of day-to-day command to his lieutenant – he was able to justify by these equestrian studies.

'That 'orse got ginger up its backside, sir?' called Private Johnson, standing at the edge of the maidan one morning.

Hervey sat astride a Marwari stallion which was pirouetting and leaping as if being backed for the first time. He managed to collect it, after a fashion, and walked him over to his groom. 'I'll have you know that this animal is trained for war, Johnson. For combat with war elephants indeed!'

'Oh ay, sir?'

'Yes. And very handy he is too, for all the fire you saw in him.' Hervey made to stretch his shoulder, to relieve the ache that had been growing since he took the reins, but he stopped short. He would give no sign, even to Johnson, that he could feel the musket ball's force still.

'And 'ow's 'e fight an elephant then, sir? 'E'd not stand as 'igh as its ear.'

'*He* doesn't do the fighting; the rider does. He gets the horse to leap up and takes the mahout in the flank with his lance. Then he can deal with the howdah.'

Johnson looked sceptical.

'I'll show you what he can do.' Hervey gathered up the reins again, though nothing like as taut as he would normally for proper collection.

Indeed, the reins themselves were unusual. They were stitched double towards the end, and Hervey held this doubled length, close to its fork, in his bridle hand and almost to his chest. It showed a long and graceful length such that his childhood riding master would have admired. But that old *rittmeister* would also have been intrigued, for Hervey was not wearing spurs, nor was he carrying a whip. Johnson could scarcely believe it either.

'The weight of the reins collects him onto the bit,'

explained Hervey. 'I don't know how or why, for I've never heard of an animal trained so. In truth, I'd not have been inclined to believe it.'

After circling two or three times at a canter, he put the stallion into a pirouette, then into a reversed pirouette, then into what he knew as '*voltes* on a small compass', stopping on the hocks and turning on them, and from that he had the horse jump into the gallop. Finally, and still at the gallop, he made the animal move obliquely, as Peto would have made headway with a weather helm.

Johnson stood silent but impressed. These were 'tricks' of self-evident utility in the field. It was not difficult to imagine the lance held across the body or out wide, the horse passaging left or right to take the enemy in the flank.

But Hervey had not finished. There were what his old *rittmeister* called the airs above ground. Jaswant Sing had shown him how to perform them, though in truth, as well Hervey knew, all he had done was show him how to sit a horse that knew its airs.

First a *levade*, the horse rising on its hind legs, hocks almost on the ground. Then forward from the levade a *courbette*, with three distinct leaps – or was it four? And finally the *capriole*, the stallion leaping into the air and kicking out long with its hind legs. Jaswant Sing had called it *udaang* – flying.

'You see?' called Hervey, panting almost as much as the horse as he walked him over to where Johnson stood – and rubbing his shoulder now, and more confidently, for he knew that to work like that meant he was all but whole again. 'You see how useful *that* could be!'

There was no doubting it. 'That were a vicious kick all right,' said his groom, shaking his head. 'I've never seen owt like it.'

'You see now how useful for elephant-fighting?'

'Oh ay, sir. Yon 'orse looked as if it would've scrambled up its 'ead.'

'That was the idea,' said Hervey, slipping from the saddle and loosening the girth. 'But all that's over with – elephants and the like. Just a pretty display now. Think how you might turn heads with it in England though, eh?'

CHAPTER ELEVEN
TOWERS OF SILENCE

_____

Bhurtpore, a month later

Hervey sat on the crumbling wall of an old well, in a large straw hat and very unmilitary clothes, sketching.

'Sir David Ochterlony makes but one stipulation,' he had written to Emma's husband, before leaving Dehli:

> *He would have me do more than merely gawp at the walls*
> *of Bhurtpore; he would have me bring back a thorough*
> *knowledge of all its defences. And all this, of course, I am*
> *to accomplish without for a moment giving cause for*
> *anyone to know what I do in that city. To what end this*
> *spying may be directed I can little imagine, except that*
> *Sir David speaks darkly of the need, perhaps, of such*
> *information in years soon to come. At first I imagined him*
> *to mean that he himself, Sir David Ochterlony, might have*
> *to do what Lord Lake had been unable to accomplish.*
> *But although I believe Sir David to be game for the*
> *hardiest adventure still, I am certain he understands the*
> *circumstances would be no more favourable now than they*
> *were for Lord Lake. I have read much of his lordship's*
> *siege, and I cannot imagine that success could be*
> *accomplished with fewer men and guns, and Sir David*
> *does not have one half of Lord Lake's force at his own*

disposal. I believe, therefore, that Sir David would put
before the Council in Calcutta a proposal for the stronger
reinforcement of his command were it ever to come to a
fight, and that meanwhile he is taking all prudent steps
to acquire intelligence of any nature. He does not confirm
me in this opinion when I ask him, but he does not oppose
it either . . .

Hervey was not by any reckoning an artist, but he had been taught to draw, and his practice in field sketching in the Peninsula had made him proficient in the reproduction of landscape with correct proportion and perspective. For several days he had wandered about the city drawing anything he could see which was of no military significance in order to establish his credentials as a travelling antiquarian. No one had shown the slightest interest in him, but he had wanted an alibi – a portfolio of architectural drawings that would serve as evidence of his innocent intent when he began work on the defences.

One sketch he had been especially minded to hide, however. Its subject appalled him – sickened him indeed. He had scarcely been able to keep down his gorge as he drew. And it took him longer to complete than some of the more elaborate works of decorative detail, for he had wanted as faithful an impression as possible; one that might have the same effect on a viewer that the archetype had on him. It had been a repetitive work, a business of drawing skull after skull. He had tried to estimate how many there were: the column was as tall as Trajan's in Rome, and his guide had said it was neither hollow nor filled with sand. Here was no bas-relief of bones, but a solid pillar of Lord Lake's dead. No Christian burial or cremation according to native rites for these men – King's and sepoys alike. The gamekeepers at Longleat would string up their trophies to discourage predators and to impress by their zeal. The Futtah Bourge, the 'bastion of victory', was but the same.

How loathsome it stood by comparison with that eloquent commemoration of Trajan's victory, an affront to every decent instinct of a Christian-raised man, and a gesture of contempt for the customs of war. Peaceful Hindoostan might be, but a sight such as this said that peace was an unnatural thing. Hervey considered it well that he concealed his sketch, and thought it best that he hide it from view of his fellows too.

This next stage of his work occupied him a full week. 'The fortress of Bhurtpore is without doubt the largest I have ever seen,' he wrote to Eyre Somerville towards the end of October:

> It stands on a plain broken and rugged towards the west but otherwise bare, affording little cover, and I calculate the perimeter to be not very much short of five miles. Any siege force would have to be great indeed to invest the entire fortress. I have now been able to make a very faithful comparison of Lord Lake's dispositions, and it is at once apparent that his insufficiency in men was greater than I had supposed when reading the usual texts, for with the Maratha cavalry harassing him he was obliged to hold ready reserves to deal with them, and he had not thereby the means either to starve out the garrison in the old way or breach the walls in enough places and in sufficient strength to bolt the defenders.
>
> A broad and deep ditch runs the entire length of the perimeter, from the inner edge of which rises a thick and lofty wall of sun-baked clay and stone, flanked by no fewer than thirty-five turreted bastions. I have been able to draw in plan the location of each, though for reasons of economy in time, and so as not to appear excessively interested should I have been accosted, I was minded to draw elevations of only those I judged would command the likely approaches. The citadel itself occupies a natural height, rising above all else in the city, and is itself

enclosed by a ditch 150 feet wide and fifty feet deep. And,
as if Vauban himself had directed the fortification, there
are ravelins and lunettes, flèches and demi-lunes the entire
length of the walls.

And how blessed are the people of Bhurtpore, too, since
the moats and ditches are dry, so they are not plagued by
the mosquitoes that thrive on still water, and they may
drive their animals wherever they wish. I have learned
that water when it is needed to fill the moats comes from a
jheel to the north-west of the fortress, a very practical and
happy arrangement. This water and these walls would
pose the best engineer a test of his science. And when the
water and the walls are covered by the guns of thirty-five
bastions and countless other outworks, the infantry might
very well become so many companies of forlorn hopes unless
directed by a general of exceptional address. In the skill of
the siege artillery and the field gunners reposes their fate.
No fortress is impregnable, we must understand, but it is my
decided opinion that if ever a fortress came close to such a
condition it is Bhurtpore . . .

And then he had confided in his friend the unhappier
detail of his detached duty – unusually, for it touched only
on the business of the Sixth:

I am resolved to have Green out. He daily becomes more
awkward in his dealings with everyone. In truth I can
scarcely bear to speak to him. Every blemish in both his
character and appearance seemed magnified in Dehli,
there being no multitude of other officers to draw away
attention. I have therefore written to Joynson and advised
him that he speak severely with him about the
advisability of his remaining in the regiment, for I have
concluded that he could never make an officer, and if ever it
comes to a fight the outcome would be very ill indeed – for
himself, principally, for there could be little enough

damage he might do to any of the dragoons, such is his subsidiary role. Yet were he ever to encounter a half decent swordsman the result must be disaster.

But, on the other hand, I am pleased to say that Perry is a fine lieutenant, on whose account I need have had no fears, and I shall take leave hence, before returning to Dehli, to see the great white mausoleum at Agra, about which you always spoke so much . . .

These letters he then took with him to Agra, where there were trusted hircarrahs to carry despatches down the Jumna and thence to Calcutta, and from where he himself could take a boat back to Dehli with greater ease. He had indeed grown fond of his licence. The days were still warm, and at night it was good to sit before a fire reading or in contemplation. He lacked the company of English-speakers, Jaswant Sing having now returned to Dehli, but this gave him opportunity to practise his Urdu with a certain confidence, and in any case he had never been fretful in his own company – except at the very end of his stay in Bhurtpore, but the fever had not developed its full power, and he was abed for no longer than a day.

Five more he gave himself to see what had once been the proud Mughal capital, Agra. On the last evening he sat beside the hearth in a comfortable haveli which Jaswant Sing had arranged for him, below the red walls of the great sandstone fort. The place was strangely peaceful for so teeming a city, and he contemplated its lessons. He laid down his glass of arrack – he had come to rely on it as a faithful aid to digestion, no matter how tempestuous the dinner served him – leaned back in his chair and drew long on the mildest of cheroots. The tobacco smoke mixed agreeably with that of the sandalwood burning in the grate, and he closed his eyes for a moment the better to hear the nightjar – stranger, as a rule, to the haunts of men.

In a while he opened them again, and picked up his

journal from the table next to him. It had commanded more time than usual of an evening, for it was his sole entry at Agra:

12th November 1824

The work at Bhurtpore being done – and greatly more of it than I had ever imagined, so immense a place is it – I travelled thence to the Jumna again, under the admirable arrangements of Jaswant Sing, and reposed two nights at the ancient capital of the Moguls. The palace called the Taje Mahl, which means crown palace, is spoken of throughout India as one of unsurpassed beauty, the place of burial of the wife of a great emperor to whom it was erected in praise. I visited it the first day on arriving and was not disappointed. While it is visible in whole from the river, approached from the south through the main gate only its dome and the four minarets, at each corner, of white marble, are to be seen above the circumadjacent trees of a Persian garden, in the way that the dome of the Pope's basilica in Rome can be seen above the crowding buildings of the Borgo. Only when, like the basilica, one comes right upon it can its entire beauty be imagined. I have attempted to sketch it, but it is wholly beyond my skill to render it any justice, and I have instead resolved to find an artist hereabout who will make me a fair likeness. Last night I visited the gardens opposed to it on the other bank of the Jumna, which are in very great disrepair, yet which are called the Moonlight Gardens for here is where, legend has it, the emperor would come at the full moon each month to recall his lost love. It was planted with all manner of herbage that gave off sweet scent by night, and there is still too a night scent, though the place is very jungled . . .

Hervey's journal pretended to nothing more than being

well-kept. For the most part it was in note form, serving as a memorandum of movement, acquisition, accomplishment; or occasionally of intention, hindrance or opinion. But never of emotion, not even anger. Had it been his practice to include such feelings he would have filled pages since coming to Agra, for in that moonlight garden he had for a time begun to question the true intensity of his former love. It had been Emma Somervile's suggestion – insistence, indeed – that he visit Agra. There, she said, he would see the perfect expression of a grieving man's love. It had been no mawkish sentiment, for he had spoken with her of raising some memorial to Henrietta, and had done so with perfect calm. Henrietta was not yet dismissed habitually from his mind – thoughts of her, especially of their moments of intimacy, came on him still, and often – but he could now think of her with reason and cool judgement, quite unlike before. And Emma's suggestion had been far from unwelcome, for he had read and heard much of the white marble shrine: it would surely be instructive to see how a man who had grieved and had the means to memorialize that grieving had done so. However, the palace had seemed more and more a rebuke to him. Here stood a memorial as much to the constancy of an emperor's love as to the empress herself. Where was the evidence of his own constancy? In truth, the evidence was to the contrary – his bibi, the letters to and from Lady Katherine Greville, more sportive with each return.

Only later, on leaving Agra, as he read fitfully on the budgerow plying upstream for Dehli, did he learn that in time the emperor had abandoned the city and set up his court in the old Mughal capital – just as he, Hervey, had abandoned England and set up his domain in India. But Mumtaz Mahal had begged her husband not to pine for her, and to remarry. Hervey could not slough off his guilt so easily. And in any case his sins were mingled. He no longer honoured his wife's memory with his body, but neither did he say his prayers with system or regularity, let alone conviction. And he might as well have forgotten the offspring of their union. Somervile had been wont to say that many a man had lost his reason in India as well as his soul. But such men, Hervey supposed, had sought consolation in drink or some other opiate. He relied only on activity. No, he had no fear of losing his reason. But in India colours were brighter and shadows darker. It was not always so easy to judge things faithfully.

A noisy skein of bar-headed geese recalled him to the present. He turned up his collar against the freshening Jumna breeze, and picked up his volume on the Maratha wars again. How had Lord Lake miscalculated so? The walls of Bhurtpore had stood then as they did now. What had been the cause of so fatal a misjudgement? He must have it. And he knew he must then pray that in all his forgetting activity he could himself keep a right judgement in things, civil or military.

PART THREE

THE PRIDE OF HINDOOSTAN

GENERAL ORDER

Fort William
28 July 1825

The Right Hon. The Governor-General has learned with great sorrow the demise of Major-General Sir David Ochterlony, resident in Malwa and Rajpootana. This melancholy event took place on the morning of the 15th inst. at Meerut, whither he had proceeded for the benefit of change of air. On the eminent military services of Major-General Sir David Ochterlony, it would be superfluous to dilate; they have been acknowledged in terms of the highest praise by successive Governments; they justly earned a special and substantial reward from the Hon. East India Company; they have been recognised with expressions of admiration and applause by the British Parliament; and they have been honoured with signal marks of the approbation of his Sovereign . . .

. . . The confidence which the government reposed in an individual gifted with such rare endowments, was evinced by the high and responsible situations which he successively filled, and the duties which he discharged with eminent ability and advantage to the Public Interests. As an especial testimony of the high respect in which the

215

character and services of Major-General Sir D.
Ochterlony are held, and as a public demonstration of
sorrow for his demise, the Governor-General in Council is
pleased to direct that minute guns to the number of sixty-
eight, corresponding with his age, be fired this evening at
sunset, from the ramparts of Fort William.

CHAPTER TWELVE
MINUTE GUNS

Calcutta, October 1825

His Excellency General the Right Hon. Stapleton Lord Combermere, GCB, GCH &c., Commander-in-Chief of all the Forces in India, as he was styled, received Hervey warmly but without the same careless ease of their previous acquaintances. They had first met eleven years ago in the field at Toulouse, as Hervey lay painfully under the ministration of a surgeon. The commander of Wellington's cavalry had been all praise and warm regards then for Hervey in that culminating battle of the campaign, in his despatches writing that 'by his bold and independent action he averted what might at the very least have been an embarrassment for the mounted arm'. They had met on three occasions since then, the last being that most diverting evening at Apsley House before Hervey had come out to India, when he had met Lady Katherine Greville.

'I fancy you might care for some coffee, Hervey? It's a damnably cold morning.'

The invitation was to help himself from a pot on a table covered with maps and sketches, at which stood Colonel Macleod, who was to be brigadier of artillery, and Colonel Anburey, who was to be the same of engineers. Hervey acknowledged them both with a brisk bow of the head before pouring some of the strong black liquid into a big cup and adding a good measure of sugar.

'You set us nicely in apposition, Captain Hervey,' said Colonel Anburey, nodding with a grim, if perhaps wry, sort of smile at Colonel Macleod.

Hervey knew exactly what he meant. 'I fear the sappers will have little chance of doing their work without the support of the guns, Colonel, for the approaches to the walls are coverless. And yet the walls are so solid and thick that the guns shall have to come in close, and that can only be done by sapping from outside the range of the fort. Indeed, I wonder that it will not be better to mine one or two of the bastions, for a breach will otherwise be devilish hard.'

Colonel Anburey shook his head. 'I read your opinion, Hervey, but it is out of the question if the country lies as you have drawn it.'

'Too far to tunnel,' explained Lord Combermere.

Hervey looked puzzled.

Colonel Anburey supplied the detail. 'The greatest distance a gallery may be driven is two hundred yards. Beyond that there is insufficient air for a man to breathe, and indeed for the explosive to operate efficiently.'

Hervey was confident he had surveyed the defences accurately. 'That is indeed a pity, Colonel. It will be an affair of heavy pounding therefore.'

And it need not have been, he said to himself later. Six months ago Ochterlony might well have carried the day at a stroke, with that never-failing ally *surprise*, had the Governor-General allowed him to try – even with half the number of men with which Lord Lake had failed. At least he might by now be keeper of the gates in those great walls, thereby shutting out every freebooting Jhaut and brigand who at this very moment was flocking to Durjan Sal's banner.

But the Governor-General had dithered, fatally. Eyre

Somervile had told Hervey of how he had gone to Lord Amherst's office the morning Ochterlony's despatch had arrived from Dehli. Amherst had looked alarmed: there was ill news enough already from the east without more from the west.

'You read my earlier minute on the situation in Bhurtpore, Excellency?' Somervile had asked, careful to observe the punctilio of address for once.

Lord Amherst had looked uncertain.

'Three months ago the Rajah of Bhurtpore died, and his infant son succeeded him under the guardianship of his uncle.'

Lord Amherst's face had shown a flicker of recall.

'However, for reasons that should not detain us, the late rajah's nephew, Durjan Sal, has laid claim to the succession.'

'*Why* do you say they should not detain us, Mr Somervile?' Lord Amherst had demanded, his brow furrowed anxiously. 'We are, by your tone, very evidently to be detained by one claim or the other.'

'Durjan Sal disputes the legitimacy of the rightful heir, Balwant Sing. But by all the evidence hitherto before us this is a most villainous claim.'

'Before us? I have not heard anything of it!'

'No, my lord. Matters in this regard have fallen entirely to the resident in Dehli.'

'Ochterlony? Good God: what has he been about?'

Although Somervile shared the general opinion of Sir David Ochterlony – that his best days were long past – he had sufficient regard for his judgement in the rights of things, if not in their consequences. 'Sir David recognized the rightful claim of Balwant Sing twelve months ago by vesting him in a *khelat*—'

'What in heaven's name was he doing? Such a thing is not done without presumptions of obligation. What is Bhurtpore to us? I consider it very rash.'

Somervile had sighed to himself. 'The fact is, my lord, that Sir David has bestowed the Company's recognition on Balwant Sing and—'

'Well, he had better renounce it. We have trouble enough in Ava. Campbell's still stuck in the mud at Rangoon, and his ships gathering weed.' The Governor-General had waved his hand as if the matter was done with.

At whose door might blame lie in that regard, Somervile had been minded to ask. 'I'm afraid it is too late. It seems Durjan Sal moved against Balwant Sing's guardian some weeks ago – and very bloodily – and has proclaimed himself regent—'

'So?'

Somervile had tried hard to hide his irritation at the Governor-General's disregard of the dangers the country powers might pose. 'Sir David has already denounced Durjan Sal as an usurper of supreme authority, by which he means, of course, the Company—'

'I am perfectly well aware what he means, Somervile! He must be told at once to moderate his demands and conclude the affair by diplomacy.'

'I fear it is too late for that. He has called on the Jhauts to rally to him and announced that he will appear at the head of a British force to restore Balwant Sing!'

Lord Amherst had then, by Somervile's account, looked like a man winded by a body blow. His brow had furrowed even more, signalling his utter incomprehension. 'Where is this force to come from, Somervile?'

Somervile had raised his eyebrows. 'By all reckoning he might muster ten thousand men at most, scarcely a thousand of them white.'

Lord Amherst had fallen silent. 'Would that be enough? Sir David was – may yet be – a fine general . . .'

Somervile had put on a most determined expression. 'Opinions vary and differ. The commander-in-chief's is as yet unsettled. His deputy is of the opinion that it would be very far from sufficient. Bhurtpore, you may recall, is the fortress that defied Lord Lake more than twenty years ago, and nothing, I understand, has rendered it any less formidable since then.'

The remaining colour had disappeared from Lord Amherst's face. 'Then the consequences will be very grave. I cannot suffer humiliation in the west, at this time especially.'

Somervile had been much perturbed by the Governor-General's alarm. 'But, Lord Amherst, I understand that the commander-in-chief's opinion tends to reinforcement. If we at once send word to Bombay, and to Madras, we may assemble full three times Sir David's present number, and a proper siege train, and that shall surely be enough to subdue Bhurtpore!'

'No, no, no! We want no second campaign while Ava is undecided. It is quite impossible!'

Somervile had been taken aback. 'But Lord Amherst, the ultimatum has been given. We cannot withdraw now. The Company would suffer an irreparable humiliation. Every native power the length of India would look at once to take his opportunity. I—'

'Impossible, I say! I cannot be mired in by Ochterlony's intemperate declarations. The only alternative is to let him try with his ten thousand.'

'But Hervey's view is that victory cannot be guaranteed thereby. There must be reinforcements to carry the day if audacity fails!'

'Hervey? Hervey? Who is he?'

Somervile had at once regretted his lapse. 'The captain of Sir David's escort, Lord Amherst. He—'

'Captain of the *escort*? Great heavens, man, have you lost your senses? No, no, it will not serve. Sir David's offensive would be a gamble on his reputation for success. Yes, that is the way it shall be done. I shall send word at once for Ochterlony to withdraw. Indeed, I shall issue immediate orders for the recall of Sir David Ochterlony to an appointment of greater prominence here!'

Somervile had felt obliged to concede defeat. 'Very good, Lord Amherst. But with respect I must give my opinion that none shall see such a recall as anything but the most peremptory reprimand for the resident. Including Sir David himself.'

Colonel Anburey, the engineer, now looked pained at the thought of the heavy pounding that lay ahead, though the same thought seemed to please Colonel Macleod, the gunner. 'You give your opinion very decidedly, sir,' said the former.

'I endeavour always to speak as I find, Colonel,' replied Hervey, with absolute certainty.

'Well, so be it, gentlemen,' said Lord Combermere briskly. 'I shall, of course, make my own reconnaissance, but for the time being I intend proceeding upon Captain Hervey's admirable appreciation. The question then turns on when is launched the – as Hervey has it – *coup de main*. I am prepared to order affairs a great deal in favour of its success. However, there is no profit in seizing these dams if they are only to be recaptured before I am able to send a reinforcement. Quite the opposite, indeed, for the enemy would be at once alerted to our intention and would instantly open the sluice-gates. And yet, if I delay too long we shall anyway have full moats to cross instead of dry ditches.'

The colonels of engineers and artillery looked somehow relieved that their own decisions turned only on what was technically feasible rather than fine judgements of this order.

It was left to Hervey to speak to the commander-in-chief's dilemma. 'I have been considering this, General. The flooding of all the moats would be a great inconvenience to the population. Durjan Sal would not order the dams open until it were strict necessity. We must therefore be circumspect in our concentration. I believe that your lordship would wish to assemble his forces at Agra – and I truly cannot conceive of a better place – but any advance west of there would unquestionably signal to the Jhauts our intention to invest the city, for it is a march of but a few days, and if my own intelligence of the time it would take to inundate the defences is correct, the enemy would be obliged to cut open the bund at once.'

Lord Combermere nodded.

'I fancy that two squadrons of light cavalry with galloper guns might dash from Agra to Bhurtpore in a night, before the garrison were properly alerted. They could seize the bund before dawn, until our engineers came up, and would have the advantage of daylight to beat off the immediate sallies.'

Lord Combermere at once saw the sequence perfectly. 'And the relief to attend on them by dusk.'

'It would be hazardous if they were *not* to be reinforced by then, General. If the enemy did not overwhelm them in the darkness, they would surely mass during the night and do so at first light.'

'Very well,' said Lord Combermere, nodding slowly, as if turning over the facts one more time.

Hervey judged that his services were now done with. He picked up his shako and began making to leave.

'Thank you, Captain Hervey,' said Lord Combermere, looking up. 'Your information has been most valuable. You shall have the honour of leading those two squadrons. And you had better have the rank for the affair, too, once we take to the field.'

Hervey left the commander-in-chief's office with the promise of a local majority. It would give him the authority he needed for his limited command, but in terms of seniority it meant even less than a brevet. He wondered when that recognition might come his way again, if ever. He wondered even more when the next regimental vacancy might occur, though he could not begin to contemplate how he might find the means to buy it. Advancement in times of peace and retrenchment was a snail's gallop – they all knew that – so he had better make the most of his temporary command. He would go at once to the adjutant-general's office to discover for himself the exact order of battle for this, Lord Combermere's first sovereign campaign.

There, he was at once astonished by the scale of the undertaking. The body of cavalry was the largest, it was certain, since Waterloo: a division of two brigades, each comprising a King's regiment, three of the Company's and two troops of horse artillery, the whole under command of Lieutenant-Colonel Sleigh of the 11th Light Dragoons in the rank of brigadier-general. Hervey was content enough with that; Sleigh he knew from Peninsula days, and considered him a good man. But it was the Devil's own luck that Sir Ivo Lankester should have prolonged his furlough, for his seniority would have given him a brigade. And the only reason Sir Ivo had prolonged his stay in England was to coax His Majesty into appointing a royal colonel-in-chief to the Sixth. An expensive adornment *that* would be, mused Hervey, if it cost Sir Ivo the opportunity of the sabre's edge at the head of his regiment.

And the two divisions of infantry were strong ones, too, each of three brigades, with two King's regiments – the 14th and 59th Foot – and the Company's 1st Bengal European Regiment. There were a good many troops of foot artillery, as well as the experimental brigade with their rockets, and strong detachments of the Bengal Sappers and Miners. The strength returns were not yet received in full, said the officiating adjutant-general, but his estimate was that the army would take to the field in excess of twenty thousand combatants.

Hervey scanned the order of battle keenly. The last regiment he came to gave him especial satisfaction, and did as much to assure him of victory as any other. Two rissalahs of Skinner's Irregular Horse would accompany the army, unbrigaded. He resolved at once to enlist them in his independent command.

In the afternoon he sent Corporal Wainwright with a dozen sicca rupees to buy provisions for the budgerow which would – he hoped – soon be taking them back up the Ganges. 'Calcutta will be no place to be these next weeks,' he said, smiling wryly. 'Not for sabres, that's for sure. You haven't seen an army assembling for the field, Corporal Wainwright. It's a grand affair of adjutants and quarter-masters and serjeant-majors. Parades, lists, inspections – no end of a business!'

Corporal Wainwright hid his partial disappointment. The oldest sweat in his barrack-room had told him many things when he had first joined, not least that a dragoon should never volunteer for anything. Yet Jobie Wainwright would have liked to see the serjeant-majors and the adjutants and the quartermasters about their business, for he himself wanted one day to fill their boots, and how was he to learn if he did not see? But he was his troop-leader's coverman – *Major* Hervey's coverman, indeed, though he did not yet know it – and he went only where he might parry the cut or the thrust directed at his officer. That next meant to Dehli, or perhaps straight to Agra.

But his officer had a prior duty, one that could not possibly be spoken of between them. When Wainwright left for the bazaar, Hervey went to the Chitpore road.

The whole of native Calcutta, from nabob to bhisti, knew now that the army of Bengal was mobilizing. And every bibi knew likewise. They also knew that the army's object was what Lord Lake had failed to accomplish, and what had been the shaming cause of Sir David Ochterlony's death. Would John Company rise in triumph this time to the old taunt 'Go take Bhurtpore'? It was the talk of the princely palaces and the havelis of the Chitpore road, debated in the more modest dwellings of the Brahmins and around the bazaars. And in the bibi khanas; *especially* in the bibi khanas, for they knew all about Bhurtpore – 'the Pride of Hindoostan'. Was the fortress not impregnable? Did not the Futtah Bourge, the tower of skulls, stand as reminder to all who would forget it? No, it was impossible that a man should leave for Bhurtpore without visiting his bibi to bid her a proper goodbye, and to receive the soldier's farewell in return, and to assure her of the arrangements he had made for her well-being should he not come back.

Hervey now spoke the words that a bibi needed to hear, but they could never be enough. She loved him. She thought him the world itself. She also understood that in the army's hands lay the Company's honour and prestige, and it made her doubly fearful, for she knew what honour meant to her sahib, and the price he would be ready to pay if it were necessary. She would not say so – it would only distress him – but if his body were brought back to Calcutta she would throw herself into the flames of his funeral pyre in the duty of *suttee*. Except that for her it would not be a duty, rather an end to interminable grief.

She pleaded with her sahib to let her go with him to Bhurtpore; even to walk among the dhoolie-bearers and syces if she could not be with him. But tempted sorely as Hervey was, his soldier's duty stood all too clear: she was not welcome in the cantonment, and she could not be welcome on the campaign.

But leaving her was harder than he had supposed. He did not for one moment imagine he would not return (she would not tell him that she imagined only this) but the necessity of proceeding on that possibility gave their parting a fateful edge that all but overcame him. It was not possible for a man – a man with a soul – to see even native eyes which looked so loving, and not be touched deep. In truth, Hervey had come to love her, too, in a certain way. It was not a love which fulfilled all his needs; their minds, so differently schooled, could never wholly meet, but there was a tenderness that could make him content, for a time. He saw that period of contentment, however, only as time that stood still, not the sharing of life's time.

It was of no consequence, however. He had long known that he could only have shared life's time with Henrietta, and it mattered not how or with whom he shared time that stood still, for it was a wholly different property. As the sun began to sink in the direction to which his duty called, he rose from beside her to bathe. He was certain of one thing: he had not the will, and certainly not the heart, to sever himself from her now. It would take the lawful command of a superior to accomplish that – a return to England, alone or with the regiment. Yet did he have the desire and the will even to comply with such an order? Why should she not accompany him home?

That twisting ache which came in his vitals in such moments of apprehension hauled him back to the truth – that here in Hindoostan he might live largely as he pleased, but that in England (above all in Wiltshire) he must live as he was expected. All the Christian charity of his family combined could not accept an Indian paramour, let alone a wife. And beyond his immediate family – Henrietta's guardians and the gentry of those parts – such a thing could signal only that Hervey had announced his intention to withdraw from all society. He might even come to know what his late friend Shelley had called 'social hatred'.

Would that matter to him? As he lay in her arms he had imagined not. But now, as he sponged the cold water over his shoulders, he knew that he would always hark back – no matter how infrequently – to the earlier, sober days, and that it would begin eating at the heart of the arrangement. And his career? He would have to forgo it. *Any* arrangement with a native girl, except in a native station, was insupportable.

Perhaps he might implicate Georgiana, to appoint his bibi as ayah to her? But what passed as a decent and honourable association in India would in England look no better than the slave-owner visiting the cabins of an evening.

As they embraced at their parting, Hervey was in more than half a mind to seek a commission in the Company's forces, to make his home here, to see how long he could make time stand still, until events resolved his troubles.

In the army's hands lay the Company's honour and prestige. If Hervey's bibi understood this, how much more did Somervile. The *King's* honour, indeed, now rested in the balance at Bhurtpore, and there were some in the great houses of Calcutta – those connected with the native powers especially – who would say that the very presence of the British in India was at stake, that in Combermere's hands lay the course of history.

'There is much to speak of, Hervey,' said Somervile, welcoming him at the door of No. 3, Fort William. 'Send for all your necessaries and rest the night here. A good dinner's the very least the council might provide before you go and pay their rent for the next hundred years.'

Hervey needed no inducement to stay with the Somerviles, for besides the unflagging pleasure he took in their company he had no agreeable alternative. He could not return to the bibi khana having said his farewell, the officers' mess was at this moment being readied to lumber in a score of yakhdans and bullock carts in the direction of Agra, and his own bungalow was once again shuttered and draped with dust sheets.

Emma joined them, the ayah with her, babe in arms.

For a moment Hervey saw something – the timeless vision of mother and child, perhaps – that reached deep into his own void. And his godson – a contented baby, swaddled with affection, a child that would grow to manhood sure of its nurture. Mother and child seemed somehow to rebuke him. 'I had a mind to stay here when the Sixth is recalled,' he said, absently.

Emma read that mind, and thought better of questioning it.

Her husband was less nimble. 'Be sure to take six months' home leave beforehand, mark. It would be perilous to chance the marriage stakes on the angels who come out here.'

Serious advice, well meant as ever – if blunt: Hervey could not take offence. 'Perhaps I shall,' he said, vaguely; and then, in a tone suggesting his true thoughts, 'and I should want to know how my own offspring fares.'

Emma sensed the danger. She nodded to her ayah. '*Mehrbani, Vaneeta.*'

The ayah bowed and smiled back, and took the child to the nursery.

'When do you leave, Matthew?'

Hervey, whose eyes had followed the child from the room, turned attentively to his hostess. 'I, er . . . tomorrow. At first light. By budgerow as far as Agra. Johnson is there with the horses.'

Somervile uncorked a bottle of champagne noisily. 'Damned carriers! They must have trotted every case for a mile and more. I had a bottle blow up in my hand last week.'

Hervey smiled. 'A perilous position you occupy these days, Somervile!'

'I wouldn't trade it for a safer one, I assure you.'

Looking now at the third in council of the Bengal presidency, with his thinning hair and spreading paunch, it was difficult to imagine the defiant defender of the civil lines twenty years ago when the Madras army was in one of its periodic foments, or a decade later the angered collector going at the gallop, pistol in hand, for the Pindaree despoilers of one of 'his' villages. Hervey knew of the first by hearsay, but he had witnessed the latter himself, and he had not the slightest doubt that, after all due allowance for the increasing effects of gravity and claret, there was no one he would rather serve with on campaign than Eyre Somervile. The erstwhile collector looked an unlikely man of action, but man of action he was, at least in his counsels, as well as being a fine judge of men, of horses, of the country, and above all of its people. No, Eyre Somervile did not seek safe billets.

'I am of the opinion that it will not be a safe place inside Bhurtpore. There's a fair battering train and good many sepoys,' said Hervey airily.

'Tell me of it.' Somervile handed him a glass after Emma.

Hervey at once retailed the order of battle, including the line number of the Company's regiments. He had fixed them in his mind as if the printed orders were in front of him – a happy knack, and one he had found could endure indefinitely if he recollected the picture once or twice a day.

Emma, by her eyes, expressed her admiration.

Hervey's exposition lasted the whole of Somervile's glass.

'There was a deal of speculation in the drawing rooms as to his capability when first the news of his appointment reached here,' said the third in council when his friend had finished. 'You know it's tattled what passed when Wellington proposed it to the Duke of York? The grand old man's supposed to have protested Combermere was a fool, to which Wellington's supposed to have replied, "Yes, but he can still take Bhurtpore."'

Hervey frowned.

'You're right, no doubt,' said Somervile, though by no means contrite. 'We all know the respect Combermere's held in from Peninsula days, but now he's no longer subordinate, and it is not for him only to implement the design of the commander-in-chief. The design must now be his own.'

Hervey merely raised an eyebrow.

'So we must trust in Wellington's faith,' continued Somervile blithely. 'And I certainly take it as a mark of

Combermere's capability that he should seek out the opinion of a junior officer. How was he, by the way?'

'Cool, thoughtful. He listens very attentively, and reads too, it would seem. He had read all there was about the last siege.'

Somervile nodded with satisfaction. He liked a thoughtful commander. He considered it the prime military as well as manly virtue. But he had his fears still. 'I would wish that he knew something of India, though. The bones of a host of Englishmen and sepoys are piled in those walls, and Lake was a general of much practice. They've stood as succour to every malcontent and freebooter who thought he could tweak the tail of the Company or chew off a bit of the bone – look at how the Jhauts have rallied to that murdering usurper just because he dares hoist his colours in the place! There must be no possibility of defeat this time, Hervey. If Combermere does not take Bhurtpore, then we may as well recall Campbell and his army from Ava and hand in the keys to Fort William!'

Hervey sipped at his champagne, judging that no answer was required.

'By my reckoning there are not so many engineers,' said Somervile suddenly, and looking puzzled. 'I should have thought the requirement in a siege was for more of these, even at the expense of your own gallant arm.'

Hervey sat up again. 'I had thought the same. But it seems the engineers can't drive tunnels far enough. And Durjan Sal will have a host of cavalry to hold at bay.'

'Has Combermere good interpreters? He must have someone who is fluent in Persian as well as others for the native languages.'

It was a detail Hervey had not missed, for the officer was an old friend. 'Captain Macan, from the Sixteenth Lancers. Do you know him?'

Somervile nodded contentedly. 'Yes indeed. A most able linguist.'

'Then I regret the position appears filled.'

Somervile saw the tease. 'Believe me, Hervey, if I thought it was safe to leave Calcutta for one hour without Amherst changing his mind about this enterprise then I should take to the field at once. But you will see me there as soon as you take the place. After your gallant comrades have reduced Bhurtpore and put Durjan Sal in a cage there will be a good deal of political work to do, and quickly. The new resident will need all the help he can get in the first months, and I for one would not stand on ceremony on that account.'

Sir Charles Metcalfe's name – Ochterlony's successor – was rarely absent from any conversation in Calcutta these days. Hervey wondered he had never heard of him before, so prominent a place he now took in the counsels of state. 'I hope I shall meet him, then.'

'I think he would hope that too, for he knows your work.'

'How so?'

Somervile took the champagne bottle from its cooler and refilled their glasses. 'I shall tell you.'

It had been in July, the evening of the Ochterlony minute guns, that Somervile had declared his opinion to Emma, who had understood him at once, as she always did. 'They would do better to take yonder guns and go finish what he began at Bhurtpore,' he rasped, flinging down a sheaf of his home papers. 'This defiance by the Jhauts cannot stand!'

No one but Emma knew how much Somervile had striven those past months to conclude a satisfactory outcome to the usurpation. He had come to regard it as a rebellion against the Company rather than solely as a source of humiliation, and his object had been its crushing. 'What does Lord Amherst say? Does he feel Ochterlony's death in any measure?' Emma had asked.

'Amherst's no fool. He knows well enough that in repudiating Ochterlony's proclamation he as good as put a bullet in his head. He was decidedly ill at ease in council today, and he railed against me beforehand as if the affair was somehow of my making. He's afeard that this will play ill in London.'

'What's to be done, Eyre?' Emma had enquired in the simple certainty that her husband would know.

And, indeed, he had already weighed the options. His position in council was sometimes tenuous, but he had no desire to hold on to it through mere compliance. 'Metcalfe's here tomorrow from Haidarabad. I doubt he'll need much persuading, and Amherst'll be too fearful of going against his advice, for his stock has always stood high with the directors.'

Though Somervile would scarce admit it, Emma knew that none but her husband's stock might stand so high in council if only he would take pains to promote it a little more. She knew his manner was not best calculated to win their affection, but not a member could be in doubt of his understanding. The Governor-General had readily taken his counsel in the appointment of a successor at Dehli: as soon as Sir David Ochterlony had tendered his resignation Somervile had pressed on Lord Amherst the claims of Sir Charles Metcalfe, though perhaps that was an easy victory, for Metcalfe had held the appointment until five years before, and his judgement had been amply tested of late as resident in the nizam's capital.

And so, next morning, he had called on Sir Charles before there was opportunity for subornation at Fort William. 'You have got to make Amherst see sense in this matter, Metcalfe. Had that place been reduced twenty years ago—'

'You forget I was Lord Lake's political officer at that time,' Sir Charles had replied, frowning. 'It is a great wonder his army achieved half of what it did. Bhurtpore was never within his grasp.'

'Let us not debate it. Now the whole of India will believe it without *our* grasp.'

'It may be so. It may well *be* without our grasp. In which case we ought not to make it an objective to grasp it.'

Somervile had relied on cool relentless logic, however. 'Nothing that is made beyond the Company's territories ought to be without the Company's grasp. It is surely the knowledge that, were the Company to will it, any country power might be subdued that secures our peace. And occasionally that will must, most regrettably, be put to the test.'

'But what say the soldiers, Somervile? What was Paget's opinion?'

'We shall never rightly know, for he's been gone these several months. All we may now do is wait on Lord Combermere. He's due here ere too long. Meanwhile I should as soon ask his deputy to play the violin as ask his opinion on the matter. The man is an ass.'

'That is a very decided opinion, Somervile. Is it much shared?'

Somervile had looked astonished. 'I have never thought to enquire! I come to my own judgement in such matters.'

Sir Charles Metcalfe had shaken his head slowly from side to side. 'Then the Governor-General, and by extension you, are without sound military counsel?'

Again, Somervile had looked surprised. '*I* am not. I have had very good counsel, and from the seat of the trouble.'

'Indeed? And are we to know whose is this counsel?'

'A dragoon captain formerly on Ochterlony's staff.'

Sir Charles Metcalfe had looked dismayed. 'A captain? Are you quite well, Somervile? There are generals and colonels here, and you put your trust in a captain of dragoons!'

'I do.' The tone had been less defiant than emphatic, as though he would have pit his judgement in this against all comers.

Sir Charles had laughed. 'Then I should very much like to see this man.'

'You shall, you shall. And in the breaches of that place, I

hope. He's studied the Bhurtpore defences and drawn plans.'

Somervile now had the khitmagar open a second bottle. 'So you see, Hervey, Sir Charles was apprised of your observations, and I might say that they materially informed his judgement.'

Hervey raised an eyebrow. 'And what transpired?'

'What transpired is that Sir Charles studied the question for a full week and then gave his opinion in council.'

Emma smiled. 'And it was, Matthew, the most eloquent opinion you might ever hear. Even Eyre was much moved.'

Her husband nodded. 'I confess I was, my dear. I can read it aloud, too, for I have all the proceedings here at hand.'

Hervey did not object.

Somervile rummaged among some papers on a side table, then returned to his chair with a look of triumph. 'Hear this, Hervey:

'Your lordship, Gentlemen, we have by degrees become the paramount state of India. Although we exercised the powers of this supremacy in many instances before 1817, we have used and asserted them more generally since the existence of our influence by the events of that and the following year.'

He glanced first at Hervey and then at Emma at the mention of 1817. They had each been so embroiled in events leading to the Pindaree war, a war which, as Sir Charles Metcalfe here made clear, had changed for ever the Company's status both north and south of the Sutlej.

'It then became an established principle of our policy to maintain tranquillity among all the states of India, and to prevent the anarchy and misrule which were likely to disturb the general peace. Sir John Malcolm's proceedings in Malwa were governed by this principle, as well as those

235

of Sir David Ochterlony. In the case of succession to a principality, it seems clearly incumbent upon us, with reference to that principle, to refuse to acknowledge any but the lawful successor, as otherwise we should throw the weight of our power into the scale of usurpation and injustice. Our influence is too pervading to admit of neutrality, and sufferance could operate as support. We are bound not by any positive engagement to the Bhurtpoor state, nor by any claim on her part, but by our duty as supreme guardians of general tranquillity, law, and right, to maintain the right of Rajah Balwant Sing to the raj of Bhurtpore, and we cannot acknowledge any other pretender.

'This duty seems to me to be so imperative that I do not attach any peculiar importance to the late investiture of the young rajah in the presence of Sir David Ochterlony. We should have been equally bound without that ceremony, which, if we had not been under a pre-existing obligation to maintain the rightful succession, would not have pledged us to anything beyond acknowledgement. With regard to the brothers Durjan Sal and Madhoo Sing, the competing claimants for the office of regent, I am not of the opinion that any final decision is yet required, but my present conviction is as follows. We are not called upon to support either brother; and if we must act by force it would seem to be desirable to banish both.

'Negotiation might yet prove effectual, but if recourse to arms should become necessary, there would not be wanting of sources of consolation, since I am convinced that a display and rigorous exercise of our power, if rendered necessary, would be likely to bring back men's minds in that quarter to a proper tone, and the capture of Bhurtpoor, if effected in a glorious manner, would do us more honour throughout India, by the removal of the hitherto unfaded impressions caused by our former failure, than any other event that can be conceived.

'And then Sir Charles bowed and sat down,' said Somervile. 'And many were the sheepish looks about the place, and the oyster eyes at the memory of Ochterlony's ill-treatment.'

'In a glorious manner!' Hervey nodded, content.

'Eyre?'

'My dear?'

'You must tell what was Lord Amherst's reply.'

'Ah, yes, indeed.' He rifled through the papers in his lap. 'Here I have it – it is but brief, and rather a handsome testimony I do think. Hear this, Hervey:

> *'I have hitherto entertained the opinion that our interference with other states should be limited to cases of positive injury to the honourable Company, or of immediate danger thereof. In that opinion I have reason to believe that I am not supported by the servants of the honourable Company most competent to judge of its interests, and best acquainted with the circumstances of this country. I should therefore have hesitated in acting upon my own judgement in opposition to others; but I am further free to confess that my own opinion has undergone some change, and that I am disposed to think that a system of non-interference, which appears to have been tried and to have failed in 1806, would be tried with less probability of success, and would be exposed to more signal failure, after the events which have occurred, and the policy which has been pursued during the last nineteen or twenty years. A much greater degree of interference than was formerly called for, appears to have resulted from the situation in which we were placed by the pacification of 1818. It might be a hazardous experiment to relax in the exercise of that paramount authority which our extended influence in Malwah and Rajpootana specially has imposed upon us. Applying these general principles to the particular cases before us, and believing that without direct interference on*

our part, there is a probability of very extended
disturbances in the Upper provinces, I am prepared, in the
first place, to maintain, by force of arms if necessary,
the succession of Balwant Sing to the raj of Bhurtpoor.

'And so decided did the opinion sound that the chamber was silent for a full minute,' added Somervile, putting the papers back in order. 'And then Amherst said simply, "I perceive that no one would gainsay. I shall today cause instructions to be drawn up for the commander-in-chief to begin preparations to restore Balwant Sing to the raj of Bhurtpore."'

'In a glorious manner,' said Hervey again, shaking his head and smiling grimly. 'We must hope for more glory than Rangoon has seen. What a prospect – war on two fronts when we can scarce make war on one!'

CHAPTER THIRTEEN

IN A GLORIOUS MANNER

Agra, 1 December

Not since the first Mughal emperor, Zahir ud din Mohamed – *Babur* (the tiger) – had Agra seen such a host of men under arms. Three hundred years ago almost to the day, having taken Punjab with great but economical bloodshed, Babur had come down the Jumna from his new capital at Dehli to confront the Rajpoot federation. His army had been small by comparison with theirs, as it had been small compared with that of Ibrahim Lodi in Punjab, but Babur knew how to manoeuvre them to advantage. The martial Rajpoots, two hundred thousand and more, learned defeat at Kanwaha near Fatehpur Sikri, where Babur's grandson, Akbar the Great, would in time build a new Mughal capital. After the battle, Babur, rejoicing at becoming a *ghazi*, a killer of infidels, had made great mounds of the bodies of the slain, and pillars of their heads – models to be copied at Bhurtpore centuries later with Lord Lake's men.

Lord Combermere's army knew its history. The sepoys spoke among themselves of the Futtah Bourge, the 'bastion of victory', the great tower of skulls that stood as affront to both their caste and their calling. The private men of the King's regiments, their information learned more recently but with no less indignation, likewise spoke of the insult to be effaced – and, it must be certain, the retribution to be exacted on the defenders of Bhurtpore. That the Jhauts who now stood defiantly on the walls of the city were not the same enemy as Lord Lake's was of no moment. They were of the same country, and they dared to oppose John Company and the King.

Red was the colour that predominated in the camps, but a vivid red, scarlet, the colour of blood, not the mellow red of the great sandstone fort nearby, nor the rich deep red of the silks that clothed men and women alike in the *chaupars* and bazaars of this old imperial city. The Company's native infantry regiments were as regular in their appearance as Lord Combermere had known the duke's in Spain, save that the sepoys' legs were bare. The cavalry, too, had all the appearance of his own command at that time, except that in the hands of some was a weapon that hitherto he had seen only in the hands of the enemy – the lance, its pennants now fluttering in the ranks of His Majesty's Sixteenth Lancers, who aped their models in this part by wearing the *schapska* of Bonaparte's Polish lancers instead of the shako. Hervey could not look at their scarlet bibs without a fraction of distaste, for blue had been the colour of all who did not fight in lines, and he thought it needless show. Show in both senses, for scouting and outpost work was hard enough at the best of times without robin-redbreast display.

Hervey had been busy on his own account with matters of uniform. For some time now he had become convinced that for field service their own coats should be modified in the same way as had their horses' bridles. Early on in the Peninsula the regiment had doubled the leather browband with chain so that a sword could not cut it and make the bridle fall from the animal's head. He had listened to accounts of Maratha and Rajpoot swordsmanship and learned that a favoured device was the passing cut at the shoulder, and he had concluded that chain on the shoulder – as of old – would serve them well. Major Joynson had been persuaded, and the metalworkers of Calcutta had been engaged to fashion six inches of mail, three inches wide, for each dragoon's shoulder. Lord Combermere saw it when he inspected his troops at Agra, and much approved. And when, three days later, he went by dawk upstream to Muttra to inspect the other half of his army, and there found Hervey and his troop, he remarked on it favourably, so that Hervey was in no doubt that Lord Combermere's estimation of him was truly of the highest order.

'I intend beginning a general advance on Bhurtpore three days hence, on the ninth,' the commander-in-chief told him as he turned his horse away. 'I shall make all appearances of wanting to parley, so that they do not take steps to inundate the defences, but I shall want you to break from the force at last light and move to seize the bund. Then at dawn next day I shall send with all despatch a force to relieve you.'

It was exactly as Hervey had urged at Fort William. 'Very good, General.'

'Two squadrons, you said.'

'Yes, sir. One of the Eleventh's, and a rissalah from Skinner's Horse, they with their galloper guns. The horse artillery would only impede us.'

Combermere nodded, but slowly, as if considering. 'The Eleventh, yes – and your own troop, I should suppose.'

Hervey nodded his confirmation.

'But the irregular horse . . . are they to be so relied upon?'

Hervey smiled assuringly. 'I may say with utter certainty, your lordship, that one could do no better in trusting them with one's very life. Three years ago, in Burma, I had proof of it myself.'

Combermere nodded again, this time more definitely. 'Very well, then, I shall have Colonel Watson write the orders at once. Is there any more you would have me do?'

'No, sir. Except, of course, that our orders should not be made general.'

'Of course.'

Hervey knew he had suggested the obvious, but he had his reasons. Combermere rode high in his estimation from all that had gone before in Portugal and Spain, but this was India.

'Cap'n 'Ervey, sir, if yon farrier's sick another day I'm gooin' to 'ave to ask one 'o' t'Eleventh's to do Gilbert. Them corns are gettin' bad.'

Gilbert's shoes were a problem that Hervey could do without. It wasn't just Gilbert, either, for although Corporal Brennan's assistants were capable of admirable cold-shoeing by replacing worn iron with the stock shoes carried by each dragoon, they were not yet proficient enough to make a therapeutic set, and there were half a dozen troopers needing that attention. 'I'll speak to their colonel, then,' replied Hervey, still wondering when he might have the orders which would give him authority to address his mission.

Johnson was content. 'Lord Combermere looked 'appy enough this mornin'. I were tellin' all them green'eads that fancies themselves as dragoons about 'im at T'loose.'

Hervey looked pained. 'Not anything in connection with General Slade, I hope.'

'Of course it were about Slade. That were t'story!'

Indeed it was a story. Lord Combermere's timely appearance at Toulouse had made General Slade drop his prey – and Hervey had raced back to the regiment a free man again. But Combermere, as far as Hervey could tell, had never known how providential had been his arrival. He had known only the eagerness of the wounded cornet to be back in action. There was a time, however – and certainly at Toulouse – when Hervey would have been truly perturbed, believing that the disparaging of a senior officer, even one such as Slade, would have been inimical to discipline. Now he cared not at all. The canteen was entitled to its views, as long as it held them in private, so to speak. And if they could

242

disparage Slade they could extol Combermere, as it seemed they might. Johnson did the commander-in-chief a service therefore; Hervey ought to commend him, indeed. There were always difficulties attendant on commending Johnson, though. 'That reminds me—'

But Johnson was not finished. 'Word is in t'canteen that them walls is fifty feet thick, and made of bones and solid rock.'

Hervey raised an eyebrow. 'How do the intelligence agents of the canteen believe solid rock and bones are mixed together?'

Johnson did not consider it an impossible notion. 'They didn't say, only that the walls is so thick it'd take a month o' Sundays just to scratch 'em.'

Hervey frowned. 'They're thick, Johnson, I grant you that, but not fifty feet, and not solid rock. They'll withstand some battering, but they're bound to be breached at some point, and then it will be the bayonet in the old way.'

'Let's 'ope so, sir,' said Johnson matter-of-factly, taking the reins of Hervey's second charger as Hervey himself began picking up each of the little Marwari's feet to check for stones. ''Ave yer 'eard there've been some deserters an' all?'

'There are always deserters, Johnson,' replied Hervey, just as matter-of-fact, picking out a pebble from the off-fore.

'Ay, but they reckon these've gone over to t'Jhauts.'

'Who reckons? How do they know?'

'Corporal McCarthy 'eard. 'E always 'ears everything if they're Irish.'

Hervey continued checking his mare's feet (they looked in good shape). 'And who are they from, these men?'

'T'artillery.'

Hervey looked up. 'The *artillery*?'

'Ay, and supposed to be good gunners an' all.'

Hervey tutted. He was not disposed to think that they

could have gone over to the enemy, for he could see no inducement . . . except that as experienced gunners their services would be keenly sought, and therefore, he supposed, well rewarded. 'But surely they would not—'

'An' one of 'em was at Waterloo, even!'

That concluded it. 'Tattle, Johnson. I should sooner imagine the sar'nt-major a preacher!'

But Johnson was unmoved. 'Well, that's what they're saying, Cap'n 'Ervey. Is there owt else?'

Hervey shook his head. 'No, I believe we may offsaddle and give them some hay.' There was only grass, but hay was what they called it still. 'And we can take our ease too for an hour or so. Call me if Mr Sledge comes in. He said he might come up from Agra today. Oh, and . . . see if you can find out any more about these deserters, will you?'

There was much to do, even had he not had the assignment at the Bhurtpore jheels. The camp was beginning to look like a bestiary come alive, with every manner of creature to provide milk or flesh for the army, or muscle or a strong back. His own troop might occupy him every minute, though for the most part they were not without experience. It was strange that they had seen action – fierce action – but had not yet been 'shot over', as the saying went. The affair at the river three years before had turned them into veterans overnight, and it had been long enough past to give them the taste for more of it now. Yet there were things he must check for himself – the firelocks especially, since he expected that what would come first against them at the jheels was better seen off with the carbine than the sabre. It was not something he could leave to his subalterns. Or rather, *would* leave. It was out of the question in any case to give the duty to Green, still as ineffectual as ever. Indeed, he would not even have passed the duty to Seton Canning, had he been with him still, for certain things were properly his particular responsibility.

In the afternoon, he received copies of general and field general orders. He was keen to see the appointments to both the staff and to commands of brigades and divisions, for there had been endless speculation and not a little wagering, and he retired to the relative peace of his tent to peruse them with as much leisure as seemed apt:

GENERAL ORDERS

Head-Quarters, Agra, 3rd Dec. 1825
The following officers are appointed Brigadier-Generals
from 1st inst., subject to the confirmation of the Right
Hon. The Governor-General in Council:
Brevet-Col. J. M'Combe, 14th Foot. Brevet-Col. J. W.
Sleigh, C.B. 11th Dragoons. Col. W. J. Edwards, 14th Foot.
Lieut.-Col. Childers to be Brigadier. Capt. Hervey to be
Loc.-Major. Lieut. Maxwell to be Aide-de-Camp to
Brigadier-General Sleigh.
Division of Cavalry. – Brigadier-General J. W. Sleigh,
C.B. to Command.
1st Cavalry Brigade. – Brigadier Murray, C.B. 16th
Lancers, to Command. Capt. W. Harris, 16th Lancers,
Major of Brigade. – To consist of H.M. 6th Lt. Dragoons,
16th Lancers, 6th, 8th, and 9th Regiments of Light
Cavalry.
2nd Cavalry Brigade. – Brigadier M. Childers, 11th
Dragoons, to Command. Lieutenant G. Williamson to be
Major of Brigade. – To consist of H.M. 11th Dragoons,
3rd, 4th and 10th Regiments of Light Cavalry. – N.B. The
Brigade of Irregular Cavalry, consisting of the 1st Local
Horse, under Col. James Skinner. Troop 6th Lt. Dragoons
under Maj. M. P. Hervey.
1st Division of Infantry . . .

On went the list, specifying each and every non-permanent appointment. 'Baggage-Master of the Army', as onerous a position as any might be, was to be filled by Lieut. J. M'Dermot, H.M. 14th Foot. And 'Brigadier-Gen. Sleigh, C.B., will be pleased to select, and send in the names of three smart, active, and intelligent Non-commissioned Officers of Dragoons, for appointments as Assistant Baggage Master of Divisions.' Hervey thought he had better have someone in mind lest the general devolve one of the number on his troop. Stray would be best, of course, except that he was not from his troop. Neither was he by any standard smart.

And then, enclosed with these orders, there were others – a long exhortation, and in a style he knew from many a time in the Peninsula and France. The duke's own, indeed:

FIELD GENERAL ORDERS

Head-Quarters, Camp, Agra, Dec. 2, 1825

The Army now assembling for Service on the Agra and Muttra Frontier, being about to advance, His Excellency the Commander-in-Chief requests, that Officers commanding Regiments will impress upon their Officers, &c. the imperious necessity which exists, for each individual reducing the number of his servants to the lowest scale, and taking the Field as little encumbered with Baggage as possible; and desires that they will use their utmost endeavours to prevent superfluous individuals following the Bazaars of their respective Corps. All superfluous Baggage will be left at Muttra and Agra respectively, in the first instance, by Divisions, on advancing.

The March about to commence being through the Territory of an Ally of the British Government, and not that of an enemy, His Excellency prohibits in the strictest manner, all marauding or plundering; and desires that Officers commanding Divisions and Brigades will cause it to be three times proclaimed to their respective Corps, that

*the Provost-Marshal has received peremptory orders to
seize, and inflict summary punishment of Death, on any
individual or individuals caught in the act of plundering.
In thus publicly promulgating the decided measures to be
resorted to in support of discipline, His Excellency feels
assured, from the correct habits of the European and
Native Troops under his command, that, as far as they are
concerned, the warning above given is unnecessary; but as
the followers of Bazaars of Corps might avail themselves
of opportunities to plunder the inhabitants of the country
and others, the Commander-in-Chief deems it necessary to
promulgate thus publicly the retribution which will await
such conduct.*

It was a handsome confidence, thought Hervey, if ill-
disguised in its attempt to avoid besmirching the soldiers of
the Line. It could scarcely be otherwise, this latter, though.
His own troop he might vouch for, the NCOs certainly, but
the arousal of baser instincts was something he had seen all
too often to be so sure he would not see the same again, for
there was nothing saintly about the men of E Troop. Better to
tell them straight, perhaps with the excuse that one man
might lose his wits in the noise of battle, and that Hervey's
warning to him now might thereby save him his neck.

He read through half a dozen more routine orders and
calls for returns, alternately relishing his independent
command and ruing it, depending on the requirements of
the paper. Just as he was nearing the end, a despatch rider
from the Cavalry Staff Corps rode into the lines. Hervey
watched keenly as the red-jacketed dragoon reported to the
regimental orderly tent, whence the corporal of the day
emerged at once to bring him to Hervey's.

Hervey was obliged to sign a receipt for the contents of
the staff dragoon's sabretache. 'More, evidently, than just a
call for returns,' he said as he did so.

'Sir,' replied the man, giving nothing away, though he

hoped it was indeed more than a routine despatch. He had just risked his neck in a gallop from Lord Combermere's headquarters, and he would prefer to return there with something more than a list.

The corporal of the day watched and listened keenly for any indication of what the despatch contained. His standing in the canteen would be raised immeasurably if he brought news in advance of actual orders.

Hervey took the despatch, broke the headquarters seal and read quickly, but silently:

FIELD SPECIAL ORDER

Head-Quarters, Muttra, Dec. 6, 1825
Major Hervey, 6th Lt. Dragoons, is required to form a
mounted party for a special task, consisting of one
squadron H.M. 11th Lt. Dragoons, and one rissalah 1st
Local Horse. The party is to be ready at once to undertake
the task on orders emanating directly from H.E. the
Commander-in-Chief, along the lines already
communicated. The object and design may not
be communicated to any man, however, until approval by
H.E.
By Order of His Excellency the Right Hon. The
Commander-in-Chief,

(Signed) W. N. WATSON
Adjutant-General.

It was no more or less than he needed. 'Thank you, staff dragoon. Please return the following reply.'

The man had his pocketbook and pencil ready. 'Sir.'

'Major Hervey acknowledges receipt of the special order, and comprehends it.'

'Sir.'

The corporal of the day looked disappointed. He would have to embellish his account to the canteen considerably.

'That is all,' said Hervey, when the staff dragoon looked up again.

The man slipped his pocketbook back inside his jacket.

'Up!' said the corporal of the day.

The two right hands shot, as one, to shako peaks, and Hervey nodded to acknowledge. As the two men left, he called the troop orderly corporal waiting outside. 'Have Mr Perry come, please, Rudd.' He then mastered himself fully: 'And Mr Green. And the sar'nt-major of course.'

'Sir!'

Hervey was glad it was Rudd. Rudd was an honorary pal – more than honorary, since the original pals were now but two. And there was something that nurture in that corner of the Great Plain did by way of making comrades across the ranks. 'Corporal Rudd?'

'Sir?'

'How handy were you about your mother's shop?'

'*Sir?*' Corporal Rudd was glad there were no witnesses to this exchange; he did not like being reminded of the millinery.

'I mean, how well are you with needle and thread?'

'As good as any, sir. Have you something to be mended?'

'No. Johnson could do that. I need a more skilled needle. Embroidery.'

Rudd looked puzzled. 'I can do that, sir, if it's not too knotty. What is it you have in mind, sir?'

'I need something that passes for a major's star on these epaulettes.'

Rudd was all pleasure at the prospect.

'But you shall have to unpick it when the siege is done. Local rank only, I fear.'

'Very good, sir. But rank is rank, isn't it, sir?'

'Thank you, Rudd. You are the first to hear.'

'You mean not even Johnson, sir?'

'Not even Johnson. Go to it, then – the officers and sar'nt-major. Oh, and say nothing to Johnson.'

Rudd smiled. 'Ay, sir.'

Hervey lost no time that afternoon. He told his officers and serjeant-major the contents of the several orders, and added his own. He wanted the troop to ride at light scales, with no bat-horses (he would long remember the dismay on Cornet Green's face) save with the serjeant-major for extra powder and ball. The baggage he wanted dividing into two: field stores and other necessaries – that which could be carried by pack-animal – to be put in charge of the quartermaster-serjeant and to move with the rest of the brigade; the remainder – camp stores and general comforts – to stand ready under Corporal Stray with the bullock carts here at Muttra awaiting opportunity to rejoin them, which, he believed, there would soon be once the siege was under way. 'But it shall have to be judged right,' he said. 'I don't want the Jhaut cavalry cutting them up, which is why I want Stray with them.'

Serjeant-Major Armstrong smiled. Corporal Stray was the fattest man in the regiment. The order 'light scales' had at once precluded his riding in the first echelon, for Stray was generally now to be found on the box rather than in the saddle. And yet there was not a man in the Sixth who was more at home in the field than Corporal Stray. His economy with stores was celebrated, he could fashion any necessary from the most unpromising raw materials, and quickly too, and he was utterly imperturbable in the face of enemy and superiors alike. Once, in Paris after Waterloo, he had been posted as lone sentry on a bridge that the Prussians were intent on blowing up for solely retributive reasons. The explosive in place, the officer of engineers had asked him to quit the span and seek cover, to which the then Private Stray had replied, 'Not until properly relieved by the corporal, sir.' The Prussians had lit the fuses, but still Stray would not budge, standing on-guard with the bayonet when they tried to remove him bodily, so that in the end the engineers had had to rush about frantically pulling the fuses from the barrels of gunpowder. Corporal Stray was not a man to have in the front rank at a review, but he was without doubt a man to have at hand on campaign, and Hervey was pleased for having the promise of him for a time.

After doing what he needed with his own troop, Hervey had addressed himself to the matter of the other corps. The commanding officer, the senior major, proved difficult at first, demanding to know what was the object of the special task despite the clear injunction in the written order. At length he had given way, however, naming the captain to do duty with his squadron, and had acceded at once to Hervey's request for a farrier. The regiments of the yellow circle, as the cavalry knew themselves, could have their difficulties with each other, but these remained within the circle and were fiercely guarded. Perhaps it was the fellowship of the horse, the common essential of their arm, for the horse took no side for himself in a fight, instead submitting humbly but nobly to the bit in whichever cavalry had impressed him. Sometimes, his rider unseated, he ran away, terror-stricken, but for the most part he remained dutiful, despite all privation. Hervey looked about at the Eleventh's troopers as he left the lines. They were as mixed a bunch as any in Hindoostan, but bigger than his own in the main by a good half-hand. If they bore the field well, they would be formidable indeed when it came to closing with the Jhaut cavalry – more so than his own, he had to admit, for size told when it came to a clash.

Next he had gone to Skinner's Horse, and if he had anticipated vexations with the Eleventh, he was positively certain that they would be legion with the irregulars since Colonel Skinner was in personal command. He had never met James Skinner, he had only heard of him. Indeed, there had been times since coming to India when he had heard nothing but of Skinner and his silladar horse. Three regiments there were of these singular cavalrymen, of which the second was commanded by James's brother Robert, and the third, hastily raised for service in East Bengal five years before, had without doubt saved his own troop in the affair of the Chittagong river. The Sixth Light Dragoons, or Hervey's troop at least, regarded them as special friends. They admired their skill as horsemen, and with the lance; they admired their boldness and proud independence; and they admired their determination to see things through. Skinner's was not native horse in the sense the canteen would understand it – serviceable but inferior: Skinner's was a corps apart.

Their camp was a vivid, lively place, noisier by half than any King's regiment's, with much music and singing. It might have been Tamerlane's own, the canvas and caparisons, the silks and the streamers, and all of the richest colours. As Hervey rode towards the guard tent, the sowars of the picket began falling in under their daffadar, lance pennants picking up the merest breath of wind, men and lances otherwise like statuary.

A syce ran forward to hold Gilbert's bridle as Hervey dismounted. The daffadar saluted. Hervey turned, to find a jemadar beaming at him. 'This way, please, sahib.'

Hervey followed to the tent of the woordi-major, who explained that both the second in command and the adjutant were at exercise. Then a bearer came into the tent, and, after an exchange of words, the woordi-major said that Colonel Skinner himself would see him. Hervey put his forage cap back on and walked with him across the maidan to a yellow-striped pavilion set to one side nearest the river. The sentry came to attention as the two began walking the line of whitened stones. As they reached the beaded entrance a voice called from inside. 'You are most welcome, Major Hervey!'

Hervey noted with appreciation how nimble must be the regiment's hircarrahs. He pushed aside the strings of beads and paid his compliments.

'I know very well who you are, Major Hervey. I have

naturally heard all there is of the affair of the Chittagong river. I stand in admiration, sir,' said James Skinner, designated commandant of what was officially the 1st Local Horse. He held out his hand.

Hervey took it, and acknowledged the accolade with a bow of the head. 'But it is I who stand in admiration, Colonel Skinner.'

'Well, well, let not either of us stand long. Take a seat. You will have some whisky?'

It was a moment or so before Hervey could judge whether he was speaking to a British or a native officer. One half of Colonel Skinner was Scotch, his father's half. His voice was that of a British officer, perhaps a shade fastidious, but without all the music of the native voice, the *hanji-banji* as Somervile called it. But it was the Rajpoot half, his mother noble-born, that presented itself in appearance most. James Skinner was forty-seven years old, his hair was silvering, and his face, though benign, spoke of many years' campaigning, and for several masters (only in Lord Lake's day had he thrown in with the Company). He had raised and trained the corps himself. He had given it its creed, and thence its uniform, and had led it to victory after victory against any that would oppose those 'sworn to die'. His wealth from booty was said to be prodigious, he had three wives – one Mahomedan, one Hindoo, one Christian – yet he was no dissolute nabob. He was as much a scholar as Babur had been, speaking and writing flawless Persian, and knowledgeable in the history and art of all of Hindoostan. His men worshipped him. But why was he here, in the field, in person? Hervey wondered. He was three years older than the duke had been at Waterloo. He might easily have devolved command on an executive officer. The share in any booty, such that it might be in a campaign made in the territory of an ally, would anyway go to him as the colonel of the corps – even if London (Hervey understood) would not officially recognize his rank. Did

Colonel Skinner, who could have taken his ease in Dehli or on his jagirs nearby, crave still the sword and the saddle for their own sake? There were such men, and Hervey saluted them. Indeed, he took more pleasure in Skinner's chair and his whisky at that moment than if they had been those of the duke himself.

'Jaswant Sing tells me you have a promising seat. He says you were quick to the Rajpoot way of riding.'

Hervey was gratified, and smiled obligingly, though puzzled that Skinner should know of it. 'But I fear I had the best of attention and horses. I could not imitate those airs when later I tried them on my own horses.'

Colonel Skinner nodded slowly as if he understood. 'Woordi-major, you may go to your ledgers or you may stay and drink whisky, as you please. Which is it to be?'

The woordi-major answered in English. 'Huzoor, I have many papers to return for the Lord Combermere.'

'Very well, my friend. There will be time for us to drink whisky when we have taken Bhurtpore.'

'*Ji, huzoor*,' and he continued in Urdu, though too quickly for Hervey to catch more than the odd word.

Colonel Skinner took it up, but Hervey managed to catch even less. They seemed to be turning over an idea – about horses, he thought, but the idiom was beyond him.

When the woordi-major had gone, Colonel Skinner poured more whisky. 'Now, Major Hervey, what is it that His Excellency has in mind?'

Hervey was surprised at the connection Colonel Skinner made, but he judged it of no matter; it was just the way of things in India. 'I beg you would read this, Colonel,' he said, handing him the order.

Colonel Skinner took longer to read it than Hervey expected. At length, the commandant looked up and said, thoughtfully, 'The jheels?'

Hervey saw little point in protesting. 'May I ask how you knew, Colonel?'

'It is evident, from the size and composition of the party, that the object is detached from the fortress, for otherwise it would be futile. There can be but one such object if one has read the accounts of Lord Lake's endeavours.'

'Do you know the bund, Colonel?'

'Of course.'

'I am of the opinion that such a force as mine could hold them until relieved – within the twenty-four hours following. We should rely greatly on your galloper guns, of course.'

Colonel Skinner nodded. 'I am of this opinion, too. I cannot suppose the Jhauts will garrison the jheels until they perceive the army is moving on them. There is much industry in the Jhauts, but little imagination. They will work most fiercely to eject you once you have them, however. Who is to lead the relief?'

'General Sleigh, or perhaps even General Reynell, as I understand.'

'Good. Combermere sees its importance then.' The commandant drained his glass. 'You will stay and dine with us, Major Hervey?'

Hervey saw his duty done. 'I thank you, yes. My corporal . . .'

'He will be the guest of my daffadars.'

When dinner was finished, more hours later than Hervey had thought possible, Colonel Skinner accompanied him to the picket to see him on his way. It was a fresh night, not cold, with a full moon. Torches blazed about the camp, and beyond in the city and the many other camps about it. As they came upon the picket, Corporal Wainwright led up Gilbert. Beside him, a naik led another horse, smaller but with twice the blood.

'Marwari, Major Hervey, of very choice breeding and schooled in our classical manner. I hope you will accept him.'

255

Hervey was all but dumbstruck. In hand was as fine a stallion as he had seen in Hindoostan – black, with a white face and massive neck. 'Sir, I . . .'

'He is called Chetak. Do you know the legend of Chetak, Major Hervey?'

'Indeed I do, Colonel. I know it was Chetak's leap that let the Maharana Pratap kill Man Singh's mahout.'

'And much more, Major Hervey.'

'Indeed, Colonel. Much more.'

'But the Maharana's Chetak was a grey, Major Hervey. And I would not have you ride *two* greys. So we make you a gift of one of our best bloods, and one, needless to say, who is well schooled in the Rajpoot airs.'

Hervey was a long time in his leave-taking. He had met a man among men, and he had known the regal hospitality of the Rajpoots. These things were to be savoured and honoured, even at times like this. Especially at times like this. There was no place for a stallion in his troop, but what a saddle-horse he would make when they were returned to Calcutta. And what a sire, too.

That night, though very late, he wrote to Somervile:

I am very glad of your letter (numbered 7), and especially its intelligence of Peto. How pleased he will be to slip anchor and be up the Irawadi at last! Let us hope, as you say the gossip has it, that a treaty is near.

What a camp this is! How I wish you could see it! Each fighting man with us has more than one follower, and a large bazaar accompanies the camp besides. We carry the men's tents on elephants, and each elephant has two men, four bhistis to each troop, a cook to every 16 men, every horse has a man to cut grass for him, the men have six camels and two men per troop to carry their beds. Then come the gram grinders, tailors, bakers, butchers, calasseys, or men for pitching tents, and many others.

Each hospital has six men, and of these there are 40,
making 240, and there are 50 dhoolies for a regiment. I
should say that for 560 officers and men we must have
5,600 followers, this counting in the bazaar and officers'
servants. I have in my own service 14 men, 5 camels, and
a hackery, five horses and two ponies, and this for a mere
captain of dragoons. Although this night I have received
the gift of a magnificent Marwari stallion of Colonel
Skinner of the Native Horse. It is tempting to ponder on
the nature of the battle to come, and whether we shall see
the single combat again that was the purpose of these
great brutes. I trust not. I think there is a more glorious
manner in which to take Bhurtpore, and it must be with art
and powder in very large measure rather than with the
breasts of brave men and horses . . .

Hervey completed another page of observations, then laid
down his pen. He knew full well that many a brave man's
breast would be torn open, sepoy's and King's man's alike.
And he trusted it would be sepoy and King's man in fair
measure, since it did not do for the King's men to be preserved, like Bonaparte's *Garde*, while the legionary
Company regiments were expended. But he knew, also, that
the butcher's bill would be determined in large measure by
his own aptness – and audacity – in executing the special
order. The affair of the jheels would be decided by a few, but
the price of failure paid by the many.

CHAPTER FOURTEEN
L'AUDACE!

The early hours of 10 December

The order had come by semaphore from Agra at first light the day before. The divisions were to advance on Bhurtpore before dawn on the 10th, the cavalry brigades leading. It was not a difficult movement. Bhurtpore, Agra and Muttra formed an almost equal-sided triangle, with Muttra at the apex, and the object of operations at the base, left. The roads, the sides of the triangle (although the base itself was not straight) were good and wide, permitting easy movement of formed bodies of men. The rains had gone and there was no rutting to speak of. The country either side was more flat than not, and not too jungled, so that if the divisions found the roads blocked it would be no very great impediment to progress, even for wheels. Not that opposition was expected. Each day the divisional commanders had sent patrols as far as three or four leagues, without sign of a Jhaut picket, and a cloud of spies, in exchange for quite modest amounts of silver, had daily brought assurances that the roads beyond, all the way to the walls of the city itself, were open and empty of troops. Indeed, the only obstacle to movement would be the sacred cows that ambled with perfect liberty along the old Mughal highways, for Krishna himself had been born in

Muttra, and so the sacred cows wandered on sacred ground.

The distance they had to march was no great trial to either shoe or boot – or even to the bare feet of the sepoy. From Muttra it was but eight leagues, at a cavalry trot no more than three hours. Even at the sepoys' steady rate of three miles an hour it was only a matter of eight – an easy day's business. The light companies of King's regiments could do it by forced march in a morning (the road from Agra was a little longer, winding through Fatehpur Sikri and the battle-field of Kanwaha, but not by much more than two hours or so). And Lord Combermere's orders were clear in respect of not encumbering the columns with excess baggage, so that by Hervey's estimation there could be no doubting their relief at the jheels by last light. His only worry was the reliefs finding him. The jheels were not especially difficult to find, but they lay to the north-west of the fortress, and were therefore masked to the advance. There was always the chance that the Jhauts would cut the road nearest the fortress once the game was up, and so the relief force would have to be strong enough to force the road or else find the long way round via the south-west, through waterlogged pasture. Hervey, conferring with Brigadier-General Sleigh, had therefore decided to send back guides as soon as he had taken the bund.

The previous day had been all bustle throughout the camps at Muttra and, he imagined, at Agra too. His own troop, forewarned, had had an easier time of it, and the unprotesting Corporal Stray had received a steady flow of camp comforts into his makeshift depot. In the afternoon, Hervey had received orders by hand of one of Lord Combermere's aides-de-camp that he was to seize the bund as soon as was possible after dawn the following morning, with the limitation that he must not leave Muttra before midnight. He had at once sent word to the Eleventh and to Skinner's Horse, and their two squadrons had assembled at the Krishna Ghat a little before midnight, their captains – or jemadar in the case of the Skinner's rissalah – having spent an hour and more with him beforehand to agree the conduct of the affair.

'What is the parole, Johnson?' he asked, as he took Gilbert's reins from him. He had not asked him that in ten years. It had been their ritual – their game, almost – before any affair began. It had started in Spain when his groom had drawn the fire of the regiment's outlying picket early one morning having searched all night like the good shepherd himself, but to bring in a lost horse. His habitual reply to any sentry's challenge to state the password was 'Sheffield', to which the equally invariable response was not 'Pass, friend' but 'Pass, Johnson.' Except that that night in Spain he had stumbled on the horse-artillery picket, and since then Johnson had had a healthy respect for the daily parole.

'Dehli,' he replied, a trifle gruffly, feeling the effects of a long day. 'What a lark *this* is. Do we get t'first pick o' t'pudding?'

Even in India, where dragoons fed like princes compared with home, Johnson's metaphors were still principally of the table. Nevertheless, Hervey thought to continue with it for a while. 'There will be no pudding, certainly not one with plums. Lord Combermere made it clear: we are putting down rebels; the country is not the enemy. Durjan Sal will lose his possessions, as well as his head, but that's not likely to amount to more than a measure of grog for every sepoy.'

Johnson muttered his disappointment. He would have to rely on his own resources rather than the prize agents'. So be it. He had always had a good nose. And he always knew how to draw the line between honest booty and plain loot. He had been as condemnatory as the officers when he heard of the Fifty-ninth's men in Agra stealing across the river in the night to prise gemstones from the walls of the Taje Mahale. No, Johnson's speciality was military, things that an officer might want for his own service or souvenir, or else liquids and perishables, which might sell at an inflated price before the sutlers arrived with their stocks.

Hervey sprang into the saddle with almost the same ease as he had at first riding school. The thought pleased him, though he knew he favoured his left shoulder still, as much by instinct as real necessity; the twinges had now grown much less painful, and greatly fewer. He gathered up the reins and shortened his stirrups one hole – which vexed Johnson greatly, for he had ridden at that length since leaving Dehli. Hervey looked about him. The moon, the torches and the campfires lit up the ghat as if it were almost day. His only regret was that, in leaving so far in advance of the main body, he would not see the division drawn up, for this was an affair in the old way and he might not see its like in another ten years. He wondered for the moment if the prospect displeased him, but he could not dwell on it since he had a mind to be off at the very instant he had given his own orders to advance – as the minute hand of his watch reached twelve. They would have six more hours of pitch dark, then one of twilight until, at seven, there would be no more dark to conceal them within hearing distance of a sentry.

The luminescent face of Daniel Coates's gift-hunter told him he had but four minutes to wait. There was light enough to see even the plain face of his own bought watch, but in a couple more hours, when the moon had set, he would be glad of Mr Prior's clever work. Four minutes only – perhaps he ought to make a start? They all knew Bonaparte's lament that anything could be bought but time. Very well. He would pay them back their four minutes when the Motee Bund was theirs. No trumpets, though. They were Lord Combermere's picked men; they had no need of fanfares.

'Column, walk-march!'

He had thought very carefully about the order of march. It was not the first time he had ridden with lancers, but their handiness at night was uncertain. He would lead with his own men, therefore. The trouble was, he didn't have a

261

cornet, for Green he considered not worthy of the name, and he wished now he had asked Eustace Joynson to find him some billet in Agra. He had even thought of leaving him with Corporal Stray, with the other useless baggage, except that it might have been an affront that demeaned the whole troop. So Serjeant Collins would command the advance guard, and command it well too. And Corporal McCarthy would take Collins's place at the rear of the first division. Next would come the Eleventh, and then Skinner's with their two galloper guns. Riding with Hervey himself would be a galloper from each squadron, and a lieutenant of engineers. No man who had served in the Peninsula could have aught but regard for the sappers and pioneers. They had breached and mined, and built and bridged for the army from Lisbon to Toulouse, in baking sun and freezing rain, shot over as they worked, even as the line took cover. Hervey, for sure, had that regard in highest measure. If only they could ride, though. Then he would have been able to take a whole company of them instead of just their officer, relying on the unskilled labour of the dragoons.

Eight leagues: they would cover them all mounted – no leading – as if it were just a long point in Leicestershire. They could trot for the first hour, for the Eleventh's patrols had had orders in the afternoon to picket that night at the two-league point. Thereafter they could proceed at a walk, which would give the advance guard time to scout properly. Hervey did not know how many of his command had ridden an Indian road by night. It was not so bad at this time of year, when days were cooler, but the traffic could be greater even than by day – mounted men and pedestrians alike escaping from the sun's heat, hackeries and elephants, palanquins and dongas. And always the sacred cow of the Hindoo, couching, utterly unmoved by all he heard and saw.

But the country people of this corner of Rajpootana knew that John Company was about (they sold him all they could in Agra and Muttra), though at night they took care to keep themselves scarce, for no one knew what the sahibs would do when the time came, or even Durjan Sal and his Jhauts if they dared leave the fastness of Bhurtpore. And why, indeed, should the Jhauts do that? Bhurtpore had stood against the *gora log* before. Against Lord Lake, even – he who had dealt the mighty Marathas such a blow. Was not Bhurtpore impregnable? Let John Company try if he dare, they said among themselves – as he tried in vain at Rangoon – and here he would meet the same as there. Only let us not be about the roads when he does try, they said. Let us not run or ride to Bhurtpore to warn Durjan Sal. He has his own spies for that. Let us secure ourselves at night in our villages, with fires burning to ward off marauders, and trust in the boy Krishna, our neighbour from Muttra become a god – and all the other gods that would protect us poor country people from armies of any colour.

They made the Eleventh's distant picket at ten minutes to two. Fires burned bright, but the two dozen dragoons were all alert and anxious for their own off. They even raised a cheer as Hervey led the column past at the walk.

'Nothing to report,' called the officer, standing wrapped in his cloak by a lantern. 'Your scouts went by not five minutes ago.'

Hervey thanked Providence it was Collins in front of him. There were but three men in the regiment he could trust so. Four, properly, for there could be no doubting RSM Lincoln – or rather Quartermaster Lincoln now – even though Hervey had never patrolled with him. A year or so more and there would be another two or three: Wainwright had the makings, certainly – he wanted only experience atop his courage – and Myles Vanneck. But for the present it could only be Collins, or Armstrong, or Seton Canning. The task was straightforward enough: judge, clear the route, report. But it wasn't easy. At night the ablest of men lost their capacity to do what they did by day. They imagined too much, or else too little, they lost command of their dragoons, they failed to observe and forgot what to report. No, Hervey had formed the opinion over long years that scouting at night tested a man more than did the worst trials of the day. He cursed that Cornet Green was so worthless. He wished the man had stayed in the pretty sort of shop that his father must one time have kept. Even though he had no need of him, Collins was entitled to have an officer share the danger. He ought, indeed, to have all of Green's pay.

Hervey's orders to Collins had been few, because they were unnecessary. All that Collins needed to know was the route and rate of advance. Certain of each, he now proved the way with the surest touch. Here and there he had to make a sleeping hackery driver pull his team off the road, but otherwise his progress towards the great fortress was unchecked. For almost five hours without pause, until just before seven o'clock, at the very first intimation of the dawn, he led the Company's troops into the territory of Bhurtpore, and Hervey had not a moment's hesitation in following.

Then, as arranged, only a quarter of an hour later than Hervey had predicted, the advance guard halted at the last village before the road opened onto the plain of the fortress city, and sent word back to him. He was not many minutes coming up, and fewer still at the halt. He had his telescope out at once and made a sweep of the plain.

Nothing, not even the outline of the distant walls. That was good. He risked a great deal in cutting things so fine, but without the help of a bit of daylight he couldn't find the jheels, let alone the bund. He was counting on poor camp discipline among the Jhauts; it was, he knew from experience, a peculiarly British rule for troops to be stood-to with arms for the dawn watch. He counted here on there being but a few sentries, tired after a long night, alert only to their relief at daybreak.

He would take over the lead himself now, for they must

soon leave the obliging road. He remembered clearly that it curved in a full right angle north towards the fortress, but a curve at night, especially a shallow one, was not easy to gauge. It would all have been so much easier with a guide. That, however, he had judged impossible without somehow giving away the intention, or else having a man who happened to live in Agra or Muttra and professed a knowledge of the jheels. Either way, it was scarcely a requisite they could advertise. Instead Hervey would have to trust his compass. God bless Daniel Coates, he said to himself, as he thought to check it again – finest of men and best of old soldiers. Who would have imagined there could be so small a thing as this piece of brass and whatever, and yet so serviceable to the hour? Clever Dan Coates, an ancient who sought the innovating as keenly as any lettered man. First the percussion lock, then the watch to read by night, and now the compass to make a man see in the dark – what a testimony to him, once a trumpeter, who had learned and risen by his own exertions alone. Hervey took the compass from its case on the saddle and noted the direction of the needle. 'Very well then,' he said, squeezing his legs the merest touch to put Gilbert into a walk.

Five minutes and the needle was backing very definitely. Hervey waited five minutes more, until the needle had moved a full quarter, and then turned right off the road to make for the stream which would lead them north of the fortress and on to the jheel bund. Gilbert, his feet now on pasture, at once sensed the change of purpose and began to throw his head, hopeful of a gallop. Trumpeter Storrs's grey, the only other in the troop, began whickering. Hervey winced. If the others took it up they would soon alert the doziest of sentries. There was nothing he could do, though, and he had worries enough finding the stream. It must be there; only if he had judged the needle so badly as to be almost doubling back would they not be able to find it. Navigating by night – the officer's constant trial. And yet he had the advantage on any in Hindoostan with Coates's 'contraption', as Johnson called it. Hervey could picture Coates now (omitting to make allowance for the difference of time), rising as always before it was light to beat about the bounds of his prosperous farm, as he had risen every day before dawn as a dragoon in America, and Flanders, and a dozen other places, and then as labourer and shepherd, and now as magistrate and man of consequence in West Wiltshire. Daniel Coates would now be—

Gilbert squealed and ran to the side. Hervey pulled him back onto the bit. 'Snake,' he said to Storrs, as matter-of-fact as he could having almost dropped the compass. 'I fear we'll have more of 'em if we're near water.' He would gladly put up with the inconvenience were it the price of finding the stream. He could never fathom the horse's ability to detect the proximity of a snake. Was it by smell or by sight? It could hardly be the latter at night, and yet it was curious what a horse could see in the dark when it had a mind. Gilbert had once shied at a basking krait thirty yards away, and yet the troop had lost two others, grazing, to kraits in the last year alone. Jessye had almost died from the same, when first he had gone to India, although that had been in the black of night.

The grass was now taller. Hervey raised his hand for Storrs to halt, and pressed Gilbert on gingerly. At last he was on it – the stream. He reined about and then motioned to Storrs to follow again as he turned right and north more, sighing with relief. The rest ought to be easy enough, even if it meant the point of the sword.

Serjeant Collins, a dozen yards behind, saw Hervey turn. Rather, he saw Gilbert turn, for a few white hairs made all the difference in the forewarning of daylight. Collins knew that Hervey was onto his line. He never doubted he would be, though he too knew how tricky the simplest of things were when night and the enemy were about. And he knew that everything would change in the next half-hour. The day came on faster in these parts than ever it managed in Spain. In half an hour they would be revealed even to a sentry on the walls of the distant fortress – intruders, murderous, like the snakes in the grass. The blow would surely be swift, as it must be against a snake lest it bite the hand that strikes. Collins had no illusions as to how desperate would be their position in the hours ahead.

The column was now in a trot, an uneven one, as the ground itself was uneven, but more than double the pace of the walk nevertheless. The noise was greater too, bits jingling and scabbards clanking. It sounded like a wagon-load of tinkers on the move. Could that be what any who heard it thought it was? Some hope, thought Hervey. Bullocks didn't snort and whinny. He pressed Gilbert for more speed: get it over with, get in among whoever was between them and the Motee Jheel, cut and slice through them and get to the bund. The commander-in-chief was depending on him, countless lives were waiting to be spared by his success.

The ground was with them for a while. Between the stream and the walls, half a league distant, was a rise which hid them from all but an observer on their side of it. And it was still too dark to see further than earshot. He could remember seeing a great many hovels when he had sketched here, but they had come across none so far. They were on the common pasture, after all, and he wouldn't expect to see even a grass-cutter abroad at this time. They were trotting even faster now – Gilbert stumbled once or twice until Hervey took a proper hold and lifted him onto the bit. He reckoned there would be light enough to canter in ten more minutes. Then they could sprint for the jheel bund and be done with it.

Another three hundred yards: the sun seemed to be racing them. Hervey could now see huts all along the rise. He would risk it – no words of command, just press to the canter and let the rest follow. Gilbert struck off eagerly with his off-fore, as he always favoured, Hervey peering intently ahead, praying that a cut or a bund would not suddenly check them. Four hundred horses pounding the till – if they could not be heard, then the earth must surely be shaking enough to rouse the dead. He thought he saw the odd figure on the ridge – with luck, terrified villagers.

Now there was light enough to make out the walls, but still in the dim distance barely more than a silhouette. They had the grass and the reeds as a backdrop, the advantage yet. Would the guns on the walls be trained on the approaches to the jheel bund, shotted and run out ready? Hervey knew they ought to be. Would they have the range? A thousand yards, he had estimated, perhaps a bit more. He had heard all manner of stories about the Bhurtpore guns, massive affairs, immovable, which could send an eight-inch ball of iron with great velocity over the outworks and beyond. Such a gun, well-served, could visit terrible destruction on a battery or a sap. This was Colonel Anburey's fear, that his sappers and miners would be too exposed to develop their work, but it could be no less a concern for Colonel Macleod, who had to expose his guns to some extent in order that they might fire at all. There was bound to be ground less dominated by the bigger guns, but the whole art of fortification was the facility to rake any approach and demolish any siege device. Hervey did not envy the engineers as they dug their saps and tunnels, nor the artillerymen, who heaved shot and powder and made themselves senseless and deaf – nor, indeed, the infantry who would have to sit patiently waiting for a breach and then storm it. And all these men relying on him now.

The sun broached the jungled horizon to his right, a brilliant torch which at last signalled an end to the night watch and to stealthy manoeuvre. It was day, the time for fighting.

And fighting they would have – directly ahead, a quarter of a mile (no more), a cavalry camp come hastily to life. He could see men rushing for their horses, and others already mounted forming up. How many they were he could have no true notion. It might be the entire Jhaut host beyond them, and these a picket only. Even so, they barred his way as effectively as any earthwork.

'Left wheel into line!' he called, checking the pace to a trot to allow them the manoeuvre time.

Trumpeter Storrs blew the call perfectly: just the four notes, and a simple fifth interval – easy enough with the bugle, even at a bounce.

Hervey's own troop wheeled effortlessly, an evolution they might do in their sleep so often had they practised it. The Eleventh, behind, had a harder time of it, with more ground to make up and two ranks to form, not one. Hervey wished he were leading with lances: they were not much use to him at the rear, and the sight of them lowered might well send the enemy packing. As they stood, he could only let them pursue once the dragoons had broken the Jhauts up. He cursed himself.

He looked rear again to see if the Eleventh were close enough yet for support. His jaw dropped. Up on the rise was a line of lances and yellow kurtas. He could scarcely believe their celerity and address. Skinner's sowars had taken post as flankers, and on the commanding ground, and without a word from him.

'Draw swords!'

Out rasped two hundred blades.

Four hundred yards now, and the ground ahead was even. He put Gilbert back into a canter, glancing over his shoulder again. There was Wainwright, covering, and Perry, upright and assured. He saw Green struggling with both hands to hold his mare. This was the best time, the troop in hand, every man intent on his next word of command. In another two hundred yards or so, when he shouted 'Charge!' he would relinquish all control for a frenzied few minutes, as each man fought his own battle, self-reliant instead of, as now, knee to knee.

He glanced left. The rissalah was pulling ahead – good! They would cut off any flight to the fortress, pin the enemy against the stream. Hervey lengthened the stride to a hand-gallop. How would the Jhauts meet them? They were still standing. Would it be with the flintlock? Surely not! Yet they showed no sign of movement. Why didn't they counter-charge? It was their only hope . . .

Then the Jhauts turned.

'They're breaking!' shouted Hervey, waving his sabre their way. 'Charge!'

Four hundred cavalry at the gallop, lances couched, but swords held high. Only infantry and guns saw the sabre's point; fleeing horsemen felt its edge.

Hervey fixed on a distant tree on the centre line and pressed Gilbert for all he was worth. In seconds they were among them. There was no need of his blade at first: the Jhauts were overmatched. Skinner's sowars were doing good execution, and his own dragoons were drawing blood. Yet an unseated man, sword in hand still, received his point cleanly at the throat – foolish or determined was he? It did not matter.

He tried to estimate how many they had bolted – two, three hundred at least. Gone like chaff in a puff of wind – no need to sound recall. He could see his objective clearly now. The lone thicket of *jhow* marked it unmistakably – the bund. Another half a mile at most. Come back to a canter, he told himself – but press on. Trust the squadrons to rally and conform.

Now he had to pray the bund was intact, the moats not yet inundated. Was that why the Jhauts had run – their job done, the bund breached, nothing more to cover?

There was a thunderous eruption of smoke and flame from the north-east bastion, the same distance away to his left. Shot whistled overhead – miles too high, he sneered. Had their gunners no art? Had they not ranged in their idle moments? Could this truly be the fortress that had defeated Lord Lake?

He could see no movement at the *jhow*. Was this really to be so easy an affair, or were they too late? More guns fired their way from the smaller bastions and redoubts as they bore on, but with no greater effect. He felt only contempt for the Jhauts' perfunctory opposition, even if they *were* safe behind their water-filled ditches.

He pressed Gilbert to a final effort.

Then they were at the *jhow*. His heart sank as he saw water in the channel. He could see the breach – not large. He needed his engineer. 'Mr Irvine!'

CHAPTER FIFTEEN

SIEGE

---

10 December

To Major W. S. Beatson,
Deputy Adjutant-General

Before Bhurtpore, 10 Dec. 1825

Sir,

*I have the honor to report, for the information of His
Excellency the Commander-in-Chief, that, in obedience to
his command, I proceeded to make a reconnaissance
on the Fortress of Bhurtpore with the object of intercepting
the means of inundation of its defences at what is known
as the Mottee Jheel, with under my command one troop
6th Light Dragoons, one squadron 11th Light Dragoons
under the direct command of Captain Rotton, and a
detachment of Colonel Skinner's Horse, under Major
Fraser. On advancing in the vicinity of the Bund at first
light, I encountered an encampment of the enemy's
cavalry, which was at once attacked and the enemy driven
off without loss. The body of Colonel Skinner's Horse,
acting on the initiative of Major Fraser, made a flank
movement; by which they intercepted and cut up more than
five hundred of the Enemy's cavalry, before they could
reach an outwork in which the greater proportion of them*

took refuge. At this time the guns of the Fortress opened a
moderate fire upon the force, but without damage.

After the affair of the Enemy's cavalry, I proceeded at
once for the Bund which was found to be cut in two places,
though the breaches had not been quite completed. A
moderate amount of water, only, was judged to have entered
the channels, and this was later confirmed by
reconnaissance, the ditches of all the outworks being dry.
Work was begun at once, under Lt. Irvine of the Engineers,
to repair the breaches, and this was accomplished by late
morning. The Enemy mounted two attacks on the Bund
during this time, but they were heartless affairs and easily
beaten off. At thirty minutes past midday, the relieving party
under the command of Brig.-General Sleigh took possession
of the Jheel Bund, and, as instructed to do so, I relinquished
my responsibilities in this regard.

I beg I may be allowed to express my approbation of the
intelligence and zeal of Major Fraser and Lt. Irvine, and
that the conduct of the body of Colonel Skinner's Horse
was exemplary.

> *I have the Honor to be,*
> *&c. &c. &c.*
> *M. P. Hervey, Major*

Hervey led his troop into the Sixth's lines late that afternoon, his command now dispersed, but their feat of arms
already the talk of the army. Edmonds had turned the
regiment out in their honour, mounted ranks with swords
drawn, and the quarter-guard with carbines at the present.
Local rank Hervey's majority might be, but it entitled him
to arms presented rather than a mere butt salute, and
Edmonds would have the regiment know what a day in its
annals this would surely become.

Hervey could scarce believe the material for the siege
now assembling – the ordnance, the tentage, camp stores,
provisions, transport; the livestock, somehow driven from

Agra and Muttra with as much ease, it would appear, as a Wiltshire shepherd might press his flock along a downland drove. And the regiments, King's and sepoy, battling for good order and military discipline as they began their routine of the siege – proud, colourful, cheery, possessed of self-confidence in limitless quantity. Hervey knew that he and his men had saved them blood, and he was glad of it also because the mounted arm would after all be able to look the infantry in the eye in this affair of digging and then the bayonet.

What a scene it was. In Agra and Muttra he had known its individual elements, but only now did it appear to him as a whole. It was a scene from many a picture he had thrilled to in his youth – the Crusades, the Hundred Years' War, Cromwell and the King, the Peninsula. It mattered not where, for the principle was the same: the paraphernalia of the siege, the methodical, patient, painful marshalling of resources, and then their remorseless application, until the besieged struck their colours or had them torn down, or else the besieger, his resources exhausted, struck camp and stole away. Only the detail of the brown-skinned servants and camp followers – the sutlers, dhobi-men, sweepers, bhistis, syces, Lascars and countless others – gave the scene its place.

Hervey nodded modestly to the salutes and well-wishers. His troop were less restrained in their acknowledgements. Enjoy it for the moment, he thought; the monotony of the siege will soon dull the remembrance. But, oh indeed, it had been a very fine affair at the Motee Jheel, and nothing could take from them the rightful sense of victory, if only as local as their leader's rank.

But two days later it seemed that the monotony of the siege would have them all exchange places with any man elsewhere than at Bhurtpore. Major Joynson read the day's general orders to the captains and staff assembled in his orderly-room tent, a well-made affair the size of a tennis court, twelve feet high and lined with vivid yellow cotton – though the smoke of a wood stove and a dozen cigars rendered the lining not as striking as once it had been:

FIELD GENERAL ORDERS.

Camp Before Bhurtpore, 13th Dec. 1825

Parole – FUTTYGHUR

Officiating Assist. Surgeon, J. Douglas, 14th N. Infantry, proceeding to join the army, is, on his arrival in camp, to be attached to the Field Hospital.

A working party of the following strength, from each of the Infantry divisions, to be sent to the Engineer Park to-morrow morning, and to be in attendance there at daybreak, or as soon after as possible – 100 Europeans, 250 Sepoys.

A Detachment, consisting of one and a half Company, to be furnished immediately from the 2nd Infantry Division, for the protection of the Engineer Park, and to provide small Escorts with cattle sent out for materials. The Officer commanding the party, to place himself under the orders of Brigadier Anburey, C.B.

Lieut. G. E. Smyth, 3rd Light Cavalry, Major of Brigade Western Division, is directed to join and do duty with his regiment on service with the Army on the Agra and Muttra Frontier.

Officers in Command of Posts and Piquets, are peremptorily required to detain all persons coming out of the Fort at the Piquets or Posts, reporting the circumstance immediately to the Field-officer of the Piquet, or to the Quarter-Master-General, and not to send them, as hitherto has been the practice, into the interior of their Camp, unless desired to do so by competent authority. Individuals

also who may be bearers of Letters or Despatches from the
Fort, are not to be permitted to pass the Piquets, but to be
detained there, and their Despatches to be forwarded to
the Quarter-Master-General, for Lord Combermere's
information.

Officers commanding Corps and Departments, to which
public or hired camels are attached, are directed to
prohibit in the strongest terms, the owners or attendants,
when going out with their cattle for forage, from
advancing too far into the Jungle in the direction of the
Fort, or from proceeding too great a distance from the
Camp, as they are liable to fall in with scattered parties of
the Enemy's horsemen.

'It's all working parties and foraging, I'm afraid,' Joynson
concluded. 'And we have received orders to strengthen
patrols and escorts. Dull work, but better than labouring for
the sappers.'

The troop-captains nodded.

'I have made a roll of the duties. The adjutant is having
them copied as we speak. That is the long and the short of
it. Are there any questions, gentlemen?'

There were none.

'Very well, that is all. But let us see if we can dine together
promptly at seven tonight. Hervey, stay a while longer if you
please.'

Major Joynson sounded confident enough, if a shade
tired. When he had said, 'I have made a roll of the duties,'
Hervey knew full well the major would have done just that
– himself, and in every detail, rather than delegating the task
to the adjutant. That was what Eustace Joynson did best,
better than anyone, indeed, and such was his conscientiousness that he could not allow a task to be performed any less
well than was possible. Throughout Lord Towcester's
diabolical time in command, Joynson had tried his best in
these regards, but all too often he had counted himself a

failure – including for his part in the events that culminated in Henrietta Hervey's death. Not that Hervey himself would apportion one ounce of blame to the major, whom he had grown to respect on account of both his conscientiousness and his doggedness in the face of the most wretched personal circumstances. And there was no doubt, too, that the painstaking attention to detail occupied Joynson's mind admirably. Daily he fretted about Frances, for despite everyone's best efforts his daughter had lately become engaged to an officer of native infantry, a penniless and stupid one at that. The responsibility of allowing his daughter to embark on an unsuitable marriage weighed heavily with him. Yet he simply did not have the strength of mind to forbid her.

'Lord Combermere's express orders are that you keep the rank of major, Hervey, *pro tempore*. I should be much obliged if you would act therefore as second in command.'

Hervey was not disposed to agreeing without some qualification, for besides aught else he would have no job to do if Joynson continued to attend to every detail. 'Of course, but I must keep command of my troop.'

Joynson nodded blankly. If Hervey thought himself capable of both then who was he to gainsay him? 'I gather Combermere asked that you join his staff.'

Hervey smiled. 'A nice gesture, but a siege is a dull enough thing to be engaged in without having to watch it from headquarters!'

'No gesture, I heard. It was to be General Whittingham's deputy.'

'Yes, but an affair of paper all the same.'

'Sooner or later, Hervey, you'll have to submit to such a regime. Armies aren't run from the saddle, as well you know.'

Hervey smiled again. Joynson's paternalism was endearing, if not always deft; he was no Edmonds – not in his sureness of touch, that is. 'I know, but I would wish for the time being that it were later rather than sooner. This affair will not be at all easy.'

Joynson looked troubled. 'You doubt we will prevail?'

Hervey considered his words. 'Nothing is certain. It would be well to remember it. The engineers say they can't tunnel; they can only sap the guns forward, and General Edwards says he can't guarantee a breach of walls so thick, even with his twenty-four-pounders. The train begins arriving today, by all accounts.'

'You are well informed. Is there word of how long the engineers will need?'

'Upwards of ten days before they get the first battery into position, according to Brigadier Anburey's major.'

'I think we shall be much occupied, then, with our little escorts and the like. I've agreed with the Eleventh that we shall patrol alternate nights throughout our allotted sectors. Without a natural feature as our boundary it's too chancy to have patrols from both beating about the place. They will take duty tonight.'

(*Five days later*)

FIELD GENERAL ORDERS.

Camp Before Bhurtpore, 19th Dec. 1825

Parole – GAZEEPORE

A working party from each of the Infantry Divisions, of the same strength as yesterday, to be sent to-morrow at day-break to the Engineer Park. The Quarter-Master's Establishments, and public cattle, to be sent there as usual. A Carpenter is also directed to be furnished from each of the Corps in the 1st and 2nd Divisions of Infantry.

A Detachment, consisting of five Companies from the 1st Infantry Division, will march to-morrow morning, and take charge of 300 Hackeries proceeding from the Artillery Park, for ammunition and stores, to Agra.

*With reference to an Act of Parliament, 54th and 86th
Geo. III. On the subject of Prize Property Agents, and
claims thereto, the Field General Orders of the 16th
Instant, appointing a Prize Committee, and directing Prize
Agents to be nominated by ballot for each of the Divisions
of the Army, and by the General Staff, is hereby cancelled;
and it is now ordered, in conformity with the provision of
the said Act, that two Agents only be appointed for the
Army.*

*His Excellency the Commander-in-Chief and the Field
Officers will nominate one Agent, and the other to be
appointed by the Captains and Subaltern Officers with the
Army. The Prize Agents will be furnished with the required
letters of attorney appointing them Agents for the Army;
and they will be prepared on their part, to give security in
the sum of £2000 sterling each. The Prize Agents, on all
points of duty connected with their Agency, will be guided
by the spirit and letter of the Act of Parliament before
cited, and which is to be found in Carroll's Code of
Regulations, Chap. 59.*

*That part of the Field General Orders of 16th Instant,
which directs that all property captured from the Enemy by
any individual of the Army, be forthwith delivered up to
the Prize Agents, and imposes the forfeiture of all claim to
share, besides other penalties, on individuals who may be
discovered secreting or detaining property, knowing it to
be a Prize – and further requires the Agents to demand all
Prize Property, wherever it may be discovered – remains
in full force.*

Major Joynson took off his spectacles as he concluded.
'Well, gentlemen, from the first part it would seem that the
sappers are making good progress if powder is to be brought
forward.' The same assembly, his troop-captains and staff,
heard the day's orders each afternoon before evening
stables, and this was indeed the first intimation of true

progress. 'As to the enemy,' continued Joynson, now polishing his spectacles, 'I had expected them to be more active by day and by night, yet it appears they will do no more than beat up a few grass-cutters now and then, and they surely won't venture out at night, it seems. That being said, we cannot afford to lapse in any vigilance.' He looked at each of the captains as sternly as he could, a game effort. 'As to the last, on the subject of prize money, I cannot imagine that it will amount to much, this Durjan Sal's army being scarcely well-equipped, but we had better attend to the election of these agents. I shall ask the adjutant to canvass all officers. But let it be rightly understood: whatever prize is taken is first the prize of the regiment. If it is a worthy trophy I intend that it is kept by us.'

'Then let us hope we intercept the treasury as it makes its escape!' said Hugh Rose, smiling and blowing a great deal of smoke into the air from his cigar.

Hervey contemplated Rose's raffish mien. He thought it a not altogether helpful pose with Riding-Master Broad, his dupe (there was no avoiding the word), sitting in the rear rank. Hugh Rose's appearance betrayed nothing of the conditions they were living in – comfortable enough, but undeniably reduced – and his thick black hair and fine features, which won him the easy admiration of his dragoons as well as their women, looked the picture of grooming, as if for a drawing room at Fort William. His remark on the pecuniary spoils of war, albeit no doubt intended in some levity, required a rebuke.

'A happy thought indeed, Rose,' said Joynson, however, inclined more to punctilious attention to regulations than to scruple. 'But on that I fear we should have to follow General Orders. And in any case, any treasure in Bhurtpore must belong rightfully to the deposed rajah. That is why I said I do not suppose the prize money will amount to much.'

The captains feigned disappointment.

'Are there any questions? No? Very well, then, dinner at eight.'

When the others were gone, Hervey spoke his mind. 'I think we might propose some more active duty. The men are restless.'

'Yes, I know it. What activity do you imagine?'

'Well, we could make an effort to root out these cavalry who pick off the working parties, instead of merely trying to guard everyone and everything. They're not sallying from the fort, that much we know, and they can't be coming from the east, or north across the jheels. If both brigades put up a squadron, or better still all of Skinner's Horse, to beat all the cover to the west, and stood-to every man during daylight for three days, say, we might bring them to battle.'

'I can suggest it to Childers tomorrow. It has merit enough, even were the men not restless.'

'It would have to be done soon, however. There's a danger that once the artillery begins they may bolt Durjan Sal. He may not have the stomach for a siege. From what I heard yesterday of Sir Charles Metcalfe's treaties with him he never imagined it would come to this.'

Joynson nodded. 'Very well.'

'There is one more thing I would speak of.'

'Green?'

'Not this time. He has had his warning. *Deedes.*'

'Oh. I feared it would come.'

'He's the most blusterous serjeant-major I've seen. There've been all manner of confusions these past ten days.'

Joynson was silent for some time. 'Sir Ivo will be back in but a few weeks. He will know what to do.'

'Sir, *you* know what to do,' said Hervey, in a tone meant to be encouraging, though the words themselves accused the major of evading his duty.

Joynson shook his head slowly. 'I had hoped not to have this sort of trouble.'

Hervey sympathized, for trouble it would be. The major

did, however, have the advantage of being in the field. It was a far easier place in which to dismiss a man than the barracks. 'A word with the brigadier tomorrow?'

Joynson sighed. 'O the pleasure of the plains!'

Hervey looked at him blankly.

'Very well. But you know, it will look very ill with the other regiments.'

Hervey knew that too. But he knew it would look even more ill were the regimental serjeant-major to falter at a time less propitious. He said nothing, but picked up his cap and made to leave.

'Thank you, Hervey,' said Joynson, wearily. 'I knew well enough that Deedes was incapable, but I kept telling myself it was only by comparison with Mr Lincoln.'

The tone was a shade too despairing. Hervey turned full back. 'Sir, I know I speak for the regiment when I say that all ranks hold your stewardship in high regard. This is but trying detail, and the corrective is at hand. Sir Ivo ought to be very well pleased with what he finds.'

Joynson looked genuinely surprised.

In the event, it was very easily done. The major called for the RSM soon after first parade next day and told him that, with regret, it was his decision to relieve him of his duties. He was to report as soon as was practicable to the depot at Agra pending a further decision as to his employment thereafter. When Joynson recounted the interview to Hervey later that morning it was with surprise, still, at Deedes's reaction. 'You know, he seemed almost . . . pleased, relieved. He said he had always done his best – which I fear is true. He said he wished to serve on in some other position if it were possible. I don't know; there may be something in Calcutta . . .'

'Well, I am all astonishment. I imagined he would bluster as ever.'

'And he left camp with some dignity, too. I called in

Hairsine and told him he was to be acting serjeant-major, and Deedes treated him very decently by all accounts.'

Hervey nodded, though he had not a moment's doubt that Deedes's dismissal had been necessary. 'Well, he must have had some quality otherwise he would never have been advanced in the first instance. I imagine he felt some loyalty too, even in his exigent position.'

'That was to have been my method if it had come to it: calling on his better self to accept things for the good of the regiment. Still, it is done now.' Joynson appeared to take no satisfaction in it, however, even with Hairsine making a difference already at orderly room.

'Who is to take C Troop?'

'I've told Strickland to make his senior serjeant do duty until there's time for a proper regimental board. By then Sir Ivo should be back. I'm deuced glad Strickland postponed his leave.'

Hervey saw no reason why a board should not be held at once, but he saw no likelihood of convincing Joynson. C Troop's man would do well enough; Strickland would not have it, otherwise. 'Did the brigadier express an opinion about taking the offensive?'

'He said he would speak with Sleigh. But it seems the guns will be going in soon and Combermere's likely to want a strong cavalry presence.'

'We shall all say amen to that. It's well time the fort's guns were answered.'

The guns of two bastions in particular had caused annoyance and casualties since the army had first appeared before Bhurtpore, yet could not be answered with any effect at the extreme range of the field artillery, nor even, indeed, with the long guns of the siege train yet. Only when the engineers had sapped their way to within a thousand yards or so, and built up redoubts, could the gunners try to dislodge the enemy's cannon. And dislodge them they must, for the siege guns could not pound away with the bastions commanding the ground so. A siege was an occasion when Adye's general injunction against counter-battery fire did not hold.

'I await orders on this keenly, too, said Joynson. 'Shall we take a ride to look at the ground?'

Hervey had never before ridden ground with the major, and he was eager to do so. He wanted to learn how good was his eye for country compared with that for administration, for in spite of the banter of the camp at Agra, he was certain that the cavalry must be more active in this siege than the textbooks allowed. He had studied the accounts of Lord Lake's failure. He was certain that if the cavalry became a mere arm of the commissary then the siege would go the same way as Lord Lake's.

They rode with only their covermen, Hervey marked by Corporal Wainwright, Joynson by the senior corporal. The major was not one for panoply, and in any case he scarcely expected trouble within the ring of scarlet around the fortress.

Everywhere was purposeful activity. Hervey could not remember scenes the like since San Sebastian, perhaps Badajoz, even. Columns of sepoys tramped to and from great breastworks thrown up in a matter of days like mole-hills on greensward. Guns and ammunition wagons lumbered forward continuously, and empty wagons passed them on their way back from dumping powder, shot and shell at the batteries in anticipation of the great pounding to come. And the engineers, the sappers and miners, who opened the way for the infantry, whether by bridge or breach, worked oblivious to their surroundings, and to the enemy's guns which periodically sent hissing spheres of iron arching into the sky, then to throw up fountains of earth where they struck before bowling along the ground to knock down men and horses like skittles if they didn't look sharp.

Hervey had observed the same curious detachment in the Peninsula, the sappers working as calmly as if they were navigators at an English cut. It was a cool courage, theirs, not one fired by dash or steadied by the touch of cloth. He wondered if it could endure as the guns began to take their toll. Sapping to the foot of the walls would be hot work indeed.

'Do you think Durjan Sal doubts the outcome, seeing all this, Hervey?' asked the major suddenly. They had ridden for ten minutes and more in silence.

Hervey was unsure what he had heard. 'You mean will he ask for terms?'

'No. I mean, does he consider those walls impregnable? Does he believe we shall just go away? You could scarce call firing from those walls much of a counter-action.'

'I confess to being surprised,' replied Hervey, watching warily as another ball arched from a distant bastion towards them.

Joynson watched it too. It hit an outcrop of solid rock a hundred yards ahead of them, sending a shower of deadly shards in all directions.

'But he must think those walls solid enough. And, in truth, he might be right. I've not seen their like before, I think.'

'Do you know why it is the engineers can't tunnel?' Joynson supposed only that the ground was too hard.

'The distance, pure and simple, is my understanding. They can't get close enough to begin a gallery.'

'I can't say as I understand. If they can sap forward, why can't they then tunnel?'

'Because after two hundred yards there isn't air enough to breathe, or to make for a good explosion.'

They rode on a further half-mile in silence, or rather without a word, for Durjan Sal's guns were now speaking continually. Three of them fired at once from the long-necked bastion, the report so loud that both men looked its way. Hervey saw the homing shot first – low and straight, not plunging like the others. 'She comes our way,' he said warily.

Neither man moved a muscle more than had they been on parade. It was as unthinkable as it was pointless.

Eighteen pounds of iron grazed the rocky outcrop fifty yards to their right then ricocheted half a right angle, but chippings the size of musket balls shot their way, drawing blood from Hervey's hand and his mare's shoulder.

Joynson, on his nearside, but half a length in front, cursed as his shako was all but knocked from his head, the silver cross beneath the oilskin having stopped a stone bullet. He didn't see his mare's wound at first, looking about her legs and flanks for marks. 'Oh, God!' he cried suddenly, jumping from the saddle.

Blood spurted from her breast as if from a stirrup pump. Joynson took off his silk stock and pressed it to the wound – a neat slice like the sabre's work. 'An artery, Hervey, for sure,' he groaned.

If it were an artery there was nothing that they – or even David Sledge – could do. But Hervey got down and took the bandages from his valise.

Corporal Wainwright did likewise, and Joynson's cover-man the same. But Joynson's sleeves were soaked through, and the pool of blood at the mare's feet was spreading rapidly.

'It's no good, Eustace.' But Hervey knew the major had bought the mare for his wife years ago. Conceding would be a doubly painful business.

'Give me a pistol!'

Hervey took one of the flintlocks from his saddle holster, already loaded, tamped. He held it out to him. 'Shall I do it while you steady her?'

'No, Hervey. It wouldn't do,' said Joynson simply, taking the pistol and letting go the silk stock.

Nevertheless, Hervey took out his second pistol and made ready. He had no idea if the major had ever shot a horse. It was the Devil's own job even without sentiment.

'Offsaddle her, will you, Hervey,' said Joynson resolutely.

When it was done, the major wiped his hands on his overalls, rubbed the little mare's nose, cocked the pistol and put the muzzle gently but firmly into the fossa above her left eye, angling it so as to aim at the bottom of her right ear.

He pulled the trigger. The mare's forelegs folded, and she fell to the ground without so much as a grunt.

Hervey was impressed – a businesslike despatch, as neat as any he'd seen. It had not been two minutes since the stone had done its worst. 'She was a fine animal,' he said, with real admiration.

Tears welled in Joynson's eyes, which he did nothing to hide. 'She was. And I should have left her with Frances.' And then, with an almost bitter note, 'except that I couldn't have trusted her to see to her rightly.'

Hervey thought to say nothing.

Joynson knelt and cut off a lock of the mane. 'The last of Anne Joynson, then . . . save for Frances herself.'

Hervey still thought it best to stay silent. Indeed, he had begun wondering how they might decently dispose of the carcass.

Joynson's coverman was already resigned to walking back to the lines. 'I'd swear them guns was trying to do that, sir,' he said, making ready to hand the reins to the major.

'So would I, sir,' added Wainwright. 'Somebody in that fort knows how to shoot. That's for sure.'

Hervey frowned and shook his head. 'The way that shot ran level, the gun must be a giant. It couldn't be retrained quickly enough to aim. Anyway, I doubt they can even make us out from that distance. No, a lucky shot I'll warrant.'

That evening, however, the camp was abuzz with rumour about the accuracy of the Jhaut guns. It was confidently asserted that the gunners were Frenchmen or Italians, as there had been in native service throughout the Maratha wars. And there were wilder stories, too – that the deserters from His Majesty's artillery were directing the fire. The

287

direst retribution was sworn for any who had changed sides, nor was it clear where a Frenchman would stand in this reckoning. Hervey did his rounds that evening well pleased with the evidence of the Sixth's fighting spirit. Even the grocer – a name that Hervey found himself thinking of increasingly, if not actually uttering – seemed more animated at dinner. Joynson, certainly, had an edge not usually apparent. It had been a dozen years and more since he had been shot over. The sudden taste of gunfire that afternoon seemed to have been an exceptional tonic.

Hervey turned in just before midnight after walking the horse lines. They had been quiet, with nothing but an occasional whicker and grunt from the animals themselves, or an 'evenin', sir' from a sentry of the inlying picket. And although it was the picket-officer's job to check that the running lines were taut, he had inspected each of the troops' in turn. He had known enough times in Spain where a loose line had ended in runaways and broken legs. And he had checked, too, that the sentries knew the parole and how they were to be relieved. The men were alert, and it had given him much satisfaction to go to his tent knowing that the Sixth were as keen in their field discipline as they were in their fighting intent. He was afraid the former would be tested far longer than the latter, for what he had seen of the siege that day did not lead him to suppose there would be anything but cannonading and sapping for a month or more – save, perhaps, an obliging sortie by Durjan Sal's cavalry.

But now he was pleased for his campaign bed, and that it was the Sixteenth – Daniel Coates's old regiment – who stood sentinel. He could rest assured. Private Johnson had placed a bowl of hot water on one of the chests, but it was now only lukewarm. Hervey undressed, put on his night-shirt, washed his hands and set to work with sponge and tooth powder. Then he unmade his bed in the nightly routine of shaking out anything that might have crawled there during the time his groom had been gone, and, satisfied at last of his safety, lay down between white cotton sheets beneath two thick woollen blankets. He took care to double them and fold the edges under, for he knew he would need their warmth on so starry a night. The pillow was soft, and he had no desire to read or to contemplate anything. He turned down the lamp to the merest glow, and closed his eyes.

CHAPTER SIXTEEN

RUMOURS OF WAR

The early hours

From the depths of sleep, Hervey was called rudely to arms. To awake to the 'alarm' – the bugle's repeated C and E, unmistakable, and easy enough for the most frightened trumpeter to blow – had been a thrill in his cornet days, but now it meant only anxiety in the knowledge that there had been some failure. Perhaps his own? There was firing, too, distant but near enough to take account of. He turned up the lamp and began hauling on his overalls as Private Johnson, breathless, pulled back the tent flap.

'Major 'Ervey, sir!'

Hervey had no idea why his groom was already abroad and dressed.

'They 'ad me up cos thi mare's got a bit o' colic. All 'ell's broke loose over where t'Sixteenth are.'

'Very well. You'd better saddle up Gilbert if you will.' He began wondering who had given the order to sound the alarm.

'Bring 'im 'ere, sir?'

'No. Just where we stand to.' This was no time to be making things complicated.

Johnson picked up Hervey's boots and shook them.

'Thank you, Johnson. Now away.'

It took him but a minute more to finish dressing, fastening on the swordbelt last and picking up his pistols from beside the bed. He put on his shako as he ducked out of his tent, straining his eyes in the darkness, which fires and torches made all the darker in the unlit places. Men were hastening all about him, but with order and purpose. All they did, indeed, was the same as for stand-to before first light every day, except that it was at the double and in the expectation of action rather than merely the possibility. When he reached E Troop's line, the chargers to the right, he found Johnson with Gilbert under saddle, fastening up the bridle. He put both pistols into the holsters then made to tighten the girth and surcingle.

'Right, sir,' said Johnson, taking away the head collar rather than spending any more time looping the straps.

Hervey was not yet ready to mount, though. 'Mr Perry! Mr Green!' he called. There was a good deal of calling all around, and he was not about to enter into a competition with the corporals; but he wanted to know his officers were at their posts.

Serjeant-Major Armstrong came up with a lantern. 'Mr Perry's reporting to the adjutant, sir.'

Of course he was. Hervey had forgotten for the moment that Perry was next for picket-officer. 'And Mr Green?'

'Haven't seen him, sir. Both sections'll be ready in not many minutes more. They were quick out of their pits, I'll say that for 'em. Mind you, Collins was on picket.'

Corporal Wainwright now came up, leading his trooper. 'Sir.'

'Where is Mr Green?'

'I don't know, sir. I'll find 'is groom.'

'No. Let it be, for the moment. Come with me to the major.'

'Ay, sir. He's by the picket tent.'

'Very well. Johnson!'

'Sir?'

'Get someone to find where Mr Green is.' He turned to Armstrong. 'Carry on, then. Not to mount without the order, though.'

'Right, sir.'

Hervey strode off with Corporal Wainwright down the flanks of the horse lines, noting the state of each troop as he passed – so far as the darkness allowed him. Only A Troop looked unready. He found Joynson and the adjutant at the picket tent, the RSM standing with his notebook poised, the picket-officer just taking his leave. There was still firing from the Sixteenth's lines, but no sign of a galloper from brigade.

'Well, Hervey?' said Joynson, a touch wearily.

'Have we sent anyone to make contact?'

'No. And I'm not inclined to risk it,' replied Joynson firmly. 'Finding what's happening would be the very devil of a job. If there's a real reverse we shall hear of it soon enough.'

'Then I believe we should move up to support the Sixteenth without orders.'

'Why?' The major's tone did not so much challenge as request elaboration.

'Because – unlikely as it may seem – it might just be the sortie in strength that we were speaking of.'

'Why have we not had orders to that effect from brigade, then? I've sent Perry there, by the way.'

'Well, the brigadier will be no more certain than we are, in all likelihood.'

Joynson was clearly troubled. 'Yes, but the general must be given the opportunity to exercise a proper command, must he not?'

Hervey was becoming exasperated. This was the Joynson of past years, not of late months: the Joynson cowed by Towcester, sick headaches and the like. 'Eustace, since when did cavalry have to await an order to close with the enemy?'

There was no answer to this. The major turned to the adjutant. 'Very well, then. Have the regiment mount.'

The adjutant turned to the trumpet-major. 'Troops to mount, please.'

'Sir!' The trumpet-major put his bugle to his lips and sounded the regimental call followed by the octave leap of 'prepare to mount', then the simpler repeated Cs and Gs of the executive.

'I'd like you next to me, Hervey,' said Joynson, perfectly composed. 'It'll be a deuced tricky business in this light. Perry can look after E Troop. They can ride under second squadron.'

'With respect, sir. It might be better to keep the troop in hand. You never know—'

'Very well, very well. If you are content with that then I have no objection. Perry's able enough to have them on his own.'

Hervey would say nothing more, but he was hardly content, for the troop would be under command of the grocer until Perry returned from his galloping. Assuming, that was, that Green would actually find them. However, there were Armstrong and Collins, and he could always take the lead again before they were committed. He turned to Corporal Wainwright, who nodded his understanding and made off at once to E Troop.

Hervey had greater concerns, however. The handling of a regiment of light dragoons in troop ranks was, even by day, a testing undertaking. When the ground was unbroken, as on a review, it could pass off at the trot tolerably well, though anything beyond a couple of hundred yards led to bunching and bulging of the line to such an extent that it was difficult to recover proper dressing without coming back to a walk. When it was dark, however, and the ground broken as here, the undertaking verged on the reckless. He took out his telescope, stepped the other side of the picket tent's fire, and tried to see what was happening in the Sixteenth's lines.

Meanwhile the troop orderly serjeants were reporting to the RSM. It was only another minute or so before Mr Hairsine could report to the adjutant that the regiment was ready. Johnson had brought Gilbert up, and Hervey now pulled down the stirrups and mounted.

'Skirmishers out?' said Joynson as Hervey closed up to his side.

'I would think it better to advance with a clear front,' replied Hervey.

'Very well. "Advance", please, trumpet-major.'

That Joynson asked for such an opinion did not in the least diminish his standing in Hervey's eyes. That he accepted it only increased it, too. Seeking support for a decision already made was the true sign of the weak-spirited.

'If it is a sortie, they might just be intent on mischief,' said Hervey, having to raise his voice against the jingle and clamour behind him (it took a fair few yards, always, before the NCOs got the dressing passable in close order). 'But it sounds a determined affair. They might be making for the guns.'

'I take my hat off to them if they are,' said Joynson, matter-of-factly.

'They know the ground better than do we.'

'But it would be a desperate affair nevertheless.'

The adjective struck Hervey forcefully. Perhaps a night sortie was indeed the act of a desperate man. Had Durjan Sal already concluded that his fortress could not withstand a determined siege? He would have known why Lord Lake's had failed – not just for the want of heavy guns but because of the attacks by the Maratha cavalry on his siege forces. How many cavalry could Durjan Sal dispose on such a night? There was no telling, and neither was there telling the damage a resolute force could do if ever panic seized hold in the camps. 'We might have to make a wide front if they're really intent on breaking through to the guns. It will hardly be enough but it might check them for a while. I hope there's a general stand-to by now.'

Lieutenant Perry rode across the front of A Troop to report. His horse was blowing hard, for he had had him in a gallop, and Hervey was pleased with this evidence of boldness. Perry saluted as he came up to the major. 'Sir, brigadier's compliments, and would you be so good as to place the regiment in a position to support the Sixteenth. They were attacked by a large force of cavalry and their object is not clear. The Sixteenth have one troop only under saddle, and the rest are standing ground with the carbine.'

'Where will the brigadier be?' asked Joynson.

'He did not say, sir, but I presumed he intended remaining with the reserve.'

Joynson did not reply.

'It's no good presuming, Arthur. We have to know where the brigadier is!' snapped Hervey. Galloping was no use without a clear head.

Perry said nothing.

'Well,' said Joynson emolliently, 'it is the brigadier's duty to make his post known. Thank you, Mr Perry.'

'Take post with the troop, then,' said Hervey. 'They're not to answer but to the regiment.'

'Sir,' replied Perry, saluting and turning, trying hard not to sound cast-down. Joynson's thanks were welcome, but Hervey's reproof was deserved.

'A little sharp, Hervey,' said Joynson when he was gone. 'He did well to get orders so quickly.'

Hervey did not reply at once; an increase in firing in the direction of the Sixteenth's camp, though two furlongs away and more, commanded their attention. 'I think we had soon better extend, sir,' he said finally, the fusillade having gone on a full minute. 'It can't be long now before they break through.'

'I think we had,' said Joynson assuredly. 'Mr Vanneck,

Second Squadron to extend to the left, please. I want them to cover as much ground as they can.'

The adjutant wheeled right and put his horse into a trot. There was no trumpet call by which the order could have been conveyed, for trumpet calls by and large regulated activity rather than conveyed changes in design. Joynson put his own horse into a lateral trot so as to be at the junction of the two squadrons.

Strickland brought Second Squadron quickly into line by the simple expedient of halting them for a time so that First Squadron cleared enough ground ahead to allow Second to trot up with the merest incline left. Once his right marker was level with First Squadron's flanker, he ordered them back to the walk and called 'dress by the right', which brought the left flank wheeling smartly round. 'Ready, Major Joynson!' he shouted.

Joynson replied at once: 'Draw swords!'

Four hundred sabres came rasping from their scabbards. A regiment drawing swords was ever a sound to thrill, more so even than a battalion fixing bayonets. Hervey smiled to himself: it was the first he had heard it in earnest in ten years. He could even forget the blunting of the edges, steel on steel.

What sight daylight would present him with this instant he could not be certain. C and A Troops were in good order in front. He could only trust that D and B were keeping both space and station in the support line, and likewise E to the rear of them. It was truly no bad thing to have a third line of sabres, a second reserve, in circumstances such as these – even if no more than a troop's worth. He would just have to trust Perry to have them in hand.

Eyes were getting used to the darkness by now, especially since there were no campfires to dazzle them any more. They could see well enough to trot, thought Joynson. But if they did they would not see the enemy until they were on top of him. Did that matter? What method in the fight could there be but a strong arm and a sharp blade?

'Trumpet-major, "trot" if you please!'

The next minute was a free-for-all of stumbling and cursing. Hervey was near to using the flat of his sword a dozen times, so bad was the barging. And then they were into a good rhythm. And just in time, for the first clash with the Jhauts came sooner than expected – on the left, so that at once there was a bending of the line and a loss of direction in C Troop. Not that Joynson, or even Strickland, could see it, for the one was too far away and the other was busy with his sabre. D Troop ran into the rear of the mêlée with no idea of what was happening, but Perry sensed the trouble and took E Troop at once into the breach opening with First Squadron, himself closing with the major.

'Hold hard, sir!' he shouted. 'The left flank's engaged.'

'Halt!' bawled Joynson, heaving on his reins for all he was worth.

But the whole line was now run up against the Jhaut cavalry. With both sides in no more than a trot, the collision was gentle enough, but the shock was great nevertheless.

Joynson's sabre flew from his hand as a tulwar sliced out of the dark. His coverman, stirrup to stirrup with him, lunged forward with his sabre and fended off the follow-through. Hervey could make out nothing. He lowered his head and thrust his sabre forward in the guard. Something hit the blade, not too hard. Corporal Wainwright, beside him, reins looped over his left arm, thrust forward with a pistol and fired. Joynson, his sabre hanging loose from his wrist by the sword knot, pulled a pistol from its holster and fired just as a huge Jhaut raised an axe to his charger's head. The man somersaulted backwards like a dolly at a fair.

Joynson pulled out the other pistol and fired at a man crossing left to right, but missed, leaving his coverman to finish the job with an arm's-length shot. Firing increased the length of the line as dragoon after dragoon managed to dis-engage his sabre long enough to draw a pistol. It seemed to gain them the initiative, for there was no shooting by return.

Joynson began shouting – bellowing – '*Forward!*' They had saved themselves with steel, and turned the tables with shot. Now they would press home the advantage with the leg.

It was not long in the doing. Suddenly there was a great shout and then the drumming of hooves, and the Sixth knew they were speeding the Jhauts from the field. 'Follow, sir?' came voices from left and right.

But Joynson would not pursue in the dark. Even before Hervey could urge him not to give chase he was shouting, 'Re-form!' He intended closing on the Sixteenth's lines in good order and standing to until they could take stock at first light.

'I'm going to my troop, sir,' called Hervey, certain he was not needed in the van any longer.

'Very well, Hervey. My compliments to Mr Perry. His action was sharp.'

Hervey smiled. It was so very like Joynson to be thinking thus. The men might consider him an old woman at heart, but they would always like him and therefore do his bidding willingly.

'And have your troop look for any wounded, if you please.'

'Sir.' It went without saying that the reserve troop picked up the wounded. It would be a dangerous affair, though. A moon would be a kindness to both sides. He would send for lanterns. 'Mr Perry,' he called, as he tried to make his way through the confusion of men and horses at the rear.

Eventually he found him. 'All accounted for, Hervey, save Green.'

'Green?' Hervey sounded as worried as he was astonished.

'And his groom.'

'How? Where was he?'

'I don't think he was ever with us. I don't think he mustered. No one has seen him.'

'Good God! Where's his coverman?'

'In his place.'

'Well, he'd better go back and bring him. And he can fetch some lanterns. We're to search the field.'

'Very well, sir.'

Hervey shook his head angrily, but swallowed hard. 'That was smart work bringing up the troop as you did. The major is well pleased.'

'Thank you, sir.'

But one man's address did not make up for the lack of it in another. Hervey continued to seethe at Green's absence as they set about searching for any who had fallen from the saddle.

At first light E Troop stood to their horses in the rear of the other four troops, fifty yards short of the Sixteenth's firing line – the line they had held since their own stand-to-arms in the middle of the night. Their search had rendered up one dragoon killed – by a ball in the back of the neck, which had very probably come from a fellow dragoon's pistol in the black confusion of the fight – and three others with sword or spear wounds, none of them too likely to be fatal. They found eight Jhauts dead or dying, but any who had been less severely injured seemed one way or another to have crawled to further cover. There were a good many dragoons riding-wounded, patched up where they stood by the surgeon's assistants, Sledge himself having beat about the ground with Hervey. Of one man, or rather two, there was no sign, however. Cornet Green was nowhere to be found. Hervey was now almost beside himself with anger. Never had an officer of the Sixth absented himself so. The word, indeed, was desertion. And in the face of the enemy.

When the light of day let them see to the range of the telescope, Joynson stood-down the regiment and issued orders to return to camp. Hervey told him of Green.

'His groom as well? That is most strange,' said the major, bruised by the day's cannonade and weary from the night's exertions – and yet disinclined to see the worst in the report.

'I can't see what else to make of it,' said Hervey sharply. 'The man's unfit to command a picket, even.'

But when they returned to camp Hervey was obliged to consider making something else of it, for into the lines soon afterwards rode Green and his groom, both of them in field order. Propriety required that he held his anger in check; reproving an officer in front of the ranks did no one credit as a rule. But the tone perfectly conveyed his state of mind. 'Well, Mr Green?'

'Sir, I am afraid I became lost.'

Hervey's mouth fell open. 'Lost? Lost, Mr Green?'

'I regret so, sir.'

Dragoons were trying their best to watch without being caught too obviously doing so.

'Mr Green, you had better attend at once on the adjutant.'

'Sir, if I might explain—'

Lieutenant Perry cut him short. 'You may explain first to me, Mr Green,' he said, glancing at Hervey and hoping for his leave. 'Report at once to my tent.'

Green saluted.

'And do not ride your charger through the lines, sir!'

Green dismounted sheepishly.

Hervey looked at Perry and nodded. It was the right thing to do. There might conceivably be an explanation that rendered his offence a lesser one than a regimental court martial would dispose of – though he could not imagine it.

'Private Needham, a word with you,' said the serjeant-major to the cornet's groom. Armstrong's Tyneside conveyed an unnerving degree of affability, which fooled no one within its hearing.

Hervey concluded that his best course was to repair to his own tent to shave.

Half an hour later, as he drank one of Johnson's fortified brews from regimental china, Perry and Armstrong came to

300

his tent. They had first compared accounts of the night's wanderings and found them in essentials to be the same. 'Green admits to failing to rise at once to the alarm,' said Perry. 'He went back to sleep until Needham rousted him out, and then he had to prime his pistols.'

'Why were they not primed at evening stand-to?' said Hervey.

'Because he's an indolent officer,' said Perry decidedly. 'But he appears at least to tell the truth.'

'That, or he's very calculating in his confidences.'

Perry sighed. It wasn't the sort of remark that one officer should make of another, but Green had exhausted everyone's patience an age ago. 'By the time he was ready, it seems the regiment had moved off.'

'And he spent the whole night trying in vain to find us?' The incredulity in Hervey's voice was marked.

'He said he thought we would have ridden in the direction opposite to that from which the fire was coming, on account of wanting to fall back on the guns.'

Hervey paused to consider the notion. 'Astonishing. Why might he believe that?'

'Hervey, he is, as I said, an indolent and ineffectual officer. While you or I or any other would have ridden towards the sound of the firing, he it seems works with a different instinct. But it would be difficult to say that that instinct was any more than feeble. There is nothing to prove that he was . . . well, running away.'

Hervey thought for a while again. 'Sar'nt-Major?'

Armstrong inclined his head ever so slightly and raised an eyebrow. 'It's not for me, sir, to make comment on an officer's capability. All I can say is Needham's not a bad man. He says he kept saying to Mr Green that it seemed strange they were finding no sign of us, and saying they ought to make for the firing, but Mr Green was certain of himself. And then he says Mr Green seemed to lose his notion of where they were, so they stopped for an hour or two, and it was only at dawn that Mr Green could see which direction was camp.'

Hervey sighed. An entirely plausible story. And yet he was not inclined to believe it. He didn't doubt Needham. Nothing that he knew of him suggested he would run from a fight. The opposite, perhaps. And Corporal Wainwright messed with him regularly; that was surely recommendation as to character. 'I just can't see how an officer could think in the way Green did!'

Green was no boon companion of Perry's, but the lieutenant was scrupulously fair. 'If every officer's instinct were the same, sir, there would be no occasion for surprise.'

'That might be so, but I can't believe it exculpates Green. There must be something wrong with the logic, but I haven't the time to look for it,' replied Hervey, his irritation increasing.

Armstrong could see no other conclusion either. 'Sir, with respect, if Mr Green had been a corporal we couldn't bring any charge as would stick – save failing to turn out for "alarm".'

Hervey shook his head. 'But he's not a corporal, Sar'nt-Major.'

'No, sir, of course he's not,' replied Armstrong, looking sideways at Perry. 'But the same evidence would apply if charges were brought. That's all I'm saying.'

Hervey was silent a while. Then he got up. 'Mr Green had better pay a good sum to the widows' fund, then. And you had better put him on his guard, Arthur. I do truly believe we have a wrong 'un here; and I say thus saving your presence, Sar'nt-Major.'

Armstrong said nothing. It was a confidence he would rather never have heard, but they had been together too long for Hervey to withhold even so infamous an opinion.

Hervey looked at him sternly. Armstrong was worth a hundred Greens. No, more than that, for a worthless thing did not gain in worth by mere increase in numbers. Come what may, Armstrong and his like would never have their just desserts; no more than would Green. Hervey put down the teacup. What a powerful thing was this drink: it brought the nation to fight in Hindoostan and it paid for Green to play the gentleman. Yet Armstrong's pension, if he were to have one, would scarcely keep his family in it. But this was no time for philosophy. He nodded emphatically: 'Very well, then, gentlemen. Boot and saddle at ten.'

CHAPTER SEVENTEEN
SAPPERS AND MINERS

Two days later

FIELD GENERAL ORDERS.

Camp before Bhurtpore, 21 Dec. 1825

Parole – LUCKNOW

The nature of the operations upon which the Army is about to be employed, requiring that the Infantry Regiments should have as few calls upon them for Guards as possible, the Right Hon. The Commander-in-Chief is pleased to direct, that the following Detail only be furnished; all other Guards not included in this statement, are forthwith to be withdrawn . . .

Hervey passed the statements to Armstrong. 'They do not directly bear on us, but it's as well to know the comings and goings.'

Armstrong, sitting in a chair in front of him, with Lieutenant Perry to Hervey's right, took the papers and looked quickly over them.

Private Johnson emerged from Hervey's tent with a coffee pot. 'Any more, sir?'

Hervey gestured to the others first, then let his cup be filled with the blackest liquid he had seen in many a year. Johnson would never throw away the unexpended portion of the day's coffee ration, and so each morning he boiled up the same liquid and the same beans, throwing in more in random measure. With the addition of copious quantities of sugar, and warm buffalo milk, it was a fortifying and nourishing drink, even if only very distantly related to any that could be had in the coffee houses of London.

'But the infantry will have a longer wait than they think, by all accounts,' said Hervey, still stirring his cup. 'The Jhaut gunners have found their mark on a good number of saps.'

Armstrong looked puzzled. 'They are tunnelling, though, aren't they?'

'It seems not. They can't get close enough.'

Armstrong looked incredulous.

So did Perry, but for a different reason. 'I don't understand, Hervey.'

'They have to dig ventilation shafts once the tunnel exceeds a certain distance, which would rather give away the game.' Hervey took a sip of his coffee. 'And they're no fools behind those walls. There are counter-tunnels ready dug. I saw some of them myself. So I think we may safely say there will be no assault this side of the new year.'

The Sixth had been in worse places at Christmas. Here at least it was warm when the sun was up, they were dry, there was firewood aplenty, and the supply of rations and powder was regular. Armstrong's expression changed to a smile. 'Corporal Stray'll be here today, sir, and a full load of rum.'

Hervey smiled too. The officers' mess was well stocked with excellent claret, but rum was so versatile an additive. He was almost of the opinion that he would exchange it bottle for bottle. 'Very well, then. There are no further orders. Interior economy today, make and mend. And I am brigade field officer, you'll recall.'

Perry and Armstrong rose. 'If it's all right with you, sir, I'd like to ride over and see them sappers working later on,' said the serjeant-major.

'By all means. Don't be *too* hard on them, though,' replied Hervey, smiling still.

'No indeed, sir. But I'd like to see how many of them would make colliers.'

Hervey reported to the headquarters of the First Brigade of Cavalry at ten o'clock. There was no telling what the duty might entail. Last night had been quiet, and the siege proceeded, as they were all informed, in the usual methodical if painfully slow manner. But activity was the nature of staff work, and he could therefore expect anything. Certainly the headquarters looked well-shod. The brigade tent had yellow pennants at each end of the ridge pole, and a lance-guard at the entrance. There was no doubting that this was the post of Colonel Murray, a man fervent in holding to the cavalry opinion that everything mattered, from the patent shine on a pair of levee hessians to the edge on a troop man's sabre.

The major of brigade, Captain Harris – of the 16th Lancers like Murray himself – received him with a smile. 'Well, Hervey, we have at least seen how it is done!'

They had indeed, thought Hervey – many a time in the Peninsula. Siege after siege, it seemed in that campaign. 'I wonder if the Jhauts have.'

'I don't know what to make of their sortie the other night, that's for sure,' said the brigade-major.

'I thought perhaps they intended disturbing our sleep every night, but it seems not.'

'Thirty and more dead: they could not long afford that price.' He looked disturbed suddenly. 'I've offered you no refreshment. Where *is* that bearer?'

But the bearer was alert to Hervey's arrival, and he now came into the big marquee that was the brigade orderly room with a tray of coffee and limewater.

'Shukria,' said Harris, and then turned to the staff orderly. 'Inform the brigadier that Major Hervey is come, if you will.'

'Colonel Murray wishes to see me?' asked Hervey, taking both coffee and limewater.

Harris nodded. 'He's not long back from General Sleigh's conference. The news wasn't good.'

'Oh?'

But before Harris could make much of a beginning, the officer commanding the First Cavalry Brigade came into the marquee looking far from his usual cheery self.

Hervey and Harris stood up as one. 'Good morning, sir,' said the former.

'Good morning, Hervey.' He turned to the bearer. 'I'll have some of that coffee, if you please, Manesh.' Then he sank heavily into a leather armchair.

Hervey and Harris sat down again and waited for the brigadier to begin. They were not kept waiting long.

'How does being an infantryman appeal to you?'

Hervey could see no sense in the question, but his recollection of the late events at Rangoon provided a prompt response. 'It does not especially appeal, sir,' he said plainly, and looking bemused. 'But we are part dragoons by name, so if there were compelling reason . . .'

'Combermere is so troubled lest he has not enough infantry for the attack that he's contemplating unhorsing the division, leaving just Skinner's for patrol and escort work.'

Hervey would agree that that was a compelling reason, albeit a desperate one. 'The trick, though, would be to judge the moment to dismount. We have no true idea how strong is the Jhaut cavalry, and they won't have lost their appetite for sorties completely.'

'Just so,' agreed the brigadier. 'And Combermere's worried too about the breaching. The sappers are having a

307

deuced hot time of it. But they reckon they'll have the first parallel open in a day or so, and then they can get some of the siege train in close. We're expected to demonstrate up and down the place, to draw attention from the real activity, but it'll be a damned tedious business. And if this Durjan Sal knows his siegecraft it will not fool him.'

Hervey knew the siege design well enough, for all the field officers had been apprised of it. The principal object of the engineers' work was to dig parallels in front of each of the four most prominent bastions. The most troublesome was the one they had called the long-necked bastion, its height being such as to give the clearest view of any approach within half a mile. Sapping was a hazardous enough task at the best of times, but commanded by the guns of the long-necked bastion it was nearly suicidal. 'That would be the time for a bold sortie. Better for Durjan Sal not to let the guns come into action than to take them on in a duel, no matter how commanding a position his own may have. Nothing is certain in these things, as well we know, sir.'

'Quite. It's on this that I wanted to speak with you.' He held out his cup for more coffee. 'I have an idea we could tempt his cavalry out in strength, and if we lay the trap carefully enough we could despatch the lot of them very surely.'

Hervey said nothing for the moment. A grand fight of cavalry, on the scale of Waterloo – he had never imagined such a thing again. But he was unsure of more than just how they would tempt Durjan Sal out. 'It's a fair prospect indeed, sir. But I'm afraid I do not see its purpose, except to employ the cavalry actively – and I am all in favour of that.'

The brigadier smiled in a satisfied sort of way. 'I'm glad you don't immediately see the purpose, for that means Durjan Sal likely as not shan't.' He sipped at his coffee, clearly relishing the ingeniousness of his plan. 'Do you think that Durjan Sal is a man who would prefer to fight to the death rather than strike his colours?'

Hervey furrowed his brow. 'On that I have no true insight. I should judge, perhaps, that since he is a usurper he is at heart a hazarder, and therefore unlikely to stick.'

'Just so. And for as long as he has his cavalry he will know – or rather believe – that if the fortress were to fall he could make good his own escape.'

Hervey nodded. 'I would imagine that, yes.'

'Then what would be the purpose in destroying his cavalry?'

A smile crept across Hervey's face.

The brigade-major was not yet certain of his own comprehension. 'Do you mean, sir, that Durjan Sal would be obliged to seek terms rather than risk a fight over the walls?'

'I mean exactly that, Harris. We might never *need* a breach.' He turned back to Hervey. 'Now, you have ridden the whole of the ground, and seen inside the walls. *Guns*: where might our decoy be best placed to tempt him out?'

Hervey's brow furrowed again. 'I should need a little time to consider that, sir. I made some plans and sketches—'

'Good, good! I want you to consider it carefully and let me have your opinion. But your best estimate today, if you please. And by all means go and consult your sketches. But keep the notion to yourself, Hervey. Loose tongues would be the death of it.'

When he returned to the Sixth's camp that evening, Hervey found that the officers had already dined. Private Johnson was therefore despatched to bring food to his tent – hot food, for there was a distinct chill in the air already and the brazier was only just lit.

'Serjeant-major says 'e'd like a word when tha were back,' Johnson remembered, as he pulled open the tent flap.

'Well, you may tell him I'm at home. Did Corporal Stray arrive with rum, by the way?'

'Oh ay, sir. T'quartermaster made an issue after stables.'

'Good. He was also meant to be bringing some bottled fruit for the mess. You might see if any has survived.'

'Ah, so tha did know about it then?'

'The fruit? Why shouldn't I?'

'No, I mean . . . it sounded as though th'd 'eard what'd 'appened.'

'Happened?'

'Ay, to Corporal Stray.'

'For heaven's sake, man!'

'Corporal Stray got attacked on 'is way 'ere. They killed t'bullocks pullin' 'is cart.'

Hervey looked almost alarmed. 'And is he all right?'

'Oh ay. T'two that were wi' 'im said 'e just stood on t'box like 'e were at sword exercise. Better than Collins they said 'e were. 'E killed 'alf a dozen of 'em an' then they ran off. T'Jhauts, I mean.'

Hervey smiled. He was not in the least surprised. Corporal Stray's resolute immobility atop the hackery box might have been in part the product of his great bulk, but it was in equal part the action of an old soldier. 'The hero of the wet canteen. I hope he gets a serjeancy for it.'

'I'll be gooin', then.'

'I'd be obliged.'

A few minutes later, Serjeant-Major Armstrong came to the tent.

'Come in, Geordie; sit down. There's nothing to eat but I can offer you some good Bordoo,' said Hervey, smiling again. 'Though I gather rum is the celebratory drink tonight.'

'You heard, then? Stray? I'd 'ave given aught to see it. The big fat bugger!'

Hervey laughed. 'When was he last on parade, do you think?'

'Mounted? Lord knows. He'd never have lasted if old Soggy hadn't been quartermaster.'

Hervey poured two glasses of claret and took his seat again. 'Otherwise a quiet day, I gather?'

'Ay, sir. Farriers have been busy, and the saddlers too.'

'Well, here's to Stray and all the stout hearts like him.'

Armstrong raised his glass. 'To stout hearts.'

Hervey refilled it at once, and his own. 'Johnson seemed to think there was something in particular you had?'

Armstrong frowned and nodded. 'Ay, there is. I went to see the sappers this morning, as I said. This business of not being able to dig out a tunnel – they're not doing it right.'

'Oh?' Hervey looked sceptical, even allowing for Armstrong's aptness in all field matters.

'I talked to the artificer for a fair while and he said they'd wanted to drive tunnels under the main bastions, but they couldn't go more than two hundred yards without ventilating shafts. Then the captain came – a grand man, he were, not in the least bit bothered talking to me – and he said they'd started to drive one under the west bastion but the Jhauts had spied the venting shaft and driven it in.'

'I fear it's the same the whole way round. The Jhauts will be very wary of mining. The trouble is, the sappers can't begin close enough anywhere. And as soon as it's known they're digging, they'll blow the tunnels in by countermines. The galleries are already made. I've seen them.'

Armstrong nodded. 'Ay, but these engineers aren't miners. We drove some long galleries in Hebburn pit and got the air in. Longer than two hundred yards – a *lot* longer.'

Hervey looked even more sceptical. 'But that would have been with steam pumps, surely?'

'Not when we were digging. We got a draught going with a furnace. Anyway, I told the captain all about it, and he said he'd think on it.'

Hervey was still doubtful. 'But how much further do you think they could go, then?'

'Well, twice as far as they reckon they can now.'

'*Twice* as far?' Hervey's disbelief was clear.

But it did not dismay Armstrong. 'Ay, at least.'

Hervey said nothing, seeming rapt in thought.

'Look, sir, why not let me lend a hand to them? The sappers, I mean. There's nothing that Collins can't do with the troop as things stand. It's nowt but working parties and escorts. It'd be good for him to have some practice.'

Hervey was not easily persuaded, though he agreed Collins was more than up to the job, especially on what seemed increasingly like garrison duties but in the field. 'I seem to recall you believed colliery a sight more dangerous than life in regimentals.'

Armstrong pulled a face. 'Aw, come on sir. I no more ran from being a collier than I have from anything.'

Hervey winced at his own crassness. It was the loss of father and brothers – and indirectly his mother – that had sent young Armstrong to the recruiting serjeant. 'No, I hadn't meant to—'

'And in any case, there's no firedamp here in 'Indoostan.'

That, too, was true. 'Very well,' said Hervey, with a smile that spoke volumes for his admiration of his old friend's spirit. 'I'll speak to the major, and if he agrees I'll speak then to the sappers.'

Later that morning, after watering, an orderly arrived at the Sixth's headquarters with a most imperative request from Brigadier Anburey, the chief engineer. Joynson at once sent for Hervey.

'What is E Troop about now, Hervey?' The major's tone was just a fraction weary, but a request from a senior officer, even of engineers, was not a thing to be brushed off lightly.

'I'm sorry, sir. I had meant to speak with you about it at orders today, but it seems Armstrong's assistance is more pressing than I'd thought.'

'Just so. You'd better sit down and tell me of it.'

Hervey hardly thought it a long enough story to require

comfort, but he obliged the major nevertheless. Then he told him all he knew.

Joynson listened with especial attention, removing and polishing his spectacles several times in the brief course of the explanation – a sure sign of his interest, as well, perhaps, of his anxiety. 'Well,' he said at length, firmly placing the spectacles high on the bridge of his nose. 'Anburey wants to speak to Armstrong in person. You'd better go with him.' His tone was as incredulous as had been Hervey's earlier.

'I think I should.'

Joynson nodded several times, slowly, as if contemplating something of real moment. 'You know, if Armstrong's little scheme works, we should think about making him . . .'

Hervey's ears pricked. He looked keenly at Joynson, now polishing his spectacles for the third time.

'There again,' said the major, now shaking his head from side to side, and as slowly as before. 'Tunnels and powder and the like . . . it's not the thing I myself would choose. I imagine there to be a great degree of hazard?'

Hervey nodded, but grimly. 'I fear so. But Armstrong *will* have it.'

When they reached Brigadier Anburey's headquarters, a mile or so from the Sixth's lines, Hervey and Armstrong found a dozen engineer officers in hot debate. They saluted as they entered the marquee, and Anburey shook them both by the hand. The faces of some of the officers, however, indicated a distinct disdain; perhaps a collier in their midst was not something easily to be borne. But Armstrong was sure of his ground, even though it had not been his for twenty years. He ought indeed to be sure of it: his father and his brothers had died in a split second for the want of good method in Hebburn pit.

'Serjeant-Major, Captain Cowie has told me of the system by which you say that a tunnel may be dug beyond the normal distance without recourse to ventilating

313

shafts. To five hundred feet, you say?'

'Ay, sir. But as I recall, there was no saying a tunnel couldn't go even further. It's just a matter of keeping the draught strong.'

Heads were shaking disbelievingly, though not Anburey's. 'If it were possible to dig such a tunnel here, the question would be whether there would be sufficient combustive air for an explosion,' he said. Then he paused, appearing to think on it the more. 'But that is not a matter to trouble you with, Serjeant-Major. Now, the officers here are all engineers skilled in surveying, bridge-building, the development of the siege and such like. None of us have practical experience of underground working comparable with yours. I want you therefore to explain in as great a detail as possible the system which you have witnessed, and then we shall decide if there is justification to put that system into effect here.'

Armstrong looked not in the slightest degree perturbed as he took the stick of chalk from the brigadier and advanced to the blackboard. Hervey wondered what recognition his scheme would bring, for it was certain that Armstrong's name would come to the attention of the commander-in-chief. He could only pray that it should not come before Combermere for *posthumous* honour.

The mood at the major's orders, two days later, was beginning to reflect the coming season. The Sixth had always looked to stand down on the day itself, and for all ranks to share a good dinner, even in the late French war – although more than once they had found themselves horsed, with sabres drawn. But here the siege was well settled into its routine, the chance of alarms diminished; and supply, on short lines from Agra, was for once excellent. There was every prospect of a good Christmas dinner and sport.

Joynson, allowing himself a cheroot, most unusually, now came to General Orders. 'And today there's rather a good story, gentlemen:

'Head-Quarters, Camp before Bhurtpore, 23rd Dec. 1825

*'The Commander-in-Chief has received with much
pleasure, the report of the excellent conduct of a Jemadar
of the 4th Light Cavalry, Sheik Rangaun Ally, who was
sent out with twenty Troopers to protect the Foraging Party
on the 19th instant, and who, by his steady soldier-like
example, and the judicious arrangement of his small force,
kept off a very large body of the Enemy's Horse, saved the
Foragers he was sent to protect, and brought off his
Detachment in the face of the Enemy for a considerable
distance, with no other loss than two men and three horses
wounded. His Lordship, in consideration of the foregoing
service, as well as of the high character borne by this
Native Officer, is pleased to promote Jemadar Sheik
Rangaun Ally to the rank of Subadar. His Lordship further
directs, that his approbation may be communicated to the
whole of the Party, for their steady conduct on this
occasion. Officers will perceive from this occurrence, the
propriety of not detaching any weak parties to a distance
from Camp. The above to be explained to the several
regiments in Camp, on the first Grand Parade that takes
place.'*

Joynson looked over his spectacles at the assembled
officers. 'Well, gentlemen, as I said, a good story. And I
think the latter point is clear enough, too.'

It could hardly have been made more heavily, thought
Hervey.

'I wonder if Stray will be promoted jemadar?' said Rose,
blowing a great deal of cigar smoke towards the roof of the
marquee.

There was an equal deal of laughter.

Joynson looked wryly over his spectacles. 'Well, the
Eleventh are ruing their distance from camp these past
couple of days. They were cut about in the outlying picket

the day before last. No one killed, but the Jhauts drove them in. *Not good*.'

'I just wish the beggars would come out and face us instead of all this chopping at foraging parties and pickets, and feinting on our part.'

'So that we can send them all to hell, Rose?' said Joynson, peering over his spectacles again. 'And why should Durjan Sal be so obliging when he's got solid walls between him and us?'

'By the way, sir,' said Hervey, wanting to bring the conference back to its muttons. 'Armstrong is to begin today.'

Joynson looked grateful. 'Indeed, yes. Gentlemen, for those who do not know, Sar'nt-Major Armstrong is attached forthwith to the engineers to render assistance in their excavations.'

Hervey noted the final noun. It was entirely accurate without giving away the precise nature of the work.

'Serjeant Collins shall stand in his place, and E Troop shall stand ready to provide assistance as required. Oh, and Corporal Stray is forthwith posted to E Troop.'

Nicely done, thought Hervey. No one would be likely to deduce anything. Indeed, the odd smile and coarse comment suggested that the others pitied E Troop as having been made a fatigue party.

Joynson pressed on, modulating his voice just sufficiently to suggest that what he now relayed was unconnected with what had gone before. 'I am very glad to report that last night, it seems, there was an operation, entirely successful, to take the gardens before the long-necked bastion – known on our maps as Buldeo Singh's garden – and the nearby village of Kuddum Kundee. The heavy cannonade we heard this morning was directed on the two prizes, but, I am given to understand, to little effect. The engineers will now begin the planned parallel, and this will materially assist the sapping operations in that direction.'

There followed more routine information, lists of escorts and patrols, and orders for the night's pickets.

'Does anyone have a question?' asked Joynson finally.

No one admitted to it.

'Very well, gentlemen. I think there will soon be rapid progress. You know what is his lordship's general design; you must act on your own cognizance when it is called for.'

The assembly began to break up.

'Oh, and I have some further excellent news, gentlemen. Sir Ivo is proceeding at this time from Calcutta to rejoin us. He is expected, *Deo volente*, within the seven days following.'

This latter news displaced all else. Hervey was full of admiration for the obvious ploy – and not a little disappointed for Joynson, who would thereby be deprived of the honour of command in the hour of victory. But that was the way of things.

Corporal Stray was a practical man, and as such he was not inclined to nod to something until convinced. 'See thee, Sar'nt-Major sir,' he replied, pushing his undersized forage cap back and scratching his head. 'I can't see that owt I can make'll do t'job.' The accent was not nearly as pronounced as Johnson's, but it was marked nevertheless. 'When I were prenticed at 'Untsman's—'

'Corporal Stray, I couldn't give a fart about Huntsman's. Just do as you're told. I want a wooden duct, six-inch-square, that can be extended as we dig. As simple as that.'

Stray scratched his head again. 'All right, Serjeant-Major.'

'It'd better be. And later on I'll want a burlap partition the size of the tunnel.'

'Where do I get t'wood, sir?'

Armstrong checked himself. It was, looked at from one angle, a reasonable enough question. 'Corporal Stray, the engineers' entire field park is at your disposal. Just go to

317

the artificer over there and give him your requirements.'

'Right, Serjeant-Major.'

'But Mick, ask him nicely.'

Armstrong shook his head as Corporal Stray shuffled off. Hervey smiled. Time and place were all the same to Corporal Stray. 'How long will it take to dig?'

'If we don't hit any rock, it shouldn't take us more than five days round the clock.'

Hervey looked again at the ground. Three hundred yards they proposed to dig. 'Geordie, seven or eight feet every hour? How are you going to keep that up? How are you going to bring out all the spoil?'

Armstrong looked assured. 'That's them engineers' worry. It'd be the same if they were sapping rather than mining. A good gang of colliers'd clear that in a ten-hour shift.'

'What is it exactly that you'll do?'

Armstrong shrugged his shoulders. 'There's no need of me at all, sir. It's just that some of the officers don't believe it'll work, and Brigadier Anburey wants me to make certain it does.' He gestured to where, covered from view by half a dozen tamarisk trees, the sappers were beginning the drift down to the level at which they would drive the tunnel to the bastion's foundations. 'See, they know what they're about right enough.'

Hervey thought they looked as though they did. 'The major's asked that I keep an eye on things, but there's no use my being here, not to begin with anyway. I'll come each morning and evening. Where will you sleep – here?'

'Ay, sir. Stray's going to need a hand too. I'd like Harkness an' all if I can. He were a cooper, if I remember right. He'll be handy with hammer and nails. And a couple of others in a day or so.'

It was a growing bill, but better, thought Hervey, than the endless fatigues and working parties. He told Armstrong he could have Harkness, and any other he thought had a particular skill. It seemed the least he could do when the regiment were otherwise so cosily set up, and safely, in their distant lines. Then he set off back through the workings to find Gilbert, and quickly, for he had arranged with Johnson for his bath to be drawn by seven. He had to watch his step, though: the paraphernalia of the sappers' siege park – and the activity, so different from that of cavalry lines, could be hazardous for an outsider.

He slept little and fitfully that night. Both sides had kept up a harassing artillery fire well into the early hours, and soon after midnight there had been an alarm which saw them stood to their horses until two o'clock. It was the routine of the siege he had first come to know a dozen years before, first standing on the defensive at Torres Vedras, and then, the boot on the other foot, at Ciudad Rodrigo. Long days of boredom, occasional danger, with little opportunity for action – only the tumultuous climax, the breaching of the walls and the rushing-in of brave men bent on promotion, the 'forlorn hope', more often than not aptly named, and then the fight through the streets until the heart of the fortress struck and its flag was hauled down. It was the business of the artillery, the engineers and the infantry, the cavalry at best onlookers, at worst an appendage of the wagon train. It was true that volunteers were called for throughout the army for the forlorn hopes – and if Combermere did indeed want to dismount the cavalry they might all be in red coats soon – but as a rule a dragoon might as well be astride a screw as a blood. They had been luckier this time for sure, with the dash for the Motee Jheel and the skirmishes with Durjan Sal's cavalry, but it had been momentary and, in the greater scheme of the siege, would be quickly forgotten. Only the brigadier's *ruse de guerre* offered them sport, the chance of fighting en masse from the saddle in the old way.

After stand-down, Hervey shaved in plentiful hot water and then breakfasted on eggs and bacon, and very good toast. The coffee, too, was quite excellent, hot and without bitterness. There were even newspapers. They were out of range of cannon fire and it was as if they were at camp for the winter manoeuvres. It was the sole advantage of the siege over a campaign of movement, he considered. The only vexing aspect of these otherwise most congenial arrangements was the presence of Cornet Green. Hervey could barely bring himself to speak civilly to him, if at all. Besides his constant maladroitness with the dragoons, and – present to Hervey's mind still – the abominable affair of the night battle, the cornet's bearing in the mess was chafing him more and more. Green seemed unable to enter the marquee with any ease, usually bumping into something or stammering to a khitmagar. And his table manners . . . Once he had picked up his knife and fork he seemed unable to lay them down again until his plate was empty. It was perhaps of no great hazard to good order and military discipline (Green was hardly likely to be seated next to the Governor-General, ever), but for some reason this morning it gave Hervey increasing distress.

'Mr Green!' he said suddenly, making the unfortunate cornet cough up a part of his breakfast. 'I shall want you to do duty with the sar'nt-major today.'

'Yes, Hervey,' replied Green, his face the colour of a beetroot, though whether by way of the coughing or because of his troop-leader's attention was uncertain.

Strickland lowered his copy of the *Calcutta Journal* and looked Hervey in the eye. The transaction of any sort of business in the mess was distasteful, most certainly at the breakfast table. But that was not entirely the purpose of the gesture.

Hervey cleared his throat. 'Is there anything of interest in the *Journal*?' he asked, as matter-of-fact as he could manage.

Strickland took a sip of his coffee. 'The bishop has given a party to the ladies left behind.'

'That is very good of him,' said Hervey, in a mildly ironic tone.

'He writes very fine hymns, Hervey. Even I would concede that.'

Hervey merely frowned.

By now, Cornet Green had finished his breakfast – or rather, had finished his attempt at it – and had quit the mess, leaving just the two of them.

'Something must be done about Green,' said Strickland, folding his paper and laying it down. 'I feel half sorry for him.'

'I'm afraid I find not a single redeeming feature,' said Hervey decidedly.

'Can he not be persuaded to exchange? He's not short of money, and he can hardly be happy.'

'I imagine the subalterns have tried. I can't think for the life of me why he chose to come here.'

'Perhaps that is his single redeeming feature, then?'

Hervey raised his eyebrows. 'Strickland, I'm sorry to say but I think he's gun-shy.' He related once more the night affair.

'So you want him shot over in the trenches with Armstrong?'

'That's the idea.'

'Then you had better have a care yourself. I gather the brigadier has something in mind for us.'

Hervey looked at him keenly, but he had no intention of quizzing him on where he had got his intelligence. It seemed next to impossible to keep secret even an idea.

When Hervey got to the tunnel workings, about eleven, he found Armstrong begrimed and resting, with an empty bottle of pale ale by his side. The lines that now perma- nently grooved his forehead seemed to have been conduits for the sweat which, even on so cold a day, had evidently run freely, so that from brow to the faintly receding line of his black hair was like veined marble – and the eyes, closed, like chips in the surface exposing the creamy unpolished stone beneath. His jaw looked squarer, even if the chin were a little fuller than in years past. His shoulders, broad yet compact like a bull terrier's, their strength outlined in the sodden shirt which clung to them as he lay, looked more powerful than ever. Once, the morning of Waterloo indeed, Hervey had told Armstrong that he believed him to be indestructible. And he half believed it still. He certainly prayed it was, for Armstrong's loss would be intolerable, and not only to Caithlin.

'He has not stopped for more than ten minutes since you left yesterday,' said the engineer major. 'Even my artificer turned in for a couple of hours. And he is famous for not sleeping until the job is done.'

The exchange was punctuated by three mighty explosions a hundred yards or so the other side of the clump of tamarisk trees, as the siege battery hurled a hundred pounds of iron at the long-necked bastion. Cornet Green flinched, but no more than would any man who had not expected it.

The major shook his head. 'They may as well throw pebbles at a shuttered window. There's scarcely a mark on those walls. We'll have to get them closer.'

'You don't think mining will breach them, then?'

'Oh yes, indeed. If we can get to the foundations we can have it down. I've no doubt that if there's enough air for a man to dig with there's enough for combustion. And once packed in we could always open a ventilator shaft by night when it was too late to do anything about it. It's just the time it will take, and if the Jhauts don't find us first.'

Armstrong opened his eyes. 'Sorry, sir, I didn't know you were come,' he said, getting to his feet and fastening the neck of his tunic.

'I'm sorry to disturb you, Sar'nt-Major. You've been working all night, I understand?'

'Ay, sir. I'll give it to these little brown beggars: they can dig.'

'How far have you got?'

'Just behind the battery. We opened the venting shaft just an hour ago.'

Hervey looked astonished. They had dug the drift down ten feet and driven a tunnel four feet high and as many wide for the better part of a hundred yards. 'May I see?'

'I wouldn't, if I were you, sir. You'd only get in the way. Leave it till we've driven a bit further and got the burlap in.'

Hervey was disappointed, but he was not going to ignore the advice. 'I'll go and have a look at the battery, then. How is Corporal Stray faring, by the way?'

'He's doing a good job, sir, him and 'Arkness. They've made fifty yards of ducting, and they'll be quicker once they get the extra timber.'

'Good. I take it he's not expected to go into the tunnel with it?'

Armstrong returned the smile. 'No, he's not. The idea's for the air to flow, not block it with Stray's great arse!'

The trench was full of men from the light company of the 14th (Buckinghamshire) Regiment, their green plumes bobbing as they shuffled forward at the crouch. An ensign explained they were going up to form a skirmishing line in front of the guns; it seemed the Jhaut sharpshooters had been getting bolder in their sorties.

Hervey turned to the covermen. 'Go fetch our carbines!'

Even in the few minutes it now took him to get to the battery parallel, a dozen roundshot from the bastion flew over with the characteristic buzz of the bigger-calibre guns. The ensign smiled. 'I am pleased to hear that at last, sir! All the serjeants ever talk about is the queer noise of the shot at Waterloo. I never thought I might hear it for myself.'

Hervey resisted the temptation to look behind at what Cornet Green's face revealed. 'I should very much like to know why it's flying so high. They surely have the range by now.'

The answer came soon enough. Just as they debouched into the parallel a ball plunged into the breastworks where stood artillerymen enjoying the spectacle of the overshoots. It threw up a great fountain of earth and bodies, spreading the ordure of a dozen men about the battery.

Hervey and the ensign's men rushed at once to begin digging out the others. 'Bastards!' he cursed. 'They baited the trap good and proper.'

Two more roundshot ploughed ineffectually into the breastworks, empty now of spectators, though earth rained down in the trench again. The ensign burrowed with his bare hands for all he was worth, as did his men. Hervey searched for the battery's captain. He found him with half his head blown away, the clever Woolwich-trained grey matter exposed like brains in a butcher's shop. But he was breathing, with an eerie sucking noise. Hervey reached for his pistol, but before he need use it the man gave up the ghost.

Earth gushed high above them again like a geyser. 'Christ!' cursed Hervey, realizing what more it might be. The Jhauts had not yet sortied, and it was now that they ought. 'Ensign, get your men up ready!'

The boy – Hervey thought him not eighteen – knew at once what was wanted. In an instant he and his serjeant had a dozen men in a firing line.

Wainwright and Needham came up the sap with the carbines, followed by Johnson. Wainwright blanched at the carnage and looked about anxiously until he saw Hervey.

'Where's Mr Green, sir?' asked Private Needham, no less anxiously; a coverman should never lose sight of his officer (the rebuke from the night affair stung his ears still).

'I don't know,' said Hervey, trying to take stock of the

damage, and looking for an artillery officer on his feet. 'He was behind me in the sap.'

Johnson pushed his way past the confusion. 'Sir, is thee 'ead all right? Tha's covered in blood.'

'Yes, it's all right, Johnson,' replied Hervey, gruffly. 'Not a drop of it's my own. Why have you come up?'

'Corporal Wainwright said we was doin' a bit o' shooting.'

Hervey wondered why he had asked. 'Ensign, can you see anything?' he called.

'No, not a thing, sir.'

Hervey clambered over the debris of the revetments to stand next to him. 'What is your name?'

'Leveson-Gower, sir.'

'Is it, indeed? Your father is not, by any chance, Dean of Wells?'

'He is, sir. Do you know him?'

'I've heard tell a good deal of him. Now, do you think you can get your men out of this trench and up to that bit of a hillock yonder?' He indicated a long, shallow rise two hundred yards to their front.

A gun on the long-necked bastion belched yellow flame. Hervey spied the shot almost at once. 'Coming our way, I think, Mr Leveson-Gower. Down, men!'

They slid to the bottom of the trench, and a second or so later the big iron ball clipped the forward edge, grazed the bottom and drove itself, hissing, into the earth wall behind.

'As I was saying . . .'

'Yes, sir. Of course we can. At once.' The ensign turned to look for his serjeant. 'Detail half a dozen men to stay here until the wounded are dealt with, Sarn't Docherty. Remainder in extended line prepared to advance.'

'Sor!'

There followed a deal of shouting, incomprehensible to any but the Fourteenth, as the men fell in.

'I intend joining you as soon as I'm able,' said Hervey.

'But first I want to see the gunners recovered. Who gave you your orders?'

'The captain, sir. He's picketing the rest of the company and then he's coming here.'

'Good. Go to it, then.'

The ensign saluted, climbed out of the trench and drew his sword. 'Detachment will advance!'

As quickly as red coats were scrambling out of the trench, blue ones were coming in from the sap – drivers and ammunition numbers keen to dig. A lieutenant looked horrified.

'You are in command now, I fear,' said Hervey, briskly. 'Your captain's over there, under the blanket. There's a skirmish line out two hundred yards in front, and the bastion's got the range.'

Private Needham came into the trench, with Cornet Green behind him.

Hervey's brow furrowed deeply. 'Where in hell's name have you been, Mr Green?'

'I'm sorry, sir. I forgot my telescope.'

'Mr Green, you have a servant!'

'Yes, sir, I—'

Corporal McCarthy now appeared, breathless. 'Sor, the major's compliments, sor, and please would you return at once. There's orders from the general, sor.'

Hervey bit his lip. 'We'll speak later, Mr Green.'

When Hervey got back to the Sixth's camp he was expecting to hear orders for the brigadier's ruse, but instead he found the entire regiment standing to their horses.

'Durjan Sal's making a sortie, it seems,' said Joynson as Hervey took his place beside him. 'Or going to.'

Hervey wondered if the business at the battery was connected. 'What are the orders?'

'Childers' brigade's going clockwise about, and we're going the other way. The horse artillery will stage behind us and signal with rockets if there's a sortie when we've passed.'

'A straightforward enough drive,' said Hervey, disappointed by his conclusion that they were about to embark on a wild-goose chase. 'I wonder if our birds will leave their covert, though?'

'Well, someone has the wind up. How is Armstrong, by the way?'

'He's doing well.'

'Let's hope he continues doing well, then. Combermere's in the dumps well and truly, if this morning's anything to go by. He rode through and said the artillery had made not the slightest impression on the walls to date.'

'That much was evident to a telescope in the garden just now. And the Jhauts have some deuced big guns in that bastion.'

'Thirty-two-pounders, says Combermere.' Joynson nodded to his front. 'Well, that looks like the Sixteenth off. Trumpet-Major, regiment will advance!'

But the day went as Hervey feared. Round the fortress they rode – ten miles without sight or sign of the enemy save the odd impudent ball that flew their way. None fell within a hundred yards of them, but they signalled nevertheless the defender's constant surveillance of their progress. Why would anyone oblige Combermere with a sortie when his men paraded before Bhurtpore in such strength? The Jhauts had their walls, and these were serving them very well indeed. Why should they leave their shelter?

When the Sixth rode back into camp, it was a tired and frustrated Hervey who dismounted and handed the reins of an equally weary Gilbert to his groom.

'I said I would go see the sar'nt-major, but it's too late. We'll go tomorrow morning.' He took the pistols from the holsters on the saddle as Johnson drew up the stirrups. 'At least *they* are getting closer by the hour. *We* may as well be at Brighton for all the good we do. And I think by today's display we have put paid to Murray's ruse having the slightest chance of success.'

'Ay, sir.' Johnson had not the least idea what was this ruse, but evidently his ignorance was of no moment now. 'A merry Christmas, then, sir. See thee at gunfire?'

Hervey smiled. 'Gunfire – yes, indeed.'

CHAPTER EIGHTEEN
THE SINEWS OF WAR

Next day

FIELD GENERAL ORDERS.

Head-Quarters, Camp before Bhurtpore, 24th Dec. 1825

Parole – SECRORA

> *General for the Day to-morrow, Brigadier Whitehead.*
> *Field Officer, Lieutenant-Colonel Cooper.*
> *Major of Brigade, 2nd Infantry Division.*
> *Adjutant, H.M. 59th Regiment.*

The Advanced Posts of Buldeo Singh's Garden and Kuddum Kundee to be relieved this afternoon at three o'clock, by parties of similar strength in Infantry as directed in yesterday's Orders, from the 1st and 2nd Divisions respectively. H.M. 11th Dragoons, and 4th Light Cavalry, will relieve the two Troops at present on duty at the Posts; and the Officers commanding them, to consider themselves placed under the immediate orders of the General of the Day, to whom they will report accordingly.

The remaining Guns of the Light Field Battery (from which a portion has already been attached) on duty at the Advanced Posts, are to be ordered down to join this afternoon, and to be considered as placed under the orders of the General of the Day.

One hundred Sepoys (Goorkas) from the Sirmoor Detachment, with a proportion of Native Officers, to be sent to Buldeo Singh's Garden at three p.m.; and the Officer in Command is instructed to report himself to the General of the Day.

Working parties for the Trenches will parade in front of H.M.'s 14th and 59th Regiments, this afternoon at four o'clock, and to be furnished as follows: by the 1st Division, for the Posts of Buldeo Singh's Garden, 200 Europeans, and 450 sepoys; by the 2nd Division, for the Post of Kuddum Kundee, 100 Europeans, and 400 sepoys. An Engineer Officer to attend at the hour appointed.

Officers proceeding in charge of working parties, are to be strictly cautioned to pay particular attention to the conduct of the men under their command, whilst employed on working duties, and to prevent fires being lighted in the Trenches, and any unnecessary noise being made . . .

. . . The Hon. Lieut.-Col. Finch, Military Secretary to the Commander in Chief, is appointed Prize-Agent for His Excellency and the Field-Officers of the Army.

The second Agent, authorized to be nominated by the Captains and Subalterns, is to be selected from the Hon. Company's Service, and may be an officer of any rank.

The General Officers commanding Divisions, and Commandants of Departments, are requested to collect, without delay, the Votes for a Prize-Agent from the Captains and Subalterns of their Divisions and Commands respectively, and will transmit them to the Adjutant-General.

It is to be proclaimed through the several Suddur Bazaars in Camp, and Bazaars of Corps, that any person bringing in cannon-shot or shell, delivering them into the Park, to the Commissary or Deputy-Commissary of

Ordnance, will be entitled to rewards, as follows:

For every 24lb. Shot	. . .	*12 annas.*
———— *8 & 12 ditto*	. . .	*6 ditto.*
———— *6 ditto*	. . .	*4 ditto.*
———— *13-inch shell*	. . .	*2 rupees.*
———— *10-inch ditto*	. . .	*1 rupee, 4 annas.*
———— *8-inch ditto*	. . .	*1 rupee.*

The Commissary or Deputy-Commissary of Ordnance, will grant Certificates for shot or shell received, and the Commissariat is directed to pay the amount on presentation of Certificate so furnished.

To-morrow being Christmas-Day, the usual gratuity of extra Batta to be issued to the Europeans in Camp.

Joynson took off his spectacles. 'Well, Gentlemen, the orders are eminently clear, if late in the arriving. The adjutant will collect votes for prize agent at evening stables. By the by, who is field officer of the day?'

'I am,' said Rose.

'The outlying picket, only, under saddle today please.'

Rose nodded.

'I conclude, then, by extending my own good wishes for the day. The chaplain will say prayers at eleven. That is all.'

Joynson had called them together earlier than usual. Since the officers had taken gunfire to every man at reveille he had thought it best to capitalize on their wakefulness by holding his conference immediately after stand-down. The sun was now well up and taking the chill off the air, which even the braziers in the marquee had not managed to do when they first assembled, and the prospects for the festive day looked good.

Hervey stayed seated as the others left.

'I believe I may guess your thoughts,' said the major.

'It were better not to,' replied Hervey. 'Not all of them at any rate. I was wondering earlier what we might do to tempt out Durjan Sal's cavalry.'

'And what did you conclude?'

'That we couldn't.'

Joynson looked blank. 'Really, Hervey, what profit had you supposed lay in such a line of thought?'

'When I was brigade field officer the day before yesterday, Murray told me he had conceived a stratagem by which all the Jhaut cavalry could be lured from the fortress and then destroyed, which would mean that Durjan Sal, having no means to escape if the fortress fell, could not dare risk a storming and would have to sue for peace at once.'

Joynson nodded. 'That is artful. I wonder you didn't tell me of it.'

'Murray said to speak to no one. He asked my opinion as to where a demonstration would have greatest effect, and I concluded the Agra gate. But thinking the more, I believe now that nothing would tempt him out, for he can risk losing his cavalry even less than losing the fortress. And it would be folly to suppose he has not made that inference for himself. Perhaps General Sleigh thinks the same and does not approve it, therefore.'

'Mm.' Joynson nodded again, but slower. 'You're a very clever fellow, Hervey. You ought by rights to be on Combermere's staff.'

Hervey smiled, acknowledging the tease.

'You know,' he continued, putting his spectacles in their case in such a way as to suggest a conclusion. 'I've seen little enough field service, but what I've seen and read leads me to believe that there's rarely a clever way to things. Better to do well what's to be done.'

It would have been too easy to dismiss Joynson as a plodder, suited only to organizing supply for the fixed defences of the Sussex coast – which had been his former extra-regimental service. Hervey would not. Indeed, he had come to respect 'Daddy' Joynson as a man who knew his limitations to an uncommon degree, and acknowledged them. 'That would appear to be what Combermere is about, is it not – doing well what's to be done?'

'I hope so. I hope he's listening to Anburey rather than Murray. I can't see that this business will be settled other than by powder and the bayonet. You know, I've a mind to leave things here for a while and go see Armstrong and his cohort. I've a mind that Armstrong's shovel will be a deal more serviceable in this than the whole of Murray's brigade. You'll come with me?'

As they rode into the extensive earthworks that Buldeo Singh's garden had become, the battery at Kuddum Kundee, a furlong away, fired in unison – eight of the artillery's biggest siege guns laid painstakingly on the same point of the long-necked bastion, 250 pounds of iron hurled with a velocity which vastly multiplied that weight on impact. Hervey pressed Gilbert to the top of one of the earth ramparts just in time to observe the effect – a column of dust higher than the walls of the fortress itself. Were there troops ready to assault the breach?

As the dust cleared, he saw there was no need of a breaching party, nor even a sign of the gunners' work. The long-necked bastion stood as before, prominent and defiant. He frowned and turned Gilbert back down the bank, muttering about Joshua and his trumpets.

'God in heaven!' cursed Joynson, climbing from the saddle. His mare looked as if she had taken root, her legs splayed, immovable.

'It was enough to startle a seasoned trooper, Eustace. She's very green, still.' Joynson's luck with horses was evidently not great, thought Hervey. 'Give her a lead?'

Joynson shook his head crossly. 'No, no. I'll walk in, damn it! Serjeant Lightfoot!'

The major's covering-serjeant took the reins. Hervey dismounted and handed his to Private Johnson.

They set off through the tamarisk grove with Joynson still tutting about his second charger.

'It's as well we approach on foot, anyway,' said Hervey, leading. 'The place is getting tight-packed with limbers.'

They picked their way through the siege park like sight-seers at a fair. There were piles of shot, powder kegs in dugout bays, explosive shell in others, all manner of engineer stores neatly piled, sacks of corn for the horses, tubs of salt beef, dripping, biscuit, heaps of black bread, barrels of water, firewood and quartermaster stores, and the surgeon's dressing post, empty now, though at the same hour yesterday it was a sorry butcher's shop. It all spoke of the effort and patience a siege required, the organization. *Someone* at least knew his job, thought Hervey. And it was as well, given the impotence of the eighteen-pounders that had just been demonstrated.

'Steady, man!' bawled Joynson suddenly, as Private Harkness all but ran into him.

'Sir! We need the surgeon sir! It's the serjeant-major!'

'What?'

'He's in the tunnel, sir. The roof's tumbled in!'

Joynson pointed to the surgeon's tent, then set off after Hervey, running for the first time in years.

At the foot of the drift, where the tunnel began, an artificer stopped them. 'There're too many in there, sir. It's too narrow.'

'Stay here, Eustace,' said Hervey, unfastening his sword-belt and taking off his shako. 'No use in two of us going.'

'My orders, sir,' said the artificer.

'My sar'nt-major, though,' said Hervey, pushing him aside.

The tunnel was well lit by oil lamps, but silent. Hervey moved as fast he could, neither quite walking nor running, ducking lower still every few yards to avoid a roof support. It took him a while to reach the airlock.

'Who's that?' said the crouching figure at the burlap partition.

'Armstrong's officer. What's to do?'

'Oh, Major Hervey, sir; it's Irvine. I'm officer of the day. The roof's fallen about fifty yards in. There are two of your men and Brigadier Anburey digging the sar'nt-major out.'

Hervey pulled aside the burlap.

'Sir, it's awfully tight in there.'

'Yes, thank you, Irvine.'

It was not so well lit the other side of the burlap. Hervey could see the flicker of lamps ahead, and hear voices. He crouched lower still, and pushed on as best he could again.

'Who's that? Surgeon?' came a voice.

'No, sir. It's Hervey, Armstrong's officer.' Hervey could just make out Shepherd Stent on his knees beyond Anburey, shovelling earth to one side. 'Who's with you, Stent?'

'Corporal Stray, sir.'

Hervey pushed past them both. Earth was flying back as fast as Stent could clear it, like a terrier digging out a badger. He could now make out Corporal Stray's great bulk, seeming to fill the remaining space. But it was Stray's shovel that worked like a machine.

'How long has he been buried?'

'A good ten minutes, sir,' said Stent, not checking in his own shovel work. 'The engineers had just put in another support and the serjeant-major was taking a turn at digging. And suddenly the roof just fell in.'

'I had only just arrived myself,' said Brigadier Anburey.

Buried ten minutes. Hervey bit his lip. How did they know the roof-fall they were clearing would not be replaced at once by more? Had the tunnel wholly collapsed, with a hollow in the ground above them? Should they not be digging from there too?

'I've got 'is feet, Shep!' called Stray.

'Major Hervey's here, Mick.'

'Major 'Ervey, sir, I've got 'is feet. And they're movin'!'

Hervey crawled past Shepherd Stent and laid a hand on Armstrong's boot. It was moving, very definitely moving.

'Can we pull 'im out, d'ye think, sir?'

'I don't know,' said Hervey, clawing away more earth around the foot. 'He must somehow have air under this lot. If we start to pull him out we might disturb it. How long would it take?'

Corporal Stray, breathing heavily, didn't know either. 'Even if 'e's got a bit of air, sir, it might run out soon. It can't be owt much. What else can we do? It'll take an hour to shift this lot.'

Hervey felt the desperation welling. 'We'll pull him! Keep digging while I get ropes.'

'Right, sir,' said Stray, relieved not to be the one to make the decision, and pleased to have the digging to occupy him.

'I'll get them,' said Anburey.

'Colonel, I'd be obliged if you would stay here. I am not a technical.'

Anburey nodded, and Hervey took off back down the tunnel like a bolting rabbit.

Joynson had not been idle, either. There were props, lamps, picks, shovels, all manner of stores piled at the bottom of the drift – and rope. Hervey quickly explained his intention then set off back into the tunnel with the end of a coil, Corporal Wainwright playing it out and Serjeant Lightfoot attaching other lengths with deft reef knots.

'Relay my orders, if you please, Irvine,' said Hervey as he pushed aside the burlap.

Corporal Stray had cleared to Armstrong's calves, but earth slid his way as fast as he could move it.

'There's a good fifteen feet of tunnel forward,' said Brigadier Anburey. 'It's that spoil which is falling back. I don't think the whole working has collapsed.'

'He knows we're 'ere at least, sir,' said Stray, sounding as though he was taking as much comfort by it as Armstrong himself.

The brigadier's assessment was cheering. At least they wouldn't be pulling against the weight of a dozen feet of earth. Hervey looped the rope around Armstrong's feet, binding them together tight. He thought of removing the boots, but judged it better to leave them for protection. 'Keep digging, Corporal Stray,' he said, once he had made the final hitch. 'Irvine, pull away!'

A second or so and the rope tautened. Then it began to inch back. Then more obviously. In a minute they saw the back of Armstrong's knees.

'Thank Christ, sir!' said Stray, digging for all he was worth.

'It's taking too long,' said Hervey. 'He'll soon have no air.' He started clawing away at the earth with his bare hands. 'Pull harder, Irvine!'

It was working, just. Inch by inch Armstrong's body emerged from the roof-fall, but the minutes ticked by. How in God's name could anyone go that long without air?

In five more they saw his waist. And then he was out in one, like a cork pulling evenly from a bottle.

'Stop!' bellowed Hervey down the tunnel.

The rope slackened at once.

He turned over the uncharacteristically motionless frame, desperate for some sign of life. He saw only the earth-caked shell of a man he'd once believed was indestructible – limp, like a rag doll thrown down in the mud.

'Surgeon!' He cursed himself; he ought to have called him up before.

Armstrong's mouth fell open, and then his eyes, the lids flickering perceptibly.

Hervey gasped, and Stray knew they'd done it. But it was too much like the brush with death in America, when Armstrong, alone, had taken on the war party – then, as now, beyond, *well* beyond, the call of duty. The thought of

337

that devotion, and its fruitless and terrible outcome in America, was too much for Hervey, and tears began welling.

It was left to Corporal Stray to restore matters. 'Yer gave us a right scare there, Serjeant-Major, sir,' he said, in the cheeky understatement which only a corporal of his standing was allowed.

Armstrong spat, but weakly, and closed his eyes again. 'And it won't be the last, Corporal Stray,' he croaked, barely audible. 'Be sure of it.'

CHAPTER NINETEEN
FORLORN HOPES

Three days later

FIELD GENERAL ORDERS.

Head-Quarters, Camp before Bhurtpore, 28 Dec., 1825

Parole – BOMBAY

The Commander-in-Chief is pleased to appoint Brevet-Captain Hake, of H.M. 16th Lancers, to the superintendence of the Field Telegraph. An establishment of one European Non-commissioned Staff, one Lascar, and three coolies, is authorized to be attached to each Field Telegraph in use. The above appointment to have effect from the 22nd instant.

The three Senior Field Officers of Infantry without Brigades, viz. Lieut.-Col. Commandant Fagan, Lieut.-Cols. Nation and Price, are brought on the Roster of Generals of the Day, until further orders.

The Advanced Posts to be relieved this afternoon at three o'clock . . .

A working party of 100 men from . . .

A relief working party of a complete Regiment of Native Infantry . . .

The Infantry Piquets to mount, till further orders, at five

P.M. and to be withdrawn from their position at day-break;
and permitted to return to their tents. The Infantry Piquets
to remain in readiness to turn out at the shortest notice, as
directed.

A Foraging Party of the usual strength in Cavalry and
Infantry . . .

The Commander-in-Chief has received with much
pleasure, the report of the excellent conduct of a serjeant-
major of the 6th Light Dragoons, John Armstrong, who
was engaged in work in the field defences at Buldeo
Singh's garden in most hazardous circumstances, and who
suffered burial for half an hour following the collapse of
his trench, whereupon he was brought out upon the
exertions of his fellow Dragoons, notably Corporal Stray
of that Regiment, and after the shortest period for recovery
and examination by the Surgeon, returned to his post to
continue with the same hazardous work as before. His
Lordship, in consideration of the foregoing service, as well
as of the high character borne by this Non-commissioned
Officer, is pleased to advance Serjeant-Major Armstrong
one year in Service and Seniority, and likewise Corporal
Stray to be advanced six months in Service and Seniority.
His Lordship further directs, that his approbation may be
communicated to the whole of the Party, for their steady
conduct on this occasion.

'Well, gentlemen, a handsome testimonial, if necessarily somewhat recondite in its description of events.' Major Joynson laid down his copy of the orders beside him and rubbed his hands together. 'By God, it's cold today. Are there any questions?'

'You were going to tell us of progress,' said Strickland helpfully.

'Indeed, I shall,' replied Joynson.

'Where does the telegraph run?' asked Rose.

'Agra and the two divisions of infantry.'

There were no further questions.

'Very well, the siege,' said Joynson, cupping his hands together and blowing into them. 'There is nothing I may say about the progress of the saps and mines. Indeed, there is nothing I *can* say, for that intelligence is very properly kept privy to the divisional commanders. We do, of course, know that Armstrong's tunnel has now reached almost to the long-necked bastion – further, so I understand, than the engineers have ever known a gallery driven in such circumstances. There are others being driven now from the third parallels, but they are highly susceptible to countermines. One indeed has already been blown in.'

'Have the guns made a breach anywhere?' asked Strickland.

'Not that I'm aware of.'

'I'm beginning to wonder if powder is going to have any effect if solid shot hasn't.'

'Well,' said Joynson, not entirely unsympathetic with the proposition, but mindful of the need not to show it, 'I should imagine that if the foundations are attacked . . .'

There was a degree of nodding. It seemed a sound enough observation. None of them was an engineer, after all.

Rose, who had managed at last to relight his cigar, blew his habitual cloud of smoke towards the roof of the marquee. 'Pigs are the answer.'

There were smiles all round, save from Joynson. 'Not now, Hugh!'

'I don't think I'm entirely jesting,' replied A Troop's wounded buck. 'Our seat is in Kent, close to Rochester.'

Hervey had some distant recollection now. One or two others looked as though they might. But Joynson did not. 'I am none the wiser. You had better spell it out.'

'When King John laid siege to the castle there they tunnelled under the keep and then packed it full of brush-wood and fat pigs and it was like the burning fiery furnace.

341

It brought down a whole corner of the place.' He blew another cloud of smoke upwards as if to illustrate the feat.

Joynson smiled. 'And yet, Hugh, I am not minded to ask the chief engineer what is the relative combustive value of pigs and powder.'

They all enjoyed the diversion. Things had become very tedious.

'But I may tell you this,' he continued, taking off his spectacles and placing them in their case. 'The commander-in-chief does not intend that any part of the cavalry dismount, save of its own volition.'

Smiling faces turned puzzled-looking.

'I mean simply that his lordship is calling for volunteers for the storming parties.'

All were at once energized.

'We shall do it in the old way,' said Joynson, holding up his hand. 'And a ballot.'

The hubbub continued. 'Useless to ask when we shall be needed?' said Rose.

'Yes,' replied Joynson.

The adjutant cleared his throat in such a way as to bring the conference to order.

'One more thing, gentlemen. This shall be my last with you in command. Sir Ivo will be here this evening. Thank you for your forbearance this past year. That will be all.'

There was silence, and then a buzz that somehow managed to combine the keen anticipation of the lieutenant-colonel's return with genuine regret at Joynson's supersession. There was scarce a man who would not say that the major had grown comfortably into the habit of command.

When the others had left, Hervey stood up and put on his forage cap. 'Sir, I speak for myself, but I don't doubt that were I not here any of the other captains would say the same. It has been—'

'Yes, yes, Hervey. Likely so, but we have much to be about. There are loose ends I would tie up before Sir Ivo arrives. It wouldn't do for the regiment to appear to any degree careless.'

Hervey smiled. 'Eustace, I hardly think—'

But Joynson would have no compliments. 'And you shall be able to return your attention wholly to your troop.'

That, of course, was a blessing. 'Do you want me to do anything preparatory to Sir Ivo's arriving?'

'I think not. But I should like you to be here when he does arrive. He will need to be apprised of things, and yours is the greatest knowledge of what went before.'

Lieutenant-Colonel Sir Ivo Lankester, Bt, had returned to the executive command of His Majesty's 6th Light Dragoons from his post-nuptial leave amid several thousand acres of Hertfordshire by way of Calcutta, where his bride, the second daughter of Sir Delaval Rumsey, a man of greater acres even than Lankester himself, had been hastily lodged with the Governor-General. To Hervey he looked not a day older, very content (but then, he had always appeared so), and keen to gather up the reins.

'Eustace, I heard a great deal of the regiment even in the short time I was in Calcutta, and all of it the highest praise. I really cannot thank you enough, especially since my furlough was longer, in the event, than anticipated.'

'You have our congratulations on that account, Colonel,' replied Joynson.

And at dinner Sir Ivo would see those sentiments in tangible form, for the officers would present him with a fine silver statuette of a mounted officer of the regiment, a wedding present executed by one of the best native silver-smiths in Hindoostan.

'Thank you, Eustace. Thank you very much indeed.' He nodded to his orderly, who advanced on him with a small box. 'And I should like you to have this, just a little token of my gratitude.'

A silver-mounted horn snuff mull – Joynson looked genuinely abashed. 'It is very handsome, Colonel. Thank you.'

'Well then. I will tell you what I know – which is only that which the brigadier has told me – and you may then tell me how little I know.'

They all smiled. And then Sir Ivo began.

It was more than an hour by the time Joynson had related the signal occurrences, incidents and events of the past year. Here and there Hervey added some detail or opinion, but it was largely the major's occasion, and one which admirably suited his eye for detail.

Sir Ivo was well pleased both by what he heard (on the whole) and by how Joynson related it. At length he smiled again, expressed himself ready to reassume command, and called for wine. 'One thing more I would hear about, though it is a curious interest only: how did Armstrong survive his entombment?'

Hervey inclined his head and raised an eyebrow as if to acknowledge the singularity of the ordeal. 'There was a duct which conveyed air to the end of the tunnel – which was itself of Armstrong's doing – and it seems that this was somehow close enough to ensure a sufficient quantity of air, even amid the debris of the roof. But how there remained sufficient air once we began to pull him free is unclear. Certainly, Armstrong has no recollection.'

'Well, let us not speculate on the science of it. But I am intrigued to know of his design.'

'The principle appears very simple, Colonel. The duct extends the length of the working, and about eighty yards in, just behind one of the siege battery earthworks, there is a narrow ventilation shaft – masked from the enemy, of course – and the tunnel is sealed by canvas, but which the duct passes through, just to the rear of the shaft. There is a fire at the foot of the shaft which draws air from the tunnel, and this in turn draws fresh air along the duct.'

'Most ingenious,' said Sir Ivo. 'I wonder the engineers didn't think of it themselves.'

'Oh, Colonel Anburey, their brigadier, is full of praise for Armstrong,' said Joynson. 'And Combermere's made special mention in his orders.'

'Capital! Now, leave us, if you will, Hervey. I have one or two matters I would discuss with Eustace in private. And do be assured that I am most especially obliged for all you have done, too, in my absence.'

Hervey was gratified, if, like Joynson, a shade abashed. 'Honoured, Colonel.' He saluted and left them to the privacy of the orderly room.

'In truth I should have been lost without him on any number of occasions,' said Joynson when he was gone.

Sir Ivo nodded. 'I saw Combermere on the way up. He said he would have him for his staff. I think we might contemplate that when we return to Calcutta. It would be greatly to his advantage.'

'I agree.'

'Very well. Now, the storming parties you spoke of – the volunteers.'

Joynson smiled. 'A very full manger.'

'And you'll draw the names in the usual fashion?'

Joynson hesitated. 'I have had two representations.'

'Indeed?'

'Well, three indirectly. Rose for one, for obvious reasons.'

'I should be very much inclined to accept that, Eustace. He will feel it keenly that he should restore his honour in the breaches. It could only serve the regiment's *esprit de corps*.'

'The other is Hervey and his cornet, Green, who really is a most execrable tick. Hervey believes him to have shown cowardice on two occasions, which he cannot of course substantiate, and wants to determine his mettle.'

Sir Ivo's benign expression changed. 'Good God! Never did I think to hear we should have a coward in the mess again.'

'I fear so.'

'Then I am inclined to accept Green's bid. The fact that he's made one would indicate there might be some doubt as to his infamy.'

Joynson raised an eyebrow. 'We must hope so. However – I do not know this, officially, of course – but Hervey gave him no practicable option.'

'How so?'

'Better you do not know, Colonel.'

Sir Ivo sighed. 'Why does Hervey have to go too? To bear witness, I suppose?'

Joynson nodded.

'Very well. And there is a fourth representation, Eustace.'

'Indeed, Colonel?'

'Yes. *I* shall join one of the parties. I think it only proper, my having been absent so long.'

'No, Colonel, I protest. That would be most irregular. The brigadier would surely not allow it.'

Sir Ivo smiled. 'I've spoken with him already. Oh, I'm not going to play the subaltern thrusting for promotion. I'm happy to let Green or whoever else lead. I think it right, though, that I go into the trenches and watch, at least. And you can sit in front of the regiment, where you deserve to be.' He smiled again. 'In any case, Murray says there'll not be a thing for the brigade to do!'

After boot and saddle next day, Hervey rode to Buldeo Singh's garden. He could only marvel at the difference between the Sixth's lines, with their comfortable order, and, not a mile away, the ant-like activity of the siege park, battery and earthworks. Indeed, it reminded him of nothing so much as a schoolboy's picture again – the building of the pyramids – so many were the brown-skinned labourers and so endless seemed the task.

He imagined that his purpose in going there was, however, an utterly vain thing. He had tried to persuade Armstrong that, his method proved, there was no purpose to his remaining there. To which Armstrong had replied that he was remaining for precisely the reason that Hervey himself would have stayed had the latter found himself in the same circumstances. Hervey had even spoken with Brigadier Anburey, but the chief engineer had only reinforced Armstrong's request, applauding the serjeant-major's sentiment but, further, stating that Armstrong was of the utmost material assistance. Hervey had reluctantly conceded, therefore, but hoped this morning to hear when his serjeant-major's work might eventually be at an end.

'Collins is standing your duties well,' Hervey now assured Armstrong, as they sat drinking what Johnson called a bad-mashing of tea – a drink which in any circumstances but those they now found themselves in, with periodic explosions from the siege guns and the returning cannonade whistling and buzzing overhead, would have been undrinkable.

'Are they about much?'

'No. For the last week there's been only one troop at a time under saddle. We had to have bending yesterday to keep them keen. Sir Ivo has decided to inspect the entire regiment. That at least will be something for them to work to.'

'Ay. Not a bad move.'

'He intends coming down here.'

'He's been missing the smell of powder, has he?'

'I suspect so. He's going with one of the storming parties into the trenches.'

Armstrong's face showed surprise.

'And so am I.'

'Good. I've cause to be there, too, then. I'd like to see what this 'ere tunnel does.'

'That's the reason I'm here now – to say that as soon as it's finished I want you back with the troop. The only reason I shall be in the trenches is Cornet Green, as you might imagine. There's no call for anyone else. All it will take is one lucky shell and we'll both be under the surgeon's knife. I'm not having you risk more than you have already.'

'Aw, there's not likely to be a shell – any more than anywhere else.'

Hervey smiled wryly. 'Geordie, I am not going to be the one who has to explain to Caithlin why you're peppered with shrapnel after being buried alive. Have some compassion!'

Armstrong took another gulp of the tea, grimaced, and started rummaging in his small pack. 'Lord knows I've no ache for rum at this time of a morning, but . . .' He poured some into Hervey's mug and then his own. 'Just as you say, sir.'

Hervey did not like the tone, for it suggested the matter was not concluded, though he knew there was little enough point pressing it. 'How much further have you to dig?'

'It's gone slower than I thought since the collapse; fifty or sixty yards – three days, four at the most. Do you know when Lord Combermere's planning on an assault?'

'No, I don't. But we all know it can't be long. There's a full muster any day now, I hear.'

'Brigadier Anburey was saying the guns have brought down the major part of yon bastion's facing, but the heart of it's too solid an affair. He reckons they must have weakened it, though. He intends putting ten thousand pounds of powder under it.'

'Great God!'

'That's why I'd a mind to see it. But believe you me, sir, I've no intention of feeling it!'

The week following passed in a curious mix of tedium and fever for the army of Bhurtpore. The tunnel – or rather

Armstrong's tunnel, for a second was now being driven into the north-east curtain from the sap under the great ditch, an unexpected opportunity as yet unchallenged by the enemy – made steady but slow progress, unknown to all but a few. The divisional musters, though they signalled to every man that the assault must truly be near, were nevertheless thorough affairs of inspection and repair which occupied all ranks for days before and afterwards. The names for the storming parties had been forwarded to the respective headquarters, but no choice had yet been made, or at least communicated, by the general officers commanding. Daily orders were scrutinized and discussed endlessly with a view to what they revealed of the keenly awaited date. On the second day of the new year, they announced that a lack hospital would form immediately, to the charge of which Assistant-Surgeon Murray of His Majesty's Sixteenth Lancers was appointed, and this was taken by the sweats to be proof positive of assault within the week. However, there seemed only the same requirements for working and foraging parties, for guards, pickets and advanced posts – 'of the usual strength in Cavalry and Infantry' – so that by the seventh of this first month of the new year there was an edgy listlessness to the camps.

That night, at Sir Ivo Lankester's invitation, Lord Combermere dined with the officers. He arrived at seven, just as it was dark and the night pickets had been posted, ate heartily, drank sociably and remained late. He appeared wholly content, as if events were entirely within his command. General George Stapleton Cotton, Baron Combermere, looked not unlike the Duke of Wellington himself – as Hervey had once observed in more exigent circumstances – except that the hooked nose and spare features never quite took on the duke's hawklike countenance, never quite gained the ruthless look that Hervey had noted as the hallmark of the best Peninsular generals. Yet Combermere had undoubtedly proved himself in Spain and Portugal, and indeed in Flanders and Mysore before that. And even if, as he well knew, the drawing rooms had it that his intellect did not fit him for the highest commands, were Combermere to take Bhurtpore then his name would go down in history as greater than Lake's.

Hervey studied him long this evening. He could reach no firm conclusion, however, unlike his most decided, and approving, opinion in the Peninsula. But there, of course, he had been but a cornet. Too much had passed since then for him to be wholehearted about a man he could not know more intimately. He was past hero-worship; long past. What did his opinion matter anyway, local major of King's line cavalry?

'Are you able to tell us, General, how things proceed?' asked Sir Ivo as he removed the stopper from a decanter of best port.

They were twenty at table, and though Sir Ivo's question had not been posed any louder than his conversation hitherto, his fellow diners fell silent in keen anticipation of a substantive reply.

Lord Combermere lit his cigar and leaned back in his chair. 'I am among friends, Ivo. I think I may tell you a little of how things have gone.'

There was now an almost tangible hush.

'Five days ago I concluded that the batteries were not sufficiently effectual to breach the walls, and so a mine was commenced in the escarp of the ditch on the northern face. The engineers, however, fearing a discovery should they continue their operations during the day, sprung it at daylight on the following morning when not sufficiently advanced to have any material effect on the wall. This unfortunately alerted the enemy to our designs, as I had always feared, and so when a second attempt was made our miners were countermined from the interior before they had entered many feet. We were, of course, alert in general terms to the possibility of countermines thanks to the work beforehand of Major Hervey.' He nodded in Hervey's direction across the table.

'I'm obliged, General,' said Hervey, bowing in return.

'So this second gallery was at once blown in by us,' Combermere continued. 'I was compelled therefore to delay the assault, waiting upon the result of two mines which the admirable Brigadier Anburey is now driving into the curtain from the sap and under the ditch. Much as I regret this un-expected delay, I feel a consolation in the hope that the place will be eventually stormed with comparative facility to the troops.'

The diners all nodded in agreement.

'I have not spoken, of course, of all our activities in these respects, for to do so would be – even among friends as here – an unpardonable indiscipline. But I may tell you that I have today sent Durjan Sal a letter laying out the general extent of our preparations, the hopelessness, therefore, of his position, and calling on his surrender of the fortress – upon generous terms, I might add, to his own person. But if he should refuse the terms – and I do not believe, gentle-men, that he will – I have laid upon him other wholly reasonable terms for the *laisser aller* of the women and children of the fortress, who must otherwise, I fear, suffer grievously soon from our mortars and when the assault itself begins.'

'Hear, hear!' said Sir Ivo, tapping the table with his palm.

With the third tap there was a huge, distant explosion. Combermere looked puzzled rather than troubled. Hervey felt a wrench at his gut, which might not have been as great had he been forward, as Armstrong. He made to rise. 'If you would excuse me, my lord . . .'

He did not wait for a reply. In any case, he was field officer of the day. He left the marquee, straining for his night vision, but it was not necessary. Flames and more explosions from the direction of Buldeo Singh's garden confirmed the worst. He raced to the charger lines, stumbling two or three times, and called out for saddle and bridle. Much fumbling and cursing followed before he was able to mount and leave camp – alone and at greater speed than any would have thought prudent in the direst of alarms. But it still took him a quarter of an hour to reach the garden.

As he neared the earthworks behind the engineer park, he could see quite clearly, for it looked as though everything combustible was alight, and blazing with a great noise punctuated by more explosions. It was at once obvious what had happened. There had been a single explosion – occasioned how, it did not matter – and then the fires had spread like ripples in a pond as successive explosions sent burning residue on a search for something else to ignite – charges for the guns, torpedoes, carcasses, rockets. And that initial explosion, massive as it was, could have been only one thing: ten thousand pounds of corned powder.

Gilbert stood the explosions well, neither did he shy from the flames. But Hervey would not take him any closer. He looked round for a horse-holder. Men were running everywhere, white and sepoy, equally dazed, but he could see no one into whose hands he could place the reins, and there was nowhere to tie a horse. He wished he'd a spancel, or even something to fashion one with. Instead, he knotted the reins and slid from the saddle, patted Gilbert's shoulder and said, 'Stay there' – as hopeless an arrangement as it was a command.

He ran through the park and into the zigzag, but he couldn't get through for sepoys carrying out the wounded. He climbed out of the trench and over the breastworks, but he couldn't see beyond the battery for there was so much flame. And all the time the noise – like a roaring wind and cannonade.

He turned back to go to the mouth of the tunnel. There was yet another explosion and he felt the air punched out of him as surely as if he had been struck by a pug. He hit the ground hard. His forage cap was gone, and his crossbelt was round his neck. He cursed loud and long, but he was not hurt.

He picked himself up, gave up the search for his cap and climbed back down into the trench. The flow was now against him again, as sappers in good order doubled through towards the battery. He flattened himself against the trench wall to let them pass, then rushed through the zigzag and out through the park to find the other way into the tunnel workings. Gilbert was standing where he had left him, head up.

''Ello, sir,' said Corporal Stray, changing hands with the reins in order to salute.

'Where's the sar'nt-major?'

''E's gone lookin' for yer, sir,' said Stray, as if the affair was nothing more than a night in the feringhee bazaar. 'We came across yer 'orse. T'serjeant-major were worried.'

'*He* was worried! It sounded as if an arsenal had blown up in camp. Was it the tunnel?'

'I don't think so, sir.'

'So you weren't in it at the time?'

'Oh ay, sir, we were in it. On us way out. But I don't think it were that.'

Corporal Stray's phlegmatic disposition – indeed, his utter and habitual indifference to all about him – was a byword throughout the regiment. Even so, Hervey found it difficult to credit with a siege battery and an engineer park blowing themselves to oblivion close by. Yet so relieved was he at learning that Armstrong was alive that he smiled and shook his head.

'Would yer like a wet, sir?' said Stray, holding out a flask.

Hervey had had more than his fill of champagne and claret – and port – but he felt a powerful need of the medicinal properties of Stray's flask. He took a good draw.

'This fell from the back of your hackery, I suppose?' He smiled again.

'Ullage, sir, we calls it in the trade.'

'There were no bloody ullage in *my* establishment, Corporal Stray!' came the serjeant-major's voice. 'Good evening, sir,' he added, throwing up a sharp salute. 'I heard the officers were dining with Lord Combermere?'

'*I* heard the sound of ten thousand pounds of powder, Sar'nt-Major. I think we should have a word.' He handed the flask back to Stray. 'Hold on to him a little longer, if you please, Corporal,' he said portentously, and then led Armstrong into the shadows.

'I know what you're going to say,' said Armstrong once they were out of earshot.

'Well then?'

'I can't slip the lead-rope now. Not just as they're coming to the end.'

'It seems to me that's a very good reason. Are you telling me they can't complete the tunnel without you?'

'No, I wouldn't say that. I just think they'll do it better if I'm there. And I want to see it through an' all.'

Hervey sighed. 'Look, Geordie; you're exposing yourself to unnecessary hazard. You've already had one very lucky escape, and tonight looks like a second.'

'Aw, come on sir! What are we supposed to be about, then?'

That was not the point, Hervey knew, but it was the point on which Armstrong was going to dig in his heels. 'I could say that you were E Troop's serjeant-major for one thing.'

'And you'd know that I knew that Collins were doing it fine. And good for him to do it, too.' He put a hand on Hervey's shoulder. 'Sir, I know what this is all about, and I'm grateful. But I'd rather stay, and I'm sure you wouldn't just resort to *ordering* me to leave!'

'I ought to, Sar'nt-Major. I really ought to.'

'No you oughtn't, sir. And you oughtn't to concern yourself another minute. Jack Armstrong's not going to 'ave 'is 'ead blown off by owt in *these* kegs,' he insisted, gesturing with a thumb to the engineer park behind. 'Yon Stray's kegs'll be a sight more trouble to me when we're done!'

CHAPTER TWENTY
THE STORM

Ten days later

Camp before Bhurtpore 17th January 1826

My Dear Somervile,
You will forgive me for having left these several weeks
empty of any communication, and it is not as if by that you
might rightly infer that I have been so engaged as to
exclude aught else, for the last weeks especially, though
not without incident, have been but a trial of labouring and
waiting. Rather, I hesitated in placing on paper anything
which, were it not to reach you, might be of material
advantage to the enemies of the Company and its officers.
All the preparations are now made for the storming of
The Pride of Hindoostan. And in this I must tell you of the
part which our Corps has played of late, for besides the
seizing of the jheels, whose possession has kept the ditches
dry before us, it has fallen to no less a man than Sjt.
Major Armstrong, together with a detachment of dragoons,
to drive a gallery at great length – greater, indeed, than
the Engineers had thought feasible – under the strongest
part of the enemy's citadel, and this is now tight-packed
with not less than ten thousand pounds of powder. It shall
be sprung at Eight o'clock in the morning, tomorrow, and

356

*shall be the signal for the storming of the fortress in as
many as six places. Armstrong's exertions, and his
devotion to duty, have been without equal. He has been so
near killed these past weeks that I begged him to quit
so exposed a place when the gallery was dug, but he
would not.*

*And so tomorrow we shall be through and over those
infernal walls and be done with Durjan Sal and his
usurping band. There shall be two breaches, if all is
carried off, and two storming parties are formed of
volunteers, in which the Cavalry shall play a distinguished
part, I am glad to say. Lord Combermere had at first
thought to dismount a large part of the Cavalry, but the
arrival of the 1st Europeans lately had rendered that
exigency unnecessary. I shall be with the party that storms
the main breach, at the Cavalier, along with our
Lieutenant Colonel, Sir Ivo Lankester, who rejoined but a
fortnight ago and is full of ardour, and Hugh Rose and
others.*

*Then let me tell you now of the particulars of His
Lordship's design for battle . . .*

Hervey penned two pages more on the vellum foolscap
which he reserved for correspondence that would travel a
good distance inland, then put down his pen, picked up the
last sheet and began to wave it about gently. The air was
cold, with not an atom of moisture: it would not take many
minutes for the ink to dry. He took up the first page meanwhile and began to read.

When he was done, he picked up his pen again and
reached for a fourth sheet. He did not imagine anything, but
on the eve of such a battle – in which the Company must
prevail, whatever the cost – there were certain 'arrangements' he felt obliged to mention, arrangements which,
though the regimental agents in Calcutta and London were
perfectly able to expedite them, needed the supervision

of someone of sensibility, sensibility of Hervey's own situation.

These things now occupied a good three-quarters of the page – nine or so inches of Hervey's small, neat hand to arrange the future for his daughter, sister, parents . . . and bibi. On this latter he was doubly insistent:

You who know so much of these things, of my own circumstances as well as the travails that might come to a destitute bibi, will appreciate my imperative wish that no scruple should stand in the way of my will in this regard.

And now, if you will forgive my overlong trespass into sentiment, I must say how it has been my very great pleasure in knowing you both, and in the friendship you have unfailingly shown to me. I am proud to be godfather to the offspring of your perfect union, which duty, I most fervently trust, I may discharge to its ultimate purpose.

> *Believe me,*
> *your ever grateful friend,*
>
> *Matthew Hervey.*

*

The sap was quiet, voices hushed, no lights. It was a little before eight, with the merest hints of daylight in the sky behind them. Hervey had not slept. On finishing the letter he had left his comfortable, warm tent and walked the troop lines and then the picket – 'the little touch of Hervey in the night' – before setting off on foot with Green and the others to the place from which they would storm the long-necked bastion. There was a deal of time to wait still, for as they slipped into the trenches in the early hours the word was passed that the mine would be sprung not at eight but at half-past. In order, they were told, to have just a little more light to carry the breach with.

Hervey thought he would rather have a half-hour of dark than of light for such an enterprise, but then he was not an infantryman. If that was Major-General Reynell's wish – he personally was to direct the storming of the main breach – then be it according to his will.

There were so many senior officers in the sap that Hervey wondered if they might yet see Lord Combermere himself. There was General Reynell, commanding the first division of infantry, a fine, whiskered foot soldier who had seen more campaigning than most men in his thirty years with the colours, and whose appetite for the fight was no less diminished by it. There was Brigadier-General McCombe of the 14th Foot commanding the first brigade, and Brigadier Paton of the 18th Native Infantry commanding the fifth. There was said to be a wager between them as to who would be out of the trench first.

And there was Sir Ivo Lankester, wearing his pelisse coat still, feeling the chill a little but as determined as McCombe and Paton to be out of the trench at once when the mine was sprung. He exchanged a few words with Hervey and Hugh Rose when they were settled, waiting, and then said he would see if he could get a few more yards forward to be next to the brigade commanders for a better view of the explosion.

'He's a spanker all right, sir,' said Armstrong.

The consolation in letting Armstrong remain with the sappers was that E Troop and his serjeant-major now stood side by side at the point where must come the decision in this battle. 'I wish *we* might have a better view of it,' complained Hervey. 'I'd no idea the sap was going to be this deep.'

'We'll be grateful of it when yon mine's sprung, sir. I never saw so much powder in my life. They only got the last keg in just before midnight.'

'We must hope for a good pile of stones to scramble up,' said Hugh Rose. 'It'll be the very devil if all it does is rearrange the wall.'

Hervey raised his eyebrows. It would not be the first time

if that happened. 'Yes, indeed.' He turned and looked over his shoulder. 'Mr Green?'

'Sir?'

'The lieutenant-colonel has gone up the trench to be with General Reynell. You had better go up and be with him in case he has any orders.'

'Yes sir. Which way is "up"?'

Hervey was momentarily speechless.

'This way, Mr Green, sir,' said Armstrong equably, making to lead him past Hervey and Rose.

Johnson now wholly recovered the situation, whether intentionally or not. 'Tea, Mr 'Ervey?'

Hervey smiled – though it was still too dark for any to see. 'Do you think it is why I got a ball in the shoulder at Rangoon, Johnson? Because I'd not had your tea at daybreak?'

'Ay, 'appen tha did, sir,' replied Johnson, uncorking his patent warming flask. 'And for you, sir?' he added, directing the question at Rose, having a care to use the less familiar second person.

'Mindful of its possible properties, I should indeed. Thank you,' drawled Rose. 'Do you think we might smoke, Hervey?'

Hervey smiled again. 'I rather think not, Hugh.'

There were a dozen or so of the Sixth in the trench. Their function, along with the fifty other volunteers, was straightforward – to rush the breach as soon as it was made and to hold on to it until the infantry could come up in proper order. It was ever a precarious enterprise. By rights, if the engineers and artillery did their work, it was but a headlong dash into a devastated space and then a few exchanges of fire with those of the garrison not too stunned to raise a musket. The work of carrying the fortress was then the business of the assault columns. But if the breach was feeble or incomplete it was theirs still to take it. And then they might face disciplined volleys, or the raking fire of guns not overturned in the blast. It was vulgarly called 'the forlorn hope', but no one really knew why. One or two were always killed, subalterns usually, well in the van and hoping for the reward of field promotion. But for the rank and file it was not a bad gamble: a good breach was worth a year's reckoning of service.

Not that Hervey or Rose would be in the van. Command of the party was the prerogative of an ensign, always, and today it fell to one of the Fourteenth's, the senior regiment of foot in the army before Bhurtpore. It was Ensign Daly's eighteenth birthday, and he had shaken hands with each man of the storming party, as was customary, before taking his place next to General McCombe at the head of the sap, together with Lieutenant Irvine of the Engineers and, just behind, Sir Ivo Lankester and Cornet Green.

There was more method in Hervey's sending Green forward than merely to give Sir Ivo a galloper. If Green showed a moment's hesitation in leaving the trench then the lieutenant-colonel would see it for himself, and all would be up. But Hervey was not entirely closed to the notion of redemption. He thought it possible that Green, with so many brave men about him, and his blood heated by the occasion, would find after all that he had the resource to do his duty, and that once it was done he would then have appetite for it in the future. However, he had determined one thing: if Green did hesitate to leave the trench – if he were still not out when he himself came up – then he would have him out at the point of the sword.

'A bit confused, I'd say, Mr Green, sir,' whispered Armstrong to Hervey as he rejoined them.

Hervey sighed. 'Well, Sar'nt-Major, there'll be no doubting which way to advance once the mine's sprung, so that's one thing he needn't concern himself over.'

'No, that's true. But I gave him some wadding to put in his ears, and told him to cover them if he got a chance. I've known sound enough men become a mite addled in a thunderstorm.'

* * *

Elsewhere about the fortress were other storming parties
braced for the assault. But all would take their cue from
the springing of the cavalier mine, or what was now
known in the Sixth – the secret at last out – as the
cavalry mine, or even 'Armstrong's mine'. What Hervey
had written to Somervile the evening before was as much as
he knew, and a good deal at that, for Lord Combermere's
staff had been generous in their information in the final
waiting days. But he supposed that only Combermere
himself had in his mind a complete picture of the assault,
the commander-in-chief having appointed no deputy,
the major-generals being with the assaulting divisions.
If he should fall, it would likely as not be his quartermaster-
general, the veteran cavalryman Sir Sam Whittingham,
to whom the reins would pass and in due course the
laurels be given. But Hervey hoped that when the fortress
was taken, Armstrong's part would receive its due
recognition – more so, even, than it had already. And, of
course, that of Brigadier Anburey, for it had been he
who had directed the preparations for the assault and had
ordered the cavalier mine to be driven under Armstrong's
supervision.

And even now Anburey courted oblivion by attending
the mine like an anxious midwife with her charge. He
had assembled ten thousand pounds of the coarsest-grained
powder – 'corned' powder, as it was known, as opposed
to the fine 'mealed' sort – which, because of the air
between the bigger grains, burned faster and therefore
produced an explosion of greater force. But he did not
know if this depended on a normal supply of air in the
atmosphere in which the powder burned. The only way
that he could be sure there would *be* an explosion was
to have air at the end of the tunnel, and this required
Armstrong's fire to be lit and Stray's duct to function.
He would not, of course, ask either man to see to the

work. He would not even ask one of his own. He did it himself – lighting the fire and then crawling to the end of the tunnel to be sure that air was being drawn through the duct.

And so he stood now at the mouth of the gallery in the knowledge that all he could do he had done, yet still uncertain that it was enough. The lives of so many men depended on that powder. He had emptied the Company's arsenals in Hindoostan of the coarsest, and he had put bellows into the middle of the pile of kegs – *and* he had doubled the quantity first calculated in order to make up for any slowness in the burn, whether through damp or poor air. But he remained as fearful in his way as the ensign in command of the storming party.

He looked at his watch. It was time to seek cover. He had lit the quick match fifteen minutes ago and it was timed for twenty. Its accuracy he was in no doubt of, for he had made it himself, sending to Calcutta for isinglass, and he had tested two others in the tunnel before they had brought in the powder.

In the sap, Hervey looked at his watch too – the luminescent hunter that Daniel Coates had given him. It said the time was past eight-thirty, but no watch or clock agreed with any other to within five minutes, except when the noon guns fired, and so he could not know if the mine was live or not. The sky was rapidly lightening. Now would be best, while they could still cross the hundred yards to the walls without the defenders seeing all. He made to draw his sword, but the sap was too tight-packed. He pulled the pistol from his belt instead.

'Sar'nt-Major, do you think—'

The mine went off like the crack of doom. The earth shook as if the trench sides would fall in, splinters of stone whistled overhead like bullets, rocks showered into the sap. A dragoon standing only two feet behind Johnson was felled dead instantly. Ahead there was shouting and moans. Hervey began to push forward, but he could not get past the men in front waiting to debouch from the end of the sap. The artillery had opened fire, on the signal, making it difficult to communicate any sense of what was happening. But it was clear the mine had somehow gone off ill.

'Help me up!' he barked, raising his hands to the side of the trench.

Armstrong and Johnson hoisted him high, then scrambled out themselves, followed by Rose and the covermen. He ran only a dozen yards before coming on Sir Ivo. The sap was all but blown in and covered with debris from the bastion. 'Christ!' he groaned, seeing his lieutenant-colonel a mass of blood. 'Johnson!'

One of the surgeons got to him first. The assault was nothing if not well provided for. 'I have him. On you go!' rasped the Glasgow voice.

'Stay with him, Johnson,' said Hervey, firmly.

He got up, only to see Cornet Green a few yards away, and in a worse state. 'Christ almighty!' he spat, kneeling by his head. But it did not take a practised surgeon to know there was no life whatever there.

He now saw General McCombe lying almost as bad, and Brigadier Paton. And Irvine, the faithful lieutenant of engineers. A few yards further on was Ensign Daly sitting upright, as if in a stupor. His right leg was unrecognizable as a limb, attached only by the thinnest thread of flesh and bone. 'Jesus!'

Up came Colonel Nation, commanding the 23rd Native Infantry. He took in all with one glance, drew his sword and shouted 'Forward!'

Then came General Reynell, shouting, 'Go to it, Fourteenth!' and running on with them.

Hervey cursed worse than he might remember, drew his sabre and followed.

There should have been cheering; that was the old way.

But there wasn't. Or perhaps he just couldn't hear it, for his ears rang like the bells on Easter Day. He glanced behind – just a mass of men running at the crouch, mainly red-jacketed. Wainwright was with him, and Rose, and he could just make out Corporal McCarthy.

Now they were clambering over fallen masonry, the bastion no more – a great hole in the side of the Pride of Hindoostan. He looked up and saw Colonel Nation in the breach, and then he saw him fall – to what, he couldn't tell, for the artillery fire of both sides was drowning all.

The storming party was now thoroughly mixed up with the Fourteenth's assault columns. He saw their two majors urging them on. Everard knew how, thought Hervey: he'd led the forlorn hope at Monte Video. And Bisshop – he'd been at Badajoz.

He saw the first bodies of the defenders – bits of them, rather, the primitive butchery of the mine. An arm stuck out from the debris; a private of the Fourteenth, huffing and puffing as he struggled up the broken ramparts with a scaling ladder on his shoulder, took the hand and shook it before plodding on.

At the top an ensign was triumphantly planting the Fourteenth's colours. But the regiment was not intent on consolidation. Without seeming to check, a company set off at once along the wall to the left, and two more under Major Bisshop to the right. And Bisshop's were almost at once hurling themselves at a bastion whose guns the Jhauts were desperately trying to re-lay for enfilade instead of sweeping the ramparts.

Hervey glanced left and right as if trying to choose, but Major Everard was even now mustering the rest of the regiment to press into the fortress. Hervey looked about him to rally any of the Sixth who had made it to the top: Rose looked game, Armstrong was with him, and Wainwright; McCarthy, his instincts still a foot soldier's, had picked up a musket.

They set off after Everard's men, half-tumbling down the shattered ramparts. Bodies and pieces of bodies lay thicker than before, scattered like winnowed chaff, the harvest of Armstrong's method. Even as they slid and stumbled over rock and flesh, brick and bone, Hervey hoped the army would indeed remember its debt.

Now there was the rattle of musketry, and to the smell of powder which had hung in their nostrils since the springing of the mine came that other stench of battle, of ordure and evisceration. Always it nauseated some men and excited others.

Soon they were doubling. There seemed no resistance despite the musketry. They were soon into the streets of the town, mean though it was. Hervey had his bearings now: the citadel lay straight ahead. An easy affair this was, his pistol and sabre as clean as a whistle.

They debouched suddenly into the maidan before the citadel. Hervey at last got a clear view ahead as the Fourteenth's companies spread left and right. He saw the great gates swinging closed, and he groaned. What an opportunity was gone!

Then he saw what the gates had also shut out – hundreds, four or five perhaps, of Durjan Sal's legionaries, who now turned back in desperation.

Everard had his men ready in the space of two words of command: '*Extend! Present!*'

One hundred muskets levelled at the host not fifty yards in front.

'*Fire!*'

The citadel and all before it was at once masked by a wall of black smoke.

'*On guard! Charge!*'

It was not his fight, this, but Hervey would not hold back – not when the citadel itself stood within their grasp. He raced forward, barging ahead of the bayonets even, sabre thrust out like a lance.

He saw only a mass of limbs and faces in the seconds before they clashed – no 'pick your man, recover sabre, ride through, rally'. The infantry had their science too, but it didn't amount to much when it came to steel on steel. Only brute strength and will atop a certain skill. He felt the sabre jump in his hand as the point found a mark. But his grip was tight, and in deep went the blade. Then up came the pistol, the flash and the smoke, and the ball striking the same chest as the sabre, point-blank, throwing the man from off it, freeing the sabre to begin its proper work – the cutting and slicing and blooding of its razor edge. In seconds, red ran the length of the blade.

He was gasping for breath. There were only bodies now within reach of him. Wainwright closed to his side, Armstrong was already reloading a pistol next to him, McCarthy stood on-guard with the bayonet. Only Rose was still fighting, determined to force his way past friend and foe alike to get to the citadel gates. 'Hold hard,' said Hervey to the three of them. It made no sense to press forward when there were formed ranks of redcoats doing their work so efficiently.

At first it had been a fight. Now it was merely slaughter. The Jhauts who had not fallen to the Fourteenth's volley had stood their ground until the first clash, but without order they had soon collapsed, while those in the ranks behind sought in vain to escape. There had been no time for quarter, either to beg it or to give it. The Fourteenth – and the Sixth's men – had gone at their quarry with brute strength and a will. Some of the Fourteenth's bayonets had run two men through at once, and some had broken with their wielders' ardour. Not a Jhaut was spared in the maidan that hour. Not one.

Hervey had not stood back, but he was ever thankful for the infantry's skill at execution. These men were now so heated they could surely escalade the walls of the citadel! But that was asking too much, for there was increasing musketry from the high walls, and they had but a few scaling ladders, and those inadequate. Instead, Major Edwards coolly retired with his company to the cover of the havelis across the maidan and sent word back to General Reynell for the engineers to bring up longer ladders, and powder to blow in the gates.

Rose now rejoined them. He agreed it was an affair of redcoats, with little they themselves could do. Instead they would explore: if the other breaches and escalades had been successful, there ought now to be attempts on the stronghold from a number of directions.

'South, I think, towards the Agra gate,' said Hervey. 'That's where General Adams's brigade should enter.'

Armstrong shouted for McCarthy and a couple of the volunteers from B Troop to join them, and they slipped away down one of the narrow streets running parallel to the citadel, not quite at the double, but breaking into a jog-trot here and there when it seemed right.

They saw no one at first, either alive or dead. The havelis must be empty, thought Hervey – and thank God, too, knowing what might happen. And then, round a corner, they ran into the pitiful flotsam of any siege. Half a dozen women, children in hand, some with babes in arm, were evidently trying to flee the place that had sheltered them during the bombardment. They were young women – girls, some of them – handsome, dressed well. Their fate in even the best-regulated siege would be uncertain.

'Christ!' spluttered Hervey. 'What in God's name do they think they're doing? Get inside!' he shouted, gesturing with his sword.

They were now terror-struck.

Armstrong and McCarthy ran forward, taking off their shakos and making a show of courtesy. It seemed to work. The party started back indoors. Armstrong made a sign to them to draw the bolts and hide themselves.

Hervey saw their chowkidar trying to slink away, and

tried to make the same reassuring gestures as Armstrong. Then he had a suspicion – just something in the man's look. He took a step towards him and the man turned to run. He followed – not long – and then it was out. There was the Khombeer gate, and before it was Durjan Sal – there could be no doubt. He had just paused long enough to collect his zenana, and now he would make his escape. Hervey could have spat with contempt as he thought of the men left to fight and die, ignorant of their prince's craven course.

One of the spearmen turned his horse and ran at him. Hervey raised his pistol and waited for the certainty of hitting, but a shot from behind brought his adversary down instead. He glanced round, to see Corporal Wainwright already reloading his carbine. And there were Armstrong, McCarthy and the two B-Troop men.

The carbines brought down three more before the gates swung open and Durjan Sal and his coterie – it looked like fifty – dashed for their freedom.

Hervey rushed for the nearest horse, a stallion that defied its gender by standing still. He sheathed his sabre and vaulted into the saddle, turned quickly to see how many would be with him, then kicked hard, for he wore no spurs.

The guards were too slow. They tried to close the gates and bring him down, but two well-aimed shots from the B-Troop men set them to ground, while Armstrong and Wainwright began a struggle to unseat two of the rearguard.

Hervey met a ragged fusillade outside, which stopped as quickly as it began, and then cheering as the sepoy picket realized their mistake.

He kicked on for all he was worth, the stallion flattening into an easy gallop.

He glanced behind as he began to narrow the lead. Armstrong was following, half a furlong, and he guessed the other was Wainwright.

He kicked and kicked. The stallion lengthened more and was fair eating the ground. Hervey's only thought now was to finish the business of Bhurtpore once and for all, to take the usurper himself and put an end to his insolence. But Durjan Sal had fifty horsemen about him – more, perhaps, for some were joining him from the little jungled patches that dotted this side of the plain. Hervey knew he could not overpower so many, even with Armstrong and Wainwright at his side. What *could* he do?

Now they changed direction, to make for the scrubby dhak half a mile in front of the Anah gate. He would lose them there, and all hope of ending the affair decisively.

The sepoy picket before the gate volleyed as best they could, but the target was hopelessly beyond range. Durjan Sal's ardour was checked, though. The party slowed just a little, seeming to hesitate over direction, before deciding to make for the dhak after all. But half a dozen of the escort now detached themselves to form front against their pursuer.

Hervey saw he could not evade them. He glanced back again: Armstrong and Wainwright would be up with him in less than a minute. But he couldn't wait that long: Durjan Sal would escape into the dhak, and—

Three of the Jhauts sprang to a gallop and made straight for him. He drew his sabre and brought it up to the guard: he wanted nothing so much as to get by them and on to the others – Armstrong and Wainwright could deal with them as they turned after him.

As they closed, Hervey flattened, and screwed up his face waiting for the passing cut. The three Jhauts lost nerve, however, opened too far to let him through, and the nearest misjudged the timing of the backwards cut.

Missed by a mile, thought Hervey. Would his luck hold?

There were four now, barring his way. Another hundred yards – what would they do? Then he saw their pistols rise as one.

At a dozen lengths they volleyed. He felt the ball strike. The stallion squealed but hardly checked before Hervey himself reined him in. He couldn't afford to stumble at that speed.

Two tulwars met him, fearsome-looking blades and wielded skilfully, the other two fallen back in echelon behind. These were men who could fight as a team. Hervey knew he had but an instant to judge his manoeuvre.

He put the stallion in a line for the further two, to pass just right of the nearer pair – a desperate evasion, since they would be on him at once from the rear as the second pair engaged him. But a few strides short he pulled the reins up and left, but loose, across the stallion's neck, in the Rajpoot manner, and pressed his right leg as firmly as he could behind the girth. The native saddle, with neither tree nor flaps, gave him more leg than usual, in closer contact with the horse's flank as if riding bareback, and the stallion responded at once, passaging left extravagantly to career into the closer Jhaut's nearside.

The tulwar came too late into the guard, and instead the man took the point of Hervey's blade in the shoulder. The Jhaut's horse turned on its quarters in response to the unintentional rein and collided with the second horse, giving Hervey precious seconds to deal with the other pair.

He loosed the reins and squeezed with his legs, and the stallion leapt forward like a cat to meet the first opponent on the nearside again, the other man masked on the off. The Jhaut, surprised by the length and direction of the leap, failed to get his guard in place quickly enough, and 'Cut One' all but severed his bridle arm.

Hervey pressed the stallion on, but the horse faltered, then stumbled, throwing him forward. He swung his sabre left and rear instinctively to 'Bridle Arm Protect'. The Jhaut cut too soon, and the tulwar struck the sabre with only a few inches of blade; but his horse had more impulsion, and the tulwar carried down from the sabre onto Hervey's shoulder. He felt the blow, but the mail stopped the blade, and he was able to slice the back of the Jhaut's neck with Cut Two as the man overran.

Then his stallion stumbled a second time, the forelegs folding, and fell dead, throwing him hard to the ground, but clear. He heard a shot – Armstrong serving notice with his pistol at a hundred yards – and scrambled for the protection of his downed horse.

He searched the distance for his real quarry, and cursed: now Durjan Sal would make good his escape. Where was the cavalry cordon?

Armstrong and Wainwright were at last bearing down. One of the Jhauts had already made off, the two wounded had fallen from the saddle, and the fourth now threw down his tulwar. Corporal Wainwright, pulling up hard, unclipped his carbine and began reloading calmly. Eight seconds – no more – and he raised it to the aim. The Jhaut was a hundred yards away, but the ball struck him square in the back and he fell dead before his horse could cover another ten. Hervey smiled grimly.

But it made no difference, Durjan Sal would give them the slip and—

'Why ay, sir, look at that!' called Armstrong suddenly, pointing. 'I thought those black buggers must be in their charpoys still. Why weren't they standing this side of the cover?'

Hervey all but gasped. He could even see who they were – the 8th Light Cavalry; the blue and the white of their Company uniforms could have been the Sixth's own. More and more of them appeared from the dhak, extending line so rapidly that it was impossible to evade them.

Durjan Sal saw it was thus, too. In a minute more the usurper of Bhurtpore, his most favoured wife and jewels, and his worst henchmen, would be prisoners.

Hervey wished he had his telescope to see the moment. Durjan Sal was as good as bagged, though – that was what mattered.

But Durjan Sal would not be put in a bag by brown faces from Calcutta! He was a Jhaut. He did not submit to effete Bengalis. He turned back and began trotting instead towards the King's men, sword held high in both hands as a gesture of submission.

Hervey took the reins of the loose horse which Armstrong now led up, sheathed his sabre and sprang into the saddle. He would receive Durjan Sal's sword with proper ceremony. But he could not trust him, even now – even with two hundred of the Company's best cavalry trotting up fast behind. Wainwright took post left and rear, his carbine cradled, loaded ready. Armstrong drew and sloped his sabre, taking post on the right.

Durjan Sal, his tulwar now sheathed, and those of his followers, brought his horse to the walk and then to a halt in front of them. He bowed his head – not submissively, but in acknowledgement that he was beaten – drew his sword again and held it out in both palms. Wainwright brought his carbine to the port, lest the usurper have second thoughts. Armstrong took the tulwar – a fine, jewelled piece – and handed it to Hervey. The two dozen followers could wait for the Eighth to close.

Hervey looked Durjan Sal in the eye, searching for a clue. He saw only a mean-featured man, who could not hold a candle to those who had fought so senselessly for him on the maidan just now – and who were dying still, no doubt, in the citadel. He looked at his charger, a sleek Marwari stallion, blood about its mouth and flanks from its rider's hard hands and ruthless spurs. He would have this horse, in the old fashion. He would ride it, as victorious generals had their adversaries', and show the usurper what it was to defy the King's authority. He looked at the favourite wife, a beauty by more even than Jhaut measures. There was a time when she would have been his too, to submit like the charger to the victor's will. He had the urge to revive the custom now. He had the *greatest* urge to revive it.

'Take the lady Durjan Sal into protection, Serjeant-Major,' he said. 'Corporal Wainwright, have the prisoner ride another, and take possession of his mount!'

CHAPTER TWENTY-ONE
REGIMENTAL MOURNING

Three days later

Despite the laurels that had daily come the regiment's way since the fall of the fortress, there was a distinct air of discouragement about the Sixth. The death of Sir Ivo Lankester had gone hard with all ranks. Not surprisingly though, for despite his absence of a year and more, and his return only very lately, there had been something about Sir Ivo that seemed to win the absolute trust of a subordinate. It was perhaps the same easy, patrician manner with which he went about his command – nothing in the least dilatory, yet breathing a calm assurance that said all would be well. Hervey thought him superior even to his brother, and Sir Edward Lankester had been a paragon. Sir Ivo, though he had come late to the regiment – direct to the lieutenant-colonelcy, indeed – had been an officer in the true Sixth mould nevertheless: he did not flog, he spent his money generously but unostentatiously, and he gave his time as unstintingly. He did not have to come to India in the first place. He was rich enough to have sold out and bought command of another regiment more agreeably posted, as many did. And he had died because he felt he had not shared enough of his regiment's perils.

And to all this was added a curious and entirely illogical sense of failure: the regiment had lost its commanding officer – by some dereliction it had brought about his death. Even Joynson, who of all men knew the circumstances of Sir Ivo's being in the trenches, could not escape the mood.

With Hervey discouragement was made worse by apprehensiveness. It was uncertain what the succession of command would be, and it seemed only yesterday, still, that the regiment was made unhappy by the imposition of an unworthy lieutenant-colonel. Combermere had been quick to give Joynson a brevet, but that would not do with the Horse Guards for long. But for now there was little business to be about but that of a garrison – and little enough of that, since the occupation was the business of the infantry.

'I wish that budgerow could have been but half a mile faster in the hour,' said Eyre Somervile, picking his way carefully over the loose masonry of the citadel's walls. 'It's a poor business to hear accounts only.'

Hervey unfastened his pelisse coat a little. The sun was warm, and the wind that had shaken the Sixth's camp so much the day before had gone.

'And Amherst had particularly wanted that I accompany Sir Charles Metcalfe when he installed Bulwant Sing,' continued Somervile, himself wrapped in thick woollens.

'Well,' said Hervey, sympathetically, 'I can see that he might have thought the siege would go longer. But you were right to be elsewhere in the hours after the citadel struck. I'm afraid it was the old rules of war for many, and the sepoys the worst. The officers were not nearly active enough. I do believe that many of them were so intent themselves on loot that – do you know I once had to put a bullet in a man in Spain? He was in such a craze of lust and murder. They get their blood heated in a storming, and it takes a time to cool, especially if it's full of drink. That's when an ensign shows his mettle, in my view.'

'I heard something about men from the artillery, gone over to the Jhaut side.'

'Oh, yes – two, and able gunners they were.'

'They are to be executed, I imagine. Is their reason known?'

Hervey smiled grimly. 'They were hanged at once for all to see – from the walls.'

Somervile looked surprised. 'Was that lawful?'

Hervey shrugged. 'I suppose it was justice. They danced a full two minutes.'

They walked on in silence another fifty yards.

'I should so much have liked to see the assault,' declared Somervile, now having come to terms with its aftermath. 'You know, Bhurtpore has been a name to me since first I came to India.'

'Well, it is better that you come now than a month hence. The engineers say there'll be not a thing to see by February. They blew up the Futtah Bourge two days ago. You really should have seen it – the most monstrous heathen edifice! Though I'm half agreed with those who say we should erect one of our own.' He gestured to where the column had once stood. 'But what an affair it was. You know, we took the place in the end with remarkably little loss compared with these things in the Peninsula. It was all done very scientifically. I'm daily more of a mind that there's so much that could be done to better the business of campaigning. We went to this business, you know, with the same weapons of a hundred years ago.'

Somervile nodded gravely. 'But in the end, it is the breasts of brave men that win the day, is it not?'

'In the end, yes,' said Hervey, reluctantly. 'Though the end has too often been close to the beginning. And for want of imagination by those whose design the battle is. Of that we had ample evidence in Rangoon. But I'm glad to observe also that it was officers' breasts in higher proportion here. General Edwards is killed, and a good many brigadiers and field officers wounded.'

'I am truly sorry in Lankester's regard,' said Somervile, stopping and shaking his head. 'You know I believed him a most admirable fellow.'

'The best,' replied Hervey, simply.

'And I'm sorry that events did not prove you wrong about your cornet.'

'Green, yes. I confess I feel no remorse at having placed him in the position whence he met his death, but I heartily regret the circumstances, for his mettle was not truly determined. But then perhaps it was the best way. If he had dishonoured himself and the regiment, what would follow now? No, it's better, surely, that the regiment believes he died doing his duty, having volunteered for the hottest place. And there's the letter, of course. I've no notion of Green's father, a tea merchant in Lincolnshire as I understand it, but he has lost a son, and it will doubtless go heavily with him.'

'And I imagine,' said Somervile, helpfully, 'that having invested so much of his provincial fortune in making a gentleman of him, he would want to be able to tell his family and friends that he had died like one. It is ironic, is it not, that the profits of tea should send a man to die in the very place the profits originate?'

Hervey sighed.

'What of Rose, by the way? I did not see him this morning.'

Hervey brightened. 'Oh, Rose. I confess I was wrong there. He's been the very best of troop-leaders. He was in the storming party. He fought like a wildcat. "Death, or honour restored" I think his motto was.'

'I am pleased to hear it. A regiment cannot afford to cast aside a talent for battle at such times – even a flawed one as Rose's might be.'

'No, indeed. And the further question in this regard is what shall be Armstrong's reward.'

Somervile nodded. 'Ah yes. Just so. His doings are, by your account, wholly exceptional.'

Hervey smiled. 'Not for Armstrong. But, yes, they are singular for a man whose schooling and obligation are so limited.'

'Then I trust he shall have a prize.'

Hervey frowned. 'Prizes. Now there is a matter for attention.' He reached inside his coat and took out a package of papers. 'General orders; listen: "Officers commanding Corps and Detachments, are directed to have it particularly explained to the men under their command, and also have it proclaimed in their Regimental Bazaars by beat of Tom Tom, that the Prize Property of every description, taken within the Walls of Bhurtpore, is immediately to be sent and delivered over to Lieut.-Col. The Hon. J. Finch, Prize Agent; and any person found secreting or detaining Prize Property, will be placed in confinement, and punished accordingly."'

Somervile looked puzzled; it was but the usual way with prize money.

'The point is, there has been far too great an expectation of prize money in the army. Durjan Sal's property isn't likely to amount to much, nor his instruments of war either. The real wealth of the place is Bulwant Sing's.'

'Indeed so,' said Somervile, still looking puzzled. 'I am presuming that the agent will determine what is for restitution.'

Hervey looked doubtful. 'That is not my sense of it. The order makes quite explicit that anything taken is, by that fact, *prize* property. But perhaps that was not the intention. Perhaps the order was written with too pressing a haste.'

'Is there anything else?'

Hervey turned to another of the sheets. 'Indeed there is. The commander-in-chief's thanks to the army.' He began scanning it for the titbits. ' "The arrangements which fell to the share of Brigadier-Gen. Sleigh, C. B., Commanding the Cavalry, not only during the Assault, but from the commencement of the investiture of Bhurtpore, are to be appreciated by the fact, that none of the Enemy escaped from the Fort but on the conditions of surrender; and that the Capture of the Usurper Durjan Sal, with his Family, and almost every person of rank or authority under him, has been effected through the vigilance and gallantry of the several Corps employed under his command." '

'Handsome, indeed,' said Somervile. Then his brow furrowed. 'You know, Hervey, we had a very particular fear for you. Emma and I, I mean.'

'Oh . . . I should not—'

'I mean that your name at the head of any casualty list would have gone hard with us. There are too many senior officers on that list for it not to be perfectly apparent how the fight went.'

Hervey nodded. 'Indeed,' he said quietly. 'And thank you for those sentiments. It is appreciated, I do assure you.'

'And speaking of senior officers,' added Somervile, brightly, 'you say that Anburey is perfectly well?'

Hervey shrugged and smiled. 'Not a mark on him. He is much grieved, however, by how the mine went. He blames himself for the excess of powder.'

'Not for long, I hope,' said Somervile, his usual cool detachment returned. 'It sounded like science of the most experimental nature, from all you've told me.'

'Indeed it was. And I hope Anburey is duly fêted for it.'

Somervile narrowed his eyes a little. 'And what, might I ask, shall Local-Major Hervey expect for *his* address?'

Hervey shrugged matter-of-factly. 'A brevet, I would hope. Combermere's as good as said so. He wants me to join his staff in Calcutta.'

'You will say yes, of course?'

'I'm very much inclined to, but there's a deal to resolve in the regiment first. There'll be promotion without payment if Joynson gets Sir Ivo's half-colonelcy, but besides Strickland there are two who are senior to me serving on the staff in England, so that will not be mine.'

'It seems unfair since you were the one in harm's way.'

'It is the system.'

CHAPTER TWENTY-TWO

PRIZES

Calcutta

GENERAL ORDERS
BY THE RIGHT HON. THE GOVERNOR-GENERAL
IN COUNCIL

Fort-William, 29th Jan. 1826

A Royal Salute, and Three Vollies of Musketry, to be fired
at all the Stations of the Land Forces serving in the East
Indies, in honor of the Capture, by Assault, of the Fortified
City of Bhurtpore, on the morning of the 18th instant, by
the Army under the Personal Command of His Excellency
the Right Hon. Lord Combermere, Commander-in-Chief,
and the Unconditional Surrender of the Citadel of
Bhurtpore, on the same day.
By Command of the Right Hon. The Governor-General
in Council,
GEO SWINTON
Secretary to the Government.

A month after the salute was fired at Fort William, Hervey
and the Sixth returned to Calcutta. It was a good homecoming. Europeans and natives alike welcomed them, and

'Lo, see the conquering hero come' was played so frequently that it began to pall. Hervey, as Joynson's second in command once again, confined himself to the regimental lines and the voluminous administrative detail that accompanied the end of a protracted period in the field. In addition, there was the matter of the church parade for Sir Ivo Lankester. His remains lay with the others who had died in the assault – interred close where they had fallen, with the simplest of ceremonies and yet to be memorialized in marble – but his memory had still to be hallowed in the regimental fashion. To Hervey fell the duty of making the arrangements, and not least in accordance with the sensibilities of Lankester's widow.

On the third evening he dined with the Somerviles. Eyre Somervile had told his wife everything of Bhurtpore when he had returned a week earlier, and she had read, too, Lord Combermere's despatch to the Governor-General. Emma was as much apprised of events as any woman in Calcutta; there were but a few details awaiting Hervey's personal explanation. And she had, with great delicacy, attended on Lady Lankester several times in order to supply answers to such questions as the widow could conceive, she knowing so little of affairs in India. Besides the obvious pleasure in their reunion, therefore, both Emma and Hervey expected the evening to be of material advantage in the question of regimental mourning.

'I am to call on her tomorrow,' said Hervey, nodding his thanks to the khitmagar who held his chair for him as they sat down to dinner. 'With Joynson and the troop-captains. I hope then to gain her general approval for the form of service. It's a pity the bishop is off on one of his peregrinations. Our chaplain shall just have to rise to the occasion.'

'You will find her very composed, Matthew. That, I think, I can assure you. She was very grateful for your and Colonel Joynson's letters especially.'

'Joynson is trying to discover what her intentions

are with regards to a passage home. Has she said anything?'

'Only that she did not intend travelling at once.'

'I am surprised.'

'She will have her reasons, I'm sure, which doubtless will become apparent with time.'

'Indeed, my dear,' said Somervile, anxious to begin their dinner.

Emma nodded to the khansamah for the soup to be brought.

'Now,' continued Somervile, draining his first glass of hock faster than Emma's glance suggested approval of. 'Laying this matter to one side for the moment, what have you decided about the appointment to Combermere's staff?'

Hervey raised his eyebrows. 'I am offered a brevet – a lieutenant-colonel's brevet, I mean. I can hardly decline the promotion.'

'Excellent!'

Emma smiled too. 'And my congratulations, Matthew! Lieutenant-colonel – it sounds exactly *comme il faut*, and very deserving, I'm sure.'

'Thank you. Thank you both,' said Hervey smiling, but not as fully.

'You have some reservations?' asked Emma.

He did not answer. Indeed he did have reservations, though they were not easily put. He was thirty-five years old (his birthday had been but a few days ago, unobserved except in the bibi khana, to where he had escaped for a few hours of forgetfulness) and the proprietor of a troop. Who would salute his prospects if he did not take the brevet? And yet . . .

'Matthew?'

'Oh, I . . . the regiment is recalled to England, don't you know. We learned it only today.'

'Ah, I see.' Emma glanced at her husband. The news seemed not to disappoint them both as much as it might.

383

'I, too,' replied Somervile, half-emptying his refilled glass. 'Not recalled as such . . .'

'Eyre has been invited to join the Court of Directors,' Emma explained.

Hervey did now smile without reserve. 'That is capital news, is it not? My congratulations to you too!'

Somervile nodded. 'Capital indeed. And yet I am in two minds. I have spent so long in the Indies.'

'I think, Matthew,' said Emma, glancing at her husband again, 'that Eyre believes that if you take the position here with Lord Combermere, his own choice will be the easier.'

Somervile said nothing.

'A really very agreeable thought,' replied Hervey, much heartened. 'Though I fail to see how my being Lord Combermere's military secretary should facilitate your business with the Governor-General and the council.'

Hervey's reply presumed which decision it would be, but Somervile was not minded to observe on it. 'Just wait until you have seen the workings of Fort William, my good friend. Then you will understand.'

The prospect sounded not altogether inviting.

'So you see, Matthew,' said Emma, laying a hand on his. 'You shall make the choice between you.'

Next day at ten o'clock, Brevet-Lieutenant-Colonel Joynson, Brevet-Major Hervey and Captains Strickland and Rose stepped down from the regimental calèche at the residence of the Governor-General. They wore levee dress and together presented a picture of the utmost smartness, as was their intention in order to display their greatest respects.

Lord Amherst's major-domo showed them into a sitting room hung with bright Indian silks, and Sir Ivo's widow entered soon afterwards with a female companion some years her senior. The officers bowed, as one, and Lady Lankester curtsied.

'Permit me to introduce myself, Lady Lankester,' said Joynson stepping forward. 'I am Eustace Joynson, your late husband's major. May I present, also, Major Hervey, Captains Strickland and Rose.'

Each nodded in turn.

'Gentlemen,' she said by reply, softly.

Hervey observed a beautiful woman, for all her mourning weeds. Neither did the pain of her loss line her face excessively, so that she appeared no older than the twenty-five years which Emma Somervile had asserted. But the reason for her delaying passage home was easily apparent. To a skilled observer her complexion told, and to one less so the swelling at her skirts. Hervey had known of it, through Emma, and had told the others. Nevertheless, the appearance of widow with child was more a trial than any of them had expected. Lady Lankester was now, if not before, 'on the strength'.

Three weeks later, on a bright, hopeful spring morning, Emma Somervile walked the Sixth's lines with Hervey, probing him for some intimation of his decision on the appointment to Combermere's staff.

'I think Joynson is of a mind to quit India sooner than I thought,' he said at length, as if it had some special bearing.

'I believe I may know why.'

'Oh?'

'Frances. I spoke with Eyre about her only a little time before you all returned. I do believe she will very soon make a spectacle of herself. *More*, for she has in truth made herself so on several occasions. It was a blessing when the army left for Bhurtpore.'

'I feel very sorry for him. There's no word yet from the Horse Guards about whether the regiment can be his.'

'And your own decision will be consequent on learning it?'

'I'm bound to say that it could. I'm being pressed almost

daily by Lord Combermere's military secretary for an answer.'

'You surely cannot turn down promotion, Matthew?'

He smiled. 'Do you want me to say "yes" so that Eyre might take his post in London with ease?'

Emma squeezed his arm. 'I confess I do not know what would be the right course for Eyre. I myself have no very great inclination to return to England, and Eyre is so very suffused by all that there is in this land that I fear he might decline in spirits. You know, Matthew, he prizes your society greatly. I do believe that whatever your decision now, his would be to do likewise.' She laid a hand to his arm. 'And I should be very happy too if that were so.'

Hervey was greatly touched by the continuing evidence of his friends' affection. But he was as yet unable to give any undertaking. 'Well, I may tell you that I must give an answer to the military secretary within the week. But I tell you, Emma, I have scarcely ever found a decision so troublesome.'

Emma simply raised an eyebrow and inclined her head, a gesture to say she understood perfectly but could be of no help.

'But how is Somervile today?' asked Hervey, determined now to be bright. 'In good spirits, I trust. Shall he dine with us in mess, as we arranged?'

Emma brightened too. 'Oh, he is in excellent spirits, though he is angered by the commander-in-chief.'

'Combermere? How so?'

'He had a letter this morning from Sir Charles Metcalfe, who complains that the prize agents are appropriating property by rights the rajah's. He says it's little better than outright theft.'

Hervey sighed. He had imagined it might be so, though he supposed it was nothing entirely new. 'And the bulk of it, I fear, will find its way down the throat, though the widows will be glad of their share.'

Serjeant-Major Armstrong stepped from the forage store as they drew parallel. He saluted and hailed them in a model combination of propriety and familiarity.

'Mr Armstrong, I am sorry we have not met since your return,' said Emma, beaming wide. 'Let me shake your hand. I am all admiration for your exploits. The whole of Calcutta is!'

Armstrong glanced at Hervey, who nodded. 'Ah, *them* exploits, ma'am!'

'I believe Mrs Armstrong may have told me of the others, Serjeant-Major,' replied Emma, with just the right note of mystery.

'Well, ma'am, it felt queer to be on me hands and knees again after all these years, but it worked in the end.'

'And I hope it is rightly esteemed.' Emma looked at Hervey.

Armstrong had no doubt of it, however. 'It is indeed, ma'am. Advanced in seniority and service by three years no less. As I was saying to Mr Hairsine, I'm only a molehill from being RSM.'

Emma smiled again, and turned to her companion. 'Are there moles in India, do you know, Major Hervey?'

On the Saturday morning following, after the customary weekly parade, Hervey sat down at his desk in regimental headquarters and began at last to compose his letter to Lord Combermere's military secretary: 'Sir, I have the honour to . . .'

The clerk had lit a fire, but Hervey did not expect the letter would take him many minutes to draft.

He was scarcely begun when a red-faced Joynson marched in and began angrily waving a sheet of paper in front of him. 'Look! Unspeakable! Infamous!'

Hervey could not suppose what on earth might bring so equable a man to such a rage. He stood up, took the sheet and began to read. There were a good many words, and figures, before he came to the offending ones. 'I cannot believe it!'

'Hah! My thoughts too. Read on!'

Hervey continued to the second page. 'I am astonished. Wholly dismayed,' he said, shaking his head, still half incredulous.

'Is this what we were about at Bhurtpore, then?' Joynson sounded like a man betrayed. 'Is this what Armstrong risked making a widow with three orphans for? And Lankester?'

On the other side of the door to the orderly room, Private Johnson's ear was pressed as close to the keyhole as it could get. 'What's it about, Smithy?' he said quietly, turning to the clerk behind him.

The clerk frowned. 'It's about the prize money. An order's come. It says what the Company will pay us.'

''Ow much do we get?'

'You and me get forty siccas.'

'It's better than nowt. What's wrong wi' Major 'Ervey and t'colonel?'

'I think it's because it says Lord Combermere's going to take all his share.'

'That's not right. Everybody knows that's not right! 'E ought to give 'alf of it to us!'

Private Johnson pressed his ear to the door again, straining hard to make out what else was to come.

Brevet-Lieutenant-Colonel Joynson took up the order and began looking at the figures again. 'It's plunder, Hervey – plunder, pure and simple. As I recall, Cornwallis gave away half his share after Seringapatam. That's the *way*.'

'*All* of it,' Hervey corrected. 'He gave away every last rupee.'

Joynson threw down the orders contemptuously. 'I have a mind to make protest. Do you suppose there is anyone with honour left in Calcutta to take note?'

Hervey shook his head slowly, without a word. Then he

picked up his sheet of writing paper and tore it in half. 'Eustace, my mind is now made up. I stay with the regiment.'

THE END

The adventures of Matthew Hervey continue in
RUMOURS OF WAR
– now available from Bantam Press

HISTORICAL AFTERNOTE

The Burmese war dragged on until the end of February 1826, with Campbell's force getting within fifty miles of Ava before King Bagyidaw conceded defeat. Of the 3,500 British troops who originally landed at Rangoon, only a couple of hundred survived the campaign. All but 150 or so died from disease and sickness rather than by the enemy's hand. The sepoys fared little better, twelve thousand of the twenty-seven thousand who eventually landed at Rangoon failing to return. It was, simply, the worst-managed campaign in the long history of the British army.

Maha Bundula deserves further mention. He was, even allowing for the generally atrocious quality of his peers, a very fine commander. His feats of forced marching through jungle and swamp in the midst of the monsoon were remarkable. He had a shrewd mind too. He early came to the conclusion that the British could not be beaten: they could deploy more troops in both Arakan and Burma itself then he could possibly counter, and he was quick to recognize their technical superiority as well. On first encountering the explosive shell he is said to have gone into deep meditation for a whole day. When he realized that Bagyidaw would not sue for peace, he put himself in the front line and openly courted death. He was killed by a rocket in April 1825, and from then on both Bagyidaw's and the army's spirit seem to have ebbed.

The controversy over the Bhurtpore prize money was very real. Lord Combermere was held in high regard for his Peninsular record and for his determined conduct of the siege – he had to be physically restrained from taking part in the final assault – but there was first a widespread belief that the army had looted Bhurtpore rather than merely taking the legitimate spoils of war. And then the news that Combermere would retain all his share – close on £60,000 – provoked almost universal disgust when a private soldier received £4 and a sepoy half of that.

The haul of ordnance at Bhurtpore was great too: 133 guns, and a further 301 'wall pieces' firing a one-pound ball. One of the biggest guns can be seen today at the eastern end of the parade ground at the Royal Artillery barracks, Woolwich.

The battle was the first time the lance was used in action by British cavalry, and the first time that Gurkhas fought on the British side.

Of the great fortress itself, 'the pride of Hindoostan', nothing remains but a small and derelict part of the citadel. The walls were blown up or pulled down almost at once, and the jheels are now a spectacular bird sanctuary.

Bhurtpore fell to mines and the bayonet as my narrative recounts, but Serjeant-Major Armstrong's innovation was in truth that of a slightly later military generation – and in America. The credit must go to the splendid men of the 48th Pennsylvania Infantry, recruited from the coal-mining districts of Schuykill County, who achieved devastating surprise over the Confederate defenders in the siege of Petersburg, 1865, prelude to the famed 'battle of the crater'.

The medal inscribed 'To the Army of India', perhaps the most romantic of all, bears last among its twenty-four clasps that for 'Bhurtpur'. The cavalry received especial praise from Lord Combermere, in marked contrast to the, at best, grudging recognition that the Duke of Wellington had usually bestowed, since 'none of the Enemy escaped from the Fort but on the conditions of surrender'. Of Skinner's Irregular Horse, Combermere said that 'nothing could exceed the devotion and bravery of this valuable class of soldiery'; and James Skinner was granted an honorary King's commission as a lieutenant-colonel and appointed Companion of the Order of the Bath.

Brigadier Allan Mallinson is a serving cavalry officer and currently the British Military Attaché in Rome. Besides the Matthew Hervey series, he is the author of *Light Dragoons*, a history of four regiments of British Cavalry, one of which he has commanded. He is also a regular reviewer for *The Times* and the *Spectator*.

The Sabre's Edge is the fifth book in Allan Mallinson's series featuring Matthew Hervey. The first four novels, *A Close Run Thing*, *The Nizam's Daughters*, *A Regimental Affair* and *A Call to Arms*, are also available in Bantam paperback, while the sixth novel in the series, *Rumours of War*, is published in Bantam Press hardback.

A CLOSE RUN THING
by Allan Mallinson

'An astonishingly impressive début . . . convincingly drawn, perfectly paced and expertly written . . . a joy to read'
Antony Beevor

As the war against Bonaparte rages to its bloody end upon the field of Waterloo, a young officer goes about his duty in the ranks of Wellington's army. He is Cornet Matthew Hervey of the 6th Light Dragoons – a soldier, gentleman and man of honour who suddenly finds himself allotted a hero's role. . .

'Now at last a highly literate, deeply read cavalry officer of high rank shows one the nature of horse-borne warfare in those times: and Colonel Mallinson's *A Close Run Thing* is very much to be welcomed'
Patrick O'Brian

'Allan Mallinson has a splendid feeling for period and for soldiers. His tale of Waterloo will delight all those who share his enthusiasm'
Max Hastings

'Effortless and impressive . . . it is a pleasure to read a book based on so much genuine knowledge, no doubt painstakingly acquired, but lightly worn'
Spectator

'O'Brian's equal in accurate knowledge of the equipment, methods, weapons and conditions of service of the fighting men of whom he writes . . . An imaginative feat of high order, owing as much to thorough scholarship as it does to compassion and sensibility . . . Brilliantly conveyed'
Country Life

A Bantam Paperback

0 553 50713 3

THE NIZAM'S DAUGHTERS
by Allan Mallinson

'A marvellous read, paced like a well-balanced symphony . . . full of surprises and excitement'
The Times

Fresh from the field of Waterloo, Matthew Hervey, newly appointed *aide-de-camp* to the Duke of Wellington, is dispatched on a mission of the utmost secrecy. Leaving behind his fiancée, Lady Henrietta Lindsay, he must journey across tempestuous seas to India, an alien, exotic and beguiling land that will test his mettle to the very limit. For the princely state of Chintal is threatened both by intrigue from within and military might from without, and Hervey, sabre in hand, finds he is once more destined for the field of battle. . .

'Mallinson writes with style, verve and the lucidity one would expect from a talented officer . . . His breadth of knowledge is deeply impressive even if it is modestly entwined in the fabric of this epic narrative. Kick on, Captain Hervey, we cannot wait for more'
Country Life

'An exciting, fast-moving story, full of bloody hacking with sabre and tulwar'
Evening Standard

'An epic adventure . . . with a texture as rich as cut velvet, and a storyline as detailed as a Bruges tapestry. Patrick O'Brian may no longer be with us, but Mallinson has obviously taken up the historical baton'
Birmingham Post

A Bantam Paperback

0 553 50714 1

A REGIMENTAL AFFAIR
by Allan Mallisnon

'Confirms his undoubted talents and marks him as the heir to Patrick O'Brian and C. S. Forester'
Observer

THE SPLENDID SEQUEL TO *A CLOSE RUN THING* AND *THE NIZAM'S DAUGHTERS*. . .

The year is 1817, and Captain Matthew Hervey has returned from India to an England in economic and political turmoil – close, perhaps, to revolution. The onerous task of policing falls increasingly to the army, especially the cavalry.

And there's unrest too within the 6th Light Dragoons. Their new commanding officer – a wealthy, arrogant and cruel man – takes an immediate dislike to Hervey who must somehow earn promotion while retaining his integrity and the loyalty of his men. The trauma of a regimental flogging is swiftly followed by action against the Luddites and it comes as something of a relief when the 6th are dispatched to Canada. But there, in the aftermath of war with the United States, tension along the border is still high and although Hervey doesn't know it yet, he and his commanding officer are on a collision course, and the consequences for them both will be devastating. . .

'Assured and capable . . . a fine read'
The Times

'Enthrallingly informative . . . beautifully told . . . in Hervey, Mallinson has a character worthy of comparison with Forester's young Hornblower'
Punch

'A riveting tale . . . Matthew Hervey has now joined Bernard Cornwell's Sharpe and Patrick O'Brian's Jack Aubrey'
Birmingham Post

A Bantam Paperback

0 553 50715 X

A CALL TO ARMS
by Allan Mallinson

The fourth splendid Matthew Hervey adventure. . .

It is 1819 and Matthew Hervey, in mourning for his beloved wife and disillusioned with military life, is kicking his heels in Rome when a chance encounter with the poet Shelley leads hem to rethink his future.

Spurred on, he is reunited with his much depleted regimented, the 6th Light Dragoons, and immediately charged with raising a new troop, for India beckons once again. But what begins as a relatively simple operation becomes a dark and dangerous march through the jungle as Hervey and his ill-equipped and inexperienced soldiers race to confront the Burmese warboats massing on the borders. . .

'The heir to Patrick O'Brian and C. S. Forester'
Observer

'Wonderfully vivid . . . the real delight of Mallinson's books is their authenticity. His portrayal of his characters, as well as his vignettes of historical personages . . . show a rare and thoughtful understanding of the human condition and the mind of the soldier. It all makes for a thoroughly satisfying and entertaining read'
Lyn Macdonald, *The Times*

A Bantam Paperback

0 553 81350 1

RUMOURS OF WAR
by Allan Mallinson

1826: Napoleon Bonaparte is dead, the Congress of Vienna's work is done, and there is peace in Europe. However, in Portugal there is the scent of civil war in the air following the death of King John VI. And with Spain, and perhaps even France, threatening to take sides, England's historic treaty with Portugal is set to be invoked. Newly returned from India, Matthew Hervey joins a party of officers sent to make an assessment and lend support to the Portuguese queen. His place on the expedition is secured with the help and influence of his new friend, Lady Katherine Greville.

But the Peninsula is a place redolent with memories. For it was here as a seventeen-year-old cornet that Hervey had his first taste of military action. The French had forced the British army into a gruelling and ignominious retreat until, under the leadership of Sir John Moore, they made a defiant stand at Corunna. In the epic battle that followed, Hervey and the Sixth Light Dragoons played their part in one of the Napoleonic War's most famous military scenes. As the wave of the French onslaught broke against the solid rock of British resolve, the tide of war was turned once and for all in England's favour.

Now, with the Spanish threatening the fortress at Elvas, and as Hervey makes ready for battle once again, the sights and sounds of the Peninsula bring back a flood of memories. But it is not only Spanish aggression and ghosts from his past that Matthew must confront.

Lady Katherine has arrived in the Peninsula, and with very determined intentions.

NOW AVAILABLE FROM BANTAM PRESS

0 593 04729 X